## THE ELFESS CLIMBED TOWARD THE GOLDEN LIGHT—

Heedless of the enemy, Riatha climbed. Suddenly she called back to her companions, "Quickly! Aid me!"

Leading Aravan, damman Faeril and buccan Gwylly scrambled up through the slithering mass of ice, coming at last into the luminance. The bulk of the glacier loomed high above and the light from within suffused through the myriad splits and cracks, shining as would the Sun through a fractured glass window. And even as they stood up to their knees in the sliding shatter, stood in that fragmented golden glow, Elfess and buccan and damman, Riatha with the Lastborn Firstborns at her side, overhead the Eye of the Hunter streamed crimson through the sky.

But neither gold nor crimson caught their sight. Instead, it was what they saw in the center of the scattered light: for out from the shattered wall jutted a hand, a large Man's hand . . .

. . . and the fingers moved!

# The Eye of the Hunter

## Dennis L. McKiernan

RoC

A ROC BOOK

ROC
Published by the Penguin Group
Penguin Books USA Inc., 375 Hudson Street,
New York, New York 10014, U.S.A.
Penguin Books Ltd, 27 Wrights Lane,
London W8 5TZ, England
Penguin Books Australia Ltd, Ringwood,
Victoria, Australia
Penguin Books Canada Ltd, 10 Alcorn Avenue,
Toronto, Ontario, Canada M4V 3B2
Penguin Books (N.Z.) Ltd, 182–190 Wairau Road,
Auckland 10, New Zealand

Penguin Books Ltd, Registered Offices:
Harmondsworth, Middlesex, England

First published by Roc, an imprint of New American Library,
a division of Penguin Books USA Inc.

First Printing, October, 1992
10  9  8  7  6  5  4  3  2  1

REGISTERED TRADEMARK—MARCA REGISTRADA

*Design by Leonard Telesca*

*Library of Congress Cataloging-in-Publication Data*

*McKiernan, Dennis L., 1932–*
    *The eye of the hunter / Dennis L. McKiernan.*
        *p.     cm.*
    *ISBN 0-451-45229-1 (hc.)*
    *ISBN 0-451-45179-1 (pbk.)*
    *I. Title.*
    *PS3563.C376E94    1992*
    *813'.54–dc20*                                              *92-8544*
                                                                   *CIP*

PRINTED IN THE UNITED STATES OF AMERICA

*To Martha Lee McKiernan:*
*Helpmate, Lover, Friend*

# Acknowledgments

Appreciation and gratitude to the following: to Daniel Kian McKiernan, without whose help the transliterated ancient Greek used as the magical language would have never been; to Dr. John Barr, whose advice on sleds, sledding, and sled dogs proved invaluable; to Al Sarrantonio, who pulled me from slush; to Pat LoBrutto, who launched a career; to Janna Silverstein for planting a seed; to John Silbersack for his faith; and to Jonathan Matson, who moves mountains.

And to Chief Seattle and all the others who heed the words of Elvenkind.

# Contents

# Foreword

At times I've been asked, "Where do you think legends come from? Was there ever a time that the tales were true ... each perhaps in a simpler form, before some tale-teller's imagination embellished it beyond recognition?"

Along with those questions come corollary probes: "Do you think there ever were Elves, Dwarves, Wee Folk, others? If so, what happened to them? Where are they now? Why did they go? Did iron drive them out?"

I am a tale-teller, perhaps guilty of embellishing tales beyond all recognition ... but then again, perhaps not. Perhaps instead I am working on a primal level, unconsciously tapping the ancestral memory embedded in my Irish genes. Mayhap in the telling, or in the dead of the night, ancient fragments bubble up, knocking on my frontal lobes for admittance, or slipping over the walls of disbelief like heroes in the darkness coming to rescue a consciousness entrapped within humdrummery.

If it is ancestral memory, then mayhap there once *were* Elves, Dwarves, Wee Folk, others. Mayhap they *did* live on earth ... or under ... or in the air above or the ocean below. If so, where are they now? Integrated? Separated? Hidden? Extinct? I would hope that they are merely hidden, at times seen flitting at the corner of the eye. Yet deep in my heart I fear they are gone. Where? I know not.

There have been times when surely I have glimpsed what

my ancestral memory has safely locked away, visions which come in the depths of the darktide when the sleeper sleeps and the walls are less patrolled. Mayhap these are the fragments which help shape the tale in the telling, glances of the visions seen in the fathoms of the night.

Come, let us together explore the latest ancestral fragment, this midnight stormer of the bastion, for embedded within *The Eye of the Hunter* we may find answers to our questions, can we just riddle them free.

—Dennis L. McKiernan
*August 1991*

# Notes

**1.** The source of this tale is a tattered, faded copy of the *Journal of the Lastborn Firstborn*, an incredibly fortunate find dating from the time before The Separation. Printed by an unknown printer (the frontis page is missing), his claim is that he took it from Faeril's own journal.

**2.** There are many instances in this tale where, in the press of the moment, the Warrows, Elves, Humans, and others spoke in their own native tongues; yet to avoid the awkwardness of burdensome translations, where necessary I have rendered their words in Pellarion, the Common Tongue of Mithgar. However, some words and phrases do not lend themselves to translation, and these I've left unchanged; yet other words may look to be in error, but are indeed correct— e.g., BearLord is but a single word though a capital *L* nestles among its letters. Also note that waggon, traveller, and several other similar words are written in the Pendwyrian form of Pellarion and are not misspelled.

**3.** From my study of the *Journal of the Lastborn Firstborn*, the arcane tongue of magic is similar in construction to archaic Greek, but with a flavor of its own. With help, I have rendered the language into transliterated eld Greek, with uncommon twists thrown in here and there.

**4.** I have used transliterated Arabic to represent the tongues of the desert since no guide was given in the *Journal*.

**5.** The "Common Tongue" speech of the Elves is extremely archaic. To retain a flavor of this dialect, in the objective and nominative cases of the pronoun "you," I respectively substituted "thee" and "thou." Also, in the possessive cases, I included "thy" and "thine" in the Elven speech. However, I resisted inclusion of additional archaic terms such as hast, wilt, durst, prithee, and so forth.

**6.** To avoid minor confusion, the reader is cautioned to pay heed to the dates denoting the time frame of each chapter. In the main, the tale is told in a straightforward manner, but occasionally I have jumped back to a previous time to fill in key parts of the story.

**7.** This tale is about the final pursuit of Baron Stoke. Yet the story is tightly entwined with three earlier accounts concerning the hunting of Stoke; these prior tales are recorded among others in the collection of stories known as *Tales from the One-Eyed Crow.*

*"Auguries are oft subtle . . . and dangerous—thou may deem they mean one thing when they mean something else altogether."*

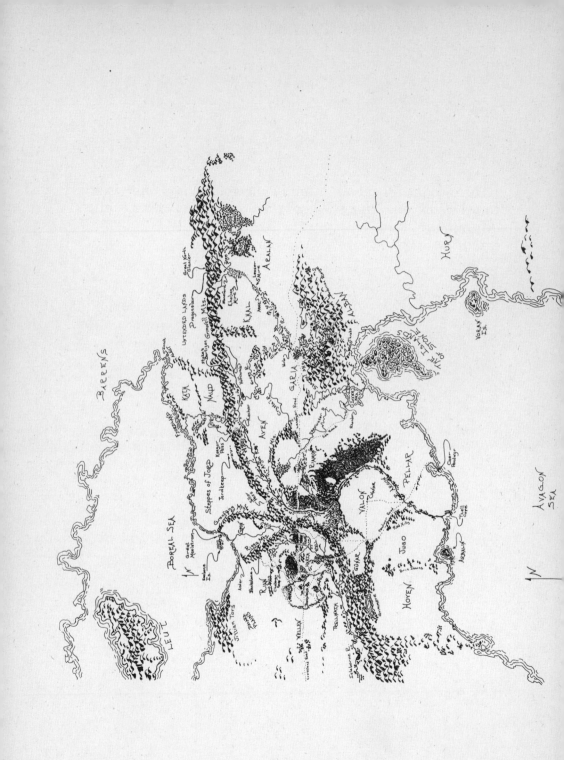

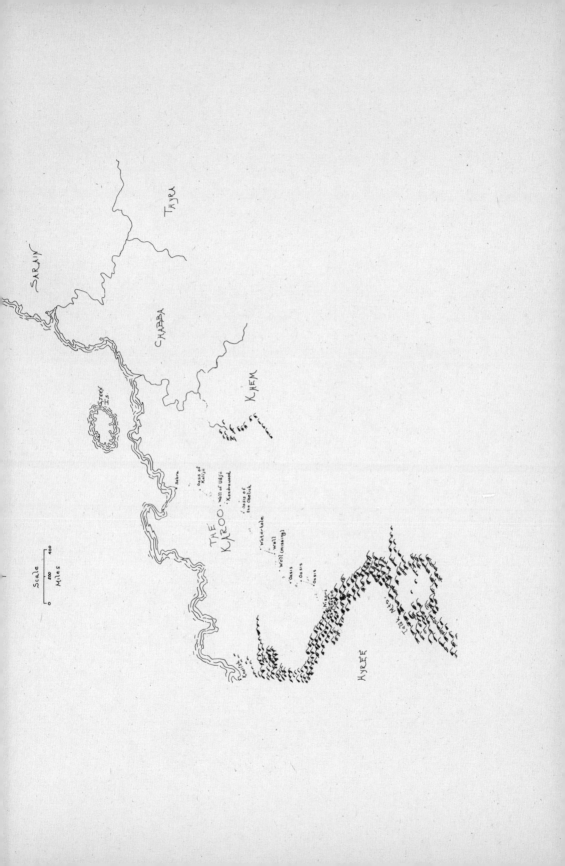

# CHAPTER 1

# Out of the Storm

**Late Winter,
5E988**

*[The Present]*

**P**redator and prey: the sudden blast of snow interrupted the race for life, the race for death, the boreal owl taking to the swirling branches of a barrens pine, the arctic hare scuttering under the protecting overhang of a rock jut. And driven before the wind, a wall of white moaned across the 'scape, while both hunter and hunted sheltered, waiting for the storm to end, for the race to begin again, for flight and pursuit, for life or death.

But now the race was suspended as snow and ice hurtled across the land, hammering upon anything standing in its way, the wind sobbing and groaning and filling the air with the sound of its agony. And the hare crouched beneath the rock and closed its eyes against the snow pelting inward, while high in a distant tree, a furlong or so away, the owl blinked and turned its head northerly, and deadly talons gripped tightly, disputing the lash of the branch.

And they waited.

Yet these two were not alone there in the Untended Lands, there along the north face of the Grimwall Mountains, for something deadly raced across the icy waste.

Perhaps the owl sensed it first, or mayhap the hare—who can say?

Out from the north it came, there where the owl stared:
*Dark shapes bobbing in the distance, obscured by the storm. Nearing.*

And an eighth of a mile north of the owl's tree, under the rock the hare felt the vibrations, not the occasional shaking of this unstable land, but a ragged drumming upon the ground:

*Feet pounding, furred, clawed, racing southward, down from the north. Killers.*

In the thrashing branches the owl peered at the oncoming running shapes, ready to take flight should the need arise.

*More than one. Through the storm. Coming swiftly. Still obscured.*

The hare opened its eyes but made no other movements, relying upon snow and white fur and utter stillness for protection.

*Thudding paws. Many. A pack. Racing, running.*

Onward they came, the owl watching.

*Three of them. In a line. One after another. Long, flowing shapes. Each with something large racing after.*

And mingled in with the sound of the wind came strange cries and a sharp cracking, and the ears of the hare twitched.

*More than a pack. Several packs. Killers all. One after another. Hammering. And something calling out.*

Now the first was close enough for the owl to see.

*Wolves, or the like. Running in a line. And behind, another pack. Or so it seemed. And another pack after.*

Past the hare's shelter they raced, mere yards away.

*Flashing legs. Wolf legs. Killer legs. All running. Grey fur. Black. And silver. Bound together. Running before something large. Something gliding upon the snow.*

One after another they passed the hiding place of the motionless hare. First, nineteen racing animals, then another nineteen, and another. And something *crack!* snapped in the air, and something called out *Yah! Yah!* as they thundered past, killers running through the wind and snow and hauling the gliding things after.

And though they had hammered past and away and were gone, the storm swallowing them up, still the hare remained motionless.

And a furlong beyond in the wind-tossed tree, the white owl watched as the three teams emerged from the whirl and hauled the sleds across the frozen white, the drivers behind standing on the runners and cracking their whips and urging the part-wolves, part-dogs onward, the passengers on the sleds bundled against the chill.

The owl's head rotated 'round as they came on and past and away, racing through the blowing snow and toward the south, through the blowing snow and toward the looming Grimwall Mountains standing ominously in the distance, barring the way.

Swiftly the sights and sounds of the intruders faded away, lost in the storm.

And only the yawl of the wind and pelting of the snow remained.

And time eked by.

Still the owl gripped the branch.

Still the hare crouched below the stone. . . .

The storm blew itself out sometime after nightfall. And the Moon rose and cast its argent light across the snowy 'scape. In the silvery luminance the white hare warily sniffed the air, its long ears twitching, listening for danger.

Nothing.

Cautiously, the hare emerged from under the rock jut. After a hop or two, again it stopped and listened, ears turning this way and that, eyes wide and gazing.

At last it set off for its burrow, some distance away.

And from the high branches of a remote tree, a white owl quietly launched itself into a long, silent glide.

# CHAPTER 2

# Mygga and Fé

**Late Winter, 5E988**

*[The Present]*

"Y*ah! Yah!"* called the sledmaster, urging the dogs onward, Shlee in the lead, maintaining the pace.

Gwylly leaned out and squinted past Faeril sitting before him. *How can they see where to run?*

Snow blew horizontally across their direction of travel, and Gwylly's vision ahead was baffled by the storm. He could see all the dogs, swift and true, tails straight out, ears laid back and flat, running hard against their tug lines fastened to the gang; but ten yards or so beyond Shlee, Gwylly could make out nothing but whirling white. Glancing back, the Warrow could see Laska, lead dog of the team behind, and he could barely see Riatha's sled gliding after; but of the third team, the one hauling Aravan, there was no sign, although now and again he could hear the *crack!* of Tchuka's signal whip.

Leaning forward, he called out to Faeril above the steady *shssh* of the runners. "The dogs—I hope they know where they are going."

Behind, B'arr, the sledmaster, laughed, a sharp bark. "Shlee know, little ones. Shlee know."

Both Gwylly and Faeril twisted about in the sled basket to look back at the Aleutan's smiling face, with its bronze features and dark eyes and straight black hair and moustache and beard. The sledmaster was dressed in a fur-lined parka with matching breeks and mukluks, his mitten-gloved hands firmly gripping the hide-wrapped handlebar, his feet well-planted on the sled runners.

In turn, the Aleutan saw before him two beings of ancient legend, dressed in quilted down: *Mygga* he had named them, though they called themselves Warrows. A small, slender folk, with tilted, jewel-like eyes, and pointed ears, and a ready smile—eyes and ears and pale skin much like that of the *Fé*, the "Elves," in the sleds behind. But unlike the *Fé*, the *Mygga* were small, child size, no bigger than six- or seven-year-old Aleutan children, standing as they did somewhere between three and three and a half feet tall, with the male *Mygga*, Gwylly, being slightly larger than the female, Faeril; why, they were barely taller than Rak or Kano, B'arr's great power dogs at the back of the team.

The *Fé*, the Elves, on the other hand, with their tilted eyes and pointed ears, stood slightly taller than an adult Aleutan, perhaps five foot five or six for the female, Riatha, with the male, Aravan, a hand or so higher.

But no matter their height, both *Mygga* and *Fé*, they were *proud*, like Chieftains, standing erect and walking with purpose and looking you straight in the eye, as if they owned the world.

And they were *dangerous*, with weapons of steel and silver and starlight and crystal:

The Warrows, the *Mygga*, bore missile weapons: The *Myggan* female was armed with two belts of throwing knives crisscrossed over her torso, five steel blades to a belt, ten steel knives in all; but there was more, for one belt held a silver blade—yet, strangely, on the other belt was an empty scabbard where the silver one's mate should have been. The *Myggan* male, too, bore a dagger, yet his weapon of choice seemed to be a sling, and he carried two pouches of bullets at his waist: one filled with steel spheroids, the other, smaller one with bullets more precious, bullets of silver.

On the other hand, the Elves, the *Fé*, bore weapons suited to close combat: The *Féan* female was girted with a long-knife and with a splendid sword whose blade glittered like starlight. The *Féan* male also wore a long-knife at his waist, yet the long-knife seemed insignificant when compared to his black-hafted spear with its marvelous crystal blade.

But it was not only the features and bearing and stature and weaponry of the *Mygga* and the *Fé* that told the Aleutan these were folk of legend, for even more telling was that the dogs allowed these strangers, *these strangers*, to approach and pet them, ruffle their fur, fawn over them—even Rak and Kano, feral savages that they were, even haughty Shlee. The same was true of Ruluk's and Tchuka's teams, with their leads, Laska and Garr, and with their power dogs, Chenk and Darga and Kor and Chun, and with all the others, too. Yipping and yammering in excitement whenever the *Fé* and *Mygga* came near. Rolling on the ground. Nuzzling. Bouncing. Dropping down on their forelegs, inviting play. Savages acting like puppies! Aye, these were the folk of legends told by the lore tellers while gathered 'round the fires; of that, there was no doubt.

*"Yah, yah!"*

Onward hammered the team through the storm, the sled *shsshing* after.

Faeril looked at Gwylly, her gaze of amber capturing his of emerald. "Shlee knows," she said, smiling, glancing up at B'arr and then back to Gwylly. "Shlee knows." Then the damman turned to face front once more.

Out before her ran nineteen dogs, two by two, except for Shlee alone in the lead, the dogs of each pair running on opposite sides of the tow line, each fastened to that gang line by their individual tug lines. Had Faeril measured, she would have found that the team was evenly spread out over a distance of nearly eighty feet from the first dog to the last, giving them room to run, and Faeril could see at most ten yards beyond the lead dog ere her vision gave out. Hence she knew that if the eyesight of Shlee in the lead was like her own, then the dog could be seeing no more than thirty or forty yards beyond into the storm, and the wee damman wondered what would happen should there be a crevasse in the way?

They came to the old stone ring atop the low hill within a half hour, Shlee somehow finding it in spite of the storm,

Ruluk's sled with Laska in the lead, and Tchuka's with Garr, running in on their heels. Still the snow blew and swirled in the moaning wind, and the stone wall of the ruin was but a vague darkness on the crown of the tor.

And as the Aleutans separated the three teams a distance from one another, and began driving widely spaced individual stakes into the frozen ground and tying a dog to each, Gwylly and Faeril were joined by Riatha and Aravan, and they began unloading the sleds, carrying goods through the blow and into the tumbled remains of a small round building, the ruin open to the sky, snow swirling in.

Her voice nearly lost under the groan of the wind—" 'Tis from the eld days," murmured Riatha, setting down her burden, the golden-haired Elfess running her hand over the stone, her silver-grey eyes gazing hither and yon, her head turning this way and that, as if seeking unseen sights and listening for unheard voices.

"A watchpost, I would say," responded Aravan, placing his bundle next to Riatha's, the Lian Elf slender and dark, his hair as black as a raven's wing, his eyes deep blue, as were those of other Elves of his kindred.

A faint tremor ran through the earth, and Faeril placed a hand against the rock. "Dragonslair?" she asked, receiving a nod from Riatha.

"Aye, wee one. From Kalgalath's ruin thousands of Spring-days agone. As a bell remembers its ring, so too does the world remember the Dragon's destruction."

Faeril said nothing in return, for she had read the ancient diary of her long-dead ancestor, some thirty generations removed, and the faded writing spoke of a region of quakes, there in the Grimwalls. Even so, to actually feel the earth shudder gave her pause. And words from a thousand years back rose up in her mind and her heart raced, for she knew that when they reached their goal they would be at a place where, now and again, the world shook even more violently than these faint echoes from afar. And that would be soon now, for they were but a day or so from their destination: the Great North Glacier, a wide, deep river bound forever in ice, imperceptibly flowing out of the Grimwall. And though it lay only a day or so away, time was of the essence, for she knew as well that in the dark of the night the Eye of the Hunter now streamed overhead, and an eld prophecy stood due, the augury of a seer cast more than a millennium past. Faeril shivered at the thought.

Aravan raised up his hand, reaching for the top of the standing wall, falling a foot or so short. "Not very tall, this guardpost, yet the land about is lower. A platform atop or mayhap a tower would give a place to stand and yield warning enough should foe draw nigh."

Gwylly cast back his hood and looked up and about, his red hair tumbling out, the coppery color in sharp contrast to his eyes of green. "Foe?" The Warrow gestured out toward the storm-swept plains. "What foe? It's deserted out there."

Aravan smiled down at the Wee One. "Look not to the empty plains, my Waerling. Instead, thine eye should be turned toward the Grimwall, for there it is that the Foul Folk dwell, there in the mountains ahead. And it is that which this post once guarded against: *Spaunen*. For those were the days before Adon's Ban, and the *Rûpt* ranged far and near, and this land was at risk. Yet the Great War changed all, and now the Foul Folk remain in the grasp of the Grimwall, nigh the places where they take shelter when the Sun rides the sky."

Gwylly knew that Aravan referred to the Great War of the Ban, when Gyphon had sought to challenge Adon for dominance over all. In the struggle Gyphon had been aided by the folk of Neddra—the underworld—and by minions on Mithgar—the Kistani, the Hyranians, by some Dragons, and by a few Wizards, as well as by Foul Folk and others. In contrast, Adon had been aided here on Mithgar by the Grand Alliance of Men, Elves, Dwarves, and Warrows; and some even claimed that the Utruni—the Stone Giants—had been part of the Alliance as well.

In any event, the struggle had been mighty and the balance in doubt, yet at the last the Alliance had prevailed, and Modru, Gyphon's lieutenant upon Mithgar, had been defeated and the rebellion collapsed.

As punishment, Adon set His Ban upon the Foul Folk, signalled by a blazing star where none had been before, a star which burned brightly for weeks, a star which faded and was nevermore seen. Yet during the time that the Ban Star burned, the Foul Folk began to suffer from a sickness whenever they stepped into the light of day; and the longer the star burned, the more deadly became this sickness, until in the end the touch of daylight upon one of the Spawn would bring on the Withering Death; even the briefest exposure meant a deadly collapse, the victim turning into ashes in mere moments.

All Foul Folk suffered Adon's Ban; other creatures as well, including some Dragons—those that had sided with Gyphon—now Cold-drakes, for Adon reft them of their fire as punishment.

But of the Men who had aided Gyphon, none suffered the Ban, for they had been misled by the Great Deceiver and Adon spared them in the end.

And *this* was what Aravan referred to when he spoke of the Great War changing all: for now the Ban drives the Foul Folk into hiding, into places of concealment in the Grimwall Mountains when day is upon the land. Hence even at night Foul Folk would not range this far, would not come unto these ruins, unless driven by great need or by great fear, for the Sun would find them and slay them should they be caught out upon these plains after dawn, should they not discover a crevice or cranny to hide in during the day, a place free of Adon's light.

And so Gwylly peered at the ruins, while thoughts of Wars and Bans and ancient days skittered through his mind.

As the wind moaned and snow blew over the rock wall and swirled in through the tumbled doorway, the buccan looked up at Aravan. "How would this place be defended? I mean, it's not more than ten of my strides across—six of yours—certainly not large enough to house any great force. I would think that it would easily fall."

"Aye," responded Aravan. "But a place such as this is not meant to be defended. Should foe be sighted, then the sentries would ride from here and give warning, or perhaps light a beacon fire and then ride."

"Like Beacontor?" asked Faeril.

Gwylly shook his head, *No.* "Beacontor, love, was meant to be defended. The towers of the Signal Mountains were ringed 'round by walls. This place, though, has no fortress walls. Just a tower . . . and a small one at that."

Riatha turned her silver gaze away from the stone and

toward Gwylly. "Should we look, I deem we would find the remains of a stable, or mayhap a kennel—a place used long ago for housing a steed or a team for quick flight across the land when the need arose. They would light the signal fire, then run."

Faeril brushed a stray lock of coal black hair from her eyes and looked through the door gap and out at the spinning snow. "Who would they have warned? I mean, who lived in here and out there when the tower was built?"

"Aleutani, I think," answered Aravan. "For even then they brought their herds of *ren* here in the long summer days when the grass is lush and green, even as they do unto this day."

Faeril nodded, for she had seen some of the antlered *ren* in their winter pastures in the deep, sheltered vales along the rim of the Boreal Sea.

Again the land trembled, and Faeril stepped to the tumbled-down entrance. "Will it be safe to sleep here tonight? I wonder, with the quakes . . ."

Riatha smiled at the wee damman. "Safe enough, little one. The land out here on the edge of the foothills is yet a distance from the Grimwall, and farther still from Dragonslair."

Glancing up at the Elfess, Faeril nodded, then turned and stepped out into the storm, leading the others back to the sleds.

It took one more trip for them to transfer the needed supplies into the stone ruins. While the Elves busied themselves with the bundles, Gwylly and Faeril set about trying to find wood for a fire. Although the Warrows did find a stable of sorts out to one side—it, too, fallen into ruin—they found no wood to burn.

No sooner had the Warrows returned than B'arr stepped in through the doorway, with Tchuka and Ruluk behind, the sledmasters having staked their teams. B'arr laughed when Gwylly asked what they would do for firewood, and so, too, did the other two sledmasters when the buccan's query was translated into the Aleuti tongue. As B'arr and Ruluk unwrapped whole frozen salmon and, using hand axes, began hacking the fish into great chunks, Tchuka disappeared outside, returning in a moment with what appeared to be slabs of dirt. To Gwylly's amazement, the sledmaster set these afire.

"Turf," said Aravan, as if that explained all.

At the blank look on Gwylly's face, Riatha added, "Some call it peat. Yet by any name, it burns."

Gwylly shook his head in rumination. "I saw the mound near the stable, but I thought—"

"—that it was just dirt," Faeril finished for him, for it had been her assumption as well. "But I should have known," she admitted, "for I am from the Boskydells, where there are fields of fireplace turf, near Bigfen and Littlefen both."

"Hah!" exclaimed B'arr, saying something aside to the other Aleutans that brought smiles to their coppery faces. Then he turned to Aravan. "No, not firedirt, *Anfé*; it is *ren møkk* . . . you name, dung. From *ren*."

Now Aravan laughed. "Fewmets! Deer fewmets! Dried dung. Ah, Sledmaster, thou show me the errors of my ways." Great grins crinkled Gwylly's and Faeril's features, for Warrow and Elf alike had been fooled.

Riatha too smiled, fleetingly, then grew somber, distracted, turning her gaze toward the unseen Grimwall. "What appears to some as one thing is oft completely different to the eyes of another, and even then its true nature might not be known, might be something else altogether."

Gwylly stared into the glow of the dung fire, his thoughts miles away. He watched as the writhing white plume of the pungent smoke was borne swirling upward above the wall, where it was shredded by the moaning wind. And the buccan wondered at what else they might encounter that would fool them all, something perhaps deadly in its deception.

B'arr stood, interrupting Gwylly's bodeful thoughts. "*Mygga* feed *span*?" he asked, gesturing to a bag of cut salmon, his black eyes glittering.

Gwylly's face lit up, and he bobbed his head. Faeril, too, nodded animatedly.

At this indication from the *Mygga*, Tchuka and Ruluk grinned widely, their strong teeth showing white against their black beards and moustaches and bronze-like features.

B'arr took up a frozen slab of axe-hacked salmon. "Then

wait. I call." And he stepped out into the wind-blown snow. The other two Aleutans also took a chunk of salmon apiece and followed B'arr outside.

They were each heading to their lead dogs, for as Gwylly, Faeril, Riatha, and Aravan had come to learn since setting forth some twelve days past, some six hundred miles agone, the lead dog of each team was the first to be fed, the last to be harnessed, and the first to be unharnessed. Each was the dominant dog in its team, in its *span*, and the sledmaster maintained that status by treating the lead dog with the deference that was its due, and by displaying that treatment to all the other dogs in the team.

As B'arr had explained in his broken Pellarion: "Life depend on *span*. *Span* depend on lead. Lead depend on sledmaster. I am pack leader, Shlee is *span* leader. His life in my hands, my life in his. I treat him as leader, he treat me as master. All dog see. All understand. All stay alive. All dog. Shlee. Me."

After but a moment or so, B'arr's whistle sounded above the storm. Gwylly, dragging two bags of cut salmon, and Faeril, hauling one, stepped out through the doorway and into the whirling snow. And after a moment there sounded the yipping and yammering of excited dogs.

The storm abated sometime after nightfall, and the Moon rose argent in the clearing sky.

And in the night Faeril awakened to see Riatha standing in the moonlight, her silver gaze turned upward. Faeril, too, looked up and out, her sight flying through the open roof. And her heart ran chill. For high in the silent vault above, she could see the Eye of the Hunter, its long, fiery tail streaming across the spangled sky.

# CHAPTER 3

# Faeril

"Ooo, the Eye of the Hunter!" exclaimed Lacey, looking up from the small leather-bound journal. "Sounds positively ominous. What is it?"

Faeril paused, balancing the throwing knife in her hand, and glanced over her shoulder at the ginger-haired damman. "Just keep reading, Lacey," she said, then turned and whipped her arm forward and down, the steel glittering as it tumbled through the air to *thunk!* into the wood next to the other blades.

As Faeril strode toward the fallen log to retrieve her knives, Lacey returned to the finely wrought script, one hand straying out and fumbling about upon the picnic cloth to find her cup, her eyes never leaving the page. The damman took another sip of tea and a bite of bread, though whether she tasted either is another matter, so absorbed in the reading was she.

Dappled shadows drifted across the pages as the day passed through the noontide, Faeril's knives *chnking* into the log, adding to the murmur of the woodland: birds calling afar, the faint rustling of leaves in the wafting air, the occasional hum of a bee hurling past, the burble of the moss-banked rill tumbling down the nearby slope.

At last Lacey closed the diary upon itself and looked up

at her distant cousin, once again collecting her knives from the fallen tree. "Oh, Faeril, these old words make me feel as if a doom is soon to fall."

Faeril stood at the log and slipped the knives back into the leather sheaths on the two bandolier belts crisscrossing her torso: six scabbards to a belt, twelve in all, ten now filled with steel, one with silver, one empty. A determined look on her face, Faeril turned and approached Lacey.

Lacey glanced from the damman to the diary and back again. "Faeril, you look positively grim. I think you are about to tell me something that I do not wish to hear."

Faeril sat at the edge of the picnic cloth. In a ritualistic gesture that she and Lacey had used since childhood, she reached out and captured Lacey's right hand between both of hers; then right to right, she pressed her open palm against Lacey's. "My best friend, I give you a secret to be held under lock until the time of unlocking."

Slowly Lacey curled her fingers and clenched her fist, as if holding tightly to something invisible. Then she pressed it to her heart and opened her fingers one at a time until her hand was hard against her breast. "My best friend, here it is locked until the time of unlocking."

Faeril took a deep breath. Even so, her voice quavered with emotion. "I'm leaving the Boskydells, Lacey. And I wanted someone to know. Someone to tell Mother."

Tears sprang into Lacey's eyes. "Leaving? Leaving the Bosky . . . ? But why, Faeril? Why?"

Faeril's eyes, too, filled with tears. Yet with her secret told, the trembling left her breath.

Again Lacey asked, "Why?"

Faeril lifted the crossed bandoliers over her head and held them out before her, steel and silver glinting. "Because I am the firstborn dammsel of firstborn dammsels, reaching back through time to Petal herself."

Shaking her head, Lacey blinked away her tears and glanced at the diary. "Yes, I know. As was your dam and her dam and— But-but, Faeril, what's that got to do with your leaving the Bosky?"

Faeril lay the belted knives on the cloth. "Tomorrow is my birthday: I will pass from my maiden years and become a young damman. I will then be of an age to set forth upon the way charted for me by my upbringing—a path ordained a thousand years ago. A path that only I can tread."

She reached out and took up the journal. "Lacey, this diary tells a centuries-past tale of the pursuit of a monster—Baron Stoke—by four comrades: Riatha, Elfess of Arden Vale; Urus, a Baeran Man from the heart of the Greatwood; and my ancestors, Tomlin and Petal, Warrows of the Weiunwood.

"Three times they faced Stoke, and on the third time they slew him, though Urus, too, was lost, the Man plunging to his death in order to take the monster down with him, in order to slay Stoke."

"I know," said Lacey. "Urus was very brave, very noble, and it was sad. But it is an ancient tale, an ancient story . . . and this is *now*, this is *today*."

"Ancient, Lacey, yes. Yet something from that past, something from ten hundred years ago, looms ominously in the *now*, or rather, in the near future, in *our* near future—a prophecy of doom, it seems."

Lacey's eyes flew wide at this pronouncement, but before she could comment, Faeril plunged on. "This journal tells of a rede about to fall due, one that in some fashion may be related to Baron Stoke, though how one who was slain long ago can reach down through the centuries to clutch at the here and now . . . well, it's beyond me."

Faeril thumbed through the booklet until she found the entry she sought. "And look, here, a millennium past, it says that Lady Riatha came to the Weiunwood and told Tomlin and Petal of a prophecy made by Rael, Elfqueen of Arden Vale."

*May 29–31, 4E1980: Days of joy and despair, for Riatha came . . . And this is what she said . . .*

Tomlin heard the horse coming up the path before it hove into view. He stood on the stoop and shaded his eyes against the afternoon Sun, watching the woodland way. His face broke into a great smile when a golden-haired Elfess clad in soft grey leather, sword in harness across her back, rode forth from the vault of the forest and into the glade.

He turned and called into the cottage, "Petal, it's Riatha!"

There sounded a flurry of footsteps, and rushing out onto the porch came three dammen—Little Riatha and Silvereyes, followed by Petal—all aproned, with a touch of flour upon Silvereyes' cheek and Little Riatha's fingers stained with berry juice.

Petal came and stood at Tomlin's side. "Can it be . . . ?"

Tomlin put an arm about his dammia's shoulders. "Stoke? I think not, Petal, for we both saw him borne down into the depths of the ice."

Petal cast a timorous smile at her buccaran, and they stood side by side with an arm about one another as Riatha came across the clearing.

Tomlin and Petal's dammsels, Silvereyes and Little Riatha—or as they were diminutively called, Silvey and Atha—stood beside their parents, watching the Elfess draw near, their eyes dancing with anticipation. They had never before met Riatha, though they had known of her all their lives.

And the sword-bearing Elfess rode her moon-dappled grey to the wee cottage and dismounted.

Petal rushed forward and Riatha knelt to embrace her and then Tomlin. And after but slight hesitation, Silvey and Atha stepped forward and were introduced.

Tomlin started to take up the reins of Riatha's mount, preparing to stable the steed, but the Elfess stopped him, calling him by his old nickname. "I will care for Beam, Pebble. Thou gather the rest of thy brood, for I have words of portent affecting all."

Tomlin's heart lurched, and he glanced at Petal and knew that her heart pounded, too.

Tomlin saddled his pony and rode to the fields. When he returned, the duskingtide was upon the land, and his two buccoes, Small Urus and Bear, were with him. Lantern light illuminated the porch, where supper was to be taken, for the cottage ceilings were too low for the Elven guest, and the Warrows would not have her stoop.

And so all gathered in the Maytime eve and took their meal and spoke of small things, of inconsequential things, while crickets sang in the grass. And at the end, Silvey and Atha served hot tea and huckleberry pie, as the night deepened.

A period of silence fell upon family and guest alike and stretched thin, while stars wheeled overhead.

At last, as if impelled by the same thought, Tomlin and Petal simultaneously said, "Riatha—"

—and the silence was broken.

Glancing at one another, Tomlin nodded to Petal.

The damman spoke: "Riatha, about these words of portent, these words affecting all—all my family—what ... ?" Her words tailed off; her unspoken question hanging in the still air of the Weiunwood night.

The grey-eyed Elfess looked into the face of each Waerling, seeing a resolute set of features before her, great jewel-like eyes glittering in the lamplight. "I come to tell ye of the words of Rael, Lady of Arden Vale, Consort to Talarin, my distant cousin, for she has the power at times to foresee.

"And she has done so.

"In truth, she has spoken of two separate destinies, both of which I would have ye hear:

"The first of her visions shows a darkness gathering in the north, and it will one day come sweeping forth across the land. There her vision ends. What it portends—War, pestilence, famine, plague—she cannot say. It will not come for some years. Even so, it is a dire enough portent that I would have ye remove to a safer haven—away from the Weiunwood, mayhap to the south, or to the protected Land of the Seven Dells.

"The second of her visions speaks of yet another destiny vaguely sensed in the distant winds of time, a destiny far beyond—a destiny Rael deems is for me, and I ween affects thee and thine, Petal ... thee and thine, Pebble."

Tomlin felt his heart hammering for the second time that day, and he felt, too, the irrational urge to gather his brood behind him, and to take up sling and silver bullets, for Petal to take up silver throwing knives, and for his buccoes and dammsels to arm themselves as well.

And an image of Baron Stoke rose monstrously in his thoughts.

"Stoke," he gritted, rage filling his breast, displacing fear.

The children looked with wide eyes at their sire, for well they knew of the pursuit of Baron Stoke. Twenty years they sought the monster, had Riatha and Urus and Tomlin and Petal. And the four companions had at last run Stoke down, some ten years past, there at the North Glacier. Aye, the children knew of the pursuit and its devastating conclusion, with Urus and Stoke plunging unto their death in the depths of an icy crevasse, a crevasse that slammed shut behind.

How could they not know? For in one way or another, all the children had been named after Urus or Riatha. And on many a long winter night in yesteryears, Tomlin or Petal had spoken of those bygone days, had told their buccoes and dammsels of the deeds of their namesakes, and of the monster they pursued.

And now their sire had named the fiend again: *"Stoke."*

"Mayhap, Pebble. Mayhap," replied Riatha, glancing at her sword, hanging in harness from a porch rail newel post.

"A destiny?" blurted out Bear, the youngest. "This Lady Rael, she foresaw a destiny affecting us? A destiny far beyond?"

Riatha turned her silvery eyes upon the stripling. "Aye, Bear, a prophecy."

Now Atha spoke: "What—what did she say, this Lady Rael?"

Riatha looked at her namesake, the Waerling no bigger than an Elfchild, though no Elfchild was she. Even so, Waerlinga resembled Elfchildren in all respects . . . but for the eyes, for those of the Wee Folk were large and jewel-like, holding deep glints carried by no child of Elvenkind.

Nevertheless, Riatha looked upon these Waerlinga and wondered if it was this resemblance between them and the children of Elvenkind that caused these Folk to be so beloved by her own kindred. For children of Elves had not set foot on Mithgar for more than four thousand years, since the Sundering during the Great War, since the last Dawn Ride, and this filled Riatha's breast with a great sadness. Here on Mithgar, no Elfchild could be conceived, none could be born; only upon Adonar was this possible for Elvenkind. And although the Twilight Ride would bear an Elf out of Mithgar and unto Adonar, the way back into this world was sundered. Hence to leave Mithgar was perhaps to leave it forever, for only at the end, in the last days, was it said that the Dawn Ride would be restored. Even then it was not certain whether the way would be open for any and all to come once more to Mithgar, or open for but a single rider, a rider of impossibility, a rider bearing the Silver Sword.

Regardless, there was now no way for any to come from Adonar unto this Plane, and so, Elfchildren were no longer seen upon Mithgar. And the Waerlinga were a poignant reminder of what had been lost.

Riatha shook her head to clear her mind of these fey thoughts as Atha spoke again, the young damman rephrasing her as-yet-to-be-answered question: "What did Lady Rael say in this prophecy of hers, Lady Riatha?"

One by one, Riatha again looked into the faces of each, faces reflecting curiosity and concern but not fear. "We were sitting in Arden on the banks of the Tumble, Rael and I, playing at scrying through crystals. Of a sudden Rael looked at me, or rather, through me, for her eyes were focused elsewhere . . . beyond. And she spoke a rede, for they come at their own time and not at will. Even so, it seemed that her words were aimed at me and none else. And this is what she said:

> "When Spring comes upon the land,
> Yet Winter grips with icy hand,
> And the Eye of the Hunter stalks night skies,
> Bane and blessing alike will rise.
> Lastborn Firstborns of those who were there,
> Stand at thy side in the light of the Bear.
> Hunter and hunted, who can say
> Which is which on a given day?"

"Ooo," whispered Silvey, glancing about, peering into the darkness beyond the lantern light as if to see what danger approached, "what do you suppose it means?"

None said aught for a while, each pondering the words of the rede. At last Small Urus, eldest bucco, sitting down upon a porch step, looked up at his sister, Little Riatha, eldest dammsel. "If, as Dad suspects, it refers to Baron Stoke, then I think it speaks of you and me, Atha, for we are the firstborn bucco and firstborn dammsel of those who were there." He pointed his chin first at his sire and then at his dam.

Fear sprang up behind Petal's eyes—not for herself, oh no, but instead for her children. She reached out to Tomlin and took his hand in hers.

But the Elfess shook her head. "Nay, Small Urus. Thy guess concerning the firstborns is a shrewd one, yet except for me, I think it speaks of no one here . . . at least, not directly."

The young buccan swept his hand in a wide gesture, taking in all the Warrows. "If not us, if not Atha and me, if not Silvey or Bear, if not my sire and dam, then who?"

The Elfess smiled down at the Waerling. "List, Small Urus, it is truly a destiny far beyond, for the Eye of the Hunter will not ride the skies above for another thousand winters— one thousand and twenty-seven winters, to be exact—"

Bear blurted out, "One thousand and twenty-seven years? Why, this is 4E1980, and that'd be in the year"—he did a quick sum in his head—"4E3007 . . . yes, 4E3007. A very long time hence. B-but here, now! None of us will even be alive then."

Petal looked at the Elfess. "Riatha will, Bear. Riatha will."

And now all the Warrow children looked at the Elfess and realized for the very first time that she was not a mortal.

Riatha shrugged off their stares. "And so will thy descendants be alive, thine Small Urus, and thine Little Riatha: the firstborns of the firstborns, or so the rede prophesies."

"This *Huntra Ëäg*," asked Tomlin, naming it in Twyll, the eld Warrow tongue, "this *Eye of the Hunter*, just what is it?"

"That I do know, Pebble," answered Riatha. "It is a harbinger, one of the hairy stars, coursing across the sky, bringing its dooms with it. Thousands of winters pass between its comings, yet always it returns, each time riding through those nights at the fading of winter, at the onset of spring; and always it first appears among the stars we name the Hunter, as the Hunter's eye, red and bloody."

Silvey's mouth had formed a silent *O* as the Elfess spoke. And she snapped it shut when Riatha fell quiet, the audible click causing all to turn and look at her, and she felt as if somehow she had made a mistake. But Atha saved her from further embarrassment, turning once more to the Elfess and asking, "The prophecy also speaks of *Lastborn Firstborns*—what does that mean?"

"And what is *the light of the Bear*?" chimed in Bear, the stripling's eyes glittering in the lantern light. "The prophecy speaks of that, too."

"And *bane and blessing*," added Silvey. "What about that?"

Tomlin cleared his throat. "Well, at least we know what the *Hunter* or *hunted* part of the rede means."

"What?" asked Bear. "What does it mean?"

"Just this, Bear," responded Tomlin. "When we sought to slay Stoke, he in turn tried to kill us, putting truth to the old saying concerning the hunting of dangerous animals, and it echoes perfectly the words of the prophecy:

> *"Deadly predator,*
> *Deadly prey,*
> *Hunter and hunted,*
> *Who can say*
> *Which is which*
> *On a given day?*

"And so shall it be once more should that monster rise again. For if he is hunted, then he in turn will hunt those who hunt him."

A silence fell over them all, broken at last by Silvey. "But who is to say that this *rede* has *anything* to do with that monster? I mean, it could concern something or someone else entirely. What is in the prophecy that points to Stoke at all?"

All eyes turned to Riatha. " 'Tis *the light of the Bear*, wee one." At the looks of incomprehension upon faces of all the Waerlinga, Riatha explained. "There where Urus fell, deep down within the ice, there is a golden glow. Why? I know not. Yet it is there, far below—an unexplained light, calling. And this I do know, Silvereyes, and so do thy parents: Urus at times took the shape of a Bear. . . ."

★   ★   ★

*May 29–31, 4E1980: Days of joy and despair, for Riatha came . . . And this is what she said . . .*

And in a glade in the Boskydells a millennium later, two dammen sat at picnic, there in the early summer Sun. And one had a secret to give the other. . . .

". . . and so it was that Riatha brought the news to my ancestors, Lacey," said Faeril, looking up from the diary.

"After the Elfess left, Tomlin and Petal moved from the Weiunwood, coming here to the Seven Dells and bringing their brood, for Riatha had warned them that a great darkness was gathering in the north, and she would have them move to a place of safety.

"They came here to have the protection of the Thornring, surrounding the Land as it does. But little did they know that the Spindlethorn would be breached during the Winter War.

"Hai! As it turned out, the Weiunwood was the safer place to be after all. Even so, they all survived—Petal, Tomlin, Small Urus, Little Riatha, Silvereyes, and Bear—though many others did not.

"The Winter War: that was what the Elfqueen Rael had seen as a great darkness gathering in the north, that was the threat which crashed upon the world back then: Modru sought to conquer the world, and he used the Dimmendark as his greatest weapon."

"Tuckerby Underbank!" exclaimed Lacey, naming the great hero of the Winter War. "He saved all." A frown came upon her face. "But what's that got to do with anything, Faeril?"

Faeril smiled at her companion. "Just this: Years past, Tomlin and Petal made a pledge to run Stoke to earth and to slay him, foul creature that he was. That pledge was renewed by Small Urus and Little Riatha, the firstborn bucco and dammsel. And they had trained in the weapon skills of their parents: sling and bullets for the buccoes and"—Faeril hefted the bandoliers—"throwing knives for the dammsels.

"Eventually Small Urus married, and so, too, did Little Riatha. And their firstborns in turn renewed the pledge and took up the weaponry skills: slings for the buccoes of Small Urus, knives for the dammsels of Little Riatha.

"Some thirty or so generations have been born since that long-ago time, and the descendants of Tomlin and Petal are scattered to the winds, moving elsewhere, marrying, having children; each generation in turn scattering farther, marrying, having children, who in turn scattered, down through time . . .

"But although firstborn damman after firstborn damman has been born, still all renewed the pledge, all were trained in the skill of throwing knives . . . just as the firstborn buccoes of firstborn buccoes were perhaps trained in the sling.

"Too, Petal had written a journal, a record of the pursuit of Stoke. It became a tradition for the firstborns to copy that record, just as I copied the one made by my dam, and she hers, and so on back to the time of Petal herself."

Again Faeril picked up the small booklet. "This is my copy, Lacey, made from the original journal, from Petal's journal, now in my dam's possession, the original that I will inherit when my own firstborn damman arrives.

"But I've known all along that I've something to accomplish before that time comes. I knew it even before I began training in the knives, even before I renewed the pledge, even before I began making my copy of the diary. It seems as if I've always known that Destiny has something in store for me."

Faeril fell silent, and in the distance a mourning dove called, and Lacey felt her heart clench with sadness. "But what's this got to do with you leaving, Faeril . . . with your going away from the Bosky?"

Faeril took up the journal and flipped it open to a particular page. "Don't you see, Lacey? Here. Petal wrote that in 4E1980 Bear ciphered that the Eye of the Hunter would come in 4E3007."

"Bu-but, that year will never come!" responded Lacey. "I mean, it's impossible! We didn't even *have* a year 4E3007. It never came. It never will. For we now stand at 5E985, and the Fourth Era is past, over, done."

Faeril smiled at Lacey's remark. "Oh, Lacey, think a moment: Bear didn't know about the Winter War when he cast that sum, for that was a calamity yet to come in his time, some thirty-eight and thirty-nine years later. I mean, the

Winter War ended the Fourth Era. And in 4E1980 Bear couldn't know the future, couldn't know that the High King would declare that Modru's defeat signalled the beginning of the Fifth Era."

Lacey looked at Faeril blankly. "So . . . ?"

"So, Lacey, there was nothing wrong with Bear's reckoning. He was right. The Eye of the Hunter was indeed due in 4E3007, and that year on the old calendar is the same as 5E988 on the new. The Eye of the Hunter is coming in 5E988—three years hence."

Lacey nodded slowly. "All right, I see that. . . . But, then, what's that got to do with you, Faeril?"

"Don't you see, Lacey, if the Eye of the Hunter will be here in three years—well, now slightly less than three years—then that means I am the lastborn of the firstborns."

Lacey shook her head in noncomprehension, and Faeril plunged on. "Look, I am not married. It's unlikely that I will bear a child, bear a dammsel of my own, bear a *firstborn* dammsel of my own, before the Eye of the Hunter rides the skies. And if I bear no dammsel, no firstborn dammsel, ere the Eye of the Hunter comes, then that means I am the last of the firstborn dammsels descending in a direct line from Petal. I am, then, the *Lastborn Firstborn*, just as foretold by the Elfqueen's prophecy, the rede of Rael.

"And I *must* leave the Bosky. You see, Lacey, I must find Riatha, to stand at her side, wherever that might be, in the light of the Bear, whatever *that* might be . . . for it is my immutable destiny to do so."

Comprehending at last, Lacey broke into tears.

The next day was Faeril's birthday, and an age-name change as well, for on this day she turned twenty; no longer would she be called a maiden, but for the next ten years would be known as a young damman. It was a day of celebration, though now and again Faeril seemed morose, and her best friend, Lacey, was occasionally found weeping.

Yet at long last the day finally came to an end. The celebrants said good night to one another, the guests departing for their homes. And finally Faeril and her family took to their beds, Faeril giving her sire and dam and her three brothers especially tender hugs.

\*     \*     \*

In the predawn hours, Faeril finished her packing. Bearing a candle, she quietly tiptoed through the wee stone cottage and out to the stables, pausing only long enough to leave a note at the kitchen table. Yet lo! at the stables she found her dam, Lorra, by lantern light saddling Faeril's pony.

"You did not think you could leave without me saying good-bye." Her mother's statement was not a question.

"M-mother!" Faeril groped for words. "B-but how did you know?"

"Oh, my dammsel, I, too, have the journal. And by your behavior yesterday—nay! not just yesterday but all the yesterdays of this year, practicing extra hours with the knives, asking your sire about living off the land, seeking knowledge of Arden Vale's whereabouts . . . well, it simply could be nothing else."

Faeril flung her arms about her mother, tears rolling down her cheeks.

"Hush, hush," her mother comforted her, though Lorra, too, now wept. "I knew, and so did you, that this day would come. And you go with my blessing."

Faeril wept all the harder.

"Shhhh, now. Weep not, child." Faeril's dam stroked her hair. "It was foretold.

"Oh, my dammsel. I *do* envy you, for did we not, each of us, every firstborn dammsel, renew the pledge? Did we not all train at knives? Did we not all *dream?* Did not each of us wish that she would be the one?

"Even so, pledges and training and dreams and desires notwithstanding, Fortune chooses its own way of fulfilling prophecies.

"Ponder this: had every firstborn dammsel been birthed but a year later each, down through the generations, all thirty of them, then *I* would be setting forth upon this venture rather than you. Then *I* would be the dammsel living out the dream.

"But Fate dictated otherwise, and even though I love you with all my heart, I envy you, for you are the Lastborn Firstborn chosen to fulfill this destiny, and not me.

"Still, I am proud, for you are *my* firstborn, and Fate could not have chosen better.

"But there is this that you should know, too, my dammsel: the prophecy says *Lastborn Firstborns.* Did you hear? *Firstborns* . . . and that means more than one."

Faeril's weeping lessened, then stopped as the import of her dam's words struck home. Sniffing, wiping her nose with the back of her hand, she stepped back and looked at Lorra. "More than one?"

Lorra smiled wanly, blinking away her own tears. "Aye. More than one. *Lastborn Firstborns* means more than one."

Faeril's eyes widened, and a look of disbelief, mingled with gladness, crept upon her features. "Mother, does that mean you get to come, too? Does that mean you get to fulfill your dream?"

"No, child. Would that it did, yet it is not to be, for I am not a Lastborn Firstborn, as are you."

Faeril's face fell. "But then—"

"There can only be two Lastborn Firstborns, my dammsel," interjected Lorra, "male and female—bucco and dammsel."

In a gesture of remembrance the young damman touched her temple, her dam's words reminding her what she already knew. "Yes, Mother, I momentarily forgot." Then she frowned. "But, the bucco—I don't know—"

Lorra gently grasped her child by the shoulders, looking at her intently. "Now heed me: Somewhere in the Weiunwood lives a young buccan named Gwylly Fenn, or so I was told by letter some twenty or twenty-five years back, when he was birthed. Lineal descendant of the firstborn buccoes back unto Small Urus and Tomlin, just as we reach back unto Little Riatha and Petal.

"Oh, by now, after all these years, after all these generations, our kinship has stretched so thin as to be no kinship at all. You could not even call him a cousin.

"Yet I deem that he is the one you must find and take with you to Arden Vale."

Faeril returned her dam's gaze in the amber light of the lantern. "But, Mother, if the prophecy says that the Firstborns will be at Riatha's side, then won't he find his own way to Arden Vale?"

Lorra genuinely smiled now. "Pish tush, child, even prophecies need help now and again."

Faeril laughed aloud, and Lorra joined her.

Together they finished saddling Blacktail, the pony looking askance over its shoulder at the giggling dammen. Faeril tied her bedroll and knapsack behind the saddle . . . and suddenly it was time to go.

Once again the dammen embraced, and this time they kissed, and then Faeril mounted up and rode away.

Behind, a mother wept and watched her daughter leave; she stood silently, not calling out, for she had always known that this day would come, and she did not protest.

And as the sky brightened, shading from grey to pink, and the ground mist swirled among the trees, Faeril rode onward, into the dawn, heading east, heading into destiny.

# CHAPTER 4

# *Gwylly*

**Mid Summer, 5E985**

*[Three Years Past]*

**W**hrrr ...! sounded the wings of the woodcock, veering among the trees. *Zzzzz* ... The sling bullet sissed through the air, missing the bird altogether.

"Bother!" cried Gwylly, vexed. "How could I have missed?" The question was purely rhetorical, for no one was there to answer it—none, that is, but Gwylly himself and his foster father's dog, Black, now slumped dejectedly before him.

The Warrow looked at the ebony dog. "How could I have missed, Black?"

Black's tail thumped against the ground a time or two, though his sad eyes looked accusingly up at the wee buccan, as if to say, *You missed!*

"I know, boyo. You were all set to retrieve this one, too. But, well, even *I* miss now and again. I'm not infallible, you know."

Black's eyes did not lose their sadness, nor their accusatory stare.

"Well, it wasn't by much, Black." Gwylly held up a thumb and forefinger, an inch or so apart. "This close, boyo. This close."

Black looked away, elsewhere, peering into the great forest surrounding them.

"All right. All right. I'm sorry! I didn't mean to miss. Besides, we'll go for another."

Gwylly bent down and caught up a string of three woodcocks. Holding them out before the dog, he shook them to get Black's attention. "See, dog, we *have* had *some* luck today."

Black snorted.

"What?" asked the buccan. "Oh, not *luck*, you say. Instead it was your skill at sniffing them out?"

Black's tail began to wag, and Gwylly smiled. "Perhaps you are right, boyo. Perhaps you are absolutely right."

Black stood and looked expectantly at Gwylly.

"Go, Black. Find bird."

With a joyful bound the black dog ranged ahead among the trees, nose alternately to the ground and then held high, sniffing the air.

Through the shaggy Weiunwood went buccan and dog, past hoary trees, great-girthed and ancient, standing silently, their leaves faintly stirring in the summer morn. Down mossy banks and across crystal rills and up the far sides ranged the pair, Black splashing through the clear water, not stopping to drink, Gwylly leaping from stone to stone after. Through stands of ferns they brushed, the green fronds *swish-swashing* at their passage. And the yellow Sun shone down through the interlaced branches above, filling the high green galleries with soft shadows pierced by golden shafts.

Suddenly Black veered, shying from a wall of dark oak trees marching off to left and right to disappear beyond seeing in the depths of the forest. As the dog ran wide of the ebon marge, steering clear, Gwylly followed, also giving wide berth to the ancient trees, though he peered into the murky interior, his sight sifting among the shadows, trying to see . . . what? He did not know.

This was one of the dark places, a hidden place, a place closed to ordinary folk. A place where no one went. A place spoken of in rumor and whisper.

Too, there were tales of strange beings within these forbidding places, shadowy figures half seen, some gigantic and shambling, others small and quick. Some were said to be shining figures of light, while others were of the dark itself.

Too, it was told that some of the dwellers within were made of the very earth, while others were beings seemingly akin to the trees and plants and greenery.

But no matter their nature, they didn't abide strangers.

Gwylly had heard the tales, tales of those who disappeared in the interior of such places, of those who had sworn to stride through such, entering but never emerging.

Gwylly had heard other tales, too. Tales of aid given to those in need.

It was said that once all of the Weiunwood was dark. Closed. But when the Warrows came, pursued as they were, flying before an implacable foe, the 'Wood let them enter. Let them take refuge. Let them hide.

And afterward, when the foe had been defeated, the 'Wood gave them the glens and glades, and parts of the treeland as well, though it kept much of the forest unto itself, closed.

The Warrows had then settled in communities within—communities called Glades. And here groups of Warrows had lived ever since, unmolested by and large. Now and again some foe would try to conquer them, such as had Modru a millennium past, during the Winter War, though he had failed.

Sheltered by the ancient forest, the Weiunwood Warrows roamed free, though even they did not enter the closed places, with its Fox Riders and Living Mounds and Angry Trees and Groaning Stones and all the other creatures of lore and legend said to dwell within.

And as Black and Gwylly ran alongside the great margin of one of these vast, dark places, Gwylly's eyes darted hither and yon, seeking to see . . . to see—

Suddenly before them a roebuck broke from cover, crashing off through the ferns. Black leapt upward, sighting the fleeing deer, the dog yelping in excitement yet not running after, waiting the command from Gwylly.

"Down, Black!" called Gwylly, his heart pounding in startlement.

Black looked at the Warrow as if in disbelief. *Not chase?*

"Not today, dog. Today we hunt bird." Gwylly felt his pulse slowing. In the distance the sounds of the red buck faded . . . faded . . . then were gone, and Gwylly wondered which of the three of them—Warrow, dog, or deer—had been the most startled.

"Bird, Black. Find bird."

Somewhat disgruntled, Black cast one last accusing look at Gwylly, then again took up ranging back and forth, searching for bird scent. And through the woods went Warrow and dog, all thought of strange forest dwellers now gone from the buccan's mind, for although Gwylly knew of these legends, of this lore, he was not part of the Weiunwood Warrows, having been raised otherwise, elsewhere, on the fringes. And so, Gwylly and Black searched woodland, hunting birds, leaving the legends for others to dwell upon.

A quarter hour passed this way, Black veering back and forth, Gwylly cutting through the dog's pattern in a more or less straight line. Then Black stopped, his tail straight out, his muzzle fixed and pointing. Sliding to a halt behind the quivering dog, Gwylly loaded his sling. "All right, Black," he whispered. "Flush."

Slowly Black crept forward, Gwylly edging softly behind, sling in hand, his eyes fixed on the place where the dog's muzzle pointed.

*Whrrr* ... Woodcock wings hammered through the air. Gwylly whipped his arm about and loosed a sling strap, the bullet flying to strike the bird, the slain woodcock tumbling down through the air and to the ground.

"Black, fetch!"

The dog bounded forward, disappearing through the ferny growth to reappear moments later with the bird in his mouth.

Gwylly knelt and took the game, and ruffled Black's fur, scratching the dog behind the ears. "Ah, Black, my good comrade, you are undoubtedly the greatest bird finder and fetcher in all of the Weiunwood. Hai! In all of Mithgar!"

Gwylly looped a slipknot into the cord, preparing to tie the woodcock with the other three. "It is your nose and my sling which makes this team so very successful. You and I, Black, we are mighty hunters. And let no one deny it."

Black sat before Gwylly, his tail thumping the ground, his brown eyes fixed upon the buccan, not knowing precisely what was being said but knowing that whatever it was, it was good. And Black was ecstatic with joy.

"Let's go, boyo," said Gwylly, woodcocks corded, slinging all across his shoulder, "time for home. Time to show Mom and Dad what we've downed for supper."

Understanding the word *home*, Black set off to the east, heading for the fringe of the Weiunwood itself, for home lay some two or three miles away on the marge of a sloping plain. The plains themselves led up into the Signal Mountains, an ancient range, timeworn by wind and rain, now no more than high tors, no more than the spines and ribs of former giants, curving in a long easterly arc from Challerain Keep in the far north to Beacontor and the Dellin Downs in the south.

Toward this ridge fared Gwylly and Black, though the forest blocked out any sight of the crags and round tops and stone rises and grassy slopes of the highland ahead.

As they wended their way among the now thinning trees, the Sun rode upward in the sky, the noontide swiftly approaching, the light and warmth of summer filling the woodland. Still they passed among hoary giants, the massive, moss-laden trunks somehow protective in their silence. Past fallen timber and hollow logs fared the two, Black stopping to sniff out scents now and again, then running to catch up to Gwylly, circling about, pausing long enough for a pat before trotting on.

At last they broke from the woods and there before them rose the fertile upland, where stood the homestead of Orith and Nelda. In the distance Gwylly could see the farmhouse, smoke rising lazily from the chimney and up into the blue sky above.

They scrambled down a creek embankment and splashed across, clambering up the opposite side to come to the grassland sloping upward. Then Black took off running, racing up the long slope, the wind in his whiskers, Gwylly running behind.

Black of course was first home, racing joyously about the yard, yelping in victory, as Gwylly, laughing, ran beyond him and to the porch.

Banging in through the door, "I'm home!" called Gwylly, unnecessarily, both he and Black making for the kitchen, whence came the smell of baking. Entering the cookery, the Warrow unslung the birds from his shoulder and cast them upward to the tabletop. And turning toward him from the woodstove, his foster mother, Nelda, greeted him with a smile, the Human female pleased to see her wee buccan son.

\* \* \*

After taking a drink from the dipper, Gwylly poured some water into a bowl for Black. "Where's Dad?" asked Gwylly, panting, the dog lapping water and panting too.

"In the field," answered Nelda. "His lunch is nearly ready."

"I've got to dress these birds first," said Gwylly, "but then I could take his meal to him."

Nelda smiled and nodded, and Gwylly caught up the birds and stepped outside, Black following.

The Woman watched him go, her heart content. Nelda turned once more to the woodstove and began stirring the contents of a pot, her thoughts elsewhere.

Gwylly was her joy, for he had come to her some twenty-two years past, in a dark hour of despair, after she had miscarried for the third and, as it turned out, final time. She had been alone the night she had lost the baby, for Orith had gone to Stonehill nearly two weeks past to trade grain and beets and onions for needed supplies.

The next day, weeping, shovel in hand, she had patted down the last of the earthen mound marking the tiny new grave—there by the other two now grown over with wildflowers and grass—when she heard Orith's hail and had turned to see the mules and waggon drawing nigh.

But wonder of wonders, Orith had had with him a wounded Warrow child, a tiny thing, three or four years old, no more, an ugly gash across his head. Feverish had been the babe, and calling out for his dam, for his sire. Nelda had taken up the wee one, bearing him inside. His parents had been slain, Orith told her, Rūck raid or the like. Killed them down on the Crossland Road 'tween Beacontor and Stonehill, looting their campsite, stripping their bodies, stealing their ponies. The wee one had been left for dead amid the wreckage where Orith found him.

Orith had cleaned the dark grume from the wound and treated it with a poultice of summer julemint, perhaps saving the babe's life, for Orith suspected that the blade which had made the cut had been poisoned. Then Orith had made straight for home, driving the mules throughout the remainder of the day and that night as well, arriving the following morn.

Nelda had replaced the poultice with another, tending the youngling day after day, sleeping at his bedside. And when the wee one's mind had cleared and he could talk, in his tiny, piping voice he had told them of the bad ones who had come in the night and had killed his sire and dam. He did know his given name, Gwylly, but not his last. Too, he knew not the names of his parents, calling them only Mother and Father.

A week or so later, when Orith returned to the wreckage of the campsite to bury the slain, he had found among the pitifully few salvageable things a sling and pouch of slingstones, and two diaries . . . or journals: one old, one new. Leaving two graves behind, Orith had returned to his stead, bearing all that remained of the memory of Gwylly's parents. The youngling yet abed had claimed the sling and stones, saying that they had belonged to his sire. Then he asked where the "shiny" ones were. What this implied neither Orith nor Nelda could fathom, and Gwylly could not tell them what he meant. And the journals had been of no help, for neither Man nor Woman could read aught of the language scribed therein—though after close inspection Orith declared that the new one appeared to be a copy of the old.

And when baby Gwylly was on his feet again, healthy once more, neither childless Orith nor barren Nelda could give him up. . . .

Twilight had come unto the steading, Gwylly, Nelda, and Orith having just finished their supper, Black asleep in the corner. Windows were open, and the trilling and croaking of the creek frogs drifted in through the still night air. Orith was speaking of shoeing the mules the next day.

Of a sudden Black lifted up his head, his ears cocking this way and that. Then he stood and trotted to the front window, rising up on his hind legs, his forepaws upon the sill. His tail began wagging, and he dropped back to the floor, his claws clicking as he went to the door.

Jumping down from his chair, Gwylly, too, stepped to the door, just as a soft knock sounded, and Black gave out with a short yip.

Gwylly raised the latch and opened the door and found

himself peering straight into the most beautiful golden eyes he'd ever seen.

The eyes of one of his own Kind.

The eyes of a damman.

She smiled. "Gwylly? Gwylly Fenn?"

Gwylly's mouth dropped open, and he could do nought but stutter.

The damman looked at this tongue-tied young buccan stammering before her, and at the two Humans behind. "Oh, I do hope you are Gwylly, the one I seek, for I've had a troublesome time finding you.

"I am Faeril Twiggins, and I've come about the prophecy."

# CHAPTER 5

# Glacier

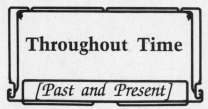

**Throughout Time**

*[Past and Present]*

In the beginning, after Adon made the stars and scattered them across the heavens above, He created the Sun and the world and the bright wanderers and set them on their ceaseless courses throughout the skies.

Although He had made the Moon, He kept it somewhere hidden, not yet having placed it along its endless path.

Perhaps the world was not then ready for light from the silver orb . . .

. . . for when the world first was made, it was harsh and molten and without life, and it heaved and churned and bubbled as if trapped in a vast cauldron of Hèl. Violent blasts of fire exploded outward, sending gigantic gouts of melt fluming up and away, as if the very matter itself were attempting to flee, to escape; yet it could not, and it fell back into the fiery wrath below to be lost in the elemental fury.

And in those days the heavens themselves seemed bent upon the destruction of the world, for immense primordial rocks of iron and stone and ice hurtled out from the frigid blackness between the stars to smash into the bubbling, boiling, molten earth, spewing melted stone and metal and matter across the heaving face of the world.

Yet the earth endured.

Aeons passed, and aeons more, and slowly, oh so slowly, the world began to cool. Down and down fell the heat and fire. Down and down.

Aeons passed and aeons more. And still the world cooled, though now and then the heavens would again hurl great missiles to smash into the earth. But still it endured . . .

And cooled. A crust formed, like slag upon molten metal. The world cooled even more . . .

And endured.

Then it began to rain. Aeons passed . . . And still it rained. Slowly the oceans filled, covering the crust, until at last in only one place was there land. A vast continent. And though it rained still, the ocean which covered all the rest of the world grew no deeper.

The continent was flat and featureless for the most part.

And then Adon sent the Moon to join the Sun in the sky.

From far off it came, the Moon, plummeting toward the earth as if it would smash into the world, just as the heaven-sent stones had done. Yet Adon had other plans in mind, and the Moon did not crash into the world, though how it missed is a wonder.

The Moon above hurled past, so large that it seemed to fill the whole of the sky. Titanic upheavals rent the crustal matter, and fire and molten rock poured forth. And the land itself broke apart, as if a mighty hammer had struck the great continent, shattering it into many pieces . . . thirty-one in all.

And great tides rose up from the oceans and rolled over the land, flooding all.

Out swept the Moon, and then back again, a silver fury causing great upheaval and calamity when it passed near.

And the thirty-one continents riding upon enormous crustal plates slid across the fiery molten core of the earth, crashing into one another, joining, fragmenting, ripping apart, melding together, raising great chains of mountains, rending open vast abysses. Volcanoes spewed out lava; rifts formed and molten stone wrenched up from the guts of the world; continents sank below others; oceans boiled and their floors hove up above the waters, forming new land.

Aeons passed . . .

And in this time the Moon fled and attacked, fled and attacked, over and again. And with each pass it rendered great destruction upon the face of the world. Yet with each pass it did not flee as far, nor did it draw as near, as if it were beginning to know the world, as if it were attempting to find a place neither too close nor distant from which to continue its dance; and with each pass its fury lessened.

Finally the Moon gentled, though on the world the fractured crusts and riven continents yet drifted upon the melt deep below, colliding, rifting, driving beneath, heaving up, creating volcanoes, raising mountains, shifting the oceans.

As the continents merged and separated, at times there were many of them, at other times few. Occasionally there was just one. But always the one fragmented into more, as the fractured crust and driving fire below shifted and churned, and the land masses hove across the face and through the gut of the world.

Aeons passed, yet over vast epochs of time, as if impelled by some hidden celestial giant, missiles of stone and metal and ice would hurtle out from the dark between the stars, some to strike the silent Moon, others to hammer upon the world. For millennia, down they would thunder, great and small, riding upon golden fiery tails; but then, as if a tide had passed, the skies above would grow quiet once more, remaining so for age upon age, until the next wave rolled.

More time passed while the earth cooled.

There came a day that snow fell, though it melted readily on what was then a torrid world. Still, it was the first snowfall.

And as the stars wheeled throughout the aeons, and the Sun and Moon and bright wanderers traced endless journeys above, still the earth cooled.

And more snow fell, far in the north at first, or perhaps in the extreme south.

Slowly life came into being. From the simple to the complex it progressed, the forces driving it causing living plants and creatures to become more and more intricate, more capable.

But even before and after life came into being, the earth continued to cool.

The continents continued to drift, and the world itself at times grew colder and then warmer, as if slowly shifting farther from the Sun, then nearer, or perhaps it was the Sun shifting and drifting with respect to the world ... who can say? Mayhap instead the Sun's heat slowly waxes and wanes, just as does the light from the Moon, though on an epochal scale rather than monthly. Regardless, weather patterns changed, for the elements depend upon the warmth of the Sun and the set of the lands to shape the world's winds and its ocean streams, the engines driving the clime.

And winter came. Snow fell. Continents drifted. The earth and Sun perhaps wandered apart—or the Sun waned—for the golden orb did not warm the land as it once had, and more snow fell. The world grew colder, more frigid. Oceans diminished as water became locked up in snow and ice. Slowly vast glaciers formed, towering, grinding across the land, until ice covered much of the world.

Weather became harsh and capricious. No longer did there seem to be seasons, or if there were, they existed at one and the same time: Spring, Summer, Winter, Fall ... each depended upon which way the wind blew—from the ice, toward the ice, or along its rim. And it was bitterly cold much of the time. Only in that part of the world where the Sun stood directly overhead did life thrive, though not well; elsewhere it grimly hung on at best, tenuous in its existence.

But then, as if the Sun waxed, or as if the world and the Sun gradually drew closer together, the ice retreated, melting slowly, until once again the oceans filled and the world grew green even in the north, even in the south.

And still the continents drifted, and still did the drift and the wander affect wind and wave, and still it seemed as if the Sun waxed and waned or the world and Sun wandered, close in some epochs, distant in others, for again the ice advanced ... and retreated ... and advanced ... and retreated ...

Many times the great glaciers formed, grinding down from north and up from south, plowing through stone and soil unto bedrock itself, forming moraines and horns and cirques and grooves and kames and domes, scraping out *U*-shaped valleys and carving knife-edge ridges, shifting great stones for hundreds of miles, the ice covering the face of the land.

Yet always they retreated, did the glaciers, leaving behind the evidence of their passage, the striae and shieldrock and vast boulders strangely perched, as well as other scars upon the land.

The last great ice age had loosed its frigid grip from Mithgar some twenty or so millennia past. Even so, far to the north and far to the south, vast stretches of snow and ice cover the land a mile or more deep. Seldom do these great caps of ice melt away. Even over the long aeons, when the continents themselves shift utterly away from the north and from the south, still the ice caps remain . . . remnant of what once was, reminder of what is to come.

Yet here and there in other realms of Mithgar, the bones of that age remain as well: in the arc of the Gronfang Mountains and in the Grey Mountains of Xian as well as on the Utan Plateau, and in the northern Rigga Mountains, and the Chulu Mountains on the southern continent—these places and more yet hold reminders of the last age of ice.

In the great chain of the Grimwall Mountains, there on its northern slope, is perhaps the mightiest reminder of all, save for the polar caps themselves. It is the Great North Glacier, flowing down from the interior of that grim range. Miles and miles of ice, locked forever in a vast frozen river. Even though frozen, still it flows, does the main body— slowly to be sure, but flowing still . . . inches a day, perhaps feet, no more, coming at last to the high north wall, where it crashes asunder on the plains far below, massive chunks calving away from the face of the glacier, to tumble down.

In the summer, at the height of the warmth, the fallen ice melts, and a glacially cold stream, a broad, shallow river, feeds the land with water, white and grey, laden with powdered stone, silt, ground from the Grimwall itself.

Too, in summer, water flows down from the surface of the ice above, seeking to forever diminish the glacier, though not succeeding. Oh, should the summer stay, then the glacier might eventually dissolve, might melt after ages have passed. But the seasons always shift, and always winter returns, bearing its burden of snow.

And along the north wall of the Grimwall Mountains, throughout winter, storm after storm rages forth from the

Boreal Sea, and during this time the snow falls as if it will never end, down on the glacier, for the glacier lies upon the prevailing storm track.

Layer after layer it accumulates, does the snow, ton upon ton, packing into ice, some white and pearlescent, some clear as frozen crystal. The weight of the mass itself causes the glacier to flow, inching along at varying speeds, depending upon the slope of the land below, and upon the mass pressing behind. And the Great North Glacier is massive, and the slope steep, and so the main body flows at an astonishing rate—for a glacier, that is. Yet here and there are immense reservoirs of frozen ice eternally trapped, for they exist at dead ends, or are slow, spinning, grinding, solid eddy currents forever caught in the grasp of mountains cupped to either side.

The flow causes deep rifts to form within the ice, narrow crevasses, opening and closing as the ice accelerates and retards, like gaping maws, opening to accept whatever falls in, closing behind, crunching, splitting, cracking, crushing.

So it has been throughout time, since winter began, since drifting continents crashed one upon the other and mountains were formed, since the birth of the Grimwalls.

So it has been until lately, that is, as glacial time flows, for something has disturbed this mass of ice, this mighty glacier: Some three and a half millennia past—a flick of time in glacial terms—a Dragon was slain in the Grimwall Mountains. 'Twas Black Kalgalath, and his destruction had caused a great upheaval in the earth. Violent shudders wracked the world, the earth trembling and quaking. And this, even the Great North Glacier felt. Mighty cracks and crevasses formed, the ice rending and splitting, the whole of it sliding forward at a rate never before experienced by the mass. Huge chunks were rent from the face, falling to the plains below, there at its terminus. Still, in time the shudders quelled, though they have not yet stopped completely, nor will they; for the very continent had been faulted, there in the Grimwall, and the drifting of the land itself yet causes the plates to grind one against the other, the resulting slips and jerks manifesting themselves as a quaking in this unstable place.

And even the Great North Glacier is affected by this rattling and racking of the land, the consequences of a Dragon's death.

Even so, the wind blows and winter comes and storms hammer forth from the Boreal Sea, snow falling upon the glacier, replenishing it, building it back unto what it once was, what it yet is, and what it will continue to be: the bones of an ice age, waiting for the resurrection to come.

# CHAPTER 6

# Grimwall

**Late Winter, 5E988**

*[The Present]*

It was yet dark when Riatha and Aravan awakened the others. But dawn came late to Mithgar in these northern climes at this time of year. Even so, Faeril felt as if she had not gotten enough sleep. Gwylly, too, seemed sluggish, groaning awake in the frigid night.

When they stepped outside to relieve themselves, both Warrows noted that low in the west the Eye of the Hunter yet rode the sky.

"Adon!" exclaimed the buccan, "makes shivers run up and down, eh?"

Faeril did not reply, her grim silence speaking volumes as she trudged through the starlit snow, her boots scrutching in the frigid white.

When the Warrows returned, the odor of freshly brewed tea was redolent on the air, mingled with the pungent smoke of burning *ren* droppings. They hurriedly ate a cold breakfast of jerky and crue, warmed by hot tea. And during the meal Riatha paced back and forth, anxious to be gone. Now and again she stepped from the ruins and peered southward through the fading starlight, toward the dark bulk of the distant Grimwall Mountains.

As they had done the previous night, the sledmasters

melted snow for water for the dogs; they used copper pans and poured the melt into the many waterskins each team carried. As B'arr had explained, "Dog no drink enough. Sledmaster make dog drink. Then have enough *makt*, enough *strength* and *lasting*, to go long. Eat snow, bad. Eat snow, steal *makt*. Eat snow, dog get cold inside. Dog need more food get warm again. More food get *makt* back. But food sometime . . . sometime little, sometime not much when hunting poor, when fishing poor, or when go long way but not carry many food. We give water. Drink water, good. Dog stay warm inside when drink water, not get cold from eating snow, not waste food to get back *makt*."

Even as snow was being melted, the sledmasters made several trips to the dogs, forcing them to drink, returning to fill more waterskins with fresh liquid, aided in this task by the Warrows.

Meanwhile, Aravan and Riatha busied themselves breaking camp, rolling up tightly the down-filled sleeping bags, packing away the supplies and utensils, bundling all.

With the dogs watered, the *Mygga* and *Fé* laded the sleds, while B'arr and Tchuka and Ruluk began hitching the teams to the tow line: the great power dogs in back, closest to the sleds, where their strength would best serve, the lighter and faster dogs fastened farther up the line, the swiftest in front, each team arranged as B'arr had said: "*Makt* in back, *hast* in front."

Last to be hitched were the lead dogs—Shlee, Laska, and Garr—each sledmaster parading the dominant dog the length of the *span*.

At a nod from B'arr, Gwylly and Faeril settled into the sled basket and covered themselves with the warm furs. The sledmaster glanced back, seeing that the others were ready, too.

"*Hypp!*" he barked, and the team surged, dogs leaping against their tug lines, lunging to get the sled in motion. Slowly it started, and then picked up speed, gliding across the frozen waste. Behind, Gwylly could hear the other sledmasters calling out "*Hypp!*" to their own teams.

And out into the vast wilderness they fared, the dogs trotting eagerly through the glancing light of the low-hung Moon, while stars yet shone dimly in the paling skies above and the Eye of the Hunter dipped beyond seeing over the rim of the world.

An hour they ran, the sledmasters calling out now and again *strak* or *venstre* or *høyre* to keep the team running straight or to swing left or right, and at last the Sun rose low in the southeast, riding a shallow angle up into the sky. Before them the Grimwall Mountains loomed in silhouette, dark and foreboding, black and grey stone rearing upward, snow-covered for the most. Faeril and Gwylly looked at each other, while their hearts pounded a desperate tattoo.

"Fear not, love," said Gwylly, his voice filled with a bravado that he did not feel. "Once we know it, this Grimwall, it'll not be so sinister."

Faeril turned about and faced the mountains once more, examining them, trying to see them for what they were, trying to gain knowledge and thereby master her fear.

Onward ran the dogs, slowly drawing closer to this place of danger, where Spawn were said to dwell.

In mid-morn they stopped to stretch their legs and rest the dogs, giving each animal more water. Too, they cared for other needs, relieving themselves as necessary. Shortly, however, they set off once more, running through cold sunlight, long shadows trailing behind.

And this was their pattern throughout the frigid day: the dogs trotting at a goodly clip, hauling sleds and passengers across the whiteness for an hour or two, then resting for long, airy minutes, while the sledmasters gave the team more water.

At one of the stops they took a meal of jerky and crue, but they did not stay longer than necessary, getting underway as soon as they could.

And all the while, the Grimwall loomed closer, rearing up into the sky.

They stopped at last in the shadow of the range, cast northeastward beyond seeing by the setting Sun, for B'arr would not run the dogs in the darkness, that time between the coming of the night and the rising of the Moon.

This time they camped in a small swale, a shallow hollow

providing scant shelter from the chill air breathing down from the Grimwall. This night the dogs did not get a ration of salmon, for they were fed only every other day.

It was a cold camp and dark, but for the moonlight and starshine, there being nothing spare with which to make a fire. Oh, they had brought *ren møkk* with them, but it would be used to melt water on the morn, water for dog and Man and Elf and Warrow alike.

And once again the Eye of the Hunter rode the darktide up into the sky, its long glowing tail streaming out behind, while now and again the land below shuddered and shivered and quaked.

Once more the predawn hours found Gwylly and Faeril lugging waterskins out to the sledmasters. Sensing the Warrows coming, eagerly the dogs got up from the burrows they had twisted in the snow and shook ice crystals from their fur, a fur so efficient that no heat escaped to melt the beds they slept in.

After a cold breakfast, again the teams began their trek toward the Grimwall, now so close that Faeril felt as if she could reach out and touch the dark mass.

*"Strak! Strak!"* called the sledmasters, and the dogs hewed straightly to the course, Gwylly and Faeril, Riatha and Aravan, borne onward, across a snow gone silver grey in the low, glancing light of the Moon. Through the platinum beams they glided, and finally the late dawn lightened the skies. At last the Sun rose, though still they could not see it, travelling as they were in the shadow of the range.

On toward the mountains they ran, straight toward the rearing walls of rock and snow, occasionally the earth shuddering beneath them, quaking in the early day. High above now loomed the Grimwall, and it seemed as if the sledmasters were aiming to drive straight into the walls of granite. But at last, at the very foot of the towering face of sheer stone, they came to a wide river, flat, frozen, the wind-scoured ice dark, grey, its surface raddled with cracks.

*"Venstre!"* called the sledmasters, and leftward they turned along this course, running atop the grey ice and alongside the massive flank, black with shadow.

An hour or so they ran, but of a sudden, *"Stanna!"* cried B'arr, stepping down on the footboard mounted between the runners at the back, the dragbrake cleats pressing into the ice, digging in, the sled gradually sliding to a halt as the dogs slowed to a trot and then to a walk and then stopped altogether, peering back and about.

"What is it, B'arr?" asked Faeril, throwing off furs, struggling to get up and out.

Tchuka and Ruluk brought their own sleds to a stop alongside, yet some distance away, maintaining a space between each of the teams, avoiding the risk of a mêlée for dominance between *spans*.

Winning free of the sled basket, Faeril stood and repeated her question. "What is it, B'arr? What's wrong?"

The sledmaster pointed at the ice, and where he pointed, a small spot was pink. "Blood."

*"Blöd!"* he called out to Tchuka and Ruluk. *"Sørge for din spans!"*

B'arr turned to Faeril, Gwylly now at her side. "I tell them to look at dogs. Ice cut feet."

The sledmaster began examining each dog in turn until he found two with pads slashed, cut by the sharp-edged cracks in the ice. He walked back to the sled and took up a bag, inside of which were—"Booties!" cried Faeril, laughing in spite of her concern when she saw what B'arr was doing. "Dog booties."

*"Renhud,"* grunted B'arr, smiling up at Faeril. He slipped the deerskin booties onto the feet of each patiently standing dog and pulled the drawstrings firm, tying them in place. "Protect from cut. Dogs no like, but wear while run."

Faeril squatted beside B'arr. The damman ruffled the fur of the dog, Kano, fending off its licks. "But you will bandage them up when we stop for the night, won't you?"

B'arr pulled another bootie onto the waiting dog's left hind foot. "No, *Mygga*. Dog no like. Bite bandage off. Lick cut, like lick *Mygga* face. Lick clean. Make well."

Then B'arr laughed as Kano took another lap at Faeril and again the damman fended him off. "Let Kano lick your face, little one; if you sick, he not make you well, but he make you feel better." Again B'arr laughed, and Faeril smiled.

Off to the side, Gwylly stooped and examined one of the cracks jagging through the frozen river. In that moment the ground shuddered, and then he knew what caused the riven ice. "Sharp," he exclaimed, drawing his thumb along the edge. "But I say, B'arr, why is the ice so grey? I mean, it looks as if it's frozen milk—milk gone bad with dirt, that is."

B'arr glanced over at the wee one and grinned. "You see good with *Mygga* eyes. It *jokel melk*—glacier milk, in tongue you speak."

As he tied the last bootie on Kano, the dog now licking at the sledmaster's face, B'arr pointed eastward with his chin in the direction they were travelling. "Great *jokel* ahead. Ice fall down from above. Ice cloudy. Full of *jokel melk*. Melt in summer. Make river. River run dark. Things grow good in *jokel* water, in *jokel melk*.

"But river get hard in winter. Land shake. River crack. River break. Make knife edge all over. Cut dog feet. What she-*Mygga* name bootie we call *sokk*. Keep dog feet from cut on ice."

Strolling over to the Warrows, Aravan arrived in time to hear B'arr's words. "Glacier milk," he murmured. "Silt-laden water. A river full of powdered stone, ground from the Grimwall itself by the ponderous ice of the Great North Glacier. And the land that drinks from this chill stream becomes rich soil. Plants and flowers and green growing grass burst forth from the bordering earth and reach up for the Sun in the long summer days."

Gwylly looked again at the grey ice, and then at the snow-laden riverbank, barren in winter, and finally at the Grimwall looming above, and he wondered how something as foreboding as this dark, ominous range could engender fertility in an ice-cold waste.

The sledmasters soon had their teams ready to travel again, *ren*-hide booties on all the dogs, and once more they set out eastward, wending along the base of the towering Grimwall range.

On they ran, following the curve of the glacier river, frozen in late winter's grasp. And as they rounded a bend, Faeril gasped, for in the distance she saw great tumbled-down blocks of shattered ice piled in a gargantuan jumble, ramping in a massive heap upward, lying against an ice-clad wall of black granite. And high above, two thousand or so feet up the sheer stone, the frozen wall of the Great North Glacier loomed white and deadly, two or three miles wide or more, and massive, an enormous frozen river, itself hundreds of feet high, poised to cascade downward.

Even as they looked, a huge section of the overhang broke away, the mass of ice falling silently for what seemed an eternity, to smash into the miles-wide ramp below. And seconds later there came a rending, a riving, a splitting *krrack!* the sound of the ice calving away just then reaching their ears, followed eventually by a thunderous *whoom!* of the mass whelming down.

And still the face of the glacier loomed above, seemingly undiminished by the gigantic fall.

Outward swung B'arr, driving the dogs on a course that would safely take them past this deadly place, Tchuka and Ruluk coming after.

An hour or so they travelled along this arc, and finally the glacier and ice fall stood off to their right. Yet onward they ran for another hour, skirting out beyond the danger to come to a broad gorge a mile or two beyond the far edge.

Again the earth trembled, and afterward came the echoes of ice rending and shattering in the distance behind.

*"Høyre! Høyre!"* called B'arr, and the dogs swung to the right in response, entering the mouth of the wide, shadowed defile.

Before them, Gwylly and Faeril could see a sheer-walled canyon twisting up into the interior of the Grimwall, its end beyond seeing, somewhere past a wrenching curve. A mile or more apart stood vertical bluffs to either side, their tops some two or three thousand feet above, crevices and crags and ledges marring the perpendicular stone. Snow and ice clad the walls, where it could gain a foothold. Scrub pine grew there as well, twisted and gnarled by the wind. Frozen snow lay on the rising ravine floor—how thick, the Warrows could not say.

Into this slot B'arr drove the dogs, aiming for a place known to Riatha and told to B'arr, a place where they could safely make their way up and to the glacier, to come to "the light of the Bear," or so she deemed.

"*Strak! Strak!*" called B'arr, now telling Shlee to follow the course, the command echoed by the following sledmasters as into the canyon they ran.

Up a gradual slope they fared, coming to the distant turn, only to find another turn before them. And another after, and more, as they wrenched and twisted deeper into the mountains.

The daytide ebbed, and shadows clustered thickly in the sheer-walled slot. And the farther they ran, the slower went the teams, despite the sledmasters' urgings.

"Is it the slope?" called Faeril to B'arr. "Do the dogs tire?"

"No, little *Mygga*," responded the sledmaster. "Dog no want to come into this place."

Another mile or two they ran, and still the dogs slowed.

And then without command, Shlee turned the full team and stopped, refusing to go any farther.

Into Gwylly's mind sprang the image of Black refusing to go into one of the "closed" places in the Weiunwood. Black had not seemed to fear the place, but simply to respect it instead.

Yet when Gwylly looked at Shlee, he saw that although the lead dog was not cowering, still his hackles were raised, and he seemed to be saying, *Bad! Place bad!*

Gwylly twisted about and saw that Laska and Garr had also turned their *spans* and would run this way no more.

"B'arr?" Faeril's unspoken question seemed to hang on the cold air.

"Shlee know, little one. Trust Shlee. He know." B'arr turned and called to Tchuka and Ruluk. "*Ikke mer. Vi vende tilbake.*"

Turning once more to the Warrows, the sledmaster's bronze features reflected the worry he felt. "We go back. You come. Not safe. Shlee know. Laska know. Garr know. All dog know. Trust dog. All know."

Riatha and Aravan dismounted from their sleds and trudged across the snow to come to B'arr's side.

Faeril struggled out of the fur blankets and stepped from the sled basket. "B'arr says that we must turn back." Her face was stricken with uncertainty. Gwylly stepped free and put his arm about her.

B'arr looked Riatha in the eye. "Shlee know, *Infé*. Shlee know. This bad place."

Riatha sighed. "I know, Sledmaster, what the dogs deem. Yet we must go on."

B'arr turned to Aravan. "*Anfé*, tell *Infé* she must turn back. All must go from this bad place. All dog, all Alute, all *Mygga*, all *Fé*. Place *vond* . . . evil. Dog *know!*"

Aaravan shrugged. "We have no choice, Sledmaster. Our way lies yon." Aravan pointed up into the defile.

Riatha turned to the Waerlinga. "Once again these mountains have become a place where evil dwells. I had hoped that it had not yet reached this side of the Grimwall." Riatha looked at the dogs. "But given the actions of the dogs, of Laska and Garr and Shlee, I deem that the *Spaunen* or worse have now come into this region as well."

Faeril's heart was hammering, and she did not trust her voice. Nevertheless, she glanced at the waning sky and hitched her bandoliers into a more comfortable position, the look on her face now resolute. "Then let us gather our things and go."

At a nod from Gwylly and Aravan, Riatha turned and made her way back to Tchuka's sled, where she began to gather up her gear, as did Aravan at Ruluk's sled, and Gwylly and Faeril at B'arr's.

Riatha slipped a waterskin under her coat where it would not freeze. She slung her sword in its scabbard across her back, and then shouldered the already prepared frame pack, settling it so that it did not interfere with the sword.

Aravan also slung a waterskin under his parka, then strapped his long-knife in its thigh scabbard onto his leg. He slipped his arms through the shoulder straps of his frame pack, buckling the chest belt across. Last, he took his black-hafted, crystal-bladed spear in hand, then turned to the others.

Gwylly's sling was looped through his belt next to the sling-bullet pouches, and his dagger was affixed to the opposite side, and so when he slung his waterskin and shouldered his pack, he was ready to set forth.

Faeril, too, prepared herself, waterskin and frame pack, the damman already bristling with knives crisscrossing her torso. She turned to B'arr when she was ready and held out her hands. "Oh, B'arr, do take care. We shall miss you, you know."

B'arr knelt down and squeezed the she-*Mygga*'s hands. "Already I miss you, little one. I know *Mygga* and *Fé* must go now. I worry you not safe. We come back when"—B'arr gestured to the night sky and groped for a word—"when star with tail gone. You stay safe till then, eh? Then we run happy back to Innuk, yes? Summer come, we fish."

Faeril managed a wistful smile and nodded and kissed the sledmaster on the cheek, then turned away.

Gwylly, too, said good-bye to B'arr, then stepped to each of the teams and ruffled the fur of Garr and Laska and Shlee, whispering something to each, his words heard by none else.

Aravan and Riatha bade each of the sledmasters farewell, and then all four—Riatha, Aravan, Gwylly, and Faeril—set forth up slope, heading deeper into the shadow-wrapped canyon, while the skies above grew dim.

B'arr watched them go, and for a long time he did not move. And he glanced down at his bone-bladed spear and wondered what perilous game, what deadly foe, the four of them pursued, a foe so dangerous that it would require weapons of steel and silver and starlight and crystal to slay it.

At last he looked up at the darkening skies, then signalled to Tchuka and Ruluk. As had been commanded, they would go back to the ruins two days north and wait until the strange star was gone from the skies. Then would they come back for the *Mygga* and *Fé*. Grasping his sled by the handlebar, "*Hypp! Hypp!*" he called, the dogs lunging ahead in response. "*Venstre, Shlee, venstre!*" Slowly the team wheeled leftward, until they were heading down slope. "*Strak! Strak!*" and down the course they fared, back the way they had come, Shlee's *span* running hard, Laska's and Garr's *spans* just as swift behind.

Night fell as up the rift they hiked, Gwylly and Faeril setting the pace for Riatha and Aravan. The Moon rose unseen, shielded by the ice-clad canyon walls. Overhead, stars wheeled in slow procession, and the four comrades knew that somewhere above the hidden horizon the Eye of the Hunter streamed.

Up the slope they walked, twisting deeper and deeper into the defile, its sheer walls looming closer in the darkness, the snow-covered floor of the vale rising up to meet them.

And now and again the earth shuddered, and snow sifted down from above, along with clattering rocks and jagged slabs of shattered ice, hammering onto the canyon floor at the base of the steep ramparts.

It was after one of these rumblings that Gwylly asked, "Hoy, Aravan, tell me about Dragons and about this Black Kalgalath. How he was slain and all."

The Elf looked down at the Waerling and smiled. "There's much to tell and little, for the life of any given Dragon is not well known. Even so, much is known concerning Dragons taken altogether.

"They are a mighty Folk, and perilous. Capable of speech. Covetous of wealth, gathering hoards unto themselves. They live in remote fastnesses, coming now and again upon their deadly raids, usually to steal cattle and other livestock, though I ween they think of it as hunting. 'All must aid when Dragons raid,' so goes the eld saying. Yet I deem that nought can be done when Dragons raid, and so the saying simply means to give shelter and comfort to those afflicted by a Drake's comings and goings.

"They sleep for a thousand years and waken for two thousand. At this time Dragons are awake, and have been so for some five hundred years.

"There are two strains of Dragons, though once there was but one. Fire-drakes and Cold-drakes they are now called: the breath of Fire-drakes a devastating flame; the breath of Cold-drakes a cloud of poison, its spittle an acid spume which chars flesh and stone and metal alike.

"Once there were no Cold-drakes, but in the Great War of the Ban, some Dragons sided with Gyphon. And after He was defeated, Adon reft the fire from these Dragons, causing them and their get to become the Cold-drakes of today.

"Too, the Cold-drakes suffer the Ban, the light of the Sun slaying them, though their Dragonhide saves them from the

Withering Death which strikes the other Foul Folk. Have thou not heard the saying 'Troll bones and Dragonhide'? It comes about because there are two things among the Foul Folk which do not wither under Adon's golden light: the bones of Trolls; the hides of Dragons. And so, when exposed to the daytide, Cold-drakes do not turn to ashes, as do the *Rûpt*, the *Spaunen*. Even so, still the Sun slays them, the Cold-drakes . . . though the Fire-drakes are unaffected by the light of day.

"But Fire-drake or Cold-, terrible are they, massive and deadly and nearly indestructible, their claws like adamantine scimitars, their hides scaled in nearly invulnerable armor. Great leathery pinions bear them up into the sky, and their flapping wings hurl twisting vortexes of air to hammer down upon a foe.

"It is said that they can sense all within their domain, and that their eyes see the hidden, the unseen, and the invisible, as well as the visible, too.

"None knows how long they can live, and in this they may be as are the Elves, though I doubt it. Some have estimated that if the waking and sleeping times of the Drakes correspond unto that of Man—that is, three thousand years for a Dragon is likened to one day for a Man—then because the lives of some Men span as much as one hundred summers, say, thirty-six thousand dawns, then the equivalent span of a Dragon would be more than one hundred thousand thousand years."

Gwylly gasped, then blurted, "One hundred thousand *thousand!*"

"Aye, wee one: one hundred thousand thousand years."

Gwylly turned to Faeril, his mind boggled by a number so large, unable to grasp even a glimmering of what it meant. The damman, seeing the confusion in the buccan's wide eyes, said, "Let me see if I can put this in terms that we can understand, Gwylly."

She thought a moment as they continued trudging up slope. "Mayhap this will serve: I have heard that there are seven thousand grains in a pound of wheat."

Gwylly nodded, for he had heard the same from his foster father, though he surely did not know who would have counted them.

Faeril continued: "And, too, I have heard that there are some fifty to sixty pounds of wheat in a bushel."

Again Gwylly nodded, for often he had helped with the harvest, and a bushel of wheat weighed nearly as much as he.

"Well, then," said Faeril, "if that's so, then a bushel of wheat contains some"—the damman did a quick reckoning in her head—"oh, say, four hundred thousand grains altogether."

Gwylly shrugged, vaguely irritated, feeling ensnared in an arcane academic exercise. "If you say so. But what's this got to do with—?"

Faeril held up a hand, and Gwylly fell silent, and buccan and damman continued striding through the snow, while she did another quick reckoning. "Then that means that two hundred and fifty bushels of wheat contain one hundred thousand *thousand* grains."

Gwylly looked at her blankly.

"Don't you see, Gwylly, if each one of those grains was like one year in a Dragon's life, it would take two hundred fifty bushel baskets full of wheat to have enough grains to number the years of a Drake."

At last this was something that the buccan could visualize, for Orith had sown and harvested wheat: In his mind's eye Gwylly saw two hundred fifty bushel baskets stretching out before him, each full to the brim with grains of wheat, each grain representing a year. He envisioned one basket spilled—for he'd spilled them—the grain spread in a uniform layer across a wide floor, the total covering a great area. Then he tried to envision two hundred fifty bushels spilled, knowing that the spread would be vast. But here his mind balked at trying to grasp it in its entirety. *To think, each grain represents one year in a Dragon's life. And as to the whole of it, well, it's quite unimaginable.*

But Faeril's thoughts, on the other hand, followed a completely different track, and she glanced up at Riatha and Aravan striding alongside. *If the span of Dragons seems so vast, then what of that of Elves? Why, all the grains of sand of all the beaches and all the deserts of all the world cannot even begin to number the years lying before each one of that Fair Folk.*

Aravan's words broke into the thoughts of the Waerlinga. "Thine example is apt, Faeril. Yet I caution thee: 'tis but speculation that the sleepings and wakings of Drakes corresponds to the days of Man. It could just as well be that they do not . . . or that they correspond to that of other beings— Waerlinga, Elves, Dwarves, Utruni . . . None that I have spoken to knows the truth of it."

Faeril looked at the Elf, weighing his words. "Then tell me this, Aravan: how old is the oldest Dragon now?"

"Adon knows, Faeril," responded the Elf. "Dragons were here on Mithgar when first we came, and that was several thousands of years apast."

For some time the foursome strode up the slope without speaking, their boots scrutching in the snow. Again the earth trembled, and more snow sifted down the face of the vertical walls looming to each side, rocks and ice rattling and shattering down as well. At last Gwylly broke the silence that had fallen among them. "All right, then. What about Kalgalath?"

Aravan took up the tale once more. "Black Kalgalath was perhaps the mightiest Drake upon all of Mithgar, though it was said by some that Daagor was mightier still. Yet Daagor was slain in the Great War as he fought on the side of Gyphon; the Drake was felled by the arts of the Wizards.

"Black Kalgalath, though, sided with no one, remaining aloof from the War.

"But there was a power token named the Kammerling, though others called it the Rage Hammer and some named it Adon's Hammer. It was said that this hammer would slay the mightiest Dragon of all.

"Black Kalgalath in his arrogance thought that the hammer was meant to be his bane, and so he stole it from its guardians, from the Utruni, from the Stone Giants, and gave it to a Wizard to ward for him.

"Yet two heroes, Elyn and Thork, recovered the hammer and used it to kill Kalgalath.

"It was in his death throes that Black Kalgalath smote the earth with the Kammerling, there at Dragonslair, whelming the world with that puissant token of power. And ever since, the land has been unstable, quaking, shuddering with the memory of Kalgalath's death here in the Grimwalls."

Onward they walked, an hour or two, then another, the night growing deeper, and the Eye of the Hunter appeared above the east canyon wall, its fiery tail streaming out behind.

Again the earth jolted, this time severely, and great rocks and slabs of ice shattered down into the deep slot below.

And Gwylly and Faeril thought that they could faintly hear the far-off ringing of iron bells. But in that very same moment there came a distant, juddering howl, long and ululating.

Faeril's heart jumped into her throat, and Gwylly beside her clutched her hand. "Wolves?" she asked, fearing the answer.

Again came the howl, louder this time perhaps, the sound echoing from crevice and crag, confusing the ear as to its direction, and Gwylly involuntarily squeezed Faeril's fingers.

Riatha looked about, sighting up the nearest wall even as debris rattled down from above. "Nay, Faeril, not Wolves," she gritted. "Instead it is the hunting cry of Vulgs on the track, and they are in pursuit."

# CHAPTER 7

# Legacy

**Mid and Late Summer, 5E985**

*[Three Years Past]*

"P-prophecy . . . ?" Gwylly stammered, staring at the young damman standing in the open doorway, she looking like a young warrior, what with the knives crisscrossing her breast. "W-what prophecy?"

Before she could answer—"Mind your manners, Gwylly" came the voice of his foster mother, Nelda. "Invite her in."

Gwylly stepped aside and the damman entered, her gaze shifting from Gwylly up to these tall Humans, Orith and Nelda, unspoken questions in the wee damman's eyes. In that moment, however, Black, wagging his tail, greeted her, attempting to get in a lick or two. The damman giggled and ruffled his ears, but fended off the wet tongue. As if suddenly recovering his senses, Gwylly leapt forward, coming to her rescue, with effort pushing Black aside, the dog a handful for one the size of the buccan.

"Black," called Orith. "Stand down." Black backed away, his tail still swinging widely.

"Take care his tail," Orith warned. "For one your size it carries a wallop."

The golden-eyed damman laughed, her voice silver, and Gwylly felt as if his heart were expanding.

Nelda gestured toward the kitchen. "Come in, my dear. Have you eaten? Won't you have some tea?" The Woman led the damman to the table. "It's not often we get visitors out this way, especially the wee ones. What did you say your name was, dear?"

"Faeril," replied the damman as she climbed up into a chair—Gwylly's chair, that is. "Faeril Twiggins."

Again Gwylly's heart leapt. *Faeril. What a wonderful name.* The buccan pulled up another chair and sat, too—though much lower since the guest was in *his* chair—and Gwylly's chin just cleared the tabletop. Orith sat, and Black flopped down beside him, the dog's tail thumping against the floor.

Nelda busied herself pouring tea and preparing a plate of food, while Orith stuffed leaf in his pipe and Gwylly stared at the damman—unable, it seemed, to look at aught else. . . .

And then she turned her golden gaze upon him.

Flustered, Gwylly tried to appear nonchalant, failing miserably.

"You *are* Gwylly Fenn, aren't you?"

Gwylly glanced away at Nelda and Orith, then back to Faeril. "My name *is* Gwylly. But as to the name Fenn, well, we don't know what . . ." The buccan's voice trailed off.

"Found him twenty years ago," said Orith, tamping down the pipeleaf as Faeril looked his way. "In a wreck. His sire and dam, well, they'd been killed. Rūcks and such, I think."

"We raised him as our own." Nelda took up the tale, pausing in her food preparation, the wild cherries and pitting knife forgotten, her eyes lost in the memory of that time. "Poisoned by Rūck blade and out of his mind—that's how he came to us."

Gwylly touched the nearly forgotten scar at the edge of his hairline, feeling the ridge running down from forehead to temple.

Faeril turned to the buccan. "Then you don't know *who* you are," she exclaimed. "And if you don't know, then how will I know whether or not you are the one I am seeking?"

Gwylly felt his heart hammering. "But I *do* know who I am," he protested. "I just don't know what last name I was born with."

Faeril slumped back in her chair, the look on her face pensive.

Black's tail stopped thumping, and he gazed up at those

about him, the tall ones and the small ones, sensing that something was amiss.

Orith stood and broke a long splinter from a split log beside the woodstove. He held it to the flames, and after it caught fire, he used it to light his pipe. The fragrance of the leaf swirled throughout the kitchen area, borne on the drifting cross breeze flowing through the open windows.

Nelda set the plate before Faeril, and the damman smiled wanly up at the Woman, yet it was plain that the Wee One's appetite had fled.

Faeril broke the silence. "There is no clue?"

Gwylly shook his head. "None."

Faeril was wakened in the night by a murmur, the voices of Nelda and Orith. But what they said to one another she could not tell, for their words were too low, too indistinct. Even so, by the cadence alone she believed that perhaps they were arguing.

On the floor beside her bed, Black's claws scrabbled on floorboards, the sleeping dog dreamchasing fleeing game.

Faeril stepped to the back porch. Pink dawn was turning blue in the eastern sky. She could hear the sound of an axe, and saw Orith at this early hour chopping wood and stacking it into cords near the byre, Black snuffling about the woodpile as if he had something trapped within.

Nodding to the Man, Faeril walked to the stables, intent upon caring for Blacktail. When she got there, she found Gwylly currying the pony while the horseling munched oats from the stall feedbox. Opposite, two great mules crunched away at their grain, while in a stall alongside Blacktail's another pony, a dappled grey, also munched oats.

Faeril took up another curry comb from a shelf and stepped into the stall with the grey. "Yours?" she asked, slipping her hand through the leather strap handle, finding that it was too large for her.

Gwylly nodded. "Dapper is his name. He's six."

"Blacktail is five."

Returning to the shelf to replace the comb, Faeril looked for but failed to find one which fit her hand. "Have you got another comb? One that I can use? Mine is in my saddlebags in the house."

"No, but I'm almost done here."

Faeril climbed up on the top rail and watched as Gwylly worked.

As the buccan moved about, suddenly Faeril drew in her breath.

Gwylly looked up. The damman's eyes were wide and fixed upon his waist. The buccan looked down at himself. "Something wrong?"

"You have a sling!"

"Uh—"

"You have a sling!" she repeated, interrupting whatever he was about to say.

Gwylly unlooped the leather weapon from his belt. "Yes, but what—?"

"Where did you get it? Can you use it?"

"Of course I can use it. And as far—"

"Silver bullets!" Faeril interjected. "Do you have silver bullets, too?"

"Silver bullets . . . ?" A vague fragment of memory plucked at the buccan's mind.

"Oh, Gwylly," cried Faeril, her voice brimming with urgency, "if you have silver bullets, then I will *know!*"

"Know what?" Gwylly was edging into frustration. "What's my sling got to do with anything? And what if I *did* have silver shot? —Not that I think silver should be wasted that way."

"Oh yes, you would," declared the damman.

"Oh yes, I would *what?*" Gwylly was ready to scream.

"Yes, you would think that silver should be used for bullets."

Gwylly slumped back against the side railings, staring up at Faeril in unalloyed bafflement. *Is this the way that all dammen act? Hopping about from idea to idea like grasshoppers in a field?* He spoke slowly and with forced calm. "And just why would I use silver sling shot?"

"Where did you get it?"

*Flp! Flp!* Gwylly envisioned a thousand grasshoppers, leaping all at once in a thousand different directions. His voice gritted out between clenched teeth. "Where did I get what? Silver bullets? I *said* that I didn't have—"

"The sling," Faeril interrupted. "Where did you get the sling?"

*Flp!* He took a deep breath. "It was my real sire's sling, or so Orith says."

Faeril's face lit up. "Oh, that's . . . that's very promising."

*Floop! Dust boiled up around haphazardly landing grasshoppers.* Before Gwylly could reply—*Dlang! Glang!*—the sound of breakfast call knelled through the air.

As the buccan and damman strode back to the house, Faeril looked at Gwylly in puzzlement, and then remarked, "It's not good that you grind your teeth together like that. Have you had the habit long?"

Throwing up his hands, Gwylly could do nought but burst out laughing in frustration.

At breakfast that morning Nelda looked haggard, as if she'd gotten little sleep. Too, she seemed to be avoiding Orith's gaze, but as the meal ended, at last she looked at him and nodded. Orith then stood and left the room. He returned moments later, bearing a small cedarwood box. Placing it on the table, he cleared his throat. "Last night, Miss Faeril, you asked if there was any clue to Gwylly's past. I didn't think of it then, but later on, I remembered:

"Gwylly, of course, was the wounded babe I found there in the wreckage of the campsite, and I brought him straightaway here to Nelda, for he was in a bad way and needed healing. Later, I returned to bury his sire and dam and to collect for him whatever I could, whatever remained of his parents' possessions. But it was mostly gone, stolen, and there were just a few things I took from that place of death:

"I found a sling and some steel shot, which Gwylly claimed. Belonged to his sire, he said. When I gave him the steel shot, he asked a most curious thing: he wanted to know where the 'shiny ones' were. At the time I didn't know what he referred to, though it *was* a puzzler that I worried over for weeks. But gradually it drifted from my mind, and I hadn't thought about it for years . . . many years. This morning, though, as I was stacking wood, I overheard you and

Gwylly talking, and you asked him about silver bullets. Oh, I wasn't eavesdropping, but I did happen to overhear that. And suddenly that strange remark of baby Gwylly's popped back into my head—'Where are the shiny ones?'—and now I know what the 'shiny ones' must have been: they must have been silver bullets.

"Of course, the Rūcks and such would have taken all things precious, and that's why I didn't find any silver shot. Else he would have had those bullets, too."

Faeril glanced over at Gwylly, her excitement growing. Gwylly thought her eyes were fairly glowing gold, and it seemed as if she were about to speak. Ere she could do so, Orith took up the cedar box and raised the lid.

"Regardless, there was something else in the wreckage which, unlike silver, had no value to those who raided the site: these." Orith reached into the box and took out two journals and gave them over to Faeril. The damman eagerly began examining them as Orith continued. "I didn't remember them until after we'd all bedded down, Miss Faeril. But you see, it's been twenty years since I found them."

Looking up from the pages, Faeril exclaimed, "This is it, Gwylly! Journals of the Firstborns, one old, one new. Perhaps . . ."

Quickly she flipped to the back of the newer one. "Yes, I am right. This one is the copy made by your sire, for here is your lineal tree, your name recorded at the end: *Gwylly Fenn*. And your sire's name was *Darby*. And before him was *Frek*. It goes all the way back to *Tomlin*, here at the top.

"Oh, Gwylly, here's the proof to show that you are indeed *Gwylly Fenn, Firstborn*."

She handed the journal to the buccan, open to the back. Gwylly looked curiously at the page, turning it this way and that, a frown coming over his features.

"And the old journal"—Faeril took it up—"yes, this is the one made by Small Urus from Petal's original nearly a thousand years ago."

Faeril glanced up at the Man. "Oh, Orith, had you only read it, there would have been no question as to who Gwylly was and is. But, then, I can't hold you at fault, what with all you did for him. Besides, it's too much for me to expect that anyone other than a Warrow would read Twyll, the Warrow tongue."

Orith glanced up at Nelda and then over at Gwylly, and Gwylly cleared his throat and closed the journal and laid it aside. "Uh, Faeril, not Twyll, not Wilderan, not Common; the three of us, well, we can't read at all."

"Can't read . . . ?" Faeril was stunned.

Gwylly nodded. "Not a word. None of us. 'Tisn't needed out here in the Wilderland."

"But all Boskydell Warrows . . ."

Orith looked at the floor. "We'd always meant to send Gwylly to Stonehill—"

"Oh, it doesn't matter," burst in Faeril. "I have plenty of time, more than two years, to teach him to read: Twyll and Common, too."

The damman turned excitedly to Gwylly. "Oh, Gwylly, you have so much before you: reading, writing, numbers."

"I can cipher," said the buccan, somewhat stung. "You have to be able to do your sums to sell or trade farm goods."

Faeril saw that she was treading on thin ice. "Well, read and write, then."

She took up the newer journal. "Here, let me read to you about your ancestors, brave souls they were. About Tomlin and Petal. And Riatha, too, and Urus. And Baron Stoke.

"Once you hear the tale and the words of the prophecy, then you'll know what brought me here and why I bear these knives, and why I have to seek out Arden Vale and find the Elfess Riatha. You'll see just why I *must* go on a long and perhaps dangerous quest, why I must travel to the Great North Glacier in the far-off Grimwall.

"And you'll see just why you must leave here, too, and go on the quest with me."

At these words Nelda gasped, her eyes filling with distress.

Once again in the night, the voices of Orith and Nelda drifted to where Faeril had bedded down. This time, though, she overheard what they said, or at least part.

"He's got to leave someday, Nelda, to find his own, to be with others of his Kind. Did you see how he and Miss Faeril took to one another? She and Gwylly were meant to be together."

"But, Orith, she wants to take him off to the Grimwall, there where the Foul Folk live."

"If that be his choice, Mother, then we cannot hold him back."

"Orith, they could kill him. They killed his kindred."

"Perhaps that's all the better reason for him to go. To revenge himself for what they took from him."

"But *we* took him in and loved him as our own. Shouldn't that count for something?"

"I am sure it does . . . I am sure it does. He was raised in love and knows we cherish him. And any can see he loves us, too. But he's got to be with his own Kind, Mother, his own Kind."

"They could just as well live here, Orith. There's no need for him to go traipsing off, for either of them to do so. Taking up with Elves. Heading into the Grimwalls. Especially after what we heard of Stoke. I mean, if he is mixed up in this . . ."

"Stoke or not, prophecy or not, it's Gwylly's to decide. No matter the danger. No matter that we would keep him safe forever, were it up to us."

"But he is so small!"

"Mother, he is full grown, full grown for his Kind."

Faeril heard the sounds of weeping, and her heart went out to the parents whose son might now choose to leave them to follow a course of his own. And as with loving families throughout time, when faced with the prospect of a son or daughter setting forth, a sadness fills the breast even though happiness dwells there, too, happiness for the bright future shining before the child. Yet there are times when sadness turns to anguish, and happiness to fear, when the future is dark and full of uncertainty and, perhaps, woe— such as when duty calls and sons and daughters think to answer, think to stand in harm's way; then souls tremble and hearts are rent in those who must let them go. And *this* is what Nelda and Orith faced, the prospect of their son standing in harm's way. That Nelda and Orith were Human and their "son" a Warrow mattered not a whit, for still he was their child, and had they a choice, they would forever protect him from all harm.

Even so, Gwylly *was* the other Lastborn Firstborn, and Faeril knew the same destiny that called to her had now spoken to him. Still, unlike she, he had not heard that voice ere now; he had not been raised knowing that he had a mission to fulfill. And unlike Faeril's mother, Lorra, neither Nelda nor Orith had known of the mission lying ahead. None in this family had been prepared for Destiny's call.

And when late in that day Faeril had finished reading the journal to them, had told them of the prophecy, had shown them her own copy of Petal's journal, and had asked Gwylly to set forth with her ere the week was out, Gwylly had not answered but instead had gotten up and looked out the window into the gathering twilight, his hands clasped behind him.

And so matters stood.

Unresolved.

And now as Faeril lay in her bed and listened to Nelda weep, the damman wondered when Gwylly might make his decision known, when he might choose to answer the voice of Destiny, and what that answer might be.

Again Black came to a point.

In a shushing gesture Gwylly put his fingers to his lips and motioned Faeril forward. Cautiously, the damman stepped through the bracken below the forest trees, her eyes fixed on the place where the ebony dog's muzzle was unwaveringly set.

Of a sudden the hare broke from cover, bounding on long legs through the ferny growth. "Go!" shouted Gwylly, and Black was swift on the heels of the running buck.

Darting after came Gwylly and Faeril, buccan and damman laughing and shouting, *"Go, Black, go!"* and *"Yah, yah!"* and running for all they were worth.

Dashing and veering, the hare hurtled among the trees of the Weiunwood, maintaining the distance between him and the ebon dog by clever maneuvers and hairpin turns, Black overrunning the track and swinging 'round and wide and back only to overrun the turn after. But then the hare bolted straightaway, no longer veering, the dark dog overtaking with every stride. Seemingly there was no escape, and Faeril shouted, "Run, rabbit, run! Else you will be a crofter's meal!"

Onward hurled the hare, Black but a leap or two behind. With great bounds, between the black oaks hurtled the buck and into the shadowed glen beyond, and suddenly Black was tumbling tail over ears, the dog unable to stop cleanly, for even in baying pursuit Black would not enter one of the "closed" places.

The dog stood and shook himself off, trotting back toward Gwylly and Faeril, the buccan and damman breathless and laughing. "Ah, Blackie, m'lad," wheezed Gwylly, "outsmarted by a hare."

The three of them made their way to a rock-shelved pool in a swift-running, moss-banked stream, where Black lapped up water as if he'd never stop, pausing only long enough to pant heavily and look about, then lap some more. Gwylly and Faeril perched above on the stone overhang and caught their breath, too.

"Why did he stop, Gwylly?" asked Faeril. "I mean, a stride or two more and the hare would have been our supper."

Gwylly pointed at the dark oaks and the dim forest beyond. "It's one of the 'closed' places, Faeril, and Black knows better than to enter."

The damman looked long at where Gwylly pointed. She shivered. "I rode through such on my way to find you, Gwylly. The trees and shadows, they seemed to just barely tolerate my being there."

Gwylly's mouth dropped open. "You rode through— But didn't Blacktail shy away?"

Faeril nodded. "She did. But finding you was more important than going the long way 'round, and so, through we went."

Gwylly shook his head. "Next time, Faeril, go 'round."

They sat without speaking for some while. Black flopped down between them, and Faeril scratched his ears. At last Gwylly asked, "What was in there, in places like that one?"

Faeril thought a moment. "Twilight," she said finally. "Green galleries and shadow. At times there is a rustling, as if someone or something watches. From the corners of your eyes, things seem to be flitting and darting among the trees. But when you look, nothing, no one is there. At least nothing or no one that I could see.

"All the time I rode among the shadows, Blacktail was shy and skittish. And as I said, the places seemed to merely tolerate my presence. Both my pony and I were glad to be out.

"Have you never been in one, Gwylly?"

"Once. Briefly," answered the buccan. "When Orith found out he bade me never to do so again. Said *things* live in there . . . not evil but not to be disturbed either. He said that only the wild things have clear passage."

Again silence fell between them. Only the murmur of a soft breeze and the purl of the stream could be heard, a bird call now and then sweet upon the air.

It was the ninth day since Faeril had come to the stead. The eighth since she had read from the journal. And still Gwylly had not answered her question as to whether he would go with her to Arden Vale.

On the five days that he had worked with Orith, Faeril had helped Nelda in the kitchen, the damman showing off her own cooking skills, giving the Woman a special recipe for a pie crust, flaky and tender. Too, she chatted about her family back in the Boskydells. And Nelda felt her own heart grow lighter on these days.

But on the days that Gwylly went hunting with Black in the Weiunwood, Faeril had accompanied him, using her skill with throwing knives to bring down small game.

Nine days had passed thus, two days more than she had allotted, and still she had no answer.

"I'm leaving tomorrow, Gwylly," she said softly, "whether or no you come with me."

Gwylly took a deep breath. "I'm going with you, Faeril. I must. I had not answered you till now because I had to give Mom and Dad a time to get used to the idea."

The buccan turned and faced her, green eyes peering into gold. "Besides, I cannot let you go alone, for you hold my heart. You see, Faeril, I am in love with you. I have been so since first I saw you standing in my doorway."

Faeril looked at him, her amber eyes gentle. Then she leaned across Black and took Gwylly's face in her hands and softly kissed him.

"Mom! Dad! We're home from the 'Wood with game to spare and wonderful news."

Nelda looked up from the beans she was snapping, seeing the glow of her son's face and the smile on Faeril's. Orith, at the wash basin, turned, his face dripping, and caught up a towel.

Black's claws clicked upon the wooden floor as the dog crossed to his water dish and lapped once or twice.

Gwylly lofted the four rabbits up to the table, then took Faeril by the hand. "Mom, Dad, Faeril and I, well, she's agreed to . . . that is, she's my dammia and I'm her buccaran."

Orith paused in drying his face and looked at Gwylly over the edge of the towel. "Dammia? Buccaran?"

Nelda laughed. "Men! What Gwylly is trying to say, Orith, is that they've become sweethearts. Any fool could have seen it was meant to be." The Woman set the bowl of green beans aside and opened wide her arms, taking Gwylly and Faeril in a loving embrace.

"Oh, my Gwylly," whispered Nelda, "you must cherish her and care for her always."

Suddenly, the smile on Nelda's face faded as a realization came upon her, and dismay welled in her eyes and her voice choked. "And oh, my Gwylly, that means you can't let her go into the Grimwalls alone."

The next morning, amid a teary good-bye, Faeril and Gwylly set off on Blacktail and Dapper, faring southward for the Crossland Road, which would bear them eastward to Arden Vale.

Behind, Nelda and Orith and Black watched them ride away. Orith had his arm about Nelda, and she leaned her head against his breast. Distress filled the faces of both, for their son and his beloved rode into danger, or so they deemed. They stood that way for many long minutes, until they could see the wee buccan and wee damman no more. At last the Man and Woman turned and made their way back into the house, while behind, Black lay down and with a sigh put his chin upon his front paws, his brown eyes gazing sadly in the direction Gwylly had gone.

# CHAPTER 8

# Journey to Arden

**Mid and Late Summer, 5E985**

*[Three Years Past]*

All that morning, southerly rode Gwylly and Faeril, following along the trace of a waggon-rut trail from long-past journeys between the farm and the distant road to the Stonehill marketplace far away, the wheel marks now faint and overgrown. In the distance to the right lay the shaggy Weiunwood; far to the left rose the tors of the Signal Mountains; before the Warrows the grassland gradually fell away toward the edge of the Wilderland, where lay the Crossland Road and Harth beyond. And down this long, shallow slope they fared, their backs to Gwylly's homestead, their faces toward the unknown.

Steadily they rode, stopping but a few minutes every hour to stretch their legs and give the ponies a breather or some grain, and to take care of other needs. Too, they stopped occasionally at streams to water their steeds and refill their waterskins, but in the main they rode steadfastly southward.

As the noontide drew upon them, they came through a gentle swale between low, flanking hills and swung their course easterly. In the distance far ahead they could see two tall hills standing against the horizon. "Beacontor and Northtor," said Gwylly. "We will camp there tonight, on one slope or the other."

Faeril gauged the distance. "How far are they?"

"Oh, twenty, twenty-five miles," replied Gwylly.

Faeril nodded. "Well, Blacktail has gone as much as forty miles in one day, though not day after day. I wouldn't wish to ask for more than she or Dapper can bear."

"We will slow down tomorrow, my dammia," said Gwylly. "I expect that twenty or twenty-five miles a day is well within their means."

Faeril twisted about and searched in her right-hand saddlebag. She pulled out a folded sheet of parchment, crackling it open. "The sketch Hopsley made in Stonehill shows Beacontor. On it he indicated that Arden is some two hundred fifty miles beyond. At twenty-five miles a day, we'll be ten days getting there; eleven, counting today."

Gwylly held out his hand and Faeril passed him the sketch. Once again the buccan twisted the printed page about, as if trying to solve the mystery of the written words by orienting the paper just so. Faeril put her hand to her mouth to cover her smile at his efforts. *I will have to begin teaching him this very night.*

Onward they rode throughout the long summer day, while the Sun passed overhead and then slid down the western sky, casting their lengthening shadows before them. Still they wended forth, the ponies at a walk, moving easterly through green rolling grassland, the Signal Mountains now marching off northeasterly, the Dellin Downs ahead and to the south.

In the late afternoon they at last came at an angle unto the great Crossland Road. Onto the tradeway they stepped their mounts, the road a major east–west thoroughfare, reaching from the Ryngar Arm of the Weston Ocean at its far terminus some eight hundred miles to the west, unto the Crestan Pass through the Grimwall Mountains three hundred or so miles to the east, where it became known as the Landover Road and stretched far across the Realms beyond.

Five more miles they fared, and evening was at hand when they stopped for the night on the southern slopes of Northtor. Slightly east and south rose the crest of Beacontor, the final mount in the chain. Between the two tors ran the road, passing up over the low saddle and on down to the east.

The skies were clear, yet Gwylly used a hand axe to cut saplings for a lean-to. "Just in case," he said.

Meanwhile, Faeril set rocks in a ring and started a camp-fire, fixing a pot of water above to make some tea.

Faeril staked out the ponies and while she curried the cinch- and saddle-swirls and -knots from their hair, Gwylly erected the shelter, using small, supple branches to tie the saplings together into a roof, the buccan chatting all the while. "Dad told me about Beacontor. Used to be where an old watchtower was located. It was part of a chain of warbea-con towers stretching from Challerain Keep up in Rian down to this end of the Signal Mountains. They say, in fact, that the Signal Mountains got their name from these towers.

"Anyway, here they'd set a fire alight atop the hill when War came, signalled from the north down the chain by the other warbeacons, or up from the Dellin Downs in the south, or whenever any sentries posted in any towers spotted ap-proaching foe nearby.

"They used this hill because it's the tallest one around, and fires from its crest raised all the land hereabout. Twice it fell during the Ban War. The first time, just two Wil-derland Men managed to defeat more than forty of the foe and set the fire alight, though one of the Men was killed. That was the time, I think, when the tower itself was destroyed.

"The second time it fell, the Black Foxes managed to free it. You've heard of the Black Foxes, haven't you?"

Faeril said, "No," and Gwylly plunged on:

"That was more Wilderlanders. A squad of Men. Other Men named them the Black Foxes because of their wiliness at defeating Modru's minions and because of the mottled grey and black leathers they wore to conceal themselves in the mountains where they fought. Dad says that eventually they took the name to themselves and had a device enscribed upon their shields: a black fox.

"In any event, the outnumbered Foxes overthrew the Rūcks and such that had captured Beacontor for the second time."

Faeril finished with the ponies and stepped to the now boiling pot of water and set it aside to steep some tea.

"Gwylly, do you know any Warrow tales, tales about those of your Kind?"

Gwylly shook his head, *No*, and a sadness filled Faeril's heart, for her buccaran knew nothing of his own Folk.

The lean-to was finished as the Sun sank below the horizon. In the twilight the buccan and damman took a meal of jerky and hard bread, while sipping hot tea and speaking of the journey ahead. Faeril took her map from the saddlebag and by firelight called attention to its features, as they examined what lay before them. And in looking at the map, Faeril began teaching Gwylly the alphabet of the Common tongue, pointing out the letters on the parchment and using a stick and scratching additional letters in the dust. She would have preferred to start by teaching him Twyll, for then he could use the journals to read from, but Gwylly spoke not the language of the Warrows, and so Twyll would have to wait.

It was late when the Moon rose to shed its glancing light upon them, and it was time for bed. And for the very first time for either, they undressed before one of the opposite sex. Gwylly's breath was taken away by the exquisite splendor of her body. Faeril's heart was pounding, and she found that she could neither look at him nor look away. As of one mind, they stepped toward one another, argent moonlight streaming all about them. He took her in his arms and she pressed herself against him, and they kissed long and tenderly. And then they lay down together. Neither knew exactly what to do, yet between them they managed to discover the pleasure of giving themselves to each other, while the stars in the vault above wheeled silently through the night.

They followed the Crossland Road through the slot between Northtor and Beacontor, and passed beyond the Signal Mountains and out upon the open wold lying to the east. Off to the south in the distance they could see the forest lining the vale of the Wilder River. Northward and east the mountain chain faded away in the distance. Westerly, the Crossland Road was the only feature breaking the landscape, wending across the rolling plains. And into this unsheltered land they went.

Three days they rode thus, the weather favoring them with clear skies and warm summer days and cool summer nights. And they spoke of their dreams and of one another and of the days to come. And in the nights they spoke in a language altogether different from that which they used in the day, though the meaning was the same.

Too, Faeril continued to teach Gwylly his letters. And the buccan was an apt learner, setting his mind to the task.

It was late on the fifth day of travel that they came into the Wilderness Hills, the road meandering among them and down the gently falling land.

The seventh day it rained a slow drizzle, and they crossed over the Stone-arches Bridge above the River Caire to come into the Land of Rhone, known by some as the Plow because of its share-shaped boundaries, the Realm lying between the Caire on the west and the River Tumble to east and south.

Before them, the Crossland Road disappeared within the dark clutches of Drearwood, and into this haunted forest rode the pair.

"In the eld days," said Gwylly, "this was a place of dire repute. But the Wilderland Men and the Elves of Arden Vale purged it of its deadly denizens, or so my dad tells me. Even so, deadly foe here or gone, safe or not, still it causes creepy crawlies to run up my spine."

Faeril looked about and shivered, for even now an ominous atmosphere pervaded the woodland, its dark trees and shadowy environs made all the more drear by the leaden skies above. "Not at all like the Weiunwood. Not even the 'closed' places felt like this."

Gwylly looked at his dammia. "How many of them did you ride through? The 'closed' places, I mean."

"Oh, I don't know, Gwylly. Several, I suppose.

"You see, when I came looking for you, I knew nothing of the Weiunwood. Only that someone named Gwylly Fenn had been born there.

"I lived in the Northwood in Northdell in the Boskydells. And so when I came looking, I rode out across the Spindle River at Spindle Ford. Then it was through the Battle Downs and into the Weiunwood, searching for the Glades where Warrows dwell.

"I found several, but when I asked where the Fenn family lived, where Gwylly Fenn lived, none knew. And so, alone, I rode through the Weiunwood, going from Glade to Glade, searching for you.

"Someone—Mr. Bink, I think—said that I ought to go to Stonehill, for there were Warrows living there, and sooner or later everyone in the region comes to trade.

"To make a long story short, Mr. Hopsley Brewster, the proprietor at the White Unicorn, remembered that a Warrow named Gwylly lived with a Man and Woman some fifty miles east along the Crossland Road, then twenty miles north, in a steading 'tween the 'Wood and the Signal Mountains. He drew me this map of how to get there, and when I asked him, he added the route to Arden Vale beyond; that very night I was on my way.

"And *that's* how I found you, my buccaran, hiding out among Humankind."

Gwylly barked a laugh, and Faeril smiled, yet she glanced into the darkness of Drearwood and shivered, and her smile faded.

"But as to how many of the 'closed' places I rode through, I cannot say. No one thought to warn me of them; they just assumed I knew. But several, Gwylly. Several."

They rode on a bit, cold rain drizzling down through the dark shadows of the Drearwood. Finally Gwylly broke the silence that had fallen between them. "They say that in the north part of the Weiunwood lies a great oak maze, confusing to the mind, and it is told that a person can wander for days and weeks and months in bewilderment, lost, perhaps never to find a way out. They even tell that one of Modru's Hordes was defeated there during the Winter War, at least Orith so says. I do not know whether this is one of the closed places, Faeril, but regardless, I am glad you did not venture therein."

Faeril mustered a wan smile, as chill rain mizzled and the dark clutch of the Drearwood enveloped them, sucking at their souls.

The next day was brighter, the Sun at last breaking through the cast, and soon fleecy clouds rode above.

On the tenth day, they passed from the Drearwood and

crossed Arden Ford along the River Tumble, to come into the wolds of Rell, a Land known as Lianion unto the Lian Elves. Eastward and northward fared the two for a league or more, finally to camp in the night.

On the afternoon of the eleventh day of travel, they came to the slot of Arden Vale.

Out from between close-set high canyon walls roared the River Tumble, the mist boiling upward, obscuring the view into the valley beyond. The falls themselves stretched the width of the narrow slot, and neither Gwylly nor Faeril could see how to enter.

"Let's ride up as close as we can," suggested Faeril, and Gwylly nodded, for that had been his thought as well.

And so they urged their ponies forward, riding through a pine wood and crags and toward the roaring water. As they approached, a figure upon a dark grey horse rode out from the shelter of the trees to bar the way. Gwylly reached for his sling, and Faeril's hand went to one of the knives at her breast. But then the rider called out to them and stepped his mount forward from the shadows and into the sunlight.

It was an Elf.

Andor led them by hidden road under thundering Arden Falls, the mist from the cataract swirling about them as they passed along the wet stone way and up through a carven tunnel and out into the gorge beyond. Behind them, the River Tumble raced through the narrow cleft and over the linn, mist whirling up and obscuring the land whence they had just come, acting as a white curtain shielding the view into and out of the cloven vale.

Ahead, the Warrows could see an enormous tree, towering upward hundreds of feet, as if to touch the sky itself. Its leaves were dusky, as if made of the stuff of twilight.

"*Ooo,*" breathed Faeril. "It must be the granther of all trees."

Andor smiled. "Nay, small one. 'Tis instead the Lone Eld Tree, brought here as a seedling from Darda Galion by Talarin when first we came to settle in this hidden vale."

"Seedling!" exclaimed Gwylly. "But that tree must be thousands of years old!"

Andor nodded. "Yes."

Gwylly was dumbfounded, just now beginning to realize that Elves were ageless.

Beneath the sheltering branches of the behemoth tree lay an Elven campsite where stayed the Arden-ward. Into this camp rode the trio, other green-clad Lian Elves hailing Andor, and coming forth to see the wee Waerlinga, so like unto Elevenkind themselves.

Dismounting, the two Waerlinga were each offered a bowl of stew, which they eagerly accepted, for they had been long on the journey and without a substantial hot meal for all that time. As they settled down with bowl and spoon and bread and stew, Andor spoke to Galron, the Elven watch commander, repeating what the Waerlinga had told him of their mission. Both Gwylly and Faeril nodded in confirmation but said nought 'round full mouths, shovelling venison stew inward as if it were pure ambrosia.

Sitting cross-legged opposite the two, Galron waited, noting that their jewellike eyes scanned hither and yon, taking in all, missing nothing, even as they ate. He smiled as he saw Faeril gaze at the banner flying on the staff—green tree upon grey field—and then the damman looking up at the immense tree above them, a look of comprehension dawning in her golden eyes even as she spooned up another bite of stew. "Aye, Faeril, thou have the right of it. This tree *is* the symbol of Arden Vale, and has been since Talarin and his party found this place."

Now Gwylly looked at the sigil on the flag, his own eyes glancing up at the tree, as Galron added, " 'Tis said that when the tree is no more, then we, too, will no longer dwell in Arden Vale."

Faeril's eyes filled with dismay upon hearing these words, and her appetite fled. Gwylly, too, set aside his bowl. Galron's hand reached out as if to comfort them, but then fell back to his side.

"*Kesa, vixi*— Ye came not here to speak of the eld days, nor of the days yet to come. Instead ye would see Dara Riatha, and she is"—Galron glanced at Blacktail and Dapper— "two days north by pony."

\*　　\*　　\*

Slowly the two Waerlinga travelled through the pine-laden vale, following alongside the rushing waters of the River Tumble. With them rode Jandrel, the Lian assigned by Galron to escort them north unto Dara Riatha. High stone canyon walls rose in the distance to left and right, the sides of the gorge at times near, at other times two or three miles distant. Crags and crevices could be seen here and there, though for the most part the lofty walls were sheer granite. In the places where the canyon narrowed dramatically, they would fare upon hewn rock pathways carven partway up the side of the stone palisade that formed the west wall of the valley. Jandrel remarked that in these straits when the river o'erflowed its banks, the vale below became a raging torrent, and so these courses along the wall were made for safety's sake. On up the canyon rode the three, easing along high pathways above or passing through the soft green galleries of the shadowy pine forest below.

That night in camp, Jandrel glanced up from his cup of tea and said, "Ye are the first Waerlinga I have set eyes upon since the days of the Winter War. Then it was that I saw the one named Tuckerby Underbank, the Bearer of the Red Quarrel."

Faeril's eyes flew wide. "You saw Tuck?"

Gwylly, too, looked up in surprise, for even this orphaned Warrow knew the tale of Tuckerby Underbank, Hero of the Winter War.

"Aye," responded Jandrel. "Sir Tuckerby and Alor Gildor and Galen King rode through Arden Vale on their way to Pellar to gather the Host, yet those plans went awry, forcing them to do otherwise.

"In those days I was the Captain of the Arden-ward, and the Dimmendark was upon the land."

"What was he like, this Tuck?" asked Gwylly.

Jandrel sipped the last of his tea, then set his cup down. "Small, as are thee, Gwylly. His hair was black, though, and not aflame as is thine. Black, as is Faeril's. And his eyes were sapphires, or as blue as. All in all, not much different from thee, or any of thy Kind."

For some unknown reason a flush came upon Gwylly's face.

Faeril drew up her legs and clutched her knees. "And so you saw three of the four Deevewalkers." Her statement was not a question.

"Nay, Faeril, not three but four instead."

Faeril looked surprised. "But I thought Brega was south—"

"He was, wee one. Yet after the battle in Kregyn, and when the War was ended, once again they came unto Arden, the Deevewalkers and others, returning from Modru's Iron Tower. Then it was that I saw Brega. Then, too, I saw Patrel in his golden armor, and Merrilee as well. Five more Wee Folks were there, among the survivors, heroes every one.

"And so in all, eight Waerlinga did I see a thousand summers past, each nought but a chit next to Elf, Dwarf, or Man, yet without whom we would not have survived.

*"Hai! Ealle hál va Waerlinga!"*

Later that night, Gwylly lay awake, his arm wrapped 'round sleeping Faeril, his thoughts returning ever and again unto the words of Jandrel, wondering at their validity. *". . . All in all, not much different from thee, or any of thy Kind."* Gwylly watched as the stars wheeled above—*"All in all, not much different from thee"*—the words echoing in his mind— *"not much different from thee . . . from thee . . ."*

When the crescent Moon set, Gwylly was fast asleep.

After breaking camp the next day, northward they rode, Jandrel leading the Waerlinga through the fragrant pine.

At a break, Gwylly asked, "I do not mean to pry, but yestereve you said that you had been Captain of the Arden-ward, yet now you are not. How so, Jandrel? How so?"

Jandrel laughed. "Among the Lian none remains long at one calling—several hundred summers or so at most. Even the Warder in Arden, even the Coron over all of Elvenkind, even they ultimately tire of that which they do and move on to other duties, to other tasks, to other activities, interests, crafts.

"Aye, I was the Captain of the Arden-ward a time apast, and may be again someday. After the Winter War, I turned my hand to gardening, and thence to caring for distressed animals.

"I came back to the Arden-ward for a short tour, ten years

or so, as does each and every member of the Lian, male and female alike.

"Next, I expect to be in the mountains, studying their texture and substance, where I will remain for a hundred summers or thereabout.

"And so, Gwylly, read nought into my former and present station until thou come to know the ways of the Lian, until thou come to appreciate the span of our lives."

"But your lives are—are endless!" blurted Gwylly.

"Just so," responded Jandrel. "Just so."

Onward they rode through the forest, travelling some twenty-five miles more before making camp.

That night Gwylly and Faeril whispered softly to one another, speculating upon how a person's life might be changed if it were eternal, and what effect that might have on a society filled with such folk.

Some distance away, his back to a tree, the Lian Elf smiled unto himself.

It was nigh noon the next day when Jandrel led the two Waerlinga in among the thatched dwellings of the Elves of Arden Vale. Lian looked up from whatever tasks they labored at, or from wherever they sat or stood, their eyes delighting at the sight of the Wee Folk. And for their part, Faeril and Gwylly gazed about in wonder, for here was where Elven Folk dwelled. And everywhere they looked was grace and beauty and subtle color.

After an enquiry, the trio rode another mile north to come at last to a wide field of oats, where Lian labored. And plying a scythe there was a golden-haired Elfess.

"*Kel, Riatha, Dara!*" called Jandrel. "*Vi didron ana al enistori!*"

Riatha turned from the grain and shaded her eyes and looked at the three at field's edge. She handed her scythe to one of the gleaners and began walking toward the Waerlinga, for even though she did not know their names, she knew who they were and why they had come.

# CHAPTER 9

# *Riatha*

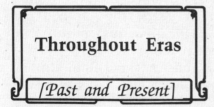

**Throughout Eras**

*[Past and Present]*

Long ago in Adonar, an Elfess and her sire and dam walked on the banks of a crystal rill dancing through a bright green glade, while high above in the branches of the ancient Eld Trees, Silverlarks sang their songs of joy. And the Elfess and her progenitors spoke of many things, past and present and future, for she was soon to set forth for Mithgar, riding upon the dawn. It was near the end of the Second Era, though few, if any, knew it at the time—for to see into the future is a rare and precious gift, given to only a few. It was mayhap one or two hundred years before the Era ended, or more, none can precisely say—for dates have little meaning to Elves, who perhaps note only the passage of the seasons. But even if Elves do not keep close track of days and dates, still they always seem to know where stand the Sun and Moon and stars—and this, too, is a precious gift. Regardless, on this last day in Adonar, Riatha walked in a glade with her mother and father, and they spoke of many things.

Riatha, then as now, was a young Elfess, just beginning her life. But so too was her sire, as well as her dam. What their actual ages were, of Riatha and Daor and Reín, is not told, for no matter the age of an Elf, he or she is always at the beginning of a never ending life. What matter if they had lived twenty or two hundred or two thousand years or more? For when compared to all of eternity, no matter the count of years, an Elf is but a step or two along an endless path.

Oh, not that Elves cannot die, for they can be slain by weapon or poison, by accident or malice, or by another living creature fighting to survive. Too, Elves can starve, die of thirst, drown, burn, and perish any other number of ways as well, a handful of rare but fatal diseases among these. Yet without these interventions, Age passes them by and Death gives them not a second's glance.

Hence, with all eternity waiting to be trod by these splendid souls, is it any wonder that to Elvenkind the death of one of their own is cause for great grief? It matters not the number of seasons that have passed since the fallen one's birth, for whatever the count of years, the Elf had but stepped across the threshold of life, had just begun, and Death has quenched an endless existence.

But that bright day, as Riatha and Daor and Reín strolled among the Eld Trees, thoughts of death and dying were not upon their minds. Instead they spoke of Riatha's impending journey to Mithgar, the mortal world, alluding to what she might find, referring to her responsibilities thereupon.

They stopped in the glade and sat upon the bank above the sparkling bourn, diamond lights scattering from its dancing surface. Daor looked at his golden-haired daughter and broached a familiar theme:

"What does it mean to live forever?"

Elven scholars had often posed this very same question to their students, there in the bowers of learning, Riatha among these. This time it was her sire who asked the rhetorical question, and she waited for him to continue.

And so they sat, there at brookside in the greenglade, while Daor spoke on.

"What does it mean? How does it affect ambitions, quests for power, for glory, the search for knowledge, the search for truth?

"How does an endless life make us differ from mortals? In strivings, in relationships, in day-to-day living?

"Consider the mayfly: its sudden birth, its frantic life, its instant death. How does the fleeting existence of the mayfly differ from that of any other mortal creature or being? Of Man? Of Waerling? Of Drimm? Of the many other dwellers upon Mithgar, the mortal, middle world?

"When seen through the eyes of an immortal being, when viewed from that perspective, are there significant differences? These answers and more I continue to ponder, daughter, just as must thee. Ponder, too, how the answers would differ if seen from the view of the mayfly.

"Heed! The mayfly is driven by the strongest urge of all: to mate, to reproduce. Survival of the species. No questions asked. No heed given to other needs.

"But as we look away from the mayfly and toward other creatures, still that urge to reproduce holds sway; yet among the various creatures, as the span of life increases, other drives, other needs, other desires begin to surface: survival of self, shelter, comfort, well-being, pleasure, curiosity, and more, much more.

"And the longer the life, the more important become these other, later needs, wants, desires, even at times displacing the more primitive drives.

"Heed! The needs, wants, and desires of the immortals are as different from those of most mortals as are their own needs, wants, and desires different from those of the mayfly.

"Even so, still we must ask these questions which will give us a view into the lives of mortals, questions which will allow us to see through their eyes. For the deeds of mortals can profoundly affect the lives of Elves, just as the deeds of Elves profoundly affect the lives of mortals.

"It is this effect upon one another—of Elf upon mortal, and of mortal upon Elf—which I wish thee to consider, Riatha, for thou are about to step unto Mithgar, unto the mortal world. There, thou will meet mortal kind for the first time. And thou will find them both strange and surpassing.

"Here, then, is another thing to ponder: What does it mean to have a mortal acquaintance, a mortal friend? What does it mean to love a mortal? Man, Waerling, Drimm, others: if thou should accept one as a friend, soon he will be gone, and if thou loved him, thou will grieve. Think upon this, too: just as is the mayfly, while thy friend lives, he, too, will be driven by his nature. A nature different from ours. Yet is this cause to shun friendship with mortals?

"Seldom do most mortal creatures rise above themselves to take the long view, or to even delve into the most fundamental questions: Why are we here? What is our purpose? What is the nature of the Creator? What is real? What is not? How do I know?

"Even the Allfather, Adon Himself, searches for answers, though His questions are far different from ours. He smiles when we name Him God, saying only that there are those as far above Him as we are above the mayfly.

"And now I ask thee: How can this be?

"And perhaps, daughter, *that* is the most important question of all, a question to be asked of everything—How can this be? . . . How can this be?

"Yet, being what we are, perhaps we have been given enough time not only to ponder these mysteries, but to ultimately find an answer or two.

"Even should we not succeed in discovering these basic truths, still, the striving seems worthwhile.

"Think, too, upon this: we believe Elwydd created Elvenkind first, though She will not say.

"But this we do know: Long did we live in Adon's worlds without the presence of other Folk. And in that time, that long, long time, mighty were our conquests. We warred, we pursued endless pleasure, we sought dominance, power, glory—and all was achieved, *all* . . . and all was vain, all turned to ashes in our very mouths even as we tasted success. In our greed we sought and found ultimate power within our sphere, over the land, over the seas, over the air, over all living things, over others of our own Kind. Aye, we strove for ultimate power, only to discover that it was and is a hollow ambition, full of emptiness when realized.

"Then we sought peace, solitude, small pleasures, truth, and beauty. These are the things we long had ignored in our quests to be mighty, yet in the end we found that these things were all that had any lasting meaning. And so, these are the things we yet pursue—along with nurturing and protecting Adon's creations.

"Can it be that Elwydd gave us those long, long years

alone upon the worlds so that we could discover these things for ourselves? Time to grow, to mature, to find for ourselves a better path through life?

"Perhaps it is so, for only after our feet were irreversibly set along this latter course, only then did she bring forth her other creations: Utruni, Drimma, Waerlinga, Man, and the Hidden Ones. In doing so, in creating these others only after we had found our way, she protected them from our cruel excesses in a time when we knew no better.

"Given all that we now know, all we have deduced, this we deem to be true: it is our lot to subtly guide others away from vanity and greed and dominance, away from those empty and deadly and barren places where we have already trod to our sorrow, and instead attempt at key moments to point them toward those places we have found to be full and fruitful and life-affirming.

"And, Riatha, my child, that is the mantle thou take unto thyself upon Mithgar: to ward the world, to be a Guardian, and to gently guide others toward the ways of life."

Daor fell silent, and none said aught for a while. These were not new thoughts posed by the Elf, but were instead deep enigmas pondered by Elvenkind throughout much of their existence, once they had survived their disastrous beginnings thousands and thousands of years agone, once they had set aside petty ambitions, turning instead toward truth and enlightenment, toward insight and wisdom. At last Daor stood, raising up Reín and Riatha, and onward they strode alongside the dancing brook, sire, dam, and daughter, graceful in their presence there in the bright green glade, while overhead among the twilight branches of the Eld Trees high above, the Silverlarks sweetly sang.

That same evening, in the clearing before her dwelling, Riatha sat on the verge of the swale and watched the distant sky transmute from azure to cerulean to lavender, the high clouds above glowing peach and rose and shell pink. And as day fell toward night, Reín came down across the soft sward to speak with her daughter, the dam bearing a gift as well as advice.

Reín handed over that which she had brought, long and

narrow and wrapped in silk. "As a Lian Guardian, thou will need such upon Mithgar, for it is at times a dangerous place to be."

Riatha unwrapped the gift. It was a sword. A magnificent sword: it was housed in a green scabbard, with tooled harness for back sling or waist, and the grip was inlaid with pale jade, crosshatched for firm grasp, while the pommel and crossguard were of dark silveron, rare and precious. Yet when Riatha withdrew the blade from its sheath, she gasped, for it too was of dark silveron, and starlight seemed captured deep within.

"Mother, I . . ." Riatha struggled to find words fitting for such a priceless bequeathal. Tears in her eyes, she took her mother's hands in her own and kissed them softly.

Reín's eyes, too, glistered, and her voice came gentle. "Hush, now, child, it is only fitting. 'Tis the same sword I bore when I was a warder upon Mithgar. Here, upon Adonar, there is no need. But there, on the mortal world, thou will find it necessary."

Riatha stood, blade in hand, cutting the air. "What marvelous balance, Mother. Has it a lineage?"

"It was crafted upon Mithgar, in Duellin, and has a Truename—Dúnamis—a name which I have never called, a name which thou should keep to thyself and not invoke lightly, for it draws strength and energy from allies nigh and yields it up to thee. And if thy need is dire enough, it will draw *life* as well. Grasp it by the hilt and Truename it— *Dúnami*—and it will glow with a blue light and serve thee; Truename it again and it will return to plainness. Yet, 'ware in its calling, for it will extract a terrible price from friends about thee—they will be weakened and mayhap be unable to defend themselves. And mortals may lose years from their span should *life* itself be drawn."

Now with eyes of apprehension, Riatha studied the weapon. After a moment she asked, "Has it a common name?"

"Dwynfor, who forged it, said that its public name should be Vulgsbane, though he did not say why."

Riatha carefully resheathed the blade. "Dwynfor? Dwynfor of Duellin in Atala on Mithgar?"

Reín nodded.

"Mother, Dwynfor is reputed to be the greatest bladesmith of all."

Again Reín nodded.

Riatha held the sword out to her dam. "Mother, this is too precious for one such as I—"

"Hush, child," admonished Reín, gently pressing the gift back onto her daughter. "Did I not say that it is useless here in Adonar? Too, I cannot think of one more fitting to bear it than thee. Dispute me not, daughter, for I would have it no other way. Besides, I did not come to argue over who should possess the blade. Great as is Dúnamis, still I came on a matter of even greater import."

Sitting once more, Riatha gently lay sword in scabbard across her lap, then looked at her mother.

"Riatha, thy sire said much in the glade today, yet he did not touch upon all, nor could he have, for wisdom comes with experience and not with words."

Riatha nodded, noting a touch of sadness in her mother's eyes. Even so, she did not comment upon it but waited instead.

Reín paused, as if searching for words. "Thy sire asked, 'What does it mean to love a mortal?' Heed, I know not whether Daor ever loved a mortal, yet this I do know: I, Reín, thy mother, I *do* know what it means to love a mortal, and I weep in that knowledge."

Riatha saw tears spring into her mother's eyes, and she felt her own heart clench.

Reín looked down at her hands folded in her lap. Her voice came softly in the twilight. "When I was a Lian Guardian, I loved a mortal Man.

"He was strong, gentle," she said quietly, then looked up at Riatha with eyes glimmering with unshed tears. "He could make a harp sing as could no other.

"And we loved. Oh, how we loved."

Of a sudden tears ran freely down Reín's face, and she could not continue speaking.

Her own eyes flooding, Riatha set aside Dúnamis and took her mother's hands in her own, gently unclenching the fists, smoothing out the fingers, stroking the backs of the hands, lending love and strength.

After long moments, Reín regained her composure, and though tears still stood in her eyes, again she spoke. "We survived the destruction of Rwn, did Evian and I, though but barely.

"But we did not survive the destruction of time."

Once more Reín's eyes flooded, and through her tears she looked imploringly at Riatha. "Oh, daughter, love not a mortal Man, for if thou do, then thou will see his youth slip out on the tides of time; thou will see his strength ebb away from him, his vigor wane. Thou will love him still, yet thou will watch his slow descent into age, and it will shatter thy heart.

"And e'en as he ages, thou will not change. Thou will remain as thou are today, just as I remained as I was.

"I could look into Evian's eyes, and behind the love that shone therein, still there was envy, perhaps e'en hatred, for I did not walk with him down the descending path he trod through time. Instead my path was level, not heeding time's call.

"I watched as he became an ancient, enfeebled Man, though but moments had passed in my count of the years.

"And when he died, so did my heart. Winter came into my days, no matter the seasons, and life was not worth living.

"Years passed uncounted, and still I mourned for Evian, for what once was, for what could never be.

"In those days I would have been consoled only by children born of Evian and me. But with him gone, I had no desire for children. Or rather, the only children that I wished for were children of impossibility.

"Yet even when Evian was alive, I knew, as do thou, that no issue may come of matings between Elfkind and Mankind, hence no children would come from our love—not only because I was Elf and he was a Man, but that we were upon Mithgar, and upon Mithgar no Elfchild may be conceived at all. Only here upon Adonar do such blessings befall Elvenkind. Yet even were Man and Elf to find themselves together upon Adonar, still I think that nought would come of it— children of such are impossibilities.

"And so I was inconsolable, and I did not think that I would ever love again.

"And I nearly did not. Yet thy father and I came to an understanding. At first I was merely fond of him. Yet slowly, slowly, I came to love him, too.

"But even as I took thy sire as my mate, I swore that should I someday be blessed with get of mine own, I would shelter them from such heartgrief as I had suffered.

"Seasons passed without count, and your sire and I hewed to the Elven way, bearing no sons or daughters, for Elvenkind was then in balance. There came a day, though, when our numbers had dwindled such that Daor and I and other couples could beget young. And in our family, first thou were born, and then thy brother, Talar.

"It was with thy birth that joy at last came back into my life. The rest thou know.

"But never will I forget Evian, and I weep for him still.

"And this is what I would warn thee of, Riatha: never love a mortal Man, for time will come to claim him, slowly yet inexorably, and it will shatter thy heart, perhaps beyond all mending."

Reín fell silent, her admonition said, tears yet sliding down her cheeks. In the Eldtree vaults above, Silverlarks sang their evensongs as twilight stole upon the land, the sky shading from lavender to violet to deep purple to velvet black, revealing wheeling stars glinting gold and copper and silver, while the argent light from a quarter Moon streamed down through the interlaced leaves, casting drifting filigree shadows upon the forest floor. At last, grey-eyed Riatha looked into Reín's eyes of grey. "I heed thee, Mother, and shall ward my heart against such."

Dawn came, an in-between time, neither night nor day, but something of each. Morning mist curled across the glade and among the trees, the mist an in-between state, neither water nor air, but something of each. And the marge bordering wood and glen was an in-between place, neither forest nor field, but something of each.

Dressed in grey leathers, Dúnamis affixed in shoulder harness, Riatha embraced her sire and dam and gave them a last kiss. Then she leapt astride the grey stud, the horse skittering and sidle stepping, eager to be underway.

Daor and Reín stepped back, the sire placing a comforting arm about the dam's shoulders.

And with a final good-bye, Riatha began chanting her journey unto Mithgar, her voice rising and falling, canting, neither singing nor speaking, but something in between, her mind lost in the ritual, neither wholly conscious nor unconscious, but something in between.

Off moved the horse, pacing in an arcane pattern, hooves flashing in a series of intricate steps, neither a dance nor a gait, but something in between.

Into the swirling mist they moved, there on the margin 'tween wood and field in the pale dawn light. Grey fog slowly becloaked them as they stepped the intricate steps and canted the arcane chant, rider and horse gradually fading into the mist, Riatha's voice becoming soft, then faint, then no more.

And in the silence left behind, Daor embraced Reín.

Their daughter was gone.

Out from the mist and into the dawn rode Riatha, still chanting, the grey stud yet pacing the arcane pattern. And when the Elfess could see the land about her, her voice fell silent, and the stud stopped his intricate stepping.

"Well done, Shadow," she murmured. "Thou has borne me unto Mithgar."

The horse nickered, bobbing his head up and down as if he understood.

About them, morning mist yet swirled. They were on a marge between forest and field, as was to be expected, for the anchoring points for crossings are fair matched unto one another, else no journey could be made. And the better the match, the easier the steps between. Yet with but rare exception, always would the chant be needed and the ritual steps be necessary, for perfect matches between stately Adonar and young, wild, untamed Mithgar are uncommon and scattered and for the most part unknown. And so, Riatha's journey followed the traditional rite, the arcane chant and precise movements driving her set of mind to that deep state necessary to make the transition, to go between.

And she had come unto Mithgar.

Even though it was still dawn—the in-between time—had Riatha desired to immediately return to Adonar, she could not have. For journeys to Mithgar must be made upon the dawn, whereas travel to Adonar could only be made at dusk. Dawn Ride, Twilight Ride: there was an ancient benediction among Elves upon Mithgar: *Go upon the twilight, return upon the dawn.*

But Riatha was not thinking upon this eld saying as she emerged from the mist and into the Mithgarian dawn. Instead, she looked about at the wild tangle of greenery and listened to the unfettered singing of Mithgarian birds, her eye spotting unfamiliar shapes and colors winging through the dawnlight, while here and there an animal slipped furtively among the undergrowth or ran along branches above. *Wild and untamed indeed are thee, Mithgar.*

She sat and drank in the air and light and sounds and sights of the forest and field and of the sky above, finding all new yet familiar. At last she turned her horse north and spoke softly to him, urging Shadow into a canter. And as the Sun rose, her heart laughed, for she was on Mithgar, and she was riding toward her brother, Talar, and his wife, Trinith, who lived among the Elves of Darda Immer, the Brightwood of Atala.

A century passed, or perhaps more than one, for Time and Elves are somewhat strangers unto one another, and season followed season without close count, and years fled into the past. In the passing decades Riatha and Talar and Trinith stayed in the Brightwood, learning the lessons of first aid and herblore and healing.

There came a day when Talar and Trinith moved to Duellin, some ten leagues hence on the eastern shore of Atala. Talar was to take up the art of sword making, apprenticed to the legendary Dwynfor himself, while Trinith was to take up a harp. But Riatha took on another duty, standing watch upon the slopes of Karak, while the firemountain slept, seeking signs of when it might awaken again, if ever.

Seasons changed and changed, and now and again Riatha would journey to see her fair-haired brother and his ebon-haired wife, or Talar and Trinith would visit her. And in the evenings they would gather 'round the hearths of Darda Immer, or those of Duellin, where Trinith would join with other harpers to sing the Elven songs that reached back to the beginnings of time itself.

There came a season when word was borne across the sea that *Spaunen* in great number seemed to be mustering in the Grimwall, there in Mithgar to the east. Something was afoot, and warriors were wanted.

Then it was that Riatha came to the seaport of Duellin a last time and bade farewell to Talar and Trinith and set sail for Caer Pendwyr, an Arbalina ship swiftly bearing her and her steed eastward across the Weston Ocean and through the Avagon Sea to the Land of Pellar. And in shoulder sling rode Dúnamis.

Then came the Great War, the War of the Ban.

Riatha rode with the Elves of Darda Galion, that mighty Elvenholt there alongside the Grimwall.

Fierce were the battles, and long the struggle lasted. And there was great loss and grief during the strife. Many were the Death Redes—those final messages somehow sent from a dying Elf unto another of his Kind in the moment of death, defying time and distance to reach the one for whom it is intended, benumbing the Elven recipient with the knowledge that a beloved companion has died, one who had just begun life.

But as devastating as is a single Elven death, the demise of hundreds is overwhelming, as was the case on the Day of Anguish, when Atala plunged beneath the sea in cataclysmic ruin—by Gyphon's hand, it was claimed.

Thousands were lost and thousands more in that monstrous catastrophe, as Humans and Drimma and Waerlinga and Elves perished. And everywhere on Mithgar, Elves were whelmed unto their knees, all Elves upon Mithgar without exception, stunned by the disembodied deathcry of hundreds and hundreds of their kindred in the moment of their dying, their passing like a ghastly wind blowing chill through the very souls of all Elvenkind.

The effects of the destruction of Atala did not end with the sinking of the land beneath the sea, oh no, for other realms of Mithgar suffered mightily with its passing, as great tidal waves rolled over the Weston Ocean, rising up into vast walls as they approached land, smashing into distant seashores, inundating all, sweeping away villages and cities and dwellings and lives alike. Too, a thunderous sound rang 'round the world, as if from a mighty explosion, and the sky grew dark, filled with a pall, while ash fell onto lands beyond the sea.

And in one of those lands, Riatha, too, had fallen stunned, for so many of Elvenkind had died in the destruction of Atala that no Elf on this Plane had escaped the consequences. But though she had been bedazed, hammered to her knees by this vast last cry of desolation, still no Death Rede had come to her from Talar, and so he might have survived, given that he had not instead sent his Rede to Trinith, for if that were the case, then Riatha would not know of his passing.

And of those whose anguished cries she had felt, they were dead, all dead; and Riatha wept for them, the Elves whose lives had just begun, no matter their ages.

Slowly her grief subsided, for the Great War continued and she had battles to fight regardless of her distress, and War waits for no one. She fought on, a hollowness in her breast whenever she thought of Talar or Trinith.

Yet there came a day when Talar rode into the wooded site where the Lian Guardians were encamped, Riatha among them. She wept to see him, and he wept, too, for when Atala had sunk without warning, Trinith had been swallowed by the sea. Talar had been waiting for her aboard a ship in the harbor of Duellin, a ship that was set to sail the very next day, bound for Hovenkeep, there in the south, he and she coming to join the Lian in Darda Galion. She had gone ashore to bid farewell to Glinner, the Harpmaster, when Karak exploded and Atala sank. The ship that Talar himself had been on was destroyed in the blast, and he remembered nought until he had found himself floating amid wreckage the next day; how he had escaped the hideous suck as the great island had plunged under the sea, he knew not, yet survive he did.

Some days later—nine, he thought—he had been rescued by a passing ship. It bore him to a port in Gothon, and from there he had made his way to Darda Galion, and thence to

Darda Erynian, following after the Lian company Riatha rode among.

And even though he had been whelmed by the shattering of the ship, still he had received Trinith's Death Rede: *I love thee*, was her sending. *I love thee*, nothing more.

And so as Riatha and Talar were reunited, Joy and Grief stood side by side in the forest glade that day.

The War dragged on, Talar and Riatha battling shoulder to shoulder and back to back. Then word came that the High Plane itself had been invaded by Gyphon's *Spaunen* from the Untargarda, from Neddra, from the Underworld on the Lower Plane.

With this dire news Riatha bethought to take Dúnamis back unto her dam, for surely now it was needed upon Adonar. Yet even as she prepared for the Twilight Ride, foe fell upon her company, and she fought instead of passing between the Planes. A running battle, it lasted for ten days— and during that time more word came from the High World, from the Hōhgarda: Gyphon's army now marched across Adonar, aiming, it seemed, for one of the places of crossing in between, preparing to invade Mithgar. To prevent such a disaster, Adon Himself declared that he would sunder the ways between the Planes, and although any could yet use the rituals to return unto the realms where their blood permitted, once there, they would not be able to venture forth unto other Planes again.

Hence, Elvenkind could return to Adonar, to the High Plane, to the realm of their blood, but then could not afterward step unto the Middle Plane and Mithgar, or to the Lower Plane and Neddra, for neither of these was of their blood. Likewise, *Spaunen* and the Cursed Ones could step to Neddra on the Lower Plane, but once there could never again venture to the High and Middle Planes. And any who were of the Middle Plane could return from High or Low, but never pass to them again.

One day later, by Adon's doing, the open ways between the Planes were sundered, and only the ritualistic blood-ways endured. To the Elves the Dawn Ride was no more, though the Dusk Ride yet remained.

After agonizing over whether to return to Adonar and aid in the battles 'gainst Gyphon there, or to stay on Mithgar and oppose Gyphon's lieutenant, Modru, and the vast Hordes hammering upon the Alliance, Riatha and Talar finally chose to remain upon the Middle Plane, for here the need was known and seemed greatest, here where the Grand Alliance of Men and Elves, of Drimma and Waerlinga, and eventually of Utruni, grappled with Rucha and Loka, Trolls, Ghûlka and Hèlsteeds, Vulgs, and other creatures dire. Too, Modru was aided by Men—the Lakh of Hyree and the Rovers of Kistan, as well as the Hordes of Jūng. Here on Mithgar, too, Wizards fought against Wizards, and against Gargoni and Dragons as well.

These were the days before the Ban, and the Foul Folk could range the land in daylight as well as dark, though it was said that even then they preferred to do their deeds in the pit of night.

Vast battles were fought across the face of the world, and many were slain.

Riatha and Talar with other Lian ranged along the eastern flank of the Grimwall, warding Darda Galion, warding Darda Erynian and the Greatwood, and warding the open wold between.

It was in the Dalgor March, there where the River Dalgor flows into the mighty Argon, that they met Aravan, bearing his crystal spear, following after Galarun, son of Coron Eiron, Elven King upon Mithgar.

Galarun and his company rode at haste, for he bore with him a mighty token of power—the Dawn Sword. And Galarun was bound for Darda Galion, where he would make the Dusk Ride to Adonar, taking with him the silver sword, for it was said to have the power to slay Gyphon, the High Vûlk Himself.

Riatha and Talar and their company of Lian Guardians joined with Galarun, his mission vital beyond compare. Yet as they passed through the Dalgor March, unexpected fog rolled o'er them, and Foul Folk rose up out from the clutches of the fen and whelmed into them. A pitched battle was fought, and many were felled, Galarun among them.

And when the *Rûpt* were routed at last, the Dawn Sword

was gone. Whether it was borne off by Foul Ones or instead had disappeared beneath the mire, none could say.

In the end, Modru lost, the Battle of Hèl's Crucible crushing him entirely. With his defeat Adon prevailed, banishing Gyphon unto the Abyss beyond the Spheres.

As well, Adon caused a bright new star to appear in the heavens above, burning fulgently, furiously, rivalling the Moon itself in brightness. A week or so it flared, and when it died, disappearing back into the blackness whence it had come, the Foul Folk were banned from the light of day, suffering the Withering Death should daylight fall upon them.

Too, Adon reft the burning fire from the breaths of those Dragons who had arrayed themselves against Him, and they became Cold-drakes, their male get thereafter as well. Sunlight was also death unto them, though they did not turn into dust, their Dragonhide proof against such.

With the Sundering, the Vani-lērihha—the Silverlarks—had disappeared from Darda Galion, had disappeared from the Eldwood. No more were their songs heard warbling down from the lofty branches, sweet songs that Riatha had studied. And when it became apparent that they would not return, Riatha came to live in Arden Vale.

Centuries passed, and centuries more, and in that time Riatha took up silver smithing, music and singing and harping, gardening, the sewing and reaping of grain, stone carving, animal husbandry, painting, weaving, and a host of other skills. She had, after all, forever to learn, and she was just beginning.

Throughout the centuries as well, she would occasionally take a lover into her bed. She was nonetheless a young lady, given at times to lusts and desires and gentle longings, as all young ladies are; too, it must be remembered that this young Elfess would live forever, and still she would be young; it is not, then, unexpected that she would have a lover or two as each century passed and the seasons fell. Even so, she had not yet fallen in love.

More Wars came unto Mithgar, though most were skirmishes and of little import in the long scheme of things.

And so Riatha in Arden Vale and Talar in Darda Erynian had little to do with such.

Even the War of the Usurper did not engage their interest, though other Elves were involved—perhaps it was *because* other Lian were involved that neither Riatha nor Talar rode to War, for only a subtle, gentle guidance of Humankind is called for.

At times, however, Riatha *did* take up Dúnamis and fare forth upon some mission or task.

And so, too, did her brother.

But this was to be expected, for the Lian Guardians warded the world, preserving Adon's creations from depredation.

Yet these ventures Riatha undertook were but way stations along the journey toward her prime destiny. And had she been counting the measure of time, more than four thousand years had passed since she had come to the Middle Plane, some forty-one centuries—or mayhap as many as forty-two or -three, who can say?—had elapsed for her on Mithgar ere the events occurred which ultimately were to lead to the shaking of all creation. But as with the rest of her Kind, she had little noted the passage of time; after all, even though more than four millennia had elapsed, she had just begun her life's journey, not realizing the critical juncture that she now was beginning to enter.

For the Great Weaver had all this time been gathering together many disparate threads and now began weaving them into the patterns that were necessary to shape the fate of the world yet to be.

There came a day when a messenger from Darda Erynian fared into Arden Vale, and he bore word to Riatha from Talar. And the slender, golden-haired Elfess looked upon the scroll from her slender, golden-haired brother, and she was glad.

Yet when she broke the seal, his words were grim:

*Riatha,*
*There is a monster somewhere within the Grimwall,*
*and he preys upon the innocent and unprotected. I do*
*not speak here of the* Draedan *in Drimmen-deeve, but*

*instead of a butchering fiend. Sister of mine, should aught happen to me, seek out Baron Stoke, for he is the evil I hunt.*

*Talar*

Riatha felt a cold hand grip her heart, and to her came a vision of her brother's face, a steely glint in his grey eyes.

Two years passed and then another, twelve seasons in all, and no word came to her from Talar. Where he was, what he did, was unknown.

Summer was upon the land, and Riatha and the other Lian Guardians were readying for combat, and her mind was occupied with stratagems and plans. Yet as she took up her sword, she noted Talar's scroll within the chest. Once more she read it, and again a dread premonition skittered across her heart, but she told herself that it was merely concern for his welfare. She set aside the scroll to finish her preparations, for the Elves of Arden, allied with the Men of the Wilderland, were setting forth this day to purge Drearwood of the Foul Folk who lay waste to caravans and bands of travellers along the Crossland Road passing through the dread forest. Peopled as the Drearwood was with Rucha, Loka, Ghûlka, Trolls, and other such *Rûpt*, it was expected that the campaign would take months.

Too, it was rumored that among the *Spaunen* in Drearwood dwelled one of the last Gargoni, deadly fear casters, as was the *Draedan* of Drimmen-deeve, and the Lian had no Wizards among them to deal with such.

She was just buckling Dúnamis in its shoulder harness across her back when Aravan, bearing his crystal spear, stepped through the doorway of her thatched hut. "Ready?" She nodded, and they stepped forth into the sunlight, where stood their steeds.

Wending past were mounted Lian Guardians, making their way ahorse across the vale and up the face of the western bluff, entering the carven tunnel to pass through, where they would emerge along the northeastern reach of the deadly forest. And into this grim procession merged Riatha and Aravan.

After the summer of the Purging of Drearwood, autumn came, and Riatha was occupied with the harvest. Still she had had no word from Talar, yet he was a skilled warrior and would not take undue chances. Even so, this was the longest that she had gone without word.

And then came that dreadful day.

Riatha was striding up from the fields, returning from a day of scything, when she was whelmed unto her knees, her skin afire, her heart hammering, a dread horror washing over her. And through eyes not her own, she saw the face of what appeared to be a Man, a narrow, pale, wolfish face with yellow gaze, laughing madly, the face of a fiend.

And in a long-fingered hand was a thin-bladed flaying knife.

*Stoke!* came a wordless message.

Pain started at the soles of her feet and lanced up her legs, as if flesh were being stripped from her. She shrieked in agony, her hands covering her face, and other Lian rushed to aid her, yet they could do nought.

Unbearable pain ripped upward, from her feet and ankles to her legs to her thighs as her flesh was rent from her, from her back, from her shoulders and arms, from her hands; then flesh was torn from her forehead and face and neck, ripping down her chest, her stomach. Yawling, shrieking, screaming, she was flayed alive, agony exploding throughout her entire being. Mewling, she fell down and down into a bubbling, blood-red Hèl, her mind erupting with horror and fear and hatred and fury and unbearable pain.

And then she was pierced through, impaled, a hideous instrument bursting outward from her abdomen.

A final drawn-out cry flared silently in her mind: *Stoke . . . !*

And then no more. The pain gone. The horror remaining.

And the hatred and fury.

And Riatha wept and raged and cried out in anguish and desolation. For this was a Death Rede: Talar had been murdered.

By Stoke.

Three years passed, thirty-eight Moons, and Riatha searched for Stoke.

Along the Grimwall she ranged, listening for rumors of a fiend but finding nought.

But with the onset of winter came a whisper: *Vulfcwmb, in Aven*, it was hissed. *He's back. The Baron.*

But with the onset of winter came a whisper: *Vulfcwmb, in Aven*, it was hissed. *He's back. The Baron.*

A blizzard raged as Riatha came upon the wreckage of wagons, horses slain. Yet trapped under an overturned wain she found an unconscious Waerling, Tomlin—Pebble.

Their tale is told in full elsewhere and will not be repeated here. Suffice it to say that she bore the wounded Waerling to shelter in Vulfcwmb. There he was revived and told that Vulgs and *Rûpt* had attacked the wains and had borne off his sire and dam, his dammia Petal, and her sire.

Riatha and Tomlin were joined in Vulfcwmb by Urus, a Baeran, who was himself seeking Stoke—Urus's quest one of revenge also.

Together they managed to find Stoke's strongholt, but were captured and thrown into a cell with Petal, for she yet survived. The other Waerlinga, though, had been flayed alive by Baron Stoke, the Vulgmaster.

Stoke came to slay them, changing into a great Vulg. But they managed to win their freedom, though it nearly cost them their lives, especially Urus.

Stoke escaped their vengeance that night, and in the shape of a leathery-winged *thing* he flew beyond their fury and into the Grimwall. But they pledged to one another that they would hunt him down, wherever he might be.

Two years passed, and once again rumor of Stoke's whereabouts surfaced.

They traced him to Dreadholt, but the monster escaped their wrath a second time, though Riatha came within a sword stroke of slaying him ere she herself was nearly slain. Again he went to ground, and they lost his trail.

Seventeen more years passed, and at last word came of mysterious disappearances nigh Inge in Aralan, there along the Grimwall. Perhaps Stoke was near.

Once more the four set out to slay a monster. And there in a monastery above the Great North Glacier in the unstable land near Dragonslair, again they found Baron Stoke.

He nearly escaped, a leathery-winged *thing* again, but Tomlin wounded him with a silver sling bullet, and with damaged wing, down the creature spun and down, landing at last upon the white glacier below.

It was on Springday night, the anniversary of Black Kalgalath's death, and the land was wracked by violent shudders.
The glacier itself was heaving and cracking, crevasses opening and closing.

Still, they managed to make their way to where Stoke had
landed, and when they spread out to search for him, Stoke
nearly killed Riatha, smashing her senseless with a great
jagged chunk of ice. But ere he could behead the Elfess, from
the limit of her range Petal hurled one of her silver throwing
knives and struck him fair in the upper left arm. Howling
in agony, for silver weapons were his bane, Stoke took the
shape of a Vulg, preparing to leap a yawning crevasse that
had opened in the glacier. But just as he sprang, Urus came
running and leapt as well, intercepting the fiend, and locked
together in combat they plunged down into the black depths
below, and the crevasse slammed shut.

Five years passed, or perhaps it was six, who can say, for
Elves keep not precise count as would mortal Man. Riatha
returned to the monastery above the glacier, there in the
juddering land, her memories wrapped about her, memories
of Vulfcwmb and Dreadholt, and of the abbey standing tall
and grey and somber before her.

> "... Ai oi! This ain't no child! 'Tis a Waldan!..."
> "... Tomlin. My name is Tomlin. But everybody calls
> me Tom or Tommy ... or they call me Pebble because
> of these slingstones I carry about ..."
> "... Again I ask, will any come with us?..."
> "... I am Urus, and I will go ..."
> "... I am Urus ..."
> "... and I will go ..."

Taking a deep breath, Riatha crossed the stone courtyard
and stepped to the closed wooden double doors of the great
rectangular building with a central tower jutting up into the
dark sky. Drawing Dúnamis, she pushed the left-most panel
inward, recalling voices from another time.

> "... 'Ware, though it seems abandoned ..."

Through an empty vestibule and past another set of doors she stepped softly, entering the great open chamber.

"... *A hall of worship* ..."

At the far end of the shadow-wrapped gallery stood an altar to Adon. Visions of a past time filled her mind.

*... Behind the altar, lying on the floor was an asper-gillum, a small handheld device for the ceremonial sprinkling of blessed water. Urus took it up. Ivory and silver, it seemed; yet if Stoke were here, why would he let such a treasure lie? ...*

The Elfess looked up at the balconies above. A tremor thrummed through the floor.

*... Snarling Vulgs; yawling, scimitar-bearing Rucha and Loka; the* shang *and* chang *of steel on steel; Petal running along a rope high above, spanning from balcony to balcony ...*

Yet now, nought but abandoned silence filled the enshadowed chamber.

Turning from these memories, Riatha passed back through the wooden doors, coming out 'neath gloomy skies, a soughing wind skirling. Again the earth trembled.

Leaving her horse stabled behind, the Elfess made her way down from the monastery and onto the crevasse-raddled ice, her thoughts now upon the one she had come to mourn.

*... Darkness gathering at the back of the cell, enveloping Urus, his shape changing, dropping down on all fours, long black claws and ivory fangs, and where Urus had been stood a great Bear! ...*

Riatha scanned the distant ice. *I came to grieve at thy death site, yet I know not that I can find where thou fell, my Urus.*

Out onto the vast frozen river she trod, wending her way

past great cracks and crevices in the ice, glancing back now and again at the monastery to get her bearings. At last she came to the point where she deemed Urus had plunged with Stoke down into the crevasse, now gone. She sought some sign that *this* was the place. Yet search as she would, nought came of her efforts. At last, heartsick, she made her way back to the monastery.

In the night, Riatha fell into the meditative state that Elves rest within, though even Elves sleep true sleep at times, and her mind wandered through memories, some pleasant, some ill.

*". . . Never love a mortal Man, for time will come to claim him . . ."*

*". . . I heed thee, Mother, and shall ward my heart against such . . ."*

*". . . I am Urus, and I will go . . ."*

*. . . Whoom! A burning overhead beam crashed down upon her . . .*

Riatha startled awake.

In the stable below, the mare slept standing. A chill wind eddied in the rafters above. The Elfess shrugged the blanket from her shoulders and climbed down from the loft. Stepping outside, she scanned the sky above. It was still cast over with clouds, and no stars shone.

Leftward, the monastery tower loomed upward. *Perhaps I can see from there where Stoke landed on the glacier. And thence find where Urus fell.*

Riatha buckled Dúnamis across her back, for she would not enter the dark interior unarmed . . . not here in the Grimwall.

As she strode for the building, again her mind turned on memories past.

*. . . Strong arms took her up. All about, fire raged as Dreadholt burned. The falling beam had broken her left arm and left leg, but the Waerlinga had dragged her free as Urus lifted up the burning truss. His arms burnt,*

*Urus bore her through the conflagration, while ceilings collapsed and timbers fell and flames raged ...*

Riatha entered the hall of worship, making her way past the altar and through the sacristy beyond, coming to a spiral stairway winding upward through the blackness and to the bell tower above.

Up these steps she twisted, remembered visions preceding her.

> *... Urus leapt up the stairs, she in pursuit, and high above she could hear Stoke fleeing toward the top. Below, the Waerlinga pelted after. Dúnamis was in her hand, and she knew that if Stoke came within her reach, he was dead.*
>
> *Up she ran and up, hard on Urus's heels, the Baeran charging after Stoke in grim silence.*
>
> *Up through a trapdoor they came, into a chamber where massive wooden yokes held great iron bells now silent.*
>
> *And Urus roared his fury, raging out into the night. Off in the bright moonlight she could see a dark-winged shape flapping—Stoke was getting away.*
>
> *But Pebble appeared at her side, and loosed a silver sling bullet ...*

Riatha came to the top of the tower. Making her way past the silent iron bells, she stepped to the archway overlooking the glacier, her gaze sweeping, seeing—

—*A light! On the glacier!* Out in the distance upon the white field, a soft glow shone. Faint, as of a firefly in the night, but a glow still. And it moved not, but remained motionless upon the ice.

Taking a sighting, her heart hammering, Riatha hurried down from the tower and out through the hall of worship. Once again she made her way down to the glacier, veering this way and that to avoid crevasses and splits. Crossing the great jumble, she came at last to the place she had seen from the bell tower.

Here the ice was nearly transparent, and a soft golden glow shone up through the glacier, coming from deep, deep below.

Riatha looked back up at the monastery in the distance, knowing that a short way from here was where she had spent the day searching. *Surely that was where Urus fell, as near as I can say. Yet I was closer to the monast— The movement! The glacier moves! Urus fell there, but in the years after, the ice moved.*

Riatha's heart cried out for her to *do* something. But what? If this light truly marked where Urus now lay, then his body was hundreds of feet below, trapped forever in the translucent depths. *Nay! Not forever! Just until the ice comes unto the great north wall. And when that happens, my Urus, I will be there to find thee and see that thou are given a fitting burial.*

Riatha wept, tears coursing down her cheeks. And she knelt on the ice and held her hands out in the golden glow, seeking . . . comfort, solace. And the world trembled now and again, the land yet shaking from Kalgalath's ruin.

It was dawn ere she returned to the monastery, having well marked the place where glowed the golden light, its soft radiance tugging at her heart.

She rode away that day, leaving behind the monastery, whose iron bells had last rung in the great quaking on that Springday night when Urus had fallen.

Years passed, some four or five. And came the day when Rael spoke a prophecy, and Riatha journeyed to speak of it to Pebble and Petal, the Waerlinga grim with the portent, yet pledging to instruct their firstborns down through time.

More years fled, and the Winter War came upon the land, and with it the Dimmendark. Riatha was in Riamon at the time and joined the Lian Guardians there to once again battle Modru's minions.

Many a Death Rede blew coldly through the souls of Elves from the fields of conflict, especially from the Battle of Kregyn, yet everywhere the survivors fought on, risking death despite the fact that they were just beginning their lives, no matter their ages. To do otherwise was to surrender unto Modru's and Gyphon's eternal damnation.

When that War ended, again the Elfess returned unto Arden Vale.

Time and years retreated into the past, and word came

that Tomlin—Pebble—had died, two years less than four decades after the end of the Winter War. Riatha journeyed to the Boskydells and played her harp and sang of Tomlin's deeds at his gravesite, keeping faith with words said years past at another wake: the Baeron Gathering in The Clearing in the Greatwood, where Tomlin and she had told and sung of Urus's deeds; then it was that Tomlin had remarked again that he would be pleased should someone sing of his deeds at his own passing. And so Riatha stood at his graveside and plucked the shimmering strings of her silver harp and lifted her clear voice into the gentle air, and sang Tomlin's soul up into the sky.

Then she took Petal with her back to Arden Vale, where the wee damman lived in honor.

Another sevenyear passed, and Petal succumbed to her own mortality. Riatha again journeyed to the Boskydells, to bury Petal at the side of her lifemate, there in the rich earth of Eastdell. Once more she sang above the grave of a loved one and played her silver harp. Too, she carved a headstone and placed it thereupon, its words in Sylva, the language of the Lian; it said merely, *Beloved friends.*

Over the next centuries, Riatha oft made the long journey to the Great North Glacier, each time finding the soft golden glow in the night. Through the years the light slowly drifted north and eastward, driven by the mass of ice, flowing, ever flowing, yet never seeming to hurry its journey through the centuries. And always Riatha wept for her lost Urus.

In these same centuries Riatha learned the ways of forestry and of the use of a bow; too, she sharpened her climbing skills; and she studied the arts of stealth and stalking and of concealment, for the Grimwall was again becoming a dangerous place to be, *Rûpt* and such once more beginning to venture forth after the crushing defeat centuries agone at Winter War's end and again in the War of Drimmen-deeve. And Riatha's visits to grieve at the Great North Glacier became more hazardous with the passage of time.

In spite of the danger, the Elfess continued each quarter century to make a pilgrimage to where Urus had fallen, once taking Aravan along, for he would see the abandoned monastery with its iron bells that rang whenever the earth quaked heavily, the Elf yet searching for the lost silver sword. Too, she took him to the ruins of Dreadholt and to the rubble of Stoke's bartizan near Vulfcwmb to look for the sword in those places as well, to no avail.

But as decade after decade elapsed, eroding away the centuries, she neglected not her studies in music and painting, in decorative gardening, and in the weaving of silken fabrics, as well as her delvings into the mysteries of crystals, of gems, of precious metals.

And she kept up her skill with the sword, practicing with other Elven Masters.

All these skills she gathered unto her, knowing that more, many more were to come. She was, after all, just beginning.

Winters came and went, winters when the earth slept, centuries of such passing seasons, each winter followed by the awakenings of spring—spring after spring. Summers followed—bright, bright summers, with their seasons of growth and growings. And then came the autumns, the harvest times, the times of gathering the earth's bounty.

The centuries passed, ticking off the count of their years. And all the while the stars wheeled their arcane courses across the skies above, forming omens and portents for any with the skills to read the shifting patterns. And still the glacier flowed, gradually moving downslope, the light deep in the ice below drifting, drifting, north and east, drifting outward, away from the main flow and toward the eastern edge but moving still. And slowly, slowly, the time drew nigh when the Eye of the Hunter would sweep through the nighttides to come, these drawing nearer and nearer until they lay but some two and a half years hence.

And upon a harvest time nigh a millennium past the Winter War, Riatha scythed in a field of grain. There came a call from behind, from field's edge. And when the Elfess turned and shaded her eyes, there ahorse was Jandrel, with two Waerlinga mounted upon ponies at his side.

Riatha handed her scythe to one of the gleaners and walked toward the visitors. Although she knew not the names of these Waerlinga, still she knew who they were . . .

. . . The Lastborn Firstborns had come.

# CHAPTER 10

# Deliverance

**Springday Night, 5E988**

*[The Present]*

A *aooouu* ... Again the distant yawl of Vulgs on the hunt sounded, echoing from crevice and crag. Riatha looked at Aravan as if for confirmation.

Beneath Aravan's jerkin at his throat was a blue stone on a thong, a stone now icy chill. "Aye," he agreed. "I deem as do thee—'tis Vulgs, a pack, and they are in pursuit."

Faeril peered down the slope of the twisting canyon, shadowy and dark in the starlit night, the damman staring toward where the defile wrenched out of sight. "I don't see them."

Gwylly looked the opposite way, up the slope hemmed in by towering stone. "Neither do I."

Rocks and ice yet rattled and shattered down from the steeps above, loosed by the quaking of the unstable land. Still the faint tintinnabulation of far-off iron bells sounded.

Faeril turned to Riatha. "Perhaps they are on our trail, yet with these echoes I can't tell which way the sounds come from, the direction of the Vulgs."

The risen Moon was yet hidden beyond the high eastern rim of the deep canyon, though its pale silver rays now splashed against the wall to the west. Weighing their options, the Elfess fixed her gaze on this moonlit stone and glittering ice rising sheer in the near distance. "Whence come the Vulgs—from ahead or behind—I cannot say. Yet this I do know: up slope or down, still we are not fleet enough to escape them afoot should we run."

As if to underscore Riatha's words, wrauling howls rebounded along the twisting granite slot, louder still, closer still.

Faeril reached for a throwing knife. "Do we make a stand? Battle?"

"Nay," gritted Riatha. "Vulgs are a savage foe and a pack would o'erwhelm us."

Nettled, Gwylly jammed a sling bullet back into his belt pouch, exasperation in his voice: "Well, if we don't run and we don't fight, then *what?* What do we do? Where do we go from here?"

"Up!" declared Riatha, deciding at last. "Up the moonlit wall. We must climb."

Gwylly gasped. "Climb? Up that? But the ice, the falling rocks—"

"Dispute me not, Gwylly," interrupted Riatha. "Afoot we are certain dead. But up the sheer stone and ice, we mayhap live, for Vulgs cannot climb such."

In haste they set out for the western rampart. Still, now and again a rock or shard of ice plummeted down. Yet the Vulg howls neared, ringing loudly.

The Elfess led, scanning the wall as they drew closer, while the Elf brought up the rear, his crystal-bladed spear at the ready. Trying to maintain the pace, the two Waerlinga floundered in the middle, their breathing harsh as they struggled, the snow deep for ones of their stature. Again howls juddered through the night. Aravan's next words were ominous: "I am reminded that where run Vulgs, so run the *Rûpt.*"

Gwylly's features were pale, and Faeril's lips were pinched into a thin grim line. Overhead, the Eye of the Hunter streamed across the spangle of stars. "If *Rûpt* there be," replied Riatha, "then we must ascend swiftly, for unlike the Vulgs, Rucha and Loka *do* climb."

"If maggot-folk come, will they have archers among them?" gasped Gwylly.

Aravan answered: "If there be Rucha or Loka among the

Vulgs, then likely some will bear the twisted bows and black-shafted arrows."

"Then indeed we had better climb swiftly," panted Gwylly, his legs churning through the snow.

"Less talking and more running, my buccaran," hissed Faeril, keeping pace beside him. "Save your breath for the climb."

As they reached the western wall, the rim of the Moon could be seen clearing the eastern stone rampart. Up a slope of rubble and scree and ice and snow they scrambled, the ramp piled high against the base of the wall, made of debris rained down during the shivering quakes. When they reached the top, Riatha shed her pack, directing the others to do likewise. Quickly they withdrew their climbing gear: harnesses, snap rings, rock nails, jams, ice hammers, and other such.

As Gwylly belted on his gear he glanced down the defile and gasped. "Here they come," he gritted, pointing at dark shapes loping into view 'round the twisting curve, flowing one after another like a long disconnected creature.

Hearts thudding, Gwylly and Faeril seemed transfixed by the sight of the black Wolf-like beasts, but no Wolves were these, for each was nearly as large as a pony, yet sleek and swift and savage.

"Haste, Aravan," barked Riatha, her voice firm, controlled, "rope the packs together. We'll pull them up after."

Aravan backslung his spear and began to lash the packs to his rope, while Riatha quickly knotted the remaining three lines to one another and clipped the four comrades at intervals on the resulting length: she first, Faeril next, then Gwylly, and finally Aravan. And as the Vulgs gave voice to long, ululating howls and raced up the slope, the Elfess turned to the craggy face of the bluff, seeking a safe route. Choosing, she began to climb.

Onward came the Vulgs, now less than two furlongs distant, their speed frightening. Still kneeling at the packs, "Climb!" hissed Aravan to Gwylly and Faeril. "They'll be upon us in ten heartbeats."

Up scrambled the Warrows, following Riatha's lead, the Elfess climbing rapidly.

Now the Vulgs sighted their quarry and hideous wrauls

shattered the air, echoing and reverberating in the high-walled canyon, the savage creatures leaping forward, rushing to the kill.

Yellow-eyed, poison-fanged monsters plunging toward him, Aravan cinched the last knot and then turned and leapt to the stone wall and began climbing. Ahead, Gwylly and Faeril clambered upward, and beyond them climbed Riatha. The land shuddered; ice and stone fell; yet up they went and up, ignoring all, Aravan coming last, the Elf now but some twenty feet up the stone, not safe, for the lead Vulg was even then bounding up the ramp of scree and ice and snow, mere yards away, mere strides away from the quarry above, and with a guttural snarl he sprang. *"Anchor!"* cried Gwylly, and Aravan thrust outward and sideways from the stone, trusting to the Waerling's skills, the Elf leaping away just as the Vulg crashed against the rock wall where he had been. Yelping, the black beast fell back among the pack rushing after and tumbled a way down the slope ere scrambling up. Above, Aravan ran in a shallow arc across and up the face of the perpendicular cliff, suspended by the line anchored by Gwylly. At the far extent of his run, the Elf managed to grasp a rock projection, halting his pendulum-like dash up the plumb surface. Below, snarling Vulgs leapt upward, claws scrabbling against vertical stone, the great beasts falling inches short of Aravan, for they had not the advantage of a running start. Swiftly Aravan climbed upward and across, now clearly beyond the reach of the slavering beasts raving below, though they raged and leapt still.

When the Elf reached the ledge where Gwylly stood, he found a trembling Waerling. Hands shaking, Gwylly pointed to the jam anchored in a crevice, the climbing rope cinched to the attached ring. "I didn't know," Gwylly's voice quavered, unshed tears glistening in his eyes. "I didn't know if it would hold. I snapped it taut and threw the clinch, but I didn't know."

Aravan looked into the viridian eyes of the buccan and smiled. "Thou did well, wee one. Thou did well."

Of a sudden, from below came furious snarling and the sounds of rending. "The packs!" cried Faeril. "They are shredding the packs!"

Quickly Aravan snapped a retaining strap to the ring of

the jam in the wall. Then he turned about on the ledge and grasped the line affixed between his belt and the packs below, reeling it in hand over hand. Above, Riatha and Faeril clambered downward to help, for all the packs together weighed over a hundred pounds. Gwylly on the ledge beside the Elf was out of position to lift, though he took up the drooping slack, coiling the excess. The line below snapped taut and Aravan grunted and hauled, and up came the packs, out from the Vulgs below; yet they in turn jumped and clamped long fangs down upon the canvas and leather and lunged back, pulling Aravan off balance, and he fell. The belt strap fastened to the jam stopped him from plunging downward, though Vulgs below raved and leapt upward at the dangling Elf, trying to reach him, abandoning their rending of the packs.

Aravan twisted about and clutched at the wall, and heaved himself back onto the ledge.

Once again the Vulgs began mauling the packs, dragging them down the ramp of scree at the base.

"Aravan," barked Gwylly. "Loose the pack line, else they'll pull you down." But even as Gwylly spoke, Aravan perceived the danger and unclipped the rope from his belt.

"If three of us could draw them away," called Faeril, "one of us can stay behind and haul the packs up."

Slightly above the damman, Riatha said, "Too late. We must abandon the supplies and instead climb, for Aravan was right: where run Vulgs, so run the *Rûpt*." The Elfess pointed down the defile.

In the glancing moonlight, dark against the snow came a lone figure loping 'round the twisting turn of the canyon below. It was a Rūck, or a Hlōk—in the shadows at this distance neither Faeril nor Gwylly could say, though Aravan called it a Ruch. Clearly he was following after the Vulg tracks. He stopped and raised his head and howled an ululating call, and was answered in kind by the Vulg pack below.

Again he howled, and again was answered, the wrauling yawls glancing off the walls of the canyon, echoing, confusing the ear as to the direction of the source. Even so, it was plain that the pack was nearby, and the Rūck raised a horn to his lips and blatted a brazen call. And after long moments, a faint brazen blat answered.

"Swift!" hissed Riatha. "Let us go. Foul Folk are upon our track."

Up over snow and ice and rock, past a gnarled scrub or two, they ascended through the moonlight, following along a wide crevice, using knobs and ledges and cracks and rifts for hand- and footholds. They had climbed a hundred feet or so when wild blaring came from the horn of the Rūcken tracker.

"He has seen us," gritted Aravan.

From the near distance, blatting horns answered the tracker's call. "And more *Rûpt* come," added Riatha.

Now and again Gwylly looked back at the turn in the canyon. And after they had climbed another fifty feet or so, he saw more shapes loping into view—more Rūcks, more Hlōks. Twenty or so he counted, all bearing pikes. Too, he thought he could see bows and scimitars, though at this range he was not certain. They milled about the tracker a moment, then howling, raced toward the wall where clung the foursome. From the foot of the cliff, Vulgs wrauled, raging for the blood of the climbers above.

"Take care," warned Riatha. "Let not the presence of these *Spaunen* cause one of us to slip and fall through haste."

In that moment the unstable land jolted, and rocks and ice rained downward. The four pressed themselves against the sheer face, hands gripping, hearts pounding, and prayed that none would get hit.

And in the distance, onward came the yowling Foul Folk, some handing their pikes to others and unslinging their twisted-wood bows even as they ran.

The trembling stopped, and Riatha clambered upward, the other three right behind. But now and again a late-falling stone or chunk of ice clattered down, and the four clutched themselves up against the wall until it hurtled past.

They had climbed perhaps another fifty feet when the first arrow shattered against the cliff, the black-shafted quarrel striking rock ten feet to the right of Faeril.

Glancing back down, Gwylly judged that he was some two hundred fifty feet above the floor of the canyon. Standing out away from the wall some fifty feet or so were the Rūcken archers, even now loosing their deadly bolts. The dark missiles flew up through the moonlight, some shattering to left and right, most falling short. Below, Aravan clambered upward. "Go on, Gwylly. Climb. For e'en a Ruchen archer can court Dame Fortune."

Gwylly turned and continued his ascent.

Up they went and up, over ice and snow and stone, arrows shattering about them. But shooting at a target overhead requires great skill, though luck takes a hand now and again. Yet Fortune favored not the Spawn, and for the most part the shafts fell short, though one or two came within inches of Aravan. Even so, after the four had climbed another fifty feet, the Foul Folk stopped wasting their black-shafted arrows.

Again the land trembled, rocks and ice plummeting down, crashing below, driving the Vulgs and Rūcks and Hlōks back away from the base. This time debris rained down upon the climbers as well, and a chunk of ice thudded upon Gwylly's arm, the buccan crying out in pain, the jagged fragment nearly jolting him loose from the wall. And as he tried to scrabble at stone to regain his grip, he found his right arm numb and useless. But Aravan climbed up from below and boosted the Waerling to a safe ledge.

Faeril, too, climbed down to her buccaran, worry etched in her face, yet there was nothing she could do to aid him. Even so, he was comforted by her presence.

A time passed and slowly his arm regained feeling, first tingling pins and needles, and then throbbing in intense pain. He could not yet resume the climb, and so all waited as the buccan sucked air in and out between clenched teeth, and Faeril spoke softly to him of other days.

And as they clung there, they heard a sharp cracking in the distance, as from a lash, and around the bend in the canyon below twenty Rūcks hove into view, hauling a sled piled high with cargo, a Hlōk riding on the runners, lashing a whip upon the backs of the dog-harnessed Rūcks.

Faeril gasped. "You don't suppose . . ."

As the haulers came 'round the bend, the maggot-folk at the base of the cliff shouted and jeered, their calls ringing from the walls of the canyon. Gwylly glanced down at the Spawn directly below, the Rūcks and Hlōks now standing in the bright light of the Moon above. And for the first time he truly looked, at last seeing that the Foul Folk bore not pikes, as he had first surmised, but instead carried poles hacked from the scrub pine and sharpened. And affixed atop each pole was—

Sickened, the buccan averted his eyes. "Don't look, Faeril," he gritted, reaching out to her. But she began to weep, for she, too, had seen the heads of sled dogs impaled upon the poles, as well as the heads of three Humans.

Rage rising inside his breast, Gwylly's voice came guttural. "They will pay, B'arr. They will pay. This I swear."

Slowly the Aleutan sled was hauled up to the group below, and Rūcks and such milled about. But after a moment twenty or so broke away from the group and began jog trotting up the canyon, bearing their weapons, accompanied by the Vulg pack, all twelve of the savage slayers loping ahead. And below, Rūcks and Hlōks jeered up at the four clinging to the wall above.

"Can thou yet climb, Gwylly?" asked Riatha. "I fear that the Rûpt and Vulgs seek the end of the canyon to reach the rim and come at us from above."

Wincing, Gwylly flexed his arm. "Let's give it a go."

And so up they started once again, more slowly this time, for one of the climbers was injured and the ascent arduous.

Over ice-clad rock they clambered, as well as bare stone. Up crevices and ledges and up through narrow chimneys, past scrub pine clinging tenuously to the cold granite walls, the wood wind-twisted and gnarled, slowly they ascended, while the land shook and ice fell and rocks tumbled down. The higher they went the more they felt an icy chill oozing over the lip of the canyon and flowing down upon them, as if something intensely frigid lay high above. And somewhere beyond the wrenching turns in the canyon, Rūcks and Hlōks and Vulgs sought to head them off, while overhead the Eye of the Hunter streamed remote and blood-red and ominous.

They had just passed the halfway point, some five or six hundred feet up the wall, when again the world jolted, a long, shuddering quake. At the onset a great *crack!* sounded from above, followed by a massive thud, as if a chunk of the mountain itself had split away and fallen to the ground. But the quake continued, the land jolting and heaving, while tons of rock and ice rained down. Yet the four were in a shelter of a sort: moments before they had entered a shallow, dead-ended chimney and had paused to give Gwylly's arm respite from climbing, and were resting on a long, narrow ledge at its base. But now as the world rattled and shook, the four grimly hung on, barely protected by the negligible crevice, and they pressed back into the wall as tons of debris thundered past, plummeting into the depths below. And after it had all crashed down, again there came the faint sound of iron bells ringing in the distance.

When quiet fell, Gwylly whispered, "Lor, if we'd been out there . . ." He said no more, for all knew what he meant.

After a short rest and a long drink of water, once more they girded themselves for the climb. Below, the *Rûpt* waited, blocking escape by that route.

"Why don't we find a deep crevice or a ledge under an overhang, one safe enough to shelter us till the Sun rises?" suggested Faeril. "Then the Foul Folk will be gone."

"That has been my hope since we started, Faeril," responded Riatha. "Can we find such, we will do so and wait for the day to come and drive the *Spaunen* into their sunless holes. Yet until then we must climb, for this wall is too dangerous a place to remain."

Aravan spoke. "Even so, Riatha, as dangerous as is this wall in the quaking land, Vulgs and Rucha and Loka are more dangerous still. And just such *Rûpt* are seeking to come unto the rim above us, if we have rightly guessed their foul intentions."

"Garn," growled Gwylly, "here we are in the middle of the night beneath the bloody Eye of the Hunter in the Spawn-infested Grimwalls, with no supplies, clinging to a sheer, frozen wall some six hundred feet up, with tons of rock and ice hailing down on us while the Dragon-damaged land rattles and quakes and tries to shake us loose, with Foul Folk below ready to kill us, and Vulgs and maggot-folk somewhere above, also preparing our death, and we've no safe place to wait until the coming of the Sun drives 'em off."

Faeril looked at her buccaran and smiled. "Gwylly, my

love, I am reminded of that which Patrel said to Danner in the dark hours of the Winter War."

Gwylly cocked an eyebrow at the damman. "And what was that?"

"He asked," responded Faeril, " 'What are you going to do when things *really* get bad?' "

Gwylly gaped at Faeril, and a tremor shuddered through the cliff. Then the buccan began to laugh, and Faeril giggled. Riatha and Aravan looked at one another in amazement, and then smiled. And as ice and stone shattered down from above, the four clung to the rock wall and laughed.

They resumed their climb, slowly inching upward. Still the icy chill from above flowed down over them, getting colder with every foot they advanced. An hour or so they climbed, ascending another two hundred feet, stopping now and again to rest, desperately clinging to stone when the land trembled and rocks and snow and ice tumbled down.

It was Faeril who observed: "It diminishes. The higher we get, the less there is above us to come crashing down."

From below, Aravan added, "Yet the higher we get, the closer we come to the *Rûpt* who mayhap even now wait for us."

"Perhaps we can—" Gwylly's words were chopped short by a bone-chilling howl from above. Vulg-like it was, yet . . . it was a howl starting deep and strong, but trailing off thinly, as if a Vulg were injured or weakened in some manner.

"Look!" exclaimed Faeril. "The Rūcks and such below!"

On the canyon floor, Foul Folk milled about in confusion.

Again came the howl. And it was answered by a chorus of distant Vulg voices, Vulgs afar, up on the canyon rim somewhere to the south.

From below came voices shouting in jubilation. Gwylly looked down. The Spawn were leaping about as if in celebration.

"Quickly," gritted Riatha. "We must climb."

"But—" Gwylly's words were cut off by the Elfess.

"Now!" she commanded.

And up they went.

Below, Foul Folk rifled the cargo on the stolen sled, and

then began jog trotting away, up the twisting canyon, abandoning their vigil of the climbers overhead.

And above, in the distance, on the rim, howls grew louder as a running Vulg pack drew nearer.

"Riatha!" called Gwylly, even as he haled himself up the stone. "The maggot-folk below have left. But above, they draw near. Downward is safety, but upward is danger. Why do we climb?"

Again the chill howl sounded from overhead.

"Do thou not hear, wee one?" answered Riatha. "That call? Once apast, I heard such a cry—not the same, but near—and it came from the throat of Stoke, summoning aid. And if Stoke is above, and can we come unto him ere the *Spaunen* arrive, then a vile monster we will slay."

Up they climbed, as swift as Gwylly's injury would allow. The Vulg howls from the rim drew nearer and nearer. Still the land shook, and debris rained, but it was as Faeril had said: the higher they climbed, the less there was above to come crashing. And still the icy drift of raw air flowing over them and down grew more chill as they ascended. Even so, their labor was such that perspiration runneled beneath their clothes as up they went, straining mightily, hearts hammering, breath coming in gasps, using their skills to the uttermost to climb rapidly.

They were some one hundred feet from the top when the chorus of Vulg howls seemed to come from directly above.

Riatha stopped. "We have lost the race," she panted.

Yawls and howls, wrauls and yammering rang through the night, while the four below tenuously clung to rock and ice, and a frigid drift of air flowed down across them, chilling them to the bone. They set jams into crevices and clip-belted themselves to these anchors, taking the strain from arms and legs, taking respite, for they were weary beyond measure.

Time eked past, and still the Vulgs above gave clamoring voice. But then came the sound of ironshod boots tramping as the Foul Folk arrived, soon followed by shouting *Rûptish* voices and cries of jubilation.

After some time, a hundred or so paces to the south of where the foursome clung, a Hlōk came to the rim and shouted down below. What he called is not known, for he

used the Slûk tongue, a language that none of the four on
the wall below knew. And they clung to the stone without
moving, hoping that their stillness and Elven clothing would
keep them from detection.

The Hlōk was joined by several Rūcks, and they ranged
along the lip above, peering downward, shouting out to
one another, obviously searching for the four comrades.
Hearts hammering, the climbers remained utterly still,
now looking down so that the whiteness of their features
and the glitter of their eyes would not give them away.
And now they could hear Foul Folk directly overhead. And
still the four pressed into the wall and moved not, and
kept their faces hidden.

The land trembled as another quake shuddered through
the mountains. Rock and ice showered down, falling into
the depths below. The Rūcks drew back from the edge, fearing that the shivering would cast them off the wall or bring
down sections where they stood.

Once more the Hlōk shouted, moving southward, away
from the comrades, drawing the searchers with him. Southward, too, receded the clamor of the remainder of the Rūcks
and Vulgs and Hlōks on the rim, slowly diminishing, as if
they marched off in a band.

As the voices faded, the four cautiously raised up their
faces and scanned overhead, seeking foe, finding none. Even
so, they remained still, waiting. Time passed, and yet there
was no movement above. At last Riatha quietly murmured
that it was time, and they unsnapped the harness straps and
recovered the jams and cautiously began ascending again,
trembling from fatigue and cold but moving as stealthily as
their dwindling strength and skill permitted.

The Moon had passed beyond the lip of the wall and they
clambered upward in shadow.

Finally Riatha came to the rim and cautiously peered over.
Signalling that all seemed safe, up and beyond the edge she
climbed, disappearing from view. After a moment she reap-
peared and motioned them upward, the rope growing taut as
she took up the strain to help.

As Faeril, then Gwylly, and finally Aravan clambered over
the lip and onto the flat, in the near distance before them

they saw by moonlight a vast, looming wall of white extending beyond seeing to north and south. The frigid air pouring over the brim and down into the canyon below flowed from this mass. It was the eastern edge of the Great North Glacier.

With chary eyes they quickly scanned the landscape, seeking foe, sighting none. Yet southward, a furlong or so distant, silhouetting an enormous mass of ice that had calved away from the glacier, there came a faint golden glow.

All four felt themselves pulled toward the light, as if called.

Even so, " 'Ware," said Riatha softly, drawing Dúnamis from her shoulder scabbard. Aravan swiftly untied the three climbing ropes from one another, and Faeril coiled and bound them in hanks to be hung from their climbing harnesses. As the damman affixed the lines to her belt and Riatha's and Gwylly's, Aravan unslung his crystal-bladed spear. Then the foursome set forth, moving toward the light, Riatha leading, Aravan trailing.

Faeril loosened her daggers in their scabbards, drawing one of the steel blades to carry, ready for throwing. Gwylly set a bullet in his sling and attempted to swing it about, failing, inhaling sharply with the pain, his injured arm unable to complete the motion. Replacing sling and bullet, he unsheathed his dagger instead and held it in his left hand.

Steadily they drew near the glow, cautious in their advance. Towering above them to their right loomed the eastern wall of the glacier. Ahead lay the vast chunk that had cleaved away, lying midst the shatterings of its breaking. 'Round this huge mass of calved ice they fared, Riatha whispering that it was freshly split from the pack. "Mayhap that great cracking and thud we heard . . ." murmured Aravan. Between calf and parent they stepped, moving toward the golden light.

Now they could see the radiance before them, shining from the wall of the glacier, brightest at the source, some fourteen or fifteen feet up from the level, there where the ice was cracked and crazed, up a slope of shattered ice. Even as they looked, the earth trembled and a mass of frozen shards fell away and slithered down the ramp of glittering scree. Of a sudden, Riatha moaned and rushed forward, clambering up through the sliding rubble, heedless of foe or other danger that might be present.

"Riatha!" barked Aravan, but she did not stop. Swiftly they scrambled after.

Riatha climbed to the golden light and called, "Quickly! Aid me!"

Leading Aravan, Faeril and Gwylly scrabbled up through the slithering mass, coming at last into the luminance. The bulk of the glacier loomed high above, white and glittering, but before them at the top of the ramp, the ice was clear though crazed from the calving, and the light from within suffused the myriad splits and cracks, shining as would the Sun through a fractured glass window. And even as they stood up to their knees in the sliding shatter, stood in that fragmented golden glow, Elfess and buccan and damman, Riatha with the Lastborn Firstborns at her side, overhead the Eye of the Hunter streamed crimson through the sky.

But neither gold nor crimson caught their sight. Instead it was what they saw in the center of the scattered light: for out from the shattered wall jutted a hand, a large Man's hand . . .

. . . and the fingers moved.

# CHAPTER 11

# Aravan

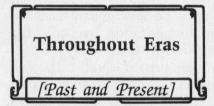

**Throughout Eras**

*[Past and Present]*

Aravan rode out of the dawn and into Mithgar in the early days of the First Era, coming to the youth and wildness of this new world, leaving behind the stately grace and beauty of ancient Adonar. When he emerged he found himself in a misty swale, the grassy crowns of mounded hills all about. He was not surprised by the cast of this terrain, for the crossings in between are fair matched to one another. But unexpectedly to his ears came the distant sound of *shsshing* booms. Intrigued, the Elf turned his horse toward the rolling roar, riding southerly among the diminishing downs. Upward his path took him, up a long, shallow slope, the sounds increasing, the wind in his face, a salt tang on the air. And he found himself on a high chalk cliff, the white bluff falling sheer. Out before him as far as the eye could see stretched deep blue waters to the horizon and beyond. It was the ocean, the Avagon Sea, its azure waves booming below, high-tossed spray glittering like diamonds cast upward in the morning Sun. Aravan's heart sang at such a sight and his eyes brimmed with tears, and in that moment something slipped comfortably into his soul.

Although Aravan had not before this day come unto the midworld, perhaps he was home at last.

Enamored of the sea, Aravan settled along that shore, and for a century or more he was content to walk the sands and study the tides, driven as they were by the Moon, influenced somewhat by the Sun. Often would Aravan stand all day on the high, chalky headland, fascinated by the ocean's shifting hues and shades: the dark, dark blue so nearly black of the waters above the deeps; the jade and turquoise and crystal and foaming pearl of breaking waves curling translucent; the sapphire of tides ebbing and flowing. Too, he marvelled at the ocean's ever changing ways, slow and undulant or wild and thundering, savage or mild, long rolling combers or short chop or mirrorlike smoothness, ever changing, ever changeless, fickle in its constancy.

A century passed and a century more, and at last Aravan was drawn to see what lay in the waters beyond the distant horizon. He sailed as a navigator with a captain from Arbalin, the island Realm just then coming into its own as a Nation of seagoing traders. Although Aravan had neither maps nor charts of the seas, still he knew as do all Elves the courses of the stars and the Sun and Moon, and so the Arbalina captain signed him on as pilot and taught him what he needed to know: of espying shoals and judging currents; of gauging drift and speed; of the reading of wave patterns, reflecting the resonances of islands standing athwart the ocean streams; of rowing through irons, skiffs towing the ship; of riding out storms with sails reefed partially or in full, the ship tethered to sea anchors cast astern; of masts and sails and sailing, and of making the most of whatever wind there was; of maneuvering asea or in harbors or near docks; of ship's routine and standing watches; of traders and trading and the lading off and on of the precious purchased cargo.

A century or two, or perhaps more, he plied the oceans among the Arbalina sea merchants, learning their ways and learning as well the ports of their then limited world: of the Avagon Sea and of the coastal waters of the Weston Ocean, and of the westward course to Atala.

Too, he sailed on a whaling ship—just once, no more, for he could not abide the slaughter of the lords of the sea.

While he was in Diel, a northern port of Jute, the city was assaulted by Fjordlanders, and after the battle the raiders fled from the burning town in their swift Dragonships. The Arbalinians put to sea to give chase, but were quickly left behind by the longboats of the northland warriors.

Upon enquiry, Aravan was told that no other vessels were as fleet, and that the Fjordlanders sailed their sleek ships to far-off shores, shores of lands unknown to other Nations. Captivated by the speed of these Wolves of the deep and the lure of lands afar, Aravan made his way to that northern Realm, to learn their ways and sail the distant seas with them. After some hesitation these Men of the North took him into their confidence.

The Boreal Sea was their realm, the Northern Ocean, too, and they sailed with Aravan across these waters, trading, raiding, and exploring.

West they sailed as well, to the then new lands beyond the blue known sea. Islands of fire and lush lands green unfolded on their long, long voyages. New shores they found and traded for furs with strange-speaking Men, clannish but unaggressive. Too, it was said by the Dragonship crews that Aravan traded with *others*—a tiny folk, a wee folk, seen riding foxes among white birches in silver moonlight. Whether or not these tales were true, Aravan did not say, yet he did wear a strange blue stone on a leather thong 'round his neck thereafter, saying only that it was a gift from a Hidden One.

It was in Fjordland during the long cold winters that Aravan took up the art of shipbuilding, spending a century or so learning the crafting of longships. When he had mastered the ways of the Dragonships, Aravan set out in a small sailboat, plying along the coastal waters to the west and south: down the shores of Jord and Gron and Rian he fared, and around Leut on the Boreal Sea, stopping in ports along the way, learning the shipwright arts each city and yard had to offer. Into Weston Ocean waters he sailed, turning southerly: along Thol and Jute and Wellen, along Gelen and Gothon and Tugal as well.

And in all these Lands he learned what each had to offer about ships of the sea.

As he sailed away from each, he left behind fast friends as well as longing hearts, for he was well liked, especially by the ladies, representing to them as he did a strange and exotic male, full of mystery and excitement and hidden danger. Lithe and slender and handsome, he was—some would say beautiful—with his black, black hair and deep blue eyes and high cheekbones. Standing nearly six foot high, he was tall for an Elf, and he had a voice of silver. And his long-fingered hands were made for caressing, as many a Woman discovered, ever desiring more. At times, however, with one last kiss and a soft word, he would make a hasty departure, exiting the way he had arrived, out through a window or down from a balcony, avoiding hostile confrontations with husbands or brothers or the like. His dalliances were many, his loves few, yet none of the ladies involved begrudged him his pleasure—or theirs—and no issue came of his amorous adventures, for matings between Humankind and Elvenkind bear no fruit.

Among the Men he was popular as well, joining them in their cups and labors. Too, he went sporting with them— not only afield with bow and hound, but also among the back streets and taverns of the towns.

Yet always he became restless, and eventually some dawn would find him down at the docks slipping away, sailing outward on the tide.

And gradually he fared back to warmer climes, plying alongside the shores of Vancha and Hoven and Jugo, until he once more was in Arbalin there in the Avagon Sea. In the Arbalina shipyards, he studied their ways, too, mastering that craft as well. Centuries had passed, five or six or more— who can say? for none kept count of them, especially not the Elf, for to him what mattered time?

At last, aided by Drimmen artisans, Aravan set about building a ship of his own, incorporating all he had learned of the craft. Strange timbers he chose, of teak and blackwood and yew, of oak and larch and cypress, of ash and ebony, and of woods unseen until then, red woods and yellows and whites, and black woods as well as rich browns; and all were treated with oils most precious and rare. Slowly the ship formed, keel, ribs, strakes, wales, decking, cabins; a silvery auger was used to drill holes, and all wooden parts were carefully oiled and pegged together, and neither nailed nor screwed; and caulking was done with a substance most strange, never before seen, or since. Metal alloys from Dwarven forges were shaped into chains and an anchor, and the same alloy was used to make the cleats and other metal parts. And lo! below the waterline the hull was coated with a rare paint into which *Starsilver* had been mixed. Spidery soft ropes of various gauges formed the rigging, easy upon the hand and strong beyond measure. And as it was assembled, a docksman remarked that the ship would last a thousand years, and Aravan and his Drimmen shipwrights laughed and shook their heads, and one Drimm said, "Nay, Man, not a mere ten centuries, but more, much more."

At last it was finished and ready for sea. Neither sterncastle nor fo'c's'le did the hull bear, but instead it was long and low and slim and rigged for speed. Three masted, with lofty silken sails, square and triangular both, this was a ship meant to ride the wind as no ship had done before. The *Elvenship*, Men called her, but she was christened *Eroean*, an Elven word whose meaning is obscure, though it is thought to be related to the wind.

Aravan took on a mixed crew of Humans and Drimma, and two or three Waerlinga, and set sail.

They say he plied all the seas, learning their ever changing ways. It is also said that he sailed the entire world, visiting strange Lands afar, anchoring at times for years, for centuries say some, exploring—for he had the time to do so, being of Elvenkind. Yet it is also said that he oft returned to Arbalin, releasing old crew, taking on new, whenever there was a need. Too, it is certain that he brought back peculiar and wonderful cargo, unseen heretofore: shell necklaces, unknown gems, bolts of silken cloth, and the like; exotic birds, peculiar animals, and visitors from far away; fruits and seeds and beans and grain, spices, teas; jades, ivories, opalescent gems, emeralds, gold and silver; all these and more did the *Eroean* carry from distant Lands to the insatiable markets of Arbalin.

And there were maps and maps of the world afar, of continents and islands alike, to the west and south and east and north and all points in between, some wild and savage, others with Nations of their own. How he kept from sailing off the rim of the world none could say, yet he managed to remain alive, bringing ship and crew back to port time and again.

When in port, Aravan's crew of Human sailors and Drimmen warriors and Waerlinga scouts would tell of adventures beyond the wildest dreams: of temples and tribes and deadly creatures; of opulent cities and bejewelled potentates and Women and other females of surpassing beauty; of dark jungles and frozen wastes and mountains disappearing into the clouds; of rivers without end and deserts dire and isles like jewels in the sea; of oceans and oceans, boiling and frigid, hideous monsters within; of enchantments and glamours and creatures rare; of abandoned cities peopled by undead beings and living statues and worse; all these and more did they tell, to the delight and awe of the listeners. Around the entire world, they claimed, had sailed the *Eroean*, but who can believe such? Surely they exaggerated in this boast, as well as in all other of their unbridled imaginings.

That the *Eroean* was swift there is no doubt, for she showed her fantail to many a merchant and to many a pirate as well, all sails set to, the braw ship heeling over in a spanking breeze, Aravan at the wheel laughing, the sleek vessel cleaving the waters, leaving a foaming wake aft, for she was an Elvenboat—enchanted, claimed many—the likes of which had never before been seen, nor since, either.

Two thousand years or three did Aravan fare the world in his Elvenship. Yet of a sudden he stopped, and the *Eroean* disappeared from the waters of the world. Why? It is not told, though some claim that it was a lost love that caused Aravan to yield up the oceans, while others claimed that the ship was drowned in a maelstrom and Aravan would sail no other. Still others claimed that the *Eroean* was yet at sea, her rigging burning with green witch fire, sailing ever sailing, haunted by a ghostly crew. Regardless whether one or the other or another of these tales is true, or something entirely different, Aravan left the sea and came unto Darda Erynian to live among Elvenkind.

But now his ready smile was more subdued, and a tormented look dwelled deep within his eyes.

And he bore with him a crystal spear.

\*     \*     \*

Centuries passed, and centuries more, and Aravan learned the ways of woodcraft and renewed his acquaintance with horses and riding. Too, he cultivated crops, and mastered tanning and leather working. Hawking he studied, learning of raptors and of their training—from swift kestrel to golden-eyed hawk to soaring eagle, as well as owls—and though he did not presume that any of these lords of the air would ever be tamed, still he used these savage birds to do his bidding—hunting, fishing, espying game and movement, standing watch. He widened his sphere of study to include other bird-kind—ebon ravens and black crows, bright songbirds, brown woodland thrushes, scintillant hummingbirds, and other birds grey and brown and raucous and timid and yellow and red and black and blue and green and white, birds gaudy and dull and small and large, birds of the sea and forests and fens and fields—and he learned their habits and manner of living and mastered their calls; he studied their structure and the types and shapes of feathers and the patterns of wings, and he deduced much concerning flight and flying.

All this and more did Aravan take up while living among the Elves of Darda Erynian. Seasons passed uncounted, millennia, yet Aravan was just beginning, the Elf but a step or two along an endless path.

War came, the Great War, and Aravan joined forces with other Elvenkind. And they stood athwart harm's way and opposed the cruel *Spaunen* running roughshod o'er Mithgar.

It was during the War that Aravan became comrade to Galarun, son of Coron Eiron, Elfking on Mithgar. And Eiron sent his son on a mission unto the forges of the Mages, there below Black Mountain in Xian. To bring back a silver sword was the charge of Galarun's Company—an argent blade named the Dawn Sword, a weapon which perhaps could slay the High Vûlk, Gyphon Himself. Galarun was to carry the blade unto Darda Galion, for there in the Eldwood was the chosen place to cross over to Adonar, bearing it where it would be needed: into the very camp of the Elven forces upon the High World.

Long was the journey of Galarun and Aravan and company to the distant Land of Xian, and they were opposed by many.

It was as if the foe knew of their mission and sought to bar the way. Twice did Aravan save the life of Galarun, the crystal spear a deadly weapon, *burning* foe where it pierced, fuming and sizzling and charring.

Unto Black Mountain they came at last, following the broad paved road to the wide gates there embedded in the ebon stone. And only Galarun entered, while Aravan and the company remained without, champing at the bit, fretting, for they knew not what transpired within. Yet at last Galarun emerged, shaken by what he had seen, and in his grasp was the silver sword. Grim was the face of Galarun, as if he knew of a dire fate awaiting, yet up he mounted on his horse and rode away in silence.

They had set forth from Darda Galion some four months past, in early spring, riding easterly to come to Xian; and four more months would it take to return, for the journey was long, very long, and would be made more so by foe along the way. Nevertheless they set out for Darda Galion, faring westerly through Xian and Aralan, across Khal to Garia and into Riamon. And every step along the way was fraught with danger, *Spaunen* lying in wait. At times they fled the enemy, while at other times they stood and fought, and slowly their ranks dwindled as comrades fell among them. Yet always did they bear the sword westerly, ever westerly, and Galarun would let no other touch it, not even his boon companion, Aravan. Along the Landover Road they fared, and through the long ring of the Rimmen Mountains, emerging in Darda Erynian, where they were given respite from the harassing pursuit. A day they spent resting but no more, for their mission was urgent, and they rode away upon the following morn. West they fared, crossing the mighty River Argon to come into the wide wolds 'tween river and mountain, where they turned south for Darda Galion, the Grimwalls on their right, the Argon to their left.

Three days they rode down the wold, coming unto the Dalgor Marches, where they were joined by a company of Elven warriors patrolling the fens. Here it was that Aravan first met Riatha and Talar, riding among that company.

The next dawn, into the fens they rode, horses splashing through reeds and water, mire sucking at hooves, the way slow and shallow, arduous but fordable, unlike the swift, deep waters of the Dalgor River upstream flowing down from the high Grimwalls to the west. Deep into the watery lowland they fared, at times dismounting and wading, giving the horses respite.

It was near the noontide that late fall day when Aravan warned Galarun that the blue stone on the thong grew chill, and so the warning went out to all that danger was nigh. On they rode and a pale Sun shone overhead, and one of the outriders called unto the main body. At a nod from Galarun, Aravan rode out to see what was amiss. He came upon the rider, Eryndar, and the Elf pointed eastward. From the direction of the Argon, rolling through the fen like a grey wall rushing came fog, flowing over them in a thick wave, obscuring all in its wake, and Aravan and Eryndar could but barely see one another less than an arm's span away. And from behind there sounded the clash and clangor and shout of combat.

*"To me! To me!"* came Galarun's call, muffled and distant in the fog in the Dalgor Fens, confusing to mind and ear.

Though Aravan could not see, he spurred his horse to come to his comrades' aid, riding to the sounds of steel on steel, though they, too, were muted and remote and seemed to echo where no echoes should have been. He charged into a deep slough, the horse foundering, Aravan nearly losing his seat. And up from out of the water rose an enormous dark shape, and a webbed hand struck at him, claws sweeping past his face as the horse screamed and reared, the Elf ducking aside from the blow. *"Krystallopýr,"* whispered Aravan, Truenaming the spear. He thrust the weapon into the half-seen *thing* looming above him; and a hideous yawl split the air as the blade burned and sizzled in cold flesh. With a huge splash the creature was gone, back into the mire.

Still, somewhere in the murk a battle raged, clang and clangor and shouts. Again Aravan rode toward the sound, trusting to his horse in the treacherous footing. Shapes rose up from the reeds and attacked—*Rûpt*, they were, Rucha and Loka alike—but the crystal spear pierced them and burned them, and they fell dead or fled screaming.

Of a sudden the battle ended, the foe fading back into the

cloaking fog, vanishing in the grey murk. And it seemed as if the strange echoing disappeared as well, the muffling gone. And the blue stone at Aravan's neck grew warm.

"*Galarun!*" called Aravan. "*Galarun! . . .*" Other voices, too, took up the cry.

Slowly they came together, did the scattered survivors, riding to one another's calls, and Galarun was not among them.

The wan Sun gradually burned away the fog, and the company searched for their captain. They found him at last, pierced by crossbow quarrel and cruel barbed spear, lying in the water among the reeds, he and his horse slain—the silver sword gone.

Three days they searched for that token of power, there in the Dalgor Fen. Yet in the end they found nought but an abandoned Ruchen campsite, one used less than a full day. ". . . Perhaps they went back to Neddra," suggested Eryndar.

At last, hearts filled with rage and grief, they took up slain Galarun and the five others who had fallen and rode for Darda Galion across the wide wold. Two days passed and part of another ere they forded the River Rothro on the edge of the Eldwood forest. Travelling among the massive boles of the great trees, the following day they forded the Quadrill and later the River Cellener to come at last unto the Coronhall in Wood's-heart, the Elvenholt central to the great forest of Darda Galion.

Aravan bore Galarun's blanket-wrapped body into the hall, where were gathered Elves waiting, mourning. Through a corridor of Elvenkind strode Aravan toward the Elvenking, and nought but silence greeted him. Eiron stepped down from the throne at this homecoming of his son, moving forward and holding out his arms to receive the body. Desolation stood in Aravan's eyes as he gave over the lifeless Elf. Eiron tenderly cradled Galarun unto himself and turned and slowly walked the last few steps to the dais, where he lay his slain child down.

Aravan's voice was choked with emotion. "I failed him, my Coron, for I was not at his side when he most needed me. I have failed thee and Adon as well, for thy son is dead and the silver sword is lost."

Coron Eiron looked up from the blanket-wrapped corpse, his eyes brimming, his voice a whisper. "Take no blame unto thyself, Aravan, for the death of Galarun was foretold—"

"Foretold!" exclaimed Aravan.

"—by the Mages of Black Mountain."

"If thou knew this, then why did thou send thy son?"

"I did not know."

"Then how—"

"Galarun's Death Rede," explained Eiron. "The Mages told him that he who first bore the weapon would die within the year."

Aravan remembered the grim look on Galarun's face when he had emerged from the Wizardholt of Black Mountain.

Kneeling, slowly the Coron undid the bindings on the blankets, folding back the edge, revealing Galarun's visage, the features pale and bloodless. From behind, Aravan's voice came softly. "He let none else touch the sword, and now I know why."

Coron Eiron stood, motioning to attendants, and they came and took up Galarun's body, bearing it out from the Coron-hall.

When they had gone, Aravan turned once again to Eiron. "His Death Rede: was there . . . more?"

The Coron sat on the edge of the dais. "Aye: a vision of the one responsible. It was a pale white one who slew my Galarun; like Man he looked, but no Mortal was he. Mayhap a Mage instead. Mayhap a Demon. More I cannot say. Pallid he was and tall, with black hair and hands long and slender and wild yellow eyes. His face was long and narrow, his nose straight and thin, his white cheeks unbearded."

"And the sword. Did Galarun—?"

Aravan's question was cut off by a negative shake of Eiron's head. "The blade was yet with my son when he died."

Frustration and anger colored Aravan's voice. "But now it is missing. Long we searched, finding nought."

After a moment Eiron spoke: "If not lost in the fen, then it is stolen. And if any has the Dawn Sword, it is he, the pallid one with yellow eyes. Find him and thou may find the blade."

Aravan stepped back and unslung his spear from its shoulder harness; he planted the butt of the weapon to the wooden floor and knelt on one knee. "My Coron, I will search for the killer and for the sword. If he or it is to be found—"

Aravan never finished, for the Coron began to weep. And so the Elf put aside the crystal blade and sat next to his Liege Lord, and with tears in his own eyes, spoke to him of the last days of his valiant son.

Long did Aravan search the Dalgor Fens for the silver sword, to no avail, for no blade did he find. The Great War dragged on, and Aravan's spear was needed. He fought in battle upon battle, until the Grand Alliance arrayed its surviving Legion against Modru's Hordes at Hèl's Crucible, where the War ended.

But still did Aravan clutch unto himself blame for Galarun's death, and he continued to seek the one responsible, for if he could find that one, then perhaps he would also find the Dawn Sword. Coron Eiron had sketched for him an exact likeness of the yellow-eyed Man, and into his mind, his memory, Aravan burned the image of the killer. As a trader, a wayfarer, as a bard, Aravan travelled across Mithgar, following legend, rumor, and myth, always asking after any who might have seen the pallid one with yellow eyes: Galarun's slayer.

Centuries passed and centuries, until all told a thousand years had fled, and in all those seasons Aravan discovered neither killer nor sword. Yet in Arden Vale the Dara Rael, the Consort of Alor Talarin, divined a sooth of baleful portent:

> *Bright Silverlarks and Silver Sword,*
> *Borne hence upon the Dawn,*
> *Return to earth; Elves girt thyselves*
> *To struggle for the One.*
>
> *Death's wind shall blow, and crushing Woe*
> *Will hammer down the Land.*
> *Not grief, not tears, not High Adon*
> *Shall stay Great Evil's Hand.*

Upon hearing of the sooth, Aravan travelled to the Court of Arden to speak with Dara Rael. There in the great hall, hung with bright silks and satins, lambent with yellow lamps glowing in cressets and fires burning on the hearths, redolent with the fragrance of pine and wood spices and foods, Aravan met Alor Talarin and his Consort, the lovely Dara Rael. Fair was Rael, and graceful, with golden locks and deep blue eyes. Dressed in green with her hair bound in emerald ribbons, she looked upon Aravan and smiled. Talarin, too, had yellow hair, though his eyes were green; he was tall and slender, and wore grey trews and jerkin.

Aravan feasted among his kindred that night, and it had been many years since he had come to Court. And though he found joy that eve, still the tormented look deep within his own blue eyes did not vanish.

The next day, the audience he sought with Rael was granted. Aravan and the Consort sat on the banks of the River Tumble, watching the water dashing through Arden Gorge, and they spoke of the sooth.

"Dara, thy words would have it that the Dawn Sword is to be found upon Adonar."

"Nay, Alor Aravan. The sooth speaks only of a silver sword; it does not name it the Dawn Sword. Still, I think thou must be right, for what other blade would be borne forth from Adonar?"

Aravan looked down at the swift-running water cascading over rocks, its turbulence reflecting the state of his mind. That the Dawn Sword perhaps could be on the *Hōhgarda* defied reason, and he said as much. "If the sword is upon Adonar, why was it not used against the High Vûlk, Gyphon, as it was meant to be? Nay, if the blade is not on Mithgar, then more likely it rests in Neddra, with the *Rûpt*, for they were the ones who raided, who slew Galarun, and then fled; and afterward, the sword was missing."

Rael, too, was puzzled by the sooth, for although she had voiced it, sooths and redes come at their own behest and are not summoned; and those that speak them oft are not privy to their meanings. "Then it is thy judgement that Rucha or Loka stole the sword and bore it from this world and unto Neddra?"

Aravan leapt up and began pacing agitatedly. "I know not, Dara. Mayhap so. Their leader, the pallid one, does not seem to be upon Mithgar, for I have searched—lo! how I have searched.

"But heed me, if the sword is indeed to come from Adonar, thy sooth requires a rider of impossibility, for the ways between the Planes are sundered."

"Not entirely, Alor Aravan. Not entirely. Elvenkind can yet go unto Adonar."

Aravan stopped his pacing and looked at Rael. "Aye, Dara, that we can do. We can go unto Adonar just as Humankind can come from there to Mithgar. But once at our separate destinations, neither of us can return to the world of the other.

"List, when first I heard thy sooth I bethought that the blade could be borne here by Man, yet any Mithgarian who was upon the High World at the time of the Sundering is long past dead, for they are mortal and four thousand seasons have fled. Nay, a Human could not bear the Dawn Sword from that world unto this. And were we to go to fetch the blade, we would not return. And that, my Dara, is why I say thy sooth requires a rider of impossibility."

Millennia passed, and Aravan continued to seek both sword and Galarun's slayer, without success.

In the Fourth Era came the Winter War. And Aravan and a squad of Drimmen warriors crept along the coast of the Avagon Sea, slipping through the invaders' lines, coming at last unto Jugo, where they stole a small sloop and sailed to Arbalin. There Aravan collected a skeleton crew, and by small boat at night sailed with them unto Thell Cove in Pellar.

Forth from a hidden cave in the cove there came the sleek, swift *Eroean*. For contrary to the tales, the Elvenship was not burning with witchfire, plying the midnight seas, haunted by a ghostly crew nor had it perished in the suck of a maelstrom. Instead it had been concealed by Aravan in a secluded grot where none would ever look.

Running at night through enemy patrols, back to Arbalin he sailed, where he took on a full complement. And the Elvenship with its crew of Human sailors and Drimmen fighters harassed the shipping lanes of the Rovers of Kistan, boarding many an enemy hull, conquering the foe thereupon, scuttling ships and War cargoes and setting the surviving enemy adrift.

Aravan was at Hile Bay when in the north the Dimmendark collapsed and the Rovers fled. The *Eroean* gave chase and with her engines of War—ballistas casting balls of fire— sank many an enemy ship, for none could outrun or outmaneuver the swift and nimble Elvenboat.

After the Winter War, Aravan once more sailed the *Eroean* to the cave in Thell Cove, where again he secreted away the swift, sleek vessel.

Time passed—some six hundred years or so—while Aravan fared across continents, still searching. When returning from Jūng afar, Aravan paused in Darda Erynian, renewing old acquaintances. It was from Vanidar—known as Silverleaf—that he learned of the War of Drimmen-deeve, for Vanidar had been the only Lian involved in the Battle of Kraggen-cor, the name that the Drimma—the Dwarves—had given to that cataclysmic conflict.

It was also from Vanidar that he learned of Talar's death at the hands of Baron Stoke six hundred fifty years past. Aravan was saddened to hear of Talar's murder, for he had liked the Lian. He asked after Talar's sister: ". . . Riatha, she is called."

"When last we spoke, she dwelt in Arden Vale," responded Vanidar, "and may dwell there still. But that was long apast. Then it was I met her as she journeyed unto the Greatwood, accompanied by two Waerlinga, to sing the deeds of Urus. He had aided her in her quest for vengeance for Talar. For thou know she is a warrior, and she pursued the Baron, she and the Waerlinga and Urus. After many trials, the four of them finally came upon Talar's slayer within the Grimwall, and Stoke met his doom on the Great North Glacier . . . borne down to his death by Urus. Urus himself was slain in that encounter, and that is why she would sing of his deeds.

"Afterward, she said, she intended to return to the Hidden Stand. Whether she did so I cannot say, but that is where I would seek her should a need arise: Arden Vale."

Some months later, Aravan's course carried him to Arden

Vale, and he sought out Riatha to extend his condolences. They walked among the ornamental gardens, with its still pools among the drifting dappled shadows, stopping now and again to watch the golden fish lazing among the green cress. And they spoke of many things, including Aravan's quest for the silver sword and vengeance for Galarun. Too, Riatha spoke of Talar and the pursuit of his killer. To Aravan's surprise came Riatha's description of Stoke: a Man with pale skin and yellow eyes. *Could this be the one who had slain Galarun?* In the several thousand years of his quest, Aravan had often pursued pallid Men with yellow eyes, only to discover they did not match the image of Galarun's killer, and to discover as well that they were mortal and could not have been involved in Galarun's death and the loss of the silver sword for entirely too much time had passed. But Stoke was different: He was a Cursed One, a shape changer; he was a leader of *Rûpt*, commanding Loka and Rucha and Vulgs; and he had lived many more years than the span of a mortal.

Riatha told Aravan of Rael's rede concerning the Lastborn Firstborns, of the light of the Bear, and of the Eye of the Hunter. Mayhap the words of the prophecy foretold that Stoke would somehow return from the dead.

"I would join thee on thy mission," said Aravan at last. "I know not whether Stoke is the one I seek, whether or not he is the one responsible for the death of Galarun, but if he is, then I have need to see with mine own eyes that he is dead. Too, there is the disappearance of the Dawn Sword, and if he took it, then we must discover what he did with it.

"Riatha, thou were there when the sword was lost. Can we recover it, then should aught happen requiring its use, it will be at hand.

"Rael's sooth speaks of a silver sword borne forth upon the dawn. She is now gone from Mithgar, having ridden the twilight back unto Adonar with Talarin. Yet were she here, I deem that she would be the first to say that it is not certain that the silver sword of her sooth is the Dawn Sword.

"Likely it is, yet should it not be, then I say we must follow all threads to where the Dawn Sword may lie. And perhaps one of those threads leads to Baron Stoke.

"Regardless of the whereabouts of the sword, there is the death of Galarun to avenge. And on the chance that Stoke is responsible, I would join thee on thy quest."

Riatha, of course, agreed.

But then the Elfess suggested that perhaps the silver sword might lie hidden at one of Stoke's strongholts of old: at the bartizan beyond Vulfcwmb, or in Dreadholt near Sagra, or at the monastery above the Great North Glacier. And so she and Aravan made long journeys to the places she named: First to Dreadholt in distant Vancha, where they discovered caverns behind the burnt-out ruins there at Daemon's Crag; long they searched but no sword did they find. Then they fared to Vulfcwmb and north, unto the destroyed bartizan which once was clutched upon the high cliff walls, ere it was brought crashing down by the Drimma of Kachar. Once again a thorough search of the ruins and caverns—those which were not collapsed—revealed nought. Lastly they went through the Grimwalls north of the ruins of Drag-onslair, the land quaking and unstable, coming at last to the stone monastery above the glacier, a monastery whose iron bells rang whenever the juddering of the land became vio-lent. Again they found only an abandoned dwelling, and no silver sword.

While they were at the Great North Glacier, Riatha took Aravan with her to the golden glow emanating from deep within the ice. Standing in its soft radiance, Aravan felt strangely drawn to the luminance, as if he were being called. Yet it was deep, very deep, far beyond reaching.

Riatha's words came softly. "It has drifted, ever drifted, toward the eastern edge," and Aravan saw that she wept.

By the time they came back unto Arden Vale, two years had passed. Aravan's quest for sword and vengeance was as yet not fulfilled and mayhap would never be, but he was driven to continue seeking. As he took his leave, he prom-ised to aid Riatha in the time of the prophecy, vowing to return in the years just prior to when the Eye of the Hunter would ride the night.

Time passed and centuries fell, the seasons ever changing. But three winters ere the Hunter's ruddy harbinger would course through the dark nighttides, Aravan came back unto Arden Vale, his quest for silver blade and red revenge still unrealized. At this time Aravan had been on Mithgar for more than twelve thousand years . . .

. . . His life was just beginning.

# CHAPTER 12

# Equinox

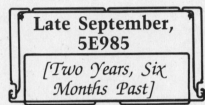

"Kel, Riatha, Dara!" called Jandrel. "*Vi didron ana al enistori!*"

Riatha turned from the unshorn grain and shaded her eyes and looked at the three there at field's edge: Jandrel ahorse with two Waerlinga mounted upon ponies at his side. She handed her scythe to one of the gleaners, and walked toward the visitors . . .

. . . the Lastborn Firstborns had come.

As the Elfess approached, the wee Waerlinga dismounted and led their ponies forward. Riatha's heart welled up within her, for in spite of their dress and the weapons they bore, once again she saw before her what at first glance looked to be two children of Elvenkind. Yet it was not so, for no Elf had e'er conceived a child on Mithgar, and no Elfchild had set foot upon this world for more than five thousand years, not since the time of the Sundering. But even though her mind told her that these were not the children of Elves, her heart said otherwise, and she found unexpected tears running down her face.

As Riatha stepped to the edge of the field, the damman bobbed a slight curtsy and said, "I am Faeril Twiggins, and this is Gwylly Fenn. We are the last of the firstborn descendants of Tomlin and Petal. . . .

". . . And oh, Riatha, you are even more beautiful than I had imagined."

And with that, Faeril dropped the reins of Blacktail and rushed forward, her arms outstretched, and smiling past tears, Riatha knelt down to embrace her.

Riatha led Gwylly and Faeril among the pine trees and past widely scattered thatch-roofed cottages, with walls made of woven withes and white clay and supported by wooden beams. "After we stable thy ponies, I shall find each of thee a dwelling—"

"Oh, no, Lady Riatha," interjected Faeril. "I mean, well, Gwylly and I are now mated to one another, though we have not yet said our vows in public."

Riatha smiled to herself. "Oh, I see. One cote, then, shall ye have."

Onward they walked, Elves pausing to look at these Waerlinga—remembering. Suddenly Gwylly piped up: "Say, d'you think that we could say our vows here? I mean, d'you have a mayor or a kingsclerk or other such?"

Riatha smiled once again. "Nay, Gwylly, no mayor or kingsclerk, but ye shall have better. I shall arrange a pledge-giving ceremony."

As they entered the stables, Gwylly looked up at the tall Elfess. "Pledge-giving ceremony?"

"Aye. 'Tis a thing we do when we wish to enter into a more lasting relationship. And a pledge-giving ceremony is a cause for celebration among Elvenkind, for it is not often that we commit unto an oath."

"Not often?" asked the buccan.

"Thou must know, Gwylly, that each of us of Elvenkind is . . . very long lived . . . very—"

"Immortal," supplied Faeril.

". . . Aye. Immortal," agreed Riatha.

The Elfess opened two stalls, and the ponies were led within. As Gwylly and Faeril removed their gear and saddles and bridles, Riatha put a scoop of oats into each feed bin and fetched water.

"What does a long life have to do with the giving of pledges?" asked Gwylly, rummaging through his saddlebags for his curry comb.

Riatha set a bucket of water in Dapper's stall and another in Blacktail's. "Just this: Each person follows an individual path. At a given stage in life, a person may find his path running side by side with another's. At a different stage, paths grow apart as the individuals change, as interests change, as common ground becomes less and less. Then other paths, new paths, may begin to parallel these new directions, as new common ground forms between different individuals.

"Friendship is an example of this: Friendships grow, become fast, then drift apart as interests change, while new friends are made. It does not mean that all friendships are fleeting, just as it does not mean that all friendships are lasting. Both fleeting or lasting: some are; some are not; most fall in between.

"Because individuals' paths change, sometimes in unforeseen directions, one must take care when taking an oath or giving a pledge. For interests change. Common ground disappears.

"Elvenkind is most aware of such, for we live . . . forever. An oath taken today in pleasure may become an unbearable burden in the future—and heed, for Elves the future is forever. Hence, oaths, vows, and pledges given or received by Elves must take this into account.

"But even among mortalkind, within a mortal's limited span of years, oaths taken and pledges made can in time become burdens too heavy to bear."

Gwylly paused in his currying. "Surely, Riatha, you are not saying that it's all right to break oaths."

Riatha hefted first one saddle, then the other onto a low rail, draping blankets over as well. "Nay, Gwylly, I am not counselling oath breaking. Among all Folk, including Elvenkind, oaths are not to be taken lightly. I am, however, counselling prudence. Think long, very long ere taking an oath, for the common ground where the pledge was made may one day become too small to stand upon."

Blacktail placidly munched oats as Faeril lifted each of the pony's hooves and examined them, scraping a blunt tool along the edge of the iron shoes to dislodge caked dirt. "Oh, I think I see, Riatha. Should the conditions for making the pledge change appreciably, well then, perhaps the pledge no longer applies."

"Such as . . . ?" asked Gwylly.

Faeril straightened, releasing the last of Blacktail's hooves. "Well, such as making a pledge of fealty to someone, someone who later changes, becoming, say, unsavory in his deeds, perhaps even asking you to commit foul acts as well. In that case the person has changed and therefore the common ground has changed, perhaps has disappeared altogether, becoming something that no longer can support you in your pledge."

Gwylly nodded, saying nothing, but Riatha spoke softly. "Aye, 'tis the common ground which supports all oaths. And conditions may change in ways unforeseen, enriching or depleting the soil nourishing a given vow. Hence, it behooves each of us to carefully examine the earth between ere planting a pledge therein."

Finished with Dapper, Gwylly stepped forth from the stall, latching the gate behind. "You make it sound as if an oath is but a fragile seedling to be sewn only in fertile ground."

"Aye, Gwylly, 'tis indeed that. And just as seedlings need tending and watering to survive and become strong and bear sweet fruit, vows, too, need cultivation and nourishment to keep them from withering."

Faeril scooped up her saddlebags and bedroll. "That must be why some friendships die—they are not nourished."

As Gwylly, too, took up his gear, Riatha smiled a sad smile down at the damman. "Aye, Faeril. Without nourishment all things wither—be they seedlings or vows or friendships or matings or aught else."

Leaving the stables, once again they trod through the pine forest and past widely scattered thatched cottages nestled therein. Soon they emerged from the trees and into a tiny sunlit glade cupped on the edge of a slope, grass and wildflowers all about. And in the center of the glade stood another cote overlooking the vale to the east. Pines ran down to the banks of the Tumble and on up the slopes beyond, and the craggy bluff of the far wall of Arden Vale was visible in the distance a mile or more away. Riatha led the Waerlinga across the glade, while bees buzzed among the wild blossoms and gathered the last of summer's bounty, sensing, perhaps, the onset of fall and the coming of winter beyond.

The Elfess stepped to the stoop of the cottage. "This will be thy dwelling, though I deem that the furnishments within are not fitted to thy sizes." Raising the latch, she opened the door.

Faeril and Gwylly stepped inside, and as Riatha went from window to window, opening shutters and letting the daylight shine in, the Warrows set down their belongings and looked about.

The cottage held two rooms: one a combination kitchen and living room, containing cupboards and tables and chairs and a fireplace for heating and cooking with two cushioned chairs for sitting before the fire, as well as a small pantry and cabinets, a washstand, a bench, and a writing desk; the other room held a bed and a wardrobe as well as a dresser and a chest of drawers, and two chairs for sitting, and a third chair before a small writing desk.

Gwylly looked out the back door, espying a nearby well, while off in the distance to the side stood a privy. Just beyond the back stoop was a small plot of land for a vegetable patch, and garden tools were neatly arrayed on the rear cottage wall.

"Oh, Riatha, it's a splendid cote," breathed Faeril, "and we shall cherish our time here."

After Riatha left them to settle in, saying that she would be back in the eventide to take them to a banquet, Gwylly and Faeril unpacked their meager belongings and explored the cottage and its surroundings. Gwylly was uncommonly somber, though, and as they sat among the flowers on the slope and gazed across the vale, Faeril at last asked him why the brooding brow.

"Just this, my dammia: I love you more than life itself, yet I wonder if we have enough 'common ground' between us to support vows to one another."

Faeril's heart clenched. "What are you saying, Gwylly? What more do we need than love?"

Gwylly took Faeril's hands in his and looked into her eyes, as if seeking something deep within their amber depths. "My dammia, I do not know if I am worthy of you." He held up a hand, stilling the protest that sprang to her lips. "You can read; I cannot. You were raised among our Kind; I was not. You knew about the prophecy; I did not. You trained for this mission; I did not. You—"

Faeril laughed and took Gwylly's face in her hands and silenced him with a kiss. "Oh, my love," she said, "let us examine these things you cite:

"Indeed, I can read. And so will you within the year—"

"But I barely know my letters," protested Gwylly.

"Faugh!" snorted Faeril. "Already you can write your name and mine, and spell perhaps a hundred words. No, love, within the year you *will* be reading and writing in the common tongue. And within two, you will be speaking, reading, and writing Twyll, the language of Warrows."

Gwylly merely grunted, not convinced.

Faeril went on: "And as far as being raised among 'our Kind,' by the time you get to know the language of the Warrows, you will by then know much of Warrow lore, for I will use lore and legend with you to practice the speaking and writing of Twyll.

"As far as not knowing the prophecy, you will read all about it in the journals we brought.

"As to training for the mission, we have plenty of time to do so ere we set out.

"Too, by the time we finish this venture with Riatha, you and I will have more common ground between us than nearly anyone else I can think of.

"And as far as being worthy . . . oh, Gwylly, you are a kind and gentle soul with a heart as big as the world. Had your Warrow parents lived, they could not have raised a better buccan than did Orith and Nelda, Human though they were.

"Oh, my buccaran, don't you see that the ground we have in common is as rich and as fertile as any could wish, and will only grow?"

Gwylly stood and pulled Faeril to her feet. He took her in his arms and gently kissed her. Together they walked through the wildflowers—bees rising up from the blossoms at the Warrows' passage and then settling back to gather more nectar and pollen—the Wee Folk returning to the cottage and stepping within, closing the door behind.

\*　　\*　　\*

Dressed in green silks and satins, jade ribbons wound among the pale golden tresses of her hair, Riatha came for Gwylly and Faeril as twilight settled upon the vale. The Waerlinga had donned their own finest clothes—the finest they had brought with them—and though the fabric was homespun and sturdy, still they were quite presentable: Faeril in black breeks and a grey jerkin, a black ribbon with long, loose ends dangling down tied 'round each arm high above the elbow, her black hair unbound; Gwylly in a rust-colored shirt and dark brown pants, and a narrow leather headband across his brow and tied behind; both wore dark brown boots of brushed leather.

Westward across the glade they walked, meadowlarks calling as evening fell. They stepped in among the shadowy pines, treading on a yielding carpet of fallen needles, the forest about them silent but for the soft susurration of slow-moving air in the crowns above, or the occasional scritching of a small animal scurrying away in the darkness. Too, in the tree branches now and then a bird would sound a gentle chirp, as if murmuring one last thing to itself while settling down to sleep. As they walked, Faeril and then Gwylly became aware of the faint echo of silver harps and voices singing in the twilit distance. A glimmer afar shone through the trees, and another, and more still, yellow and amber and soft. Closer the trio came and closer, stepping at last past a line of boles and into a small open glade. They came forth into amber light cast by candlelit paper lanterns hanging from limbs of the encircling trees, each lantern bearing an arcane sigil or rune, their colors various. As they entered the glade, the voices rose up joyously, and they found themselves among Elvenkind, dressed in silks and satins and leathers of varying hues—blacks and greys and whites, yellows and oranges and reds and browns, blues and greens and violets and lavenders—the Fair Folk gathered in celebration.

Elves smiled and gave way as Riatha led the twain across the greensward and unto glade center. Back and back moved the Fair Folk, yet singing, until they were ringed 'round, yielding a space so that all could see the visitors. Riatha took Faeril's hand in her right and Gwylly's in her left and slowly turned about, letting all view the Waerlinga. And as she turned, the singing slowly faded, subsiding until it was but a gentle murmur and then not at all. Harp strings rose and then fell in a last silvery glissando, the final notes drifting among the shadowed pines. Silence descended, and overhead stars emerged as the gloaming dimmed to darkness. Riatha faced north, a Wearling at each hand, and called out in words of liquid silver: *"Alori e Darai, vi estare Faeril Twiggins e Gwylly Fenn,"* and a shout of welcome rang through the woods as again Riatha turned the Waerlinga about so that all could once more see them.

Facing north again, Riatha led the Waerlinga toward the arc of the be-ringing Lian, toward the point where stood a tall, flaxen-haired Elf. To his left and right were planted standards, the flags hanging lax in the still night air. Even so, as they approached, the Warrows could see the design thereupon—green tree on field of grey—and knew at once that they beheld the sigil of Arden Vale, the Lone Eld Tree standing in twilight, a flag that had been borne with honor upon many a field in Wars cataclysmic.

Riatha came to a stop before the flaxen-haired Elf. *"Alor Inarion, vi estare Faeril Twiggins e Gwylly Fenn, eio ypt faenier ala, Faeril en a Boskydells e Gwylly en a Weiunwood. Eio ra e rintha anthi an e segein."*

The Elf smiled down at Faeril and Gwylly, and winked, and his words came softly: "I would be greatly surprised if ye spoke Sylva."

Faeril, her eyes glittering in the lambent yellow glow of the lanterns, shook her head *No*, but added, "We could learn."

The Elf laughed. "Dara Riatha—that is, Lady Riatha—has presented ye unto the Host of Arden Vale. Too, she has spoken thy names unto all gathered. She has also presented ye unto me. I am Alor Inarion, Lord Inarion, Warder of the Northern Regions of Rell." The Elf Lord bowed.

Returning the courtesy, Faeril curtsied and Gwylly bowed. Then the buccan grinned up at Inarion. "Even though we don't speak, uh, Sylva, I did hear my name called . . . Faeril's too. But it seemed to me that Riatha said much more as well."

Inarion's eyes widened slightly at Gwylly's canny observation. "Aye, she told that ye both came afar, Faeril from the Boskydells and thou from the Weiunwood. Too, she named ye the Lastborn Firstborns of the prophecy.

"But we can speak of that later. For now, let us conclude these formalities and resume our celebration. Here, stand beside me and turn unto the gathering."

With Faeril on his left and Gwylly on his right, Inarion called out unto the assembly: *"Darai e Alori, vi estare Faeril Twiggins e Gwylly Fenn, vala an Dara Riatha e an doea Lian."*

Once again a shout rose up from the gathered Elves, and as it rang out through the shadowed pines, Inarion said, "I have named ye a third time, and told that ye are the companions of Lady Riatha and of all Lian."

Even as Inarion spoke, silver harps began a soft melody, gradually intensifying as Elven voices slowly joined, singing in roundelay, harmonies rising upon harmonies. And the Alori and Darai began to drift across the greensward past one another in a shifting complex pattern, or perhaps in random movement, pacing and pausing, a given Elf or Elfess passing among other singers pacing and pausing too, voices blending and adding, singing point and counterpoint, all the while stately stepping, stepping, Riatha among these.

Neither Faeril nor Gwylly had ever heard such magical singing, and they looked at one another, quite overwhelmed by the concord. Too, they glanced up at Lord Inarion standing between. "We sing to the harvest and to the autumnal equinox," said the Elf. "And to the rising Moon."

Easterly, just now visible above the crowns of the trees, a full yellow Moon rode upward, its white-gold beams glimmering among the pines.

"Come," said Inarion, taking a Waerling in each hand. Singing, he stepped the twain among Elvenkind, pacing slowly pacing, following a ritual reaching back through the ages. And down among the rustling silk and rippling satin and brushing leather, enveloped by melody and harmony and descant and counterpoint, trod the Warrows, their hearts full to bursting.

Step . . . pause . . . shift . . . pause . . . turn . . . pause. Slowly, slowly, move and pause. Voices rising. Voices falling.

Liquid notes from silver strings. Harmony. Euphony. Pause
. . . step . . . pause. Inarion turning. Waerlinga turning. Ladies
passing. Lords pausing. Counterpoint. Descant. Step . . .
pause . . . step . . .

When the song at last came to an end, voices dwindling,
strings diminishing, movement slowing, until all was silent
and still, Gwylly and Faeril found themselves once again
between the standards flanking Inarion, Riatha before them.
The motif of the pattern they had paced was beyond the
Warrows' comprehension, but now at ritual's end they knew,
somehow, that the movement was not random but had some
design, some purpose. They had been lost in the rite, for
when it was over, the Moon was up full, having covered a
quarter of the sky in its journey across during the dance.

Inarion smiled down at them and then looked out at the
gathering. *"Darai e Alori, ad sisal a ad tumla ni fansar isa
nid. Ses ti qala e med."* A joyous shout greeted this pronouncement, and as Elves began streaming out from the glen
and westward, Riatha stepped forward. "Alor Inarion."

Inarion moved from between the standards and took Dara
Riatha's arm, glancing back at the Waerlinga. "Come, my
friends, the ritual is ended for this night, and food and drink
awaits us."

Gwylly offered his arm to Faeril, and as would two children pretend, they followed Inarion and Riatha, mirroring
their every move.

As they strode southwesterly, they came among the Elven
cotes, passing them by, heading for the central gathering hall
in the distance ahead. But ere they reached it, a horn cry
sounded from the nearby western canyon wall, and in the
fulgent moonlight they could see a band of riders wending
down a narrow pathway from a dark opening on the face of
the bluff above. Again the horn sounded.

" 'Tis Aravan and the others," said Riatha, "returning from
the hunt."

Inarion barked, "Hai! They have a stag. It portends well
for morrow night's fest."

Accompanied by Riatha and Gwylly and Faeril, Inarion
turned from the gathering hall and strode to the stables. No
sooner had they reached the mews than the line of Elven

riders drew nigh, led by a tall, dark-haired Lian on a black horse. His dark leathers as well as his face were bespattered by mud. The black horse, too, was slathered with grime. Across the steed's withers was an arrow-slain stag. "Hai, Fortune favored thee, Aravan," called Inarion.

Swinging down, Aravan gestured back in the direction of the following Lian. "Not only me, Alor, but She smiled down upon Alaria as well."

An Elven rider with dark brown hair, her leathers and her mount also covered with muck now dried, rode to the byre. Another stag lay across the withers of her steed.

"Hai!" called Inarion. "Now we feast doubly!"

Gwylly moved out from the shadows and into the moonlight, Faeril still clasping his arm. All the band paused, smiles playing across their features as they looked upon the Waerlinga. Aravan's eyes widened slightly at the sight of the twain, and he glanced at Riatha, the Elfess nodding in answer to his unspoken question. And when the other riders had dismounted, Riatha called: *"Alori, vi estare Faeril Twiggins e Gwylly Fenn. Eio ra e rintha anthi an e segein."*

Leading his horse, Aravan stepped forward and made a sweeping bow to the Waerlinga. "I hight Aravan."

Gwylly bowed in return. "I hight Gwylly and this is Faeril." The damman curtsied.

One by one the other mud-spattered Elves introduced themselves as they led their begrimed horses past the Waerlinga and into the byre.

The hall brimmed with light and color. Tables and benches were filled to capacity as the feast continued, Elves serving Elves, carrying platters laden with the bounty of the harvest as well as with baked fish and roast fowl and spitted game.

Faeril and Gwylly sat at a table with Inarion and Riatha. During the feast Riatha's silver-grey eyes ever and again strayed across the faces of the Waerlinga, her thoughts carrying her back a thousand years or so, recalling the images of Tomlin and Petal, and she was startled by the resemblance of Faeril and Gwylly to their ancestors of days long past: Faeril with black hair and amber eyes, just as Petal's had been; Gwylly with red hair and emeraldine eyes, as had been

Pebble's, Tomlin's. Even the shapes of their faces were nigh the same: Faeril's oval; Gwylly's squarish. Their slimness and quickness and deftness seemed identical to those Waerlinga of long ago as well. Riatha closed her eyes in memory, then again looked at the twain. *Were I a Drimm, then would I think that Petal and Pebble were now reborn.*

She was wrenched from these thoughts as Aravan and his hunting party joined the fest, having dressed the deer and cared for their horses and having made themselves presentable. The black-haired Lian sat beside her and soon was regaling the party with the tale of the hunt for stag in Drearwood: of the dash through a swampland; of the near miraculous casting of an arrow by Alaria at the very moment when it seemed as if the first stag would ne'er be brought to earth; of another wild dash through thick pines on the way home as a second stag jumped up before them; of being knocked from his saddle by a low branch at the very moment the stag doubled back; and of nearly being run down by the beast even as he loosed his own arrow point blank, the stag collapsing at his very feet.

"Hai, Aravan," crowed Inarion, "indeed Dame Fortune rode before thee on this day."

"Nay, Inarion, more like She clung to my leg, dragging alongside," rejoined Aravan. Inarion burst out in laughter, as did they all.

The tables were cleared and once again music filled the air, Elf and Elfess alike taking turns with pipe and flute and drum and harp and lute and timbrel. And the singing, oh the singing, silver voices on the air as an Alor or a Dara or sometimes more than one would take up a melody. And there came a dance, with a male and female whirling and gyring, advancing and retreating, laughing and mock arguing, fleeing and chasing, catching and escaping, dancing far apart and independently, then sensuously together. At last the dance came to an end, amid applause and voiced approval.

Faeril was enthralled, Gwylly, too, for neither had ever seen such grace and beauty in a dance before. " 'Tis the mating dance they did, for Seena and Tillaron are lovers," explained Riatha.

Faeril sighed. "Well, though Gwylly and I have yet to say our vows in public, we are mates and lovers, yet never could we dance thus."

Inarion turned to the Waerlinga. "So ye contemplate a pledging to one another?"

Gwylly looked up. "We would, can we find a kingsclerk or mayor or the like."

Inarion laughed, and Riatha smiled as she spoke. "Did I not say that I would arrange a pledging for ye? Of kingsclerk or mayors we have none. Yet beside ye sits the Lord of all of Arden, as well as the Warder of the Northern Regions of Rell. And who better than Alor Inarion to lead ye through the ceremony?"

Faeril turned to Gwylly. "Oh yes, Gwylly. Who better?"

Gwylly merely shook his head.

The damman faced Riatha once again. "My Lady Riatha, we would be honored to have Lord Inarion conduct the ceremony."

At the next lull in the entertainment, Inarion stood and called for quiet, and the hall fell to silence. He then turned to Riatha, and she stood, her green silks and satins bright in the lantern glow. *"Alori e Darai, va da Waerlinga brea tae e evon a plith."*

A shout of approval rose up at the announcement.

Inarion stepped to a dais and held up his hands, again calling for quiet. Then he motioned for Aravan and Riatha to stand to either side facing him. Last, he called for the Waerlinga to step before him.

Gwylly turned to Faeril, seated beside him still. "My dammia, will you have me with all my faults?"

In response Faeril kissed him, then stood and pulled her buccaran to his feet. Taking him by the hand, she led him to stand between Riatha and Aravan, facing Alor Inarion.

Inarion looked down upon the two Wee Ones. "Ye have come before me to make a pledge of mating. I understand that among mortalkind mating pledges attempt to bind a pair until Death comes between. Yet heed, 'Till Death do us part' is not a term used in an Elven vow, for Death was ever meant to be a stranger unto Elvenkind.

"Too, we have become wiser in our long lives than to

believe that things stay the same: change is a rule of existence.

"All things change with the passing of the seasons, though for some things the change is imperceptible, whereas for other things, change is swift, sometimes deadly. Individuals, too, change with the passing of seasons, and vows should not bind one in a relationship in which the common ground no longer exists, no matter the type of oath, be it for mating, fealty, vengeance, or aught else. For just as Death may part one from a vow, so too does the loss of common ground.

"This concept of common ground is no abstraction, for 'tis common ground which drives all relationships, be they simple acts of working with one another as well as working against one another . . . or be they more formal, such as lovers' vows, or oaths of fealty, or compacts among friends, or even vows concerning foe, vows of vengeance and retribution.

"Hence, common ground is the key to a relationship. And for a relationship to become strong, to remain strong, both parties to an agreement must work more or less in equal measure in tending the common ground and nurturing the vows between. For when but one tends the ground and the other does not, the ground suffers, becomes less fertile, the things planted in common weaken, mayhap to wither altogether. After a span of this behavior, when but one nurtures and the other does not, a time will come when the ground will lie fallow, perhaps becoming barren, as those involved go their separate ways, or perhaps it will become ground supporting nought but bitter weed should they sow enmity thereupon. Too, there may be times when the ground disappears altogether, when individuals no longer have aught in common. And so, to keep the ground fertile and the vows planted therein robust, each must do a goodly part of the work to make it so.

"Even in the best relationships, there are ofttimes onerous or tedious duties involved, most recurring time and again. Heed me, on Mithgar various Folk have long-held beliefs that some things are females' work, while other things are the males' to do; these Folk usually separate all tasks along these lines, with a rigid boundary between. Those who well and truly consider this division of tasks eventually come to realize that there are but a very few things which fall only into one domain or into only the other—but this we can say: males seldom give birth to babies; females seldom are as strong as males; at times males are more fleet; at times females endure surpassingly; all else merely requires the skills or talents to perform the tasks. Hence, among Elvenkind, on Mithgar and upon Adonar, all duties are shared—except for those requiring strength or speed or endurance or other physical attributes beyond one's capacity, and those requiring the birthing of a child and its suckling, and those requiring skills not yet acquired or talents beyond reach. By sharing all else, we keep the common ground among us fertile and everlasting.

"Hence, to keep thine own relationship strong ye must share equally in the cultivation of the common ground and in the nurturing of the vows between; and ye must sort among all duties and participate willingly and fully in all which can be shared."

Inarion knelt down and took each Waerling by a hand, his voice soft. "Do ye understand the meaning of that which I say?"

Both Gwylly and Faeril looked into one another's eyes and then to Inarion. *Yes*, they said in unison.

"Then speak true: Do ye vow to one another to tend the common ground and to nurture the pledges given and received?"

*I do vow*, they said in unison.

"Then speak true: Will ye plight thy troth to one another, forsaking all who would come between?"

*I do vow.*

Inarion then placed Faeril's hand in Gwylly's and clasped their joined hands in his. "Then Gwylly Fenn, then Faeril Twiggins, each having spoken true, go forth from here together and share thy joys and thy burdens in equal measure until thine individual destinies determine otherwise."

Inarion embraced each Waerling, first Faeril, then Gwylly, and then stood, calling out to all. *"Alori e Darai, va da Waerlinga, Faeril Twiggins e Gwylly Fenn, avan taeya e evon a plith."* And a great shout went up from all.

Riatha and Aravan then turned and escorted Gwylly and

Faeril through the gathering, harps and lutes and pipes and flutes and drums and timbrels began playing a merry tune, and Elven voices were raised in song.

Out from the hall they went—Riatha and Aravan in the lead, Gwylly and Faeril directly behind, Inarion and all the others following—out into the moonlight and among the white cottages and into the woods, song filling the air. Easterly through the forest fared the procession, Riatha and Aravan drawing the Warrows after, with a long train of Elvenkind following behind. They came at last to the glade where was the cote of Gwylly and Faeril. Three times 'round the cottage they marched, or danced, circling deosil, the long promenade curling after, Elven voices lifted in joy. At last they stopped before the stoop, and Riatha and Aravan led the Waerlinga to the small porch, the dwelling glowing white in the platinum moonlight, the rest of the procession remaining in a ring encircling the cottage, the elegant hues of their silks and satins and leathers muted in the silvery beams. And all Elven voices were lifted in a final song whose melody filled the heart near to bursting. And when it was done, Riatha and Aravan each hugged the Waerlinga, then all the host quietly left, moving away to the notes of a silver harp drifting on the air, leaving the Wee Folk unto themselves.

The next evening came the second night of the celebration of the equinox, and the evening afterward held the third. And on this final night Gwylly and Faeril found Riatha in a communal kitchen helping dozens of others prepare the meal. Aravan, too, was there, up to his elbows washing pots and pans.

" 'Tis the sharing of duties," responded Raitha to Gwylly's question. "Three nights do we celebrate, each taking turn on one of those nights serving others."

"Oh," exclaimed Gwylly. "I understand. This way, all get to enjoy the singing and dancing."

Riatha smiled. "Aye, for two nights of the three, 'tis so. But even more so, all get to share the joys of the labor."

Faeril rolled up her sleeves. "Well then, Gwylly Fenn, it's time we did our part."

And so, that third evening of the equinox celebration,

Elves were treated to the sight of two Waerlinga carrying platters of food and jugs of wine and ale and *wela*, a heady Elven mead. And later, the twain aided in clearing away the trenchers and platters and jugs and cups and flatware.

After the hall had emptied, Gwylly and Faeril and Riatha, as well as several others, worked at cleaning the tables and floors—Gwylly pushing a broom, Faeril and Riatha wiping down tables.

Faeril took advantage of this time to seek an answer to a puzzle. "Riatha, I was told by my dam that during the Winter War the Elves of Arden Vale were led by Lord Talarin and by Lady Rael, yet I find now that Lord Inarion is the leader."

Riatha paused in her wiping. "Aye, my mother's brother, Alor Talarin, was the Warder during the Winter War. And indeed Dara Rael was his Consort. Yet they have ridden the twilight and are again in Adonar." The Elfess resumed cleaning.

"Talarin was your uncle?"

"Aye, though the Elven name for uncle is *kelan*."

"Why did they go back to Adonar?"

A look of sadness came over Riatha's features. "My *sinja*, my cousin, Vanidor, was slain at the Iron Tower in the early days of the Winter War. And near War's end many Lian of Arden fell at the Battle of Kregyn, the place you call Grūwen, and their Death Redes were like unto a cold wind blowing through the souls of Elvenkind. Neither Talarin nor Rael ever recovered from the loss of one of their sons, nor from the loss of so many who fell at Kregyn. However, they did not take the twilight ride immediately, for they had pledged fealty unto the then High King, Galen. Yet when Galen died some forty or fifty years after War's end, Talarin and Rael journeyed unto Darda Galion, and with Coron Eiron and a retinue of like-minded Lian, they rode the twilight. Ere setting out, however, Talarin asked Inarion to become the Warder of Arden Vale."

Finishing the wiping down of the table, Faeril and Riatha moved to the next. . . . And then the one after. . . . And the next.

"He was named after our *kelan*."

Faeril looked up at Riatha's words. "Who?"

"My brother, Talar," answered Riatha, her eyes grey and glistering with unshed tears. "Talar was named after Talarin—his *kelan*, my *kelan*, our uncle."

Riatha brushed at her eyes with her sleeve, then looked with a clear gaze at the wee damman. "On the morrow we begin preparing. On the morrow."

Faeril nodded, and together they moved to the next table.

That night, when buccan and damman fell into bed they were exhausted by worthy work. Gwylly turned to Faeril. "Truth be known, my sweet, these Elves have the right of it—sharing the burdens as well as the joys."

"*Mmmm*," responded Faeril from that state halfway 'tween wake and sleep.

Gwylly smiled at his love and brushed a lock of hair from her forehead. *Rest well, my dammia, for as Aravan told me, on the morrow we start training in earnest for the mission ahead, for he intends to go with us.* The buccan turned over and blew out the candle, then rolled back and snuggled spoonwise unto Faeril.

*On the morrow we begin. . . .*

# CHAPTER 13

# Honing the Edge

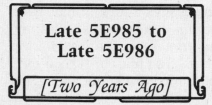

Late 5E985 to
Late 5E986

*[Two Years Ago]*

Winter came swiftly upon the heels of fall, and snow fell thickly down. Time and again the prevailing winds drove churning storms to crash upon the steeps of the Grimwall Mountains above the Elvenholt, for the long ravine of Arden Vale lay at the foot of the western climb to the Crestan Pass. And snow fell and fell again and pressed deeply upon the land and bent the boughs of the pine tree forest, and more snow fell as the days and weeks went by. The surface of the River Tumble froze, and hoarfrost and rime glittered upon the vertical walls of the deep gorge. Aravan took the winter opportunity to teach the Waerlinga the art of snow shoeing, and the making of shelters using cut blocks of snow or using pliant pine branches bent and woven into bowers and anchored upon the ground with pegs or rock nails and covered over with insulating snow. Too, he and Riatha began training Gwylly and Faeril in the skills of climbing rock and ice. Time and again did the four of them clamber up and down and across the sheer walls of the hemming bluffs. The Waerlinga learned of ice axes and picks and crampons; of jams and rings and rock nails; of climbing harnesses and ropes and belaying and rappelling; of free climbing and hoisting goods. And Gwylly and Faeril and Ria-

tha and Aravan drilled at aiding one another in ascents and
descents and crossings. Aravan showed them a technique
named "swiftswarm" by the Drimma who had taught him,
where a strong-gripped climber could come hand over hand
up a rope while at the same time companions above haled
the rope upward, hence the climber ascended at double rate;
as could be expected, this technique worked particularly well
with a Waerling climber and Elven halers.

Drilling in all that they had learned, they climbed in the
night as well as the day, for who knew what Fortune held
in store? And this training was cold and frigid, yet necessary
given their goal and the time of year they planned to arrive.

The Elves fashioned winter clothing for Faeril and Gwylly,
light and supple yet exceedingly warm, with boots and
gloves to match, all mottled in greys and whites and blacks
to blend with a winter 'scape. Too, for summer wear they
clad the Waerlinga in soft leathers crafted to their stature,
these too mottled of pale greys and greens and browns and
tans to conceal. Raincloaks were made, reversible, browns
and tans on one side, greys and greens on the other; and
even Elven eyes were fooled by such.

They drilled in knife throwing and slinging, in swordplay
and spear casting and wielding. They practiced supporting
one another in combat, studying tactics 'gainst Rūck and
Hlōk and Vulg and other such, for where they would go was
fraught with Foul Folk. The Waerlinga began learning the
skills of plying long-knives as swords, though these weapons
would be last used by them should it come to combat, their
deftness at hurling blade and bullet being considered more
valuable.

And Gwylly's lessons in reading and writing continued,
Faeril teaching him not only on a regular basis but at every
opportune moment as well. His progress came swiftly, for
the buccan seemed to have a natural aptitude for such. And
both buccan and damman took up the Elven tongue, living
among the Lian as they did. At times Gwylly's speech became entangled among Sylva and Common and Twyll, yet
always did he unravel the words, and his flair for apt expression grew.

But it was not all lessons and learning, training and practice, for the Elves oft held celebrations, Winterfest among these. At times Gwylly and Faeril participated in the dancing and singing and other ceremonies; at other times they cooked and served and cleaned alongside Elves doing the same, sharing in the burdens as well as the joys. And in their own cottage they worked together or took turns doing the chores, be it cooking, cleaning, or aught else, for they had fully embraced the Elven way. Gwylly learned to sew, Fearil to chop wood; both learned to cook a variety of dishes, crowing over their successes, laughing over their failures. These and more did the Warrows share, and their common ground grew as did their love.

The first eve of Winterfest—Year's Long Night, the night of the winter solstice—found Gwylly and Faeril in the kitchen standing on overturned crates, washing pots and pans, while the sounds of music and singing and dancing and gaiety drifted in from the great room of the gathering hall. Even so, at mid of night all labor stopped and everyone took up a cup of pure water and assembled to see Inarion raise his own cup and hear him speak the invocation. And though his words were in Sylva, still Faeril and Gwylly understood what he said:

["Darai e Alori an Arden Dal . . .]
"Ladies and Lords of Arden Vale,
     now is the longest night.
On the morrow again begins
     the long march unto the Sun.
As grows Adon's light,
     so may grow the bright spirits of each and every one.
May the renewal of the seasons
     bring renewed joy to all the world.
Let us here affirm our guardianship
     o'er Adon's creations:
The sweet earth, clear air, pure water,
     and all the creatures which live thereon
     and crawl and fly and swim therein.
Let us not forget to aid
     those in our charge whom we guide most gently
     along the paths of wisdom.

*But let us remember as well*
  *that even the most humble or young or*
    *inexperienced*
  *may show wisdom beyond their years,*
  *wisdom beyond our own, for which we should be*
    *grateful.*
*Hence we must ward our hearts against pride,*
  *e'en as we ward the world 'gainst evil,*
  *for knowledge alone is not wisdom.*
*Ladies and Lords of Arden Vale,*
  *now is the longest night.*
*On the morrow again begins*
  *the long march unto the Sun."*

Inarion then raised his cup and called out: *"Hai, Lian Guardians, hai! Protectors of the world!"*

*Hai!* shouted the gathered assembly, Faeril and Gwylly among them. And each and all drained completely their cups of pure, sweet water.

Spring came, and with it the snowmelt, water running everywhere, and the River Tumble roared throughout the days and nights. Green grew the land, flowers bloomed, and the birds returned and sang their songs of territory and mating. Animals began stirring, Bear and deer and elk and mountain sheep and goat. Small animals, too, came forth from their winter's lay-up, badger and hare and squirrel and marmot and otter and many others as well. Not all of these had slept in the winter, not fox nor Wolf nor wildcat nor others who roam the snow as well, but spring brought a renewal of energy unto them, and so they were active in preparing dens and in rearing young and in their unending quests for food.

And with the vernal equinox came the Elven celebration of the change of season. And just as did the festival of the autumn, so too did the festival of the spring extend over three nights, with singing and dancing and music and feasting, as well as sharing the joy of the labor. For the occasion Elven seamstresses fashioned for Faeril a silken gown of scarlet and gold, with just a touch of black. And Elven tailors made for Gwylly dark satin breeks of emerald green and a pale silken shirt of jade. Slippers there were of ruby for Faeril and shoes of black for Gwylly, with gold and silver buckles respectively, and Gwylly had a belt to match, while Faeril was accented with ribbons. Oh, how their eyes did sparkle in the light of the gathering hall, and after the feast the twain waltzed alone to the joy of the assembled Elvenkind.

After the Springday festival, the training continued, as Gwylly and Faeril, as Riatha and Aravan, taught and acquired skills and drilled—in snow and slush and water and mud, o'er wet rock and dry, among pines and crags and open fields, on slopes and banks and on ground flat, on soil smooth and rough, and on open stretches of stone, for none could foretell what conditions would prevail when a given skill would be called upon. And so in all conditions, day or night, fair or foul, they practiced: stalking and hiding and other skills of stealth, learning to blend with forest and field and stone, learning how to catch a foe unaware, learning, too, the deadly skills of silent kill and more. Ambushes they lay, and overhead drops, and deadfalls and other traps. Still they climbed vertical rock, and climbed trees as well. They practiced walking a rope, Faeril teaching the others. All this and more did they do as spring moved toward summer.

But not all was training and practice, not all was learning and drill, for there was the spring tilling to do and the planting of crops and the tending of flocks and herds: sheep, cattle, horses, swine, ducks, geese, chickens, and the ponies of the Waerlinga. They sheared sheep for the wool and aided with foaling. They drove cattle to the high fields, and the sheep higher still.

It was while she and Gwylly were tending sheep that Faeril spoke again to Riatha about the prophecy, a topic often speculated upon in their free moments. But this time Faeril asked about Dara Rael and how the prophecy came to be.

As the Elfess and damman perched on a large rock in the high meadow, Riatha cast her thoughts back, recalling that distant day. "We sat on the banks of the River Tumble, not far from the cote, and Rael had a long crystal"—Riatha held thumb and forefinger some three inches apart—"clear it was, with six sides and faceted ends that came to a shallow point. I, too, had a crystal, somewhat smaller, but one I had prepared long ago.

"Rael had been trying to teach me scrying, though it seems I have little talent for it. Ai, now and again would I seem to catch an inchoate glimmer, a confused flash, but no true redes or sooths came to me.

"Nevertheless, we were playing at scrying when she seemed to slip into a trance, and then spoke the prophecy.

"Afterwards, I went unto thy ancestors—Petal and Pebble—to tell them of the rede . . . but thou have read of that in thy journal, neh?"

Faeril nodded. "Yes, Petal wrote of it." The damman fell silent and the two sat together and watched the sheep grazing in the grassy ways among the rounded boulders and smooth stretches of partially exposed white stone of the high mead, Gwylly in the distance trudging up a high slope, intending to retrieve a lamb that had somehow become separated from the flock. After a long moment—"Someday, Riatha, would you teach me to scry?"

Riatha's eyes flew wide. "What little I know was said to me a millennium agone, Faeril. As a teacher, thou could find one better than I."

Faeril laughed and caught up Riatha's hands in her own. "Oh, Dara, I am merely curious as to how it is done."

Riatha smiled back at the damman and nodded her assent.

During their stay in the high meadow cabin, Gwylly's reading and writing plunged ahead apace, and Faeril began seriously tutoring him in Twyll, speaking as much as possible only in that tongue, keeping her phrases short and simple, translating only when necessary. With Gwylly's natural aptitude for tongues, he took to Twyll as a duck takes to water— or rather as an *akkle chinta vi*.

The days of spring lengthened and summer drew nigh, and a week or two before the solstice their relief came, and the buccan and damman returned to the Elvenholt below. The training with Aravan and Riatha resumed, though every third day or so, they disengaged from it to aid in the labor of the Elvenholt.

It was on such a day, on Year's Long Day, that Riatha and Faeril broke off from hoeing rows of vegetables in the Elvenholt fields and strolled down to sit on the banks of the River Tumble, preparing to take a midday meal. And as they sat, the Elfess gave over a long crystal to the damman. Clear it was. Pellucid. Six-sided down its length, each end blunt-pointed with six facets. Some three quarters of an inch across from flat to opposite flat, and perhaps four inches from tip to tip.

Faeril drew in her breath, clearly taken by the transparent stone. She held it up in the sunlight and turned it and peered through the shifting panes. "Oh my, this is splendid."

" 'Tis a gift, wee one," said Riatha after a moment of watching.

Faeril was astonished. "Oh, no, Riatha. This is too precious for one such as I." She held out the crystal to Riatha.

"Hush thee, Faeril." The Elfess refused to take back the stone. "Thou place too low a value upon thyself. Too, Inarion would be puzzled by thy refusal."

Faeril's eyes flew wide. "Alor Inarion? This is a gift from him?"

Riatha smiled. "He was most happy to give it over."

Faeril looked down at the crystal, shifting sunlight flashing as she slowly turned it. "I suppose it would be an insult to refuse a gift from the Lord of Arden Vale, neh?"

Riatha laughed her silver laugh. "Indeed, wee one. Indeed."

They sat and took their meal of oatcakes and berries, drinking tea, Faeril's eyes turning ever and again unto the crystal, while below the River Tumble *shsshhed* over falls and burbled over round rocks. Somewhere in the distance birds sang. At last the damman said, "Is this the same one you and Rael used when she spoke the rede?"

"Nay, Fearil. That one was Rael's alone. But heed, these stones are not uncommon, though one of this size and clarity is seldom found.

"Most come with flaws. Some with threads of gold or silver or other metals. Some are tinged rose, while others are smoky or blue or green, ruddy or faintly gold.

"Rael told that those of color had particular uses, depending on the tint"—Riatha took up the stone and turned it aglitter in the sunlight—"but crystals clear, such as this, could be used for all."

Again Riatha handed the stone to Faeril. The damman held the crystal and looked into its structure. "Riatha, is it . . . magic?"

The Elfess's answer was long in coming, as if she pondered an enigma. "I know not what thou mean by such a word as 'magic.' But this I do know: it is *special*, for to some it provides the focus for them to unleash their own . . . power."

Faeril looked up at Dara Riatha. "Does everyone have this . . . this 'power'?"

Riatha sighed. "Mayhap, though for some it comes in greater measure than for others. At least that's what Dara Rael believed. And perhaps I subscribe to that view as well, for never did I succeed in scrying. Perhaps, though, it was because I could not meet Rael's criteria."

"Her criteria?"

"Aye. 'This is the way of it,' she would say. 'Empty thy mind of all distraction, and concentrate first on cleansing the crystal; then thou can charge it with light: sunlight, moonlight, starlight, dawn light, twilight, candlelight, lanternlight, firelight, forgelight, torch-light, spectral light, gem light, and light from other sources—each has a purpose, each.' "

Faeril looked again at the crystal. "And just how does a person go about this 'cleansing'?"

Riatha hearkened back, remembering. "It must be submitted to the five elements: buried in fertile earth; washed in clear water; breathed upon by a natural breeze; passed through a living flame; and aligned to the six cardinal directions of the aethyr—north, east, south, west, up, down.

"Then it must be kept wrapped in a black silk cloth and stored in an iron box to protect it from the fluctuations of the aethyr until time to charge it with the light and seek the vision." Riatha took a small iron container, one inch by one inch by four and a half inches, from her pouch and opened it along a lengthwise seam, hinged opposite. The interior held a square of black silk, clearly marking this box as the container for the crystal that Faeril held. The Elfess gave over the receptacle to the damman. "Once cleansed by the one who will use it, the crystal is . . . attuned. It not need be cleansed again unless others have touched it or have otherwise greatly influenced it in some manner . . . or so said Rael long past."

Faeril looked in at the iron box, the silk cloth, and the clear crystal. "All right, I understand how it might be cleansed. But how is it, mmm, used?"

Riatha again took the crystal and held it up into the sunlight. "Charge it with the light by bathing it in the desired illumination. And in the same light hold it before thee. Clear thy mind of all else but the crystal and the light and look deep into the stone, and let thy consciousness fall within. Ask it what you will, and perhaps answers will come.

"I remember not all Rael said, yet this I do know:

> *Moonlight to see the future;*
> *Starlight to see the past;*
> *Noonlight to see the present;*
> *Twilight to see tomorrow;*
> *Dawnlight to see yesterday;*
> *Firelight to see afar;*
> *Candlelight to see loved ones;*
> *Forgelight to see allies;*
> *Torch-light to see foe;*
> *Spectral light to see Destiny;*
> *Darkness to see death;*
> *Sunlight to see all.*

"Rael also told me of many things which at times can be seen by viewing light through various jewels, yet these I do not remember in any great detail.

"But heed, one must be wary of such visions, for some are but imaginings—wishful and fearful both—while only a few are otherwise. Only at times unpredictable do true visions or redes or sooths or prophecies come through the crystals, and even these must be viewed with caution—for not always is revealed what immutably *must* be; instead thou may be shown that which merely *might* be."

Ere Faeril could ask aught else, workers began streaming back to the fields. And so she wrapped the crystal in the black silk square and placed all in the iron box and closed it tight, the clasp clicking into place. She slipped the container into her own pouch, then she and Riatha took up their hoes and returned to the fields as well.

Summer came in full with the celebration of the solstice, and Aravan began teaching Faeril and Gwylly and Riatha the

calls of birds—birds of the night as well as those of the day—
for he had long studied the avians and had mastered this
craft. And slowly they gained skill in the many whistles and
chirps and trills and coos and chirks, learning how to use
them as signals to one another. They also gained some facility at imitating bat shrills, for such calls were within the
range of hearing of Warrows as well as Elves. Too, Riatha
taught each of them the patterns of silent hand signalling.
And before the days of autumn came, they were able to carry
on long conversations without speaking a word.

Too, in a large eddy pool of the River Tumble, Faeril learned
to swim, aided by Aravan. And although Gwylly had some
skill in the side stroke and in treading water and in diving—
having been taught by his Human father, Orith, in the farm
pond—the buccan also heeded Aravan's lessons, gaining skill
in several strokes, including swimming underwater.

In this time of training and learning, Gwylly began to read
from his copy of Petal's journal, for his progress in Twyll
had moved apace. Slowly at first, groping for meaning, did
he read the words, often failing, needing guidance. Then
swifter and swifter did he read, needing less and less aid.

In the evenings as he studied, so too did Faeril. But her
studies were far different, on untrod ways, for she sought to
master the crystal. With care she had "cleansed" it, seeking
to "attune" it: a day she left it buried in fertile soil, choosing
a rich loam; another day it was washed in the clear water
of the nearby running rill; she dried it in the soft northerly
breeze that blew down the vale, taking another day to do so;
carefully and swiftly she passed it through the flame of a
white candle, bathing the full length of each and every side
in the fire, and bathing the facets at the tips as well, but not
letting the crystal dwell long in the flame for fear of cracking
the precious stone; and last, at midnight, and at dawn and
noon and twilight as well, she aligned the crystal to the
cardinal points of the aethyr—north, east, south, west, up,
and down—breathing a new prayer to Adon as she held it
steady along each direction. And she wrapped it in the black
silk square and stored it in the iron box in between the
stages of cleansing, and afterward as well.

As Gwylly slowly read through the journal, Faeril held the

crystal in the moonlight and tried to clear her mind of all distraction, looking deep into the stone, attempting to let her consciousness fall within, seeking to see the future and the events it held . . .

. . . to no avail.

Summer waned and autumn approached, and when they were not sharing in the labor of the Elvenholt, still the foursome continued preparing for the unknown challenges and perils of their venture.

There came a day that Gwylly asked Aravan about the Elf's crystal spear. It was after a strenuous drill at long-knife wielding, and the two sat at leisure in a glade among the pines. The spear lay on the ground at Aravan's side, for it was never far from his reach. The smoky blade caught a noontide sunbeam shining down through the boughs, fragmenting it into shards of light.

Gwylly's eye was caught by the glitter, and he looked at the blade and the length of the black haft and wondered at its making. Tentatively he reached out to the shaft. It was cool to the touch.

"I say, Aravan, just where did you come by this?"

Aravan looked at the Waerling and said nought for a long while. As the silence between them grew, Gwylly decided that the Elf would not answer. Yet at last Aravan spoke:

"It was made for me by the Hidden Ones long past." The Elf fingered the blue stone on the thong 'round his neck.

"A gift?"

"Aye, thou could call it that, or mayhap a remembrance."

Gwylly glanced at the spear and then back to Aravan. "A gift by the Hidden Ones? Who are they? And why—?" Gwylly's words jerked to a halt as he saw a look of anguish spring up in Aravan's eyes.

Again a long silence fell between them.

"I was once a master of the sea," said Aravan at last. "Rather, not of the sea, but of a ship of the sea.

"In those days there was an island called Rwn, a place of Mages far from here. There, too, dwelled some Hidden Ones—these were wee folk, smaller even than the Waerlinga." Aravan held his hand a foot or so above the ground, indicating their height.

Gwylly's eyes flew wide. "Surely you jest, Aravan."

"Nay, Gwylly, I do not."

"B-but, wee tiny Folk are merely myths ... or so I thought."

A sad smile fell upon Aravan's features. "Thou has heard of them, then. Fox Riders. Tree and hummock and hole dwellers. Fen swimmers and forest runners. Others."

"In hearthtales, I have," responded the buccan. "But I always believed that they were only legends."

"Not legends, Gwylly. Not legends." The Elf gazed long at the Waerling, then finally spoke. "There are Hidden Ones in thy Weiunwood, and not just the tiny folk."

"But I've spent nearly every one of my days in that forest," protested Gwylly, "and I've *never* seen a Hidden One."

Again Aravan smiled. "That, Gwylly, is why they are named Hidden Ones."

Now Gwylly smiled. "Even so, Aravan, surely someone would have come across them."

"Mayhap some have stumbled upon a Hidden One or several, Gwylly. Yet who would believe them? And mayhap none have come across the tiny ones, or others, for they have ways of protecting themselves, as well as ways of discouraging trespassers in their domains."

Suddenly to Gwylly's mind sprang the image of Black in full pursuit of a hare, and the dog tumbling tail over ears to keep from running into one of the "closed places" in the Weiunwood, a place only open to the wild creatures. "Perhaps I know where some Hidden Ones dwell, Aravan, there where legends speak of figures half seen, some gigantic, others small and quick—figures of light, figures of dark, things of the earth, things of the trees and greenery, things named Fox Riders and Living Mounds and Angry Trees and Groaning Stones, and other creatures of lore and myth.

"Why, Faeril rode through such places, places that seemed to just barely tolerate her, places her pony did not want to go. She told that they were full of twilight and shadow and watching eyes, and a rustling. She said that from the corners of her eyes, things seemed to flit and dart among the trees, but when she looked, no one was there."

Aravan nodded. " 'Tis likely that Faeril did ride through domains of the Hidden Ones."

Once more silence fell between the two. At last Aravan took up his spear and stood, looking down upon the buccan.

"I rescued a band of Hidden Ones from the destruction of Rwn. They fashioned this spear as a token of their gratitude." Aravan said nought for a moment, his face a stoic mask. He looked again at the weapon. "Yet the cost of that rescue was nearly more than I could bear."

Aravan turned and walked away, and Gwylly watched him go, knowing that the Elf wished to be alone.

That evening, when Gwylly told Faeril of his conversation with Aravan, Faeril said little, yet a sadness filled her own eyes, for she knew somehow that a great sorrow lurked in the core of Aravan's heart.

Later, Faeril said, "In the Boskydell we, too, have legends of people like Aravan's Hidden Ones. They are said to dwell within the Thornwall. Of course, no one knows the truth of such, for even birds find it difficult to penetrate the fangs of the Spindlethorn."

Came the autumnal equinox, and the Elven ceremony in the glade seemed especially auspicious, the dancing and feasting and singing and the sharing of the labor particularly joyous, for Faeril and Gwylly celebrated the first anniversary of their vows. Too, they celebrated the anniversary of their arrival in Arden Vale. And the occasion was publicly noted by Inarion and hailed by all.

Autumn aged and winter drew nigh, and still did Gwylly and Faeril and Riatha and Aravan prepare.

Snow began to fall, and now the Warrows spent some eventides before their fireplace, Gwylly reading from the copy of Petal's journal, Faeril studying her crystal.

"I say, Faeril," remarked Gwylly, "listen to this." The buccan began reading aloud, his voice hesitant but managing to speak the passage as written, his words in Twyll:

["*Ve din á lak dalle . . .*]
    "*As I sat there waiting for Tommy to return with the horses, sat there holding Riatha, she bleeding from the great chunk of ice slammed down onto her head by Stoke, in the distance the iron bells of the abandoned*

*monastery were ringing, as if tolling a death knell for Urus, or celebrating the demise of Stoke. Yet I knew that it was the great quake that set them to clanging so, the quake that had riven the ice and opened the deep crevasse, the crevasse that Urus had borne Stoke into. As the bells rang, even though I wept for dead Urus, there was another thought which ran over and again through my mind, and it was this: Stoke is a werebeast—Vulg and flying creature and Man—and he once claimed that nought but silver or the like could ever slay him. And now he lies far below in the ice, the crevasse no more, slammed shut by the very same quake that had opened it, Stoke and his killer trapped perhaps forever; yet I wonder, if nought but silver can slay him, then is the monster truly dead?"*

Gwylly looked up from the journal. "*Brrr!* Rather spooky, isn't it? I mean, thinking of Stoke down there trapped alive all of these hundreds of years, frozen in the ice, unable to move."

Faeril set aside her crystal. "Perhaps Petal was more right than she knew. Or so the prophecy would seem to say."

Gwylly turned a page. "Come the spring a year and a half from now, we may find out, love."

The buccan returned to his reading, Faeril to her crystal, emptying out her mind, staring into its glittering depths.

# CHAPTER 14

# Dangerous Journeys

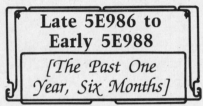

**Late 5E986 to
Early 5E988**

*[The Past One
Year, Six Months]*

During that long winter, as snow once again deeply covered the land, Riatha, Aravan, Faeril, and Gwylly carefully laid their plans. Given the state of the Grimwalls—teeming with Foul Folk, the region near the Great North Glacier made unstable by a Dragon's death long past—Aravan advised that in the coming autumn they should travel through Rian unto the coastal waters of the Boreal Sea and there take passage unto Aleut, where they would winter over. Then, come late winter, when spring drew nigh, they would travel overland by dogsled to the glacier, making their way through the Untended Lands and a short way up into the Grimwall to the place Riatha would take them. This, Aravan argued, would expose them the least to the *Spaunen* and to the quaking land.

As an alternative plan, they considered wintering over in Jord, there among the scattered settlements, there where the Vanadurin once dwelled ere migrating unto Valon at the end of the War of the Usurper. When the time was right, they would travel from Jord east along the Grimwalls to the Great North Glacier.

But current skirmishes between the Jordians and the alliance of the Naudrons and the Kathians made the crossing of the borders unsafe.

Last they considered wintering in the village of Inge in
Aralan, and journeying through the Grimwalls to reach the
glacier. This was the way that Riatha traditionally fared—
across the range past Dragonslair—the route she knew best.
Yet by the same token it was the most dangerous of ways
because of quakes and *Rûpt*.

After examining the alternatives, they decided to follow
Aravan's advice and sail to Aleut in autumn, ere the stormy
season; there they would winter over, and then use dogsleds
to fare across the Untended Lands to the Great North Glacier
on the arctic flank of the Grimwalls.

Spring came, heralded by the vernal equinox, and again the
Elvenholt set aside three days to celebrate.

Snow melted in the vale as well as high on the mountain
slopes, and the River Tumble roared. Again the cattle were
driven to the high meadows, and the sheep higher still, as
life went on. Things crafted in the long winter nights were
displayed: smithed silver and woven silk and jewellery set
with gemstones dear; carven wood and chiseled stone and
fire glazed pottery; paintings and poems and tales of delight
and wonder as well as heartbreaking odes; and music for
flute and lute and harp and drum and timbrel, as well as for
woodland pipes. There was weaponry rare of forged steel,
chased with runes and filigree; these were not *special* weapons, for much of that art had been long lost, though some
yet remained. Even so, these weapons were valued, for they
were well balanced and true, and those with blades were
keen and held an edge. Bows of carven wood with arrows to
match were also crafted over the winter. All these and more
were made by the Elves—items most precious and rare—
while the cold pressed down on the land.

When spring came, caravans laden with Elven goods set
out from Arden to trade for needed things: salt and spices
and condiments; herbs not found nigh the vale; fabrics and
raw gems; worthy ingots; these and the like did the Elven
traders seeks, travelling to far away Lands to barter and bar-
gain and exchange, gathering items and goods to bring in
return.

Among these caravans was one faring to Challerain Keep,
the High King's citadel in Rian. Of the Elven wayfarers, one

bore a message from Aravan to a friend at the Keep, asking him to send a messenger north to the sheltered port town of Ander along the Boreal Sea, there to arrange for a ship to bear the foursome unto the village of Innuk in the Land of Alute.

And the days marched on.

Still Gwylly continued to read and write, gaining skill and confidence, acquiring words in Twyll, and in Sylva and Common as well. Faeril wondered how he could keep it all straight, yet his natural facility seemed to somehow sort all out, and he managed to juggle all three. Too, he spoke the languages more fluently than he could read and write, though now and again he would mix the tongues, often with amusing results.

Faeril, too, continued her studies in Sylva, and both Waerlinga gained skill and comfort in the Elven tongue.

Faeril also continued her attempts at scrying the future, so far with little success. Yet one warm spring evening she sat in the moonlight on the stoop of the cote, the crystal in her hand, emptying her mind of all distraction, peering into the depths of the crys—

—*She fell through glittering space, silvery glowing crystal panes tumbling past, or was she tumbling and the panes still? . . . she did not know. Mirrored reflections from angled, crystal surfaces sparkled about her, and the whole of creation was filled with the ring of scintillant wind chimes, tinkling, pinging, chinging, the sound surrounding all. Down she spun, into a shimmering sea of argent light, of luminance and glimmer and flash, and there came the peal of crystal bells ringing near and far. And as she tumbled past crystal panes, over and again she saw reflected a glow of golden flame—at times multiple images, at other times but one—a steady and slender shaft of light; and suddenly she realized that it tumbled as did she, and knew it to be her own reflection, showing perhaps her very soul.*

*Still she fell endlessly, down and down within, glittering hexagonal panes turning about her as crystalline chimes chinged and tinked in the nonexistent wind . . . in the blowing aethyr.*

*And even though falling, she felt no fright, her spirit steady, her soul filled with chimes and light and wonder.*

In the glittering crystal surfaces where glowed her own reflection, beyond the golden light, beyond the multiple windows of sparkling crystal, she could discern images, some vague and unformed, as if unfocused, others sharp and strange. They flashed past rapidly as she fell down among the scintillant panes—shadowy armies marching, a field of roses red, a murky black pool rippling, a great bear, enormous pillars looming, stars glittering, water whirling, grey mist swirling, and more, much more, images vague and distant, others near and sharp, and all fleeting, all nought but glimmers and glances.

Of a sudden she glimpsed an Elfess—Riatha?—she could not say, and standing behind was a huge Man. Next came a rider—Man or Elf?—on horse, a falcon on the rider's shoulder, something glittering in his hands.

And Faeril felt words echoing from her mouth as she called out something. What? She did not know, even though the words were in Twyll, for she could not hear them, and she knew not what she said—the words were not her own.

> "Ritana fi Za'o
> De Kiler fi ca omos,
> Sekena, ircuma, va lin du
> En Vailena fi ca Lomos."

And onward she fell, endlessly, down and down, the images of Elfess and Man and rider and falcon left far behind, Faeril twisting and turning among a myriad of golden reflections of her soul as crystal panes tumbled past, shapes and forms and figures glimpsed beyond.

But then there came a voiceless cry, someone inaudibly weeping, and she listened, knowing that somehow it was important, and somehow familiar, this mute voice calling noiselessly, this unheard grieving, this silent—

—Even as Faeril opened her eyes she could hear Gwylly weeping and whispering her name. And he was holding her hand and stroking her fingers. His visage swam into view and steadied. "Don't cry, beloved," she murmured.

Gwylly started, clutching her hand tightly. "Faeril, oh Faeril, you're awake." He kissed her and clutched her other hand.

She was in a bed, not her own, but a stranger's instead. Her throat was dry. But before she could say anything, Riatha moved into view. Aravan, too. The Elfess held a chalice to Faeril's lips, and a minty aroma wafted up from the cool water. Eagerly she drank, easing her terrible thirst. Riatha gave her another cup, and then another; this last the damman took in her own hands and sipped.

"Where?" she whispered, setting the chalice aside.

Gwylly answered. "You are in the healers' quarters, love. We brought you here three days ago."

Faeril's eyes widened. "Three days?"

Riatha nodded. "Thou were as if fevered, though no fever had thee. Thy consciousness was fled from thee. Gwylly found thee so, on thy doorstep, three evenings apast."

"Oh, Riatha, I was in the crystal"—her voice gained strength—"it was beautiful."

Gwylly squeezed her hand. "Oh, love, I thought . . . well, I didn't know what to think. But you are back, and that's all that counts. You've returned."

"In the crystal?" Riatha looked at Aravan. The Elf shook his head, for he had not heard of such in all his years.

"Yes, Riatha. In the crystal." She pulled Gwylly's hand to her lips and kissed his fingers. "Oh Gwylly, I tried to see what the future held for us. But I failed, my buccaran, for though images glittered past, no vision of the future did I see."

Gwylly stroked her fingers again. "Perhaps not, but you *did* call out something."

"I did?"

"Aye. In Twyll."

"What did I say? Did you understand it?"

"Oh, yes, I understood the words, though I don't understand their meaning. It was as Riatha first examined you. You opened your eyes and looked straight at her and said:

> 'Ritana fi Za'o
> De Kiler fi ca omos,
> Sekena, ircuma, va lin du
> En Vailena fi ca Lomos.'

"If my Twyll is correct, it means:

*"Rider of Impossibility,*
*And Child of the same,*
*Seeker, searcher, he will be*
*A Traveller of the Planes."*

Faeril looked at Riatha, hoping for an explanation. Riatha slowly shook her head. "I know not, wee one. It would indeed require an impossible rider to travel among the three Planes. The ways are sundered for those not of the blood and pattern, and none has the blood of all three Planes."

Aravan fell into deep thought but said nothing, keeping his counsel unto himself.

The next morn, Riatha came alone to speak to Faeril. "Heed me, wee one: I know not how to counsel thee true, yet this do I say: What seemed but moments to thee in the crystal was three days of time without. The journey thou took was mayhap a most dangerous one, and though thou did safely return, I would ask thee to refrain from stepping along those pathways again without a learned guide . . . one who knows the ways of crystals and seeings, else thou may get lost within and not return at all."

Long was the damman silent, reflecting, remembering the beauty of the crystal, the feeling of peace and well-being, the golden images of her soul and the visions beyond, remembering as well the look of anguish upon her buccaran's face. Sighing, at last she agreed.

Faeril rapidly recovered from her days of entrancement, seeming no worse for the experience. The damman was eager to take up the crystal again; even so, still she resolved to heed Riatha's warning, intending to wait until she could find someone experienced in the ways of a seer. But though she resolved to wait for a teacher, her thoughts were ever and again drawn unto the glittering, shifting luminous panes and to the tinkle and ting of wind chimes.

Summer came with the solstice, and the days waxed toward the harvest and then waned toward fall. In the month that summer began, word came to Aravan that a ship would be awaiting them at Ander to sail on the autumnal equinox and bear them to Innuk. And in the waning weeks of summer, some thirty-five days ere the first of autumn, they took their leave of Arden Vale to begin their journey to Aleut.

On the day they prepared to go, as they saddled their mounts and bundled their goods on a pair of packhorses as well as their steeds, Inarion sought them out. And he gave unto Gwylly a leather bag of silver bullets for his sling, the shot crafted by Inarion's own hand, saying, "I deem thou may need such, whither thou are bound."

Gwylly accepted the bullets and bowed to the Elf and said in Sylva, "*Vi danva ana, vo Alor.*"

Inarion then gave over to Faeril a silver dagger in a tooled black leather sheath, these too made by his own hand. "This will give thee a blade somewhat like unto the one the Dwarves made for thy ancestor Petal, long past."

Faeril smiled and with a curtsy accepted the knife, saying in Sylva, "*Alor Inarion, vi eallswa danva ana.*" Faeril then hefted the dagger and compared it to the ancient blade of the Dwarven smiths. Although the new was not identical to the old, still they were a fine pair; even so, she slipped the dagger and sheath onto the belt at her waist, leaving the one scabbard empty upon her crossing bandoliers.

Inarion then addressed both. "Heed, ye will always be welcome in Arden Vale, be it for an hour, a day, or a thousand years."

The Warder of the Northern Regions of Rell then knelt and embraced each Waerling. And with a nod to Aravan and Riatha, he stepped back.

As they rode up and out of Arden Vale, packhorses trailing behind, following the path up the west wall of the gorge and through the tunnel, they heard the horns of Elves sounding in farewell. And when they emerged, all was silent, and the vast stretch of Drearwood lay before them.

They fared across the Land of Rhone, following along the northern fringes of Drearwood, passing over the River Caire at Drear Ford. Then northerly they swung, up into Rian, riding up the plains lying between the river in the distance to the east and the far Signal Mountains to the west.

The golden time of summer lay upon the land, and long,

lazy days and pleasant nights accompanied them on their way. On the fourteenth day of travel it rained, and as the chill drizzle fell, they passed through the Argent Hills, the high-mounded tors running from the Dalara Plains in the west to the Rigga Mountains in the east. There in the Argent Hills they came to the trade road between Challerain Keep lying southeasterly and the Dwarvenholt of Blackstone to the north, and they set the hooves of their mounts along this way.

And as they rode, Riatha mentioned that Blackstone had been besieged by one of Modru's Hordes during the Winter War, yet the Drimma—the Dwarves—had held out to the end, when the Dimmendark collapsed.

Faeril then began telling Gwylly the various legends of Sir Tuckerby Underbank, the Bearer of the Red Quarrel. And thus they whiled away their time as they fared toward the Boreal Sea.

Two weeks and four days after leaving Arden, they came to where the trade road swung sharply east, running straight for Blackstone in the Rigga Mountains, and there the foursome left its track, continuing on northerly across the Realm of Rian.

There were few settlements along their journey, though now and again they passed through a hamlet. When they could, they stayed in an inn, luxuriating in whatever beds it offered, taking hot baths as well. At other times they put up at farmsteads, usually sleeping in byres, where their beds were made of hay. And always the innkeepers and farmers would goggle at these fey folk, at the Warrows and the Elves, for seldom did they get even ordinary visitors, much less travellers such as these.

But for the most part they camped—in thickets or coppices or stands of forest trees, though now and again they slept in the open, while hoping it would not rain.

And slowly they wended north, covering some twenty to twenty-five miles a day, some seven or eight leagues 'tween sunrise and sunset by Elven measure.

Twenty-six days had passed in all in the waning summer when the Boreal Sea came into view, the waters seeming cold and grey in the distance. Even so, Gwylly and Faeril were stunned by the sight of water reaching unto the very horizon and beyond.

Down they rode toward a small port town in a sheltered harbor along the shores of the sea; they had come to the town of Ander, where Aravan's messenger had arranged for a ship to meet them. And there was yet a week and a day ere the autumnal equinox would come.

The ship they sailed on was a round-bellied *knorr*, a cargo vessel of the Fjordsmen making its last run of the season, for soon the Boreal Sea would rage with winter storms. Even in the best of times the Boreal was fickle, but in the worst she was brutal.

The day they sailed was pleasant enough, with a brisk westerly wind. Still the waters were chill, and the air scudding across the waves blew cold, and rope and canvas and timbers creaked and snapped and groaned in response.

Faeril and Gwylly stood at the rail and watched the land recede, while Riatha and Aravan spoke with Captain Arn.

"I hated to leave Blacktail behind," said Faeril. "Dapper, too. But I suppose the place where we go is too cold for horse or pony."

Gwylly put his arm about the damman. "Worry not, my dammia, for they will be waiting for us at Arden Vale when we return."

Faeril nodded, saying nothing, for she knew that Aravan had arranged for a rider to take the horses and ponies to Challerain Keep and deliver them to an Elven caravan master to be taken to Arden Vale. Even so, she had tended to Blacktail since the filly's birth and did not wish to part from her.

Northeasterly they sailed, the ship wallowing and groaning, faring along the coastal waters of Rian and then Gron. They turned northerly after a full day to pass around the Seabane Islands and avoid the suck of the Great Maelstrom, there where the Gronfang Mountains plunged into the sea. Throughout this second day it rained, and the bosom of the sea rose and fell. Below decks neither Gwylly nor Faeril felt well, a dull nausea rising in their throats, and they ate and drank most sparingly. For two more days they felt thus, though walking about the deck and breathing in the brisk salt air helped. The following day their appetites returned with a vengeance and stayed with them thereafter. Their course had hewed northerly and then easterly, along the coast of the Steppes of Jord and toward distant Fjordland.

During this time the crew of the *knorr*—*Hvalsbuk* was her name—looked upon the Warrows and Elves with wide eyes, for these were Folk seldom seen. It was Faeril who broke the ice, however, by asking what *Hvalsbuk* meant.

A crewman scratched his head, searching his mind for the Common tongue words, then replied, "*Whale's Belly*, miss, that be her name. *Whale's Belly*."

Faeril doubled over laughing, as the *Hvalsbuk* wallowed and creaked and groaned and bore her cargo easterly.

In late afternoon of the eleventh day, they docked at last in Vidfjord, sailing 'round the curve of the wide-mouthed bight and into the high-walled fjord, travelling some six miles in all to come to the fjordside town.

The very next morning again they set sail, this time in a swift Dragonship, the *Bølgeløper*, which Faeril discovered meant *Waverunner*. Eighty feet long and open-hulled she was, with twenty oarlocks down each side. Her sail was square and could be angled to catch the wind by a long whisker pole, called a *beitass* by the captain. Crewed by forty, they rowed down to the sea, then set sail east-north-east for a day or so, then easterly for another.

Fleet was this ship running o'er the waves, like a Wolf loping o'er the snow. Yet no Wolf this, for she never grew weary and ran as long as the wind blew. Aptly was she named, for running day and night, in just over two days she crossed some four hundred miles of water, to swiftly come to the shores of Aleut.

Winter came, frigid beyond expectation, at times the wind hammering for days on end. The land froze and the sea as well, as far as the eye could see. Ice covered all, that or snow. And Faeril and Gwylly and Riatha learned what Aravan already knew: the arctic was not a fit place to dwell, given nearly any other alternative.

Yet the Aleutans thrived on this land, if land it could be called. But even they in the long winter months seldom ventured far. For storms came unexpectedly, savage in their fury, and to be trapped or lost in such often led to death. And so they sheltered in coastal vales in earthen houses crafted from sod and stone and logs of vale pine, smoke hole in the roofs, bare dirt floors within. Also sheltered in the deep vales were the gathered herds of *ren*, deerlike and antlered, wealth of the Aleutans. But even among the pine forests in the vales, winter was harsh and living hard.

Even so, still the foursome learned to cope, living among the Aleutans in the sod and stone huts as they did, lacking the amenities of life they had become accustomed to in Arden. And swiftly they discovered that even the winters of Arden had been mild compared to wintering in Aleut, where the brumal wind of the Boreal Sea hammered harshly down upon them and hurled blinding snow and stinging ice horizontally across the land. Here it was in these conditions that they learned arctic survival, taking lessons from the villagers—elders and youths alike.

And as the short days and long nights passed, they came to know the Aleutans, and the coppery-faced folk treated them with deference, for these were *Mygga* and *Fé*, straight out of the legends. Did they not have the bearing of Chieftains? Did they not charm the dogs? Did they not carry upon their persons weapons of terrible might, weapons of steel and silver and starlight and crystal? Surely only the *Mygga* and *Fé* would have foe so powerful to need killing with such.

Shortly after their arrival, they spoke with the elders and arranged for transportation by dogsled unto the Great North Glacier, some seven hundred fifty miles away, the trip to be made in the waning days of winter ere spring came to the land. And the elders gathered and considered who would be chosen—who the tribe would honor by assigning them to bear the *Mygga* and *Fé* on their mysterious journey. B'arr and Tchuka and Ruluk were selected, for they had the best three teams.

In the long, long nights they made their final plans, seeking the advice of the three sledmasters. As the foursome had discussed in Arden Vale, they did not wish to arrive too early, for then their wait would be extended and they would risk discovery by the Foul Folk there in the Grimwalls. On the other hand, they knew that some time during the days of spring the words of the prophecy would fall due, and so they wished to be on the glacier by the time of the vernal equinox, on the glacier some seven miles north of the abandoned monastery. For that is where the "Light of the Bear" last had been seen by Riatha, the glow now trapped in a slowly grinding eddy of the glacier, a vast, creeping churn of solid ice trapped in a wide, shallow col along the eastern edge of the ice field, an eddy turning once every seventy years or so, as it had been for the past two centuries. Here the foursome intended to set watch until the prophecy was fulfilled—assuming that they would know. When not at the eddy, the comrades intended to stay at the monastery, the cloister providing shelter as the winter passed and throughout the spring.

B'arr told them that the terrain was such that the dogs could make the journey in fourteen or fifteen days, barring storm delays. Tchuka and Ruluk agreed, holding up seven fingers and announcing *"Sju synskrets hver isaer dag . . ."* and B'arr translating, "Seven horizons each day . . . can dog do long." Faeril concluded that given the height of the Aleutans and the distance they could see to the horizon, they meant fifty miles a day was well within the capability of the dogs over many days' time. Then she laughed, saying, "I'm glad it's Human horizons and not Warrow horizons, else we'd be twice as long on the trail." Hence, it was decided that the trip would begin in the final month of winter, some three weeks ere Springday. This would give them a sevenday buffer for storm or other things unforeseen, and should the journey be swift, then they would only be a week in the monastery ere spring commenced. Of course, exactly when the prophecy might fall due no one knew, though as Aravan said, "The Eye of the Hunter will not ride the night sky for the full spring. It comes some twenty nights ere Springday night, growing brighter and longer with each darktide. Then comes the equinox, and the harbinger lasts for twenty nights more. Then does it course into the day to run invisibly with the Sun; where it goes thereafter is not known, for it cannot be seen, but surely it must flee back whence it came and dwell there among the millennia until it is time to bring its dooms again. Hence, if the rede be true, then we should spend but some twenty or thirty days at the glacier, no more. Then will the sledmasters and dogs return from their place of safety two days north, when the Eye of the Hunter can no longer be seen."

And so their plans were laid in the long nights of winter as ice and snow hurtled over the land and the north wind howled in savage fury.

But there were other nights as well, when the wind blew not and the skies were clear, and spectral lights draped in folds of shifting color across the vault above. And on these nights when the ghostly light shimmered and shifted o'er-head, Faeril's thoughts were strangely drawn to the silk-wrapped crystal shut in a box of iron. Yet she yielded not to the temptation, but left it tucked safely away.

And on one of these boreal nights as the skies above ran red and the four stood beneath and marvelled at the display, Aravan canted an ancient chant of the Fjordlanders, one that had been sung by them for as long as their Dragonships had roamed the seas:

> "In the long and icy winter nights,
>     when the skies above run red,
>     and Men dream their dreams
>     and scheme their schemes
>     of vengeance for the dead,
>     of great deeds of derring-do,
>     and of feats of arms and skill,
>     of the gold and silver they will win
>     with each and every kill . . .
> Aye, these are the nights that the Women fear,
>     when their hearts run cold with dread—
>     for their Men dream their dreams
>     and scheme their schemes . . .
>     and the skies above run red."

The cruel winter eked toward spring, the Longnight at last coming to an end, the Sun returning, the long, long nights thereafter gradually growing shorter. With the return of the

Sun, hearts lifted, and each day was a bit longer as the Sun slowly climbed upward in the southern sky. Faeril, Gwylly, Riatha, and Aravan continued to learn from their Aleutan hosts, discovering that these Folk had several hundred names for snow alone, though none of the four tried to master the list.

Steadily spring drew nigh, and finally came what was to be their last day in the village; on the morrow they would leave. But an elder seeking an augury cast a handful of carven ivory shapes and then shook her head, saying that the bones told of a bad storm, and none would be able to move for some days to come.

In the darkness of the night the storm yawled out from the Boreal Sea and whelmed upon the land, the blizzard fierce beyond measure and to venture forth was to court suicide. And so they waited, fretting, trapped, while shrieking days passed. Seven howling days and nights the wind and snow and ice hammered through the vales and into the barrens beyond. And seven howling days and nights Riatha and Aravan and Faeril and Gwylly paced the dirt floor and spoke of their plans going awry and checked their supplies and checked them again and snapped crossly at questions and . . .

Late on the eighth day the storm blew itself out, blessed quiet falling upon the land. The foursome pushed aside the layers of musk ox hides weighted at the bottom which served as a door, and they stepped out into the night. A light snow drifted down, and high clouds still covered the sky, moving swiftly eastward, driven so by unfelt winds aloft. To the soddie of B'arr they went, finding the sledmaster awake, and it was apparent that he had been playing with his two children as his wife looked on. Yet all scrambled to their feet and smiled and bowed as the foursome was invited in. But in the flickering light of a seal-fat lamp Riatha wasted little time on formalities, saying, "We must leave in the morning, B'arr, for even now we are seven days late."

B'arr looked at the commanding *Infé*, then at the *Anfé*, and finally smiled down at the wee *Mygga*, and bobbed his head, agreeing, for were they not Chieftains all? "B'arr ready. Tchuka ready. Ruluk ready. Sled ready. Dog ready, too."

The four then returned to their own sod dwelling, preparing to rest, for on the morrow they would begin an overland journey of some seven hundred and fifty miles, a journey lasting some fourteen or fifteen days. And they were late. Seven days late. They had planned on staying in the monastery and waiting, but now they would barely reach the Glacier by Springday, assuming no more storms delayed them along the route. And Faeril wondered if the prophecy would come true or not, and she remembered the words of her dam: *". . . even prophecies need help now and again."* Yet the damman did not see how she could aid this prophecy; only the sledmasters and their dogs could do so. With these thoughts running through her mind, Faeril bedded down next to Gwylly.

Buccan and damman tossed and turned, trying to sleep but failing. Now and again Faeril would look to see Riatha and Aravan sitting quietly in the shadows as Elves are wont to do, not sleeping but nevertheless resting. But the damman knew that she and her buccaran would not sleep this night, and even as she thought this, she drifted into slumber.

It was well after mid of night when Faeril awakened once more and saw Riatha standing. The Elfess motioned to the damman, and quietly they stepped outside. The sky had cleared and the stars glittered in the frigid darkness. Without speaking Riatha pointed, and Faeril looked and her heart jumped into her throat, for there streaming high in the east was the Eye of the Hunter, its luminous tail long and bloody.

Ere the Sun rose the next morning they set forth from Innuk, B'arr's team in the lead with Tchuka and Ruluk coming after. Faeril and Gwylly sat in the first sled, along with supplies for Man and dog and *Mygga*. Riatha rode in the second, and Aravan in the third, their sleds, too, laden with food and goods for the journey. The village entire turned out to see them go, and there was a small ceremony of leaving. Yet even the elders could sense the impatience of *Fé* and *Mygga* to be on their way.

At last *"Hypp! Hypp!"* called out B'arr, and Shlee eagerly lunged forward, all dogs in the team leaping, setting the sled into motion. Tchuka's and Ruluk's teams followed as those two sledmasters each cried *Hypp!* in turn, Laska surging forward, Garr, too. And up out from the vale and away from Innuk ran the dogs, sleds gliding after, sledmasters running alongside, then stepping onto the runners as the *spans* reached their strides.

They crested the lip of the vale and headed out into the Untended Lands, into the barrens beyond—sleds, dogs, passengers, sledmasters. And on board, Faeril, Gwylly, Riatha, and Aravan each felt that they might be too late to fulfill the prophecy, yet they would try regardless. East-southeast they fared, toward a goal afar, *Mygga* and *Fé* and B'arr and Tchuka and Ruluk, not knowing what the future held, but knowing that they coursed into danger.

# CHAPTER 15

# Monastery

**Early Spring, 5E988**

*[The Present]*

'W are, Riatha!" cried Aravan, shivers of ice slithering down the shifting ramp of shatter as he clambered up behind Gwylly and Faeril and into the golden glow. "It may be Stoke."

Desperately, using nought but her hands, Riatha began digging away at the fragmented wall, great splinters and shards clattering down the icy slope of sliding scree. "Nay, Aravan, were it Stoke, then the fingers would be long and grasping. 'Tis the hand of Urus! Now aid me!"

Again a faint twitch rippled along the fingers of the huge Man's hand jutting forth from the glacier, central to the light shining out from the wall.

"Surely he cannot be alive," breathed Gwylly. "It must be the quaking causing—"

"Faeril, Gwylly," barked Aravan as he backslung his spear and climbed up beside Riatha, "ward us, for though the blue stone grows warm, foe may return."

Hearts hammering, buccan and damman turned to look out over the 'scape. The view was blocked by the great piece that had calved off from the glacial wall. "Quick, Gwylly," urged Faeril, pointing at the mass, "let us take a stand on that."

Up to their knees in sliding fragments of ice, they made their way down the heap, shards and splinters chinking and chinging as would shattered glass, cascading before them as they descended. At the base of the mound, they gazed at the solid mass rearing up, searching in the bright moonlight for a way onto the calved bulk. Behind them, more ice clattered down as Riatha and Aravan dug away at the wall. Gwylly turned right and Faeril left, as each scoured the gigantic block for a place to climb. "Here, love," called Gwylly, seeing a way up.

Ascending a series of jagged ledges, the Warrows made their way up to the cloven surface of the shorn-off mass. "You stand at that end, I'll take this one," directed Faeril, knife in hand, heading south.

A dagger in his left grip, Gwylly started north, his track taking him across from Riatha and Aravan, the Elves now reaching up and back into the wall, casting broken ice out, taking care to remove it from the upper part of the zone of shatter downward so that none would come crashing atop them or on the one trapped within. And just as the buccan came opposite the Elves, his eye fell upon—"*Ai-oi, Faeril!*" he called softly. "Love, come here and see."

Faeril, some distance away, cast a glance southward and, finding no foe in sight, turned and came to Gwylly's side.

"Look, love," breathed Gwylly.

Faeril gasped, for at the bottom of a cusp in the ice was impressed the hollow of what could be nought but the shape of a Vulg, now gone. And in the moonlight shining upon that hollow, there where a Vulg once lay, something glittered. "Gwylly, it's a knife!"

Her heart racing, the damman scrambled down into the cusp and reached into the hollow and took up the blade. It *was* a knife, a silver knife, the mate to the one in her bandolier. "Gwylly!" The damman looked up, her eyes shining. "It is Petal's knife. The one she hurled into Stoke."

Gwylly looked at the hollow. "Then that shape in the ice . . ."

Fearil drew back from it. "It was Stoke. He was here. Right here."

Gwylly looked up and southward, in the direction that the Rūcks and Hlōks and Vulgs had gone. "Riatha was right:

that howl of a wounded Vulg—that was Stoke we heard. Calling for aid. And now he's gone with them . . . or has been carried off by them."

Overhead, blood red and ominous, the Eye of the Hunter gashed the skies, its long tail blazing behind. And the earth shivered below.

As the quake rattled the land, Faeril sheathed the silver dagger in its long-empty bandolier scabbard and then scrambled back up and out from the cusp. Across from the Warrows, shards clattered out from the glacier face, slithering down the ramp where Riatha and Aravan worked, the judders loosening more ice around the trapped figure. And now the Warrows watched as the Elves backed out from the hole they had cleared. And hauling, straining, out from the glacier Riatha and Aravan drew the body of a huge Man. A broad Man. A giant of a Man.

It was Urus.

Riatha wept as they dragged him down the slithering mound of shards and to the bottom.

Now all could see what caused the glow, for at his belt was an aspergillum—a device used by monks and clerics for sprinkling blessed water upon a congregation. And it was this object which gave off the illumination.

Even as they looked, a wondering Aravan reached out and touched the glowing dispenser. Instantly the light faded and was gone, leaving behind what appeared to be nought but a religious device, though a precious one, for it was made of ivory and silver.

Riatha lifted her ear from Urus's chest, and on her knees she rocked back and forth, keening, her arms clutched across her breasts. Her face was twisted in anguish, and wrenching sobs racked her frame, as if she had been withholding her grief for a thousand years. And 'midst her sobs she called his name—"*Urus . . . oh, my Urus!*"

Faeril's face fell, and tears rolled down her cheeks and she turned to her buccaran. "Oh, Gwylly, I was hoping against hope . . ."

Gwylly embraced her and held her close and stroked her hair, his own features stricken. Aravan knelt beside Riatha, and put an arm about her and spoke softly. And still overhead, the Eye of the Hunter streamed through the sky, and again the earth below jolted violently and trembled for a time after, and from a distance came the sound of iron bells ringing.

And *lo!* in that same moment, Urus drew in a great, shuddering breath of air, and exhaled again, and did not move afterward.

Riatha flung herself forward, her ear against his chest. This time she remained listening long. At last, without lifting her head, she spoke. "He lives, but only by a thread. We must get him to a place of safety. A place where we can warm him, tend him."

Gwylly looked at Faeril as the echoes of the iron bells diminished. "The monastery?"

Faeril called down from the height of the calved mass. "The monastery, is it close?"

Riatha lifted up from Urus's form, and still kneeling, glanced at the damman above. "Nay, 'tis some seven miles o'er rough terrain, broken land . . . but thy words are worthy—it is the only proper place of care for league upon league."

Aravan stood and loosened an ice axe at his belt. "We cannot carry him for a lengthy distance. I will find a tree or two and make a travois."

Gwylly turned about and from his vantage spotted a stand of scrub. "This way, Aravan."

The buccan scrambled down from the mass and led the Elf southward.

Faeril clambered down as well, coming to where Riatha tended Urus. The Elfess examined the Man for broken bones, finding none, after which there was little she could do until they got him to a place of shelter and warmth. "Perhaps if we could move him away from this ice . . ." suggested the damman.

"I would rather wait for the litter, wee one," replied Riatha.

They waited without speaking, watching, and after a long while Urus for the second time slowly took a breath, one breath, no more. Again Riatha put her ear to his chest. "He yet lives," she murmured.

Removing a glove, Faeril reached out and took the Man's huge hand in her own. His fingers were like unto the very ice itself. "How can this be . . . that Urus is still alive after a thousand years?"

Riatha's answer was long in coming. "I know not," she said at last, lost in thought, absently gazing at the silver and ivory aspergillum. "Perhaps—"

Gwylly's hail interrupted whatever Riatha was about to say.

Using ropes and climbing harnesses and limbs chopped from an arctic pine, they fashioned a travois. Carefully, they rolled Urus onto the litter, and Aravan slipped the makeshift harness onto his shoulders. Aided by the others, the Elf dragged the Man out away from the glacier, and following Riatha's lead, they set off southward, intending to bear west as soon as the terrain would permit, heading for the abandoned monastery.

By the platinum light of the overhead Moon the Warrows could clearly see the Man, and how like Petal's description in her journal he looked: he had dark reddish brown hair, lighter at the tips, giving it a silvery, grizzled look, and his face was covered with a full beard of the same grizzled brown, both beard and hair were grown long, very long, reaching to his waist and beyond. He was dressed in deep umber, and wore fleece-lined boots and vest, and a great brown cloak. A morning star depended from his belt, the spiked ball and chain held by slip-knotted thongs to the oaken haft. And although they couldn't see them, they knew by Petal's journal that his eyes were a dark amber.

Indeed, it was Urus . . .

Alive . . .

Barely. . . .

After some moments of march, Gwylly said, "We must be wary, for this is the way Stoke was borne."

Startled, Riatha swiftly questioned the Waerling, her voice sharp. "How know thee this, Gwylly?"

The buccan looked up at Riatha. "Above you, in the ice where we stood, we saw where Stoke had lain trapped all these centuries, for his impression was yet there—a Vulg-shaped hollow at our feet. And in that hollow Faeril found her lost knife, the one Petal winged him with.

"You yourself said that the howl of the wounded Vulg we heard was Stoke. Calling for aid. Well, they came and got him and carried him off, or so I think.

"And while Aravan cut branches for the travois, I looked about and discovered the track where the Rūcks and such went with him, bearing him . . . or so I surmise. For if Stoke is damaged, as we think he is, then I would expect to find evidence of a limping Vulg, or tracks of a Man . . . if Man he be. Yet none of these things did I come across. Only Rūck and Hlōk and loping Vulg tracks did I find, running south, there to the left a hundred or so paces away."

Riatha groaned, indecision upon her face. "If he is indeed helpless, as is Urus, then now is the best time to halt his murderous madness."

Gwylly protested: "But he is warded by many maggot-folk."

"Vulgs, Rūcks, Hlōks," added Faeril.

"Nevertheless," began Riatha, "if he regains his strength—"

Riatha was interrupted by Aravan, the Elf speaking even as he pulled the loaded travois across the snow, his words labored. "Hearken, two demands lie before us: we must not lose Stoke; we must tend to Urus. These two goals are not incompatible, but it means we will have to divide our forces.

"This I propose: Riatha and Faeril will track Stoke; Gwylly and I will bear Urus to the monastery—"

Gwylly began to protest, as did Riatha, the Elfess speaking first: "To divide our force is to court disaster. And I have the best skills to treat Urus."

"I would not be separated from my dammia," added Gwylly.

Aravan continued dragging Urus. "List, and list well:

"First, we know not what the weather has in store. But should a spring storm come, it will erase all trace of Stoke's trail, and in this season storms are likely. Hence, to not begin tracking him immediately risks all.

"Second, only I have the strength to hale Urus any distance, especially o'er rough terrain, and he must be taken to a place where he can recover.

"Third, Gwylly is hampered, there where his shoulder was struck while climbing, and he cannot wield his sling. To

send him tracking after the *Rûpt* is to send a wounded, de-
fenseless warrior into combat. Yet he can aid me greatly, by
ranging to the fore in the broken land ahead to find the
least arduous trails, those with the easiest passage unto the
monastery, and once there he can aid in the treating of
Urus.

"Too, we are without food and other supplies, and by going
in pairs, while one forages or hunts, the other can tend to
the task at hand.

"In Gwylly's and my case, one will hunt and forage while
the other tends the Man.

"In thy case, it will take two to track Stoke for any length
of time: one to guard while the other rests; one to forage, to
hunt while the other tracks; one to bring back word if and
when Stoke goes to ground. And heed, I deem that he *will*
go to ground, and soon, given that he is impaired as is our
newfound comrade, Urus.

"Now *if* ye wish to risk losing Stoke, then let us all fare
to the monastery; mayhap after reaching there and treating
Urus, we will later discover Stoke's location. Yet I remind
ye that once long past he escaped for nigh twenty years,
years in which he committed his foul deeds.

"But if ye would of certain not lose him now, then here
we must divide, and two follow Stoke unto his hiding place,
while two others hie Urus unto the monastery."

Aravan's arguments were unassailable, and in the end Riatha, Gwylly, and Faeril had no choice but to accede to his
logic. And so, after Riatha described the location of the monastery to Aravan and Gwylly, and spoke to them of the treatment for Urus, handing the Elf a packet of herbs taken from
a pocket in her down jacket, she and Faeril were shown by
the buccan to the track of the southbound *Spaunen*.

Then Gwylly embraced Faeril and gently kissed her. "Take
care, my dammia. Come to me soon with news of Stoke's
bolt-hole. But should Stoke not go to ground, then leave trail
sign, and we will follow as soon as we may."

Saying nothing, Faeril only hugged Gwylly tightly, then
stepped back, her eyes glittering, but Riatha spoke. "I pray
that Urus recovers swiftly."

With a glance at Faeril, who nodded that she was ready,

the Elfess and damman slipped away into the moonlit night,
while again the earth trembled. Gwylly watched them go,
anguish in his eyes, then turned and trotted toward Aravan,
the Elf yet hauling Urus across the snow.

Gwylly could see Riatha and Faeril for some time, as
slowly the two courses diverged from one another, Elfess and
damman tracking southerly, Elf and buccan veering southwesterly. Gwylly had overtaken Aravan with Urus on the
travois, and then had pressed on, seeking the best route
through the rugged land ahead, toward the abandoned monastery whence they were bound.

To their right loomed the wall of the glacier, its edges
rounded and sloping and raddled with great cracks and ravines, eroded by weather. Huge ridges of ice extended outward from the interior mass, like titanic fingers on a vast
hand. Skirting the tips of these ridges, Gwylly went slowly
forward, the jumbled terrain rising up to meet the massifs
of the dark mountains beyond.

Now and again Aravan would stop to rest, the Elf perspir-
ing freely, for the task was arduous. And Gwylly always returned to the Elf's side during these pauses, describing the
land to come, advising Aravan as to the easiest way, though
at times there seemed to be only hard passages ahead. And
on this difficult terrain, often would Aravan have to hale the
travois and Urus up rough steeps, and at times they were
beyond the Elf's strength; even with Gwylly helping, some
places could not be traversed, and another way would have
to be found.

And when they rested, they did not speak of the dire
straits in which they found themselves—stranded in shuddering, icy mountains teeming with foe, Gwylly himself unable for the moment to use his sling, the party split, all of
their food and most of their supplies lost, an incapacitated
comrade on their hands, the route to the monastery all but
impassable burdened as they were. Instead they spoke of the
trail ahead, of finding the monastery, and of Urus.

During one of these stops, Gwylly looked down at the
huge Man, and Urus drew in a breath and exhaled, then was
still. "I say, Aravan, Urus's beard reaches below his waist,

and his hair is long enough to come to his belt. Do you think that they've been growing all these hundreds of years?"

Aravan glanced at Urus. "If so, wee one, then it has grown very slowly."

Gwylly thought awhile. "Slowly, slowly, like his breathing."

Aravan nodded. "It is said that extreme cold will slow the pulse of life."

"How so, Aravan?"

"That I do not know, Gwylly. But heed, things go to ground in winter. Growth stops. E'en those things which do grow throughout the year—pine trees, some shrubs and grasses, lichen, and the like—all slow to near imperceptibility in the winter season. Some animals go to ground as well, sleeping as do the plants."

Gwylly looked at the Elf. "Like Bears in the winter, neh?"

"Exactly so, Gwylly. And in this case, thine example is most apt."

Gwylly again looked at Urus, remembering what he had read—that Urus at times took on the form of a Bear.

Aravan stood and shouldered the harness, and Gwylly once more clambered through the land ahead, leading the way.

Again they paused, and this time Gwylly examined the aspergillum affixed to Urus's belt. Some eight or ten inches long it was, and made of ivory and silver: a hollow ivory cylinder joined to an ivory handle, sparsely decorated 'round with heavy silver wire crisscrossing in an open geometric pattern. A silver chain was attached to the tip of the handle, forming a wrist loop. The top of the cylinder had tiny holes in it for dispensing contained liquid, though Gwylly's inspection saw no manner by which it could be filled, other than perhaps submergence. Along the top rim of the cylinder, carven into the ivory, were some runes. "Ho, Aravan, look at these."

The Elf peered at the runes. "Ai, this is in the language of the Mages of Rwn!"

Gwylly's eyes widened. *"Magic,"* he breathed.

Aravan cast his mind back thousands of years, recalling. At last he translated the ancient markings: *"Adon, I ask for aid—my need is great."*

The Warrow looked at Aravan. "When Urus was trapped in the ice, then did the dispenser glow. But as soon as aid came to him and he was set free, it stopped."

"Nay, Gwylly," responded Aravan. "The glow disappeared when I touched it."

Gwylly made a negating gesture with his hand. "Nevertheless, Aravan, it did summon aid, and when aid came . . . well, the glow ceased. Like blue stones that grow cold or swords that glimmer when enemy is nigh, or rings that render the wearer invisible or strong or swift, this, too, is a thing of *magic!*"

Aravan slowly shook his head. "Wee one, that glowing swords do exist I'll not deny. And I wear the blue stone. But rings? I have never seen such. I think you speak of hearthtale fables.

"Even so, this aspergillum is indeed *special*, though how it came to be in Urus's possession, I cannot say."

"Oh, that," replied Gwylly. "I can explain that, for it is recorded in Petal's journal. Urus found it . . . in the monastery."

Onward they moved across snow and ice, struggling up and westerly through a trembling land. Still they had some three miles to go through the rugged terrain, and the Moon slid down the sky.

At the next stop, Gwylly sat at Urus's side, feeling for a pulse, finally locating it, though the time between beats was amazingly prolonged. "Tell me, Aravan, though Urus is alive, still his life is slowed beyond compare, made so by the cold, or so you deem. Yet Baron Stoke was in the ice, too. But we heard him howl—that is, Riatha said it was him. Why is it that Stoke was able to howl and yet Urus remains unconscious, his life hanging by but a feeble thread?"

Aravan shook his head. "I can only guess, Gwylly, I can only speculate, for we move through a realm of knowledge unknown to me. What thou say is true—Urus wakes not, while Stoke howls. Possibilities spring to mind, and they are these: Stoke was in animal form, while Urus was not, and in the wild, feral animals seem to have great capacity to survive damage and to recover quickly, as perhaps has happened to Stoke, for I can think of no animal more feral, more savage than a Vulg; or mayhap Urus is in a sleep beyond our ken, as thou did liken unto that of a wintering bear; or, Urus may be damaged in a way that is not apparent, a hurt to the head, though no sign of such can I find."

Again Urus took a breath and exhaled.

Up a long slope they fared and through a col, emerging onto a narrow plateau above the glacier, the ice in the distance below gleaming whitely in the remaining moonlight. But it was not down at the glacier they peered; instead Gwylly pointed across the flat. "There." Yon where his outstretched arm indicated, a mile or so away, on a rocky slope above the glacier, there stood a tower and several large buildings and some small, walled about, all made of stone.

It could be nought but the monastery.

Suddenly Gwylly blanched. "I just thought of something, Aravan: what if the Rūcks and Hlōks and Vulgs are bringing Stoke here? What if they already have?"

The earth juddered beneath their feet.

Aravan glanced at the eastern sky. "It will be dawn soon. Even so, we must proceed with caution. Thou must wait here with Urus while I range ahead, scanning for spoor."

"Nay, Aravan, this is mine to do. You stay, I'll range ahead. Should you go and aught happen, then Urus will die, for I have not the skills to tend him and I am too small to haul him to a place of aid. But should I fall while seeking tracks, then Urus will live, for you will be with him and can take him elsewhere."

Aravan objected. "But thou cannot use thy sling—"

The Elf's words were cut short by the buccan. "To do elsewise risks more than just the scout. Besides, I am no hero. I can run and hide."

"Thou cannot outrun a Vulg, wee one. Nor can thou hide thy scent from such here in this barren land."

"Even so, Aravan, it is you who must stay with Urus."

Now it was Aravan who was forced to bow to the logic of another, and he nodded at last. "Then go, Gwylly, yet 'ware, for e'en though we've seen no tracks, thou may be right— Stoke and his band may be nigh, having come by different route."

Aravan removed the blue stone from 'round his neck and handed it over to Gwylly. "Here. Wear this. It is now warm, yet the monastery is a distance away. At first sign of chilling, of danger, flee. Go with caution, though, for the amulet does not detect all."

Gwylly, his heart leaping about in his chest as would a caged bird, left Aravan behind and set off across the snow, swiftly ranging back and forth, seeking sign of foe. Slowly he drew near the monastery, dark stone in the night. But a furlong or so from the buildings his feet came upon wind-swept barren rock, where no track could be made. Despairing, for here on stone any sign of passing Spawn would end, Gwylly ranged along where the snow ended and the stone began, running the perimeter of an area kept scoured clean by fierce winter winds, winds channelled through a slot in the mountains above. At the moment, though, the air blew steadily down toward the glacier beyond and only occasionally twisted in eddies. Still the Warrow found no tracks in the snow along the edge of the bare expanse.

Keeping low and following what cover there was, he slipped to the wall of the monastery. Some fifteen feet high it was, and made of stone. Sheltered from the wind by the bulwark, a wide, irregular band of snow fetched up against it. Gwylly saw no tracks as he worked his way 'round to the high wooden gate—it was closed. Before the gate lay more snow, again without tracks, yet he well knew that swirling wind could have erased any sign of passage, not only here but in any of the expanses that he had scanned.

Gwylly pressed against the heavy planks and remained still for a long while, holding his breath, listening—hearing nothing but susurration of mountain air and perhaps the beat of his own heart. He felt the amulet at his neck—*Is it chill?* It felt cool—*How cold would it be if foes were within the stone buildings?* The Warrow peered through the narrow crack between wooden gate and rock wall. Within, he could see a bit of the main building and the bell tower above. No light shone from that part of the darkened stone structure within his restricted view, and no light shone onto the stone courtyard from the parts he could not see. Too, glancing up— his heart leapt into his throat—through the crack he could see fetched up against the planks on the opposite side of the portal a silhouetted portion of what had to be a large horizontal wooden beam, in place, barring the gate.

Gwylly dashed back across the stone plateau and snow, coming to where Aravan waited with Urus. "I found no tracks, and the monastery seems deserted, but the gate is closed and barred—*from the inside!* Someone is there!"

Aravan touched Gwylly at the throat. "Did the stone grow icy?"

Gwylly shook his head, *No.*

Aravan fell into thought. "Then mayhap the gate was left so by Riatha years past."

Gwylly shook his head. "Petal's journal says that she and Riatha and Tomlin left it standing open when they departed. And granted, Riatha has been here since, yet why would she have left it barred from the inside? She would have had to clamber over the wall after doing so. And if she knew that it was barred, why did she not tell us?"

Aravan's eyes were lost in thought, and he slowly shook his head.

Urus took another breath, then was still.

Aravan looked easterly. Dawn was on the horizon. "Let us go forth, Gwylly. We dare not delay any longer, for Urus needs our aid. I deem the Sun will lip the horizon ere we arrive, and *Rûpt* cannot abide such. If they are in there, we shall use Adon's light as our protecting shield and as our avenging sword."

Exhausted, Aravan stood and again took up the travois harness, and following Gwylly, set off across the snow and stone and toward the dark buildings looming in the distance ahead. Behind, the skies began to pale as dawn brightened.

They stood before the heavy wooden gate, Urus on the travois lying on the snow beside them. The final mile had been relatively easy, for the plateau was nearly flat. Even so, both Warrow and Elf were weary beyond measure, for they had journeyed up through a rugged land, the Elf hauling a wounded comrade, the Warrow ranging back and forth, clambering and scaling, finding the way.

And now Gwylly looked up at one more wall, this one he hoped the last. Loosening the small grapnel from his belt, he clicked the tines into place and began affixing a line to the haft ring. Aravan glanced at the Waerling, nodding his approval. "I'll climb over, Gwylly. The beam barring the gate may be too heavy and high for thee to remove."

Gwylly cinched the knot and then let dangle the hook at the end of a foot or so of slack. "It should catch better on the wood of the gate," he said, and with a whirl or two, let fly, the grapnel sailing up and over the headbeam and beyond, the rope uncoiling behind. With a *thnk!* the hook swung back to strike the planking somewhere opposite, and Gwylly slowly reeled in the line, pulling the grapnel upward, a tine digging in as the hook reached the top of the gate. First Gwylly and then Aravan set their weight against the line, sinking barb into wood. Then Aravan shed his cloak, preparing to ascend.

In that moment a metallic scrape sounded from the stone wall to the left, and Gwylly's heart leapt as he saw silhouetted against the paling sky the shape of a crossbow slide over the edge and catch them in its aim.

"Who goes?" called down a voice, that of a male.

"Friend!" answered Aravan immediately.

"Friend you say, yet you stand in the dark and one of you is small, as small as a child . . . or a Rutch!"

"No Rukh," declared Aravan.

"Faugh! Who would bring a child into this wilderness?"

Gwylly threw back his hood. "I am a Warrow!"

"We shall soon see," responded the voice, the crossbow aim unwavering.

"Friend, we urgently need thine aid," called Aravan. "Our comrade is nigh death."

"You will wait," snapped the voice, "till the Sun comes. Then we shall see."

Behind, at that moment on the edge of the brightening sky, the rim of the Sun came into view between mountains eastward.

The crossbow remained upon them for a moment longer as light fell on the land, then the weapon disappeared. Gwylly and Aravan heard footsteps clambering down from above. The wooden bar of the gate slid on its tracks, and then the leaves of the portals swung inward. Before them stood a grey-bearded Man dressed in coarse brown robes.

"I had to make certain," he said, beckoning them inward.

He turned and took up his crossbow from where he had laid it aside, and stepped out to peer across the 'scape beyond. Apparently satisfied that no enemy was upon the land, he grumbled, "Except for Gavan and me, they've killed all the rest."

Wearily, Gwylly scooped up Aravan's cloak while the Elf settled his shoulders into the travois harness. Pulling Urus, through the gates they went, pausing as the grey-haired Man set aside his crossbow to close and bar the gate once more. Gwylly flipped loose the grapnel now that he was on this side of the barrier.

As the Warrow coiled the line he looked about, his gaze gritty with fatigue. They stood at the entrance of an open yard ringed 'round by grey stone buildings, most appearing to be storage sheds, though some were dwellings. Directly ahead, standing in the morning sunlight, was the main tower, backed against the wall. Forty or fifty feet high it was, and round, some eighteen feet across, and made of stone as well; and it was capped with a steep-canted slate roof. The tower bore window slits, shuttered, winding up and about, as if following a spiral stair—except nigh the very top, where wide archways ringed darkly 'round, archways through which Gwylly thought he could see the shapes of bells hanging.

The tower itself jutted up on the mid line of a large squarish building, a building perhaps eighty feet wide and twice as many deep, and two or three storeys high, itself with a slanted slate roof all way 'round. Window slits there were, shuttered over, along its high stone walls. And facing into the courtyard, up a step or two, stood a joined pair of great wooden doors, closed.

A tremble juddered through the earth.

With the gate barred once more, the old Man turned and peered at his visitors. "Why, you really *are* a Waldan!" he exclaimed to Gwylly, then looked at Aravan. "and a Deva!"

He turned to gaze at Urus on the travois. "Adon, he's a wild-looking one." Again he took up his crossbow and started across the courtyard. "Come. Come. In to where it's warm. Then we'll see what needs doing."

No sign of life did they see as they trudged across the courtyard toward this main structure, the dragging sound of wooden travois poles echoing back from the hard stone walls within. Up the steps they went, the Man swinging the left-most panel inward upon oiled hinges.

A vestibule they entered, the hallway short, and before them stood another set of closed doors. The Man motioned them to stop, then opened one of the doors, the panel swinging outward.

They stepped into a large open chamber with a high-vaulted ceiling, unlighted but for the daylight seeping inward, pressing back the gloom. Off to the sides in the shadows loomed pillars buttressing overhead galleries to left and right hugging the walls, narrow, enclosed stairs pitching upward immediately at hand, to either side, east and west, leading up to those balconies. Across the chamber, near the far wall, stood an altar, with Adon's glyph carven thereupon. And farther on, at the back wall, off to left and right, again enclosed stairs led upward unto the galleries.

The old Man bowed toward the altar and then led them on inward, across the stone floor, the scrape of the litter poles resounding in the great hollow space. Behind, the portals they had entered slowly swung to, hinged as they were to close without an aiding hand, deepening the darkness within. And now only the light streaming through the large window above the western balcony pressed against the gloom.

A tremor thrummed through the floor as the earth shivered again.

The old Man spoke, his words resounding in the cavernous hall. "We are Adonites, monks of the mountains. We came here last year to reopen the cloister. But Rutch and such discovered us and raided. So far we have managed to repel them, but no more, for all are slain but Gavan and me, and now he is wounded. Next time they will prevail."

"My name is Gwylly Fenn," said the buccan. "My comrade is named Aravan. Our unconscious companion is called Urus."

The robed Man turned. "Forgive me. I am Doran, former prior, now abbot of this retreat."

Doran led them through a concealed door behind the altar. Past the panel was a sacristy, hanging with robes and vestments. A door led out one side, and beyond was a hallway, with rooms left and right.

Down the corridor they went, Doran remarking, "The privy's at the end of the hall." They entered a modest room on the right—"The infirmary," announced Doran—where a smokeless fire burned in an iron stove, chimney behind. In a bed lay another Man, a younger Man, clean shaven—presumably Gavan—sleeping, his head bandaged, his arm in a sling. Five other beds were ranged 'round the room, and into one of these they managed to lift Urus, requiring all three of them to do so.

Aravan then took out the packet given over to him by Riatha. Opening it, there were golden mint leaves within. "Gwynthyme," said Doran, the abbot recognizing the herb. "As a tea, it serves as a stimulant. As a poultice, it draws poisons."

Aravan looked at the old Man. "Thou are learned in the ways of healing?"

"Somewhat," replied Doran, glancing at Gavan, "though chirurgeon and physician I am not . . . would that I were. But herbs and simples I understand."

Urus drew in another breath, then exhaled.

"Then, Doran, while I prepare a brew of these leaves, would thou examine this Man for hurt?"

Gwylly, upon hearing Aravan's words, turned and found a kettle sitting beside the stove. And even as the abbot shuffled to Urus's bedside, the Warrow began filling the container with water from a bucket on a stand.

It was nearly sunset when Doran wakened Gwylly and Aravan, and the smell of stew was redolent on the air. Aravan stood and stepped to Urus's side; the huge Man was breathing regularly now. Gwylly groaned and levered himself up and swung his feet over the side of the bed, feeling as if his body had been hammered, feeling the after effects of last night's difficult climb up the canyon wall and the exhausting trek to the monastery. After a moment the buccan made his way out the door and toward the privy.

When Gwylly returned, Aravan was holding Urus's wrist, taking measure of the Man's pulse. "The beat of Urus is very strong. I think his life no longer hangs by a thread."

Gwylly felt the Baeran's hand. It was warm. "When will he waken, Aravan?"

"I know not, for I have never seen such before. Mayhap soon, mayhap on the morrow."

Doran, spooning stew into bowls, spoke up. "And mayhap never."

Gwylly turned and looked at the elder. "Why do you say that?"

Shuffling forward, the abbot brought the filled bowls to Gwylly and Aravan. "I have heard of those who fall into a prolonged sleep, never to be aroused. Liquid they take, and sometimes food, yet they do not awaken. They must be cared for until they die. If such is the case here, then mayhap 'twould have been better had your friend died cleanly, for then he would not dwell in a living death the rest of his days."

"Oh," protested Gwylly, "do not say such a thing. Surely Urus will awaken."

Gavan was awake, but had been silent until this moment. "I will pray for him," he said softly. "Mayhap Adon will show mercy in his case."

After they had eaten, again Aravan brewed some gwyn-thyme tea for Urus.

Gwylly, his belly full, lay on his bed and watched Aravan tending Urus.

The buccan awoke in the night. But for the breathing of other sleepers, all was quiet. Again Gwylly made his way to the privy. When he returned, he saw that Urus was yet asleep, Doran and Gavan as well. Of Aravan, there was no sign.

Quietly, Gwylly dressed, then stepped through the door and into the corridor. He made his way out through the hall of worship and into the courtyard. The night was cold and clear, though wisps of clouds scudded across the face of the Moon. Gwylly walked the length of the bailey and to the gate. A ladder led up to the banquette. Climbing to the walk-way, he found Aravan standing watch.

"Get thy rest, Gwylly. This night shall I ward."

"But you need your rest, too, Aravan," protested the War-row. "I can take the watch."

"Nay, wee one. I slept well this day, and this night I have been resting my mind in memories—a talent of Elvenkind. Nay, Gwylly, argue with me not, but return unto thy bed. On the morrow thou can take thy turn, but this night is mine."

Without further debate Gwylly climbed back down the ladder.

The overcast morning found the Warrow well rested, ready for the day. About the monastery the wind moaned. "Storm coming," grunted Doran, shuffling out of the room, returning with firewood.

Aravan again was at Urus's side, and at last the huge Man swallowed the gwynthyme tea freely, though he still did not awaken.

Doran observed the ministrations, watching Urus drink. "Even so, he may never regain consciousness," mumbled the abbot, and Gwylly's heart sank.

Gavan came back from his morning prayers and fell weakly into his bed. It was obvious that the young Man had taken a debilitating wound, though his injuries appeared rather light. "Took a Rutchen arrow on the arm," he had said. "Poisoned, we think. But the poultice took most of it out, and I am getting better."

Gwylly, on this day, slowly worked at loosening the muscles in his damaged arm. Doran soaked cloths in hot water and applied them to the Waldan's shoulder. The muscles atop the joint were bruised, but now that he had gotten warm and had slept and had eaten, and after the hot cloth treatments, his arm was much improved. But he felt as if his heart were clutched by a chill hand as he paced the floor and fretted about Faeril and Riatha, wondering at their plight. The groaning wind outside only served to remind him that unless they had managed to take cover, the two of them were out in the elements.

Doran shuffled to a cabinet against one wall, and after rummaging about, pulled forth a large packet of gwynthyme, giving some over to Aravan. "We have a goodly store of herbs," he explained. "Food and other supplies as well. More than enough. We numbered sixteen when we came, and now but two of us are left." In response to Doran's words, Gavan bowed his head in prayer.

Nigh midday the blizzard came upon the land, the howling wind lashing hard-driven snow onto the grey stone of the cloister. " 'Tis a spring storm," said Doran. "Unpredictable. It could quickly blow past, or stay a week."

Again Gwylly's heart sank, for somewhere out in the yawling wind was his dammia—and for all he knew, she and Riatha were without food or shelter.

All afternoon the storm battered the monastery, but as evening drew nigh, the wind began to abate. And as darkness fell, the storm ended.

"I think I'll go stand watch on the walls," remarked Gwylly. "Rūcks and such know the monks are here, and I'd rather not be taken by surprise."

Aravan looked up from Urus. "Here, take the amulet. I'll relieve thee in four hours or so. Too, we must talk, for there are plans to be made."

Doran nodded gratefully at the buccan as the Wee One prepared to leave. "There's an iron hoop hanging on the wall walk up by the gate lantern. Sound the alarm should foe be sighted." The abbot patted his crossbow. "We'll give them a battle.

"Needless to say, light not the lamp, for it would serve only to announce our presence."

Gwylly slipped his hands into his gloves, then stepped through the door. Crossing the courtyard, he mounted up the ladder. When he got to the sentry walk, he discovered that the wall was too high for him to see over. Yet he found a ledge partway up running the length of the wall, and he clambered up to it.

The wind still blew from the south, driving the remnants of the storm before it. High in the sky, rifts appeared in the clouds, and now and again a star could be seen. The drift of air was raw, and Gwylly shuffled back and forth to keep warm and to stay alert. Behind the clouds the Moon rose, its glow diffuse.

Back and forth marched Gwylly, and except for the tread of his feet and the soughing of the wind, a silence descended upon the world, broken by the occasional shuddering of the land. Even so, the iron bells remained silent, for they only rang when the quakes were severe.

The hours passed slowly, and just as slowly the skies above cleared. At last the Moon shone down on the 'scape, the snow pearlescent in the platinum beams. And Aravan trod through the silver night and climbed up to stand beside Gwylly.

"Wee one, I think to leave thee with Urus while I take supplies and find Riatha and Faeril, and send the Dara back."

Aravan held out a hand to still the protest springing to Gwylly's lips, but what the Elf was about to say is forever lost, for in that moment they heard the yawls of Vulgs on the hunt, the baying unmistakable. They turned and peered out beyond the walls in the direction of the howls.

Gwylly gasped, for a furlong or two away, fleeing across the snow came an indistinct figure running. And down the slopes far behind raced howling Vulgs after. Even as he loosened his sling, the blue stone at his throat began to grow chill. Gwylly glanced back and forth between the savage beasts and their quarry, judging speeds. His heart hammered in his breast, and he shrieked, *"Run! Run!"* for he did not think that whoever fled would escape.

Then Aravan beside him gritted, "It is Faeril."

And at that instant she fell.

# CHAPTER 16

# Bolt-Hole

As Faeril and Riatha set off down the wide track left by the Rūckish band, the damman could not keep her thoughts on the trail, and instead time and again she looked at Gwylly in the distance as her path and his diverged. *He said to me, "Take care, my dammia," and I just stood there mute. Oh, my buccaran, take care of yourself as well, and of Aravan and Urus, too.*

Riatha also glanced often at the comrades afar, her own eyes following the figure on the travois. Yet at last they disappeared from view, rounding the shoulder of a hillock between and were seen no more.

"We shall track for some time longer, Faeril, then stop and sleep. Day will be the time to come upon their lair, for they must take to the splits and cracks in the earth ere the Sun rises. Then we shall see what can be done."

Faeril nodded, pausing long enough to notch a solitary tree, leaving trail sign for the others to follow should it become necessary. "We will need food, too. I'll set a snare before we sleep, baited with a crumb of the oatcake I have in my pocket."

On they strode, treading the track of the Foul Folk. The path Faeril and Riatha followed was level or down slope and crossed relatively smooth terrain, unlike the generally up-slope trend of Gwylly's and Aravan's and Urus's route into the broken land leading to the monastery. And so, down fared Elfess and damman, coming into a sparse forest of arctic pine, first encountering lone trees, then occasional stands, and finally moving among widely scattered pines. Still the route wound downhill, aiming, it seemed, for a deep slot between mountain flanks east and west. Every so often Faeril or Riatha would blaze a score on a tree trunk, or would interlace boughs, or cut branches just so, leaving trail markers for their comrades, just as they had practiced months ago in Arden Vale.

Yet at last, in the shelter of a thick coppice, Riatha called a halt to their march, saying, "Ai, wee one, we must rest. Thou sleep. I will set watch."

Faeril took a cord from her remaining climbing gear. "First, Dara, I would set a snare, for we must eat."

The damman found evidence of a stream, though all water was now frozen, and she walked toward a small stand of trees cupped in a curve of stone of the mountain flank. First cutting a peg, she sharpened and notched it, then used her ice hammer to pound it into the frozen soil below a small pine. She cut another peg and fashioned it into a trigger. She tied a snare noose in the cord, then bent the tree, tying the line to its top and knotting the cord to the trigger peg as well. She tied a very short trip line to the trigger peg, too, then set the trigger into the anchor peg. Spreading the loop, she affixed a chunk of oatcake to the trip cord and lay it on the snow in the center of the loop. She covered the noose and line with a light dusting of snow, concealing the snare, leaving the bait in the open.

Returning to Riatha, the damman settled down on the pine boughs that the Elfess had cut and fashioned into a bed. "Well, Riatha, the snare is set. Perhaps tomorrow we will have captured some game. I do hope so, for I am hungry."

Riatha may have replied, but Faeril, weary to her bones, heard nothing, for she was already fast asleep.

The light of morning was on the land when Riatha awakened Faeril. A small, smokeless fire burned. Speaking softly, the

Elfess handed the damman a section of root. "Here, Faeril, 'tis tannik root. Thou will find it somewhat bitter, yet it is nourishing." Riatha took a bite of her own piece.

Faeril sat up. "My snare . . ."

The damman started to get to her feet, but Riatha waved her back, pointing to the pegs and cord lying on the snow beside her. "Sprung without game."

Faeril shook her head. "Then all I managed to do was give up a bit of our only oatcake, neh?"

Riatha smiled, taking another bite, while heating her dagger blade above the tiny flame; she then took up some snow and held it against the metal, and melt ran down the warm steel, dripping from the tip into the open waterskin. Faeril stood and made her way into the pines to relieve herself. When the damman came back, Riatha said, "Nay. Thy efforts were not entirely without reward, for 'twas when I went to see what had sprung the trap that I did espy the tannik bush along the way."

"Did you see what tripped the snare?"

"I found traces of a vole. She came under the snow to take the bait. The noose snapped upward above her."

Faeril shook her head. "Clever vole." The damman then took a bite of the root, and her face twisted into a grimace, her eyes squeezed nearly shut, her lips clamped into a tight, thin line. Still, after a moment she began to chew, swallowing at last. "*Whoo!*" she exclaimed. "Bitter is right." She took another bite.

"Say," she remarked, working her words around the acrid taste, "you did not waken me for my turn at watch!"

The Elfess held the dagger blade in the flame. "Thou needed thy sleep, wee one, and I can rest and yet keep watch."

Faeril knew that Riatha referred to the talent inborn to Elvenkind wherein they could rest their minds in gentle memories, benefitting from such meditation nearly as much as if they had slept. Yet Faeril knew that even Elves must take true sleep eventually, for peaceful contemplation alone did not serve all the needs of body and mind and soul.

Riatha and Faeril each ate their entire share of the tart root, for they knew not what the coming events of this day would call upon them to do, but they did know that hunger-weakened warriors could not sustain a prolonged effort. Too, they gambled that they had the skills to obtain more food along the way.

Riatha at last finished her replenishment of the water-skins, handing Faeril's back to her. "Let us be gone, wee one. Day is upon the land and the *Rûpt* will have gone to ground."

Again they set forth, following the wide trail down slope. An hour or more did they travel thus, the terrain gradually falling. The spare forest around them gradually thickened, arctic pine for the most part, though here and there grew whin and other low piny shrubs. All along the way Faeril blazed a trail for Gwylly and Aravan to eventually follow—and Urus, too, should he live. Riatha also paused now and again to forage for foodstuff alongside the trail. She gathered pine nuts from the few cones she could yet find on the trees; too, she discovered another tannik bush, and with her ice axe harvested the root; last, she collected some yellow lichen growing on the underside of a rock overhang, scraping it free with her dagger. At one point an arctic hare sprang up practically underfoot, startling both damman and Elfess, but before Faeril recovered enough to draw a knife, the hare was gone. "Garn, Riatha! There went our supper."

But never were these pauses long, for the trail of the *Spaunen* drew them ever onward.

At one place where Riatha stopped to gather cones and pry open the scales and collect more of the small nuts, Faeril softly asked, "Tell me, Dara, why did the Foul Folk not de-file Urus when they were at the glacier? I mean, he was helpless and all. They could have dug him free, as we did, and made certain that he was dead. So why did they leave him undisturbed?"

Riatha shook her head. "I know not why, Faeril. Mayhap they did not despoil him because he was still in the ice, for only as we drew nigh did the quake strip away the outermost cover—though thou are correct in that the *Rûpt* could have drawn him forth. Mayhap they thought him dead. Mayhap if they did find Stoke, he commanded them to leave Urus be, though I think that Stoke would gladly have murdered

Urus had he known. Mayhap their prime aim was to get Stoke to safety. Mayhap they could not abide the golden light of the aspergillum." Riatha took up the cloth onto which she had shaken loose the pine nuts, tying it with a cord. "There are too many imponderables, Faeril, and likely we will never know."

At another stop, this time to rest, Faeril examined the long-lost silver knife that Gwylly had discovered in the hollow. It was identical to its mate in her bandolier. She handed the blade to the Elfess. "Riatha, it is said that this knife is made of silver, and I have always believed so; yet look, it is not tarnished though it has lain in a glacier for a thousand years. How can this be?"

Riatha turned the knife over and again in her hands. "It is Drimmen work, Faeril—Dwarven made. How they forge such I cannot say, yet this I do know: silver this is, and pure, yet in its forging lies a long-held secret of the Drimma." Riatha handed the knife back to the damman.

Faeril sheathed the blade and drew its mate. "Well, I don't believe that the other one tarnishes either, though I'm not at all sure that it has ever been given a chance to do so—it seems to me as if we polished it every day. I suppose by now it should have been rubbed to a nubbin, but I can't see any wear on it at all." Faeril glanced at Riatha. The Elfess shrugged. Faeril resheathed this blade, too. "I know, Riatha, I know—another Dwarven secret, neh?"

It was late mid-morn when they came to the canyon, the land slowly dropping down between sheer walls. The track they followed plunged down and in. Onward paced the two, following the footprints in the snow. A mile or more they went, the canyon walls sheer above them, rising some two or three hundred feet overhead, the slot growing narrower until it was but forty or fifty feet wide. Ahead, they could see that the ravine flared outward, and soon they came unto an open area, roughly circular, perhaps three hundred feet across, the hemming vertical walls raddled up and down and roundabout with crevices and holes. Opposite the way in, it appeared the canyon continued onward, exiting through another narrow slot, spanned by a snow bridge high above.

Whether or not this way led outward and into the mountains beyond, they could not see—for all they knew, it could be a dead end.

" 'Ware, Faeril," hissed Riatha. "Here I ween is Stoke's bolt-hole."

Cautiously in the daylight, they followed the tracks inward. These led to the center of the amphitheater, and there the two could see that the snow had been tramped down in a wide area, as if the *Rûpt* had milled about. From this central point, tracks led outward in all directions unto the sheer walls ringed 'round, going into various shadowed cracks and dark crannies and black holes. None led onward into the slot under the snow bridge.

"Now we can see just how many *Spaunen* are in this band," breathed Riatha. "Thou count the tracks on thy side, separating Vulg from others, and I will count them on this side. But 'ware, step not on the untrod snow, for we would not leave our scent where it can be found by Vulg when darkness falls."

Staying within the large beaten-down area, Faeril counted the number of individual trails that she could see heading for the wall. Riatha did the same. Then they traded sides and counted again. Their tallies were consistent: the Rūcks and Hlōks totalled twenty-seven, the Vulgs thirteen. Neither Elfess nor damman espied what could clearly be identified as Stoke's tracks—although as Riatha pointed out, any one of the Vulgs' trails could be his, were he in that form. Faeril suggested that if Stoke were in fact impaired, he might have been carried by Rūcks or Hlōks, perhaps even on a litter, though no evidence of this was seen.

Riatha scanned the rim overhead. "Let us backtrack, hiding our scent among the traces left by the *Spaunen* band. When we can safely do so, we will circle to the west wall above and, when night falls, see what we can see."

Faeril removed her glove and wetted a finger, holding it up. A chill breeze swirled within the arena. "What if the wind is such that our scent will be borne down from the west wall? Can we cross over the snow bridge and take station on the east wall? The span must be sturdy to exist in this shaking land."

Riatha shook her head, glancing up at the white arch. "Nay, Faeril, though thy words ring true, still snow bridges are treacherous, even for one of thy slightness; only when there is no other acceptable choice should they be tried. If the wind is against us, we will backtrack and come at the east wall in the same manner that we now assay the west."

Faeril nodded. "If we do this, we need to change the markers, too, so that Gwylly and Aravan avoid the canyon and find our true trail."

"Aye," agreed Riatha, and the two started back the way they had come.

Moving swiftly, Riatha and Faeril hiked up the trail some three miles or so, pausing now and again to notch through each of the blazed trail signs pointing into the ravine.

At last the Elfess found what she was seeking: an expanse of bare stone rising steeply. As Faeril blazed a new sign, Riatha loosened the small grappling hook from her belt and fixed a line to it. Casting the hook and setting it, up from the trail she and the damman ascended. From atop the stone, Riatha looked back down. "There. If *Rûpt* should find our trail this night, then that should give them a riddle to read."

Faeril's heart leapt into her throat. "Oh, Riatha. Should they find our trail, then it will lead them back to the glacier—back to the tracks of Gwylly and Aravan . . . and Urus."

Riatha stood long in thought. "Mayhap, yet there has always been the danger that Vulgs will find their scent, just as they found the four of us last night. Too, the *Rûpt* may stumble across any of our tracks, including those of Aravan and your beloved Gwylly. The *Spaunen* of certain know that we are in the region, even though they abandoned their search for us yesternight—to aid Stoke, we deem.

"But heed: they would have forsaken their pursuit of us regardless as soon as day drew nigh, else they would suffer the Withering Death. I judge that where we stand is some twenty miles from where Stoke was found, and they were hard pressed to reach yon bolt-hole ere light of day. Even so, though it is a distance back to where we were, there is a chance they may return to the glacier to hunt us again—yet I deem it unlikely they will do so."

Riatha glanced at the Sun, now nearing the noontide. "Rest thy heart, Faeril, for even now our loved ones must be at the monastery. I know of no better place to be, should Foul Folk come upon them."

Even though the Elfess seemed confident, still the damman wished that there were some way to make certain that her buccaran was safe. "Is it always like this in times of peril, Riatha? I mean, I am so afraid for my Gwylly."

Riatha squatted and loosed the grapnel and began coiling the line. "Aye, wee one. 'Tis always so. Yet list—thy loved one afar has the same concern of thee, and thou must take all honorable precaution to guard thyself for his sake, just as he must do for thee. Thou and he can do little else. He knows this, as do thou. Take comfort in this knowledge, as well as in the knowledge that he is with steadfast companions, just as are thou."

Faeril threw her arms about the Elfess and kissed her on the cheek, receiving an embrace in return. Then Riatha stood and hung the hook and line on her belt. "Let us away."

As the Sun set, Faeril and Riatha were in place atop the bluff above the circular amphitheater in the canyon below. Before taking up their places, Riatha had marked the direction of the wind, and they had positioned themselves as well as they could to avoid their scent wafting into the canyon. They had carefully brushed away the snow and loose rock at this place so that none would inadvertently fall from their own movement there on the rim, alerting the foe. To their left was the canyon the *Spaunen* had followed into the arena below. To their right, the canyon continued onward, sloping downhill, the walls of the hemming bluffs diminishing as well as receding, the ravine widening and becoming shallower until it was no more, having merged with the broad valley beyond. Be-ringing the entire rim of the arena stood the sparse forest of arctic pines, the trees marching away unto the mountain slopes on either side, covering the width and length of the canted vale.

Darkness fell, and with it came the sound of Foul Folk. Riatha and Faeril eased themselves belly down and peered over the rim. The arena below was deep in shadow, yet

Waerling and Elven eyes could just make out the floor of the amphitheater. And as they watched, torch-light flickered from many of the splits and cracks and holes below. Dark shapes emerged, bearing burning brands, fluttering shadows cast against the snow. Vulgs and maggot-folk there were— Rūcks or Hlōks or both—and they milled about in the center, speaking their guttural tongue. At last a small band broke away, Vulgs in the lead, running south, into the canyon beyond. A short moment later, another band formed, and this one went north. Yet some Vulgs and others remained behind, and these disappeared back into their holes.

Hours passed with no activity. The Eye of the Hunter scored the sky, and the Moon overhead shone down into the pit. Then there came a great hubbub from the south, and again Riatha and Faeril lay belly down at the rim. Even as they watched, Vulgs, Rūcks, and Hlōks came marching in through the slot, and they bore a slain deer with them. Vulgs yawled, and answers echoed out from the splits and cracks of the stone walls. Rūcks and such emerged from within, and the deer carcass was hacked into meaty chunks, *Spaunen* squabbling over choice parts. Of a sudden there came a howl from on high, and all quarrelling stopped. All eyes swung toward the east wall, and there, halfway up, in the ebon mouth of a cavern, there was a shadow of movement, but no form could be discerned, for no light shone therein.

There came a Vulg-like snarling, and the band below gathered up the rendered carcass and trooped to the east wall and within.

Riatha sucked in her breath and clenched her fist, but otherwise made no move, for there was no way in which she could bring a weapon to bear upon the shadow opposite.

Beside her, Faeril looked across at the dark arch, her heart racing in her breast. She could not even tell the shape of the shadow, yet she had no doubt who it was. And she found that she held a silver dagger in her hand; when she had drawn the weapon, she could not say.

Then the darkness within the hole changed, as if whoever, whatever had been there was gone.

The Elfess turned to Faeril, Riatha's voice grim and deadly. " 'Tis Stoke!" she gritted. "He is alive! Once apast at Dreadholt did I hear him speak as would a Vulg, and this was the same." Riatha gazed intently into Faeril's eyes. "On the morrow, under the safety of the Sun, thou must bear word unto the monastery, for Aravan and Gwylly need to know that Stoke of a certain walks upon the world again."

Faeril protested. "But you will be left alone, Riatha! I cannot—"

Riatha's hand chopped downward in a negating gesture, stilling the damman's words. "Thou *must* go. We are in a precarious position as it is, and as thou did observe, the *Rûpt* may stumble upon our track. Gwylly and Aravan—and Urus, too, if he lives—must be warned . . . for the slayer is resurrected and once more will seek to begin his deadly harvest of innocent victims."

"But what about you, Riatha?"

"Faeril, one of us must remain behind to track the monster should he decide to move."

"That could be me as well as you, Dara."

"Aye, Faeril, it could. Yet I have more experience than thee, and I have less need of sleep, and my stride is longer should it come unto an overland trek.

"Nay, Faeril, 'tis I who should stay while thou gather our companions."

The damman said nothing for a moment, but at last she spoke. "I will do as you say, Dara, and bear the word to them, but as soon as I have done so, I shall return."

Riatha reached over and squeezed the Waerling's hand, saying nothing.

More hours trickled by, and sometime after mid of night, the second band returned. Riatha wakened Faeril, and together they watched the scene below. This band, too, came with game of a sort: arctic hares mostly, although Riatha glimpsed what she took to be some kind of a large burrowing animal, mayhap a badger. This time a Hlōk came forth from the caverns below to meet them, and again the game was taken within.

In the hour before dawn, Rūcks and Hlōks and Vulgs boiled out from the east wall, streaming across the arena and into individual splits and crannies and holes. It was as if Stoke had sent them unto separate places to spend the daylight hours. And neither Faeril nor Riatha could fathom why.

\* \* \*

Day came, wan and bleak, a grey sky casting a pall over all. A chill wind blew up from the south, bringing with it roiling dark clouds. And under the lowering skies Faeril set out cross-country for the monastery, even though both she and Riatha knew that a storm seemed to be in the offing, for her mission and message were urgent. Too, Faeril had been trained in arctic survival, and should a blow come, she would endure. And so, under the gloom the damman set out, following the directions given to her by Riatha.

The Elfess had gauged that the cloister lay some four or five leagues northwesterly of Stoke's bolt-hole, some twelve to fifteen miles across the rugged scape. Of course, Faeril could have backtracked all the way to the glacier and then southwesterly for the retreat, but that would have added miles to the journey, and perhaps hours to it as well. Too, there was always the chance that if she followed a route frequented by Spawn, the Vulgs would scent her passage, leading to disaster for all. Thus, Faeril trekked toward the col to the northwest, beyond which she should find Gwylly and Aravan and perhaps Urus as well.

She used a pine bough to erase her tracks behind, not wanting Riatha to be discovered by backtracking maggot-folk. A mile or more did she brush away her traces, praying that the snow would not hold her scent for Vulgs to follow back to the Elfess. Espying a vertical rock face, Faeril swept until she reached the stone. Then, placing her back to the wall, she walked straight away. Looking over her shoulder, she saw that the footprints in the snow seemed to emerge from the rock itself. *There. Let the Rūcks and such cipher that. Mayhap they'll think a secret door lies therein.* Giggling at the prospect of maggot-folk seeking entry into solid stone, Faeril trekked onward.

The land was rough, broken, and splits and ravines barred the way. Often was the damman forced to backtrack and find a different route, a route skirting 'round the obstacle, whatever it might be. At times she had to break out her climbing gear, to clamber up or down or over. At other times the way was too sheer and smooth, and an alternate path was called for. And slowly did she progress, while the sky grew ever darker and the south wind ever more chill.

Up she went, and up. She came to another crevasse, its black depths lost to sight. Ranging leftward, she espied a snow bridge spanning the gap but passed it by, for she had listened well to Riatha's words that such were dangerous, even for one of her slight weight. She moved onward, until she fetched up against a high stone bluff. *No passage that way, unless I climb.*

To the right the crevasse ran on a goodly distance, yet at last she rounded its far extent and slowly, slowly went on upward through the shattered land, the wind skirling bodefully under blackening skies.

The blow came sometime after the noontide, though exactly what the hour was, Faeril did not know. She was perhaps a mile from the crest of the col when a wall of white came boiling up after her, snow hurtling horizontally across the 'scape, borne on a shrieking wind.

The damman took shelter in a crevice in the rocks. And as she peered out at the hurling white, gone grey under the dark skies, for the first time it occurred to her to wonder what she would do if she came to the monastery and no one was there, not Gwylly, not Aravan, not Urus. *What if Urus has recovered and they are already following our trail? What if they never reached the cloister at all? What if the maggot-folk got them? What if they are all dead?* She felt a great hollow in her chest at these dark thoughts, and there was little she could do to shake them, storm-trapped as she was.

*What if this storm lasts for days? What then, my dark-haired damosel?* Faeril began to ration her water, knowing that she had not wood for a fire to melt more snow, and knowing as well that to eat frozen snow would rapidly sap her energy. She recalled B'arr's words: *"Eat snow, bad. Eat snow, steal* makt. *Eat snow, dog get cold inside. Dog need more food get warm again."*

Remembering B'arr brought a lump to her throat. *B'arr, this dog won't eat snow if she can help it, for I plan on avenging your death.*

Faeril jerked awake sometime after nightfall. *Oh lor', I've been asleep!* Though a wind still blew, it had stopped snowing. Groaning to her feet, the damman hobbled from the crevice.

The storm had blown itself out and the skies were clearing. Here and there a star twinkled through rifts in the cover. Low in the east, the Moon illuminated the clouds from behind. Still the south wind blew, now more gently, driving the cast before it. A fresh fall of white snow covered the land. *Good! Now all trace of my passage is gone.*

Ahead and upward about a mile hence lay the crest of the wide col, and somewhere down the far side she hoped to find the monastery. Fumbling in a pocket, Faeril drew out the last of her tannik, and chewing on the bitter root, she set forth.

Up and up she clambered, at times finding the way easy, at other times difficult, for in this broken land were crevices and cracks and bluffs and ridges. And for one who stood but an inch or two above three feet tall, the terrain was formidable. Yet Faeril persisted, slowly making her way unto the crest of the col.

It had taken the damman nearly two more hours to reach the summit of the pass, and during this time the wind bore the clouds away. Above and behind her the Moon was bright, and stars glimmered overhead. Too, the Eye of the Hunter scored the sky, its tail long and bloody. In the distance down below her, Faeril could see a narrow plateau, and a mile or so away at the far end of the flat lay her goal—the monastery, its buildings dark, showing no light, standing starkly on the broad 'spanse above the glacier gleaming beyond. *Oh, my Gwylly, are you there within?*

Down she started, down from the col, the slope before her shallow. Even so, the way was difficult, for cracks and seams in the stone yet stood across her way, seeking to bar her passage. But these she managed to traverse or go around and head once more for the buildings afar.

She had come some three quarters of a mile, the monastery now but a furlong or two away, when dreadful yawls sounded behind her, the howls of Vulgs on the hunt. She spun about, looking back, and her heart leapt into her throat, for in the silvery moonlight she saw them coming across the col, running on her trail. And then the howls changed tenor, for the creatures had sighted their quarry and leapt forward in pursuit.

Faeril turned and fled toward the dark monastery, knowing

that she would not reach it ere the monsters overtook her. Heart hammering, breath coming in sobbing gasps, Faeril ran a race she could not win. A furlong or so away stood the high stone walls ringing the cloister, and the gates were closed.

And then she tripped over something hidden under the new-fallen snow and fell sprawling.

# CHAPTER 17

# Awakening

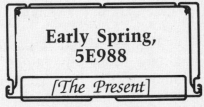

**Early Spring, 5E988**

[The Present]

"Faeril!" cried Gwylly as the damman scrambled to her feet to fly toward the monastery.

"Swift, Gwylly," shouted Aravan, "a rope over the wall!"

As Gwylly loosened the line at his waist and clicked the grapnel tines into place, Aravan snatched up the iron rod and—*Clang, clang, clang, clang . . .*—began hammering the alarm hoop.

Gwylly tossed the coil over the side, glancing away from the fleeing damman long enough to lodge the hook into a crevice.

"Now take this," commanded Aravan, handing the rod to the buccan. "Strike the alarm! It will guide her and she will know we are here, and it may give the Vulgs pause to think the walls are warded."

As Gwylly began hammering the hoop, Aravan hastily lighted the gate lantern and swung it on its pivoting arm out above the anchored line. "She will need to see where to run to, as well as a light to see the rope."

And across the snow came Faeril fleeing, now angling toward the light on the wall. And behind raced Vulgs, five hurtling beasts, gaining with every stride.

"Run, Faeril, run!" shouted Gwylly, yet hammering the iron hoop, his voice lost in the clangor.

But of a sudden he dropped the rod and started to clamber over the wall there where the rope dangled. Aravan grabbed him by the arm and hauled him back. "No! You cannot prevail on the ground. Ready your sling."

Footsteps sounded behind them, and Doran clambered up the ladder, crossbow slung over his shoulder.

Gwylly moaned in desperation as he loaded a steel shot, for he knew that the Vulgs would overtake his dammia ere she could reach the wall. But even should a miracle occur, even should the ravers falter, even should Faeril somehow reach the bulwark first, still it was fifteen feet high, fifteen foot up to safety.

Now Aravan rang the alarm hoop, hoping the clangor would cause the Vulgs to sheer away. But on they raced, within yards of overhauling Faeril, the damman a hundred or so feet from the wall.

Of a sudden—*thunn! ssss . . .*—a flaming quarrel flashed from the wall, a bright red streak sissing through the icy air to graze through the fur of the lead Vulg, the black slayer flinching aside, stumbling, the other Vulgs momentarily shying away, Faeril gaining, the Vulgs again hurtling after.

Doran levered the crossbow, cocking it again. "They don't like fire." He snatched another rag-wrapped quarrel from his quiver and thrust the oil-soaked cloth toward the lantern.

In spite of his injured shoulder, Gwylly whipped his sling 'round—*"This way, Faeril! This way!"*—and let fly the steel bullet. Behind the running damman a pursuing Vulg howled, the missile glancing from the beast's tough hide. Yet on it came with the others, in full cry.

*Thunn! zzz . . .* Another bolt of fire sissed across the space, but this one struck true, and howling, the lead Vulg thudded into the snow, quarrel embedded deeply in its chest, flames burning.

Faeril dashed toward the wall, running now for the rope, Vulgs again hurling after.

Aravan dropped the iron bar and grabbed hold of the line. *"Swiftswarm! Swiftswarm!"*

Another steel bullet crashed into the Vulgs, cracking into the leg of one, and it yelped, but continued in pursuit, though limping, trailing the others as yawling on they sped.

Footsteps came up the ladder.

Faeril grabbed the line, and up she swarmed as Aravan hauled. Behind a great Vulg lept upward, slavering jaws wide. *Zzzzzaaak!* A flaming quarrel sprang full blown from the Vulg's eye and it tumbled down. Other Vulgs leapt. *"Petal!"* bellowed a voice, and a great dark form—changing, altering— hurled outward over the wall and down atop the leaping Vulgs, bearing them backwards to smash into the ground under its massive weight.

And boiling up from the pile came three Vulgs *and a Bear!*

A huge, savage Bear!

*RRRAAAWWWW!* Claws slashed. A Vulg fell slain, its throat torn out. Aravan hauled Faeril upward. *Crkk!*—a steel bullet smashed through the skull of a Vulg circling behind the Bear, the Vulg crashing to the snow. Doran lit another quarrel and dropped it into the groove of the crossbow and he took aim. *"Shoot not the Bear!"* shouted Gwylly. *Zzzzzk ... tssss!* The bolt flashed past the Vulg to hiss into the snow.

Yelping, the Vulg spun 'round and fled, the Bear roaring in rage. Yet the black raver, though favoring a leg, was too fleet to be overhauled from behind, and swiftly was beyond reach of claw, bullet, and quarrel.

Aravan swung Faeril over and down to the sentry walk. Gwylly took one last look at the Bear snuffling and pawing at the Vulg corpses, then leapt down from the shelf and embraced his dammia, tears of relief running down the buccan's face. "Oh, Faeril, I thought you would be slain."

Faeril's heart was hammering, and she sobbed and gasped for breath at one and the same time. She could not speak, so winded was she. But her eyes, too, were filled with tears.

"Oh, Adon," breathed Doran, averting his face from the scene outside, scribing a warding sign in the air. Glancing over the wall, Aravan swiftly climbed down the ladder and slid back the bar on its tracks and opened the gate. And through the portal came limping a huge Man, a Baeran: Urus.

Looking up to the walkway above, "Well, Petal," called the Man, his voice deep, rumbling, "are you all right? Come down, let's have a look at you. And what were you doing out among Vulgs? For that matter, how come you and I and

Tomlin to be back here at the monastery?" And then, without warning, Urus fell to his knees, collapsing sideways into the snow.

Urus held out the bowl. "Another, please."

The Baeran sat on a stool, a cloth wrapped 'round his shoulders. On the floor all about was shorn hair. Behind stood Gavan, holding comb and shears, his wounded arm no longer in a sling. He set aside the shears and took the wooden vessel from Urus and again filled it with stew and smiled. "Why don't you just eat straight from the pot, Urus? I mean, this is the fifth one."

Urus grinned and tore off another great hunk of bread. " 'Tis enough of a struggle keeping hair from my food in that tiny bowl, Gavan, much less the struggle it would take to protect the pot. Else believe me, I would."

Color had returned to the Baeran's face, so pale when they had carried him in. Though they had feared he had taken poisoned Vulg bite, upon examination they found no wound. Urus had merely fainted after the battle, having awakened to hear the alarm and rushing to render aid, his health and constitution not yet ready for such. And so the fight had drained him of what little energy he had summoned up from Adon knows where, and he had collapsed afterward. When they had revived him, he had asked for food and drink, downing copious quantities, eating as would a starving Man.

"I'm hungry as a—"

"Bear," interjected Gavan, handing the bowl to the Man. "A Bear that's just wakened from a long winter's sleep."

Gwylly nodded. "A very *long* winter's sleep."

Urus shook his head. "It's hard to grasp that a thousand years have . . . have passed"—the Baeran looked at Gwylly and Faeril, the damman applying the last of a minty salve to the buccan's tender shoulder—"and that you two are not Petal and Tomlin . . ."

A hard glint came into Urus's eye. ". . . and Stoke is alive."

Faeril leapt to her feet. "Oh, where is Aravan? I mean, we've got to go from here. Even now Riatha sets watch over that monster . . . and she is alone."

Gavan held up his right hand in a soothing gesture. "Adon will protect her."

Urus set his bowl aside. "Mayhap so, priest. Yet I've noticed that Adon protects those best who protect themselves."

Gavan sketched a sign in the air, its meaning unknown to the Warrows. "You speak as would a strong Man, Urus. Yet Adon watches over the weak as well."

Urus growled. "Just as he watched over you and your comrades, eh?"

Gavan's face fell.

"Argh, priest, I am sorry. I had no cause to say such."

The door opened and Aravan came in with another armload of supplies, followed by Doran, the abbot's arms also filled. "This should do us," said the Elf, piling all upon a table. He then swiftly divided the goods into four stacks, and set each stack next to partially filled frame packs.

"There," said Gavan, laying down the shears and removing the sheet from 'round Urus's shoulders. "All done."

Urus, beard and hair trimmed, drained the last of the stew, then stood and thanked Gavan and stepped to the scullery basin to wash the bowl and spoon.

Doran shuffled back from the herb cabinet, bearing several packets. "Here, Aravan, you may need medicines in the days ahead. Know you the uses of these?" The abbot and Elf opened each packet, discussing the herbs within, their uses and preparation, Gwylly and Faeril watching and listening.

As Doran divided out the herbs and wrapped individual doses into separate packets, Urus came to him and unhooked the aspergillum from his belt. "Friar, I would return this to you."

The abbot looked at the silver and ivory relic. "Nay, lad. You go into peril, where dwell the Spawn, and the Rutch and such are loath to come into the light of this holy vessel. If you are beloved of Adon, it shines forth at great need, repelling your enemies and calling allies unto your side."

Urus set the aspergillum down on the table. "I am done with it, friar. It served me once when I was in need. 'Twas only by accident I had it with me, and now I return it to its rightful keepers."

Aravan looked up from the frame packs he was filling. "Abbot, thy need is greater than ours, for we will be five when we join our companion, whereas ye are but two"—the Elf held out a hand, forestalling Doran's protest—"and ye must survive to take word unto the Aleutani that B'arr and Tchuka and Ruluk are dead, slain by the *Rûpt*. Too, I would have ye deliver my letter unto a Fjordlander ship captain, to find its way back unto my kindred in Arden Vale. And though I know that driven *Spaunen* can o'ercome the golden glow of yon device, still I think that they will not come at you without a driving hand.

"Hence, keep the aspergillum as Urus advises, and use it to ward ye twain in the long nights ahead. And come the summer, go down unto the grasslands where the *ren* herds graze, and there find the Aleutani. They will escort ye back unto the Boreal, and ye can go from there unto thine order and report on what has passed here. Mayhap they will again wish to occupy this monastery; if so, then let it be with warrior-priests, for such is needed in this perilous place.

"We would stay and ward ye both, had we the choice. Yet we do not, for our Dara waits."

At last Doran bowed his head and took up the aspergillum. Long he held it reverently, then passed it on to Gavan. The young priest clutched the artifact to his breast and fell to his knees, giving thanks to Adon.

For long moments did Faeril gaze at the praying monk, then she turned to Aravan. "Let us go from here, for Riatha is alone."

Stowing the last of the goods and shouldering the frame packs, the four stepped through the door and passed down the corridor and out through the hall of worship, Doran and Gavan following. Day was on the land, early morning, and pale light shone through a greying sky. Chill wind gusted and swirled among the stone buildings, and Gwylly wondered if another storm was in the offing. At the gate they stopped, and Urus drew the bar.

Beyond the open portal lay nought but snow. Of the slain four Vulgs there was no sign, and none expected, for with the coming of the daytide the dead creatures had withered into dust which the swirling wind scattered even as the Ban took its toll on the corpses.

Gwylly stepped out into the snow and looked, finding three crossbow bolts.

Faeril turned to the abbot. "I thank you for my life, Doran.

Had it not been for you and your crossbow, I would now be dead."

"*Hai!*" called Gwylly, returning, holding high the quarrels. "It was one for the buccan and one for the Bear, but two of the five did Doran account for. Would that I had his skill!"

Doran gave a negligent wave of his hand, yet it was apparent to all that he was pleased as Gwylly handed him the bolts.

"Take care, priest," rumbled Urus to Gavan. "Protect yourself and Adon may watch o'er you."

A smile tugged at Gavan's mouth. "I will pray for you and yours," he answered.

Doran sketched a warding sign in the air. "Adon's blessings on you all."

Aravan raised his own hand in farewell. "And may He keep ye both safe as well."

The four set forth, following Faeril, and behind, the Adonites watched them go. At last they closed the gates and slid the bar into place. And then the old Man and the young Man turned and trudged through the swirling wind across the courtyard and into the hall of worship beyond. And as they entered, the ground rumbled and trembled, as if shivering in fear.

Up to the col fared the four, and at the crest of the pass they paused. Urus looked back at the pearly glacier behind, the miles-wide river of ice coming into view down the long slope of the mountains to the south and passing from view in the distance to the north. "Long was I trapped, though it seems but yester."

They turned and in single file crossed through the gap and started down into the broken land beyond.

Down they fared and down, climbing over ridges and crossing 'round crevasses and lowering themselves down rock faces both slanting and sheer, the stone snow-covered or wind-scoured or ice-clad. Often did they stop and rest, for all were weary, especially Faeril, who had clambered up these same slopes only the night before. Additionally, they all were burdened with full backpacks, both Urus and Aravan carrying extra, that which would be given to Riatha when they came to her side. Too, Urus was weak, his frame gaunt and his clothing loose, and none knew, not even Urus, how he had managed to survive a thousand-year entrapment within the glacier. Gwylly considered it a miracle that Urus was alive at all, though neither Faeril nor Aravan ventured an opinion.

And so, weak and weary and burdened, down and down the land they went, under lowering skies. And somewhere in the distance before them they hoped to find an Elfess standing watch o'er a monster's lair.

It was late that drear afternoon when they came nigh the cliffs above Stoke's bolt-hole. Cautioning silence, Faeril led them among the pines and through the newly fallen snow to the place where she and Riatha had set watch . . .

. . . but the Elfess wasn't there.

Instead the snow was moiled with the spoor of Rūcks and Hlōks and Vulgs!

His heart pounding, Gwylly wanted to shout out in anger, yet he clamped his lips tightly and forced his rage to remain within. And as they bent to examine the tracks, all was silent there 'mid the pines, but for the occasional *chrk* of a distant arctic ptarmigan and the soft sound of Faeril weeping at his side.

# CHAPTER 18

# Elusion

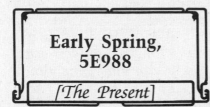

The wind blew chill as Riatha watched Faeril move off among the pines, the damman bearing word to the monastery that Stoke was of certain alive, bearing word as to the location of his bolt-hole. Slowly, Faeril went, backward up the slope, and with a pine bough swept out the traces of her passage as she threaded her way across the snow.

Riatha continued to gaze in the direction Faeril had gone long after the damman was beyond seeing—*May Adon protect thee, wee one*—the Elfess's heart torn between going with the Waerling and staying with the *Rûpt*, torn between protecting a friend and keeping close watch o'er foe. And so, long she looked up the slope, wondering if she had made the right choice.

At last, however, Riatha turned her attention to the pines, her eyes seeking cones, for she had sent all the food with Faeril and needed to replenish her own stores. The boughs above swayed to and fro, snow sifting down from the branches. *'Tis likely a storm will fly on the wings of this wind. Would that Faeril reach the cloister ere it comes.*

The Elfess spied a cone among the branches, its scales yet closed—any seeds would still be held within. She climbed, the limbs her hand- and footholds, and plucked the cone, finding two more hidden among the needled boughs. Clambering back down, she trudged to the next tree, and the next, and the one after, slowly moving among the forest, finding more cones as she went. When her pockets were full, she stopped and pried open the scales, shaking out the small nuts, no larger than a fat grain of rice or wheat, her mind returning to the discussion between Faeril and Gwylly concerning the span of a Dragon. *How many cones would it take to yield up enough pine nuts to number the Dragon's years ... and how many trees, what size forest, would hold that many cones, my Faeril?*

On went the Elfess, collecting more. *Had I a fire, then these could I roast ... had I a pan. Too, I could use the inner bark of a pine to make a hearty soup ... had I a fire and a vessel in which to hold the broth.*

The wind began gusting harder, and dark clouds ran across the skies. *A two-edged sword is this blow, for I can use it to carry away the scent of a fire, yet at the same time I doubt not that the wind indeed bears a storm—Oh, Faeril, make haste, for I would have thee sheltered ere it strikes.*

Riatha walked north along the canyon wall, leaving Stoke's bolt-hole behind, the Elfess moving with the wind and away. Far downwind a mile or more she found a shelter between a mountain rise and a great rock slab that leaned against it. There she built a small fire, out of the blow, and used it to melt more snow, replenishing her depleted water supply. She sat in the shelter and took a meal of pine nuts, the seeds nutritious and tasty. *I will grow weary of such after a time, yet for now I savor them.*

All the while she sat, the fury of the wind grew. At last Riatha quenched the fire, hauling snow into the shelter and piling it high, until the ashes were deep under, all evidence hidden, all scent extinguished. Then she started back.

Riatha had reached the high rim of the sheer-walled basin when the full storm fell upon her, the wind howling, snow hurtling horizontally. The sparse pines yielded little shelter, and the Elfess shielded her face and turned away from the arena below and made her way outward among the trees, pressing toward a nearby jumble of boulders up slope. In the shelter of the rock she found a crevice just wide enough to admit her, and she crawled within to a place where she could sit with her back to the stone. And as the wind shrieked all about, Riatha prayed that Faeril was not caught out in this blizzard, but instead had reached the safety of the monastery; the noontide had just passed, and if the way to the cloister were not too difficult, Riatha gauged the damman should even now be within those sheltering walls. But if the way were hard . . . *Oh, Adon, let her be safe.*

Struggling, the Elfess sought to calm her fears. After a while she managed to slip into the meditative state which Elvenkind substitutes for sleep.

Night was falling when the storm blew itself out. Riatha crawled forth from her tiny refuge and made her way through the new fall to the brow of the circular pit, arriving just as torch-bearing *Spaunen* far beneath began emerging from their splits and cracks and crevices. Taking care not to cause snow to cascade down, Riatha lay on her stomach and watched as the *Rûpt* streamed from the holes to gather in the center. And even as she looked upon them assembling, suddenly she knew when to come at Stoke and slay him.

She watched the Foul Folk milling below, her heart pounding in excitement at her abrupt illumination. She could do it alone, if necessary, search him out and slay him, but with her comrades at her side the outcome seemed more certain. *Hurry, Faeril. Bring them to me, for now I know the way.*

Again she wondered at Faeril's success at reaching the monastery. *Even were she storm delayed, likely she is on her way once more, now that the blizzard is gone.*

Then dark thoughts intruded. *She could be injured, even dead;* Rûpt *may have come upon her. —Nay! Not* Rûpt, *for she went in the daytide.*

The Elfess shook her head to clear these ominous musings. *Fie! for all I know, she could be safely holed up in some rock shelter, as was I, and if so, she may even be asleep. No matter, for if she is, she will awaken to go onward. And the* Rûpt *are here below; surely she is beyond their rangings this darktide.*

As they had done the previous night, the *Spaunen* divided

into two hunting parties, leaving a third group behind to stand ward on the bolt-hole. One party headed northward up the canyon, the other southward. The remainder trooped into a single passage in the wall opposite, into the wall where Riatha deemed Stoke was holed up.

When all were well beyond sight, Riatha cautiously began clearing away the snow from where she lay on the brim, once more providing a place from which to observe below without fear of causing a cascade of white to betray her. As she worked, the wind yet blew to the north; overhead, a solid cloud cover slid across the skies, obscuring all. Now and again the land would tremble, snow showering down from trees and from the walls of the canyon, and Riatha would pause to see if *Rûpt* came forth from the holes below to look about—but they never did.

Just as she finished clearing the landing, her keen Elven hearing heard the baying of Vulgs, coming down from the north, along the top of the canyon wall, on the hunt. She cocked her head and listened, straining to hear, for the wind blew from behind her, bearing the sound away. Of a sudden she realized, *Adon! 'Tis me they hunt, for the wind carries my scent unto them!*

Riatha leapt to her feet. *Which way?*

Suddenly the choice was taken from her, for the wind stilled momentarily and Vulg howls mingled with yawls of *Spaunen* burst upon her full. And she could see their torch-light and hear them running, iron-shod boot and clawed paws slamming into the snow.

Whirling, Riatha fled southward along the rim, but as fleet as she was, she knew that she could not long outrun the pursuit. And even as she realized this, the howls behind her broke into a chorus. *Adon, they see me! I am fordone!*

On she sped, howling creatures swiftly closing the gap, overhauling her with every stride. And at the very moment Riatha decided to make a stand, she saw—

*The snow bridge! Allfather, let it serve my need!*

She skidded to a halt at the rim even as ravening beasts thundered toward her. Taking a deep breath and marshalling all her discipline, all her training, Riatha ran lightly across the span, running as if she were trying to keep from touching the snow, her feet but barely in contact ere they were gone onward.

Behind, baying Vulgs raced on her track, and as Riatha gained the far side, the lead Vulg bounded onto the span and hurtled toward her—*I am lost!*—a second Vulg pounding onto the span after.

Whipping her sword from its backslung scabbard, Riatha braced herself for the onslaught . . . and in that moment the span collapsed, unable to bear the weight of both Vulgs, the beast in the rear wailing as it plummeted downward, the creature in the lead, its front claws digging into the stone of the rim, rear claws scrabbling at the vertical wall, struggling to climb onto the plateau.

Riatha stepped forward and slammed the beast in the muzzle with the flat of her blade, jarring the slavering monster backwards off the rim to fall yawling, to plunge some three hundred feet down to its death.

On the rim opposite, five more Vulgs ravened, a canyon between them and their quarry.

*Sssshhh . . .* A black-shafted arrow sissed past her face, and howling, Rucha and Loka pounded nigh.

Riatha whirled again and ran southward, angling outward into the sparse pines, running for the shadows within.

More arrows hissed past, whispering of death in their flight. Yet none struck Riatha, and onward she plunged, fleeing southward into the forest beyond. She could see torch-light flickering among the trees and hear the *Rûpt* shouting in victory, as south along the opposite rim they ran, for they knew that the walls diminished and soon she would be out in the valley before them, where they would run her down. Ahead of the clamoring *Rûpt* sped the Vulgs, their savage howls ululating among the stone of the mountains.

When Riatha was certain that they could no longer see her, she stopped and listened as the pursuit hurled on southward. The Elfess then doubled back, racing again for the brow of the steep-walled arena. Overhead, rifts could be seen in the cast. *Adon, let it stay dark. Let it stay dark. Nearly the entire night lies before me, and I have no hope of outrunning the hunters throughout the full darktide, no hope of running until the light of dawn comes to my rescue. In-*

*stead I must outwit them, and I need moonless darkness to hide me until I am safe.*

Riatha came to the rim. In the distance behind, she could hear the far-off baying of the hunt.

Even though pursued, she stopped and carefully scanned the wall and rim opposite, seeking certain refuge. At last she espied what she sought, and marking it well in her mind, she fled atop the eastern brow and toward the slot at the north entrance into the arena below, toward the gap where stood a large pine on the opposite side.

Reaching her goal, she unhooked her grapnel and line, and flung it across the width of the canyon, the tines hooking into a limb some fifty feet away. Behind, howls grew louder, the *Spaunen* drawing nigh, having rounded the end of the canyon south. Taking up all the slack, Riatha leapt from the brink and swung across to the far wall. She poised her legs before her to take the shock, yet she slammed hard into the stone, knocking the wind from her. Even so, she managed to hang on, and hand over hand she clambered up to the lip above.

Ululating yawls came echoing through the pines, and still the riven clouds above continued to cleave apart, moonlight now and again glancing through. Riatha flipped loose the grapnel and swiftly coiled the rope. Out into the snow she ran, until she came unto the wide track of the *Spaunen*, the track they had made when they had first come upon her.

Following this path, south fled Riatha, mingling her steps with theirs. She did not believe that her scent would be lost in theirs, for her spoor was too fresh. Yet it was vital for her to come once more unto her own trace, closing the circle.

Up the vale came the hunters, running among the pines on the plateau opposite, closing the distance to the canyon arena, yowls and yawls growing louder.

At last Riatha closed the circle, and now she ran to a bent tree on the brim and dashed on past, joining the track again. Backtrailing in her own footsteps, she returned to the tree and, snaking her line about the trunk and casting both ends beyond the lip so that a loose double line dangled down the wall, over the edge she went, rappelling some forty feet or so, down to the mouth of a cavern. And just as she swung into the dark opening, the Moon broke through the clouds. Onto the rim opposite howled the hunters, racing along her distant trace.

Riatha waited until the next cloud drifted across the face of the Moon, then snaked her rope down and in. *There. Let them find me now, if they can, hiding in their very own caves.*

A time passed, the Moon gliding across the sky, and Riatha heard loping footsteps on the rim above her, running past. Cautiously, she peered out the mouth of the cavern. At the south entrance, Vulgs sniffed the snow, there where the bridge once had spanned the gap. *Rûpt* came, shouting, pointing across.

*Well and good! They now run in circles. Let them do so till dawn.*

The Vulgs returned to the rim above her, snuffling in the tracks.

More time passed. Of a sudden, yawls cried out, Vulgs howling on a trail. *Ai, they have now found my steps from the shelter where I waited out the storm.* The howls grew fainter as the beasts raced away. *'Twill be nought but another dead end for them. That track merely leads up slope a distance. Hah! Mayhap they will chase phantom footsteps up the mountain, up to—*

Suddenly a chill ran up Riatha's spine. For up that slope was where Faeril had gone, and if those five Vulgs ran far enough . . . *Adon, let them not stumble upon her tracks; keep them from the monastery.*

A deep foreboding fell upon Riatha's heart, while above, *Rûpt* split their forces, half to stay on this rim, half to cross to the other, each to hunt the elusive intruder.

By reflected moonlight Riatha explored the extent of her cavern. Some five feet high and perhaps eight feet wide at the mouth, swiftly it narrowed down to a thin crevice some twenty feet back. *Mayhap a Waerling could get through such, but not I.*

She returned to her watch, sliding slowly, cautiously on her stomach to peer out into the arena below and at the brim above, taking care that her golden hair was well hidden beneath her cloak hood, and that her white face was completely scarf-covered but for a narrow slit to peer through, for she knew that watchful eyes opposite might otherwise espy her in the gloom.

Time passed, and still the *Rûpt* searched the rims above, cursing at one another, or so it sounded, raging to find the stranger who had just *vanished* before them.

*Mayhap they have never before hunted fox.* Riatha smiled. *Certainly not this vixen.*

As before, some two hours ere dawn, hunters returned to the arena below. This time, though, none had captured any game. Yet they dragged the dead Vulgs from the south canyon entrance, the Vulgs that had fallen from the collapsed snow bridge. These they butchered for food, the living Vulgs just as eager to get at this meat as at any other.

And once again a shadowy figure lurked in a cavern opposite, an archway well marked by Riatha.

An hour or so later, the *Spaunen* emerged from the eastern wall and spread out among the splits and cracks and caves 'round about. Riatha counted the foe: still there were some twenty-seven Rucha and Loka, but only six Vulgs. *Two Vulgs fell at the bridge, and five more ran up slope following a false trail, and six I number below. That would account for all. If the five have not yet returned, may the Ban find them running this way!*

Another hour passed, and in the last few moments ere dawn crept over the mountains, a single Vulg, somewhat favoring a foreleg, came racing into the pit through the north canyon and hobbled into the cavern below where Stoke had stood. *Could this be one of the five? If so, then four have not returned. Mayhap they encountered more than they bargained for.*

Riatha remained in the cavern until full day fell upon the land. The other four Vulgs were still unaccounted for. *May they all have perished!*

She surveyed the wall above, and free-climbed to the rim. *Spaunen* tracks tramped down the snow. Moving cautiously to stay within their beat, Riatha trekked through the woods, verifying that the Vulgs had indeed gone up the slope, the way that Faeril had fared. Riatha's heart thudded in apprehension. *Let her be safe. Let them all be safe.*

Once again a chill wind blew from the south, and above the skies fell drab with cloud cover. *Cast, thou herald another storm being borne on the wings of the wind.*

Riatha hiked back along the canyon rim, heading north, returning to the place where she had built the fire yester. Her water was depleted and she needed to refill the skin. Too, she needed to relieve herself and did not wish to leave fresh sign. *Let them think this vixen long gone and not yet lurking about.*

After replenishing her water, the Elfess spent the day foraging for pine nuts, sweeping away her tracks with a pine bough broom, and resting in the stone shelter where she had made the fire, wishing to keep her scent to a minimum near the canyon rim. She had decided to wait one more night for her companions to return, and if they did not arrive on the morrow, she would go after Stoke alone.

In mid-afternoon, again she buried all evidence of her stay and started back along the *Spaunen* track for the rim high above the circular pit. Striding, now and again she sounded a *chrk* as would an arctic ptarmigan.

As she drew nigh the rim of the canyon, she heard a *chrk* in response; and her face broke into a wide grin, and her legs broke into a run.

# CHAPTER 19

# Reunion

**W**iping the tears from his eyes, Gwylly reached out and took Faeril's hand in his own. "Weep not, my dammia. Surely Riatha will have found a way to thwart the maggot-folk." In spite of his words, Gwylly's heart thudded in apprehension, for he did not see how anyone could escape Vulgs and Rūcks combined. *Yet wait! We did so just three nights past—Has it been only three nights? Seems as if we climbed up that cliff years agone.*

Urus looked up from where he knelt next to the track. "These are muddled and run both ways. And I do not see Riatha's prints at all."

"Likely lost under the steps of the *Rûpt*," gritted Aravan, his features grim.

Urus stood and began shedding his pack. "Aravan, you go north with Tomli—with Gwylly. Faeril and I will scout south." The Baeran glanced at the grey cast above. "There is precious little more time to search ere nightfall—"

Urus's words were cut short by Aravan flinging up his hand for silence. The Elf cocked his head and listened. Then he faced north and sounded a *chrk*.

Almost instantly came the answering *chrk* of a ptarmigan. Sudden understanding flooded Gwylly's face, and he turned to Faeril. But the damman had started running northward, shedding her pack even as she went. Gwylly followed, dropping his pack as well. Urus looked on in puzzlement. Aravan glanced over at him, the Elf's visage no longer grim but smiling instead. "The ptarmigan. 'Tis Riatha." Aravan turned back. *Chrk!*

Again it was immediately answered.

Urus bowed his head and took a deep breath and exhaled slowly, and when he looked up again, his eyes glistered.

In the distance, Faeril clutched a kneeling Riatha, the damman's arms about the Elfess. "I thought you slain, Riatha. I thought you slain." Tears ran freely down Faeril's cheeks.

Riatha's embrace took in Gwylly, too. "Ah, my wee ones, there was a time when I, too, bethought myself slain. Yet I eluded them in the end."

"And now, Gwylly, thou must tell me . . ." Riatha's voice fell silent, for toward her came Aravan and one other, one whom she had thought gone from her life forever. Disengaging from the Waerlinga, she stood, her heart hammering. Slowly the Elfess walked toward the two, her silver-grey eyes glittering with unshed tears. And then they came together, and Urus wrapped his huge arms about her and held onto her tightly, and she clutched him unto her, her face buried in his chest, softly weeping.

And Aravan looked on in consternation.

Riatha pointed. "There. The dark hole shaped as a cathedral window. A hundred or so feet up from the floor. There is where Stoke has stood in the shadows two nights now."

The five were on the western brim of the circular pit, peering across to where Riatha pointed. "We can lower ourselves from above to come at him."

Gwylly looked up at the Elfess. "How far to a place where we can cross over?"

"Half a league," responded Riatha. The Elfess glanced at the sky. "But not today, Gwylly. Not tonight. We know not what lies within that hole—a simple cavern or a twisting maze—and there is not enough day left for exploring a maze, not enough light ere night falls and the others join him.

"Yet I do have a plan. Heed, in the hour before dawn, Stoke sends the *Spaunen* away from him and unto splits and cracks and crevices spread wide. Then is Stoke most vulnerable, for should aught come at him in the daylight hours, his warders will be unable to answer his call, for, because of the Ban, they cannot leave the blackness of their holes to cross the arena below to come to him when Adon's light is in the sky.

"And so, this I advise: that we wait till morn, and at sunrise go in after Stoke, trapping the viper in its lair. Then will we have time enough to search for him, be his bolt-hole a complex labyrinth or a simple cave."

Urus growled. "I like not this waiting, yet I have no better plan."

Aravan nodded his agreement. "I would see this Man with the yellow eyes, and so I, too, would wish that it were now rather than on the morrow. But thy plan is sound, Dara, and I follow thee."

Gwylly spoke up. "What about tonight? Where do we go? Where do we stay?" The buccan gestured at the tracks of the maggot-folk. "I mean, we can't just stay out in the open, at least not on this rim. Look, it's plain that the Rūcks and such were here last night and they are likely to come again. And so, what'll we do about them?"

Riatha looked at the sky. "E'en though it seems a storm is in the offing, hence hiding all trace of our presence, we cannot rely on the fortunes of the weather. List, ere we go to ground, first we must lay a false trail, one the *Spaunen* will follow this night, for I deem thou are right, Gwylly— they will come this eve once more, searching for me again.

"Yet if they do, they will not find us, for we will be well hidden in the *Rûpt's* own caves, where I spent yesternight."

Faeril's eyes widened in amazement. "You spent last night in the caves? These caves?"

Riatha smiled. "Aye, in one they do not use. Where else to hide but in a place they think not to look?"

Aravan barked a laugh as he laced the last thong on the spare frame pack they had brought with them, a pack now filled with a share of the supplies. "Where else, indeed?"

Riatha stepped to the pack. "Come. Let us lay that trail for the *Rûpt* to follow, and I will tell ye all of my adventure as we go."

After shouldering her own gear, Faeril turned to the Elfess. "False trail you say, Riatha? Let me tell what I did to fool the maggot-folk." Faeril giggled, remembering her vision of Rūcks and such searching for a secret door in solid stone. "Perhaps we can use the trick here."

Riatha raised a questioning eyebrow.

Again Faeril giggled, then grew sober. "Here is what we can do. First, let us cut some pine boughs and then backtrack up the trail we made coming from the monastery to here, walking out beside it, taking care not to step in our old footprints. About a mile from here we will pass a sheer stone face. We will go on beyond the face a furlong or two, now on top of our track from the monastery. A furlong beyond we will stop, start back, and brush out all tracks heading toward or coming from the monastery, thereby keeping the Foul Folk from going there. Instead, when we get back to the stone face, we stop brushing and walk from our trail to the face, as if there were a secret door hidden therein. Then we lay a trail from that stone back to our original trail, and step in our own prints back to here.

"Only you, Riatha, will need to lay a new trail on the return while we step in our original tracks, for you were not with us as we came from the monastery.

"Now think how what we do will look to the maggot-folk. If we are careful, they will not be able to tell which tracks were laid first, hence will believe that we came out a secret door concealed in the stone, walked to the pit, looked about, and then returned to the secret door and went within.

"Perhaps they'll knock for admittance."

All burst out in laughter, and Riatha clapped her hands. "Hai! Another clever vixen in this band."

And so, carrying out Faeril's scheme, the five set forth from the pit, moving back up the trail, taking care not to step in the tracks.

One after another, down from the bent tree they rappelled, swinging into the mouth of the cave high above the floor of the arena. They had laid the false trail and had returned to the rim of the sheer-walled pit. Evening was on the land, the overcast had grown darker, and snow began to flurry. Wind moaned through the mountains, driving south to north, up the main valley between hemming massifs, wailing into and over the canyon and pit and beyond. And now the five entered the cave high on the sheer western wall, its dark interior swallowing them whole and sheltering them from the blow.

Being the smallest, Gwylly and Faeril moved all the way to the back of the hole, there where the roof and walls came together. Ere taking a seat, Faeril explored the narrow crevice at the rear, discovering that she could squeeze into the crack, finding that beyond a turn it twisted away into the darkness, but she did not explore any farther.

Hooded, with his face covered, Aravan lay at the mouth of the cave and peered outward, standing watch.

Between the Elf and the Warrows, Urus sat on one side, his back to the wall, Riatha on the other, her back to the stone as well.

And they waited.

Riatha gazed across at Urus, the Baeran leaning against rock, his eyes closed, resting in shadow. He was a giant of a Man—easily two or three hands taller than Aravan—with broad shoulders and trim waist and slim hips. And his strength was enormous. His face was covered with a close-cropped full beard, reddish brown, lighter at the tips, grizzled, and his hair was the same. Though his eyes were closed, she knew them to be a dark amber. He was dressed in deep umber and wore fleece-lined boots and vest. A morning star depended from his belt, the spiked ball and chain held by slip-knotted thongs to the oaken haft. He was wrapped 'round with a great brown cloak. He was exactly as she had remembered him. He was Urus.

And as she drank in the sight of him, the Dara's mind drifted back to a time long past. *Ah, Reín, my mother, thou did warn me long ago in Adonar when thou did say, "Love not a mortal Man . . . it will shatter thy heart." Mother, perhaps it is the fate of daughters to walk in the tracks of their dams. Thou and thine Evian, me and mine Urus—*

*Adon knows, I do love this mortal Man. Yet I cannot tell him so, for I could not bear to see the anguish in his eyes as he grows old and I do not.*

Outside, the wind moaned. Urus shifted, opening his amber eyes, looking directly into Riatha's gaze of silver.

# CHAPTER 20

# Urus

**4E1911 to 5E988**

*[The Past Millennium or So]*

"Oi!" called Beorc. "Did y' hear that?"

Uran cocked his head in the wind and listened, hearing nought but the sound of air swirling among the crags of the Grimwalls. But then—*wrauu*—came the faint cry. "Sounds like a cub. Lost."

"Aye," responded Beorc.

Uran shouldered his gear. "Well, there's nothing for it—we've got to see that it's all right."

Beorc, too, shouldered his goods. "Take care, Uran. The sow may be about."

Nodding, Uran led the way, the two Men moving higher among the crags.

*Wrauu!* "There is no mistaking that call," grunted Uran as the two clambered up slope. "It is a cub, indeed, for nought else squalls so. One in distress, too, if my ears hear straight."

The Men were in the mountains west of Delon Isle, there in the River Argon. Scouting for the spoor of Spawn, for reports had come to them that the Grimwalls once again had become a dangerous place to be. Yet the Wrg had not begun raiding; it was as if they were waiting for some signal, or for some leader or event to come. Yet Modru was said to

be in exile in the Barrens, and had been since the Great
War some thirty-nine hundred years past. And Gyphon was
banished beyond the Spheres for those same thirty-nine centuries. And none else had been capable of assembling the
entire Nation of Spawn, hence the renewed numbers of Foul
Folk here in the Grimwalls at this time was a mystery. And
so, in the spring the Baeron had come from the Great
Greenhall and had set up station on the Isle of Delon in the
clear waters of the Argon, and had begun sending scouts into
the mountains to keep track of the Wrg.

Dressed in varying shades of brown, Uran and Beorc,
brothers, were a pair of these scouts. Typical of all Baeron
Men, they were tall and muscular. Uran, the elder of the
two, stood some six feet six and weighed a jot over sixteen
stone. Beorc, the younger brother, was mayhap a half inch
taller but weighed a bit less, coming in at fifteen stone and
some. Both had brown eyes and dark brown hair, and Uran
sported a beard, while his brother was clean-shaven. Uran,
at twenty-four, was married; Beorc, at twenty-one, was not.

And now in the early morning sunlight of a late summer
day they climbed to see what was amiss with a Bear cub, a
cub wrauling in distress. That these Men did so was not
surprising, for Bears were *special* to the Baeron—Bears and
Wolves, alike—some folk even claiming that there was a
mystical bond 'tween the Baeron and these beasts. Why,
some claimed that the Baeron were able to *talk* to Wolves
and Bears. As to the actual truth of the matter, few knew,
if any, and none would say for sure.

*Wrauu!*

"Up there," called Beorc, pointing. "No cub, but still a
Bear." Uran looked, and indeed he did see what appeared to
be the dark form of a large Bear lying on the edge of a
boulder-laden flat above.

Higher they climbed. "Fox!" called Uran. "No, two! —
Three!"

A flash of red fur betrayed a fox scrambling away among
the stones of the rocky 'scape.

Uran stood with his mouth agape. "Adon! My eyes must
be playing tricks. I thought I saw . . ." He fell silent, reflec-
tive, and resumed climbing.

"What?" No answer came to Beorc's question.

"Well, no matter what you saw, Uran, foxes couldn't bring down a full-grown Bear, be it sow Bear or boar."

*Wrauu!* The wraul of the distressed cub sounded near.

"Mayhap they were after the younker," replied Uran, clambering upward.

"Hola! Look!" Uran pointed up slope at what appeared to be another felled Bear farther back on the flat.

Beorc held up his hand and tested the wind. " 'Ware, Uran. The wind blows that way. Mayhap they are but asleep; it would not do to startle them."

Uran loosened his morning star from his belt. "Something is not right, Beorc."

When Beorc had taken his mace in hand, the two Men resumed climbing, going more slowly, more warily.

They came up level with the downed Bears. Now they could see that altogether there were four of them, slain, feathered with arrows, the Bears lying before a low opening in the rocky slope.

*Wrauu!* The wraul of the distressed cub came from the dark slot.

Carefully, the Men approached. "Look!" hissed Uran. "Armor. Weapons. Abandoned."

Scattered across the flat was what could be construed as evidence of battle—chain mail, helms, cudgels, bows, arrows, boots, clothing—abandoned, or so it seemed.

*"Rach!"* cursed Beorc, taking up a black-shafted arrow. He stirred the clothing, finding ashes, dust. *"Forbanet* Wrg! No wonder there are no corpses."

*Wrauu!*

Uran examined one of the slain Bears, the beast pierced with black-feathered, black-shafted arrows. "This is Rutch work. At least they didn't get the cub.

"Stand awhile, Beorc. Let the wind carry our scent into the cave. Mayhap the cub will come out once it smells who we are."

Beorc squatted, stirring ashes with the arrow. "Hola! What is this?"

He held up a tiny arrow, no more than five inches long. Its point was discolored, as if coated with something. Taking care not to touch the darkness, Beorc handed the minuscule shaft to Uran. " 'Ware the point. Mayhap it is poisoned."

While Uran examined the arrow, Beorc sifted through the remains of other Rutcha, their corpses turned to ashes by the coming of the Sun. "Uh," he grunted. "Here is another . . . and another. What manner bow—?"

*Waa* . . . The tone and tenor of the cub's cry changed pitch dramatically, climbing upward, becoming less of a hoarse wraul and more of a plaintive wail. *Waaahh* . . .

Uran leapt to his feet. "That's no Bear cub," he gritted, moving to the low cave mouth. Cautiously he peered in, then reached. "Aye, no cub this! Instead, it's a wee bairn!"

Uran turned to Beorc, and in his arms he cradled a squalling child, perhaps six or eight months old, male, unclothed.

Beorc dropped the tiny arrows and whipped off his cloak, handing it to Uran to wrap the baby in. "You've good lungs, my wee Manchild," said Uran above the yowling as he enfolded the bairn in cloth.

Beorc squatted down and looked into the enshadowed cave, finding that it was but a shallow hollow. "No cub at all. No place for one to hide."

While Uran gently rocked the baby and rumbled a wordless tune, Beorc examined the slain Bears, then studied the ground up slope and down, carefully reading what he could from the tracks.

When he returned, the child was asleep. Uran continued to rock the baby. "Well?"

Beorc took up the tiny arrows. "All these Bears, they are boar Bears. Not a sow among them. And for boars to travel together . . . well, it's—it's unnatural!

"The tracks tell that they came downhill from the col above, four boar Bears and a cub! D'y' hear me, Uran? I said that boars, *boars*, came with a cub! And that's not all: there were foxes—three, maybe four—and the overlap of prints tell that they walked among the Bears!

"The signs say the Rutcha lay in ambush. When they attacked, the cub took to the cave, and the boars stood before it.

"Whether the Wrg were slain by the Bears"—Beorc held up the tiny arrows—"or by these, I cannot say, for Adon's Ban destroyed the evidence of such.

"That Rutcha would lay in ambush to slaughter Bears is not surprising, for Foul Folk revel in such butchery. Yet,

Uran, I ask you this: Why would boars travel together? Why would they tolerate a cub? Why were foxes among Bears? Who cast these arrows? And where is the cub?

"The only answers that I can think of are . . . are . . ."

Uran spoke. "Are perilously strange, aye. Heed, Beorc: as to your first four questions, I deem the foxes were among the Bears, for they were ridden by those who cast the arrows: the Hidden Ones—in this case, the Fox Riders. And that's what I thought I saw on the back of the fox as we climbed—a tiny person astride—a Fox Rider." Beorc's eyes widened at Uran's words, for even though they followed his own line of reasoning, conjecture was one thing—confirmation, another. Still, he remained silent.

After a moment Uran added, "It is my thought that the Bears and Fox Riders were escorting the cub, taking him to a place of safety, or to his kindred."

Beorc looked over his shoulder and up slope, as if he suspected that even now eyes were upon them. Seeing nothing untoward, he turned back to Uran. "And the cub?"

Uran sighed, looking down at the sleeping babe. "Beorc, I deem I hold the cub."

While they waited, Beorc stirred through all the ashes of the slain Foul Folk, gathering diminutive arrows, taking care not to touch the dark smear on the minuscule points. He laid the tiny shafts out side by side on a flat rock. "They'll want them back, I shouldn't wonder."

The Sun climbed up the sky, and Uran sat in the shade of a great boulder and rocked the sleeping babe. "He is exhausted, Beorc."

"Mayhap he travelled through the night."

Uran nodded.

Beorc came and sat beside his brother. "If the Fox Riders are proportioned to their stature as we, then by the length of the arrows, those Folk stand no taller than my foot is long."

Uran grinned. "A small Folk, but a large foot."

Beorc barked a loud laugh, quickly stifled, for he would not wake the babe. The sleeping child stirred but slept on.

At last Uran stood. "They are not coming for him."

Beorc looked up at his elder brother. "You would take him with us?"

"Aye, we can't leave him here."

Beorc nodded, gaining his feet. "Then let us go. And a surprise we'll be bringing to the camp."

Uran looked down at the babe. "Only temporarily, Beorc. I'm of a mind to surprise Niki."

Beorc's eyes flew wide. "You'd take this wee one to your wife?"

"Aye."

Shaking his head in bemusement, Beorc scrambled down from the flat and reached back up, and Uran handed the child to him, then descended after. And in this manner, down the slope they went, when necessary, passing the babe from hand to hand as they clambered down each ledge.

Now and again they would scan back up slope, and when they had gone a furlong or so, Beorc called in a low voice, "Hola, brother. Look and see."

Carefully cradling the babe, Uran turned about.

High above on the brim of the flat stood *five* foxes gazing down.

"Given to us by the Hidden Ones, you say."

"Aye, Niki," responded Uran. "That they did."

Niki bent over the child, spooning warm milk into his mouth.

"Followed us all the way, they did," chimed in Beorc. "Flitting through the woods, through the shadows of the Great Greenhall. Every day for five days . . . till we got here, till we came to the village."

"Well, what did you feed him for those same five days?"

"Well-chewed rations, love," answered Uran. "I took my lessons from the Wolves."

"Don't forget the berry juice," added Beorc.

Niki glanced up at the Men. "No wonder his stomach is upset. But I judge there was little else you could do.

"I don't suppose he has a name."

*Cub!* both Men said simultaneously.

"*Cub?* What kind of a name is that for a child?" Niki spooned more milk into the baby's mouth, the tot grinning from ear to ear at the Woman's face, reaching out to clutch at her russet hair. Niki smiled back, and the babe laughed, his amber eyes sparkling.

"He shall be named Urus, after your grandsire."

And that settled that, though Beorc and Uran often called him Cub.

Urus was a happy child, and he prospered under Niki's care and Uran's guidance. He developed swiftly, seeming to go from crawling to walking overnight, and likewise from babbling to talking, though when Niki and Uran looked back on it, they realized that winter had come and gone. Another year passed and another, and Urus ran through the forest with the other children, playing in the leafy galleries of the Great Greenhall, the child tall for what they guessed to be his age.

When Urus was perhaps four, there came a clamoring from the glade center, and the boy threw open the shutter and looked out. Waddling across the sunlit sward came a great Bear. Calmly in its path stood Niki, water pail in hand, the Woman still.

Niki was unafraid, for Bears and Baeron had long held each other in respect, but she was astonished when a cub came bolting from her cottage, squalling, thundering across the grass toward the boar. The boar raised his muzzle and snuffled the air, then sat back on its haunches and waited, and was bowled over by the younker Bear. There was much shrill growling by the cub, matched by deep rumbles from the boar, and they rolled about on the sward in mock battle.

Niki laughed to see such, for she had never witnessed a boar Bear playing with a cub. In fact, it was well established that boars would at times harm cubs, were it not for the sows' fierce protection. Yet here were two who proved to be the exception to the rule.

The cub yawled and the boar roared, and the entire village came to see. But at last the boar Bear stood and shook himself, as did the cub, and together they ambled off into the woods.

"What do you mean it was Urus?" Niki's question seemed to fill up the entire cottage.

Uran sloshed oil into the lantern. "Love, there's some that I never told you about the day we found Urus." He stoppered up the jug and set it aside.

"What? What didn't you say?"

Uran scrabbled under the bed and withdrew his morning star. "I've no time to tell you now. I've got to find him. Night's coming on, and he's out there, mayhap with a boar, mayhap alone." He hooked the weapon to his belt.

"I'm coming with you."

"Oh, Niki, there's a large boar involved, and should he go mad—"

"I said, I'm coming with you!" Her tone brooked no refusal.

Niki caught up another lantern and threw her cloak about her shoulders.

Uran took a deep breath and let it out. "Well then, let's be off."

Niki following, Uran stepped to the door and flung it open.

And before him was Urus, the lad just then stepping onto the stoop, returning home. "Where we going, Da?" piped up the child.

Her chair creaking gently, Niki rocked back and forth, holding Urus, the younker asleep. "I don't care if he is a Cursed One, still I love him. Even though he is not of our blood, he will always be my baby, my child . . . our child.

"Oh, Uran, even had you told me this the first day you brought him home, still would we have kept him. We had no children of our own, though Adon knows we have tried"—Niki smiled—"and still do."

In the flickering candlelight she gazed down at Urus's face, brushing a lock of his reddish hair back from his forehead. "Cursed or no, we would have kept him, for he is precious. He is precious."

Uran whittled on a block of wood. "They wanted him raised where he could learn the ways of Man."

Niki looked up at her husband.

"The Hidden Ones, I mean," continued Uran. "They were bringing him here . . . well, mayhap not *here* exactly, but to the Baeron, I'm certain."

Niki said nought, the rocker creaking, the knife whittling. After a moment—"I wonder who his sire and dam are."

"Most likely they are dead," answered Uran. "Else they'd raise him on their own."

The Man stood and placed his carving on the mantel. It was the likeness of a Bear. "Let us to bed, love."

As they lay Urus in his bunk, Uran advanced one more opinion. "The Wrg are thick as thieves in the Grimwall. Why? None knows. Yet I think that they are responsible for making this lad of ours an orphan. What happened and why . . . well, like as not we'll never know. One thing is clear, though, this lad is an orphan no more."

They blew out the candle and the silver Moon shone in the open window, lighting their way to bed.

Years fled, and Urus grew toward his Manhood, and when he came into his fullness, he towered some six feet, eight inches high and massed nearly twenty-two stone.

The fact that he occasionally transformed into a huge Bear did not seem to cause great distress among the Baeron. In truth, when Urus took up border duty in the Grimwalls, his ability became an asset. Wrg had continued to gather in the mountains and several skirmishes had been fought at night, and Urus as a Man was a mighty fighter, but as a Bear he was devastating. And though often wounded, weapons did not seem to do him lasting harm, and his healing rate was phenomenal. It was told by the loremasters that only silver pure could do his kind permanent harm—that or starsilver.

His prowess was sung of often at the Gathering, the annual Mid-Year's Day convocation of the Baeron in The Clearing in the Greatwood to the south of the Great Greenhall Forest. There it was that tales of heroism were told, and songs of valor sung, and among these were stories of the Man who at times became a Bear.

Still, he *was* cursed and knew it, and though he longed to love a Woman and to be loved in return, he held himself aloof from Women and made no advances, for he did not wish to pass his curse onto a child. And perhaps because of his aloofness, or perhaps because of his curse, Women made no advances to him.

His foster parents, Niki and Uran, had never withheld from him that he was a foundling, not that it lessened their love for him or his love in return. But even though he was happy, Urus had always wondered at his origins, and resolved to one day find his roots somewhere in the vastness of the Grimwalls above Delon Island. Yet time and again, skirmishes against the Wrg prevented him from going on this quest, for his fighting skill was needed along the borders.

He had been found in 4E1911, and thirty years later, in 4E1941, he was hailed as Chieftain by the Baeron of the Greenhall nigh Delon. Oh, he was not Chieftain over all the Baeron—Rau in the Greatwood held that honor—but Urus was made leader of his clan. When the Council announced their decision, Niki, her russet hair showing strands of grey, embraced and kissed him, saying. "Your father is likely to burst with pride." And Uran was indeed proud, and he hugged Urus a fierce bear hug and slapped him on the back, and that night Uran and Uncle Beorc, both now in their fifties, drank themselves sick.

Well and good did Urus lead the clan for the next three years. And then, one night . . .

Urus and his Warband of thirty had come upon the survivors camped at Haven, the long-abandoned way station on the Landover Road near the eastern rise up to the Crestan Pass, the stopover point nought but crumbling ruins. These people had been part of a waggon train attempting to cross over the pass in early winter. But snow had come, and the train had turned back, only to be ambushed by Wrg. Several had managed to hold out until sunrise, but Men and animals alike had been slaughtered, and now Women and children and the wounded were all that were left. The survivors had come back down on foot as far as these ruins, but as night drew nigh, they feared another attack.

Urus and his Men tended the wounded as best they could, then set pickets about the perimeter of the camp as it began to snow.

Four hours or so after sunset—"Who goes!"

"I need help! I need help! They've got my wife!" A Man staggered out from the dark, out from the swirling snow. He was tall and gaunt and dressed in black, with black hair and a thin, straight nose and long-fingered hands. His skin was stark white against his ebon cloak, and his eyes were yellow.

The guard led the Man to the Baeron campfire. "He came in from the southwest, Urus."

"Urus, are you the leader of these Men?"

Urus nodded.

Other Baeron had gathered 'round, and the Man jumped up onto the remains of a hut floor, the ruins acting as a platform. "I need help," he appealed. "The *Drik*, they have my wife."

"*Drik?*" rumbled Urus. "Do you mean the Wrg, the Foul Folk?"

"Yes, yes, that's right, the Foul Folk. Six or eight. They attacked my steading. I fled. I thought she was behind me, but when I looked, they had her. I trailed them. They're in a cave not far from here. Come with me. Oh, Urus, bring your Warband and come with me, or at least send some of your Men."

The hair on the back of Urus's neck stood up. *There's something wrong here, as if—*

"Hurry, before they do something awful."

Arag turned to Urus. "Send me, Urus. They killed my wife and I would take my revenge."

More Men surged forward.

"Wait!" called Urus. "We cannot leave the Women and children and the wounded unguarded.

"Man, give me your name."

"Béla," replied the yellow-eyed Man. "Oh, hurry."

"Béla, you say that there are six or eight Wrg in the cave?" At the Man's nod—"There are thirty of us. Arag, choose nine to go with you. The rest will stay to defend should the Wrg raiders come down from the pass. I will remain as well, for the raiders number many, and I would serve better here.

"And, Arag. Take care, for there may be more than just six or eight."

Arag nodded and chose nine of the volunteers. Within moments they were gone into the night, following Béla away from the camp and into the spinning snow.

\*    \*    \*

The night passed without attack, and toward morning the snow stopped falling. Dawn came, and as the Baeron and members of the waggon train prepared to follow Landover Road to the Great Greenhall, Urus scanned the hills to the southwest. He saw nothing but empty white 'scape rolling up to the dark Grimwalls in the distance.

"Where be Arag?" he growled, but there was no answer.

Raff came to his side. "They are ready to march, Urus."

Urus sighed and turned away from the mountains. "Then, let us away. Arag and the Men are seasoned warriors and can follow when they will. But if aught has happened . . ."

Raff waited, but Urus did not complete the thought. "If aught has happened," concluded Raff, "then Waroo has seen to it that we cannot track Arag and the others."

"Aye," agreed Urus, knowing that Raff spoke of the hearth tale White Bear who claws his way over the mountains to bring snow unto the lands below. And now Urus looked across the unmarked 'scape, pristine white under the morning Sun. "Waroo has indeed seen to that. "

And so they set off, escorting the survivors to the Greenhall, Urus's heart filled with anxiety.

*"Drik?"* Uran turned to his son. "Why, I believe that is the Wrg word for Rutcha."

"Wrg word? You mean Slûk?"

"Aye, the Slûk tongue."

"Damn!" Urus slammed a clenched fist into his palm. "Damn! I *knew* there was something wrong! The stranger, Béla, if that's his true name, *he* said *Drik!*"

"If he did, son, Adon knows what he might be up to. The Men who went with him mayhap are at grave risk. I think we had better gather up a party and go looking." At Urus's nod, Uran added, "I'll get Beorc."

Two days later, again Urus led a Warband to the sparse ruins of Haven. On the march they had seen no sign of Arag and the nine others. It had been five days since Urus was here last—it had taken three days to escort the survivors unto shelter in the Great Greenhall, and but two days to return—

five days in which disaster could have befallen those who had followed Béla into the night.

"From the Grimwall he came, did Béla," rumbled Urus, "there, to the southwest, and though it may have been a ploy, southwest shall we search."

Urus divided the Warband into four groups of ten each, and they fanned out 'cross the open wold. The rest of the day they searched as well as all of the next. But mid-afternoon of the following day, the group led by Beorc came upon Regar, one of the nine, fleeing through a stand of woods, running away from the dark stone of the nearby mountains. The young Man fell into his rescuers' arms and wept uncontrollably.

Beorc sounded his ram's horn, and within the hour all had gathered, and Regar, his lips drawn thin with distress, his voice choked with fear, told his horrid tale to Urus.

". . . into the caves we went, and Stoke managed to drug us all. How? A vapor, I think, though it could have been otherwise. When we awoke, we were in chains, to be used in his—his—" Regar burst into tears.

Uran clutched Regar unto himself, shushing the Man as he would a child.

"His *experiments*," supplied Beorc, his eyes hard as flint, repeating what he had gotten from Regar earlier. "To be used in his *experiments*."

Urus ground his teeth in suppressed rage. "This Stoke, he is Béla?"

Regar was in no condition to answer, so again Beorc spoke for him. "Aye, lad. He's one and the same."

Pushing away from Uran, Regar turned to Urus and gritted, "Aye, Baron Stoke he names himself. And, yes, he performed his *experiments* on the others."—Regar's eyes went wide in remembered horror. "Urus, the Baron, he . . ."—Regar clenched his fists so tightly that blood seeped where his nails cut into his palms, and the timbre of his voice steadied— ". . . he started at Arag's feet and began flaying him, *skinning him alive!* while all the rest of us watched and tried to cover our ears to shut out the shrieks.

"But that's not all, Urus, that's not all . . . for after he had flensed him, flensed Arag, then he *impaled* him, with this— this . . . Arag was not dead. He was not dead. He was not—"

Again Regar broke.

Urus glanced at the sky and at Regar's trail leading back to the Grimwall. "Before this night is done, Regar, we shall avenge Arag." Urus motioned to Kael and Bora, and the two forward scouts nodded and shouldered their packs and took up their spears, readying themselves for backtracking.

Urus turned to Beorc. "What of the others?"

"Like Arag, all dead."

Urus gripped Regar by the shoulders; the young Man stood withdrawn into himself. "Regar, we are going back into those caverns, all forty-one of us if you'll come. If you do not wish to go, I will understand. We will all understand. I will send some Men with you if you wish to leave this place forever, if you wish to return unto the safety of the Greenhall. But if your heart cries out for vengeance . . ."

Regar raised his head and looked Urus in the eye. Fear dwelled deep within Regar's gaze, yet rage was held therein as well. "He must die, my Chieftain. He must die."

Regar held up his hands. His wrists were raw and bleeding where shackles had been. "I managed to kill my jailor, him with the key. And I escaped, the last one alive. I do not easily go back into that Hèlhole, nor readily, but Stoke must die." Regar raised his right hand before his face and clenched his fist so hard that it shook, and his voice grated out, "Stoke. Must. Die."

"Get this Man a weapon," called Urus, and three warriors stepped forward to offer up one of their own.

Day was almost done when they came to the cavern, the short winter twilight on the land. "There it be, Urus," said Bora, one of the forward scouts, his voice low.

"Then let us go," gritted Urus, "while all are yet within."

Into the caves they went, to find the Wrg stirring. Mighty was the battle, forty-one Baeron 'gainst more than twice that many Foul Folk. Spear and mace, morning star and axe, all clashed with scimitar and cudgel, iron bar and tulwar. Too, fang and claw slashed and tore as a raging Bear faced Rutcha and Vulg alike and rent them asunder. Black blood and red stained the walls and slickened the floor, and when it was over, twelve Baeron lay dead, one of whom was Regar. Of the Foul Folk, eighty-nine Rutch and four Vulgs had been slain.

But of Baron Stoke there was not a sign. He had fled into the night.

After binding their wounds, the surviving Baeron found the flayed corpses of the nine. They were laid out on slabs; each had been impaled, their abdomens burst open.

Weeping, the Men took Stoke's victims and those slain in battle, and they built a great funeral pyre, the flames roaring up into the sky. And that night, heeding no protest, Urus stepped down from the Chieftainship of the clan, turning the responsibility over to his father, Uran, until the Council decreed otherwise.

"Sire, I pledge myself to ridding the world of this evil monster who calls himself Baron Stoke. Tell my mother that I shall think of her often."

Urus would not allow any to accompany him, for he held himself responsible for the death of all who had fallen, both to Stoke's madness and to the Wrg. And that night he disappeared, and seven years were to pass ere he would return unto the Great Greenhall . . .

As to the Baeron, the Council made Uran Chieftain of the Clan, though this time there was no celebration by he and Beorc.

The following year, word of the slaughter spread throughout the Great Greenhall, a forest named Darda Erynian by the Elves who lived therein. And one of those who heard of Stoke's monstrous deeds was a golden-haired Elf named Talar, a Lian Guardian who felt it his duty to run the Baron to earth. And so he dispatched a scroll unto his golden-haired sister, Riatha, in Arden Vale, telling her of his quest.

Talar began his search in the late spring of 4E1945, six months after the night of slaughter.

Baron Stoke had fled that bloody night in November of 4E1944. Where? None knew. For seven years Urus followed every rumor: into Riamon, into Gûnar, into Jord, and finally in the winter of '51, into Aven, into the Grimwalls north of Nordlake, then south and east to Vulfcwmb.

There in Vulfcwmb, in the Red Weasel tavern, he met an Elfess named Riatha and a Waldan named Tomlin, also on

the track of Baron Stoke. Riatha's brother had been slain by
Stoke, and that's why she sought him. As to the Waldan,
Tomlin's sire and dam and his dammsel, Petal, and Petal's
sire, had all been kidnapped that very night by Stoke's lackeys. And those in the tavern knew of Stoke's whereabouts,
for he had returned to his old haunts to once again terrorize
the region.

At last Urus knew that he drew nigh the monster.

Tomlin, Riatha, and Urus banded together, and the next
night came upon Stoke's holt, a black bartizan high on the
face of a sheer cliff.

But again Stoke escaped, and Urus was nigh slain. Yet they
discovered that Stoke was a shapechanger—into Vulg and
flying creature could he shift his shape. Like Urus, Stoke,
too, was a Cursed One, though unlike Urus, Stoke was truly
a monster.

They had managed to free Petal, and she joined their quest,
for she had witnessed the deaths of her sire and of Tomlin's
sire and dam. Stoke had flensed them and impaled them as
well.

Two years passed, and in 4E1953 again they followed a
rumor, this time to Vancha.

In Dreadholt nigh Daemon's Crag they cornered Stoke, and
believed that he perished in a raging fire.

This time it was Riatha who nearly died, and Urus discovered that he was by now hopelessly in love with her; but
she was Elven and immortal, and he was Cursed and a Man,
and so he kept his feelings unto himself, returning to the
Great Greenhall without speaking his heart to her.

Years fled, and in this time Urus's father, Uran, died, and
three years later, Niki passed away. After his mother was
gone, Urus moved south to the Greatwood, and there he
tutored the sons of Kings, teaching them the ways of the
Baeron, the ways of nature.

Among his princely pupils, the very last was Aurion, son
of Galvane, High King of all Mithgar. And even as he tutored
the Prince, chilling rumors came from Aralan of disappearances, like those of Stoke's day.

And so, Urus sent messages to Riatha and Tomlin and Petal, for all were pledged to run Stoke to earth and slay him, and if there was a chance that he had survived the fire . . .

Tomlin and Petal and Riatha all came at his summons, and Urus felt his heart clench in his breast at the sight of Riatha. But still he said nought, and they prepared to go.

Prince Aurion, but ten at the time, came unto the four of them and pledged that the High King himself would aid them if need be. The four accepted the warranty, saying that perhaps there would come a day when they would redeem the pledge.

North of Inge across the Grimwall above the Great North Glacier, again they discovered Baron Stoke, in a monastery. And this time Urus bore him down into the depths of a crevasse, a crevasse that slammed shut on both Cursed Ones.

And a thousand years passed. . . .

And in the intervening years:

Rael in Arden had spoken a prophecy, one concerning Last-born Firstborns, the Eye of the Hunter, the Light of the Bear, and the rise of friend and foe.

The Winter War came and went, revealing why Foul Folk had gathered in the Grimwall, for they had done so at the behest of Modru, who once again was defeated.

Some thirty-eight years after the Winter War, Tomlin had died, having reached the age of one hundred twenty-nine. Seven years later, Petal passed away at one hundred thirty-three.

The War of Kraggen-cor was fought, and the Dwarves regained their ancient homeland.

Dragons wakened from their thousand-year sleep.

Aravan, in his quest to recover the Dawn Sword and to avenge Galarun's death, had come unto Riatha and pledged his aid in fulfilling the prophecy, for he would see for himself this yellow-eyed Man who was called Baron Stoke . . . if he indeed rose from the dead.

And Gwylly and Faeril came, uncanny in their resemblance to Tomlin and Petal.

And the Great North Glacier at last disgorged its prisoners. Resurrection.

How had Urus survived? He did not know. Perhaps it was the cold; perhaps it was his Curse, a Curse to be a Bear.

Yet Stoke had survived as well, and had escaped unto a bolt-hole. But Riatha had conceived a plan to come upon him in the caverns shortly after sunrise in the morn, some thirteen or fourteen hours hence.

Outside the wind moaned, now driving snow before it. Urus awakened. Momentarily he was disoriented. And then he remembered: they were in a cave high on the sheer wall above the pit. Gwylly and Faeril sat at the back whispering; Aravan lay at the mouth, peering out; and across from Urus, her silver eyes glistering in the shadows, there sat his love. . . .

Aravan slid backwards a few inches. "Night has fallen," he hissed, "and the *Rûpt* begin to stir."

# CHAPTER 21

# Flight

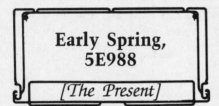

**Early Spring, 5E988**

*[The Present]*

Snow swirled before the mouth of the cave, borne on a twisting groan of air. Still Aravan lay on his stomach and peered out at the pit floor some two hundred fifty feet below. Now and again the unstable earth trembled as night came full upon the land.

"They gather in darkness," Aravan hissed at last, his Elven sight making out silhouettes moving across the snow.

Gwylly felt his heart hammering, and he reached out to take Faeril's hand, finding her reaching for his.

Urus shifted his bulk and drew up his legs and sat with his hands draped over his knees. Except to turn her head toward Aravan, Riatha moved not. "In darkness?" she asked, her voice low. "Are there no torches among them?"

"Nay," responded Aravan.

Puzzled by this new tactic, Riatha looked at Faeril, seeking answers, but in the darkness of the cave neither could see the face of the other. Even so, Faeril said, "Perhaps they do something in secret."

The wind moaned, and snow raced past, thickening. Above the sob Aravan's voice hissed again. "They mill about, as if waiting."

He sucked air in between his clenched teeth. "And in the bolt-hole . . . someone, some*thing*—"

*Skraww!* A harsh skreigh split the air.

Gwylly's heart jumped into his throat, and Faeril tightly clutched his hand. Riatha's eyes flew wide, and she looked at Urus. *"Stoke!"* he gritted, scrambling toward the entrance, Riatha following, Gwylly and Faeril coming after.

And opposite, issuing forth from the bolt-hole, a large leathery-winged black *thing* flapped out and upward, rising through the moaning wind and hurtling snow.

*Skraww!*

Like some creature from the time ere Men walked the world, out and up it came, wings flapping, its long, fang-filled beak wide and shrieking, its eyes glaring yellow, clawed feet trailing after.

Only Aravan saw it well, the rest arriving too late to see aught but a dark blot rising up through the storm. Even so, they saw its span—twenty feet from wing tip to tip, fifteen from beak to whiplike tail—as southward arrowed the hideous creature.

*Skraww!*

Below, Rūcks and Hlōks and Vulgs turned and streamed southward, too, into the canyon slot.

"They're leaving," said Aravan.

Riatha started to scramble out, but Aravan caught her by the arm—"Dara! Wait! Thou will betray us to the *Rûpt!*"—holding her back.

"Stoke!" she spat. "He's getting away!"

Aravan did not release her. "What would thou do, Riatha? We have not the weaponry to bring him down. Were Gwylly or Faeril or both on the rim above, mayhap they could achieve such . . . but they are not! And we must climb to come to the rim. He will be gone by then.

"Nay, Dara, reveal us not to the *Spaunen*. Instead we must follow in secret. Else he will know he is pursued."

Distressed, the Elfess looked at Urus. The Man's teeth ground in suppressed rage. "Aravan is right, Riatha. Aravan is right, damn it!"

The Elfess burst into tears of frustration. "Mayhap I could have slain him yester had I only tried. And now he is fled."

Urus reached out to her, but she would not be comforted. And still the wind moaned past and snow swirled and tremors shook the land.

Aravan peered outward, seeing nought in the pit below; the arena was obscured by the white fling. "Let us be gone. I will climb to the verge and lower a rope."

Out and upward he went, free climbing the stone, a line fixed to his harness and payed out by Urus in case the Elf fell, the wind battering at him as if trying to dislodge an intruder in its domain. A time passed, but at last a signal came from above and another line snaked downward, lashing about in the blow. Urus leaned out and after two attempts managed to catch it.

One by one they sent up their packs, Aravan hauling them upward. When that was done, with the Baeran anchoring, Faeril climbed first, Gwylly after, then Riatha. And the angry wind howled, yet could not stop their ascent. Last came Urus, the huge Man clambering up and over the brim.

Aravan coiled the lines as the others shouldered their gear. When he had buckled his own pack in place, southward they headed, into the teeth of the growing storm. "We must hurry," urged Riatha, "else their tracks will be buried."

Pressing against the wind, the snow pelting into their faces, along the western rim of the canyon they fared, the brow slowly descending to meet the wide vale beyond. Gwylly carried a shuttered lantern, the hood tightly closed to prevent detection from afar, yet enough light leaked out to show the way.

Soon they came to the valley floor and, in the lead, Aravan called a halt, and he bent down to examine the trail in the snow. Gwylly cracked the hood of the lantern, illuminating the track, a track even now being eroded by the wind and covered over by the new fall. The Elf stood. "We must make haste, else we will lose their trail under the storm. Yet we must not come upon them until day arrives, for they travel in a force that will overwhelm us with their very numbers."

Southward they went, three hours or more, the Warrows setting the pace. Wind-borne snow spun down, thicker by the moment, as if to bury these interlopers.

Burdened as they were with their packs, a few minutes every hour they stopped to rest, for they could not keep this pace endlessly. And so they sheltered in thickets or against rock outcroppings when they could find them in the thickly swirling snow, trying to evade the wind. As they rested, Faeril sought the elusive answer to a question that had been tugging at the back of her mind, an answer that she thought she should know. *Why had the maggot-folk gone forth in darkness, issuing out from their splits and cracks without torches to guide them?*

But each time ere she came to any conclusion, Aravan called for them to take up the march, and once again the exigencies of the trek drove the search for the loose thread from her mind.

Again Aravan signalled for a resumption of the march, for the tracks they followed were now but dimples in the snow, and if they did not begin, the trail would be lost. Faeril wrapped her scarf tighter and pulled the drawstrings of her hood to shield her face from the stinging white, and along with the others, shouldered her goods and set out once more into the buffeting wind.

Onward they hurried, Gwylly and Faeril walking on either side of Aravan as he tracked the diminishing spoor. *Why did they go without torches?*

*Why . . . ?*

Suddenly Faeril remembered the thought that was lost; she remembered what she had said about the maggot-folk's lack of torches just before the *thing* flew up and out from the pit: *"Perhaps they do something in secret."* That *was what I had just said, ". . . something in secret."*

*What would they do in secret? Escape? Do they lay a trap for us ahead? An ambush? If so, then they know we follow . . . or suspect so. And if they suspect such—*

"Wait!" exclaimed Faeril, stopping, reaching out to stay Aravan, too. All five halted. Urgency filled the damman's voice. "Aravan, how many maggot-folk left the canyon? Did you count them? Did you count them, Aravan?"

"Nay, Faeril, I did not. That black flying thing . . . it—it took my mind from doing so."

Faeril's heart pounded in her breast. "They did not bear torches. Do you hear me? They did not bear torches."

By the faint light of their hooded lantern, Gwylly peered through the blowing snow at Faeril, her face hidden in the blackness of her hood. "And the meaning . . . ?"

Faeril's voice was grim. "If Stoke plans something in secret, he would issue forth in darkness, where spies such as we could not count the strength he takes with him. And if some had been left behind—"

Urus's growl cut through the shadows. "—then they were held back to see if Stoke is followed, and if so, he would want to know who is it that pursues and how many."

"Thou are not saying that we must wait to see if we are followed, are thee?" Riatha's voice was filled with distress. "If so, then surely Stoke will escape us."

Ere Faeril or Urus could answer, Gwylly spoke: "What if they all went? I mean, there may be none left behind. If so—"

"Gwylly is right," interjected Faeril. "To assume that Spawn follow us doesn't make it so. They may simply have wanted to slip away in secret. There may have been none waiting while the others left, waiting to follow later and see if anyone trails Stoke. There were twenty-seven maggot-folk and thirteen Vulgs, last I knew—"

Riatha interrupted. "There are but seven Vulgs now—two fell to their deaths in pursuit of me, and four others disappeared."

"Oi!" exclaimed Gwylly. "Those four that disappeared— we killed four at the monastery."

"If the four ye slew are the missing ones, then that would account for all," responded Riatha. "Of the thirteen Vulgs, seven are left. And of the twenty-seven Rûpt, Faeril, thy count still holds true."

The damman turned to Aravan. "Can you count the tracks and say how many we follow?"

Gwylly opened the hood of the lantern slightly, illuminating the trail, but at a gesture from Aravan he closed it again.

"Nay," answered the Elf. "The trace is now too faint to do so. There could be that many ahead, but I cannot say. Thou may have the right of it, Faeril—all may be ahead, or only part: even as we follow Stoke, Rûpt may follow us."

Urus growled in frustration. "Regardless as to whether some follow or none, we must go onward, for as Riatha says, Stoke will escape if we do not. But this I say: we must be ever vigilant for those who may come at our backs, as well as guard against traps laid by the foe ahead."

Again they started southward, trekking onward in the blowing wind and the ever thickening snow, the trail becoming fainter and fainter as they went. They struggled down a twisting valley, wending among unseen stone massifs rearing upward, hidden by the blizzard. Earlier, the choice had been simple: follow the plain track. Yet now the trail grew perilously dim, and at times disappeared completely. And they knew that Stoke and his lackeys could make for unrevealed canyons and hidden vales split off to left and right, or could go up slopes to either side where lay storm-concealed cols leading to other vales. And so, whenever the trail vanished completely, all would search for trace of the spoor, casting about for which way the faint dimpled track ran, finding it eventually, and going forward.

Finally the trail disappeared, and they could not find any traces at all. Long they searched by lantern light without success. At last Urus growled, "We will lose them altogether lest we change our tactics."

The Baeran began shedding his pack. "Here, Aravan, you and Riatha carry this between you. I am going ahead. Follow the tracks I shall leave in my wake."

Before any could object, a dark shimmering overcame Urus, enveloping him. His shape changed, his form dropping down on all fours, growing huge, with long black claws and ivory fangs and coarse reddish fur grizzled at the tips. And where Urus had been stood a great Bear!

Gwylly's heart was hammering, and Faeril clutched his arm as if he were an oak in a storm. Aravan stood stock still, as if made of stone, and Riatha's eyes glittered in the night.

The great Bear shoved his nose into the snow and snuffled until he found faint traces of Spawn. Moving forward, again he burrowed his muzzle and breathed. Then he looked over his shoulder at the four behind, and with a deep *Wuff!* he turned and lumbered away, moving at a pace that none of those left behind could match, burdened as they were.

Onward trekked the four, now following the spoor of the Bear, fresh tracks in the snow. Even so, the storm intensified, and this trail, too, began to dwindle under the onslaught, yet for the moment it was clear enough to follow.

An hour passed and then another, and on they marched, occasionally resting awhile, by faint lantern light the snow spinning about them as a whirling wall of white. Now they could see no more that a stride or two ahead, and their progress slowed to a virtual crawl. "Stay close," cautioned Aravan, "else we will need rope ourselves together."

Still they wound their way among the unseen mountains, with canyons and valleys and cols concealed to either side. Often they came to where the Bear had cast about for traces of those he followed, at times the pattern of his search showing that it took a long while to relocate the spoor. Yet always he found it, or so they deemed, and they trailed after.

Following another short rest they resumed the trek, Riatha and Aravan in the lead, carrying Urus's pack between them, breaking trail in the deepening snow, Gwylly and Faeril coming after. Of a sudden Aravan held up a hand. "Wait! The blue stone grows cold. *Rûpt* or other such are near."

"Which way?" asked Gwylly, peering about, seeing nothing but the whirling blast.

"I know not," responded Aravan. "The stone only tells me whether far or near, and these draw nigh."

Riatha and Aravan put their common burden down.

"Let us take refuge," said Gwylly.

"Where?" asked Faeril. "I can see nought."

As Riatha turned to answer the damman, her eyes flew wide and she shouted, " 'Ware!" the Elfess wrenching her sword from its shoulder harness.

Aravan whirled about.

Faeril heard a horrendous snarl, and she started to turn, but someone or something crashed into her from behind, slamming her facedown into the snow, smashing atop her.

After the transformation, when he was no longer Urus, the Bear snuffled the snow and caught the acrid traces of *Urwa*, the Bear's name for Foul Folk. He turned to the two-legs behind, those companions he befriended, and called out for them to follow: *Wuff!*

Deep within this savage creature, reason prevailed, but barely, for the Bear was driven by other urges, other needs from those of the Man he once had been. He was now a thing of the wilds—not some Man in the shape of a Bear, but a Bear cunning beyond all others, a Bear who at times had strange un-Bearlike urges, urges and motives akin to those of Man, perhaps even akin to those of a particular Man, a Man named Urus. Yet the Bear who once was Urus only occasionally thought along those paths, and although he might again *become* Urus, there was no guarantee he would. And *that* was a danger that the Bear and Urus both lived with: Urus might never again become the Bear; the Bear might never again become Urus. The Man Urus was aware of this danger; the Bear was not.

But now the Bear followed *Urwa*, hated foe of all Bearkind, and he would not be swayed from this task. And so, down the track he lumbered, knowing that the others followed in his steps. How he knew this was beyond his ken—but he did not question, for he simply *knew.*

Miles he went, and miles more, the scent of the *Urwa* growing fainter. Often he had to root about for the spoor, and at times he raged in anger, roaring loudly in challenge, slashing the snow with his claws. But he found dim trace of the scent again and again, though it was now all but gone.

The pelting white all about him grew thicker until he could not see more than a Bearpace or two, and it tried to hide the *Urwa*. It would fail.

The blowing air tried to stop his walk. It would fail. He *knew.*

The Bear had no concept of time, and little of distance, only knowing that light came, then dark, only knowing that something was near or far.

He lumbered far. He *knew* far.

He lumbered until the white and the blowing air erased all *Urwa* spoor. He roared and bit the white, clawed the white, bit the blow, clawed the blow. The scent of the *Urwa* was gone.

The Bear sat on a hillock, the last place he had smelled *Urwa.* Here he would wait until the two-legs came in his footsteps.

White howled about him. He waited.

White grew thinner. Howl grew less. He waited.

The blow stopped pushing and just breathed little. He waited.

The white stopped. Light would come. He *knew*.

Light did come. The two-legs did not come. Something was wrong. He *knew*.

He thought of Urus. . . .

And a dark shimmering came upon the beast, and swiftly it *changed*, altering, losing bulk, gaining form, and suddenly there in the deep snow sat a giant of a Man: Urus.

Urus stood and looked at the sky. Dawn had come. He remembered much of what the Bear had done, for Mankind has the capacity to do so, whereas Bearkind has much trouble envisioning the acts of Man.

Mountains loomed about, and from the knoll Urus could see five ways that Stoke and his minions might have gone, five ways they could have escaped.

And where were Riatha and Aravan, Gwylly and Faeril? Surely they could not have fallen that far behind.

The Sun rose.

Urus scanned up the vale until it twisted from sight. *Where are they?*

A sudden foreboding filled his heart, and he *knew* that ill had befallen his comrades. And Urus the Man roared his anger, wrath twisting his face beyond all recognition as he raised his clenched fists unto the sky and bellowed the name of the enemy—*"Stoke!"*

His shout flew out among the mountains, and the mountains hurled it back—

*Stoke! . . . Stoke! . . . stoke! . . . stoke! . . . stoke . . . stoke . . . toke . . . oke . . . o . . .*

# CHAPTER 22

# Stoke

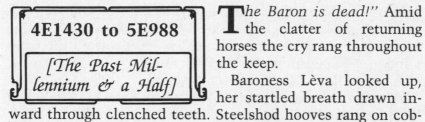

**4E1430 to 5E988**

*[The Past Millennium & a Half]*

"The Baron is dead!" Amid the clatter of returning horses the cry rang throughout the keep.

Baroness Lèva looked up, her startled breath drawn inward through clenched teeth. Steelshod hooves rang on cobbles, and the shouts of stable men and riders alike echoed in the bailey. Voices rose and fell, intelligence lost amid babble. *Boom! Doom!* The massive outer doors of the main keep boomed open, echoing throughout the great building like the knelling of doom, even in the remote chamber of the Baroness. Lèva set aside pen and parchment and composed herself, turning from the desk to face the doorway. Approaching footsteps rang upon flagstone, and she braced herself.

A knock sounded. "Enter," she called. A tall, rawboned Man dressed in begrimed hunting garb, a smear of dried blood high on one cheek, trod into the room, his hard stride bearing him across the stone floor. As he stopped before her and bowed slightly, his silver-shot dark hair fell 'round his bearded face. "Lady Stoke, Baron Marko is dead. Slain by a boar."

Lèva's heart leapt for joy—*At last!*—yet in no manner did she let such pleasure cross her thin-faced features. Instead, her voice was cold. "How, Kapitain? Through what dereliction of your duty did you let him die?"

Janok's eyes flew wide at this deliberate accusation, yet he swallowed his anger as he looked upon this ice-eyed, black-haired bitch. "The Baron ordered us to stand aside and he faced the boar alone. But the shaft on his spear snapped, and the beast slew him."

"I would have that spear, Kapitain. I would see the weapon which failed to serve. I would have it destroyed before my very eyes."

Janok bowed his head in assent.

"And the boar, what was its fate?"

"Dead, Baroness. Slain by my own spear as it gored the Baron."

Drifting up from the courtyard came the clatter of horses ridden out through the gate, and then hooves pounded off, galloping down the reach of the high mountain road leading away from the keep. Lèva turned her head toward the open window. "Kapitain, where do they ride?"

Janok smiled. "They ride for Aven and Vancha."

Her thin lips drawn white in fury, the Baroness wrenched her face toward the Kapitain. "I gave no orders!"

"Nay, madam, but I did. As Kapitain of the Keep, it was my duty. The Baron's brothers, his *heirs*, must be informed."

*"Out!"* Lèva spat. *"Out!"*

Again, Kapitain Janok bowed slightly. As he withdrew, a sardonic smile tugged at the corners of his mouth.

When he was gone, the Baroness swept the papers from the desk in rage. *Meddler Janok! Sending word to the brothers! Lenko now Baron lest I somehow ... somehow ... Oh, why did I not anticipate this and take measures?* Lèva leapt to her feet and paced the floor. *What to do? What to do?* She stopped before the fireplace and stood staring at the grating. *Calm down! Calm down! First things first: when the broken boar-spear is burned, the evidence will be destroyed.* Lèva knelt at the hearth and with her own hands she kindled a blaze. Flames leapt upward. *But what to do about Lenko?* Lèva crossed to the bell cord.

When the maidservant appeared, the Baroness stood at the open window. "Pick up that mess at the desk. Then send a runner to bring to me the foul weapon that failed to protect my husband. And tell Madam Orso to attend me here," she ordered, not shifting her glacial blue gaze from the surrounding massifs of the dark Skarpal Mountains.

"She wishes to bear a child within six months."

Pale, long-fingered hands reached up, lifting cowl back and away from a white face, the shaven head giving it an ugly, skull-like aspect. Yellow eyes stared forth from beneath hairless brows, sight shifting from mother to daughter and then to mother again.

Lèva felt her blood run chill, and she looked away from the gaunt Man, if indeed Man he was, summoned here by her mother, though how, Lèva could not say.

His voice was whispery, seeming somehow ancient, belying his youthful frame. "*Tji* need an heir to Baron Marko." His words formed not a question, but a statement of fact instead. "Else *tji* cannot control the estate, the lands, the wealth."

"Yes. We need an heir," answered Koska. The older Woman was somewhat shorter than her daughter but otherwise as narrow-faced and thin, her hair black as well, though her eyes were dark—black as a pit, said some.

Again his voice came soft. "To control the estate."

Koska shifted uncomfortably. "Yes. Yes. To control the estate."

"A male child," added Lèva, glancing at her mother but not at the Man, turning away from his yellow-eyed countenance. "In Garia, a girl child has no status as heir."

"What would *tji* give?"

"What do you ask?"

"For *tji*, Madam Orso, what *tji* have given before when summoning me."

Lèva shivered, as if spiders crawled across her flesh. Koska gritted her teeth, then jerked her head up and down once, no more, agreeing to his terms.

"For *aun* daughter, a place to stay as long as *jai* desire, and to be tutor to *mai* son."

Lèva gasped and turned to the Man, the dregs of her soul shuddering at the sight of him. "*Your* son? It will be *your* son?"

The Man nodded. "Baron Marko Stoke is without heir. His

brother Lenko is next in line of succession. None else but *jai* can give *tji* a child, a male child, to be born within six months. To go to a *Human* Man and get with child will depend on chance: first, that *tji* and he are fertile together, as *tji* and Marko were not; second, that if *tji* do bring forth a child from such a mating, that it be a male. Regardless, a child born of Humankind, even if it were a male, would come entirely too late to be the fruit of Marko's loins, and *tji* would lose the estate to Lenko in any case.

"Nay, if *tji* would have a male child arrive in such time that it could have been sired by Marko, it will need be *mehr* who sires it."

Lèva turned to her mother, fear in her eyes. Madam Orso slowly shook her head. "There is no other way, Lèva. You must truly be pregnant, for Lenko will bring his own personal physician to verify such. And the physician will be present at the birthing as well, for should the child be stillborn or female, then Lenko will be heir.

"You must submit to Ydral if you would keep the estate."

Revulsed, slowly Lèva nodded, agreeing.

Ydral smiled, then stepped forward and savagely rent the clothes from Lèva's body, hurling her naked to the stone floor, holding his long-fingered white hands over her mouth, muffling her shrieks.

. . . And when he was done with her, he turned to the waiting mother.

Lèva spent much of the next six months locked in her room, all sharp instruments forbidden. At night her yowls and yammerings filled the keep, and in the day she wept uncontrollably and babbled in unalloyed fear of something or someone hideous and grasping, but what or who it was none knew or would say. That she was pregnant was plain, and by the size of her it could be no other but Baron Marko's get, as Madam Orso claimed.

Baronet Lenko came from Aven, and among his entourage was his personal physician, who verified that in spite of her madness Lèva was indeed pregnant and would deliver in a few short weeks. Lenko was enraged, yet would stay for the birth.

On the other hand, the younger brother, Baronet Marik, remained in Vancha, not bothering to come to pay his respects to his dead sire, and instead sent word that if aught happened to Lenko, then and only then would he return to Garia.

And in the isolated chambers atop the east tower of the keep, a strange Man came to live: a Man who kept to himself and was never seen in the day, though sometimes at night he was espied stalking the shadowy halls and high ramparts of the keep, and some said they saw him coming down from the roofs above; a Man who always wore a cowl, and none ever saw his face; a Man who filled the rooms with scrolls and tomes and arcane instruments and peculiar animals; a Man who performed strange experiments in the nighttide, the animals shrieking in terror. Yet Madam Orso, mother to the Baroness, said that the Man was physician to Lèva and would assure a live birth and ordered that he not be disturbed, and so he was let be.

The weeks dragged by, the Baroness shrilling in the ebon dark, lamenting in the wan light, growing larger with child even as she sunk deeper into madness. She was attended by both Ydral and by Lenko's physician, Brün: Ydral at night, Brün in the day. And Ydral gave her concoctions to drink, some clear and sparkling, others dark and bubbling; while Brün tried to soothe her with herbs.

Lèva went into labor in the nighttide, and amid wild shrieks gave birth in the pit of the dark. It is said that the birth of the child was marked by two ominous events: an attending midwife ran screaming from the birthing chamber, babbling of demons and a mouth filled with fangs—she was never seen again; white-faced and shaking, Brün came forth from the room, and at the very moment he reported to Lenko that it was a male child, Brün fell stone dead. Whether none, one, or both of these tales are true, it is not now known. What *is* known, however, is that Lenko stalked into the chamber to see the child for himself. Lèva, pale and trembling and quite mad, cowered in the corner of the childbirth bed, the sheets drenched with sweat and birth water and blood. Madam Orso bore a cup of liquid to her gibbering daughter. Hooded Ydral held the child, wrapped in soft blankets, and as Lenko approached, Ydral passed an arcane hand over the child's face. When Lenko lifted the blanket to see for himself the visage of the newborn Baron, what he saw was a babe seemingly normal in all respects but one: the child had yellow eyes.

Béla, they named him—the new Baron Stoke.

The year was 4E1430.

After Béla's birth, Ydral called upon guards to surround the child, and Kapitain Janok was made personally responsible for the newborn Baron's safety. And at Ydral's suggestion and Madam Orso's orders, Lenko's entourage was forbidden to approach the babe, for if little Béla died—through whatever means, natural or contrived—Lenko would then be Baron. The Baronet himself was not permitted to see the child alone, and in fact was guarded whenever he was in the same room as the baby. Raging, Lenko stormed from the keep the very next day, setting forth for his bartizan in the Grimwall above Vulfcwmb in Aven.

Within a week Mad Lèva was dead. How she died is a mystery, yet rumors were rampant. Poisoned by her own mother, said some. Slain by Ydral, claimed others. Yet the most prevalent rumor of all was whispered by those who had heard the shrieks of the fleeing midwife: the new Baron was born with a mouth full of fangs, and as a result he suckled blood mingled with mother's milk, draining unto death his own dam. Adding credence to this rumor, in the following months wet nurses also vanished, and so the tale persisted throughout the years, gathering strength with age.

But even though Lèva died and nurse maids disappeared and none knew the fate of the vanished midwife, others ridiculed this tittle-tattle—for had not Madam Orso herself said that the mother had been too weakened by the birth of such a healthy son? Was it not a common occurrence in Garia that Women died in childbed? Besides, Baroness Lèva had been quite mad. And had not Koska also told that the nurses had run dry and had returned to their distant homes? *Faugh!* any could see that little Béla's mouth was normal, though his yellow eyes did give pause—*Eyes of a demon*, it was whispered.

With the death of her daughter, Madam Orso became the child's Regent, holding court at night, ruling in the name of Baron Béla, though many muttered that Ydral was the *true* power within the Barony, for it seemed that no decision of importance was made without Koska leaning over to the hooded one to receive his whispered advice.

It was said that Madam Orso was a wanton harlot, cavorting with any and all, taking Man after Man unto her bed, sometimes more than one at a time, and debauching Women as well. Whether or not these tales are true, it is a fact that as Béla grew, his maternal granddam aged at a rate faster than her years.

Ydral became the child's tutor, taking him under his wing. Béla was an apt pupil, spending long nights within the tower, there where the animals shrieked in rage and fear and pain.

Rumors bred rumors as Béla grew, whispers of cruelty and torture and acts of perversion. Servants crept about the keep as if fearing for their lives, scuttling from view whenever Koska or Béla or Ydral drew nigh. Doom and oppression rode in the haggard eyes of the staff, and many longed for the old days when Baron Marko ruled with an iron fist, for if a job was done right, then he let be, and if done wrong, a lash or two or a kick in the face wasn't all that bad, eh?

But Marko was dead, and Koska ruled in name though Ydral ruled in fact, and little Béla was a yellow-eyed monster.

The Skarpal Mountains 'round about became a place of terror, a place where Vulgs howled in the dark where no Vulgs had howled before, a place where *Gritchi* and *Durdi* now dwelled, Foul Folk of yore. Landowners locked themselves in at night, driving their livestock into byres and cotes and sleeping alongside the beasts. And although they asked the Regent for succor, she sent none, telling them to fend for themselves. But even though the keep sent no protection, still the tax collectors came for their due, backed up by the force of arms.

All agreed that even dead Marko, hated as he was, had been a better ruler by far than what now sat on the Chair of the Barony.

Slowly, slowly, the Barony slid into dissolution. Just as did

Koska. Just as did Béla. Driven by a yellow-eyed Man . . . if
Man he was.

When Béla turned fourteen, Ydral showed the young Baron
his true nature, and thereafter *Vulp* howls—Vulg howls—
echoed from the tower, to be answered by like calls from
the surrounding mountains. And some of the servants reported seeing a hideous winged creature flying through the
night.

And in the surrounding countryside, people began to disappear in the darkness, only to be found the next day,
murdered.

At age fifteen, almost sixteen, someone wounded Bèla, ran
him through with a sword. The next morning the terrified
servants awoke to discover Kapitain Janok's remains strewn
across the battlements, as if he had been torn asunder by a
wild beast. Yet his eyeless, earless, tongueless head they
found mounted on a pole.

It was rumored that an assassin had attempted to slay Béla,
yet whether it was Janok who had tried but failed, or had
merely failed to prevent the attempt, none knew, and certainly none would ask.

Béla healed rapidly, for he was a Cursed One. Yet thereafter, none of the servants or soldiers were permitted to bear
weapons in his presence—that is, none of the *Humans* were
permitted to do so.

There came a night when he realized his terrible pleasures
were not enough to sate him, and in the shadowy chamber
atop the tower he confronted his mentor.

Ydral turned from the tome he was studying to look at
Béla, yellow eyes staring into eyes of yellow. "My son, there
are things even more delightful than *tji* have done so far.
There are things more . . . complete."

Béla stood and waited, his eyes glinting in the lantern
light.

"I call it . . . the harvest." Ydral rose and walked to a chest.
From it he took a narrow, flat, leather-covered box. Opening
the clasp and raising the lid, he withdrew a long, thin-bladed
knife. "Had we a victim, I would show you how to flense
flesh, how to flay. And yet delay death for the most exquisite
time. . . . Had we a victim."

At that moment Madam Koska Orso stepped into the room.

After Madam Orso's disappearance, Béla took the reins of the Barony into his own hands.

*Now*, by all the demons, said some, now that a *true* Baron Stoke sits on the Chair, *now* things will be different.

And they were.

Different.

Dwellers from nearby steads and villages began to disappear at an alarming rate. Over the next five years, delegations went to plead with the Baron for aid, and he blamed all on the *Gritchi* and the *Durdi*. But after the audience, those who stayed until the safety of dawn returned to their villages and steads and told of distant tortured shrieks in the night, shrieks sounding like those of people in pain beyond imagining.

Servants fled the keep. Soldiers, too. And they told of demons in the tower, the tower where Ydral dwelt. They told of seeing *Gritchi* on the walls and in the bailey. They told of *Durdi* and Vulgs, too.

An exodus from the Barony began: first it was but a few families who left, then a flood. And the population dwindled.

Baron Stoke raged, but there was little he could do to stop the flight, for within ten years all his soldiery was gone. And now the *Drik*—the *Gritchi*, the Rūcks—served him. Too, there were the *Ghok*—the *Durdi*, the Hlōks—serving him as well. And *Vulpen*. All summoned by Ydral.

All manner of Foul Folk would serve Baron Stoke, for such was his power.

Some five years went by, and Baron Stoke's minions ranged wider and wider afield to capture victims for his insane pleasures and mad experiments. For by this time Ydral had introduced him unto necromancy.

But then there came a night when the Baron discovered Ydral hastily gathering together some of his possessions, preparing to flee.

"There is a *Dolh*, an Elf, who has pursued me for more than three thousand years—since the cursed War of the Ban. I have word from one of my own that he draws nigh, and I would not face him, for he wears a token that I cannot overcome, and bears a weapon that will slay even me. This, too, do I know: it is my destiny to perish at the hands of one in whose veins courses *Dolh* blood, and I would stay such fate, forever."

Béla tried to persuade Ydral to remain, offering his mentor the protection of the keep, to no avail, the yellow-eyed tutor leaving that very night, riding a Hèlsteed easterly into the Skarpal Range. And at last Baron Stoke was alone, but for the Spawn.

Three years passed, and Stoke decided to travel away from this empty Barony and unto Aven, unto the bartizan of his Uncle Lenko, unto a place where the harvest would be rich.

Two years after, an Elf bearing a crystal spear rode into the Skarpal Mountains, into the abandoned keep, searching for a yellow-eyed Man.

None were there to greet him.

Following the murder of Lenko and all his get, Baron Stoke remained in the hold north of Vulfcwmb for a number of years. He harvested the region of Humans until it was nearly barren of game.

Then he fared south through the Grimwalls to come to Marik's estates in the mountains above Sagra in Vancha. Baronet Marik was an old man by this time, giving Béla but little pleasure as he flayed his uncle. The others of the household, however, had youth and vitality. Thus they lasted longer.

Over the next years, the estate came to be known as Dreadholt, and the mountain behind as Daemon's Crag. And it was a place of horrid repute. Even so, people were slow to react to the danger it represented, and more years passed ere the harvest became sparse.

Stoke and his minions then made their way unto Basq, and then Gothon, and a number of other Lands, remaining at each for ten years or so, until the game payed out, and then they would move onward to fresher pastures, where the herdfolk were not yet wise.

And so went Baron Stoke's existence down through the decades, hunting, capturing, flaying, experimenting in necromancy. And still he appeared to be a yellow-eyed Man in his middle thirties, though by now he was more than a hundred years old; given what he was, he aged not, and only silver or starsilver rare could do him permanent harm, that and perhaps fire.

He was some two hundred fifty years old when he at last perfected the potion that would sustain the life of the one being flayed, sustain it until all the skin was gone, sustain it and keep the victim awake and aware, sustain it but not deaden the pain.

Then he began impaling them.

Although he retained the looks and physique of a Man in his mid-thirties, Baron Stoke was five hundred fourteen years old and had just established a new chamber within the Grim-wall when his scouts told of a waggon train crossing the Crestan Pass. A sudden snowstorm caused it to turn back. His raiders failed to harvest herd victims, and so Stoke took it upon himself to lure several unto their doom. Baeron, they were, a vibrant Race of Men, and with a few well-chosen words he managed to fool the Chieftain. Ten were sent into the night, following Stoke to a hideous fate ordained by him.

But the Baeron were more than Stoke had bargained for, and one managed to break free. The escapee brought back a force of these powerful warriors and what appeared to be a savage, trained War-Bear. Stoke fled for his life, for surely they had silver weapons at their disposal.

This was the first time that Baron Stoke had been hounded from his dwellings. At all other times it had been his choice to move on to more fertile harvesting grounds. But this time he had been forced to flee. His rage at such was nigh bound-less, yet there was nothing he could do against so powerful a foe as the Baeron Men.

Stoke fled to the Rigga Mountains in Gron. Over the next four years, he experimented upon the *Drik*, yet they did not seem to satisfy his unholy passions.

And then he and his minions captured a male Elf.

Compared to a Human, the flaying of one of the immortals

was delicious, and the impalement of the Elf was beyond Stoke's wildest imaginings.

He was driven from the Gronfangs by his rekindled lust, and he returned unto the bartizan above Vulfcwmb, for he had not been there for several decades, and so the harvest promised to be fruitful.

After a number of months of reaping victims, some Men of Vulfcwmb had the temerity to try to oppose him, coming at his fortress with the intent to slay him. They screamed most delightfully.

And then his lackeys brought to him some of the Wee Folk, with the jewel-like eyes and Elven ears. Two elder males there were and an elder female, but also there was a young female, and Stoke saved her for last, slaying the others before her horrified eyes.

But ere he could harvest the young damman, three would-be rescuers came into his holt: another Warrow, a young male; an Elfess, the *sister* of the Elf he had slain in the Rigga Mountains; and Urus, the Chieftain of the Baeron, the Man he had so easily deceived.

It seems that these *fools* were *hunting* him. Hunting Baron Stoke!

Stoke and his minions captured them all. *What a glorious harvest!*

But then the Man, Urus, changed into a great Bear and burst down the door of the cell!

Stoke almost died that night, nearly slain by the fangs and claws of another so cursed as was he. Yet he managed to escape . . . barely.

He fled to Vancha, to Dreadholt upon Daemon's Crag. It had been many years since he had last harvested in the region, and Sagra was once again populated.

But two years after fleeing Vulfcwmb, again his holt was invaded—by the very same four who had nearly proved his undoing there in the bartizan!

This time he came even closer to dying—by a starlight sword most dire, borne by the Elfess; by silver bullet, hurled by the buccan; and by fire.

Dreadholt burned to the ground, yet once again Stoke managed to escape.

\* \* \*

He fled to the distant eastern reaches of the Grimwall, there on the border of far away Xian. But within ten years the harvest became sparse, and so he drifted westerly, remaining in the grip of the mountains, reaping new victims as he went, deriving his perverse pleasure from flaying people alive and impaling them, and from practicing his mad necromancy.

Some years later, he had drifted as far as the ruins of Dragonslair, in the quaking mountains above the Land of Aralan. He sent his lackeys down to reap victims from farms and villages of the region, to raid caravans, to capture the fourteen folk living near the river crossing known as Stoneford.

In the mountains north and east of Dragonslair, Stoke discovered a monastery above the Great North Glacier, and he flayed and impaled the twelve priests he found living therein.

He made the monastery his lair, but again his holt was invaded, *by the very same four pursuers:* two Warrows, the Elfess, and Urus—twenty years had passed, *and they were still after him!*

Stoke hid in the underground rooms of the monastery, but their search revealed him. He fled to the belltower and *shifted.* Yet as he flew away, he was severely wounded: a silver sling bullet cracked a bone in his left wing, and he spiraled down unto the glacier below.

Still they pursued relentlessly, as they had done for two decades. They overtook him on the ice. Even so, he nearly slew the Elfess, she with the starlight blade, but as he prepared to behead her with her very own sword, a silver knife was thrown by the damman, embedding in his shoulder.

The pain was hideous, yet he could not bear to touch the silver to withdraw the blade. He *shifted* again, but the knife remained. In the form of a *Vulp* he sprang from the lip of a wide crevasse, leaping for the far side to escape, but that *fool* Urus intercepted him in mid-flight, and together they fell down into the frigid black depths below.

And the crevasse slammed shut, locking *Vulp* and Man eternally together in frozen battle.

When they crashed into the ice in the depths of the abyss, the silver knife was jarred from Stoke's shoulder, and over the millennium the ice held them, slowly, ever so slowly, the *Vulp* healed—he was, after all, a Cursed One, and rapid healing was one of his traits, though here in the cold, the process was greatly retarded.

A golden glow bathed both the Baron and the Baeran, *Vulp* and Man, and even though his life was suspended, still Stoke felt the cursed light.

A thousand years passed—deep in the ice the *Vulp* and the Man were caught in a slow, grinding eddy, an eddy drifting ever closer to the edge of the pack.

At last came a night that the wall of the glacier split, calving, disgorging the *Vulp*. Hours passed, and still Stoke did not move. Yet given his powers of regeneration, ultimately he regained consciousness, and he heard the far-off voices of yammering *Drik* and *Ghok* and the distant howls of *Vulpen*. Stoke yawled for help, and when it was answered, he *shifted* again, becoming once more a yellow-eyed Man, if Stoke could be called a Man.

As he waited, he saw a hairy star scoring the night sky, and by its position among the stars he deduced that it was the Eye of the Hunter and that he had been locked in the glacier for more than a thousand years.

At last, aid came to him. And when he was lifted up from the ice, he could dimly see the form of Urus yet trapped in the glacier, but only inches deep, silhouetted by a cursed golden glow. Stoke ordered the Foul Folk to dig Urus free and behead him, and to burn the remains. Yet none could withstand the auric luminance, and so Stoke had to let the Man be, for Stoke, especially Stoke, was repelled by its holy aura.

That night the *Drik* bore Stoke to the canyon caverns. And there he laired, regaining his strength.

Two nights later, his hunting parties reported the scent of strangers, and they told of an Elfess who vanished into thin air. And just ere dawn, a wounded *Vulp* came limping from the monastery bringing news of a damman Warrow that had escaped, and of a savage Bear that slew.

And then Stoke *knew* that he was yet pursued—by Elves, by Warrows, by Urus. He deduced that likely this place was watched, and so he laid a plan.

And the next night, as he and his band left the canyon, remaining behind were *Drik* and *Ghok* and *Vulpen*. If Stoke was followed, those who hunted him would in turn become the prey.

A hideous winged *thing* flapped southward through the falling snow, knowing that the white would cover the tracks of its lackeys, knowing also that even if someone managed to trail them, the trackers themselves would be slaughtered from behind.

And so it flapped onward through the night, the savage storm howling 'round not matching the cold fury within.

# CHAPTER 23

# Vanishment

**Early Spring,
5E988**

*[The Present]*

Hurtling out from the spinning wall of white, the snarling Vulg crashed into Faeril from behind, slamming her facedown into the snow, smashing atop her, driving the breath from her—*"Unhh!"* Only the deep snow and her backpack saved her from instant death. All she could hear was a wild wrauling and footsteps thudding past. And the creature bearing her down sought to savage her. Struggling, Faeril attempted to roll, but she could not escape the mauling weight crushing her. She could not reach the knives in her bandoliers, but she jerked the silver Elven blade from the scabbard at her waist and slashed at the creature's leg, gashing it. With a howl it leapt aside, and Faeril managed to scramble to her knees even as it plunged at her again, savage mouth agape. Without thinking, the damman jammed the blade past its teeth and straight down its throat, silver slamming home even as slashing fangs tore into her flesh. Yawling, it jerked away, wrenching the blade from her grasp. And of a sudden it collapsed.

Gaining her feet, Faeril threw down her backpack and drew a steel throwing knife and looked into the swirling whiteness whirling all about in the howling wind. And at that very moment, all was plunged in blackness. *The lantern! It's out! Oh, Gwylly!*

She could hear sounds of combat, the skirl of steel on steel and the shrieks of the dying, and vague shapes hurtled past in the blackness, more sensed than seen, but who was fighting whom, she could not tell. *I cannot see to throw!* She jammed the dagger back into the bandolier and drew her long-knife—a sword in the hand of a Warrow.

Before her, a torch sputtered into life, and she could momentarily see dim figures lunging through the blizzard, a tall one plunging toward the torch bearer, merging, a loud shriek, the torch falling in the snow, *sissing*, blackness returning.

A figure loomed before her. *"Adon!"* she cried. She could sense the figure turning, and she stabbed out with her blade, feeling it scrape bone, the figure gasping, collapsing, nearly wrenching the long-knife from her hand. But she hung on grimly, and grinding, it came free of the downed being.

Faeril fell to her knees and groped. *Oh, let it be foe!* Her hands fumbled across the body, the torso clad in leather sewn with steel ringlets. *Rūck!* she thought just as she put her hand atop spurting blood from a heart pumping its last.

Revulsed, Faeril scrabbled backwards, only to slam into someone behind. Snarling, the being fell over her akimbo, thudding into the snow. Blindly the damman slashed, making contact, the being howling in agony. Faeril jammed the long-knife at the sound, but whoever, whatever it was rolled away, scrambling up and running through the blackness, a blot of darkness disappearing into the raging ebony storm.

Another came near, gasping harshly. Faeril readied her blade. *"Adon!"* she called, starting to plunge the long-knife.

*"Adon!"* came the instant reply.

*"Gwylly!"*

*"Faeril!"*

"Oh, Gwylly, I almost—"

"Back to back, love," interrupted her buccaran. "Back to back, though I won't be much help. I've taken a wound."

"Oh, Gwylly—"

"Back to back!"

And so the two Warrows stood back to back, facing into the blackness—Gwylly breathing harshly, coughing now and then; Faeril trembling in fear for him.

In the distance, another torch sputtered into life, to be extinguished moments later amid shrieks of dying.

Still the black blizzard howled, dark snow hurling past—ebon ravens' feathers flying in the nightwind. Occasionally there sounded steel on steel, occasionally a dying scream, occasionally footsteps ran past. Nought could be seen in the blackness, and little could be heard above the squall of the storm. And Warrows stood back to back.

"The darkness and wind alone save us," hissed Gwylly. "Without the blizzard hiding us, the wind flinging away our scent, we would fall to the maggot-folk."

And then Gwylly collapsed.

Faeril spun about and knelt, feeling for his wound, discovering nothing.

But even as her hands fumbled over Gwylly's form, from nearby there came a guttural growl, and a snuffling, and then a yawl of a Vulg. Faeril crouched above her buccaran, her long-knife at the ready, praying that the beast would not find her, would not find Gwylly. Yet that was not to be, for the rasping snarls sounded louder, the creature casting about, coming nearer. And then black on black loomed before her, wrauling. "Adon!" she shrieked, leaping up and across, hurtling forward over Gwylly. But in that same moment another plunged inward, spear piercing the Vulg's unprotected flank, Aravan crying "Adon!" even as Krystallopŷr burned into and through the howling beast, even as Faeril's blade took it in the throat, chopping short its agonized wail.

Now Elf and damman stood back to back, Gwylly lying in between. In the darkness by feel alone they could find no wound, and so they took up station above him, for there was nought they could do in the midst of battle to aid the buccan.

Now and again they heard the skirl of steel on steel, at times coming from two different directions simultaneously. "They fight themselves," hissed Aravan, "though surely Riatha engages them as well."

Suddenly a harsh voice yawled above the howl of the wind, his call taken up by others. What he cried, neither Aravan nor Faeril knew, for Slûk was the language. After several moments, again there sounded cries, farther off, southward. Then again, growing faint in the storm. Then no more.

"Perhaps they've gone," said Faeril

"Mayhap 'tis but a ruse," responded Aravan.

Still they waited in the blackness, ebon snow whirling about. The world spun 'round, and Faeril's stomach heaved, a sudden nausea whelming upon her. She staggered a step or two and fell to her knees and retched.

From far off a hollow, booming voice echoed in her ears. "Faeril, what passes? Are thou wounded?"

The damman could not answer, for her ears rang and her entire body seemed aflame—she *burned*. Icy perspiration exploded from her skin. And as she toppled into the blackness, she managed to whisper a single word: "Vulg."

*Stoke! . . . Stoke! . . . stoke! . . . stoke . . . stoke . . . stoke . . . toke . . . oke . . . o . . .*

As the echoes of his cry slapped and rang among the mountains, in the morning light Urus turned and set off northward across the trackless snow, heading up the wide, twisting vale, the Man moving back towards where he had last seen his companions.

Seething rage and cold apprehension warred within his heart: rage, for Stoke had eluded him; apprehension, for his comrades had not arrived. *Is it possible that Stoke has them in his vile grasp?* Urus did not know, could not know, and he roared a wordless shout in anger, his stride carrying him onward.

*If they are within his grasp . . . where?* Urus glanced about; within sight he could see a handful of cols and canyons that Stoke could have taken, yet he knew that just beyond, a thousand avenues of escape branched forth among the Grimwalls, and a thousand bolt-holes lay within. *Stoke could lair in these mountains forever! And the wide world lies beyond!* Again Urus shouted his anger, but only dying echoes answered.

His wrath cooled to a deadly determination, receding into that secret place where he stored his rage, leaving his heart filled with deep foreboding. *If not captives, then what? Is it possible that Peta—she is not Petal! She is Faeril! Yet she is Petal's very image. And he is Tomlin's—Gwylly. . . .*

*Is it possible that Faeril had the right of it? Was a band of Wrg following? If so, could this be the cause of the delay?*

*Oh, my Riatha, are you . . . are you . . . ?*

On he trekked, his mind and heart filled with anxiety and rage and foreboding and logic and wrath.

And he shouted unto the mountains, "Stoke! Bastard! Monster! Filth! We shall destroy you just as the Dwarves destroyed your bartizan! Destroyed the caverns beyond! Just as we burned Dreadholt!"

The snow lay deeply in the vale, at times coming to the Man's mid-thigh—*This will be hard for the Waldana to broach, yet I can break trail for them . . . if they yet live—* but in spite of it Urus made good time, and onward he trod.

At last he rounded a curve and in the distance saw a thin tendril of smoke rising up from a sparse coppice. His heart leapt. *Let it be them!* As he trudged closer, he could see what appeared to be a lean-to among the trees, its backside toward him. Urus slipped his gloves from his hands, and placed two fingers in his mouth and emitted a piercing whistle—*Tweee . . . !*—high-pitched echoes shrilling back from the stone flanks rearing upward all about.

There was no movement. *Nothing!*

Again he whistled, and as the echoes died, a tall figure stepped out from behind the shelter—*Aravan! It is Aravan!*—and raised a hand and slowly waved.

Urus waved back, increasing his pace, but Aravan disappeared behind the shelter once more. *Where is Riatha? And the Waldana?* Dread clutched at Urus's heart.

Now Urus came in among the sparse trees, the snow shallower, and he broke into a trot. In but moments he reached the lean-to, and out before it by a small fire squatted Aravan, stirring a liquid in a container suspended above the flame. Yet Urus only glanced fleetingly at the Elf, for stepping forth to greet him was—*Riatha!* Urus crushed her to him, his heart hammering in his ears, fierce joy singing through every fiber of his being as she clung tightly to him.

But then his heart plunged into despair, for within the shelter, their faces pale as death, laid out in repose were Faeril and Gwylly.

"They came at us in the night," said Riatha as she and Urus sat at the edge of the lean-to. Riatha was spooning tiny amounts of liquid between Faeril's lips, the damman not awakening but swallowing. "From behind, just as Faeril suspected they might. The howling storm prevented us from perceiving their approach. But by the same token, the storm prevented them from overwhelming us, for they could neither see nor hear us, and the Vulgs could not easily catch our scent.

"Faeril was Vulg bit, but gwynthyme and sunlight have burned the poison from her, though she will yet be fevered throughout the day.

"Gwylly took a blade in his lung, though, and will not be fit for travel for a week or so, and even then but slowly.

"Fortune favored both Aravan and me, he taking nought but one or two cudgel blows, and I a slash on the wrist."

Gently Urus took her left hand and looked at the bandage. "Did you cleanse it thoroughly? Wrg blades are often—"

"Poisoned," interjected Aravan. "Aye, we let it bleed, and applied gwynthyme as well. I made poultices for all who took cutting wounds."

Riatha did not recover her hand from Urus's. "What of Stoke?" she asked quietly.

A hard look came into the Man's eyes. "Lost! The storm— Five ways could he have gone from the last place I—where last the Bear scented him."

Aravan glanced at the mid-morning sky. "Have we time, thou and I, time to find traces? Traces of their passage?"

Urus gently placed Riatha's hand back in her lap. Then the Man leapt to his feet and began pacing as would a caged beast. "Traces? Nay! The storm took care of any traces. If Stoke moves tonight, then there will be tracks. Then will I follow . . . alone."

Riatha started at this declaration. "Alone?"

"Aye," interjected Urus. "Alone. The Waldana cannot pursue them. And they will need caring after. You are wounded—"

Riatha leapt up. "*Akka!* 'Tis but a scratch! 'Twill not keep me from Stoke."

Of a sudden the ground trembled—Dragonslair shuddering in the distance. After long moments the shaking stopped.

Urus had reached out for Riatha, steadying them both. As the shocks died away he asked, "What of the Waldana?"

A voice piped up from the lean-to. "What about us?" Gwylly started to struggle to a sitting position, but a spasm of coughing overcame him, and he fell back, crimson stains on his lips.

With a cry Riatha spun about and swiftly knelt at his side. "Oh, Gwylly, move not. Thou are sorely wounded. Pierced through by blade."

His eyes closed, the buccan groaned. "Oh, is that what it is? I feel as if I've been dragged by my heels through the very pits of Hèl."

" 'Twas a hard fight, wee one."

Gwylly's eyes flew open. "Faeril! What of Faeril?"

"Hush, hush," soothed Riatha. "She sleeps at your side."

Gwylly turned his head. Then he reached out a hand and took hers in his. "Is she . . . all right?"

Riatha nodded.

"What happened to her?"

Riatha glanced up at Aravan. He knelt beside the Elfess. "Well, Gwylly, she killed a Vulg, that's what." Aravan reached over and took up a silver knife, holding it for the buccan to see, the argent edge flashing in the sunlight. "Stabbed him in the throat with this, Talarin's gift. I know because I went back to retrieve our packs and aught else, and I happened to be looking at the dead beast when the Sun turned the slain creature to ashes. I saw the glitter, and when I stepped to where the Vulg had lain, there was the blade."

Gwylly gasped. "And I thought I had done well to bring down three Rūcks, or Hlōks—in the darkness I couldn't tell. But Adon, a *Vulg!*

"It proves one thing, though," he said, faintly smiling, "it doesn't pay to cross a Warrow—especially a damman."

Aravan laughed. "Thou have the right of it, Waerling."

Gwylly tried to roll onto his side, but gave it up as Riatha objected. "She looks flushed," said the buccan. "Are you certain—?"

"Aye, Gwylly," responded Aravan. "She's completely out of danger. She took a gash from the Vulg, that's all. We used a gwynthyme poultice—"

"*Vulg* bite?" Gwylly tensed, and that brought on another fit of coughing. After it subsided, Gwylly turned to Riatha. "The black bite, the poison—did the gwynthyme get it all?"

"Yes. That and the Sun."

Riatha took the buccan's hand in her own. "She sleeps off the dregs of the fever, Gwylly. When she wakes, all will be well."

The Elfess moved to the fire and began preparing an herbal concoction, flaking bits of a dried root into a small container of water, heating all. As Urus sat beside the buccan and began speaking softly, Aravan squatted by the Elfess, his voice low. "Dara, thou will have to remain with the Waerlinga while Urus and I trail Stoke and his lackeys. Only thou have the deep knowledge to tend the Wee Ones' wounds should aught go awry."

Riatha looked at the buccan and sleeping damman, and gazed at Urus as well. And then, sighing, she glanced over at Aravan and nodded, and continued to stir the liquid.

That night, a savage Bear prowled the perimeter of the camp, warding the ones within.

The next morning as dawn lightened the sky, Urus and Aravan set out for the last place the Bear had scented *Urwa*, the Man and Elf hoping to find traces of the Foul Folk. Should there be tracks, Urus and Aravan would leave clear trail sign for Riatha and Gwylly and Faeril to follow when they could travel.

An hour after sunup, Faeril wakened, the damman trembling from residual weakness brought on by the fever— that and lack of food. Riatha began spooning up a plate of lentil beans to go with a biscuit of crue.

Faeril looked in Gwylly's face and listened to his breathing, assuring herself that he merely slept. Then, groaning, she tottered to her feet and stumped into the trees to relieve herself. When she returned, slowly she hunkered down on her haunches and took the plate of food from Riatha.

"Gwylly, how is he? What wound did he take?"

"A thin blade 'tween the lower ribs and into a lung. A dagger, I suspect, though it could have been a sword. He will heal, can we but give him rest.

"But thou, Faeril, how fare thee?"

"Garn, but I feel as if I had been sat upon by a horse."

Riatha smiled. "Nay, Faeril, no horse, but Vulg instead."

"Well, horse or Vulg, I have the bruises to prove it. My body's gone all blue."

" 'Tis not surprising. Vulgs have nearly the size of ponies, though not the weight."

Faeril shifted about, trying to ease her sore muscles. "How heavy are they?"

"I know not. Mayhap four hundredweight. Mayhap five."

"Well, it felt like a thousandweight, though had it been, I would now be but a flat spot in the snow. I think it did not put all its heft upon me."

Spooning up a mouthful of beans, the damman looked about the campsite as she chewed. "Where is Aravan? And have you heard from Urus?"

"Aye. Urus returned yester. He tells that the storm erased all traces of Stoke and his lackeys. Yet Urus and Aravan now fare south, seeking fresh tracks so that once again we may run Stoke to earth."

Satisfied, Faeril took a bite of crue and fell silent, concentrating on eating.

Later that morning, Gwylly awakened. He would have nothing of this lying abed, demanding that he be allowed to go into the trees to relieve himself. Supported by both females, he leaned against a tree to do so, coughing gently.

Afterward, Riatha brewed a moss tea and insisted that Gwylly breathe the pungent aroma. " 'Twill aid thy lung to heal from the inside." Additionally, she removed the gwynthyme poultice from the wound at his ribs and replaced it with a bandage soaked in the same brew, murmuring, "This for the outside." And she made him drink the rest in spite of its terrible bitterness, the buccan screwing his face into a horrid mask. " 'Twill pull the fluid from thy lungs."

"*Gack!* 'Twill curdle my insides, if you ask me," protested Gwylly, shuddering.

The Elfess laughed and Faeril giggled, yet both watched the buccan closely to make certain he drank it all.

The Elfess then turned to Faeril. "Thy bandage as well needs changing." Together they unwrapped the old, revealing a deep gash on the inside of Faeril's right arm, running from elbow to wrist.

"Oi!" exclaimed Gwylly. "Bad wound. But, I say, it looks as if some stitchery has been done."

"Aye," responded Riatha. "Sewn with fine gut. Else the wound is open to ill vapors. Four and twenty stitches, whereas yours, Gwylly, took but nine."

Gwylly looked down at his chest, unsuccessfully trying to see the wound beneath the brew-soaked bandage. "I'm sewn up, too? Like an old coat?"

Again Faeril giggled, and Riatha laughed outright. "Aye, Redtop. Like an old coat."

Gwylly smiled. "Redtop? Better were I called 'Patch.'"

Grinning, Faeril looked up from her arm. "Patch it is, Gwylly, if you insist, even though it does sound like the name of a dog."

Now Gwylly laughed, but his humor was cut short by another coughing fit.

All that day they waited, speaking in hushed tones, as if the mountain stone were listening. While Faeril oiled and sharpened their long-knives—both weapons retrieved yester from the deep snow at the battle site by Aravan—Gwylly told of downing his three foe and how confused and desperate and frightening it had been, fighting in near total blackness, taking a wound in the second engagement, "... Like a lick of fire hitting me between the ribs."

Riatha, it seems, with her Elven vision had fared slightly better at seeing the foe, and when combined with her acute hearing, altogether she had slain seven of the enemy. Aravan had told Riatha of four *Rûpt* he had killed, and the Vulg that he and Faeril together had dispatched. And when added to Faeril's other Vulg and the slain Rūck, well then—"Oi!" said Gwylly, "that totes up to two Vulgs and *fifteen* Rūcks and Hlōks!"

Faeril glanced at Riatha. "Why, that means Stoke has only five Vulgs and twelve maggot-folk left in his band."

"Mayhap, Faeril, yet heed, we are in the Grimwalls, and other *Rûpt* will flock to him should he call."

Throughout the day, their conversation ranged far and wide, and they spoke of family and hearth and home and told of simple meals of bread and stew, which now seemed a luxury. As Riatha melted snow for water to boil the used dressings, they spoke of taking baths, and Gwylly told of his dog, Black, as a pup chasing ducks at the pond, the fowl taking to the water, Black leaping after, and the goose that came to the rescue of the ducks, forever curing Black of the notion of hounding barnyard fowl. They spoke of riding ponies and horses, of gardens and growings and other such, but always did their talk return to Baron Stoke and to speculations as to whether Urus and Aravan now tracked the monster.

An hour or two after dark, their speculations were answered, for a distant whistle announced the return of the Man and Elf.

"No tracks did we find, no traces," said Aravan, warming his hands 'round a hot cup of tea.

Urus growled. "Aravan and I separated, and I took one canyon while he took another. Miles I covered, to no avail."

Riatha spooned lentil soup into shallow tin bowls. "No cracks, crevices, caves?"

Aravan reached out, taking his measure of soup. "Nay, though the stone hides much."

Urus shook his head. "I saw none either."

They ate in silence, frustration and buried rage evident. At last Urus spoke: "Tomorrow we will search two more routes, and if we are unsuccessful, that will leave but one."

"Mayhap," said Aravan. "Yet there is a chance that we overlooked his new bolt-hole in the canyons we searched today."

Urus stopped. "Garn! The blizzard hid all."

Riatha looked up at him. "Yet it saved our lives.'

That night, Aravan and Riatha took turns standing guard, their Elven heritage allowing them to rest and watch at one and the same time.

Now and again the earth shuddered. And the Eye of the Hunter running its course rose late and ran lower down in the sky.

The next night when Urus and Aravan returned, the Baeran sat with a bitter scowl on his face. "The canyon I followed came to a dead end some eight miles inward. But the route Aravan followed went up through one of the cols, and beyond the pass he discovered six or seven more ways that Stoke could have gone. Garn!" He slammed a fist into open palm.

"Six," said Aravan, frustration in his eyes. "Six more routes he and his lackeys could take."

Gwylly sat propped up by a backpack. "Say, it just occurred to me: Stoke could abandon his maggot-folk and simply fly away, leaving no trail at all. I mean, even if we find tracks, what's to say that Stoke's with 'em? There is this, too: he could have his band—"

"Lay a false trail," interjected Aravan. "Thou are correct, Gwylly. Urus and I have discussed such. Yet we have no choice but to try to find tracks. To do otherwise assumes that Stoke has already flown, with all the wide world his to alight within."

Ten more days they searched, finding no traces at all, the canyons and vales beyond the cols branching and branching again, yielding hundreds of ways Stoke could have gone through this shuddering land.

Every night Aravan and Urus returned to camp, vexation and ire written in their every glance, in their every move. And every night the Eye of the Hunter rose later and rode lower, disappearing with the dawn.

At last in the night they held long council, and 'mid oaths and tears of frustration and bitter invective they slowly came to the conclusion that for now Stoke was lost to them. He had escaped.

But what to do about it? Where to go next?

Then Faeril dug through her garments, drawing forth her copy of Petal's diary. And in the flickering firelight she read to them, translating from Twyll to Common as she went:

*The following day, a small force of warriors, armed and armored, clad in scarlet and gold, came riding across The Clearing and into the village. It was Aurion's escort, come to accompany him back to Caer Pendwyr. And five days after, they rode out again, the Prince in their midst.*

*But ere he went, he came unto Tommy and me. "I am but a Prince of the Realm," he said, "yet I deem my sire will hew to the pledge I make this day, and it is this: Should you or Urus or Riatha need the aid of*

*the High King, come unto Caer Pendwyr or to Challer-*
*ain Keep and ask. We will help in running unto earth*
*this monster you seek. So do I pledge in the names of*
*all High Kings of Mithgar, forever."*

*Though he was but ten, every inch a Prince he was,*
*and both Tommy and I knew that aid would come if*
*we but asked. We each hugged and kissed him, and he*
*mounted his horse.*

*We all watched—Tommy, Riatha, Urus, and I—as*
*Aurion rode away, southerly, out across the wide Clear-*
*ing, the Princeling mounted on a dappled grey, amidst*
*chestnuts and bays and blacks all about, spear-borne*
*pennons snapping in the breeze, rampant golden griffin*
*on scarlet field.*

*And when we could see the future King no more,*
*when the last standard passed beyond the horizon, we*
*turned and strode back into the forest, where awaited*
*mounts of our own.*

Faeril closed the journal.

Riatha looked up at Urus, her silver eyes glittering in the firelight. "Well do I remember that day."

Urus nodded, for he, too, had been present when Aurion had made the pledge, even though it was a millennium agone.

One at a time Faeril's gaze took each of them in, and her voice came softly. "I think it is time we went to Caer Pendwyr to see the High King."

That night, as Riatha stood her watch, she at last accepted the fact that for now Stoke was absolutely lost to them. And as the night slid by and when finally came the dawn, she realized as well that the Eye of the Hunter, too, was gone.

# CHAPTER 24

# Trek

**Spring, 5E988**

*[The Present]*

When they set out, the buccan rode on the back of a great brown Bear. The Bear was also laden with two frame packs, roped 'round so that they rode one on either side. The Bear did not gladly suffer such burdens, yet seemed to understand that they were necessary, for Gwylly had been sorely wounded, and though his healing had progressed, deep breaths were painful, and he was unable to sustain long hikes through the heavy-laden snow, and so the Bear bore the wee two-legs cub.

It had been thirteen days since the combat, thirteen days since Faeril had been Vulg bitten and Gwylly had been stabbed, thirteen days since they'd had an inkling of Stoke's whereabouts. And when they had broken camp that morning to begin the long journey southward, an air of failure, of dejection, rode like a hag on their shoulders, and their faces were glum, were chapfallen. Yet none thought to abandon the search, to give it up, for each was driven to go onward, to run this monster to earth: two were compelled by the history of a time long fled, and bound by a pledge given therein; three by distant events they had lived millennia agone, and the vengeance they would wreak in return; all were impelled by Destiny.

Even the Bear.

In the council of the previous night, Riatha had unrolled her maps, all trying to divine Stoke's goal. . . .

In the near distance lay the remains of Dragonslair, a firemountain blasted into ruins. "Too unstable," commented Riatha, "for I have passed it often and have seen and felt how the earth wrenches, and any underground haunts are likely to collapse."

To the north lay the Great North Glacier, and the monastery on the slope above. "Unlikely he will return to that place," said Urus, "for there he suffered defeat at our hands. But as to farther north . . ."

Aravan made a negating gesture. "Unlikely as well. There is nought but barrens beyond, sparsely populated, and then only in summer when the Aleuti bring their herds of *ren*."

Riatha traced their route on one of the maps. "His track went southerly. . . ."

Gwylly pointed at the map, his finger stabbing into a shaded zone. "What's that?"

"The Khalian Mire," answered Aravan. "A place of dire events in times long past."

Faeril raised an eyebrow. "Dire events?"

Aravan nodded. "I will tell thee another time, Faeril, for our task here is to anticipate Stoke's goal and not to recount history."

"Well, if the mire is such a dreadful place, then surely Stoke might hide within."

"Aye, Faeril, he might at that; yet were he to seek its clutch, like as not we would ne'er find him. Heed"—Aravan's finger traced across the map—"the mire is fully forty or fifty leagues from north to south and twenty from east to west. It is a vast tangle, with unnumbered bolt-holes. Too, the land holds no tracks, the seeping muck backfilling, steps disappearing even as they are made. Lastly, Stoke knows that we pursue him, else he would not have laid an ambush. Hence, I deem he will hie far from these environs ere stopping, and when next we hear of his depredations, they will be"—Aravan gestured at the maps—"remote . . . not nearby as is the mire."

Faeril reluctantly nodded and turned her attention back to the maps. "East lies the Wolf Wood."

Riatha shook her head. "Nay, Stoke would not go there—for that is where Dalavar the Wolf Mage dwells, he and his Draega and other such. Evil ranges wide of those woods, for Dalavar tolerates it not."

Gwylly's eyes went wide. "Draega?"

Aravan answered. "Silver Wolves, Gwylly. Foe of *Rûpt*, especially Vulgs. Trapped here in the Mittegarda by the Sundering. Exiled here forever, unless of course they can find enough Folk of the Hōhgarda to pace the pattern and cant the chant and lead each and every one of them back, for they are a blood-loyal pack and will not abandon one of their own."

Here was another tale for the telling, and though Gwylly was about to burst with curiosity, now was not the time. Again all turned their eyes to the map.

Riatha pointed to two areas. "There is the Skög . . . and the Lesser Mire."

Urus growled in ire, his hand sweeping diagonally across the length and breadth of the maps. "*Hèl!* There is the entire Grimwall, running thousands of miles east and west. Stoke favors mountains."

"In that case," added Faeril, "I can see many mountain ranges on Riatha's charts: the Rimmen Mountains in Riamon; the Skarpals in Garia; the Grey Mountains in Xian; the Gronfangs and Rigga, bordering Gron. Down here is the Gûnarring, and over here the Jillian Tors. There's the Brin Downs and the Red Hills and the Signal Mountains and—"

"*Arrgh!*" Urus leapt to his feet. "*Stoke!*" he shouted to the stone of the mountains. Echoes slapped back.

Frustration filled Riatha's face, for Stoke's goal could be anywhere in the wide, wide world.

And that had been when Faeril had read to them of Prince Aurion's long-ago pledge, and they had decided to seek the aid of the High King. . . .

And now they trekked southward: two Elves, two Warrows, and a Bear.

\*     \*     \*

They covered some twenty miles that day, trudging through the deep snow, the Bear breaking trail, the five of them wending among the stone massifs of the Grimwall, Riatha directing them, for she had often come this way to visit the Great North Glacier when Urus had been trapped within.

Southward they had gone faring in a long westerly arc, the Elfess aiming for the village of Inge in the Land of Aralan, where they would rest and recuperate and purchase mounts for their journey to see the High King. And as they had pressed ahead, the earth beneath their feet shuddered and trembled, for the ruins of Dragonslair lay among the mountains before them.

That evening, Riatha kindled a small fire with wood that Urus and Aravan brought from the coppice surrounding them. As water heated for tea, Urus glanced at the stars above. "They seem not much changed in all the centuries I slept," he rumbled. "I find it hard to believe that a thousand years have gone by. To me it was but a nearby yesterday when we tracked Stoke unto the monastery. Tell me, Riatha, of the happenings in the wide world beyond since last I knew."

Riatha sat back on her haunches. "I cannot speak for the whole world, Urus, for much of the time I dwelled in Arden Vale, separate from the doings of Men and Drimma . . . and of the Waerlinga.

"Yet there were two upheavals of note while thou slept within the ice:

"Some forty years after thou carried Stoke down into the crevasse, a great War was fought—"

"The Winter War," exclaimed Gwylly.

"Aye, wee one," agreed Riatha. " 'Twas the Winter War. The Wizard Modru acquired a token of great power, the Myrkenstone, and with it caused a vast darkness to o'ercome the world—parts of it at least.

"I was in Riamon at the time, and fought with the Men and Elves to free the Drimma of Mineholt North, who were under siege by one of Modru's Hordes.

"Aravan . . ." Riatha paused.

The Elf looked up from the fire. "I was on the Avagon Sea, striving against the Rovers."

"Just so." Riatha added tea leaves to the boiling water. "Thy Folk, Urus, they fought in the Grimwalls above Delon Isle, seeking out the hidden holts and doors of the *Spaunen* within, shutting them forever, or so it was believed."

Urus nodded, for he had fought in those same regions himself long before. "Then *that* is why the Wrg gathered long past. They readied themselves for the Winter War to come."

Riatha nodded. "Aye, though none but Modru knew it at the time."

"Tell him about Tuckerby Underbank," urged Faeril. "I mean, he was the hero of the Winter War, single-handedly destroying Modru and all of his schemes. And oh, by the way, Urus, Tuck was a *Warrow*!"

Aravan smiled. "Single-handedly, wee one? Not quite. He was aided in his venture by the High King and the Vanadurin of Valon, to say nought of the Elves of Arden and Men of Wellen who held Kregyn Pass against the Horde behind."

Faeril bobbed her head in agreement, but added, "Yet Tuck *was* the key, and as the High King later said, all the rest but aided him along his way."

Gwylly smiled a great, wide smile and squeezed Faeril's hand, and he said with quiet pride: "And he was a *Warrow*."

"Modru is dead? Hai, there's a bit of news!" Then Urus laughed, for what was news to him was but history to the others. He held forth a tin cup and Riatha filled it with tea, handing him a crue biscuit as well. The Man settled back. "This Winter War, start at the beginning and tell me all."

Long they talked into the night, Riatha speaking of the great conflict and of the darkest day at its end. Yet at last all took to their bedrolls, but for the one who set watch, each taking a turn throughout the darktide.

All the next day as southward along their arc they fared, the trembling of the land grew more violent, and in the distance they could hear a muttering of thunder and see dark plumes rising up into the sky.

The Bear did not like this jolting of the earth beneath his feet, nor the rumble of sound to the south. And he growled and snuffled, and whenever the tiny two-legs on his back dismounted, the Bear would stand erect and snuffle and peer and roar. Yet he did not frighten away whatever it was that juddered the land below; but by the same token, neither did it frighten away the Bear.

That night Riatha spoke to Urus of the next great conflict—the War of Drimmen-deeve—telling of the retaking of that Dwarvenholt, the Drimma wrenching it from the grasp of Gnar and his minions. Here, too, Faeril spoke of the Warrows involved—Peregrin Fairhill and Cotton Buckleburr—guides to King Durek's Host.

Another two days passed, the five wending among the trembling mountains, drawing nearer to Dragonslair. On the following day they rounded a shoulder of stone to come within sight of the great ruined firemountain, the shattered crater belching out roiling clouds of smoke and blasting huge rocks up into the sky, the air thundering, and here and there rivers of molten lava ran red up out of its bowels and down its stubby flanks. The Bear reared up, sending Gwylly tumbling, and roared and clawed in a display of might, refusing to be intimidated by this bellowing mountain. Satisfied that he had demonstrated his courage, the Bear dropped back to all four paws and swung his head to look hindward at the small two-legs cub in the snow, sounding a *Whuff* that he was ready to go onward. Gwylly scrambled up and clambered back onto his unruly mount, and then the five resumed their trek, Aravan chuckling at the antics of the Bear.

That night they camped within sight of the wreckage. And borne upon the wind was the smell of sulphur and brimstone. In the darkness now and then an eerie blue fire rose up from the crater. " 'Tis Kalgalath's ghost-fire," said Riatha. "They say that every Springday, Kalgalath's ghost rises up from the fire and flies beyond seeing up into the sky, only to come plummeting at last down the very throat of the firemountain, whelming the Kammerling into the world, blasting Dragonslair to ruin, all but that eastern slope yon."

Like a maimed hand, the middle slope of the eastern slant yet stood, rearing upward into the air, a wall that had somehow survived the ruin of Kalgalath. For here it was that the mighty Dragon had met his doom, here at the hands of Elyn and Thork, the great Fire-drake plummeting down to destroy the very mountain in which he lived.

And still the land juddered and shook, here along the Grimwalls, e'en though the firemountain had detonated nigh three thousand, four hundred years agone. Here was the epicenter, here at the ruins of Dragonslair, for as Riatha put it: "Yet unto this day the earth remembers that destruction, that mighty whelming, as a bell remembers its ring."

That the land had shuddered off and on for such a long while was a mystery in and of itself, or so Riatha said, remarking, "The Loremasters say that the Utruni—the Stone Giants—were here at Kalgalath's doom centuries past and remain unto this day. And yet it was at this time of destruction the land became unstable, and it has shaken for lo these many years; and that is a riddle: For Utruni work to shape the land, to raise its mountains and carve the valleys. And in this work they strive to gentle the earth, to ease the quaking of the world, quelling it. And yet, here, the Utruni have let *this* land continue to judder, even though nearly thirty-four hundred summers have passed.

"It is as if they are waiting for something to happen. . . ."

Across this jolting realm the five plodded, past the fire and brimstone and molten lava, past the rocks blasted upward and the boiling reek, past the maimed ruin of Dragonslair, past the place sung of in many a bard's songs. A week or more did the shattered firemountain dominate the 'scape, first before them, then to their right, then fading into the mountains rearward. And slowly they swung southeastward, aiming now for the village of Inge, there along the south slope of the Grimwalls, where they would take some days of rest, and hoped to find horses for the journey south.

And as they came down through the mountains, spring drew upon the land, snow melting, water cascading, plants greening. Here and there flowers thrust upward, blossoms braving the chill. And where the snow had melted altogether, new growth burgeoned.

Gwylly's healing progressed apace, and now he began walking long stretches on his own, the Bear ambling at one side, Faeril at the other.

Down through a forest they came, and the Bear snuffled and then *whuffed*; Gwylly had come to realize that this meant for him to follow. The Bear led the two tiny cubs to a great log, then casually rolled it with a shrug of one of its mighty paws. Underneath, in the rich loam exposed to the sunlight, beetles scrabbled for cover and white grubs writhed. The Bear pounced on this delicious meal, once pausing to look at the two-legs cubs, inviting them to join in. The "cubs" declined.

In camp at night, Gwylly and Faeril listened as Riatha and Aravan recounted events of history: of the destruction of Rwn; of the Great War, of the Sundering, of the banishment of Gyphon to the Abyss beyond the Spheres; of the War of the Usurper; of the Dragonstar and the Winter War; of the War of Drimmen-deeve; of Aravan's pursuit of a Man with yellow eyes; of the past encounters with Stoke.

Faeril noted that when Riatha spoke of the destruction of Rwn, a look of desolation came into Aravan's eye, and he stood and strode off into the darkness, and did not stay to listen.

Likewise on another night, when Riatha told of her brother, Talar, the Elfess could not speak of his Death Rede, but instead, weeping, she too stood and left the circle, striding out to stand in the gloom.

When Urus went to join her, Aravan spoke softly to the Waerlinga. "Riatha is the only one among us who has actually experienced Stoke's madness, Stoke's ghastly flaying of a living being, Stoke's hideous impalement." At the look of noncomprehension on the buccan's and damman's faces, Aravan took one of Gwylly's hands and one of Faeril's in his own. "Understand me well: she *experienced* it! It was as if it were happening unto *her*! It was her own skin being flensed, her own body being pierced, she and her brother simultaneously, for such was the endowment of the Death Rede sent to her by Talar."

Both Gwylly and Faeril drew back from Aravan, comprehension dawning at last. Distress welled in Faeril's eyes, and Gwylly took her in his arms. "Oh, what a terrible gift," said Gwylly, his own gaze misery-filled.

When they came into sight of Inge, Riatha called a halt. "It will not do to come upon the village with a Bear in our midst."

Turning to the Bear, she and Aravan unbound the frame packs, struggling, for the Bear sat on his haunches and scratched, not cooperating yet not resisting either; the Bear simply didn't deign to notice.

When the packs were off at last, Riatha spoke to the Bear. "Urus!" she called. "Urus!"

A dark shimmering came over the Bear—Faeril and Gwylly yet awed by the transformation, even though they had witnessed it every morning and evening throughout the preceding days—and in but moments where the Bear had been now sat Urus.

"Inge," said Riatha, pointing.

Urus nodded and stood, taking up his pack and strapping it on, reaching for Gwylly's. "No, Urus," called the buccan. "I think I am now well enough to bear my own burden." Gwylly swung the frame across his back, grunting. "Whoosh. I'd forgotten what a load these were." Yet he waved away proffered help.

And down into Inge they went.

Even though there was no Bear in their midst, still these strangers caused quite a stir among the villagers. Not because they were travellers, oh no, for Inge lay on a minor east–west tradeway, and more often than not travellers passed through. Instead, these five strangers were remarkable in that they were two Elves, two Wee Ones, and a huge Man—all travelling together. Not like ordinary visitors— mostly farmers and their wives, occasional tinkers or merchants, at times a caravan of traders—Humans all but for a rare Dwarf now and again. But these were Elven Folk! And Wee Ones! And, oh my, wasn't the Man a big'n!

They came into town, taking rooms at the inn, purchased horses and mules and supplies, then they were gone, staying but three days all told. Why, they were in and out so fast that not all folks got to see them. And the business they were on, their mission . . . well, let's just say that it was most mysterious.

As Borlo Hensley, proprietor of the Ram's Horn, the only inn in town, said after they had gone: "We welcomed them with open arms, and the first thing these strangers asked for was *information!* of all things. *Had we seen any Foul Folk? Suffered any raids? Heard any Vulgs howl? Had any* disappearances? *Seen a yellow-eyed Man? Noted any monstrous flying things? And other such nonsense.* Oh, Widow Trucen *said* she'd heard a Vulg howl some nights back, but Burd the wheelwright said 'twasn't nothin' but a Wolf or two. Set her right he did, and she hasn't forgiven him to this day, turns up her nose and passes him by.

"Strange questions, these, for it seems they were *hunting* after some'n, a Rutch or Drōk or Ogru, or even a Guul. But we couldn't help them in their folly.

"The next thing they wanted were rooms and baths, though why the baths, I wouldn't know. Said they'd been in the wilderness several weeks and hadn't bathed even once in all that time, and couldn't we smell that it was so? I told 'em they smelt just fine, and that too many baths'd make 'em sick. But they went ahead regardless.

"The Wee Ones, splashing and singing together, they were. And then after . . . well, let's just say they kept in their room to themselves a good long while.

"The Elfess, now, she had a voice like that of a evengale, playing Ella's harp and singing songs at night. *Magic* it was, that or I'm a confirmed twithead, the way she made that harp do. And the Elf, he spoke poetry, some so fierce as to make your blood boil, and other so sad that there weren't a dry eye in the house.

"Horses they bought, and mules—three of each. Made Burd right rich, I shouldn't wonder, what with purchasing this and that and the other for to go along with 'em . . . good coin all, though I hear tell that Burd says he was paid with a jewel—Ha! I'll believe *that* when I see it.

"The big Man, now, they say he's a strong one. Lifted a waggon Burd was fixin'. Like it was of no consequence. Up by the corner. 'So what?' says I when Burd was telling me, 'Dardar the smith can do that.' 'This is what,' says he. 'The waggon was carrying a load of fireturf. A whole load at that!'

"Now, it ain't that I'm callin' Burd a liar, or even a exaggerater, but a Man'd have t' be as strong as a ox to lift a load of turf, and that's no flam."

A murmur of agreement rippled among the patrons of the Ram's Horn but quickly silenced as the innkeeper spoke on.

"Something else Burd said about the big Man, though, right peculiar: seems as if the horses and mules were skittish around him, like they was afraid o' his smell or something, but they settled when he finally put a hand on them and spoke . . . gentled right down, they did.

"Be that as it may, three days they stayed, then left. South they are headed. I told 'em to steer clear of the Mire. A bad place, that, what with its bogs that'll suck a Man under in a eyeblink, and the things that live in there what'll do you in and gulp you down, to say nothing of the vipers and adders and of the nits and gnats and bloodsuckers and the poison vines and other such."

Again a mutter of agreement washed through Borlo's listeners. *Almost as bad as Dragonslair*, said some. *Worse than Dragonslair*, said others. *Full of "deaders,"* added others still. And once again the arguments erupted over which was worse—Dragonslair or the Khalian Mire—a war of words which had lasted without resolution for nearly thirty-four hundred years.

And as they debated with one another, the land jolted and juddered, timbers rattled and crockery clattered, and none paid it any heed, for living where they did, the world forever shook.

Mid-morn of the day they left Inge found three riding horses and three pack mules fording the river that marked the border between Aralan and Khal. In the lead rode Aravan, a laden mule on a tether trailing behind. Immediately after came Urus and Riatha, each with a mule following. On these last two mules, ensconced among the cargo, rode Gwylly on one and Faeril on the other, for no ponies were to be had in Inge.

The swift-running water was high and frigid, the river wide-swollen with spring snowmelt. Leaving his mule with the others, Aravan rode across, testing the depth, gauging the current, assessing the danger. On the opposite shore he wheeled his mount and rode back across, the water up to his horse's belly at the deepest. "Should a mule fall," he said to the Warrows, "cling to the pack frame. The animal will right itself, and if the water is deep, it will swim to shore. We will come after ye or throw ye lines should there be a need."

His words, though prudent, proved to be unnecessary, for the crossing was uneventful.

Southerly they rode, cutting cross-country through the rolling hills, intending to follow along the banks of the River Venn until it came to the Avagon Sea. Altogether, as the raven wings, they were some two thousand miles from Caer Pendwyr and slightly more than that from Challerain Keep, the two principal residences of the High King: the keep his summer quarters; the caer his winter home; the two Courts some fifteen hundred miles apart, the King travelling between in April and September.

Although the five comrades were two thousand miles from either residence as the raven flies, by land or by a combination of land and sea they were farther still. It would take them nearly four months to reach either place, given the choices before them.

Urus had growled when Aravan had proposed his plan sixteen days past:

*"In four months, Stoke could be anywhere."*

*"Yet we have little choice. We need the aid of the Realmsmen."*

*"Realmsmen?"*

*"Aye, Realmsmen. After the Winter War, nearly a thousand years agone, High King Galen, the son of Aurion, founded a group of Men he named Realmsmen: guardians of the Kingdom, champions of Just Causes. They range the Realm and defend the Land."*

*"When I was in the ice. . . . These rangers, how do we enlist their aid?"*

*"They headquarter in Caer Pendwyr in Pellar. It would be best to go there to describe Stoke and his deeds and have his likeness sent to all Realmsmen throughout the High King's domain. 'Twould also be best to go to the caer to seek audience with the High King, for no matter which place we go, we are months from either residence. And should we strive for Challerain Keep in Rian and be hindered along the way, then he will be gone to Pellar by the time we arrive."*

*"I like not this delay, Aravan, yet I have no better plan and we have but a short list of choices. Stoke is lost to us,*

*and we could search forever. We need aid, and mayhap in*
*Caer Pendwyr we can find it. Let us go there then and seek*
*audience with the High King . . . and contact the Realmsmen.*
*Mayhap together with their aid we will find the one we*
*seek."*

And now they travelled southerly, aiming for a port on the
Avagon Sea to book passage to the place where High King
Garan dwelled.

The next day they sighted a swamp on the horizon, and by
the noontide they rode along its marge. Large, hoary old
trees, black cypress and dark swamp willow, twisted up out
of the muck, looming, barring the morning light, their
warped roots gnarling down out of sight into the slime-laden
mud. A greyish moss dangled down from lichen-wattled
limbs, like ropes and nets set to entangle and entrap the
unwary. A faint mist rose up from the bog, reaching, clinging, clutching at those who would seek to pass through.
Though it was early spring, snakes slithered from drowned
logs into green-scummed water, and swarms of gnats and
flies and mosquitoes filled the air like a grey haze, for the
heat of decaying vegetation provided the dark environs with
the warmth to sustain such life in all but the dead of winter.
And alongside these environs they rode, out where the
cool air protected them from the swarms of bloodsuckers.
Looking in through the trees, they could see that the bog
itself was a veritable maze of water and mire and land and
wild growth. And as the Sun shone down into this green
enigma, the swamp steamed in response; and it seemed as
if the air within might become too thick, too wet to draw a
clean breath. The marsh heaved with gases belching from
slimy waters, bubbles plopping, foul stenches reeking.
South they rode as the Sun sank into the west, and lengthening shadows streamed from the hunched hummocks, from
the twisted trees, from the sharp-edged reeds and saw grass,
filling the bog with gloom. And above the barely heard hum
of the swarms of flying pests within, other noises began to
fill the air: a *chirruping* and *breeking* and *peeping* of swamp
dwellers, along with ploppings, splashings, wallowings,
slitherings.

"Lor!" breathed Gwylly. "I'm glad we're out here and they're in there."

The Sun began to set. Long shadows slanted across the darkening land and into the murky bog, filling the environs with ebon blackness, creeping shadows slipping among the reeds, past the foul moss adrip from lifeless branches, over oozing muck and above scum-laden water, the Khalian Mire taking on an eerie aspect as night fell.

And as the five set up camp along its edge, Faeril's eyes were ever drawn to the sinister galleries. Of a sudden she jumped up and pointed. "Oh my, there's someone within calling for help, for I see their lantern."

All looked where she pointed. Gwylly leapt to his feet as well, preparing to go into the mire.

"Nay, wee ones," said Aravan, "stay! 'Tis no lantern ye see, but a ghost candle instead."

Faeril turned to the Elf. "Ghost candle?"

"Aye. Said to be the spirit of one who is dead. Said to try to lure the innocent and the unwary unto their doom within the bog."

Riatha spoke. "Aravan speaks one of their names. They are called will-o'-the-wisp by others. But by any name they are indeed a danger should ye try to go in after them. They will lead ye on a chase to nowhere, mazing thy minds, getting ye lost, luring ye unto deep waters where ye may drown. So stay, for 'tis no lantern ye see, but a cunning spirit of the swamp."

Reluctantly, the Warrows resumed their seats. "Tell me, Aravan," asked Gwylly, "how came ghost candles to this place?"

Aravan looked at the firelight dancing on the faces of the Waerlinga. "Let me a tale unfold for thee, a tale of a time long past, for I have heard how the Khalian Mire came to be, though I was not on Mithgar when it occurred and did not witness the events I am about to relate, so I cannot vouch for the truth of them."

Riatha poured more tea into each of their cups, and all settled back as Aravan began:

"In the Time Before, there was a crystal castle with a rainbow bridge sitting midst a fair land, much like the rolling hills to the west, yet forested thickly. The castle with its bridge was a marvel to behold, and occupied by a folk most fair. Some say they were Elven, while others say they were Men, and none I know can say for certain which indeed they were. You see, of the Time Before little is known, except that it was in the days before Elves knew of those things worth striving for and instead sought to conquer all.

"Regardless, in the center of the forest stood a crystal castle peopled by a Race most fair. And 'round the castle and beyond the bridge were gardens of remarkable flowers and trees and running waters and dancing fountains and a sward so green as to put emeralds to shame.

"Beyond the gardens lay the wide forest, a woodland filled with game: hare and stag, deer and chuck, boar and wild kine, and more, oh more, oh very much more.

"Through this realm a clear river flowed, its waters pellucid and cool and with a taste to quench all thirst, and it was filled with fish and eels and clawed backswimmers, frogs and turtles, too. Thereupon as well were waterfowl: ducks and geese and swans and loons and colorful gallinules, and other such swimmers and waders.

"Birds dwelled in the forest as well, gamebirds and songbirds alike.

"Fruit and nuts grew on the branches and vines, and berries on the briars. Honey filled many a hollow tree, and the ground was rich with herbs and mosses and greens and mushrooms wondrous and rare. And where the soil was tilled and planted, gardens grew and fields flourished, and their bounty was plentiful.

"Cattle and goats and sheep found lush grazing, and crofters' barnyards were filled with fowl and their nests with eggs.

"Every evening, it seemed, a gentle rain replenished the soil.

"So abundant was the land that no spit was without at least a hare or a fish or a stag or a goose or other such, all so savory, so tasty . . . well, let us just say that hunger was an unknown thing.

"And the King who reigned o'er all was blessed.

"Yet there were those who coveted the crystal castle with

its rainbow bridge and lush gardens surrounding it and the rich Land beyond, with its forests and fields and clear, clear waters, and would have it all be their own.

"One of these covetous ones was a King in his own right, and he proposed a challenge to the rightful ruler. His army he would bring to the sward before the castle and there they would meet in battle, the winner to take all.

"And so knights and squires, footmen and bowmen, all gathered on the wide sward. The two great armies met and fought a mighty War. Back and forth raged the combat, the striving bloody and fierce, and tens of thousands fell. Yet the rightful King won the day, though of his great Host there remained but a pitiful few, yet his enemy had far, far less.

"But the enemy was most treacherous, and amid his ranks a Sorcerer stood, the mightiest of his day; and he was the true power behind the enemy throne. And when the Sorcerer saw that the battle was lost, that the forests and fields and remarkable gardens and the crystal castle with its rainbow bridge would not be his, he called up a mighty spell. And with a cataclysmic lurch the land fell, forest and fields all. The gardens themselves sank beyond sight, and the rainbow bridge and crystal castle shattered into shards beyond count.

"The spell was so powerful, so wicked, that all living creatures within its sphere were destroyed: all the remaining knights and squires, all the remaining footmen and bowmen, all the pages and thralls, all nobles, including both Kings, as well as their Queens, and last of all the Sorcerer himself.

"The clear river that flowed through the land continued to stream down from the mountains, and for many months it went no farther, pooling on the land instead. Slowly the great depression filled, and the forest and plants, the herbs and mosses, and the wondrous mushrooms, all were drowned. All the dead plants and animals and Men—or Elves—all rotted.

"Ages passed. Silt collected. The depression, which was shallow to begin with, the depression slowly became a great bog, a mire, a swamp. Black cypress came, and rushes, and a grey moss that hangs down to catch up and strangle the unwary. Reeds and scum and snakes and bloodsuckers came, and beasts too foul to name. And what was once the most blessed of Lands became the Land most baned, due to a Sorcerer's curse.

"They say that the spirits of the dead are forever trapped within, those who fought in the War. And that is what ye see when ye sight a glimmer in the dark, dark canopied vaults therein—ghost candles, corpse candles, will-o'-the-wisps they're called; but by any name they are the spirits of the dead, lights that'll draw ye to a watery doom if ye follow their lure.

"Yet that's not all who inhabit the mire, for there, too, are the undead. Decaying corpses riddled with rot yet curiously ever preserved lie beneath the black muck and the stagnant pools, rising up at night to stalk through the sucking mud and bubbling ooze and choking vines, o'er the decay and slime, sometimes silent, sometimes calling out for the living, seeking victims, for these are the undead reaching out to clutch whoever they can, to suck the life out of the very blood and sinews and bones of the pitiful wretches they capture.

"And that, my wee Waerlinga, that is the tale of the horrors of the Khalian Mire. Beware the call of the rotting undead, beware the ghostly lights, beware the Sorcerer's curse, but most of all"—Aravan leaned close, his voice dropping to a whisper; the Warrows' eyes were as wide as saucers—"most of all beware of those who tell such tales, for those are the ones who will *GET YE!*"

Aravan's hands snaked out, clutching at Waerlinga, grabbing each by an arm. *Yaahh!* they shrieked simultaneously, startled beyond their wits; then all burst forth in laughter, Urus's great rolling booms roaring, Riatha's silver voice trilling, Aravan belling, and Gwylly and Faeril both rolling upon the ground, mirth pealing.

The horses and mules looked about as if to say, *What fools*, and when Riatha noted it and unable to speak pointed instead, laughter rode upon laughter until throats grew hoarse and ribs ached.

Yet in the central grasp of the Khalian Mire, deep in the rotting ruins of an ancient castle, a yellow-eyed Man stood over a shattered crypt, muttering arcane words above an open sarcophagus, a sarcophagus occupied. In the guttering torch-light, *Drik* and *Ghok* shrank back in fear, trying to remain unseen, trying to slip from sight among the writhing shadows, for they knew not what next would come.

# CHAPTER 25

# *Lógoi tôn Nekrôn*

**Spring, 5E988**

*[The Present]*

Stoke stood above the ancient sarcophagus, his yellow eyes glaring down at the desiccated remains lying within. Rotted raiments clad the withered flesh. Skeletal hands clutching a scepter were folded across the corpse's chest. Brown with untold age, dried skin stretched taut across a sunken-cheeked face, as a skull covered with dark, shrivelled leather parchment. Hollow sockets stared upward, ebon holes unseeing, and yellowed teeth shone past mummified lips grinning a rictus smile. To one side lay the shattered lid of the stone coffin, the knightly figure carven thereupon smashed into a thousand scattered pieces. Feeble, wavering torch-light cast writhing shadows throughout the chamber, dark pits showing entrances to the myriad passages riddling the catacombs. In the guttering torch-light, *Drik* and *Ghok* shrank back in fear, trying to remain unseen, trying to slip from sight within the fluttering gloom, for they knew not what next would come.

There remained but seven *Chūn*—*Drik* and *Ghok*—those and five *Vulpen*—Vulgs. All told, Stoke had started his trek through the snowstorm with twenty-seven *Drik* and *Ghok* and seven *Vulpen*. Of these, twenty *Chūn* and four *Vulpen* had slipped aside in the outbound canyon to ambush those who followed; the remaining seven *Chūn* and three *Vulpen* had gone with Stoke into the blizzard, leaving a track to lure the followers on. The trap, though, had been a disaster, for the ambushers could not see through the blinding nighttime snow, and fifteen of the *Drik* and *Ghok* and two of the *Vulpen* had been slain. Of the five *Chūn* who had survived that deadly encounter, one had died of a stab wound taken in the combat, and the other four had been slain by Stoke in his wrath at discovering that they had failed. The two surviving *Vulpen*, Stoke's favorites, had been spared. And so, altogether there now were but seven *Chūn* and five *Vulpen* in Stoke's entourage.

They had evaded the pursuers by taking passage under a mountain unto a hidden valley and then another passage beyond. Southerly they had fared, the tunnels disastrously weakened by the quaking land, stone falling all about even as they fled. Twice they had spent days digging through massive blockages, even as the land wrenched and shuddered, threatening to collapse the mountains down on them. And yet they had survived, travelling aboveground at night and underground by day. Emerging at last from the Grimwall Mountains, they had bypassed the village of Inge, for Baron Stoke would leave no clue as to his direction of travel. Swiftly they had come to the Khalian Mire, and Stoke had raced on ahead with his *Vulpen*, leaving the *Drik* and *Ghok* behind, slogging after through the swamp with all of its deadly denizens. During the day the *Chūn* had burrowed beneath mucky hummocks to escape the Sun, seeking refuge but finding instead writhing bloodsucking leeches, blind mouths questing. Two nights after entering the mire, they finally had come to the ancient ruins of the castle and fled down into the dungeons and catacombs below, where Stoke and his *Vulpen* waited.

And now they had come unto this place, this ebon crypt.

Water ran from their legs, pooling on the floor, for although the chamber itself had been dry when they smashed the seal and broke in, in the passages behind they had waded through tunnels awash with bog water, the walls slime-laden, the ceilings adrip, half-seen things writhing out of sight, escaping the feeble light of the torches they bore. They had shattered open the crypt, revealing the sarcophagus, and the Baron alone had heaved the massive lid onto the floor, smashing it asunder. And now Stoke stood above the corpse and spoke the words of power, for only the dead could tell him what he wished to know:

Deadly concentration was dark on Stoke's brow. *"Ákouse mè!"* rolled out his voice, commanding the dead one to listen.

Clenching his long, grasping fingers into clawed fists, Stoke imperiously dictated, *"Peísou moî!"* commanding the dead one to obey.

Sweat beaded on Stoke's lip as he called out, *"Idoû toîs ophthalmoîs toîs toû nekroû!"* commanding the dead one to see what the dead can see, visions beyond time and space.

Stoke channelled fierce energy through his being, perspiration running down his forehead, and he spoke the next decree: *"Idoû toùs polémious toùs emoùs toùs mè nùn diokóntous!"* commanding the dead one to look through space for the enemies who now pursue.

Salt stung his eyes, yet Stoke did not wipe it away, for to do so would disastrously loosen his control; instead his chanting voice demanded: *"Heurè autoús!"* commanding the dead one to find the foe.

Now Stoke's teeth gritted and ground with the strain, yet he uttered the compelling words: *"Tòn páton tòn autôn heurè!"* commanding the dead one to discover the path of the enemy.

His body slick with effort, his hands trembling, Stoke mandated, *"Eipè moî hò horáei!"* commanding the dead one to reveal what it sees.

Now Stoke's entire being shook, for such arcane workings called for energy beyond that which most could give, his voice canting, *"Anà kaì lékse!"* commanding the corpse to rise and speak.

Sweat pouring down, muscles knotted with rack, eyes bulging, jaws clenched, mind shrieking for relief, Stoke spoke the final command, *"Egò gàr ho Stókos dè kèleuo sé!"* invoking the name of Stoke commanding the dead one.

As of a legion of voices in distant agony, the chamber filled with unnumbered whispering groans, the corpse stirring. *Drik* and *Ghok* shrank back in fear. Even the *Vulpen* warding the tunnels seemed to cower. Stoke, his yellow eyes burning with a ghastly light, called out again, *"Anà kaì lékse; egò gàr ho Stókos dè kèleuo sé!"*

A shriveled hand reached up and clutched a side of the stone sarcophagus, dust exhaling upward, brittle flesh sloughing downward. Slowly, agonizingly, the other hand reached for the coffin edge; the scepter, loosed from its millennia-long grasp, rolled aside. Tattered garments crumbled, falling away from mummified arms. Skeletal fingers gripped the rim; dry bones cracked. Again there came the massed groans of a multitude, and haltingly, falteringly, by inchmeal the corpse dragged itself upward, desiccated flesh and cartilage and sinew and bone crumbling with the effort. At last it levered itself to a sitting position, and slowly, vertebrae snapping, it turned its skull-like head, the tight, dry lips drawn away from yellowed teeth, empty eye pits staring at the one who summoned. The jaw hinged, parchment flesh crumbling away, and speaking as one voice a hideous choir of whispers filled the chamber. The *Chūn* whimpered at the empty sound, looking about for a place to flee. And the voices spoke in a language the *Drik* and *Ghok* did not comprehend.

[*"Pego an vilar . . ."*] "Why . . . why . . . why . . . hast thou summoned me? . . . *summoned me . . . summoned me . . . summoned me . . . summoned . . ."* echoed the ghastly chorus of mutterers, whispers hissing, different voices fading in and out, stronger weaker, rising falling, murmurs on top of murmurs, all asking . . . asking . . . asking. . . .

Stoke answered in the same tongue, a tongue long lost to all but those who would and will not let the dead lie buried: the scholars of the ancients, who seek knowledge for the sake of knowledge alone; and those who delve into the forbidden art of *Psukhomanteía*, of Necromancy, where such tongues are at times . . . useful. "Seek not to evade me, dead one. Instead do that which I asked! Where are the enemies who now follow me?"

Still the ebon holes stared at Baron Stoke, but his yellow-eyed gaze did not waver. At last, 'mid the creaking and cracking of bone, and the thin sound of dry parchment tearing, the corpse turned its head, searching, at last peering northwesterly and very slightly upward. A myriad whispering voices hissed answers, simultaneous agonizing echoes murmuring, rustling, mumbling, as if numberless mutterers crowded forward, all speaking, each striving to be heard, murmurers fading in and out, many voices talking at the same time through the same mouth, each whisperer describing a different event, a confusion of sissing babble.

*... Flay ... four follow ... one follows ... burn ... three ... pierce ... demon ...*

Yet Stoke listened for the dominant whisper, not easily distinguished from the multitude, for as his mentor, Ydral, had told him long past, *"Trust little the word of a dead soul, for unto the dead time has no meaning. They see the past and the present and the future all at once, all the same. Unless the* Psukhómantis—*the Necromancer—has the will and energy and endurance, the power to give focus, then the voices of the dead bring words of little use to the summoner, for they may bear a message meant for another entirely. Tji must listen carefully to find the truespeaker for* tji. *If* tji *can single out that voice, then words of value may come, as they did when* jai *discovered that one who bears Elven blood will be* mai *doom. Concentrate, dominate, else what* tji *learn will lead to disaster."*

And so Stoke listened carefully, trying to choose from among the myriad of agonized whispers, trying to pick out the voice of the truespeaker who would answer his questions. Mutterings filled the chamber, murmurings, sissings, hissings.

Yet among the whispering voices, Stoke found one that seemed to dominate, one that seemed to belong to *this* corpse. "Thine enemies ... *collapse ... Dwarves break the*—two Elves ... *she will cut* ... two small ones ... *beware the long piercer ... the ruined spear breaks ...*and a ManBear—encamp at the marge of a great mire ... *flay ... timbers fall* ... a mire this one ... *silver bullet ... silver dagger* ... hast not seen ere now."

Stoke laughed. "So, my enemies encamp at the marge of a great mire, a mire you have not seen ere now. Hah! It is *this* place, you fool! Look about and see the bog your Realm has become."

Moaning ten thousand moans, the corpse rotated its head

about, parched flesh falling away from yellowed bone, as the dry tissues 'round the neck crumbled to dust. Vacant eye sockets seemed to be staring through surrounding stone walls, through earth, seeing the tangle and scum and muck and foul waters beyond. *Aiee . . . !* shrieked the voices of the countless damned, the echoes filling the crypt with cries of anguish. *Drik* and *Ghok* shrank hindward in terror, some backing against the walls, others bolting a few steps from the chamber and into the dark tunnels, stopping, wanting to flee yet unable to face the ebon catacombs beyond. *Vulpen* whimpered and cowered, yet would not leave their master.

Stoke reveled in the agonized wail, though it did not nearly answer his unholy lust to inflict pain, to flay, to . . . impale. "Enough!" he commanded. "Answer my second question: where are my enemies bound?"

Countless sobbing moans issued forth from the gaping jaw, yet no answer came.

Now Stoke invoked the tongue of *Psukhomanteía,* of Necromancy, bidding *tòn nekròn,* the dead, to answer: *"Tòn páton tòn autôn heuré!"*

Slowly the chorus of wails subsided. Finally, as if seeking, again the corpse rotated its head about, vertebrae grinding, withered flesh crumbling, all the while thousands of voices whispered: . . . *Gûnarring . . . Gron . . . Arden Vale . . . Fjordland . . . Vancha . . . Rian . . . Wilderland . . .* Yet still the head swivelled, skritching, flaking, disintegrating. At last the corpse fixed its vacant stare southerly. Voices poured out: . . . *Karoo . . . Garia . . . Pellar . . . Sarain . . . Chabba . . .* But Stoke listened carefully, seeking the whisper of the truespeaker, and he heard: "Southerly . . . *westerly . . . northerly . . . easterly . . .* they fare . . . ride . . . ship . . . unto a great town . . . *desert . . . hamlet . . . forest . . .* where a High King . . . *seer . . . oracle . . .* dwells along the shore of the . . . *Boreal Sea . . . Weston Ocean . . . Grimmere . . .* Avagon Sea."

Air sissed in through clenched teeth. "Speak again," Stoke demanded. "To what end do they seek this High King?"

The corpse replied not.

*"Egò gàr ho Stókos dè kèleuo sé!"* commanded Stoke.

Gradually, bones crumbling, parchment skin splitting, the

desiccated head of the corpse turned empty sockets unto the yellow-eyed Man. Thousands of hollow whispers sounded. "I have given thee all that thou are due ... *are due ... are due ... due ...* Thou now attempt to reach beyond ... *beyond ...* that which thou did invoke when thou didst summon me ... *summon me ... summon me ... me ...* It is not ... *not ...* in thy power to ask ... *to ask ... ask ...* for more and receive it. I would go now ... *would go ... would go ... go now ... go now ... go ...*" The ghastly whispers fell silent and would not speak again.

Stoke's eyes flared with rage, yet he was spent and had not the energy to invoke obedience, would not have the power for weeks to come. Glaring in wrath at the withered thing before him, he hissed, "Then thou shall fall again back unto the black abyss wherein dwell the souls of the dead!" And his voice took on the incantation to make it so. *"Pése pálin eis tòn keuthmòn tòn mélanta éntha oikéousin hai psukhaì hai tôn nekrôn!"* he shouted, and with a clatter the corpse collapsed, bones shattering, skin, raiments, tissues all crumbling, a boiling cloud of dust whooshing upward, dancing motes drifting, some to settle back upon a long-forgotten scepter whose office of power was not even a memory.

# CHAPTER 26

# Pilgrimage

**Spring and Summer, 5E988**

*[The Present]*

Off and on for four days did Aravan and Riatha and Urus and Gwylly and Faeril ride within sight of the great Khalian Mire, that vast swamp some one hundred and fifty miles from its northernmost reach unto its southern extent. Fifty or so miles below lay the Lesser Mire, out of which coursed the River Venn, its waters originating in the Grimwalls, flowing by many tributaries unto the mires to spread out over the two vast swamps and drift sluggishly, torpidly, through the great bogs to funnel down and come together and rise at last as a single stream beyond. Just past the mire along the banks of the Venn lay the village of Arask, the place where the five hoped to purchase ponies for the Warrows to ride, for as Gwylly had said, "Mules are fine as pack animals, but me, I'll take a pony." Too, they hoped to trade up to a larger horse for Urus, the Baeran's weight a burden for the one he now rode, the horse in effect bearing double; and so they stopped often to rest, or to walk awhile, relieving the mount of the Man's twenty-two stone, of his three hundred and ten pounds.

After passing through Stoneford west of Inge and north of the mires, they had seen no other hamlets or villages along the way, though solitary farms and the cabins of hunters and trappers had lain in their path, and at each the companions had stopped and spoken to the occupants, seeking information that might lead to Stoke's whereabouts, finding none. And so, alongside the bogs southward they rode across the gently rolling hills, ten or twelve leagues a day.

Spring was now full upon the land, and trees were beginning to leaf out, some now showing blossoms—apple and pear trees, cherry and peach. Bees hummed among the petals, collecting nectar and pollen, disappearing when they had gathered as much as they could bear.

It was the fourth day of May when they came into Arask, ten days after they had departed from Inge three hundred and twenty-five or so miles hence by the route they had travelled.

"Here we stay a day or three," rumbled Urus. "Give the animals a chance to rest a bit. Us too."

They inquired after an inn and were directed to the Red Ox on the main street. While stabling their horses and mules out back, they found from the horseboy that indeed some ponies were to be had, though he opined that the price might be high ". . . for a pony, that is." Too, there were some larger horses, though how fleet these were was another matter. But pony purchasing and horse trading would have to wait, for uppermost on the minds of the comrades were rooms and baths and good hot meals and a tankard or two of ale.

As they took supper that night, Faeril remarked, "Gwylly and I went for a stroll. Saw some boats alongside a quay. Docked. We thought that if we all went by water, we'd get to Pellar faster."

Aravan nodded. "Aye, that we would. Yet were we to take the river, like as not we must needs leave our mounts behind, for I, too, saw those boats at the quay, and they are too small to bear the horses and mules and any ponies we might get."

Gwylly glanced up from his mutton. "And . . . ?"

"And," continued Aravan, "should we hear of Stoke's whereabouts, without mounts we would have no swift way of getting there . . . unless, of course, he were on the river as well—an unlikely event."

"Oh, right," responded Gwylly, shovelling another chunk of gravy-soaked bread into his mouth.

*　　*　　*

They spent another two days in Arask, filling themselves up with hot cooked meals, sleeping in soft beds at night, taking daily baths—to the wonder of the innkeeper and his staff—and purchasing needed supplies, including a larger horse for Urus and two sturdy ponies—promptly named Ironfoot and Buster by Faeril, who said that it would be undignified to ride on a nameless beast . . . and besides, Ironfoot *had* needed his new shoes, and Buster *had* kicked down the stall door when Urus had come near, though he had settled down after Urus had spoken to him.

And daily they pored over Riatha's maps, again studying the alternatives before them, reviewing the best course to Pellar. Urus summed up their primary choices, his finger tracing the routes on the charts:

"Here at Arask we can ferry across the river into Aralan and then follow the Venn awhile, veering from it here, where it arcs westerly, rejoining it here where it swings back to run through this slot between the Skarpal Mountains and the Bodorian Range, aiming for the port of Thrako on the Avagon Sea. From there we sail to Pellar. In all, some eight or nine hundred miles to the sea, and then a voyage of another thirteen hundred. Given the terrain we must cross, and conserving the horses and ponies and mules, that's some five or six weeks overland, and by sea, another . . ." Urus cocked an eyebrow at Aravan.

"Depending on the ship, when it embarks, its route, the number of stops, and how long it stays in any given port along the way, it could take as little as, say, a week or two, and as much as one or two months."

Urus growled at Aravan's reply. "*Arrr.* Anywhere from eight weeks to fifteen, then. Anywhere from July to September."

Aravan nodded.

Faeril spoke. "What about this river here, the Hanü? Can we ford it?"

Aravan glanced over at the damman. "Aye. I crossed it once on my way into the Skarpals. Somewhere nigh here"—he pointed—"is a ford we can ride for."

Gwylly scanned the map. "What about the other routes?"

Again Urus's finger traced across the chart: "There is this:

We follow the Venn all the way to Vorlo in Garia, here where the River Ulian joins it. Then we ride easterly, swinging southerly, passing 'round the Skarpal Mountains to come to Dask on the Inner Sea, where once again we wait for a ship to bear us, first out to the Avagon and thence to Caer Pendwyr. The journey by land covers some"—Urus used the length of his thumb to gauge—"eleven to twelve hundred miles, and then another twelve hundred by sea; here the terrain is somewhat more gentle, so the overland journey will take perhaps eight weeks or so, and the sea journey another"—Urus glanced at Aravan—"week to two months, neh?"

Aravan nodded in agreement.

Urus sighed. "July to September, again."

Gwylly pointed at the map, bobbing his head up and down. "We could go to Rhondor instead of Dask. I've always wanted to see Rhondor, the city of merchants."

Urus smiled. "Aye, we could, can we ford the River Storcha. The distance is almost the same."

Faeril traced a route overland from Rhondor to Caer Pendwyr. "It looks to be some nine hundred miles cross-country. If we went by horse, pony, and mule all the way . . ."

"I have made that journey in but three weeks," interjected Riatha. " 'Twas War, and the steeds were utterly spent at journey's end. Six weeks or seven would I recommend for us."

"What if we can't ford the Storcha?" asked Gwylly, then answered his own query. "Oh wait, I see: we could sail the Inner Sea from Dask to Rhondor."

"In all, then," rumbled Urus, "some fourteen or fifteen weeks, can we ford the Storcha, and somewhat more if we cannot. That would put it August or September when we arrive at Caer Pendwyr."

Aravan shrugged. "No matter which way, we must await the High King, for he arrives after."

Urus studied the alternatives. Finally he said, "Aravan's original plan holds the most promise for the swiftest delivery to Caer Pendwyr: we ferry across into Aralan here, ride down to the sea at Thrako, then book passage to Pendwyr."

Gwylly's face fell. "I'd been hoping to go to Rhondor. But

I suppose that it's best we get the Realmsmen involved as soon as we can . . . the port of Thrako it is."

When the five of them left Arask, Gwylly led Buster down to the ferry, and Faeril led Ironfoot, and coming after were Riatha and Aravan and Urus, their horses on leads, the mules tethered behind. And even though it was dawn, the village entire turned out to see them go: the two Wee Ones with the jewellike eyes, the Elven Bard, the Elven Poet, and the towering Baeran Man.

It was a large ferry, and one trip sufficed, the ferrymen chanting as they used the pull rope to hale the travellers across. Aravan paid the toll—a few coppers—and then the five were on their way, riding down through Aralan along the banks of the River Venn.

Southeasterly they fared, sometimes swinging wide of the course to pass beyond the great loops of the meandering stream. Yet always the river vale was in sight, and they used it to guide their way by day, though had they travelled at night they would have guided by the stars.

Thirty or so miles a day did they go, the land gently rolling, stopping often to rest the steeds, feeding them grain hauled by the mules. Buster and Ironfoot easily kept up the pace, even though they were but ponies, for they came of a hardy mountain stock, having been bred in the Bodorian Range there in the Land of Alban. And so thirty miles a day did they cover, ten leagues from Sun to Sun, camping at night on the Aralan plains or down by the River Venn. And as they went, the days grew warmer and the nights less chill, and the horses, mules, and ponies began shedding their winter shag, curry combs filling with hair. Slowly the world came green, flowers blossoming, trees leafing, grasses transforming from yellow to succulent green, and water ran in rivulets everywhere. Birds swept through the sky, some to travel onwards, others to take up residence in the surround, calling out their mating cries, challenging any interlopers who would dare trespass. Marmots and hares were often seen, and now and then a fox. And the lords of the air— falcons and hawks and an occasional eagle—would sweep o'er the plains or circle above and stoop in their deadly dives.

And as they rode through the awakening world, Gwylly's and Faeril's eyes sparkled with pleasure and their mouths flashed with grins, calling out to one another, sharing spring. And when this would happen, Riatha would smile unto herself, and her own eyes would seek out Urus, only to find him looking at her.

Seven days after leaving Arask, the comrades' path slowly diverged from that of the River Venn, it taking a slightly more westerly course, while the five continued onward in their southwesterly line cross-country. At last there came a time when the riverborder forest was no longer in sight, as down across the plains of Aralan fared the riders.

Another week went by, the companions making their way over the lush prairie, and spring rains came like long grey brooms sweeping west to east. And when this happened, through chill drizzles rode the five o'er the open plains, no shelter other than their own raincloaks to fend off the water—no forests, no thickets, in which to escape the rain, not even the makings for a crude lean-to. Too, there was no sign of civilization within sight—no hunter's lodge, no trapper's shack, no farmer's outbuildings, no soddies, not even the tents of wanderers.

In fact, they had not seen anyone for the past nine days; their last contact with civilization had been with an isolated crofter and his family. The companions had accepted a meal and had slept in the tiny barn, a byre too small to take in all of their steeds. They had sheltered the horses only, for they were the animals most likely to need the comfort of a stall. And as Gwylly said, "Buster, he doesn't like stalls."

But that had been nine days past, almost a hundred leagues ago.

The day was somber when they came upon the Landover Road, an ancient east–west tradeway still in use—though no caravans or merchants' trains could be seen along the road from horizon to horizon, no solitary wayfarers either. They were now some fifteen days and four hundred thirty miles from Arask, and as they crossed the road they swung due south, for now they fared toward the slot between the Bodorian Range and the Skarpal Mountains. Beyond the slot lay their first goal, the port town of Thrako, also some four hundred thirty miles as the raven flies, somewhat longer by the route they planned to follow, the Landover Road more or less marking the halfway point on their journey from the Lesser Mire to the Avagon Sea. Yet though they were halfway to the sea in miles, the terrain ahead was considerably rougher, and they gauged it would take some three or four weeks to reach the port. Even so, down into the land they fared, aiming for the ford across the River Hanü, three horses, two ponies, and two mules plodding stolidly under the sullen skies.

South they went across the wold, the land gradually changing from plains to rolling hills, thickets and trees beginning to appear. As they topped hills, now to the west they could see the crests of the Skarpal Mountains—grey crags jutting up from the Garian Plains—for the comrades were near that Land.

It was now late May, and the nights were warm as well as the days. The trees had come into their fullness, and as the five rode through the green forests it was as if the woes of the world were gone, gentle breezes soughing through the leaves, songbirds casting their carols for any and all to hear, animals scurrying among undergrowth and rustling through the leaves and ground cover of the woodland, other creatures running along the limbs and branches in the arbors overhead, chattering at these interlopers below. At a freshet they came across a doe and her fawn, and none had the will to bring down the game, even though it had been long since venison graced their plates.

At last they came to the River Hanü, arriving late in the eve. Twilight was descending upon the forest as they made camp alongside the mossy-banked river. Water rippled nearby, purling its endless song. And as the Moon rose and shed its light downward, Gwylly and Faeril sat facing one another and holding hands, singing softly to each other in Twyll.

Riatha glanced at them and over at Urus. *Never love a mortal Man.* Tears filled her silver eyes and she stood and walked into the darkness, and Urus watched her go, his heart pounding. *I am cursed.* His hands clenched into white-knuckled fists. *I am cursed.*

The huge Man stood and walked upriver, opposite the way Riatha had gone. Some distance along the bank he stepped down to the water's edge, there where an eddy had formed a wide pool, his mind a turmoil, slowly spinning as spun the moonlit mere before him. Urus shed his clothes, his stomach flat, his shoulders wide, his hips narrow, his physique tall, strong, well-muscled, his body completely recovered from his glacial ordeal. With a flat dive he knifed into the water, a pearlescent string of silvery bubbles flowing 'round him, the chill bite of the river driving away all doubt, all confusion, renewing his resolve. *It can never be, for I am a Cursed One.*

Across the mere he swam underwater, till the pale sandy bottom rose up from below. Silently he surfaced, silvery bubbles cascading upward in the platinum light. And there on the shore unclothed stood Riatha, alabaster and ivory and gold.

Urus was transfixed. She was so lovely he could hardly bear to look at her, yet could not look away. He could not seem to get enough to breathe, and his heart roared in his ears. He stood in the moonlight, the water waist deep, liquid running down over his body. Long-legged and slender and shapely, she walked into the crystal pool toward him, her silver eyes glistening, her voice shaking with emotion, *"Vi chier ir, Urus.* I love thee. Oh, how I love thee."

His pulse hammering, Urus stepped forward and took Riatha in his arms, and in the moonlight kissed her long and gently and then in hunger as desire exploded outward from the pit of his stomach and burned through every fiber of his being. Riatha's own racing heart singing, a wondrous fire running through her breasts and loins, through her very blood. Urus swept her up and carried her out of the water and to the moss-laden shore, lowering her to the soft brye, she pulling him down after, their two bodies joining, fusing, all thoughts of mortality and of cursedness banished.

Faeril and Gwylly awakened to the singing of the dawn-time birds, heralding the coming of a new day, calling out to one another proclaiming their territorial rights. Gwylly lay on his back and listened to the songs, softly imitating some of them, chirruping and whistling, chirking and clicking. Faeril raised up on an elbow and silenced him with a kiss, then sat up and began to stretch, suddenly stopping, nudging the buccan to look. Gwylly raised up beside her and saw Riatha curled tightly against Urus, spoonwise, his arms wrapped 'round her, the two yet asleep. Aravan sat by the small campfire feeding it twigs and branches, a brooding look upon his features.

Faeril turned to Gwylly and whispered, "See, I told you."

Gwylly rolled his eyes and threw up his hands. "My dammia, even someone as dense as I could see that they were in love. Why it took this long, weeks and weeks . . . well, I'm sure I'll never know."

Faeril peered into Gwylly's eyes, amber gold gazing into emerald green. "Weeks and weeks? *Weeks and weeks?* Oh, my buccaran, she has been in love with him and he with her for more than a thousand years!"

Gwylly's jewellike eyes flew wide in sudden understanding, and he fell back upon the blanket, groaning, "Oh dammia, you are right. And I must truly be as dense as a rock."

Laughing, Faeril sprang up and reached down and took Gwylly's hand and pulled him to his feet. Riatha stirred and opened her eyes, and started to raise up, but Urus clasped her tightly unto him. The Elfess smiled and twisted 'round in his embrace till she was face to face and kissed the Man gently, then soundly, and he opened his eyes and looked into hers.

"Let's have some tea, Aravan," chirped Gwylly, stepping to the fire. The Elf looked up and grinned, the dark brooding fading from his brow, though not entirely.

As Aravan set the pot to brew above the flames, Gwylly stepped down the mossy bank to join Faeril and splashed water over his face. "Aravan seems moody."

Faeril handed Gwylly a small cloth. "Yes, and I don't know why. It isn't as if he's jealous—"

"Jealous!"

"Yes, Gwylly, jealous."

"Of Urus and Riatha?"

Faeril shook her head in disbelief at how naïve Gwylly seemed to be, not realizing that she, too, was just as ingenuous. "Yes, Gwylly. Jealous of Urus and Riatha. It could be that Aravan himself is in love with Riatha, but I think not, for I believe he thinks of her as a *jaian*, as a sister. It could be that he is upset over an Elfess and a Man loving one another, but again, I do not believe that he holds Humans to be unworthy of Elvenkind. It could be that he is disturbed

because Urus changes into a Bear, that Urus is a so-called
Cursed One, yet again I think that enters not into his mind."

Gwylly looked back into the campsite. "Perhaps he is
upset because they are in love and he is not."

Faeril slowly shook her head. "No . . . I think had that
been the case, he would have been upset by you and me."

Gwylly smiled and kissed Faeril. "Love is all around,
neh? —Oi! Mayhap that's it: love is all around for everyone
but him."

"No, Gwylly. That is not in Aravan's nature. I sense that
it is something else altogether, but what it might be . . . I
cannot say."

They searched all day for the ford across the River Hanü,
coming upon it as the Sun was setting. Instead of crossing
in the twilight, they made camp in a glade. As with every
day, they fed and watered the steeds, and curried out the
knots from the animals' hair where saddles and pack frames
rode, assuring that no twists were left to gall and rub raw
and ulcerate.

Darkness fell as the five took their own meal, and when
they were done, Riatha and Urus walked away into the surrounding night, lovers seeking privacy, and Aravan watched
them go.

Again, Gwylly noted the brooding on the Elf's face, and
he cast about for something to lighten the mood. "I say,
Aravan, how did you know about this ford?"

Aravan blinked and shook his head, as if clearing it of
distant images and echoes. "This ford . . . ?" Aravan stirred
the fire, collecting his memories. "The yellow-eyed Man I
pursue is the one who slew Galarun and stole the Dawn
Sword in the days of the Great War of the Ban. I have since
wandered the world, seeking out yellow-eyed Men. Searching
for one. For vengeance. To recover the sword. To redeem a
sworn pledge.

"A millennium and a half agone, in 4E1461, there came
rumors of a yellow-eyed Man in the west; I was at the time
in the distant islands of Mayar, far to the east. But where in
the west dwelled this yellow-eyed Man, none knew. Nevertheless, I journeyed westward, seeking, searching, asking.

"In Jūng, I came across a name. Ydral, it was whispered,

Ydral of the yellow eyes. Whether this Ydral is the one I seek, I cannot say, yet his was the name that I followed.

"Seasons passed, and seasons more, and slowly westward I came, following whispers, following the name of Ydral.

"In Hurn, breathed some; in Alban, hissed others; in Garia, sissed others still; and westerly I came, faring wherever the rumors led.

"I crossed through the Bodorian Range in 4E1466 and found this ford, five years after hearing of a yellow-eyed Man in the west, four years after hearing the name Ydral.

"Into Garia I went, my steed and I swimming the River Venn which runs west of here, riding onward into the Skarpal Mountains, aiming for a keep said to lie deep within that chain. Through a desolate 'scape I rode, the land abandoned, dwellings empty, as if those who had once dwelt within had fled for their lives.

"Ydral, I thought, he is the cause of their flight. And on inward I rode, searching for the keep, following a rumor.

"I found it at last, yet it was abandoned, though signs told that once Humans had dwelt within. But the signs also showed that the *Rûpt* had dwelt there as well. Destruction was everywhere: buildings defaced, wells polluted, and everything that could burn had been.

"This I believe: The yellow-eyed Man, whoever he is, is in league with the *Spaunen* and drives them to acts of savagery and ruin. This I know, for he it was who commanded the *Rûpt* when Galarun was slain and the sword taken. The keep I found was in ruins, made so by *Spaunen*, perhaps at the behest of a yellow-eyed Man—Ydral, who is said to have lived there . . . a rumor at best. Yet even though it is but a rumor, even though I have no evidence of it, found no proof of it, I do believe that Ydral is the one who dwelt in the keep in Garia.

"Where he has gotten to, I cannot say.

"Mayhap this Baron Stoke is Ydral. Yet when I searched for confirmation, his bartizan in Vulfcwmb had been destroyed, collapsed by the Drimma, and his mansion in Sagra had been burned, and nothing came of it." Frustrated, Aravan's voice took on a dark tone. "If Ydral is the yellow-eyed Man I seek, if he is this Baron Stoke . . . or in league with Stoke—"

Aravan slammed his fist into his open palm, his face dark with fury. Gwylly and Faeril drew back in apprehension, and when the Elf saw this, he opened his fist and relaxed his hands and slowly let the tension drain from him.

Faeril reached out and touched Aravan's arm. "Are you all right, Alor Aravan?"

Aravan took her hand in his own and gently held it. "Aye, Faeril, I am. I did not mean to affright thee, nor Gwylly. It's just that I have been searching for so very long for Galarun's murderer and the Dawn Sword . . . and only shadows and whispers do I find."

Gwylly cocked his head, his viridian eyes glittering. "This Dawn Sword, do you really think it will be found? I mean, you've been searching for—for millennia, and if you can't find it . . . well, maybe it's lost forever. Perhaps it is a false hope."

Aravan took a deep breath. "Dara Rael gave me hope with her augury of the Silver Sword, and Faeril here has renewed my hope, for not only do we have Rael's prophecy, we now also have Faeril's."

Gwylly leaned back in surprise, and Faeril's eyes flew wide. "My prophecy? Why, I've never made—" Suddenly the damman remembered falling through the crystal.

Aravan smiled. "Rael said:

> 'Bright Silverlarks and Silver Sword
> Born hence upon the Dawn . . .'

"And thou said:

> 'Rider of Impossibility,
> And Child of the same,
> Seeker, searcher, he will be
> A Traveller of the Planes.'

"Surely ye both see the linkage 'tween these two."

Gwylly shook his head, *No*, and Faeril turned up her palms.

Aravan took a deep breath. "My interpretation is by no means certain, for auguries are oft subtle . . . and dangerous—thou may deem they mean one thing when they mean something else altogether. Yet as to the linkage 'tween these two prophecies, this I ween is the way of it: To bear the

Silver Sword forth upon the Dawn implies a Dawn Ride from Adonar unto Mithgar, as prophesied by Rael. Yet the way is sundered. Hence, for such to happen requires a Rider of Impossibility, a Traveller of the Planes, and that is what thine own prophecy foretells, Faeril."

Now both Gwylly and Faeril nodded, and Gwylly said, "So you think it likely the Silver Sword and the Dawn Sword are one and the same, and believe that my dammia's words fit hand in glove with Rael's."

Aravan smiled at Gwylly's apt turn of phrase. "Aye, that I do."

Faeril looked up into Aravan's face. "But what about the child—*The Child of the same*—what does that mean?"

Aravan laughed. "Ah, wee one, did we know that, then the world would be at our feet, for our sight would be clear beyond that of all other beings."

They forded the Hanü the next morning, faring southward toward the slot between the Bodorian Range on their left and the Skarpal Mountains on their right, the terrain rugged, their progress slow. Through foothills and craggy tors they rode, among wooded land canting this way or that and pitching up and down, and at times they had to dismount and walk, occasionally backtracking to find an easier way. Often they had to stop and give the steeds a rest. And their travel was not aided by the weather, for it rained that day and all the next, and the slopes became slippery and at times too slick, too loose, for the horses to traverse, though perhaps the mules and ponies could have gone on for they seemed more sure footed.

The following day the skies cleared, though the rain-soaked soil was yet a hazard. In the afternoon of the day after, they came down a steep grade and to the banks of a river. It was the Venn, having swung through its wide westerly arc and south, flowing on its own journey down to the Avagon Sea. And they had come to its course once again. Across the Venn lay Garia to the west; on this bank, Alban to the east; mountains before and mountains aft, and a river threading southward between.

Down the Venn rode the five, along the river's edge, at times on the bank, at times in the water along a shallow shore, following the meandering watercourse, for it was easier than riding through the steep flanking tors. Water cascaded from the mountains, braw streams leaping down the slopes, plunging, shouting in waterfalls, churning into the waters of the Venn. And whenever the comrades rode a distance in the crystal stream, Gwylly would cast out a hand-held line baited with nought but a daub of crue; even so, he managed to catch three fish this way, Faeril laughing in delight.

Urus and Riatha rode in enchantment, for it seemed to them that nature itself recognized their trothplight, for the days were cool and the nights warm, and it was as if the birds caroled paeans of joy for their ears alone. And even the animals of the forest and of the river appeared to celebrate their love, pausing to look at the Elfess and the Baeran and to be seen by them in return: otters mudsliding; beavers in their ponds on dammed-up tributaries, slapping water as the two rode by; stags standing nobly, bounding away; squirrels chattering above in the trees. . . . What a wonderment! Idyllic. Serene. The woes of the world banished. . . . Or so it seemed to the lovers.

Though Aravan rode in silence.

Seven days they followed the river, but on the eighth they left its bed, for again the Venn swung on a westerly arc, and the five cut cross-country through the foothills of the Bodorian Range, striving for direct route to the port city of Thrako. Yet once again the weather turned and wild spring storms raged, thrown against the land by the Avagon Sea. Two days they spent against a high stone bluff, sheltered under a shallow overhang, while the wind and rain lashed at them and huge strokes of lightning crashed near, great blasts of thunder whelming in after. It was all they could do to keep the animals from bolting, and they got little rest.

After the storm, they camped for two days, recovering. But on the third day's dawning, once again they took up the journey, wending down through the hills and tors, following vales and streambeds, following the paths of least resistance. Even so, the way was formidable, and there were full days they traversed but ten miles or so. Yet onward they struggled, at times riding, at other times leading their mounts through thickets and briars and up steep hillsides and back down again, riding left and right to find ways down bluffs and up, and ways to pass beyond canyons. Often they speculated that perhaps they should have continued following the River Venn even though it did swing wide westerly, for surely that easy route, though longer, was swifter. But they did not turn back, for now they were deeply committed, and Riatha's map showed that soon the way would ease. At last the hills began to diminish, and their course took them down toward a broad plain. South they continued, now veering westerly, as out onto a rolling land they came, arcing for the port town some hundred or so miles distant.

That night when they camped, Riatha and Aravan sang Elven songs and spoke invocations, and all stepped the slow, stately dance to a chant by the Elfess—Aravan, Gwylly, Faeril, Urus, and Riatha herself, all moving to her cant, celebrating the summer solstice.

Over the next three days, they began to see signs of civilization: farms, herds of sheep and cattle, growing fields of grain, roads and tradeways, steads, cotes, shacks, occasional hamlets.

At last they came unto Thrako, a port town of some five thousand—a massive city to the Warrows.

It was the twenty-fourth day of June.

Twenty days they waited ere catching a ship bound for Caer Pendwyr. A coastal freighter from Hovenkeep, it was the *Orran Vamma*, Hovenian meaning "Golden Dolphin," though the round-bellied craft was a far cry from the sleek-swimming denizen of the sea. It reminded Faeril of the Fjordlander knorr the *Hvalsbuk*—the *Whale's Belly*—and she smiled at the thought, noting that Gwylly was smiling, too. Yet the *Orran Vamma* would transport them and their steeds to Hile Bay in Pellar, landing at the port of Pendwyr.

And so it was that on the fourteenth day of July they boarded the *'Vamma* and set sail for Pellar.

The *Orran Vamma* wallowed and broached its way down the coast, stopping it seemed at every port city along the shore, offloading cargo, onloading cargo, Captain Ammor, a large, laughing Man in his fifties, trading and buying and selling.

Slowly, slowly they progressed, if progress it could be called. Down the coast of Garia and through the straits past The Islands of Stone, a place where it was said that nothing grew and arcane stone figures stood, some folks claiming that 'twas sorcery that had graved them, others claiming that they were carven merely by water and wind. Regardless, these isles had a sinister reputation, for in times past, they had been the lair of many a pirate, striking out from the hundreds of inlets between.

Past the narrow channel to the Inner Sea they wallowed, not sailing into the great body of brackish water, neither fresh nor salt, but faring onward in the coastal waters of the Avagon Sea.

Along the shoreline of Southern Riamon they sailed, stopping now and again.

It was during this part of the journey that Gwylly and Faeril discovered why Aravan brooded. During a starlit summer night, as buccan and damman strolled the deck, they came to the bow of the *Orran Vamma*, and there stood Aravan and Riatha, the two speaking low to one another in the Elven tongue.

"[. . . *Vio alo janna* . . .] I am simply saying, Riatha, that he is a mortal Man, and as such, tragedy will surely come unto ye both as he—"

"As he grows old and I do not." Riatha's voice was bitter, her eyes filled with despair. "Aravan, Aravan, think thou not that I have considered this? It has bedevilled me for more than a thousand years!"

Aravan took her hand. "I know, Dara. I know." He fell silent for a moment, then continued, "Thou are like unto a *jaian* to me, Riatha, and I would not see thy heart shattered."

"As was thine own at Rwn." Her words were an observation, not a question.

Bleakly, Aravan nodded.

They stood a moment longer, the water *shsshing* against bow and hull. At last Aravan spoke again: "There is this, too, Dara: There may come a time in our pursuit of this yellow-eyed monster that thou must choose 'tween thy love's life or death, and the lives or deaths of others—the Waerlinga, you, I, to name them—those likely to be in jeopardy. At Rwn, I chose one way. How will thou choose, Dara? How will thou choose?"

As Aravan released Riatha's hand and strode off from her, Gwylly and Faeril shrank back into the shadows. Riatha stood at the bow and watched the phosphorescent waves before them, and what she thought, neither buccan nor damman knew. After a moment they, too, crept away, leaving the Elfess standing a lonely vigil.

At last they came to the coastal waters of Pellar, and finally unto Hile Bay, ringed 'round by high sheer cliffs, towering upward a hundred feet.

As they sailed into the harbor, the city of Pendwyr could be seen above, its buildings ranged along the lengthy, steep-sided headland sheltering the bay. At the tip of the headland, separated from it by no more than fifty feet, stood a tall, sheer-walled stone island, its surface on a level with that of the city, a castle occupying the heights—Caer Pendwyr. Beyond the island holding the caer stood two more plumb-sided islands towering up nearly as high, and it could be seen that buildings were thereupon, but what they housed could not be discerned, and none aboard spoke of their purpose.

The *Orran Vamma* docked alongside other coastal freighters in mid-afternoon. Faeril and Gwylly, Aravan, Riatha and Urus, and the ponies, horses, and mules were offloaded as dusk fell across the bay.

Slowly they made their way up the cliff-side road to the city of Pendwyr, taking rooms at the Silver Marlin.

It was now the tenth day of August.

They had begun their journey on Springday Night, one hundred forty-two days ago, travelling from the Great North Glacier in the far Grimwalls unto this inn in Pellar, nearly three thousand miles in all. Yet their purpose for coming here had not been achieved, *might not* be achieved, for it depended upon a boon yet to be granted in the High King's castle a mile or so away, and relied upon redemption of a pledge made by a child of ten a thousand and thirty-seven years past.

# CHAPTER 27

# Pendwyr

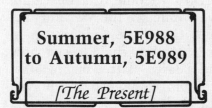

**Summer, 5E988 to Autumn, 5E989**

*[The Present]*

Gwylly came instantly awake. *What was that?*
The buccan did not recognize his surroundings, for he was in a broad bed, and the room did not rock and sway.

Again came the light tapping on the door.

"*Unh,*" he groaned. Trying to sit, he found his arm trapped under Faeril, the limb totally asleep, and he had to pull his entire body away to get free. When he had struggled to an upright position, his eyes swept the chamber. *Oh. The Silver Marlin. No wonder it doesn't rock and sway. It's not the Orren Vamma . . . thank Adon.*

One arm dangling uselessly, Gwylly slid out of bed and staggered to the door, opening it to find Aravan standing there.

The Elf smiled. " 'Tis dawn."

Without saying a word, Gwylly stumbled back to the bed and tried to get in again; with only one arm he struggled to clamber up into the great four poster, a full Man-sized bed and him nought but a wee Warrow. Aravan boosted him up, and Gwylly fell over, rolling and then lying on his back, his good hand massaging his sleeping arm.

Beside him, Faeril opened her eyes.

Aravan threw wide the drapes. Pale morning light filled

the room. "Come, wee ones, we don't wish to be last to the caer. Petitioners will line up shortly, and we must needs arrive early to get a hearing this day."

"*Ow! Ow!*" yipped Gwylly.

Alarmed, Faeril bolted upright, scrambling 'cross covers to the buccan's side. "What is it, Gwylly? What's wrong?"

"*Ooo*," he moaned. "Pins and needles, love. My arm was asleep and now wakens."

Relieved, Faeril plopped facedown on the bedding.

Aravan crossed the floor, heading outward. "I'll see ye adown shortly for breaking our fast."

"Elves," growled Gwylly, "never sleep!"

Grinning, Aravan stepped from the room and closed the door after, turning toward Riatha and Urus's chamber.

Faeril slid backwards off the bed. "Come, my buccaran. Aravan is no doubt correct. If we would see the Steward . . ."

Within a half hour, Faeril and Gwylly joined Aravan in the common room of the Silver Marlin, the Elf just now being served, the maid bringing a large platter of breakfast eggs and rashers of bacon and helpings of bread and honey. Too, there was a pot of hot tea with milk on the side. As the three were lading up their trenchers, Riatha and Urus joined them.

Aravan smiled at the glum looks on his companions' faces. " 'Twas a merry time last night, neh?"

Staring at the Elf, Riatha slowly shook her head in 'wilderment. "How thou can down glass after glass of brandy, Aravan, and yet be chipper in the morn, I'll not know. Some arcane secret gained from years at sea, mayhap?"

"*Akka!* No secret to it, Dara—I've not yet been to bed."

Urus choked on his tea, but managed to swallow most of it ere he burst out in strangled laughter. "Arcane secret!" he wheezed, coughing, grinning sideways at Riatha as she pounded him on the back. "Some secret!"

The Sun had just cleared the horizon as they strolled toward the distant caer, the summer day promising to be clear and warm. A southerly ocean breeze swept gently across the headland. They passed through a city made primarily of stone and brick and tile, stucco and clay, the buildings for the most part joined to one another, though here and there were stand-alone structures. The narrow streets and alleyways twisted this way and that, the cobblestones of variegated color. Shops occupied many first floors, dwellings above. Glass windows displayed merchandise, the handiworks of crafters: milliners, copper smiths, potters, jewellers, weavers, tanners, cobblers, and the like.

The city was beginning to come awake, a few storekeepers sweeping the flag walkway before their shops, light traffic trundling, waggon wheels and horses' hooves clattering on cobble.

"Stone and brick," Faeril commented, her eyes taking it all in. "It seems as if only the bright-colored doors are made of wood."

"Lack of water," said Aravan when Faeril remarked upon it.

Gwylly looked up at the Elf. "Water?"

"Aye. Water . . . or the lack of it, I should say."

The buccan swept his arm in a wide gesture. "But there's an ocean surrounding."

"But no wells, Gwyly. No wells."

Noting the looks of puzzlement on the faces of the Waerlinga, Aravan explained. "Fires need a lot of water for putting them out. A wooden city with buildings this close"—he waved at the surrounding structures—"would flare up like a tinderbox, were there to be a conflagration . . ."

"They could store seawater in tanks, barrels," offered Faeril.

Aravan nodded. "They could, but store fresh instead . . . and use it for cooking and drinking, washing and bathing."

Gwylly looked about. "Where do they get their water?"

"Wells yon," replied Aravan, pointing in the general direction of the plains beyond the headland.

"Too, they catch and store the rainwater that runs from the tile roofs," Riatha added, nodding at the ingenious gutters channelling water into the buildings, where stood waiting vats to collect it.

Faeril looked at Gwylly. "Not much of a place to build a city," she commented. "No water."

Aravan smiled down at her. "Thou are correct, wee one,

yet it was not meant to be a city." He held up a hand to forestall her questions. "At first, 'twas merely a fort, yon"— he pointed at the caer—"easily defended 'gainst invaders, though long sieges would eventually prevail o'er the defenders.

"The city came after, growing bit by bit over the centuries, till it is as ye see it anow." Aravan fell silent, and they strode onward, drawing closer to the caer.

In spite of the ocean breeze, an effluvia of middens rode on the air, and now and again a heavy drift of noisome odor surrounded them, raw and rank. Finally Gwylly wrinkled his nose. "*Ugh!* What is that?"

Aravan glanced at Riatha, but it was Urus who answered. "Humanity, Gwylly. Humanity. Whenever this many people are crushed together . . ."

They continued onward, passing through several market squares, for the most part just beginning to set up business for the coming day. Even so, it could be seen that some would sell a variety of goods, while others seemed to specialize: fish, fowl and meats, vegetables and fruits and grain, cloth and woven goods, flowers, and the like.

Past shops and stores, past restaurants and cafés, past inns and taverns, past large dwellings and small squares, past hospitals and chirurgeons, herbalists, tea shops, smiths, stables, jewellers, clothiers, tailors, cobblers, greengrocers, past every kind of shop and merchant that Gwylly and Faeril could even imagine and some they hadn't, past them all went the five. And for the most part, these shops and businesses were just beginning to stir.

As the comrades came into the vicinity of the caer, the buildings took on a different aspect, the face of government— a great courthouse, a tax hall, a constable station with jail above, a firehouse, a library, a census building, a hall of records, a cluster of university buildings, and other such.

At last they came to a wall, and warders stood at the gate. Several petitioners were lined up waiting, sitting on the stone benches provided.

Called forth by the guard, the gate captain was clearly taken aback by the appearance of Elves at his station, but it was the Warrows who astounded him, for throughout the ages they had rarely come to Pendwyr, and in fact had taken on an aura of being a legendary Folk.

"Well, I'll be . . ." he breathed, then realizing his station, gruffly said, "State your business."

Urus answered. "We have come to speak with King Garan, to redeem a royal pledge."

The captain looked up at the huge Man towering above him. "The High King is in Challerain and will not return for another seven weeks."

Aravan smiled. "The Steward will do for now."

"Adon, what a tale!" The speaker was Leith, Garan's cousin and Steward in Pendwyr when the King was away at Challerain. Leith was a slender, grey-haired man in his fifties, with the eyes of a hawk, some said. "What say you, Lord Hanor?"

At Leith's side sat a huge-girthed Man of perhaps forty, with dark brown hair and eyes. Advisor to the Steward and High King alike, Hanor steepled his fingers. "I won't mince words, m'Lord: were this tale to be borne by anyone other than Elves and Wee Folk, in Jugo we would call into question either the sanity of those who told it, or their honesty."

Across from the two sat the five companions: two Warrows, two Elves, and a Baeran—Folk not often seen in Pendwyr. Because of this fact, they had bypassed most of the bureaucracy and had gotten swift audience with the Steward. And now they were in one of the Steward's private chambers in Caer Pendwyr, the castle on the first towering rock pinnacle jutting up from the sea beyond the headland.

Hanor shifted his mass in the broad chair. In spite of his girth, great strength lay within his bulk. "I mean, trapped in a glacier for a thousand years? Why, look at him: he has the appearance of a Man no more than thirty. Yet are we to believe the tale, he was some sixty years old when he fell in—"

"I was fifty-nine," rumbled Urus.

"Fifty-nine, sixty, it is of no matter," replied Hanor. "By your youth, given that you are now more than a thousand years old, why, were it not impossible, I would say that you have Elven blood running in your veins.

"Mayhap, though, it was the ice that preserved you and your youth. . . ."

Aravan leaned forward. "How this Man survived is not at issue here. That he did is enough.

"What we came for was to redeem a pledge made long past by Aurion, son of Galvane, a pledge made unto this Man, Urus, to Dara Riatha, and to Tomlin and Petal, the ancestors of these Lastborn Firstborn Waerlinga, Gwylly and Faeril. And that pledge was to render aid—"

"Wait!" interjected Faeril. "Let me read his words to you."

The damman turned to Gwylly, and the buccan dug out his copy of the journal from a pocket, a journal he had constantly kept with him ever since he had begun to read.

Faeril opened it to the appropriate page.

*But ere he went, he came unto Tommy and me. "I am but a Prince of the Realm," he said, "yet I deem my sire will hew to the pledge I make this day, and it is this: Should you or Urus or Riatha need the aid of the High King, come unto Caer Pendwyr or unto Challerain Keep and ask. We will help in running to earth this monster you seek. So do I pledge in the names of all High Kings of Mithgar forever."*

Faeril closed the journal. "The words were written by Petal, my ancestor a thousand years ago, and the Prince making the pledge was Aurion. And now we come to redeem that pledge, for we need help in running the monster Stoke to earth." She handed the diary back to Gwylly, and he in turn passed it across the table to Leith.

The Steward glanced at it, leafing through a few pages, passing it on to Hanor. "*Hmph*," grunted the stout Man, cocking an eyebrow, "what language is this?"

"Twyll," answered Gwylly, "the tongue of the Warrows."

Of a sudden Steward Leith stood. "There is much to consider here, and I have business elsewhere that awaits me. Yet this do I say: Only High King Garan can honor in full the pledge made by his ancestor. However, we shall send messages to the Realmsmen that a menace stalks the land. We will ask for word as to this creature's whereabouts. Be-

yond that, the commitment of resources and Men to run this
foe to earth must await Garan's seal.

"Where are you quartered?"

"The Silver Marlin," answered Riatha.

"I would have you move your quarters to the caer."

"We have horses," interjected Aravan.

"Ponies and mules, too," added Gwylly.

"Stockade them in the enclave," answered Leith. He
crossed to a pull cord. "I will have an attendant accompany
you and arrange for rooms and aught else you might need."

A page hastened into the chamber, and after a few words
from the Steward, left. Leith turned. "We will speak more
upon this anon, but for now I have several ministers waiting,
no doubt pacing the floor in agitation. Stay here; the page
will bring you your escort. Hanor?"

Lord Hanor stood and stepped to the Steward's side, and
together they strode from the room, and Faeril overheard
part of what Hanor was saying, "... written in Twyll, a
language we've never seen. And I have never heard of this
Baron Stoke, and it seems to me ..."

They moved into the castle that very afternoon, housing
their animals in the stables in the enclave. The enclave itself
stood behind the guarded wall running across the tip of the
headland, the wall separating the enclave from the city
proper. Within this warded tract were a hundred buildings
housing agencies and offices of the Realm, providing as well
the living quarters for many of the officials and aides within.

The five comrades, though, were given chambers within
the caer itself, the walled castle occupying the whole of the
spire, the fortified island pinnacle connected to the headland
by the bridge.

Beyond the castle spire were two more sheer-sided pinna-
cles: the first containing lodgings for the King's closest advisors; the second holding nought but the High King's private
residence. Each was connected to the next by a short suspen-
sion bridge a hundred or so feet above the rolling sea.

Two days later, they related their tale to Commander Rori,
captain of the Realmsmen, and within the day the com-

mander sent horsemen galloping forth from Pendwyr, bearing details of Baron Stoke and his monstrous deeds.

Rori, a tall Vanadurin of forty-five or so, his yellow hair and beard in braids, suggested a search through the archives to see if they held any record of Stoke or his Barony.

Following Rori, they crossed over to another of the buildings in the enclave. There they met an elderly Man, Breen, Chief Archivist. "I would not hold too much hope for such an accounting. Most of the records of that era were destroyed by the Hyranians in the Winter War, when the city fell to them," said the eld archivist.

"What about the records at Challerain Keep?" asked Rori.

Breen ran his hand over his bald head. "Destroyed as well. Burnt by the Horde."

"Nevertheless," rumbled Urus, "search what you have and let us know."

Weeks passed, and in that time Gwylly and Faeril spent hours at the library, Gwylly continuing his lessons at reading and writing and ciphering, Faeril guiding him and reading as well on her own. In the caer, Riatha and Aravan earned all of their keep by entertaining courtiers, playing harp, and singing and reciting verse. And Urus, it seemed, prowled as would a caged beast.

Yet all were under tension, for Stoke roamed, and they knew not where.

They often took the horses and ponies—and mules as well—out into the plains beyond the walls of Pendwyr, exercising the animals, keeping them in condition for a journey to an unknown destination. All five companions relished these outings, for Pendwyr, though exciting at first, came to be looked upon by them as a crowded anthill, or as Gwylly once laughingly put it, ". . . a crowded dunghill."

"The odors are horrific," said the buccan. "I mean, it seems as if they merely dump sewage and refuse in the streets."

"Nay, Gwylly," responded Aravan. "Instead, they spoil the ocean below. It is the way of Humans to do so."

Faeril looked at the Elf. "That sounds rather grim, Aravan. 'The way of Humans'?"

Aravan sighed. "Aye. Mankind seems not to know that the world itself can be slain, just as if it were a living creature. It can be stripped bare, poisoned, burnt, drowned, strangled, ruined, and destroyed in any other number of ways.

"Humans are ingenious creatures, inventive, and in this they are much like unto the Drimma, the Dwarves. They make things which are marvelous to behold, yet in doing so they destroy the land.

"Look at Pendwyr: a great city, full of wonder, full of interesting items of manufacture, things of Mankind's inventiveness.

"Yet look at the ocean beneath Pendwyr, poisoned by Mankind's offal, his refuse, his swill and slops and sewage; and the very walls of the stone headland which supports the city, those walls are stained with his feces, his urine, his filth.

"And the air itself is fouled by his excretions, by the effluents of his manufacture, by the outpourings of his furnaces.

"He destroys forests, poisons waters, fouls the air, rapes the land.

"Does this have to be? That Mankind destroys the very world? Is it the destiny of Humans to drown in their own spoilage?

"In the Boreal Sea lies the Land of Leut, a vast island. On that isle lives a tiny creature, in length no more than a handspan, a rodent, called *lemen* by the island dwellers, though in Common it is named *lemming*.

"In the spring lemmings breed and breed, and breed in the summer as well. In the autumn lemmings breed. Two to five litters throughout the year, their numbers increase without bound. Yet soon the food runs short and shorter, until there is nought to eat.

"Then a great migration begins, lemmings eating everything as they go. During such migration, predators come—the Wolf, the fox, the hawk and falcon and eagle, more—and they feast without limit, lemmings falling to fang and claw and talon.

"Too, lemmings fall prey to disease and starvation, yet the march goes on, the tiny creatures devastating the land of plants and grains and aught else that they can consume. Frequently the migrations end at the sea, and with no food behind them they hurl themselves into the waters, lemmings swimming to reach distant shores, yet all drown.

"Humankind seems to be set upon this same course, overbreeding, devastating the land, rushing to his destruction. That he has not already done so is due to War and plague and pestilence, drought and floods and fires and famine, and other calamities wherein Mankind dwindles in numbers, and the world rallies somewhat from his ravagings. Yet, as do the lemmings, Humans breed swiftly, and soon their Race recovers, and the pillage and plunder of the world begins again.

"Elvenkind nearly destroyed its own world once, yet we saw in time what the outcome of our ravagement would be. We stopped, barely soon enough, for our world was greatly damaged. And now we limit our births, holding our numbers to well under that which our world can sustain without harm. And we limit our activities to those which do no permanent injury to the land or waters or air, or to the growing, living things thereon and in.

"But Humankind has yet to learn such . . . may never learn such. For Man is a short-lived creature of many appetites, and as such does not consider what sating those hungers has already done and will eventually do to his world; he thinks not of long-term consequences, but only of gratification of his current needs, no matter where it leads, no matter the ultimate end.

"Mayhap it is this short-livedness that is at the root of Mankind's destructive tendencies, for unlike Elves, who are immortal, a given Man does not exist over the centuries to witness what his and other hands have done.

"Yet mayhap not all is dark, for the children of Men provide a link from the past to the future—an immortality of sorts. Perhaps by passing knowledge from one generation unto the next down through the ages, perhaps Mankind will become aware of and will heed the distressed signals of his world.

"His very inventiveness may lead to his own destruction, for he may in time build machines and devices that will ultimately poison his world beyond redemption. Yet by the same token, perhaps his ingenuity will lead him to reverse the damage he inevitably causes.

"But now I look about and see what Man hath wrought, and I think that this world will die gasping, poisoned by Humankind."

When they rode back into Pendwyr that day, Faeril and Gwylly looked 'round at all the remarkable things within the city, at the markets and shops and sturdy stone buildings with their brightly colored doors, at the plenitude of manufactured goods all about, at weavers and cobblers and greengrocers and merchants of all sorts, hawking their goods, a hubbub of voices and calls filling the bustling streets. Through this swirl of commerce rode the Waerlinga, and as the noisome smell of middens washed over them, they did not marvel anymore.

High King Garan returned to Caer Pendwyr on the second day of October, and within the week held an audience with the five. Rather short of stature and brown-haired, Garan was a Man in his late thirties, having ascended the throne a decade past, when his sire, Orwin, had died of a seizure.

His Queen, Thayla, was a plump Woman, not quite five feet tall, with mouse-colored hair.

At the side of the throne stood Fenerin, Elven advisor to Garan, the Elf some five and a half feet tall, his shoulder length hair a deep chestnut.

Other courtiers filled the chamber with a low hum of conversation, but silence fell as Alor Aravan and Dara Riatha, as Sir Gwylly and Mistress Faeril, as Chieftain Urus were announced. Though Fenerin nodded in recognition of Riatha, it was the first appearance by the five before most of the courtiers, and a gasp flew up as the Waerlinga entered, the elfin pair smiling, their tilted, jewellike eyes aglitter, as they came forward to meet the High King.

Dara Riatha, Alor Aravan, and Chieftain Urus all knelt briefly before the King, but Gwylly and Faeril, tutored in Court protocol by Riatha, merely bowed and curtsied. As Riatha had said, "No Waerling has knelt before royalty since the War of the Ban, for it is their privilege to remain afoot, ever since Sir Tipperton requested such of the then High King."

Garan stood, sweeping his arms wide, his brown eyes alive and taking in the five of them, his voice vibrant. "Welcome to Caer Pendwyr. On the morrow we will break our fast together, and you will tell us your most remarkable tale. 'Tis not often that we get to set aside the humdrum affairs of state to list to an adventure true." Queen Thayla smiled, joy and beauty filling her face.

Garan pledged resources to their cause, honoring without question the vow made long ago by Prince Aurion. Yet none knew what might be needed, since Stoke's whereabouts was unknown.

A month passed and then another, and in spite of Gwylly's fears and Riatha's warnings, Faeril spent time in the city searching for a mentor to teach her scrying . . . yet all she found were frauds and charlatans, and so her plans to locate Stoke via her crystal came to nought.

In early December, Archivist Breen told them that all surviving documents had been examined, and there was no record of Stoke or of a Barony by that name, and no record of such name associated with Vulfcwmb in Aven, or with Sagra in Vancha. And ". . . Yes, I know that you say he lived there. But there are no records of such. If ever there were any, they must have been burnt by the Hyranians." No record of such a name was associated with Garia either, though Aravan had been uncertain that Stoke was the yellow-eyed Man whispered of in the rumors, for they had named Ydral instead.

Rori, too, came to say that the last of the Realmsmen had been notified. "Now there's nought to do but wait," he said. "If this Stoke creature be anywhere in the High King's Realm, we will know. Word will come from some Realmsman somewhere."

And wait they did: Gwylly reading, writing, continuing his lessons in Twyll, and now learning as well the language of the Baeron, Urus teaching him. Too, he continued to search out Aravan and Riatha, seeking knowledge concerning how the Elves care for their world, for he did fear that one day Mankind would ruin the earth, and he sought a way to prevent such.

"What will you do if it seems likely that Man will destroy Mithgar?"

"Ere he does so, in the last days Elvenkind will leave this world, never to return."

"What about the others who are trapped here with Mankind? What about the Dwarves, the Utruni, the Warrows? What about the Hidden Ones? Will you just leave them, leave us, to the mercy of Man's destructiveness?"

"Someday, Gwylly, the Wise Ones say there will be a Separation: Adon in His own manner will divide Mankind from us all—from the Drimma, from the Waerlinga, from the Hidden Ones, from Elvenkind, even from the Utruni. This they say will be to Mankind's loss, for when we fare forth from his world, wonder and enchantment will fade from whatever is left behind."

"Wise Ones? Who are these Wise Ones?"

"I deem thou would name them Wizards," answered Aravan.

"Oh." Gwylly's face fell glum. "But I *like* Mankind, Aravan. I would rather stay. If what you say comes to pass, are we to be separated from Humans forever?"

"As long as Mankind's world is in jeopardy, 'twill be so."

"Will they remember us, Aravan? Will Mankind remember us at all?"

"Mayhap, Gwylly, mayhap. Mayhap in their legends and fables. Mayhap in nought but their dreams."

Months passed by. Winter came, and then spring. They spoke with Commander Rori often, but among the reports posted by the Realmsmen, as yet there was no word concerning Stoke's whereabouts. He seemed to have vanished from the face of the earth.

And as the days passed and grew into weeks, and the weeks into months, they cudgelled their minds for something, anything that they could do to speed the search, anything to locate Stoke, something that would allow them to go after him . . . but always they came to the same conclusions. Although it was difficult to remain at the caer while others searched, and although feelings of uselessness filled their breasts, still, if they themselves went searching, where would they go? The world was wide, and Stoke could be anywhere. Hence, the Realmsmen represented their best hope, for hundreds searched, covering more ground in weeks than the five of them could in years. They knew that if Stoke were anywhere within the High King's Lands, the Realmsmen would succeed.

And so, they waited.

. . . Yet if Stoke were not in the High King's Demesnes . . .

Summer followed, and more and more the five of them rode away from Pendwyr, ostensibly to exercise their animals, but in reality to get away from the cloying closeness and artificiality of the city. There were days that it seemed as if the stench and noise and crowding would o'erwhelm them, and Gwylly and Faeril at times could not seem to draw a clean breath of air.

Gwylly could not but help compare Pendwyr to Arden Vale, the vale a place where art and literature, sculpting and metal working, jewel carving and floral works and the growing of tiny trees and other such, occupied Elvenkind. Where elegant rock gardens with running water and crystalline pools filled with flashing fish were shaped and cultivated, Riatha once telling them that often a century or more would pass ere an Elf would finally decide upon the placement of a particular single stone or flower or shrub.

Too, he compared the businesses of the city with the growing of crops and the tending of gardens and the harvesting of fruits and berries, with the shepherding of flocks and the raising of fowl and other such.

The Warrow found much lacking in the life-style of the Pendwyrian dwellers.

Yet there was much he found admirable—though on balance he preferred the life he had known to the one he had come to know.

And so Gwylly, along with the others, scoured his mind for a way out, for a means to track down Stoke—to no avail, and yet the buccan kept trying.

It was Fearil, however, who suggested a different course of action from that of merely waiting for a Realmsman's report of foul deeds done by a yellow-eyed Man.

The two Warrows were in the library: Gwylly studying, Faeril searching for knowledge concerning divination, for still she bore her silk-wrapped crystal in its iron case, though

she had not tried to use it again. "I say, Gwylly, look here."
Faeril held out a dusty tome.

The buccan took the book, setting it on the table.

*"Oracles:"*—he read aloud—*"persons who reveal divine knowledge; persons through which a divine being speaks; places in which deities so reveal hidden knowledge or divine purpose."*

Gwylly glanced up at Faeril. "Read on," she said.

*"Throughout the Eras, mortals and immortals alike have sought answers to questions concerning the unknown and the imponderable. It is claimed that answers are given at times to these seekers by a deity, sometimes directly, sometimes through a chosen one. It is said that the gods couch their answers in obscurities, for to give clear knowledge is not the way of the divine.*

*"It is told that the gods reveal their answers through such things as the rustling of oak leaves, wind noise in a cavern, the flights of birds, the shapes of clouds, the incoherent ravings of the mad or the entranced, the forks of lightning and the rolls of thunder, the twinings of the intestines of sacrificial birds and animals, the ordering of randomly shuffled cards—"*

Gwylly looked up from the book. "No wonder the answers are obscure."

Faeril pointed at a paragraph. "Down here, Gwylly. Read this part."

Gwylly turned his attention back to the dusty tome.

*"Among the more famous oracular locations are: the Alinian Temple in the Uthana Jungle, destroyed in the Second Era by the Vudaro March; the Byllian Maze in Olor, now sunk beneath the Hyrigian Sea; the Pythian Hall of Phrygia, attested as fraudulent by Ramis the Fifth; the Oakwood of Gelen, whose oracular pronouncements were accounted among the most accu-*

rate, but when the last priest of Rūdūn died, so expired
the divine utterances; and last, the legendary Ring of
Dodona in the Kandrawood, said now to be lost beneath the sands of the Karoo. It was told that the gods
of Dodona would speak to any and all, and their utterances, though obscure, were unfailingly true."

Faeril reached out and turned two pages in the tome,
pointing now to another passage. "Here, Gwylly, now read
this."

"Spurred on by the legends of its infallible accuracy,
in the Second Era, Prince Juad of Vancha led an expedition into the Karoo to find the lost Ring of Dodona,
and neither he nor any of his followers were ever heard
from again.

"Juad's sire, King Carlon the Wise, sent a second expedition into the Karoo to discover the fate of his son,
to return the Prince to Vancha if he yet lived, or to
bring back his remains if not. This mission likewise
was lost.

"King Carlon mounted no more expeditions, believing in the words of the desert nomads that some
dire creature now dwelled in the heart of the Karoo,
where the Ring of Dodona was said to lie."

Gwylly looked at Faeril. "Well, dammia, what have you
in mind?"

Faeril pursed her lips in thought. "Just this, Gwylly: It has
been a year since first we came to the caer, a year of no
results. Commander Rori himself has come to believe that
Stoke is not in Lands where Realmsmen patrol, and so word
may never come. With the whole wide world his sanctuary,
we need a different way of searching for Stoke. If what is
written here is true, could we find the Ring of Dodona, then
we could discover his whereabouts."

Gwylly glanced back at the tome. "Aravan could find the
sword, too. . . . But I don't know, Faeril—according to this
book, the place is lost. Besides, people who go searching . . .
well, they disappear."

Faeril sighed. "You are right, my buccaran. Yet—"

"Look," interjected Gwylly, "let us talk it over with the others. I mean, *anything* is better than just waiting around in Pendwyr."

"Dodona in the Kandrawood, eh? List, to build the *Eroean* I used special wood from o'er the whole of the world. One of these timbers was *kandra*, and in only two places was it said to exist—in the Karoo, and in the Realm of Thyra. It was thought even then that the sands of the Karoo had encroached o'er the last stand of *kandra*, and so I went to Thyra instead. Yet there is an eld chart of the Karoo on which was marked a place where *kandra* once grew; I knew not that Dodona mayhap was nigh."

"Have thou that chart?" asked Riatha.

Aravan slowly nodded, reflecting. "On the *Eroean*. Yet, Riatha, I deem that thy charts will serve, for well do I remember where the wood was said to grow. Had I not gotten the wood in Thyra, I was prepared to go to the Karoo, and I found a simple means to plot the location of the stand, a means I yet remember."

Riatha stood. "I'll get my maps."

As she stepped from Aravan's chamber, where they had gathered, Urus rumbled, "Think you that Dodona truly exists?"

Aravan shrugged. "When first I came from Adonar, e'en then Dodona was but a legend."

Faeril's face fell. "Oh, Aravan. Does that mean it is but a fable?"

Aravan shook his head. "Nay, wee one, I did not say so. Heed, it seems as if all Nations have tales of old ruins, of lost cities, of ancient temples miraculous and castles beyond compare, of entire civilizations forever gone, of hidden treasures and fabulous wealth, of arcane lore and wondrous items, and of other marvels lost and waiting. Most of these tales are but fables, yet many are true, or spring from the well of truth.

"In my voyages of the *Eroean*, oft would we anchor and journey inland, seeking the truth of a legend. Much of the time would we find nought . . . yet at other times *Hai!* what adventures did I and my crew have!

"And so, Faeril, I am not saying that Dodona is nought

but a fable, yet neither am I saying it is real. All I am saying is that I know where in the Karoo *kandra* was said to have grown."

Faeril glanced at Gwylly, but the buccan merely shook his head. "Mayhap, my dammia, mayhap there is no Ring of Dodona . . . but mayhap there is. The book we read claims that there was one, and— Hoy! Wait a moment. Aravan, the book also said that the desert nomads claim that some dire creature lives in the region where Dodona was said to exist. What do you think the truth of *that* is?"

Aravan turned up his palms. "Who can say, Gwylly? Many are the legends of the Karoo, and I know but few of them. Tales of *Djinn* and *Afrit*, of haunted wells and oases filled with demons, of the skeleton of Death riding his huge black camel, of sand wyrms whose fangs are filled with poison, of jackals of fire and Hèldogs running through the air, of giant scorpions larger than horses, of hideous monsters under the dunes who become whirling winds filled with flailing sand, of phantoms and wraiths and liches and ghost snakes and other such.

"Tales such as these have always been told, no matter the Realm—sometimes true, sometimes not. Again, my crew and I oft encountered like stories, and most of the time found them to be entirely false, but at other times we barely escaped with our lives."

In that moment Riatha returned to Aravan's chamber, and they unrolled her maps on the table, anchoring the corners with daggers and pouches and knickknacks from the room.

Riatha and Urus leaned over the table, braced on their hands, while Gwylly and Faeril stood on chairs to see. Aravan pointed. "Here. See this spur of the Talâk Mountains? Follow a straight line to the fork where the River Hailé meets the Pilar. Half distance along the line"—Aravan measured it out, his finger stabbing at the map—"*that* is where the *kandra* was said to grow."

Urus used his thumb as a scale. "*Hmmm.* Two thousand miles across the Avagon Sea, and four hundred fifty miles through the Karoo. I make that some two weeks by water"—Aravan nodded in agreement—"and another twelve or so days by land. We can be there within a month of setting out. And should there be nought found, then another month returning." The Baeran paused, pondering, all others looking at the map. At last he broke the silence. "I am of a mind to say let us do it." Urus looked down at the buccan. "As Gwylly said, anything is better than waiting about in Pendwyr."

Slowly Urus glanced 'round the table, seeking consensus, Riatha nodding *Aye*, Faeril and Gwylly doing likewise. Smiling, Aravan looked Urus in the eye, his voice taking on a thick brogue. "Ha'e ye e'er rithen a camel? Ships o' the sand, they be, gang whare no harse c'n gae."

Lord Leith arranged for a ship and funds for the expedition, and Commander Rori assigned two Realmsmen to accompany the five: Reigo, a small and wiry, dark-eyed, black-haired Vanchian, twenty-eight or -nine years old, from the city of Portho; Halíd, a slightly larger, dark-eyed, hook-nosed, black-haired Man from the Isle of Gjeen, some thirty-three years old. Each had been chosen for his stature, eye color, complexion, and knowledge; given the correct dress, each could pass for a native, and each spoke Kabla, the predominant language of the Karoo.

Some six weeks elapsed ere all was in readiness, for the ship was in drydock being refitted. But on the autumnal equinox the Arbalina vessel *Bèllo Vènto* set sail from Hile Bay for the desert port of Sabra on the rim of the Karoo.

And as Faeril watched the headland of Pendwyr disappear below the horizon, gathering clouds slid over the Sun, casting a darkness upon the sea, and a cold shiver ran up her spine.

# CHAPTER 28

# Avagon

**Autumn, 5E989**

*[The Present]*

It rained for three days and the seas ran high, but the *Bèllo Vènto* cut cleanly through the waves. Faeril could not but compare the smooth running of this sleek Arbalinian ship to the wallowing and broaching of the *Orren Vamma* or the pitching roll of the *Hvalsbuk*. In these same three days, Captain Legori, a tall, slender Man with an olive complexion and dark brown hair, sailed virtually by dead reckoning, unable to see the stars at night, sighting only on the diffuse glow behind the clouds in the day, judging the position of the Sun. That Aravan and Riatha were along helped the captain immeasurably, for it is common knowledge that Elves know, without needing to see, where stands the Sun and Moon and the stars at all times. Hence, although they could not point at it, for the skies hid it, both Aravan and Riatha could tell the captain the measure of the Sun at any given moment—dawn, sunset, noon, midnight, and all points between. By Aravan and Riatha knowing the precise mark of the Sun, the Moon, or the stars, Legori was confident in his reckoning . . . and Aravan's experience at navigation added to Legori's certainty that the *Bèllo Vènto*, if not precisely on course, was not far off either.

While the rain was lashing the ship, for the most part

the seven passengers remained below deck discussing the upcoming journey deep into the Karoo. Aravan, Reigo, and Halíd all had experience in desert living, but the others had none; and so, much of the time they spoke on desert survival, as they had during the six weeks they had waited for the ship to come out of drydock.

During those same six weeks, each had been fitted with desert garb, Reigo and Halíd giving the articles their Kabla names and demonstrating their wear, and speaking of the customs of the desert dwellers, the K'affeyah, nomads of the sand. Aravan added bits here and there, for he had spent time on the fringes of the desert, speaking the Kabla tongue as well.

"This headdress, it is called a *kaffiyeh* or a *ghutrah*," explained Halíd. "It is held in place by a headband called an *agāl*. The cloak is named *jellaba*, or *abaya*. The shirt is a *brussa*. The pantaloons are called *tombon*.

"In the desert it is most important to be well covered, for not only will clothing protect you from the Sun, it will also lower your need for water, for the Sun and wind on bare skin will rob the body of moisture, causing you to drink more often, and water is the most precious commodity in the Karoo."

Reigo grunted an affirmation of Halíd's words, then continued the lesson, naming such items as *gimbāz*, *abāyeh*, *shatweh*, *kola*, *pushtin*.

They discussed the fact that a Woman of the Karoo went about covered from head to foot by a *thōbe*, and wore a veil, a *yashmak*. Yet they thought it best that Riatha pass for a male; she was as tall as most of the nomadic Men. Too, she would be bearing a sword, and the desert Women were permitted only small, decorative *jumbiyahs*, curved knives.

By the same token it was decided that both Warrows would pass for male children, hence Faeril's throwing knives could be borne in sight.

Neither Urus nor Aravan would need to disguise their nature, though Urus would be considered a giant by the small, wiry Karoo tribesmen.

Reigo and Halíd would pass themselves off as natives. Both of the Realmsmen had been deep in the Karoo, yet it was a large desert—nearly two thousand miles wide and some fifteen hundred miles deep, depending upon where one measured—and so their knowledge of the interior was fragmentary at best. Yet while they waited for the ship, Reigo and Halíd had searched the archives, and they had recovered copies of maps of the wasteland on which were denoted several wells and oases. All of the markings they had transferred to Riatha's charts, though it was by no means certain that water was yet to be found at the places so noted. Two lay on their route: the Oasis of Falídii, some sixty leagues south of Sabra; and the Well of Uâjii, some twenty leagues north of the place where *kandra* was said to have grown.

But learning of the desert and survival and the customs of the coastal dwellers and K'affeyah nomads were not all that occupied their days. Reigo and Halíd were told the tales of the pursuit of Baron Stoke, and that the two Warrows, the two Elves, and the Baeran hoped to discover the whereabouts of Stoke by finding the Ring of Dodona. This led often to speculations upon the validity of oracles and the like, with examples of success and failure and fraud. Riatha spoke of the Elfess Rael and her redes. Faeril spoke of her own "prophecy," when her mind and soul were lost in the crystal.

And as the rain beat down upon the *Bèllo Vènto*, for the most part trapping the seven below decks, Riatha told the tale of Falan the Vainglorious and of Shumea the Pythian Seeress:

"Long ago in the Land of Hurn was the famed Oracle of Telos, high on a mountain overlooking the bay on the rim of the Avagon Sea. There a great white temple was raised over a crack in the land from which invisible vapors rose. Here, by chains, a priestess of Telos would suspend herself above the crevice, inhaling the intoxicating vapors. After some moments she would begin to speak in tongues, tongues never before heard.

"Seated before her on a silver throne sat a Seeress of Phrygia chewing on a leaf of a *janjah* without which even she could not interpret the priestess's mystic words.

"At the Seeress's side sat a scribe, recording the prophetic utterances.

"Many came to Telos to discover their destiny—peasants, warriors, courtesans, Kings—people from all walks of life. At times they received an answer, at other times not, for all were at the mercy of the whims of the gods, or so it was repeatedly said.

"One of these visitors was Falan the Vainglorious, sailing his entire fleet unto Telos, seeking to see if he and his minions would conquer the whole of the world. At that time Shumea was the Seeress of Telos—the last, as it turned out.

"Falan asked his question but was not answered, for oft the response was silence. He was enraged that the gods of Telos did not deign to reply, for after all, he was Falan!

"So filled with wrath was his heart that he threatened to destroy Telos, slaying all within.

"At that moment the priestess in chains uttered her arcane words, and Shumea bit down on her *janjah* leaf and listened exceedingly well. Then she turned to Falan: 'For eleven talents of gold, Lord Falan, I will give thee all nine Scrolls of Telos on which are recorded all of the prophecies of the gods.'

"Falan refused, for he would have his answer and nought else.

"Shumea took three of the Scrolls of Telos and put them in a brazier and in spite of the protests of Falan's advisors, set them afire, burning them unto ashes.

"Shumea now turned unto Falan again, saying, 'For eleven talents of gold, Lord Falan, I will give thee all six remaining Scrolls of Telos on which are recorded many of the prophecies of the gods.'

"Again Falan the Vainglorious refused, in spite of the urgings of his counsellors, for he had not yet received the answer unto his own question.

"Once more, while Falan's advisors looked on in outrage and horror, Shumea took three of the six surviving Scrolls of Telos and placed them in the brazier and set them afire, burning them until nought but ashes remained.

"Shumea turned unto Falan a last time, saying, 'For eleven talents of gold, Lord Falan, I will give thee the three remaining Scrolls of Telos on which are recorded some of the prophecies of the gods.'

"Again Falan refused, and Shumea reached for the brazier, the last three scrolls in her hand.

"A great outcry rose up from Falan's couosellors, and they

fell to their knees before the Vainglorious, begging him to accept. Pleased by this show of entreatment, Falan at last agreed to Shumea's terms.

"Eleven talents were brought to the Seeress from the ships of the mighty flotilla anchored in the bay, and she handed over the scrolls. Falan and his entourage left, his vainglorious question as yet unanswered, though some advisors bethought the reply might be in one of the scrolls.

"That night, under cover of darkness, Falan the Vainglorious leading a force of handpicked Men came slipping through the shadows to steal back the gold. Yet, lo! the temple was deserted, the Women and treasure gone, including the silver throne.

"Enraged, Falan and his Men destroyed the temple, crashing it down unto the ground.

"And on the night tide, the flotilla sailed. . . .

"Yet just ere dawn, the earth trembled mightily, and the Mountain of Telos was destroyed. And in the wake of its devastation a great wave rushed o'er the sea, crashing headlong into Falan's mighty fleet, shattering the boats and drowning all, carrying every Man jack down into the depths below—Falan, his advisors, and minions all . . . as well as three priceless scrolls.

"Falan the Vainglorious had at last received his answer from the gods of Telos, now gone."

On the fourth day after setting sail, the rain stopped, the skies cleared, and a fair wind abeam pressed them across the water. All were glad to see the Sun, and they promenaded on the deck, or lay about in the warm light. Only minor corrections needed to be made to the course.

For two more days and nights they sailed thus, the wind slowly diminishing . . . and the seventh day found them in irons, becalmed on a glassy sea.

Captain Legori set Men in dinghies rowing, towing the *Bèllo Vènto* after, the oars plashing in pellucid water, leaving widening ringlets behind, the hulls cleaving elongated vees, the slow wedges outspreading as well.

Aravan stood aft with Gwylly, watching the mingling of patterns, the Elf seemingly entranced by the glistering ripples extending o'er the mirror.

In Sylva, at last Aravan said, ["She has a thousand faces
. . . nay, more."]

Also speaking the Elven tongue, Gwylly responded, ["The
ocean: a fickle lover, I hear."]

["Aye. Mistress of many, yet mastered by none."]

They stood quietly for a moment more, only the chant of
the rowers breaking the silence. At last Aravan spoke: ["She
is too tempestuous to be tamed by any, and always will
remain wild and free . . . though there are those who would
make her their own."]

Gwylly shook his head. ["Who would ever think she could
be owned?"]

Aravan barked a laugh. ["*Ha!* Now I know that thou are
becoming Elven in thy heart, Gwylly, for thou speak as
would a Lian . . . or as a Hidden One. . . ."]

The buccan glanced up at Aravan, questions unspoken.

Aravan's eyes were lost in reflection, and it was as if his
heart remembered the words of another . . . another from an
elden time. *Who can own the sky?* echoed his mind.

*Tarquin sat before the Elf, the Fox Rider no more than a
foot tall, his voice soft, speaking in the tongue of the Hidden
Ones.* ["Mankind is not like the People, for he seeks to lay
claim to all he touches, to all he sees and feels.

"Yet who can own the sky? Who can own the wind or the
rainbows? Who can own the rain or the waters of the world,
the laughing of brooks or the roar of thunder? Or stones and
mountains, the very bones of the earth? And who can own
the grass and the trees, the forests, the plains? Who can own
the birds of the air and the creatures of the land, the fish
that swim in the waters? Who can own any of these songs
of earth?

"Man would say, 'I. I own all. I have dominion. It is
mine! To do with as I will!'

"But the People say, Nay! None owns the world . . . or it
is owned by all, for all is sacred. Every shining leaf, every
sandy shore, every mist in the dark woods, every humming
insect. All are to be revered.

"We are part of the earth and it is part of us. And it is to
be cherished and loved and nurtured, for it is precious. It
is our mother and father, and all things upon it are our
brothers and sisters. The Bear, the Deer, the Eagle, the Fox,*

*these are our kindred, even the flowers. The air that
breathes over us, the shining waters that flow in the streams
and rivers and lap the ocean shores, this is our lifeblood.*

*"The earth does not belong to anyone; instead, we belong
to the earth. All things are entwined in the great web of
life, and whatever is done to the web in one place will cause
tremors felt throughout.*

*"Who owns the world? Might as well ask, Who owns the
wind? . . ."*]

["Why, none owns the wind, Aravan."] Gwylly's voice cut
through Aravan's consciousness, and the Elf realized that
he'd been reminiscing aloud. . . .

Aravan laughed. ["Aye, Gwylly. None owns the wind. For
if we did, then would we whistle it up to remove us from
these irons."]

The buccan turned and looked forward. ["Legori rows to
find it, though. I think I'll go forward and watch. Care to
come?"]

["Nay, wee one. I think I'll stay here yet awhile."]

The buccan shrugged, then started toward the bow.

And while Men in dinghies rowed upon the mirror-smooth
sea, haling the *Bèllo Vènto* onward, seeking the wind, Aravan leaned upon the stern taffrail gazing at the waters, his
mind lost in memories. . . .

. . . And still the glistering patterns continued to ripple and
widen.

A full day and a night was the Arbalina vessel trapped on a
glassy sea, Men slowly drawing her southerly. But on the
next morn a slight belling of the slack sails showed that the
air had begun to stir. And by mid-morn a light breeze came
upon them, and the dinghies were shipped aboard, the Men
canting a chantey, and once again was the *Bèllo Vènto* under
way.

As they took their noon meal, the wind picked up and the
ship heeled over, cutting through the waters at a goodly pace.
Faeril smiled. "At one point I thought the Men might have
to row all the way to the Sabra. I'm glad *that* didn't come
true."

"I'm glad that we're on the hunt again," added Gwylly.

"Hunting, yes; finding, no," responded Faeril. "At least not finding yet. It may take some time."

Aravan glanced at Riatha and then Urus and finally back at the buccan and damman. "The search might be a long one, indeed, wee ones. Yet for Elves a decades- or e'en centuries-long hunt is of no moment, but for Waerlinga? . . . Do ye have the time? It may take untold years."

Faeril reached out for her buccaran's hand. "As long as I am with my Gwylly . . ."

From the corner of his eye Gwylly saw Riatha reach out for Urus's hand.

On the ninth day of the voyage a school of porpoises raced before the bow of the ship, cleaving the crystal blue waters in glee. Faeril and Gwylly were delighted, laughing at the agile play. Urus and Riatha, too, stood hand in hand joyously watching. Halíd said, "My village elders tell that the *jeenja* aid the shipwrecked, yet I hope we never need discover the truth of the tale."

Aravan leaned on the bow wale and watched as well. "Aye, Halíd, they do indeed aid those whose ships have foundered, helping swimmers to keep afloat, guiding them to land, yet I deem that others aid as well—dwellers of the deep."

"Lord Aravan"—Halíd's eyes were wide with wonder—"speak you of the Children of the Sea? *Ai*, many are the Gjeenian tales of beings half seen in the glittering depths and under the rolling waves."

At Halíd's words, Reigo snorted. "Children of the Sea? Bah! My own sire swears that they are not real . . . and he should know, for he was a sailor for thirty years."

Aravan smiled. "Thirty years? Perhaps if he'd had more time . . ."

Halíd looked at the Elf. "How long did you sail?"

Aravan glanced at Riatha, as if seeking aid, then he said, "Some five thousand years."

Halíd's mouth fell open and Reigo gasped, "Five thousand—"

"Oh, look! Look!" called Faeril, pointing. The porpoises had formed up in a long diagonal chain, the last in the line had begun leaping uptrain over the others, and as soon as it

was past, the next to the last began leaping upchain as well
. . . and so it continued, porpoise after porpoise leaping and
plunging, leaping and plunging.

"Leapfrog!" shouted Gwylly.

But even a marvelous thing such as this did not take away
the cast of wonderment from Reigo's and Halíd's eyes whenever they looked at Aravan . . .

. . . and at Riatha as well . . .

. . . for they were of a Kind.

In mid-afternoon sixteen days after putting out to sea from
Pendwyr, the sleek Arbalinian vessel *Bèllo Vènto*, crewed by
Men and captained by Legori and sailing under the High
King's commission, haled into the broad harbor of Sabra,
dropping anchor in the glittering bay, the arc of the city
before them baking in the overhead Sun.

Among others on deck stood two Warrows, two Elves, a
Baeran, and two Realmsmen, all dressed as K'affeyah, wearing light blue turbans—with their face-covering cloths
wrapped 'round and fastened—and cloaked in light blue as
well, shirts, girdles, pantaloons, soft boots, and other such
beneath.

Too, they bore weapons, but not those of the tribesmen.
Instead from the north came these arms, straight swords,
morning stars, long-knives, throwing daggers, and such. Only
were two of the weapons like those of the desert: one was
a spear, the other a sling.

On the deck stood these seven, staring over the bay. On
the horizon beyond the port city, in shimmering heat waves
afar, could be seen their next goal: the sands of the vast
Karoo.

# Chapter 29

# *Karoo*

**Autumn, 5E989**

*[The Present]*

The seven came ashore and pressed through the throngs in the streets, heading for the Inn of the Blue Crescent, quarters highly recommended by Captain Legori. As they passed through the city, a babble swirled around them and then raced ahead, for when hawkers and merchants crowded forward to sell their wares, they saw tilted eyes of silver and sapphire on the two graceful strangers, and jewellike, tilted eyes of amber and emerald on the small ones, and one of the outlanders was a giant, and the merchants drew back in fear. *Djinn*, they whispered of the first two, and *zrîr Djinn* of the small ones, and *Afrit* of the huge stranger. . . . *Yet how can this be, for they wear blue, the holiest of colors? Perhaps they are Seraphim instead.*

Aravan laughed and said in Sylva, ["They think we are either agents of the demons or messengers of the gods."]

Gwylly repeated Aravan's words to Urus, speaking in the Baeron tongue. ["Good!"] replied Urus in kind. ["Mayhap it will work to our advantage when purchasing camels, for who would try to cheat an angel or a devil, eh?"]

At last the seven came to the inn, Aravan translating the ornate, filigreed letters on the signboard, though the cerulean quarter Moon depicted thereon announced the name to all those who could not read the serpentine swirls.

That evening, after a meal of bread and shishkebabbed oxen meat and vegetables, with hardtack and goat-milk cheese on the side, and dates and oranges following, they sat in the common room and from tiny cups discreetly sipped *khla'a*, a dark brown, somewhat bitter, bracing desert drink.

Again they looked at the map, and Urus cleared his throat. "Captain Legori will sail on the tide tonight, and return in a month, and wait . . . for another month, if need be. With twelve days to travel down to where we think Dodona lies, and another twelve days returning, that will give us at most five weeks to search for the oracle. Mayhap Fortune will smile upon us and we will find the ring the day we arrive on site, though I deem it unlikely. Mayhap Fortune will also smile upon us and the Oracle of Dodona will immediately tell us the answer as to Stoke's whereabouts, though I deem such unlikely as well. Hence, given the best of Fortune's favor, we *could* be back here within as few as twenty-five or so days . . . but regardless, we *must* be back within sixty days, else Legori and the *Bèllo Vènto* will sail to Pendwyr without us."

The others sipped their *khla'a* and nodded, for Urus merely reviewed what they had gone over time and again, yet it seemed necessary to all that his words be spoken once more. Silence fell on the group, but at last Reigo turned to the huge Baeran. "My heart nags me with a question, and has done so since we left Caer Pendwyr, and it is this: Even now, has word of Baron Stoke come to Commander Rori from a Realmsman in some distant Land? Has Stoke been found, even as we seek to know where he is? I have this— this *fear* that we are here on a wild loon hunt, while the real quarry, Stoke, escapes."

Each looked at the others, the same fear lurking behind all eyes—all, that is, but Halíd's, who merely shrugged in Gjeenian fatalism. "If such be the case, it is the will of Ru-alla, Mistress of the Wind."

The next morning, they passed by stables of high-stepping horses, sleek and hotblooded and swift, and went beyond the city walls and out to the camel markets, for by law camels were not permitted within the bounds of the city except to deliver or pick up goods. Why there was such an edict governing the whereabouts of camels became obvious to Gwylly and Faeril and Riatha and Urus when they came to the camel grounds: the odor was horrific. *"Whew,"* hissed Gwylly, his eyes crinkling and watering, denoting that the rest of his face, hidden beneath his fastened turban scarf, was screwed into a grimace of distaste. "No wonder the place is downwind of town." The others nodded in agreement, and it was with some reluctance that they stepped in among the noisome beasts.

Mouths moving side to side as they chewed cud, the camels grunted and groaned, as if perpetually complaining, whether or not they were working or resting, standing or lying, immobile, walking, or trotting. And as the seven strode past, camels rolled their eyes and contorted their faces into hideous masks, and some spat malodorous gobs at the strangers.

Reigo laughed. "I had forgotten!"

Faeril looked up at the Realmsman. "Forgotten what, Reigo?"

"An ancient tale, little one. It seems that the prophet Shat'weh, riding his favorite camel, Onkha, fled across the desert, ahead of pursuing enemies. Urged on by Shat'weh, Onkha galloped most swiftly and outran the pursuers and bore his master into exile and safety. As a reward, Shat'weh whispered the true name of God into faithful Onkha's ear. From that time to this, the Secret of Secrets has been handed down from one camel to another. And now, whenever any camel looks at a person who lacks its knowledge, the animal feels superior and its face twists into a supercilious sneer."

Reigo burst into laughter, and Faeril began giggling. Soon all seven were striding and laughing among hideously grimacing dromedaries, and that's how they came mirthfully into the company of the camel merchants.

Although the merchants clearly were unnerved by Elven and Warrow eyes and by Urus's towering height, still they haggled long and loudly. Yet Halíd and Reigo were highly skilled in the art of camel bargaining: examining the humps for firmness, gauging how well the animals had been fed; looking at yellow-stained teeth and even smelling each proffered beast's foul breath, both signs of ageing; having the complaining, groaning creatures stand and lie, judging their docility and response to command; looking at height and length of leg and condition of coat and other such indicators of health and endurance and speed.

In the end, they purchased five swift *hajun*, dromedaries for riding, and six *jamâl*, pack camels for haling supplies. All were females but for a gelded male, and that one was a huge dromedary to bear Urus.

Too, they acquired the needed tack, obtaining as well two special double saddles, ones that allowed a K'affeyah tribesman to ride with a child, the youngling sitting down and forward of the rider.

After a long discourse among themselves, casting many fearful glances at those who were perhaps *Djinn*, *zrîr Djinn*, and *Afrit*, cautiously the camel dealers approached the Human pair—Halíd and Reigo—and asked if they wished for the decorative blue tassels to be removed from the tack, for after all, everyone knew that blue was the holy color used to ward off imps and demons.

Reigo laughed so hard that he could not answer, but, speaking in Kabla, Halíd fixed a cool eye on the merchants and said, "The blue tassels must remain, for they will serve to enhance the powers of our masters."

Awed, the camel merchants turned to Riatha and Aravan, to Faeril and Gwylly, and lastly to Urus, and salaamed reverently and deeply.

Reigo laughed even harder.

All was obtained at a fair price, for it may have been as Urus had asked: "Who would try to cheat an angel or a devil?"

Early the next morning, camels sneering and grumbling and complaining, the seven departed Sabra, heading southerly into the Karoo. Being the most experienced camel riders, Reigo and Halíd each rode with a Warrow mounted down and before them on the lower seat of the double saddle— Faeril with Reigo, Gwylly with Halíd. Riatha, Aravan, and Urus each rode on individual dromedaries, Urus's animal protesting loudly. Too, Reigo, Halíd, and Aravan each had pack camels in tow, laden with goatskins of water, food, grain, light tent cloths, cooking gear, firecoke, and the like, all purchased in the *suq*. Although most of the water and other supplies were laden on the pack camels, the riding dromedaries also bore a goatskin of water apiece and a minor amount of other goods as well, for as Halíd had said, "If the pack camels manage to run away, we would not wish to lose all things needed to survive."

As they purchased their goods in the bazaar, Reigo and Halíd had asked about waterholes and pasturages and other such along their intended route. They had received some valuable information. But for the most part, the caravaneers had warned them of the whirling demons and haunted oases and the black camel and the vile spirits living under the sand and down in the wells and of the jackals of fire and had warned them of the evil nature of the place where they were headed; they had cited tales of caravans vanished and of travellers disappearing and even of the lost expedition of the Prince from Vancha who searched for fabled Dodona, the tale yet remembered to this day. And they had shaken their heads in disbelief when Reigo had laughed over these tales of desert truth, calling them but mere superstition, though Halíd had seemed to take them more seriously. Regardless of the heartfelt warnings, Halíd and Reigo, along with their *Djinnain* and *zrâr Djinnain* and *Afrit* had seemed determined to go into this evil part of the *Erg*, and so the caravaneers had given them amulets of blue to ward off the wraiths and liches and ghosts and other such. *Perhaps*, the Sabrinians would later speculate, *perhaps they truly were Seraphim and Cherubim and a Throne, here on earth as God's messengers, with their lowly Human servants to attend to them. For only the Lord of Wisdom would know why they went into the cursed zone, that part of the Erg all sensible Men avoided. On the other hand, if they were demons—* Mahbûl! *How could they be demons? They wore blue and took the blue amulets and asked for blue tassels for their camels. . . .* The debates were loud and tumultuous, and even the *imamîn* knew not the answers, though they often prevented hotheads from slitting one another's throats with their drawn curved knives. Long were the arguments and they continued throughout the following months, and in some quarters lasted for years.

Within two hours of departure, the seven came to the *Erg*, the great sand dunes curving away in long, graceful arcs as far as the eye could see, all the world before them a sea of sunlit beige and shadowed bronze. To their left, the Sun rose upward in the morning sky. To their right, the slow bend of the *Erg* carried it westerly veering northward. In the near distance behind them lay the city of Sabra and the Avagon Sea beyond. And before them stood the sands of the vast Karoo.

*"Hut, hut, hut, hajîn!"* cried Reigo in Kabla. *"Yallah, yallah!"* Then he switched to Common: "Onward, O sluggard bag of bones," he called, the beast protesting with a shouted *Hronk!* but padding forward into the endless dunes despite its complaints concerning the bearing of a Man and a damman, the grumbling pack camels drawn after. Behind came Halíd and Gwylly, their string of muttering camels in tow. Next rode Riatha and then Urus on his dissenting gelding, with Aravan and his two pack camels bringing up the rear. And although Reigo rode in the lead, with Aravan coming last, they were following a course set by the Elf, their navigator across the Karoo. And so went the small caravan of camels and riders, swaying into the *Erg*.

"Not like riding a pony," mumbled Faeril.

"What?"

"I said, Reigo, that riding a camel is not at all like riding a pony. No wonder Aravan named them 'ships o' the sand,' what with all of this rocking and swaying. Why, a person might get seasick."

Reigo laughed. "Some do, Faeril . . . get seasick, that is. Look at the camel's gait—it swings both right legs forward at the same time, then both left legs. When walking, this causes the swaying, for the camel must do so to maintain its balance. But when running, the gait smooths greatly."

The damman looked down at the camel's walk—"Oh, like that of the pacers of Pendwyr"—her mind hearkening back to a time she and Gwylly had attended the horse-drawn, two-wheeled cart races on the green at Pendwyr.

"Aye," replied Reigo. "But a horse has to be trammel-trained to the gait, whereas it comes naturally to the camel."

"Lurch on, gallant camel," cried Faeril, pointing ahead, "across the sandy dunes. But should I get sick, you will be the first to find out."

Reigo's hearty laughter belled forth, and his camel *hronked* in protesting response. And hearing the laughter and growl, the people behind smiled while the trailing camels grumbled, neither knowing the cause of mirth nor the cause of complaint.

During the heart of the heat of the day, they stopped and sat under hastily erected shade cloths. Out before them, the camels knelt down on the sand, instinctively aligning their bodies lengthwise to the Sun, exposing as little of themselves to its direct rays as they could. They would remain resting from late morning until mid-afternoon, resting during the time it was too hot for prudent travel.

The Sun had slid halfway down from the zenith toward the horizon when they prepared to take up the trek once more. The day was yet hot but bearable, and the loose robes and clothing in which they were swathed protected the companions from the torrid rays. Again Halíd reminded them all to down copious quantities of water. "Remember, like desert raiders the Sun and wind will rob you of moisture, and though the covering of your clothes will ward you from the worst of it, still you need to drink often. Take all you need, storing your water inside yourself instead of in your canteen. Men have died of thirst, water yet at their belts."

"What about the camels?" Faeril asked.

"Tonight we should reach a pasturage," answered Halíd. "Not all the Karoo is barren dune; some thorny bushes and grasses grow in sheltered places. There we will hobble the camels, and they will eat. They chiefly get their water from the bushes and grasses and shrubs, and for the most part do not need to drink. I have known them to go for a winter season without sipping water, especially when the grasses are rich and succulent and the mornings laden with dew.

"We will offer them a drink at dawn, but they will only take it if the grazing is poor."

They struck their shelters and bundled them back onto the camels, the ill-tempered beasts sneering and growling and trying to bite ere they got underway again. But eventually they heeded commands, levering themselves up, hind legs first, then one front leg and finally the other, an ungainly maneuver at best, *hronking* and *rrrunking* throughout.

Gwylly turned to Halíd behind, looking up at the Man. "I say, Halíd, do you feel as I do that we might as well be up in the *Bèllo Vènto*'s crow's nest, pitching and swaying high above everything? I mean, look at us up here on our lofty perch, higher than a tall Man's head. From this vantage we should be able to see all the way to where we are going to camp tonight."

Halíd smiled. "Not quite, Gwylly. Camp is some twenty miles south . . . five or so hours away."

Halíd's assessment was not far off, for they arrived at their campsite in just under five hours, well into the night.

They had gone some thirteen leagues that day, some thirty-nine miles, a good day's trip and one that they could maintain day after day, for in spite of the complaints of the camels, they were lightly loaded.

They made camp and took a meal, and poured a small quantity of *hruja* oil in a thin ring about each bed site, a line that scorpions would not cross.

That night they set watch in order: Reigo, Halíd, Aravan, Gwylly, Faeril, Riatha, and Urus.

At the breaking of fast in the dawn's light, Faeril looked at the pasturage, nought but thorny bushes and sparse grass, and she wondered at any beast that could survive on such. Yet when the camels were offered water, sneering with disdain they took none, having found the plants to their liking. Nevertheless, when offered grain, the camels ate eagerly, their appetites for such insatiable.

For four more days did they travel on a more or less south-bearing course, camping late at night, setting watch, rising at dawn, resting in the heat of the day. Depending on the pasturage, at times the camels took water, at other times none.

The land they crossed was desolate beyond redemption, filled with sand and rock and sparse vegetation. Yet there was an elusive beauty in its gaunt reach: Isolated rock towers soared hundreds of feet into the sky, as if an entire mountain had been carven down to its core by wind-driven sand, leaving behind a great monolith visible for tens of leagues. Dry *oueds* twisted across barren land, silent testimony that water once had flowed within their banks and might once again. Hills of red rock thrust up from rust-red sand, fantastic whorls and gnurlings and striations exposed to the Sun. Vast arrays of timeworn hoodoos, twisted stone pillars shaped by the wind, stood like unremembered fields of ancient obelisks dedicated to Kings long forgotten. Valleys of gravelly stone there were, the rocks rounded as if from water, though 'twas the wind and sand instead. Immense shallow circular pits gaped in the stark land, walls and floors covered with crustal salt. Towering flanges of upright stone ran for hundreds of yards, holed through here and there, huge windows for viewing beyond. In places wide stretches of bare flat rock reached for a mile or more, called beds of the giants by the K'affeyah. And now and then they came upon extended reaches of tussocky hummocks mustered in random array, and here they let the camels graze.

But always they came back into dunes, the sands of the Karoo, the face of the mighty *Erg*.

Late in the morning of the fifth day of travel the normally reluctant camels began eagerly surging up a long dune 'mid unmistakable grunts of urgency. And when they topped the rise, the comrades could see why. "Green!" squealed Faeril, for in the near distance ahead rose a sweeping arc of low, stony mountains, and cupped in its embrace was an extensive palm grove: they had come at last to the Oasis of Falídii, some sixty leagues south of Sabra.

*Hronk, rrrunk*, bellowed the camels.

"They smell the dates," called out Reigo, "but I would have a bath."

Thwacking his mount with the riding stick, *"Yallah, yallah!"* cried Reigo, then, switching to a dialect of Sarain, *"Tazuz et h'tachat shel'cha!"* and down from the dune loped the dromedary, pack camels running behind, needing no urging; and so ran all the camels, racing for the grove, as if afraid the ones in front would get there first and eat up all the dates.

As they galloped closer to the palm grove, Faeril could see

that there were several mud-brick buildings clutched against the side of a broad, boulder-laden hillock. When she pointed them out to Reigo, "I see them," he replied.

As they drew nigh, she could see that the buildings were relics, their roofs fallen in, some walls collapsed, the site abandoned. Though she knew not why, this revelation caused Faeril's heart to hammer loudly in her breast.

As the hobbled camels grazed on fallen dates, the comrades wallowed in the great watering hole they found partially hidden under the solid rock hillside, a pool sheltered by a broad overhanging ledge of stone. The basin was some eighty feet long and perhaps half that wide, the water ranging in depth from a foot or so to perhaps eight feet . . . and it was cool and crystal clear and pure. Spouting and diving down, Urus discovered a hole in the deepest part, and they speculated that the pool was fed by underground springs flowing down from the surrounding arc of low mountains.

"Perhaps the entire grove is fed by water from the hills about," hazarded Halíd. "I can see the tracks of *oueds* threading on the surface. When the seldom-rains come, water is funneled down into this valley, disappearing into the thirsty soil. But the pool itself, I would guess that its water flows down underground slopes from the mountains above."

"*Yah hoi!*" called out Gwylly, splashing, "I don't care *how* it gets here. Simply that it does is enough for me."

They pitched camp, and as the afternoon began to wane they strode up to the ruins, ancient dwellings rising up the slope above. Made of mud brick, most of the buildings had collapsed walls, and none had other than a hole where a door frame once was, their lintels fallen, the walls above tumbled down. The same was true of window openings, their structures but a memory. Open to the sky, no remnant of roofs remained, and sand had blown in and collected. It was apparent that no one had lived herein for countless ages.

Up through the ruins they explored, finding nought but wrack. Higher they climbed, seeking an answer as to why the dwellers had abandoned the oasis, finding none. At last they came to the topmost structure, and peering through the fallen-down doorway, a sweeping glance showed nought but another sand-laden ruin. Yet in one corner—"Hoy!" called Gwylly, stepping inward. "What's this?"

Lying half buried in the sand was a piece of curved metal.

Taking care that no scorpions were lurking beneath, Gwylly gingerly pulled it free.

The buccan turned about, showing his find to the others. Aravan stepped forward. " 'Tis a vambrace." At Gwylly's puzzled expression, Aravan explained. "Armor worn on the forearm. And from the look of it, ancient."

The others had gathered 'round, and Gwylly relinquished his find, returning to the corner to poke about in the sand as the vambrace was passed from hand to hand. When it came to Reigo, he looked at it carefully, then started to pass it on, but then jerked it back and held it at an angle to the sunlight streaming inward through the place where a window once had been. "¡Oiga! See the scrollwork. This is Vanchan!"

"Perhaps so is this," said Gwylly, holding up a yellowed length of shattered forearm bone.

That night, as Reigo prepared to stand the first watch, Aravan handed the Man the blue amulet. "Wear this, Reigo, and pass it on to the next warder as well, and have them pass it on to the next and the next."

Reigo slipped it over his head, then held the stone out to see, the leather thong threading through a hole in the small blue stone. "What is it, Aravan?"

"A stone of warning, Realmsman, and a stone of warding as well. Should it get icy cold, wake the camp."

Watching the exchange, Halíd's eyes flew wide, and he breathed, *"Magic!"* and Gwylly at his side nodded.

Reigo, on the other hand, raised a skeptical eyebrow. Nevertheless, he tucked the stone inside his *brussa*, next to his skin. "Why, Aravan? Why now? I mean, we've been standing watch all along and never needed it before."

"This grove is too rich to be abandoned without cause, Reigo. It has all desirable things: water, date palms, forage, shelter. Too, I deem that the vambrace Gwylly found came from one of Prince Juad's Men, or one of the Men of the expedition which came searching for him. And all disappeared.

"And there are the desert tales of haunted oases, perhaps with good foundation.

"For those reasons I give thee the stone, to wear and to pass on to the others.

"I will rest now, as Elves do, watching and sleeping at one and the same time. Yet thou will be the first line of warding . . . thou and the stone." Aravan moved some distance away and sat with his back against a large rock, easing his mind into gentle memories.

When Gwylly's turn came, the night was cool, but not as cold as in the open desert, where the temperature plummeted with the setting of the Sun. But in the grove the trees somewhat ameliorated the chilling effect of the coming of the dark, releasing heat into the surround. Yet Gwylly did not notice, so uneasy was he from Aravan's words to Reigo, words that conjured up inchoate visions of a terrible threat that had led to the abandonment of the oasis. . . .

Throughout the rest of Gwylly's watch he paced about the camp, his thoughts racing. In his mind's eye he saw a lone Vanchan fleeing upward through the ruins, seeking shelter, a place of safety, a place to hide from the pursuing . . . *what?* No matter, for "it" or "they" found him, huddling in shadows in the corner, and they— *Stop it! You incredible fool! Next you know, you'll go running screaming out across the desert, pursued by nought but bogles of the mind!*

Gwylly tried to settle down, but several times he thought he heard noises out in the dark, and twice did he deem that the blue stone grew cooler, though not icy cold.

When he wakened Faeril for her turn at guard, he handed over the stone on the thong, reminding her of Aravan's words as well, telling her to take special care, and should the stone chill, call for aid immediately.

Faeril smiled at his concern, yet she nodded in agreement, kissing him good night.

Lying down, Gwylly wondered how he could ever get to sleep, but next he knew, Urus was rousing him awake in the dawn.

As they rode from the grove, Aravan called from the rear. Turning about, the others saw the Elf commanding his camel to kneel, Aravan dismounting. He strode a step or two to a small mound, and scooping sand aside he revealed an ancient toppled obelisk, faint carving upon its flank. Casting a handful of sand back on the stele and then carefully brushing it away so that whatever sand remained lay in the groovings, Aravan revealed its message. *"Djado!"* he called out to the others. "It is a warning—*Djado!"*

Halíd sucked in his breath between clenched teeth. *"Cursed!"* he hissed.

Gwylly twisted around to peer up at the Man. "What do you mean, cursed?"

Halíd looked down at the buccan seated before him. "It is said that at a place of *Djado,* Lord Death himself comes on his black camel, and if any are found at his *guelta,* at his watering hole, they will forever ride with him through the endless dark."

A chill ran through Gwylly. "Oh, Halíd, how frightful."

The Gjeenian reached out and squeezed the buccan's shoulder. "Let us be glad, wee one, that the black camel was not thirsty last night."

Aravan remounted his dromedary, and soon the place of *Djado* was lost to sight.

Far across the *Erg* they went, endless dunes of sand, the world a torrid furnace by day and a frigid waste by night, the 'scape ever changing, never changing, as across dune after dune they trekked. Pasturage became nonexistent, and the only water to be had was held in their *guerbas,* their goatskins. They fed the camels grain, but even so, there was not enough to sustain the grumbling, complaining beasts, and so, the animals began to draw on the fat stored in their humps. Faeril and Gwylly became concerned, and even though Halíd and Reigo and Aravan each assured them that the camels could bear up under such conditions, still the Warrows fretted. Yet onward they went across the sands, aiming for their next destination, marked only by a tiny spot on the reach of Riatha's map.

Each day they rode till late morning and rested till midafternoon, then rode again until after dark. They camped on bare sand and spoke of grass and shade and running water and fields of green growing things, reminiscing. Too, they continued to pass Aravan's blue stone from warder to warder throughout the night, and although occasionally it seemed to grow cool, it never became icy cold.

Five days they fared, crossing endless dunes, seeing nought but creeping waves of sand, but on the morning of the sixth day, once again the camels surged eagerly forward. "They smell water," declared Reigo, giving his dromedary its head. Onward trotted the camels, and within a mile they came to a vast, shallow depression. Scrub grew in the wide hollow, and in the distant center were a handful of threadbare palms, parched, the fronds yellowish and sickly, among which they could see a mortared stone ring: it was the Well of Uâjii.

At Halíd's nod Reigo dropped a pebble down the well, Gwylly and Faeril watching as it disappeared into the blackness below. It seemed an endless time ere they heard the *plsh* of the stone striking water. "*Waugh!*" exclaimed Halíd. "Five heartbeats deep!"

"How much rope?" asked Reigo.

"Two hundred sixty-six cubits," Halíd answered, "four hundred feet."

Gwylly looked up, astounded. "Four hundred— Who dug this well? Who would set mortared stones that deeply? Even beyond! I mean, if it's four hundred feet to the water, then the bottom of the well is deeper still. Who would do such?"

Halíd and Reigo both shrugged, and Aravan turned up his palms.

"That much rope will be heavy," commented Faeril, "even without a bucket of water at its end."

"I will draw the water," rumbled Urus, knotting together several lines.

Riatha gazed about as if seeking something. "I wonder . . . if a traveller came unto this well and had no line, no way to draw up the water, would he die of thirst at well's edge? Look about: See ye winch, line, bucket? See ye a cover capping the well to keep the water from evaporating? Nay! Here is a riddle to read."

Down went the bucket into the well, and Halíd's judgement proved to be accurate, for Urus payed out one hundred and six ells of rope ere the bucket struck water. Weighted on one side, the bucket overturned, and Urus gave it suitable time to settle, then drew the filled bucket back to the top of the well. Time and again did the huge Baeran draw up water, replenishing first the goatskins and then pouring bucket after bucket into the trough at well's edge. Each camel drank its thirsty fill, downing nearly twenty-five gallons apiece, taking considerable time to do so. Then bloated and grumbling, the animals were hobbled and set to grazing, for other than a small amount of grain, they had had nothing to eat in the past five days, and their humps were flaccid from lack of food.

Several more times did Urus draw up water, refilling the trough to the brim. Strong as he was, Urus was wearied, for he had hauled up bucket after bucket of liquid. "Last one," he grunted as he started to hale up the final bucket. But it did not rise. "Caught," he growled.

"On what?" asked Gwylly, peering downward into the blackness, seeing nought but the rope dwindling out of sight.

"Mayhap on the masonry, or on a rock." Urus moved to the far side of the well, paying out slack. Then he drew upward, but it did not yield. *"Garn!"*

Again Urus moved, then setting one foot against the well top—*"Unh!"*—he wrenched up and back, the bucket coming free, the Baeran stumbling hindward, landing on his seat yet retaining his grasp on the line.

Gwylly laughed, and Aravan, smiling, said, "Here, Urus, let me." The Elf took the rope from the Man and stepped to the wall of the well. As he hauled upward, his eyes widened at the weight of rope, bucket, and water, and he glanced at Urus in surprise. "Hai! Thou are indeed a strong one, Urus. Better had we dragooned a camel for this work." Yet hand over hand the slender Elf continued to pull up the rope, the final bucket coming to the top at last, the side holed, water running out.

"Hoy!" exclaimed Gwylly. "Good that this was the last."

They pitched camp near the well in the tattered shade of the shabby palms. As the seven rested, Aravan studied Riatha's map. "We have come another sixty-seven leagues on our journey, one hundred twenty-seven leagues from Sabra in all. There are but twenty leagues left ere we reach the place where *kandra* was said to have grown, a day and a half of travel."

"Dodona," breathed Faeril.

"Let us hope," added Gwylly.

Urus nodded but said nought as Riatha kneaded his back and shoulder muscles, for the labor of drawing water had been difficult.

Reigo sat with his back to a tree, his chin on his chest, napping.

Halíd stood, his eyes casting about. When Urus looked up in question, the Gjeenian said, "I am of a mind to search for another stele, for this may be a place of *Djado*, too, as was the Oasis of Falídii."

Urus barked a laugh. "This place is cursed, aye . . . but only because of its wickedly deep well."

Faeril got to her feet. "I'll join you, Halíd. After what you told Gwylly, if there's another *Djado* stele, I want to know, for I would be elsewhere if Lord Death and his black camel come calling tonight." She reached down and pulled Gwylly to his feet, saying, "Come on, my buccaran, who knows what we may find?"

Aravan continued to study the map, and Riatha continued to soothe Urus's worn muscles. Reigo slept on.

Long the searchers looked, walking outward in a spiral from the wellhead, finding nought. But on the return journey, as was the case when the vambrace had been found, again it was Gwylly who turned up evidence of a deadly nature: some twenty yards on the south side of the well, he found part of a shattered Human jawbone embedded in the arid soil, some teeth yet set in place.

When Gwylly's turn at guard came, Aravan handed him the blue stone. "Keep a sharp eye and ear, Gwylly, for the chill waxes and wanes."

Gwylly took the small stone in hand, feeling its cool surface. Aravan stepped away a short distance and sat down, placing his back to a tree. Gwylly knew the Elf both slept and watched, as he had been doing since the Oasis of Falídii, the place of the *Djado* stele.

Holding the stone, Gwylly took a seat on a boulder, his senses alert to the surround, warding his companions. How long he sat thus he knew not, yet ever did his eyes sweep across the starlit sand. But he saw only the vague silhouettes of the camels grazing on the thorny brush and wisps of grass. And so, amulet in hand he sat on the rock, watching the desert, guarding his comrades, listening to the rustling of the faint breeze among the sparse palm fronds, the susurration whispering above, a soft sibilancy murmuring in his ear, almost as a faint, faint song dimly in the distance, a purling aspiration, a wafting ripple, singing, singing, insistently, inviting him to listen to its soft echo, a gentle breeze shushing, bidding him to rest, singing, singing, darkness falling, sleep, sweet sleep overcoming, blackness flowing, stars winking out, dreaming wonder drawing closer, closer, ebon darkness growing, flowing up and out and over the stone rim, followed by a thing of beauty, leaning down, gently kissing companions, joyfully receiving, lips smacking, liquid dripping, maw masticating, hand burning, fierce with cold, silent screaming, eyes open, never closed, seeing, seeing, seeing—

Struggling against the irresistible, Gwylly squeezed his hand tightly upon the burning cold amulet, his mind shrieking for him to move, yet he could not, for he was frozen in place. Still he fought desperately, striving to focus his mind on what he was seeing, praying for the fiery pain of the frigidly cold blue stone to aid him. Slowly he began to apprehend, and dimly through the ebon darkness he could see the motionless bodies of his companions lying as still as death. But at the well—at the well—he could see a black *thing*, extending up and out from the well, a thick, segmented, wormlike body, laden with glistening slime, filling the round well shaft—filling the shaft. Gripping the freezing amulet, drawing strength from it, forcing himself to *see*, Gwylly followed the arc of its shape up and over and down through the murk, the roundness tapering down, flattening, coming to a blunt end, a mouth fastened to Reigo's still form—and it was *feeding*. Slime dripped from its bloody maw, horrid sucking sounds filled the air, Reigo's body like a bag of blood being drained. The sight burned into Gwylly's mind, and he shouted in terror, but all that came out was a feeble moan.

being drained. The sight burned into Gwylly's mind, and he shouted in terror, but all that came out was a feeble moan. Straining, in small wrenching movements, he managed to turn his head slightly, and saw that next in line for the hideous creature to *feed* upon was *Faeril!*

And even at that moment the creature rose up from Reigo, blood and slime dripping from its red maw. And with sucking, slurking sounds, its glistening orifice opened and closed, and the eyeless head of the creature—nothing more than a hideous, flat, blunt tip—slowly moved back and forth, as if seeking the whereabouts of new prey. And when its ghastly, drooling, sucking mouth pointed toward Faeril, the dreadful questing stopped.

Shrieking in silent horror, with all of his might, Gwylly tried to leap up, and slowly, ever so slowly, he toppled from the stone, slamming into the ground, the crash jolting him, driving back his enthrallment but barely. Straight in front of him lay Riatha and Urus, unmoving.

Driven by desperation, grimly he inched himself forward until he came to the Elfess. Agonizingly, he forced his arm ahead, placing his hand in hers, pressing the frigid amulet into her palm, against her skin. Reaching down deep inside for his last dregs of strength, Gwylly managed to utter words, his voice whispering, croaking, "Riatha. Riatha. Help. It will kill Faeril."

And then he knew no more.

Words, like dark stones falling into a black pool . . .
*Help . . . help . . . elp. It will kill Faeril . . . it will kill . . . Faeril . . . Faeril . . .*
. . . fell into Riatha's empty dreams of dread.
Urgent words:
*Riatha . . . help . . .*
Desperate words:
*It will kill . . .*
Whispered words:
*Help . . . Riatha, help . . .*
She struggled . . . Something cold, frigid . . . and came awake, remnants echoing in her mind . . .
*Help . . . help . . . elp. It will kill Faeril . . . it will kill . . . Faeril . . . Faeril . . .*

Who called?

She did not know. But something icy burned her hand . . .

. . . and this she did know.

*Amulet!*

*Danger!*

She could not move.

She forced her eyes open. She could not see. All was blackness. Impenetrable. In the distance she heard the bellowing of terrified camels, yet at hand was a hideous *sucking* and *slurking* and *bubbling*, and she could smell the iron tang of free-running blood, overpowering all. Yet there was another odor on the air, close and dank, sickening to the senses.

She closed her hand upon the amulet, gripping it tightly, driving back the thralldom slightly.

Willing her arm to move, with tiny jerking motions she inched her empty hand downward, fingers extended, straining to reach the sword lying at her side. Sweat beaded on her brow, and she ground her teeth with the effort, all the time sweet blackness sucking at her mind. At last she touched the jade grip and managed to close her fingers 'round, and her very soul wept at what she was about to do, her mother's voice echoing in her mind—*"It has a Truename . . . it draws strength and energy and life . . . a terrible price . . . mortals may lose . . . years from their span . . . years . . ."*—yet had she any choice?

*"Dúnami,"* she whispered, Truenaming the sword, and suddenly she was filled with a burst of strength, of energy, of *life*, and could *move!* And a pale blue light streamed outward from the blade, piercing through the unnatural blackness, and she could *see!*

And something shrilled thinly.

Rolling forward to her feet, Riatha saw the *thing*, the wyrm, recoiling up and away from Faeril's body, its oval maw oozing slime and blood, the hideous, segmented black monstrosity shrinking back from the sword's blue radiance, trying to withdraw, to escape down the well. Yet more than thirty feet of it extended from the circular opening, and it was bloated, engorged, and it struggled to force itself back in.

Dread hammering through her entire being, *"Yaaahhhh!"* shrieked Riatha in a wordless yell, running forward, blue flaming sword raised high in a two-handed grip. *Shkk!* the blade sliced across the hideous *thing's* gut, black blood and red gushing out, spilling on the ground, the creature mewling. *Shlakk!* With a backhanded stroke Riatha drove Dúnamis again through the monster, opening another great gaping wound, blood and tissue and slime pouring forth.

Shrilling in agony, the monstrosity whipped back into the well, disappearing downward, the blackness collapsing, the stars shining down.

Pursuing, Riatha ran to the lip of the well and peered inward, the azure glow of Dúnamis shining into the depths of the black hole, revealing only massive streaks of slime and blood down the dark stone throat.

The *thing* was gone.

Stepping back, *"Dúnami,"* whispered Riatha, Truenaming the sword once more, and its blue radiance vanished, leaving behind the sparkle of dark silveron.

And as the light disappeared, a massive wave of weakness washed over Riatha, and she fell to her knees, nearly swooning. Struggling, she barely regained her feet, but then she saw Reigo, or what was left of him, and her hand flew to her mouth in horror. She reeled away, sickened, even as tears sprang into her eyes.

Stumbling, dry retching, she fell to her hands and knees on the ground among the companions, even now some of whom were striving to rise—Urus, Aravan, Halíd—yet failing in their feebleness. Beyond them, Gwylly lay, and right at hand was Faeril, and Riatha's heart leapt to her throat, for buccan and damman moved not.

# CHAPTER 30

# *Kandra*

Struggling, Urus managed to gain his feet, and two steps later he fell to his knees at Riatha's side. His voice croaked out, "Beloved, are you—"

"The Waerlinga, Urus," she gasped, "they move not."

Urus crawled to Faeril. A sickening mix of blood and mucous covered the damman. Quickly Urus wiped her face and stripped the Wee One of her slathered cloak and *brussa*. He could see no wounds, for Riatha had acted before the *thing* had begun to *feed* upon Faeril. Urus placed his ear to her breast. "She yet lives, but barely." The damman drew a shallow breath.

Aravan had overheard Riatha's words and had dragged himself to Gwylly. "This one has no breath . . . but faintly his heart beats still." Aravan pinched Gwylly's nose shut and put his mouth to the buccan's and breathed shallowly into him. He took his mouth away, and watched as the buccan exhaled. Then the Elf gave him another breath, and paused, and another, and paused, and another . . .

Clutching Dúnamis in one hand, knuckles white, the blade slick with slime and gore, Riatha crawled toward her belongings, hissing out, "Halíd, the fire. Boil water for tea."

"Tea?" rasped Halíd.

"Adon!" gritted Riatha, crawling on. "Question me not, Halíd! Water for tea!"

Halíd floundered impotently, trying to gain his feet, failing. Then he, too, began hitching himself across the sand, canteen in tow, aiming for the fire.

At her bedding, Riatha loosed Dúnamis from her right grip, and found that she was yet holding Aravan's blue amulet in her left; the stone was cool to the touch, not icy. How she had managed to retain it and yet take a two-handed grip on the sword, she did not know. Aravan was but an arm's length away, still aiding Gwylly to breathe, and Riatha held out the amulet to him. The Elf took it and placed it 'round the buccan's neck, and in that moment Gwylly began breathing on his own.

Riatha fumbled through her belongings, searching, finding, withdrawing a small packet. "Gwynthyme?" asked Aravan. The Elfess nodded, and she managed to gain her feet and totter toward Halíd, the Man now at the campblaze, a copper pot of water set on the stubby tripod above the burning scrub.

Halíd had levered himself into a sitting position, and he was rocking and moaning and staring toward what remained of Reigo, the Realmsman's body no longer resembling that of a Man, but rather that of a flaccid, emptied skin, covered with slime and blood and drained.

Riatha slumped down in the sand beside Halíd. "Halíd, don't look. Reigo would not wish thee to look at him the way he is."

But Halíd could not look away. "I heard you shout a Warcry. I saw the blue light pressing back the murk. I saw the . . . the *thing*. I could not move . . . I could not move! . . . I could *not* move! And now Reigo is dead!"

"Halíd, look at me. *Look at me!*" Slowly Halíd turned his face toward the Elfess. She reached out and put a hand on his arm and stilled his rocking. "There was nought thou could do, Halíd. The *thing* in the well entranced us all. I deem Gwylly managed to put the amulet in my hand. Even then—*hear me, Halíd!*—even then it was too late, for Reigo was by then dead. Without the power of . . . my sword . . . we would all have perished."

Halíd stared in noncomprehension at her, anguish filling his eyes.

The water began to boil. Riatha took the copper vessel from the tripod and set it in the sand. She extracted six of the small golden leaves from the packet and carefully crumbled them in the water and slowly swirled it, steeping the resulting tea. A minty fragrance filled the air, driving back somewhat the dank odor overlying the campsite.

Rummaging through the cooking gear, she filled a small cup and handed it to Halíd. "Here, drink this. *Drink it!* Slow sips, Halíd."

Her strength returning, the Elfess stood and stepped to Urus. Two more cups she filled. "One for Faeril and one for thou, beloved."

Urus glanced up at her, a strange puzzlement in his eyes. "Riatha, look at the Waldan. Look at her."

Urus had stripped Faeril of the remaining soiled clothing and had washed her clean of mucous and blood and had wrapped her in a blanket. Kneeling, Riatha peered closely at the Wee One and drew in a shuddering breath. The damman's turban had been removed, and underneath, Faeril's raven black hair had a narrow silver streak running through it, extending from the right brow over the back and down the full length of her mane.

In Riatha's mind whispered her mother's voice. "*. . . If thy need is great, Dúnamis will draw* life *itself . . .*"

A great hollowness filled Riatha's chest, clutching at her thudding heart. But she shoved aside the feeling, for her comrades were in need. "Give her the tea. Small sips over time. And likewise drink thine own, Urus." She looked closely at her beloved, yet she saw no apparent change in his grizzle-tipped hair.

As she gave Aravan two cups of gwynthyme tea, she examined both Elf and Waerling. There seemed to be no effect upon Aravan, but beneath Gwylly's turban the buccan's red hair had gone grey at the temples.

Back at the campfire she unwound Halíd's turban; his black hair was now shot through with strands of grey.

"*. . . Dúnamis will draw* life *itself . . .*"

Riatha buried her face in her hands. *Adon, am I no better than the wyrm of the well!*

*     *     *

The gwynthyme tea restored them somewhat, and Faeril and Gwylly slipped into a natural sleep. As soon as they could, Riatha, Urus, Aravan, and Halíd moved the campsite far from the well, Urus and Aravan gently bearing the sleeping Waerlinga out to the new site. When they had relocated all their goods, Urus returned to the well and enwrapped Reigo's remains in a blanket. With the coming of the dawn they would hold a ceremony, cremating what little was left of their companion. Aravan and Halíd walked out into the basin to find the camels, for the beasts had panicked, yet hobbled as they were, they could not have gotten far, and the Elf and Man went to retrieve them.

Urus and Riatha remained in the camp, Riatha wearing the blue stone amulet.

Once again Urus stepped to the well. The stone ring was yet slathered all 'round with slime, there where the wyrm had been. And the smell was as that of a dark mire. Even though the trough was made of stone and filled with water, Urus dragged it away from the well and back to the campsite, for he could not abide the odor the creature had left behind, and Urus would lave the filth from Faeril's garments.

As the Baeran knelt at the trough and washed the damman's clothes, beside him Riatha cleaned Dúnamis of mucous and gore, scrubbing the blade violently, as if it were befouled, corrupted by unspeakable filth, desecrated with vileness, as if it had been *violated* by the creature. In her hand she had a small brush, and she *jabbed* the brush at the blade, and *jabbed* it at the blade, and *jabbed* it, and *jabbed*. Her breath came in sobbing gasps, and tears ran down her cheeks. And she *jabbed* and *jabbed*.

And Urus reached over and stilled her hands.

Riatha stopped moving altogether and quietly wept. Urus took her in his arms and held her close, stroking her hair. *"Shh, shh, my beloved,"* he whispered.

Riatha did not answer, sobbing still, as would a child lost. Urus said nought. He held her. She wept.

At last Riatha spoke. "Dúnamis, my sword. I Truenamed it. For the first time since I have had it, I invoked Dúnamis."

Urus nodded. "I heard you say to Halíd that without the power of the sword we would all have perished."

"But it stole *life*, Urus! It stole *life!* Did thou not see Faeril's hair, Gwylly's, Halíd's? It took life from them and gave it to me." Again Riatha wept.

Urus held her gently still. "List to me, my love: had you not called on your sword's powers, we, none of us, would have life at all."

"I could have tried harder to overcome the . . . the *song* of entrapment. Mayhap I needed not Dúnamis's power, yet I did not wait to see."

"Had you hesitated, Riatha, Faeril would now be dead."

Riatha gritted in return, "Never before had I used it, never again will I. The cost is too high."

"The cost would have been even higher otherwise."

Riatha wept still. But at last she choked out, "But oh, my beloved, what have I done to thee and the others? What have I done? . . . What have I done to ye all?"

Urus's only answer was to wrap her tightly in his arms.

When came the dawn the Warrows wakened, momentarily disoriented in their new campsite, out from under the sickly palm trees, far from the well.

["Where are we?"] mumbled Faeril, speaking in Twyll, the damman sitting up, clutching the blanket about her. ["Where are my clothes?"]

Gwylly sat up beside her and fervently embraced the damman. "Oh, my dammia, you are all right! You are all right!"

He held her at arm's length and looked at her, his emerald eyes flying wide at the sight of the silver streak in her hair. But then he clasped her to himself again. "Oh, Faeril, the *thing*, it was after you and I couldn't move."

"Thing? What thing?"

"From the well. A giant leech-like thing, only worse—" Suddenly Gwylly glanced wildly about, seeking, seeing all his companions but— "Reigo! Where's Reigo?"

Riatha squatted beside the Waerlinga and handed over Faeril's freshly scrubbed clothes, now dry. "Reigo is dead, Gwylly. Slain by the wyrm."

Faeril felt as if she had been kicked in the stomach. "Reigo dead?"

Riatha nodded, saying nought, gesturing toward a pile of scrub on which lay Reigo's blanket-wrapped remains.

"Oh, Gwylly." Weeping, the damman threw her arms

about her buccaran, and he held her tightly as tears streamed down his own face.

After a listless breakfast, they broke camp.

"What about the well?" asked Gwylly. "Do we destroy it? Break down the stone sides and topple all within? Bury the monster?"

Aravan shook his head. "It contains precious water. Someday we will return and destroy the monster within. Halíd has set warning stones about, configured to say to all that they must not be within this basin when the Sun is not in the sky. I think the wyrm will not hazard the daylight."

Faeril looked at the Elf. "Another *Djado* place." Her words were a statement, not a question.

Aravan nodded. "Another *Djado* place. A place where death came in a hideous shape and slew a comrade."

Urus stared at the distant well. "A place where death dwells still."

Now they stepped to the ground where Reigo lay, Halíd with a torch in hand. The Gjeenian looked at the others, then down at the blanket.

> *"As the haft of the arrow is feathered*
> *with one of the eagle's own plumes,*
> *and loosed into the sky to fly up forever,*
> *so, too, is this one's soul loosed from its bow.*
> *May the heavens above accept this worthy*
> *  Realmsman*
> *who lived in Honor, sought Justice, and spoke Truth.*
> *Fly up, Realmsman, fly up forever. . . .*
> *Thou were cherished."*

Halíd thrust the torch into the brush, and the dry branches crackled with flames, fire springing up as the Gjeenian moved about and set the whole to burning.

Tears ran down the faces of all as they stepped back from the roaring pyre. And then slowly they walked toward the waiting camels, Gwylly placing his turban back on his head. "Oh, Gwylly," said Faeril as she watched him, "your temples are grey," and at these words Riatha turned to Urus and buried her face in his chest.

At last they rode up and out of the basin and away from a place of *Djado*, away from the Well of Uâjii, the camels trekking south into the endless dunes of the *Erg*, seeking a place where *kandra* once grew, a place where Dodona might be.

And as they moved southward, up from the desert floor hindward a plume of smoke rose into the sky.

They travelled fourteen leagues that day, encamping in the dunes for the night. And as they sat beneath the stars, they spoke of the *thing* in the well.

"Perhaps it was the creature who dug the well so deep," said Gwylly.

"A trap, do you think?" asked Faeril.

Aravan nodded. "Mayhap. Mayhap."

"Perhaps this *thing* is the reason why Prince Juad's expedition disappeared . . . and the one that came after," suggested Faeril.

Again Aravan nodded. "Mayhap, Faeril, but that wouldn't explain the vambrace and shattered arm bone Gwylly found at the Oasis of Falídii."

Faeril shook her head. "Perhaps it was a survivor fleeing from the wyrm's trap, and he died or was slain as he went for help. Or it could have been someone who died on the way *to* the well. Perhaps something else haunts *that* place . . . the oasis, I mean."

Gwylly took a bite of his crue. "Oi! Urus, when the bucket was stuck at the bottom, it could have been in the grasp of the leech-wyrm."

Urus shrugged.

Faeril glanced from one to another. "I didn't see it at all," she remarked, "though I *did* have black dreams of a dreadful thing, a thing cloaked in darkness."

Gwylly looked at the damman. "It *was* cloaked in darkness, Faeril. I had a devil of a time seeing it."

Riatha, who had remained quiet until now, exclaimed, "Thou saw it, Gwylly? But I thought that thou had swooned ere the light of the sword drove back the wyrm's impenetrable black."

"Oh, I was out, all right. I didn't see the light from your sword, though I wish I had. No, I saw the leech dimly before

I put the stone in your hand. And it was surrounded by a terrible murk."

Faeril cocked her head to one side. "Just like the Dimmendark?"

Gwylly paused in thought. "I suppose it was, love."

At Caer Pendwyr both Warrows had read the High King's copy of the *Raven Book*, an illuminated tome telling the tale of the Winter War. It described a darkness that had come over the land, a darkness cloaking Modru's Hordes as they marched south from Gron, conquering all in their path. Yet Warrows could see far through Modru's Dimmendark, and the Wee Folk had proved his undoing, or a small group of them had, one in particular—Tuckerby Underbank. It was he who was responsible for the writing of the *Raven Book*, or as it is more formally called, *Sir Tuckerby Underbank's Unfinished Diary and His Accounting of the Winter War.*

Aravan leapt to his feet. "*Hai!* Once again jewelled Waerling eyes see through a darkness dire to foil a foul foe!"

Gwylly smiled up at the Elf. "Ah, but it was your blue stone that saved us all . . . that and Riatha's sword."

A bleak look came upon Riatha's face, and she stood and walked away in the night.

After a moment Urus got up and followed.

That darktide, only Aravan and Riatha and Urus stood watch, for the others yet were drained, weary.


"It is a most distinguished look, Gwylly," said Faeril, commenting on the buccan's grey temples.

Gwylly glanced up from his breakfast. "Perhaps, my dammia, yet nothing to compare with the silver stripe in thy raven locks—a truly beautiful enhancement."

"Was it the wyrm, Gwylly, that changed your hair and mine and Halíd's?"

Riatha, overhearing, said bitterly, "Nay. Not the wyrm. Instead, 'twas I who caused such. I and my sword."

Faeril sipped the gwynthyme tea prepared by the Elfess, for Riatha had gauged that it would help restore energy to Faeril and Gwylly and Halíd. "How could you cause such, Riatha?" queried the damman.

"My sword is Truenamed, and when invoked, it draws

energy from allies, strength ... and if the need is great
enough, e'en life itself. It was meant to be a Dylvan Champi-
on's sword, to be used among abundant allies, at a time
when a War is to be settled in a battle of Champions.

"But at its forging, the blade was instead given unto my
mother, for there was sudden strife on the land and she was
in immediate need of a weapon, and the reach and weight
of the sword not only was fit for a Dylvan male, it also was
fit for a Lian female. When the War ended, the weapon was
by then my mother's, and when I came unto Mithgar she
gifted it to me. Neither of us had e'er invoked the sword ...
until the wyrm at the well"—Riatha glanced at Urus—"and
then I had no choice.

"I Truenamed the weapon, and it drew the energy I
needed, the strength, the *life*, to o'ercome the creature."
Tears filled Riatha's silver eyes. "It drew life from thee and
gave it to me, and *that* is why thy tress is silvered and Gwylly's temples grizzled, and Halíd's locks shot through with
grey as well."

Faeril stood and stepped to the Elfess and threw her arms
about her. The wee Warrow, saying nothing, simply held
Riatha. And Riatha, weeping silently, clung to the damman
as would a castaway cling to a floating spar.

They came up a long, stony slope to the wide rim of the
plumb-walled canyon in late morning, the Sun high overhead. They looked down within the deep gorge, seeing greenery on the distant floor. And in the vast silence they could
faintly hear the sound of a fall of water coming from below.

From beneath his robes Aravan retrieved the one of Riatha's maps that he had borne all the way from Sabra. He
glanced at the chart and then at the position of the Sun. "We
have arrived at the place where *kandra* was said to have
grown."

Faeril sat on the double saddle down and in front of the
Elf, where she had ridden the day before, now that Reigo
was gone. "*Dodona*," she breathed.

"Mayhap, wee one. Mayhap."

Urus rumbled, "See you a way down?"

Long they looked for a place to descend. Finally, Riatha

pointed to a distant, narrow slot cleaving full down the face of the sheer bluff opposite. "There. Mayhap yon crevice provides passage, can we find its far extent."

No other path seemed to offer itself up for the six to follow, though the wide gorge turned beyond seeing 'round a steady bend, past which there could be a route down.

They backtracked north and west, coming to the far northern extent of the wide ravine, the walls yet sheer to the bottom. 'Round this end they swung and rode southerly once more, and at last they came to the crevice Riatha had seen. They trailed it down slope back to its origin, and found that the camels could squeeze through, though if they came to any blockage, the animals would have no room to turn about.

"Hold," called Urus, then—"*Raka! Raka!*"—commanded his gelded dromedary to kneel. 'Mid *hronks* of protest, the camel reluctantly obeyed. "I will walk and see if it provides passage through," said the Baeran, dismounting.

"I will go with thee, Urus," declared Riatha, her camel, too, grumbling as it knelt.

And so did all the camels growl, as down they were commanded, the remaining companions dismounting, as well.

Leaving camels and comrades behind, Urus and Riatha stepped into the slot, disappearing 'round a twisting curve and into the shadows beyond. Faeril heard a faint *shing* as Riatha drew her sword.

Time passed, perhaps a half hour all told, and up through the slot bouncing from the walls came the echoing call of a Jillian crow.

Gwylly leapt up from the rock where he had been sitting. "Safe passage!"

Halíd looked at the buccan, questioning.

"It is Riatha," explained Gwylly. "The caw of the crow is a signal that all is well and to come ahead."

Halíd turned up the palms of his hands. "How do you know that it is not a desert crow simply calling to its mate?"

Gwylly smiled. "*This* crow is found only in the Jillian Tors, year 'round, and has a distinctive call."

Halíd nodded in understanding, moving with Gwylly to the animals, fixing the lead line of Riatha's dromedary to the last of the camels in his train, while Aravan tied the

lead of Urus's gelding to the train that followed him. And
with shouted commands of *"Kâm! Kâm!"* they got the grumbling beasts to their feet.

Into the high-walled crevice they went, Aravan and Faeril
first, three pack camels and a dromedary trailing after, Halíd
and Gwylly following, three pack camels and two dromedaries in their train, for tethered behind was Reigo's dromedary as well as that of Riatha.

Daylight faded as inward they rode, the walls cool in the
notch, and even though it was mid of day, the air in the
narrow slot felt chill. Downward they fared along a rock-
strewn floor, among boulders and fallen slabs, with ragged,
shadowed stone looming overhead. The clamor of grumbling
camels reverberated along the twisting corridor, sounding as
would a mighty caravan, but the softly padded feet of the
complaining beasts made no sound as they walked, for as
with all camels their steps moved in silence, though their
irritated *hronks* more than made up for any secrecy they
might otherwise achieve. And so, stepping silently and ob-
jecting loudly, down they went into cool shadow, along a
narrow, tortuous path, while high overhead a thin jagged line
told where the distant sky was above.

At last Faeril saw before her a great vertical cleft filled
with bright daylight, and she knew that they had come to
the end at last, and they rode out into a sweltering blast of
heat on the canyon floor, the dazzling Sun blinding, painful
to the eyes. Dimly, through tears, she could see two figures
walking toward them, and only by the sound of their voices
did she confirm that they were indeed Urus and Riatha.

Halíd and Gwylly came riding outward, and Gwylly,
squinting, called, "Hoy! Too bright to see. And it's like a
furnace out here."

The eyes of the new arrivals adjusted to the daylight as
Riatha and Urus retrieved their dromedaries, the odorous
beasts sneering and eructing accusations as down they knelt,
then stood again.

"Somewhere south there sounds the fall of water," rumbled Urus, "and southward, too, are trees in the distance.
Let us go there to pitch camp."

Down a long slope of scree they rode, down into the gorge

bottom, where sparse grass grew among thorny weeds. "Prime camel fare," said Gwylly, Halíd agreeing.

They rode a mile or so along the burning floor of the broad canyon, here a half mile from rim to rim, sheer walls of tawny stone rising up to left and right, towering a thousand feet high. As they went, the vegetation slowly changed, becoming more succulent. In the distance ahead they could see a line of trees: not palm trees, but something else altogether. Too, as they fared, the sound of a fall of water came louder to their ears, as if they were nearing the source.

At last they reached the tree line and rode into shade.

"Grass!" cried Faeril. "Real grass! I was beginning to think that the world was made of nothing but rock and sand—

"But, Aravan, what are these trees?"

"*Kandra*," declared Aravan. "This is a *kandra* wood."

Large were the trees, spreading outward like oaks. Yet no oaks were these, but of a different ilk, for the *kandra* leaves were small and bladelike, shaped as rounded stone arrow points—green on the topside and yellow on the bottom, and quaking in the slight breeze as would aspen leaves tremble. Too, the bark was smooth and dun, and the thick boles bulged somewhat at the ground, gnarled roots diving down into the soil. "The wood of this tree is golden, the grain dense, and it seems to have a natural sheen, as if it contained an oil, though it does not burn. It is a precious lumber and found only on Mithgar, and only the wood of the Eld Tree surpasses it in value."

Turning rightward, they followed the sound of falling water and came to a wide stream running clear and coursing in the shade cast by overhanging branches of the Kandrawood. Upstream a furlong or two they found a cascade falling some ten feet into a sparkling pool, rainbows dancing in the mist. Above the pool and a hundred yards beyond, the stream issued forth from a wide crevice at the base of the west canyon wall.

They pitched their camp downstream from the waterfall, down where the sound of the falling water was muted by the intervening trees. Halíd and Urus led the camels back to the succulent grasses at the edge of the Kandrawood, hobbling the grumbling beasts eager to graze. When they returned, Urus said, "I advise that we rest this day, for the journey has been long and wearisome. Tomorrow will be soon enough to begin our search."

Gwylly, sitting on the grass beside Faeril, asked, "How long has it been? How much time is left?"

Urus held up the fingers of both hands, ticking them down one at a time and then back up as he counted. "We spent two days at Sabra, and counting today, we have been thirteen days getting here. If we take the same time returning, thirteen days more, then the sum is twenty-eight. That means we have at most thirty-two days to search ere our sixty days total are gone, ere we need be back at Sabra to sail on the *Bèllo Vènto*."

Faeril's amber eyes sparkled. "Thirty-two days to search? Then we are certain to find it, I think, for Dodona was believed to lie in the Karoo, in a place where *kandra* was said to grow, and here we are in the midst of the Kandrawood. It's got to be near; I feel it in my bones."

Gwylly sprang to his feet. "Bones or not, love, it's me for a swim. Besides, I am of a mind to look behind that waterfall for a secret cave . . . for I ask you, where better to hide the Ring of Dodona?"

Faeril's eyes flew wide. "Oh, Gwylly, do you think so? Wait up, I'm coming with you."

Refreshed by their swim, it was mid-afternoon when all the companions returned to camp. In back of the waterfall Gwylly had found nothing but the slightly hollowed stone of the linn, needing a boost from Urus to clamber up behind. As Gwylly had emerged, sputtering and blowing, declaring failure, Faeril's face had fallen, but then quicksilver swift she had broken into a smile, and they had gamboled in the water. Wallowing in the pool, even Halíd's dark mood had lightened somewhat, the Realmsman still mourning Reigo's death, his friend of many years.

And now as they sat under the *kandra* trees, Halíd gazed at the stream. "*Ilnahr taht*," he murmured.

Gwylly, combing Faeril's wet hair, looked up. "What? What did you say, Halíd?"

"Oh, I was just reflecting on an old legend of the desert, the legend of *Ilnahr taht*, the River Under.

"It seems that far beneath the sands of the Karoo flows an

endless river, coming from the place beyond, going to the place afar, returning at last on its long, long journey unto its very own origin, circling forever upon itself.

"Some claim it is a river of death, while others call it a stream of life. The *imâmîn* say it is both, for are not life and death each part of the same endless circle?

"I know not the truth of it, nor whether this stream is *Ilnahr taht*, yet I am curious as to the source of this water and whither it does flow . . . for this gorge is surrounded by the Karoo. If it is not *Ilnahr taht*, coursing beneath the sands, then it imitates it well."

The morning of the next day found each of them eager to set forth to find the Ring of Dodona. As they broke their fast, Riatha suggested their course of action:

"We know not what we look for, other than it is a ring. As to what the ring may be, the legends and tales are filled with speculation, and surviving fragments of the records do not tell; perhaps those who scribed them assumed that all would know. Many icons purport to show its mein, all different: a circle of fluted columns; a temple round; a wide stone basin; a ring of dolmen; a circular cavern; a crystal chamber; an enormous pillar; a mound. It could even be a finger ring or a ring of mushrooms. Natural or constructed, we here know not. Who can say? We cannot.

"Yet this I can say: when we see it, *if* we see it, mayhap we will not recognize it as the Ring of Dodona. We must keep in mind that it may have decayed or fallen to ruin; it may even have been destroyed, deliberately or by natural forces. It may be a thing cleverly concealed, or it may be a thing in plain sight, a thing that we would not ordinarily take as a ring.

"Today I would have us ride together the length of this ravine, from one end to the other, from side to side, and measure out its extent, see its broad features. If we find not the ring, then after we have seen what these walls contain, let us devise a plan for searching out all.

"What say ye?"

For twenty-seven days they searched out the canyon, divided in teams of two: Gwylly and Halíd, Faeril and Aravan, Riatha and Urus. The gorge held the shape of a crescent Moon, running southerly and curving away to the west, seven miles from tip to tip, and three quarters of a mile at its widest. The only path inward was the one they had taken, except of course for the river, flowing in under the western wall, streaming some three miles southward, exiting out under the wall opposite. From under the Karoo it came; back under the Karoo it went; and the six of them took to calling it *Ilnahr taht*, the River Under. The Kandrawood grew the length of the watercourse, spreading out a goodly distance from both banks, filling the gorge from side to side for most of the river's length. The very horns of the crescent gorge were rather barren, being farthest from the water, the vegetation sparse and dwindling in the far ends. But the middle-most four miles were relatively lush, especially in the Kandrawood.

But twenty-seven days did they search, finding nothing that they could call a ring. A rope about his waist with Urus anchoring, Aravan even swam underwater under both walls looking for a hidden chamber beyond . . . to no avail.

They walked the flanks at the base of the high stone walls, seeking a hidden crevice.

They searched the walls of the chasm of the known pathway out.

They tapped on stones, listening for hollows beyond, and rolled aside boulders.

Halíd and Gwylly rode up and out and 'round the rim, not only seeking the ring *on* the verge above, but also seeking the ring *from* above, peering down into the canyon for any circular shape.

Again, all their efforts were futile, unavailing.

Each night they would return to camp, frustrated in their quest.

Twenty-seven days they had searched. In just five days they would have to leave.

It was after mid of night when Gwylly wakened Faeril for her turn at watch, giving over to her Aravan's blue stone. As was their wont, they sat together awhile and spoke softly. And on this night Gwylly said something which continued to echo in Faeril's mind long after her buccaran had gone to sleep: "What we need," he had declared, "is an oracle to find the oracle."

Faeril pondered Gwylly's remark, wondering why it nagged at her so. *Perhaps* . . .

She went to her pack and rummaged about, finding the small iron box with its crystal. *Moonlight to see the future. There is no Moon, only starlight. Starlight to see the past. The last time I charged it, though, it was with moonlight.*

Faeril returned to the rock on which she had been sitting. With some trepidation she opened the iron lid and withdrew the silk-wrapped crystal. *The last time I tried to use this, I was in a coma for three days. Mayhap if I merely let it guide me, mayhap I won't tumble down within.*

Faeril took the crystal in hand, closing her fingers about its long-sided, hexagonal shape. The damman next closed her eyes, her mind canting a chant: *Dodona . . . Dodona . . . Dodona . . .*

She felt a warm tingling at her throat. With her free hand she located its source, her fingers touching Aravan's stone.

*Left,* seemed to come a gentle bidding. *Left.*

Her eyes flew open. The stone stopped tingling.

Closing her eyes once more, she struggled to still her startled spirit. At last her heart quieted its wild hammering, and a state of anticipatory calm filled her soul. *Dodona . . . Dodona . . . Dodona . . .*

*Left.* . . .

Riatha wakened Gwylly, the buccan sitting up, rubbing his eyes. Darkness was yet upon the land. *"What is it?"* he whispered, not wishing to waken the others.

The Elfess whispered in return. *"Gwylly, do thou know where is Faeril?"*

Gwylly looked about, his heart thudding. He did not see his dammia, and alarm filled him. Still he managed to control his voice. "No," he replied softly.

Riatha's shoulders slumped, and she held up a small iron box and a black silken cloth. "Then, Gwylly, Faeril is missing, and I fear for her."

*       *       *

They roused the camp and weapons in hand began the search, moving softly through the night, for who knew what foe might have taken her? And when came the dawn, they had not yet found her, even though at last they had begun calling out her name, their voices echoing from the canyon walls. Finally Urus said, "I will find her." The Baeran turned to Halíd. "Halíd, fear not that which you are to see."

A darkness gathered about Urus, enveloping him, his shape changing, growing huge, brown, with long black claws and ivory fangs, dropping to all fours, and where Urus had been now growled a huge Bear.

"*Waugh!*" cried Halíd, backing away, scribing a warding sign in the air. "*Afrit!*"

"Steady," hissed Aravan, placing his hand on Halíd's, stopping the Gjeenian from drawing his knife. "There's nought to fear."

His eyes wide, Halíd glanced at the Elf, then back at the Bear. "Reigo would have laughed," he murmured, then nodded to Aravan. "I am all right now."

The Bear snuffled at Faeril's blankets, then cast about, *whuffing*, nose to the ground. Into the woods he went, away from the stream, ambling in the general direction of the waterfall, rambling back and forth across a track that only he could follow, the others coming after. Yet the farther he went, the more reluctant he became, nearly turning aside several times, as if something was resisting him, bidding him to turn away. The two-legs trailing him also seemed disinclined to go farther. But one—the small two-legs that had ridden him when there was snow—*that* two-legs seemed more determined, and though the wee two-legs nearly stopped several times, on each occasion he shook his head as if dispelling sleep and urged the Bear onward. And together, Bear and wee two-legs, the rest following, they at last came to a glade and stepped within . . . and suddenly the resistance vanished.

A peaceful quietness lay upon the dell, leaves rustling softly overhead—though strangely, the sound of the waterfall could *not* be heard even though it was but mere yards away.

Lying in the glade center was another two-legs, another wee one. The Bear ambled to her side and snuffled—this was the one he had been seeking. The Bear nosed her, nudging her, but she did not move for she was deeply asleep, a winter sleep, or so it seemed to the Bear.

The others had gathered about, some kneeling. The Bear backed away and sat down . . . and thought of Urus. And a dark shimmering came upon the beast, and again Halíd stepped back, awe in his eyes. Swiftly the shape before the Gjeenian *changed*, altering, losing bulk, gaining form, and suddenly there on the ground sat Urus.

In glade center Gwylly and Aravan and Riatha knelt beside Faeril. The damman lay on her back, her eyes closed, seemingly asleep. In her left hand resting 'cross her stomach she held her clear crystal; in her right hand at her neck she clutched Aravan's amulet on its thong.

Aravan reached out his hand and touched the blue stone, and his eyes flew wide with surprise. "Wait!" he called.

Riatha looked up and 'round, her silver eyes filling with wonder. They were in the very center of a perfect circle of evenly spaced *kandra* trees. At last they had found the Ring of Dodona . . .

. . . but at what cost?

# CHAPTER 31

# Dodona

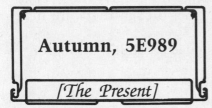

**Autumn, 5E989**

*[The Present]*

**H**er eyes tightly shut, crystal clasped in her left hand, the blue stone in her right, mentally chanting *Dodona . . . Dodona . . .* Faeril stepped cautiously forward, following the gentle bidding. Whence it came, she knew not, only that it did.

Faeril was reluctant to leave the campsite, and nearly did not, but *something* or *someone* seemed to assure her that her companions would be safe, that the entire gorge was warded, protected. Too, she did not wish to lose her *link* with the *presence.*

And so, eyes closed, crystal in her left hand, amulet in her right, she followed the vague nudgings, nudgings more sensed than felt.

That she walked in the Kandrawood she did not doubt, for leaves rustled overhead. That she neared the falling water, this she also did not doubt, the *shssh* of the cascade growing louder. That she did not stumble or collide with a tree never entered her mind, for she *knew* that she was guided in safety.

*. . . Dodona . . .*

Stepping on the soft grass, among the trees she wandered, following . . . following. At last she came to a place where, except for the rustle of leaves, all sound ceased, the *shssh* of the falls suddenly stilled. She nearly opened her eyes but did not, and instead paced forward, then stopped . . . and sat.

A voice came softly. "Open your eyes, child."

Faeril saw before her an eld Man, or so he seemed, long white hair and a flowing white beard and dressed in white robes. His face was crinkled with age lines, and pale blue eyes looked out at her from beneath shaggy white brows.

"Are you Dodona?" asked the damman.

The Man smiled gently. "I am known by many names, Dodona among them."

"What are you?"

The Man smiled. "Ever direct. Ever in a hurry. Mortals.

"I am the warder, the guardian, the keeper, the speaker. Some would call me a Hidden One, though there are many of many kinds by that name."

Faeril now smiled. "You are indeed a Hidden One, for we could not find you."

"I was always here to be found."

"But it was difficult, Dodona."

"Not all who seek, find. This ring"—he gestured about, and Faeril saw that she was seated in the center of a ring of *kandra* trees—"this ring is warded from discovery by a simple charm, and only those of sufficient need or wit can find it."

"We have a need, I and my companions."

"I know, child. You seek a death. I do not willingly aid those who seek the death of another."

Faeril nodded. "Your reluctance I can understand, Dodona, but this Man is a monster. And I travel with honorable companions."

The eld Man seemed to look elsewhere, as if seeing something beyond the circle of trees. "Yes, child, your comrades are most worthy. You travel with a Friend; this I know, for that stone at your neck is his and not yours. Too, you travel with a BearLord, and I know whence he came. You travel with one who is to bear the hope of the world, and she is worthy. You travel with one who will aid in ridding the world of a foulness, though not the one you seek. And you travel with one who loves you, one whom you love in return. All of these companions are indeed honorable."

"And the one we seek? What of his honor?"

Again the eld Man gazed elsewhere. "The one you seek has no honor, and truly is a monster upon the world. Even so, I am reluctant to aid in the death of *any*."

"But I found you, Dodona. Does that not say I have sufficient need?"

"Or that you have sufficient wit."

Faeril looked at the Man. "In either case, I seek knowledge."

The Man's blue eyes gazed into hers. "And I am bound to answer, though you may not understand my reply."

"Well and good, Dodona, well and good, for I have many things to ask you: where we can find Baron Stoke; the whereabouts of the Dawn Sword; where Aravan can locate his yellow-eyed Man; the secret of Urus's identity, of his abandonment, and of the identity of his parents; the meaning of Rael's prophecy concerning silverlarks and Silver Sword; the meaning of my own prophecy concerning the Rider of the Planes; what you meant about Riatha and the hope of the world; what happened to the expedition of Prince Juad when he came to find you; and—"

Faeril's words skidded to a halt as the eld Man, smiling and shaking his head, held up a hand, palm outward. "You may ask, but I will answer only one question of import, and it must be one you choose."

Now Faeril was nonplussed. "Only one?"

"Only one."

Her chin in her hand, long did the damman think, trying to decide. Yet at last she looked at the eld Man and said, "We came seeking the whereabouts of Baron Stoke, and though there may be more important issues that I could address, still, my companions and I are sworn to run him to earth. I suppose that I could be clever and ask where we will slay Stoke, thus gaining foreknowledge not only of his location but also foresight as to the success of our mission . . . but I will not. Instead, Dodona, I will merely ask where will we find Baron Stoke."

The Man smiled. "It is good that you did not try to be

overly cunning, child, for the answers I give are uncertain at best, and the simpler the query, the more reliable the answer.

"Yet heed, it has been long since one such as you has come, one with an innocent heart, and in giving my answer to your question, I would also reward you with knowledge you seek but did not ask for.

"You hold in your left a clear crystal, and I know that you would learn about such. I will show you much concerning that talisman, but not all.

"Gaze into its depths, child, for I would take you on a journey."

Faeril held the crystal up before her amber eyes and looked deep within. And suddenly, down she tumbled, falling among glittering mirrors and glistening panes and the tinging sound of wind chimes . . .

. . . to land . . .

. . . in Caer Pendwyr.

Dodona stood at hand.

Courtiers strolled. Pages rushed thither and yon. People sat on benches, waiting for an audience with the High King.

The eld Man bent over and said to her, "They cannot see us."

Faeril looked at the Man. "Wha— Is this real?" She could yet hear the *tink* and *ching* of crystalline chimes.

Dodona laughed. "Perhaps, child. Perhaps not."

Suddenly they were in an empty chamber of the castle.

"I brought you here to show you something. Gaze out this window. What do you see?"

Faeril looked out the window. The cerulean waters of the Avagon Sea rolled below, white caps rushing inward to crash against the base of the sheer stone cliffs. "I see the sea."

"Is that all?"

Gulls wheeled on the wind, and distant clouds drifted on the horizon above cobalt water afar. A sailing ship clove the waves. "Birds. Clouds. A ship."

"Is that all? Look more closely."

"What do you mean, Dodona?"

"Look at the glass."

"Oh." Faeril looked at the glass itself. "I see bubbles in the glass, its greenish-blue tinge, dirt on the pane."

"Is that all?"

Reflected on the glass was a vision of the chamber behind. "I see the room mirrored."

"Is that all?"

Now Faeril looked and saw her own reflected image, a golden flame, and at her side was a free-standing flame of silver. "I see you, Dodona, and I see me."

"Exactly! One window: four views. Beyond. At Hand. Behind. Self.

"We can shift to a different window"—of a sudden they were at a tower window looking over the city—"and what we see is different, the views Beyond, At Hand, and Behind. Self stays essentially the same, unless we somehow have changed.

"But most important, though Self stays the same, note that all is seen through the reflection of Self. The Vision Beyond is seen through Self. The Reflection Behind is seen through Self. Even the View At Hand is seen through Self."

Suddenly Dodona looked upward. "Wait!" he shouted. "It is too dangerous. Move her not!"

Aravan looked at the others, surprise in his eyes. "We must not move Faeril."

Gwylly looked at the Elf. "But, Aravan, she's gone into a coma again. Last time, she was unconscious for three days."

Aravan shook his head. "I know, Gwylly, yet we *must* wait. All we can do is nourish her, give her small sips of water, care for her needs. We must not take her from this glen. Else she will be in jeopardy."

Riatha glanced at Aravan. "How know thee this?"

"I touched the stone."

Faeril was startled. "Wait for what?"

"Oh, child, I was not speaking to you. It was to one of your companions: the Friend."

"Aravan?"

The eld Man nodded. "Now, where was I? Oh yes, views—"

They fell among the crystal panes, mirroring, reflecting, views Beyond and Behind, wind chimes sounding in the swirling aethyr.

"Tell me what you see."

"I see crystal panes, Dodona."

"No, child. Look in large. See the overall. What is the pattern?"

Faeril tried to take in the broad view. At first, all was a glittering confusion. But then—"Why, it is something like a honeycomb, Dodona. A six-sided pattern running throughout."

"Good, child. You have seen . . . but not all. Look again at the pattern."

Now that she knew what to look for, Faeril peered about as she and Dodona tumbled downward. "There seems to be three honeycombs, staggered, interlaced."

The eld Man clapped his hands. "Exactly, three patterns interlocked. Yet that is not all. Take my hand, I will be your guide."

As they flew downward, Dodona again called, "Wait!"

Aravan looked up at the others and shook his head. "Not yet."

Gwylly wrung his hands. "But, Aravan, it's been a whole day."

"Nevertheless, Gwylly, we must not move her."

Urus stepped from the camp and into the ring, for they had relocated next to the circle of trees. "Is there aught else we can do?"

Bleakly, Gwylly looked up and shook his head.

Aravan spoke. "All we can do is watch over her, tend to her, and care."

Dodona flew down to a corner of one of the hexagonal surfaces, the damman holding on. The plane seemed to grow as they approached it.

"Why, this is not a corner at all," exclaimed Faeril. "Instead it's a . . . a pyramid. A three-sided pyramid."

"Four sides if you count the bottom. Look up. Look down."

Affixed to one another at their points, tetrahedrons twisted upward beyond seeing, spiralling downward as well, each face a plane, a window, a mirror.

The crystal surfaces of tetrahedrons reflected their images as they flew onward, now for a point of a pyramid where something tiny glowed, pulsating; and in the pyramid's center was suspended another glowing mote, this one . . . different. At the point they found a shimmering sphere, a glittering sphere, spheres within spheres.

Passing through the shells, they came to a tight cluster of glowing globes, each made up of even smaller motes—spinning, whirling sparks, seemingly interlocked.

"Wait!"

Halíd voiced what all knew. "We are running out of time. This is the third day. Two are left ere we must start back."

Aravan merely shrugged.

"This is as far as I have gone, child. In this glitter we are looking at the marrow of creation, the core of all . . . the beginning and the end. Here is the hub of everything, all that is, all that was, all that will be. All things—fire, water, wind, earth, aethyr—all are made of this stuff of creation . . . the beat of time, the extent of space, the durance of matter, the vigor of energy."

Faeril looked at the whirling sparks. "All things, Dodona? What of the mind, the soul, the spirit, the concerns of the heart? Are they, too, made up of nothing but mere glitter?"

The eld Man paused. "Ah, my dear, now you delve into the ultimate mysteries. Those are questions I cannot answer, but ones whose answers I eternally seek."

Again the eld Man looked up. "Wait!"

Halíd sat with Riatha. "There is but one day left, yet I can gain us seven more."

Riatha turned her face to the Realmsman. "How?"

Halíd gestured northward. "If I were to take only my swift *hajîn* and Reigo's, and two goatskins of water, and a small amount of food, then, switching from camel to camel, I could make it back to Sabra in six days, or perhaps even less. *Hujun* have been known to travel one hundred miles a day for several days."

Riatha nodded. "Yes, Halíd. It is a sound plan. Should Faeril fail to waken in time, then we will use it." Her eyes focused once more into the Ring of Dodona, where Gwylly faithfully tended to his Faeril.

*       *       *

They hovered before a crystal pane, views Beyond, At Hand, Behind, Self.

Faeril could see as if through a half-silvered glass. The Vision Beyond was that of a scarlet citadel clutched within mountains; the View At Hand was that of a Man in shackles; the Reflection Behind was that of a mountain keep.

Dodona spoke. "Time is frozen here within the crystal, yet all times are valid.

"The Vision Beyond represents the future; what is shown is not that which *must* be, but only that which *might* be.

"The Reflection Behind is that of the past, often muddled through multiple images, conflicting reflections.

"The View At Hand is a look at the present, often distorted through Self.

"The Sight of Self is self, and it frequently gets in the way of seeing *anything* clearly."

Faeril looked at her own reflection, and then at Dodona's silver flame. Suddenly she knew without knowing *how* she knew that she was seeing the true Dodona, and that the oracle could take on any shape he desired, eld Man, young child, Elf, male, female, whatever he wished.

Dodona laughed. "I see that you have discovered one of my secrets."

Faeril's eyes widened. "You have a power somewhat like that of Urus, the power of shapechanging, that is."

"Much more, child. Much more. . . ."

Faeril clapped her hands. "Oh, what a wonderful gift you have. I have always wanted to fly like a falcon—"

Faeril did not hear Dodona's cry, for the transformation was already upon her.

At Gwylly's side Halíd gave a shout of alarm, for a sudden golden light flared in the glade amid a knelling of chimes. Abruptly the glare and ringing faded and Faeril was gone, and in her place a falcon stood, blue stone on a thong about its neck, a crystal lying on the ground.

It was a thing of wildness, untamed, great amber eyes glaring, and it unfurled its wings and crouched to launch itself.

In that instant a silver light blazed forth from the crystal, englobing the entire ring with its brightness, and neither

Gwylly nor Halíd could see nor hear, for the air was filled with crystalline tintinnabulations. Rushing inward, Riatha, Urus, and Aravan were blinded and deafened as well. Yet all felt an overpowering presence step into the glade and then back out. The dazzling light faded, the ringing fell to silence, and when sight and hearing returned, Faeril lay sleeping before them, clutching blue stone and clear crystal, the falcon gone.

"Fool!" lashed out Dodona. "All shapes are possible within the crystal! You could have been entrapped forever as a falcon wild!"

Faeril shrank inward upon herself at his scathing words, then suddenly flared up in anger. "Who is it you name 'fool,' Dodona?" she spat. "Did you give any warning? I did not know, and you cautioned me not."

"Ignorance is no excuse," shot back Dodona. "Fools rush where the wise pause."

Before Faeril could reply, Dodona ground his teeth and gritted, "Don't those impatient lackwits know that time steps here to a different drum?" And he raised his face and shook his fist upward and shouted, "Wait!"

Aravan turned to the others, shaking his head. "We yet must wait."

Halíd sighed. "Nine days ere Legori sails. I must leave within three."

Aravan saw that Gwylly was weeping, and he put his arm about the Warrow. "Fear not, Gwylly. Faeril is yet in good hands. *That* I can sense."

The eld Man now looked down at the wee damman, standing on a hexagonal crystal plane, her hands on her hips, fuming. Suddenly Dodona laughed and knelt down and embraced her. "Adon! What am I to do with you, daughter? You are too bold!

"Too, you are right. I gave you no warning, and I am sorry for that.

"Yet list, all within the crystal is too dangerous for you, for you are of the Middle Plane and ill prepared. Seek not to use the crystal to *see*, for you may become entrapped forever!

"Instead, you may use the crystal as a guide, to help point the way when choices are uncertain. Use it to magnify your intuition, to aid you with vague premonition, but seek not again to fall within; for you it is nought but a door to eternal imprisonment. And you are too precious to spend that way."

Faeril returned Dodona's embrace, for she had become fond of this—this Hidden One, even though she had known him for only an hour or two, or for twelve days, depending on who was marking time.

Dodona took her by the hand and looked overhead. "Yes! Now! Now you may have her back!" he called up into a sky filled with hexagonal lattices interlaced, with crystal planes and windows and mirrors, with interconnected, spiralling tetrahedrons, with glowing globes of shimmering shells and clustered spheres within, those shining orbs made up of interlocking sparks spinning in a whirling glitter.

And upward they flew into this crystalline sky, hand in hand.

"But wait," called Faeril. "What about my question? Where will we locate Stoke?"

Dodona looked at Faeril with guileless pale blue eyes, but he and the lattice began to *fade*, yet she heard his words most clearly among the diminishing chimes. "My dear, I have given you all the answer that I am willing to give, but it is you who must find it among your memories."

And then Dodona was gone, and Faeril opened her eyes. Overhead a lace of *kandra* leaves rustled against an afternoon cerulean sky. She lay in a glade on her back, clutching a blue stone in her right hand and a clear crystal in her left. Gwylly knelt at her side, weeping with joy. Urus, Aravan, and Halíd stood back, smiling. At her other side, Riatha knelt and held a cup of gwynthyme tea.

Faeril sat up and embraced her buccaran, whispering, "Oh, Gwylly, I found Dodona and asked him a single question of import, but received a thousand answers."

Faeril sat through the evening, telling all of what she had seen, what she had experienced, what she had learned. And it was in the retelling that she realized that Dodona *had* shown her at least a partial answer to her question as to where they would find Stoke.

"There was only one crystal pane that I looked through. In the Reflection Behind was a mountain keep."

"A keep?" rumbled Urus. "What did it look like? It might be Stoke's black bartizan."

Faeril described the grey stone keep, ringed about with high crenellated battlements, the stone of the mountains grey as well.

"That could be any number of places," murmured Aravan, "yet once when tracing a yellow-eyed Man, I came upon such in the mountains of Garia."

Halíd cocked his head sideways. "Did you find your yellow-eyed Man?"

"Nay. The keep was abandoned, as was the land."

Gwylly turned to Faeril. "Go on, love," he urged. "What about the View At Hand?"

Faeril shuddered. "It was of a Man in shackles. No one I knew, yet he was swart and thin."

Riatha looked at Urus. "Stoke shackles his victims for a while. It gives him pleasure to have them dwell upon their coming fate."

Aravan added, "There are many Lands where the Men are swart and thin. Hyree. Kistan. Gjeen. Thyra. The Karoo. More. They are too numerous to name."

Faeril sipped her tea. "The Vision Beyond was of a scarlet citadel clutched within mountains."

"*Aiee,*" hissed Halíd. "That could be Nizari, the Red City of Assassins, a place of ill reputation."

Aravan nodded. "I have heard of it. On the border of Hyree. South of here and west, across the sands of the Karoo. It is marked upon one of your maps, Riatha."

Gwylly turned to Halíd. "City of Assassins? Why assassins?"

Halíd's finger sliced across his neck, his tongue sounding a *kckkk*. "Because long ago it was said assassins were the city's principal export, and some say it is yet true."

Urus glanced across at the damman. "Describe it in detail, Faeril. Mayhap we can verify that it is indeed Nizari."

Faeril depicted the city as best she could, portraying the mountains as well, but nothing she said confirmed that it was Nizari, though nothing told it was not. "If I could see it, I could say," she said at last.

Urus nodded, looking 'round the circle. "At the morrow's dawning there will be but six days left ere Captain Legori and the *Bèllo Vènto* set sail from Sabra. We six here tonight must decide what we are to do: head back for Sabra, Halíd riding ahead to hold the ship; or strike out across the desert, riding to Nizari."

Riatha haled out her maps. "There is a third choice, Urus: send Halíd back to Sabra, carrying word to the High King, while the rest of us ride on to Nizari. That way, if we fail, some will follow.

"Too, the *thing* in the well must be destroyed. And Halíd can see that those who have the power to deal with that creature learn of its existence. He can go to Darda Erynian, the Great Greenhall, and find Tuon, for he bears Black Galgor. Find Silverleaf, too, for he is clever enough to lure the wyrm from the well where it can be killed."

Long did they debate their future course of action, but in the end it was Riatha's plan that was accepted. Halíd was the last to be convinced, for he would go with them to Nizari. Yet finally Riatha said, "Thou must speak with the High King thyself, Halíd, for he would hear it from the lips of one who has lived the tale.

"Too, thou must bear word to Tuon, for thou have seen the wyrm of the well and know of its deadly *song*. Thou can lead Tuon and Silverleaf and any others to the Well of Uâjii, and take revenge for Reigo's slaughter.

"Lastly, should we fail in our mission, it will be up to others to destroy Stoke. Thou can assure such by bearing that knowledge unto those who will come after.

"For those three reasons, Halíd, thou must go."

The Realmsman looked long into her steady, silver-grey eyes, and perhaps what he saw there convinced him more than did her words; finally he nodded, agreeing to the plan at last.

As they prepared for sleep, Riatha searched through her pack and located Faeril's small iron box and silken cloth, handing them to the damman. "Thou left these behind when thou went to find the Ring of Dodona."

Faeril took the proffered items in hand, staring down at them as if struggling to find words. At last she burst out, "Oh, Riatha, I left the camp unguarded, and for that I am ashamed. I should have awakened someone."

The Elfess nodded, agreeing. Silence fell between them, but after a while Riatha said, "It is past, Faeril, and should be forgotten by all but thee, to be used as a guide for thine actions in the future. Yet who knows, mayhap thou would not have found the ring had thou done otherwise than thou did. Whether it was wise or foolish, we here cannot say. What is done is done, and we cannot recall the moment and do it differently."

Pondering Riatha's words, Faeril set the iron box aside and spread the silken cloth on the grass. Reaching into her pocket, she drew forth the crystal, laying it in the center of the square of black silk. As she started to wrap the clear stone, suddenly she stopped, taking up the crystal and holding it to the firelight, staring at the quartz. The perfect crystal now seemed flawed, and she turned it 'round and 'round, peering closely, trying to see what— The damman gasped, for no flaw was this. Instead, frozen in the heart of the crystal was an exquisitely detailed form, almost as if it had been incised by a master craftsman, though no jewel carver known could do such superlative work as this—it was the form of a wild falcon, wings unfurled as if ready to spring into flight.

At the coming of the light of day, Halíd readied himself to set out northward. Urus admonished him to avoid the Well of Uâjii, and Aravan advised him to enter the Oasis of Falídii only if day was on the land. He saddled his dromedary and the one that had been ridden by Reigo, placing upon each a full goatskin of water as well as a small amount of food. He had six days and nights to ride, racing to Sabra, some four hundred forty miles across the sands of the *Erg*.

Faeril and Gwylly embraced the Gjeenian and kissed him on the cheek, and the buccan said, "Take care, Halíd, Realmsman, for we depend upon you. And, oh my friend, I will miss you."

'Mid irritated *hronks* Halíd mounted up. Riatha stepped forward. "Our journey ahead is long and arduous and will take time, as will thine own, Halíd. Yet if nought else we will try to get word to Caer Pendwyr within the coming year. If the year expires in silence, then thee and thine must decide what to do, if aught, for like as not we will be dead."

Riatha stepped back and raised her hand. "May Adon ride with thee."

Halíd unfastened his turban cloth from across his face and smiled and held up his own hand and said, "And may the strength of Adon be in your blades and may the hand of Elwydd shield you." The Realmsman then refastened the scarf and turned and rode away from the verge of the Kandrawood, riding his own dromedary, Reigo's in tow behind. Up the slope and to the slot he went, where he paused and waved to all, and they waved back. Then the Realmsman disappeared into the notch.

Two days later, on the first day of December, the five companions broke camp, for Faeril had recovered to the point that Riatha deemed the damman fit for travel.

Before setting out, Faeril stepped to the center of the Ring of Dodona. "Farewell, O Oracle of mine. I shall not forget you."

Only the rustle of leaves overhead answered her, and she stepped from the ring and into the sound of falling water.

Her companions waited for her, and when she came forth, all mounted their camels and rode up and away, passing through the narrow crevice connecting the crescent-shaped gorge to the outside world.

Facing into a hot wind blowing from south and west, they urged the complaining, sneering beasts forward, riding for Nizari, the Red City of Assassins, some twelve hundred miles distant across the mighty Karoo.

# CHAPTER 32

# *Prey*

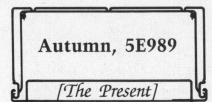

**D**eep in the mountains in the pit of the night high in the tower of the ancient mosque, Stoke ceased pacing long enough to glare out over the Talâk Range, seeing nought of consequence in the moonless dark. Stars wheeled through the black vault above, but the Baron did not use his high vantage to admire them. Instead, he resumed his caged striding, as if impatient for his *Chūn* to return, bringing with them fresh new victims, victims to fulfill his desires. Yet sating his needs was not at the root of his agitation. Nay! Far from it! Rather, he was pacing in fear and rage, for just moments before he had discovered that *they* were coming. . . .

In his *Psukhomanteîon*, Stoke lit the last black candle and set it in the fifth equidistant position on the chalked circle, the wavering yellow light adding to the glow from the other four, all joining the ruddy cast coming from the hot coals in the hammered iron brazier in one corner of the chamber. In circle center lay the corpse—flayed, abdomen bursted outward, entrails showing—its head aligned with the first candle, its arms outflung, hands pointing at candles two and three, its legs splayed apart, feet pointing at candles four and five. Once it had been a Human; now it was a thing.

Positioned between the spraddled legs but standing outside the circle, Stoke summoned his energies and began the incantation: *"Ákouse mè! . . ."*

Command after command he voiced, each one taking more energy, more power, sapping his strength, draining his will. Yet finally . . .

*". . . Egò gàr ho Stókos dè kèleuo sé,"* came the last command, Stoke straining with effort merely to utter the final words.

As with other corpses in other places, from the mouth of this one, too, came a myriad of whispering voices, all speaking simultaneously, ebbing and flowing, crowding inward, fading outward, all answering the questions of the *Psukhómantis*, all answers different, for all times and places were the same to the dead.

*Castle . . . glacier . . . Wee Ones . . . bartizan . . . desert . . . Elf . . . wyrm . . . death . . . Bear . . . spear . . . child . . . Uâjii . . . Avagon . . . Man . . . Arden . . . Greatwood . . . Rwn . . . Realmsmen . . . Atala . . . oceans . . . Elfess . . . sword . . . drapes . . . crystal . . . Falídii . . .* hissed ten thousand mutterers, their answers commingling, murmurings running together.

Stoke listened carefully to separate out the one voice, yet he had chosen a fresh corpse, his latest victim, and *he phéme*—the prophetic voice—of the dead thing in the circle was stronger than that of the rest. And when that voice fell silent at last, Stoke stood shaken.

He had *not* lost his pursuers; they were after him still! And even now they crossed the Karoo, journeying towards Nizari.

. . . And high in the minaret Stoke paced back and forth in fear, enraged that they were the predators and he the prey. Again he paused, looking north and east, as if willing his sight to fly beyond the mountains and over the desert and unto his relentless enemies.

Of a sudden he spun away, cursing, and hurtled down the spiral stairs and underground, striding through red-marbled corridors, coming at last to the workbench in his laboratory. Striving to calm his thoughts and conceive a fitting plan for those who pursued, he took up the work where he had last left off, focusing his mind on perfecting his latest ... instrument.

Golden it was, some three inches in diameter and thirty inches long, tapering to a hideous point on one end, an anchoring plate on the other. Carefully he measured, scribing short longitudinal lines in the gold where each of the many razor-sharp triangular blades would be embedded, blades to be set 'round the shaft and down its length. Here and there he also marked places where he intended to inset gems— bloodstones in particular.

When he had finished marking the gold, a plan had formed in his mind, and he set the grotesque auric stake aside and raced back to the minaret and up, and raged out into the night: "Now will the hunters become the hunted, now the predators the prey!" his shouted words echoing from the mountains 'round, Stoke laughing madly at the sound of his own voice reverberating—*hunters ... hunted ... predators ... prey.*

The following eve as twilight dimmed into utter night, from the minaret a hideous creature launched itself into the gathering darkness, its wide leathery wings bearing it toward Nizari.

# CHAPTER 33

# Mai'ûs Safra

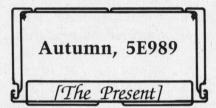

Autumn, 5E989

[The Present]

A hot quartering wind at his back, Halíd and his *hajî-nain* trotted across the desert, retracing their steps of the weeks past, travelling northward, drifting slightly easterly, racing for Sabra some four hundred forty miles away.

All morning Halíd kept up the pace, switching from one *hajîn* to the other every hour or so, the sneering dromedaries protesting at every change. Over rough terrain he transferred more often; over smooth, less frequently. Running at the speed that the camels could sustain over the given terrain, by the time they stopped at midday they had covered more than thirty miles.

Halíd and the beasts rested in the hot wind throughout the heat of the day. In mid-afternoon Halíd mounted up once more, and off they trotted, resuming the trek.

The scorching breeze continued to press upon them, driving them before its steady blow. *At least it's at our backs.*

The hours fled by, the Sun sliding down the western sky, and as the short desert evening came and went, night following, onward across the dunes and rocks ran the *hajînain*, their steady trot consuming miles. With the coming of nightfall, Halíd had expected the wind to abate, but it did not, and its breath blew warm upon them.

Halfway between sunset and mid of night, they passed the basin wherein was the Well of Uâjii. The dromedaries smelled the water and would have gone to it, but Halíd did not permit them to. Shouting *hronks* of dismay, onward the *hajînain* ran, and soon the Well was behind Halíd, though not the memories of Reigo's death.

Another six hours they pressed northward, Halíd stopping at last in barren dunes to sleep and let the camels rest. All told, some ninety-two miles they had gone, running for twenty-one hours. At this rate, in five days they would reach Sabra, one day ahead of the final day, could he and the *hajînian* keep up the pace.

And still the southwest wind blew, though now it was chill.

After but a bare three hours of sleep, Halíd awakened. Dawn was in the eastern sky. The Realmsman considered the southwest wind as he ate a small amount of food and drank a large amount of water. *An ill omen, this. It has blown for a day or more. May Rualla, Mistress of the Wind, decide it has been enough.*

Halíd roused the dromedaries and set out northward again, across endless barren sand, the *hajînian* complaining mightily, for they had neither eaten nor drunk since leaving the crescent gorge.

North they trotted, across the sculpted dunes, the hot wind rising at their backs.

Again in the heat of midday they stopped and rested, while all about them the wind stirred the sand, bearing the finest grains up and away, Halíd pulling his scarf closely across his face, dozing, trying to rest.

After three hours, once more they hurried northward, Halíd switching from *hajîn* to *hajîn*, and when they finally stopped in the wee hours of darkness, they had covered another ninety-eight miles, and still the wind blew.

On the third day of travel they entered rugged terrain, and when they reached the dunes again and stopped at last for the night, they had covered only fifty more miles. Even so, over the three days they had run some two hundred forty miles in all, and were but two hundred miles from their goal.

But the wind yet blew, and the next day, within an hour of setting out across the *Erg*, a wall of blackness howled out from the southwest, borne upon the squalling air.

Halíd dismounted and pulled the dromedaries through the dark, scouring wind and down into the scant protection of a dune, shouting *"Raka! Raka!"* above the shrieking yowl, commanding them to kneel, the Man taking his own shelter against the flank of one of the beasts, covering his full face with his scarf.

Endlessly the howling sand whelmed upon them, the dune drifting against them, threatening to bury Man and beast alike. But squinting against the hurtling sand, Halíd moved the camels, then moved them again, struggling to maintain control of the creatures.

He knew not how long the shrieking blast had blown, but faintly, above the yawling there came a *different* sound, the sound of endlessly rumbling thunder. Halíd pulled his scarf down from one eye, peering out as the crescendo grew louder, and of a sudden a huge black whirling column loomed out from the darkness and roared down upon them. *Sand demon!* Halíd's mind shrieked, even though he *knew* that it was but a fable—but then the black, spinning wind was upon them, howling so loud as to deafen, unimaginable strength tearing at them, hammering, battering, wrenching, lifting . . . then it was gone onward, thundering away.

Gone, too, was one of the camels.

Some ten hours all told did the shrieking wind roar across the *Erg*, but then it began to diminish, rapidly fading away, until there was nought but silence left in its wake.

Halíd dug out from under a layer of sand, peering 'round. There was no sign of the missing camel, but at hand was the remaining one—Reigo's former mount.

*"Kâm! Kâm!"* shouted Halíd, stepping to the saddle and mounting as the beast reluctantly complied. "It is just you and me, *sabîyi*. Just you and me."

Turning the nose of the *hajîn* northward, off once more they set, running for Sabra, some one hundred ninety-five miles away.

\*     \*     \*

They came upon the Oasis of Falídii in the late afternoon, two hours before sunset. Halíd turned inward, riding to the waterhole. After the dromedary had drunk its fill, the Realmsman hobbled it and set it to graze. Halíd took the remaining goatskin and refilled it, then shed his clothes and washed himself clean in the pool. He was weary, yet he had far to go and but little time left. Even so, he waited until the Sun was halfway below the horizon ere riding forth from the oasis, for, remembering Aravan's words, he did not wish to remain here after darkness. It *was*, after all, a *Djado* place. What made it so, he knew not. And how they had escaped evil while camped in its embrace on the journey down to the Ring of Dodona, he did not know. Yet he speculated that perhaps the blue stone amulet had some such to do with them remaining unmolested, even though the stone had proved of less worth at the Well of Uâjii.

Regardless, Halíd now had no stone of warding, and so he rode away from the oasis and into the *Erg*. And even as he rode outward, the Sun set and the hair on the back of his neck rose, as if something behind were watching, something maleficent.

*"Hut, hut, hut!"* he called out to the *hajîn*, but for once the dromedary needed no urging as it bolted forth.

When they stopped in the glancing light of the setting Moon, they had gone only forty miles in all. It was the end of the fourth day of travel, and they were now two hundred eighty miles from the crescent gorge.

There were just two days left and one hundred sixty miles to go, and Halíd now had but one camel.

The next day, the fifth day, they crossed again into rugged terrain, and that night when they stopped, they had gone only another seventy miles.

The sixth and final day found Halíd and the dromedary back in the dunes of the *Erg*, the Realmsman pushing the beast to its sustainable limits. Across the sands they raced, up and down the long, drifting slopes. And when came the noontide, Halíd did not stop as he had been doing, for altogether they had ninety miles to go that day and even though it was like travelling in a furnace, onward they went, the flagging beast trotting across the burning sand.

Night fell, and ahead they pressed, over the endless dunes 'neath a bright yellow gibbous Moon. And when mid of night came, they were yet some twenty miles distant from Sabra. Halíd knew not when the tides flowed, yet he did know that now Captain Legori and the *Bèllo Vènto* were free to sail on the next one.

*"Hut, hut!"* he called to the camel, but the weary beast could go no faster. Through the moonlight they trotted and over the lip of a high dune, and of a sudden the beast pitched forward, the sand beneath its feet giving way, and down the slope they slid, sand enveloping them, the dune behind cascading upon them. But it was not the avalanche of sand coming after that was covering them, instead it was the collapsing sand at their feet, for the *hajîn* had stepped into a sink hole and, camel bellowing in terror, both Man and beast were being sucked under and buried alive!

Even as the animal sank, Halíd scrambled up the camel's back and leapt outward, landing on the slope of the funnelling sand, his feet and legs scrabbling for purchase, the Realmsman clawing upward even as the cascade drew him backward toward death. On he went and up, barely ahead of the collapsing sand, gaining the rim of the funnel and out to safety at last. He stumbled some distance away and fell to his hands and knees. And when he turned and looked back, sand yet slithered down . . . but of the camel there was no sign.

Tumbling through Halíd's mind again were the childhood legends of the evil demons who lurk under the sands, waiting for innocent victims to draw them down unto suffocating death.

After long moments, wearily Halíd got to his feet and set out across the dunes, trudging toward Sabra, twenty miles away.

Just after dawn, a dirty, disheveled, exhausted Man staggered out of the Karoo and in through the city gates of the desert port of Sabra. He had no water, no food, no camel, having lost all to the sands of the *Erg.* Yet he had survived the *mai'ûs safra*—the desperate journey—and inward he stumbled and wearily made his way down toward the harbor, toward the quays. When he got there he asked a dock worker the whereabouts of the harbormaster, and was directed towards a portly Man overseeing the offloading of a white stallion down the ramp of a three-masted dhow and onto the quay, a group of admiring *shaikhîn* gathered 'round the prancing animal. The exhausted Man, Halíd, approached the harbormaster and spoke to him. The master drew back somewhat from this filthy wretch and pointed out to sea. There sailing away from the anchorage against the turning tide fared the *Bèllo Vènto.*

Rage flashed over Halíd, and he cursed at the sky, the harbormaster backing away in alarm. The Realmsman looked about wildly, then bulled past these desert chieftains and knocked aside the groom leading the stallion, leaping upon its bare back and thundering away northward, crying, *"Yah! Yah!"* racing through the city streets and out the north gate, shouts of pursuit lost in the distance behind.

Up along the headland he ran, galloping in full, racing for the promontory a mile or so away. In moments, it seemed, he had reached the high point, hauling the stud to a skidding halt, the horse squatting on its haunches to stop, dirt flying, dust boiling upward. The Realmsman leapt from the blowing stallion and wrenched his curved knife from its scabbard, turning the gleaming blade into the early morning Sun, light glancing from the glittering steel.

Long he stood on the promontory, holding the blade out horizontally before him, shifting and turning it in the bright rays. And as he heard an angry mob of people rushing up the hillside after him, he saw the *Bèllo Vènto* heel over in the wind and come about.

Captain Legori had finally seen the Realmsman's flashing signals.

# CHAPTER 34

# Crossing

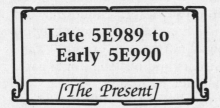

Straight into the teeth of the hot southwestern wind rode Aravan and Faeril on one *hajîn*, Riatha and Gwylly on a second, and Urus on the gelding, each dromedary trailing two pack camels after. Out into the *Erg* they fared, aiming now for an oasis marked on Riatha's map, an oasis some one hundred forty miles hence, a journey of perhaps some four days. It was but the first way station on their long trek, the distant goal being Nizari, the Red City set on the far rim of the Karoo, eleven hundred miles away as the raven flies. But their plan called for travel of some twelve hundred miles in all, their route zigzagging from oasis to waterhole to well for their passage across the sand.

As they rode, the wind blew hotter, a fine grit lashing at them. They drew thin scarves across their eyes, seeing out through the mesh. Even so, now and then a tiny grain would penetrate, seeking out an eye.

Faeril, blinking and squinting, tears washing away one of these grains, asked, "What about the camels, Aravan? Won't they get sand in their eyes, too?"

Aravan smiled. "Nay, wee one. Thou have seen their thick lashes, thick enough to stop most sand. Yet could thou get close enough without risk of being bitten or spat upon, thou would see that even should granules get through, each eye has an inner lid to protect it and push out the grit."

"I am relieved, Aravan, for I would not relish being the one to bind an ill-tempered camel's eyes against the blowing sand."

Aravan barked a laugh, and onward they rode into the rising wind.

They camped that night in the lee of a stony, rock-laden hill, the wind yet warm upon them, blowing harder still.

An hour before dawn, Urus came down from the hilltop and awoke all. Wind moaned past, and he had to shout to be heard. "A black wall comes, blotting out the stars."

"*Shlûk!* Sandstorm," cried Aravan.

While Aravan and Urus pulled the camels into the shelter of boulders, the others gathered up all the belongings at the campsite and stowed them behind the rocks as well.

Aravan just had time to call to each of them to cover their faces, when the blast was upon them. Faeril leaned her head against Gwylly's and shouted, "Oh, Gwylly, I do hope that Halíd doesn't get caught in this, too." Gwylly reached out and squeezed her hand, and they hunkered down behind their boulder, black wind shrieking past.

For ten hours the roaring wind hammered at them, but even so, both Gwylly and Faeril dozed in fits and starts. So too did the others, the *shlûk* howling them to sleep. But as suddenly as it had come, just as suddenly did it go, leaving behind a silence that seemed almost deafening in its utter stillness.

Aravan was the first to his feet, and he trudged toward the hilltop, his boots scrutching loudly upon the grit. Urus hauled Riatha to her feet, and together they followed, casting long shadows down the slope behind them, the afternoon Sun shining in a clear sky above. Gwylly and Faeril busied themselves with shaking sand from all of the belongings. "I'm hungry," said Gwylly. "What say we break out something to eat?"

It was late on the night of the fourth day of travel that they came to the oasis, the camels sensing the water first, surging forward.

As they pitched camp, Aravan said, "Here we should stay this night and the next as well, for the camels need to graze, and we could do with a respite. The next watering hole is some one hundred leagues hence, and though we may find suitable forage along the way, we should give them some time to feed before moving on."

"The circle of Elves can only grow smaller on Mithgar." Riatha stirred the embers of the fire, though the full Moon sliding down the western sky shed enough light to see far and wide. Faeril sat with the Elfess and they spoke softly so as not to wake the others. "With each one slain, we are diminished. With each that returns to Adonar, the circle here is diminished again, for the way back to Mithgar is sundered." Riatha looked at the damman. "And as thou know, we cannot bear young here on this world." Riatha's eyes glittered, and Faeril reached out and took her hand.

"Someday you will have a child, Riatha."

Riatha's gaze flew to Urus, the Man asleep. "But I would have the child of Urus, Faeril, and that can never be. He is mortal and of Mithgar; I am immortal and of Adonar. I cannot have a child here, and he cannot go there . . . and even should he somehow find his way to the High World, still we could not have a child together, for love between mortals and Elves is ever barren of offspring."

Faeril started to reply, but ere she could say a single word, Riatha's hand flew to her throat. *"Swift!"* hissed the Elfess, casting sand on the fire, smothering it, *"wake the others. The warding stone grows cold."*

Faeril awakened Gwylly and Aravan, while Riatha raised up Urus.

Long they waited in the night, a circle facing outward, peering through the moonlight. In the distance beyond the oasis, Faeril thought she saw dark shapes running across the dunes, yet when she called for the others to see, the shapes were gone.

Slowly the chill went from the blue stone amulet, the danger fading away.

After the stone returned to normal, Faeril, Gwylly, and

Aravan took to their bedrolls, Riatha and Urus remaining on guard.

But the damman found sleep eluding her, her mind shuttling between sadness at Riatha's plight and apprehension at what could have caused the stone to grow cold. After an hour or so of restless tossing, she moved over to Gwylly and curled up against him; the buccan snuggled closely and held her tightly . . . and in moments slumber reached out to clasp her as well.

In the early morning light, Gwylly climbed up a long, sandy slope to look for tracks, Faeril accompanying him. As they stood at the crest, the damman pointed at a nearby dune. "What's that, Gwylly? Looks like a . . . a toppled pillar."

"It does at that, my dammia. Let's go see." Gwylly turned and whistled at the others in the distance below, and with a series of piping signals he told them of the find.

As they trudged toward the object, they came across sets of impressions dimpling the sand, running east and west. "Well, something *was* here, all right," said Faeril, "but what it or they might be, I cannot say, for too much sand has trickled down into these prints."

Gwylly squatted beside the trail. "More than one something, love. Several, from the looks of it."

Urus, Riatha, and Aravan caught up to them, but none could say what made the impressions, though Urus hazarded a guess. "Four-legged, I deem. Running east, I would think. Smallish."

After a moment, onward they went, toward the slope of sand ahead. When they reached the dune, they found a huge, partially buried obelisk lying on its side, some forty feet or so visible before it disappeared under the sand, strange pictographic carvings in the stone. Gwylly asked, "Can anyone read this? What does it say, I wonder."

None knew the language, though Aravan said, " 'Tis my guess that it was placed here by some Human King, seeking a kind of immortality."

They brushed off additional sand, revealing more pictographs but no more knowledge. Birds, dogs, horses, camels, other beasts were carven thereupon. Shocks of wheat, boats, Humans, pottery, wheels, chariots, bows, arrows, and the like, all manner of people and items could be discerned, though no Elves, Dwarves, Warrows, or Folk other than Humankind appeared.

Aravan said, "In Khem, south and east of here, Men have erected great stone pyramids, burial chambers, memorials to their eminence, as well as stone monoliths and other structures to last for all time, conferring immortality unto their names."

Gwylly shuddered. "*Ooo*, immortality or not, I would not like to be shut up forever in hard, cold stone. Instead, bury me in soil . . . or better yet, offer my soul up to Adon on the golden wings of fire."

Faeril reached over and squeezed her buccaran's hand.

Aravan made a vague gesture easterly. "Pyramids, monoliths, monuments: all intended to confer everlasting fame, but most are as this obelisk—bearing inscriptions that no longer have any meaning unto the living."

Urus rumbled, "Immortality they may have, yet recognition they have not."

"What if Mankind were immortal, thou ask?" Riatha looked down at the damman. "*Aro!* With his lack of discipline, he would soon o'erburden the world and drag it down unto destruction with him."

Faeril rinsed the clothes she washed in the oasis waterhole. "Like lemmings? Aravan told Gwylly and me about lemmings and their rush to destruction."

"Worse than lemmings, Faeril. Much worse. Lemmings have not the intellect, the power, the ability to destroy the world. Mankind has."

Faeril handed the *brussa* to the Elfess. As Riatha hung the shirt over the line tied between trees, Faeril took up a pair of pantaloons and plunged them into the water. "Will Man ever change? I mean, will he ever see that he is part of the world, and what he harms, harms him in return?"

Riatha shook her head. "I know not, wee one. I know not. But this I do know: Man is clever, inventive, and can he extend his life, he will. Yet, adding years without also adding a sensitivity to his effects upon the world can only lead to a disastrous ending. Can Man overcome his insatiable appetites, then there is hope for Mithgar. Yet should he retain his greedy grasp, then this world will not last."

"Yah hoi!" came Gwylly's cry. "Fruit for each and all!"

To the waterhole came Gwylly and Aravan and Urus, a cloth bag filled with clusters of ripe dates. Gwylly's mouth was stained brown. "Watch for the seeds, love, they are like long, skinny peach pits and are as hard as rocks."

As Aravan squatted beside Faeril and took up clothes to wash, laughing, he said, "That buccaran of thine, Faeril, has monkey blood in his veins. Just like the one thou saw entertaining for coins in the streets of Sabra."

"Hah!" exclaimed Gwylly. "Urus alone boosted me more than halfway up."

Riatha took up a date and bit into it, smiling at its sweetness. "Had we time, we would dry some of these to bear with us across the Karoo."

As the full Moon rose above the horizon, Gwylly began humming a tune. Faeril cocked an eye at him, and he pointed at the rising yellow orb and broke into words.

*"Fiddle-de-de, fiddle-de-di,*
*The cow jumped up so high in the sky,*
*Up through the air and over the Moon . . .*
*'Oh, look there,' said the dish to the spoon.*

*The spoon stood back and upward eyed*
*Then after a moment solemnly replied,*
*' 'Tis odd, I'll agree, most unexpectedly at that,*
*As queer as if the dog were to dance with the calico cat.'*

*No sooner said that the fiddle sawed,*
*And the dog led the cat in a promenade,*
*And the cow fell down from above the Moon,*
*The frightened dish ran away with the spoon.*

*I laughed so hard that I cried,*
*The dog laughed, too, at my side,*
*The cat did wail loud and long,*
*As the fiddle screeched a different song . . .*

*. . . But the cow with a crash tumbled down on my
   head,
And that's when I woke, falling out of my bed!—
Thud! Whump!"*

Urus's guffaws belled out into the night, completely
drowning out Faeril's giggles and the laughter of Riatha, Aravan, and Gwylly.

When a modicum of quiet returned to the oasis, Faeril
asked, "Where did you learn such wonderful nonsense,
Gwylly?"

"My father—my Human father, Orith—used to sing it to
me to put me to sleep, though I laughed at it instead, and
Nelda, my mother, would chide Dad for keeping me awake
. . . though she was the one who sang it to me when Dad
was away in Stonehill. It was my favorite."

Suddenly, Aravan held up a warning hand and reached for
his spear. *"Ssst! The stone!"*

Again they took up station in a circle facing outward,
standing next to date palms.

Long moments passed, and once more Faeril saw silhouettes loping through the night. She gave a low whistle, and
her companions turned to see. In that instant, clear in the
moonlight, atop a dune a mottled, doglike animal appeared,
pausing to look down at the comrades among the palm trees.
Then it whirled and raced away, following the tracks of the
others, disappearing beyond seeing among the dunes of the
*Erg.*

"The stone grows warm," said Aravan, "the peril wanes."

Gwylly turned to the Elf. "What was it, Aravan? I mean,
it had large round ears and its fur was splotched. Yet it
wasn't very big. Why would the stone grow cold at such a
creature?"

"It was a wild dog of the desert, Gwylly. And in a pack
they can bring down nearly *any* beast. The stone knows well
the hazard of such."

Faeril looked toward the scrub growth. "Oh my! What
about the camels? Are they in danger?"

Aravan shook his head. "I think not. The stone should
hold the pack at a distance."

Riatha sat back down. " 'Tis good we leave on the morrow, for I deem we keep the dogs from their water, and stone or not, they will come when thirst drives them so."

Aravan nodded, agreeing. "Aye, Dara, thou hast the right of it. Some things are too virulent to be affected by the stone—Vulgs, Loka, Rucha, and other *Spaunen*, Drakes, monsters of the deep, to name a few—"

"The wyrm of the well," interjected Gwylly.

"Aye, Gwylly, the wyrm, too.

"Other things are too desperate for the stone to hold at bay—creatures driven by hunger, thirst, a need to defend themselves or their get, a need to escape, to flee.

"The wild dogs are among these last, for they will come regardless, when their thirst grows great enough."

Urus gazed out into the moonlit dunes. "Then I say we sleep this night away from water's edge. If they do come, they will find the way open."

Five days later, in the afternoon they camped alongside a *oued* where grew cacti and thorny shrubs, for again the camels had gone awhile without sustenance.

Gwylly and Faeril climbed up a long, stony slope to see the land about. "Hoy! Look at that!" cried Gwylly as they reached the crest, the buccan pointing at the horizon. "Ships! And an ocean!"

Faeril gasped, for there in the distance before her, two lateen-sailed boats, dhows, plied the sea. Then she shook her head. "No, Gwylly. Like the lakes we've been seeing, this too is a mirage."

"I know, love, but isn't it marvelous? Oh my, the others need to see this as well." Gwylly turned and whistled down the slope, signalling to those below.

That evening, Aravan said, "Once when my crew and I were tramping across a desert in the land to the west, from a high ridge we saw a mighty forest. Down from the ridge we marched, aiming to reach the sanctuary of the trees by nightfall. When we got to where we thought the forest stood, all we discovered were fallen logs lying in the sand. We made camp, and lo! when one of the Drimm warriors took an axe to a log for firewood, the blade chipped! The log was solid stone! All the logs lying in the sand were stone!

" 'Mayhap,' said the warrior whose axe was broken, 'mayhap a *Kötha* did this.'

"When I asked what a *Kötha* might be, he replied that it was a dire creature whose gaze could turn living things to stone.

"We left the next day, marching onward, to the great relief of all the Drimma in the company, for though most thought the *Kötha* nought but fable, they were not willing to test the truth of it.

"Yet the fallen forest of stone is not the strangest part of my tale, nor even the legend of the *Kötha*. Nay! The strangest thing of all was that when we came back through that territory, returning overland unto the *Eroean*, to ease the minds of the Drimma, we skirted 'round the region where lay the trees of stone. But when we climbed back up the distant ridge where first we sighted the forest and looked hindward along our track, once again we saw green and growing a mighty woodland afar, there where we had found nought but a field of stone."

Days and days they travelled across the endless waste, stopping to let the camels forage whenever they came upon desert grass and cacti and thorn bushes, small stands of twisted trees and other plants.

Ten days it took to travel from the oasis to the watering hole, some three hundred miles in all. And another five days were spent to reach the well one hundred nine miles beyond.

As they left that well and headed for the next, there came a torrential rain, and dry *oueds* filled to overflowing, the thundering water rampaging down into the flats below.

The desert burst into bloom, plants rising where it seemed nought but dry weeds stood, the whole world aflower. And wonder of wonders, they came to a small, shallow lake teeming with tiny fish!

"How can it be," asked Faeril, "that fish swim in the desert?"

"Adon knows, wee one" was the Elf's answer. "The world is filled with strange things, and this is but one of them."

Faeril twisted about in her saddle. "Strange things? Such as . . ."

Aravan smiled down at her. "Such as sea shells embedded in stone atop mountains."

Faeril cocked her head. "How can that *be*, Aravan?"

"I know not, Faeril. Some say that the mountains were once at the bottom of the sea, rising up long past, bringing the shells with them."

Faeril faced front once more. "Oh, you mean that just as Atala sank, so, too, could somewhere else rise?"

"Just so, Faeril . . . yet that is not the only explanation. There are other tales as to how shells of the ocean got to the mountaintops. Hear me:

"There is a small desert Kingdom to the east of the Avagon Sea. There the priests say that once long past their god, Rakka, became exceedingly wroth over his errant people and caused endless rains that flooded the world entire, the oceans rising up to cover all, their waves rolling above the inundated peaks. And during this time were the sea shells deposited upon the mountaintops, and Rakka locked them in stone as a reminder to all that his word was law.

"When I first heard this tale, there was with me a Drimm who asked several pithy questions of the priests. First he pointed out that there were some mountains that were over two leagues high, six or seven miles. He then remarked that to cover the earth over with water to that depth, it would take more water than was in all the oceans of all the world.

"His first question was, 'Whence came this volume of water?'

"His second question was, 'Where went the water after?'

"His third question was, 'Would not a god who is vengeful, wrathful, who slays old Men and Women and children, the halt and the lame, the newborn and the aged, the strength of the Nation's manhood, the flower of its womanhood, who would drown not only the people of that desert Kingdom but all the peoples of all the world, and all the animals of all the lands, and all the land birds as well—for what would they eat?—and all the freshwater fish and other water dwellers of streams and rivers and lakes, and all the trees and flowers and plants, who would kill all the life of all the world except for the creatures of the sea, and who would poison all lands with the salt of the oceans, would not such a god be evil?'

"Their responses to all three questions were always the same—'*Only Rakka knows, for his ways are mysterious, beyond the ken of any. Rakka is beneficent and he loves you, so fear him and revere him.*'

"The Drimm was disgusted with their response, and stalked away. '*You are an infidel and are lost forever!*' shouted the priests after. 'Better an infidel, O priests, than to worship such an evil god!' he shouted back, and returned to the *Eroean*.

"But I stayed awhile longer, asking questions of my own: 'When came this great flood? And if all was destroyed, whence came all the animals and birds, creatures of the fresh waters, all the trees and flowers and plants, and all the peoples of the world?'

"'*As to the when,*' they replied, '*it was some four thousand years agone.*'

"'But *I* have been on the world longer than four thousand years, and no flood o'er the whole world did I see. But e'en had I not been on the world that long, other civilizations have, and their records predate that time. How explain ye these things?'

"'*Your memories are false, emplanted by the Evil One to question our faith, just as the records you speak of are false as well.*'

"'What then, O priests, of my other question? If all was destroyed, whence came all the animals and birds, creatures of the fresh waters, all the trees and flowers and plants, and all the peoples of the world?'

"'*As to the saving of life, Rakka in his great love for all Mankind saved a single Rakka-fearing family, sealing them in a great cave, and they took with them two of each living thing.*'

"'Even the locust, even the worm? Even the fly and the flea?'

"'*Verily, even the locust, even the worm, even the fly and the flea, and all other living things as well . . . two of each. Whether they walked on four legs or slithered on their bel-*

*lies or hopped, whether they flew through the air or bur-*
*rowed in the earth, be they insect, worm, or creatures too*
*small for the eye to see, or creatures as large as the*
*elephant.'*

" 'And the green growing things, the trees and shrubs and
flowers and grains and all other possible plants?'

" *'Rakka gathered seeds from all and deposited them in*
*the cave as well.'*

" 'Even those creatures and plants which are found only
in remote places throughout the world?'

" *'Even those.'*

" 'I alone have seen thousands of different kinds of creatures, and tens of thousands of blossoming things, things of
leaves and blades, twigs and barks, branches and roots, and
other things without, all growing, each distinct . . . and I
have not seen one scintilla of all that this world has to offer.
Know ye just how many different creatures and seeds were
shut in that cave? And how large the cave would have to be
to hold such?'

" *'Nay, we do not. But Rakka knew and arranged for such.'*

" 'Where is this cave? Where did he store this vast
menagerie?'

" *'It is now lost, but hear me, O faithless one: Rakka*
*provided!'*

" 'What of this, O priests: all know that when animals
are interbred and interbred and interbred for generation after
generation, such breeding causes fatal weaknesses, dying
lines, animals with flaws beyond saving. And if but two of
each type of animal were sealed in the cave, to survive while
all others perished, then would not their descendants today
be defective past redemption?

" 'And lastly, had there been but a single family saved,
would not their children have had to intermarry and intermarry and intermarry, brother to sister, father to daughter,
mother to son, cousin to cousin, uncle to niece, aunt to
nephew? Would this not weaken their blood as well, cause
all manner of deformities, enfeeblements not only of the
body but also of the mind? And would not all be descendants
of them? All the red Men, the black, the yellow, the brown,
the white, the seal-hunting peoples of the far north, the

brown-skinned natives of the islands in the eastern sea, the small Men of the deep jungles, the tall Men of the north. And what of the Dwarves, the Elves, the Utruni, and others—whence came they?'

" 'Only Rakka knows, but to Rakka all things are possible. Hence, Rakka provided. Worship him, fear him, for he loves you.'

" 'One last question do I have, and it is this: tell me, O priests, what did the shrews eat?'

"They did not understand the import of such a simple question . . . but their answer was, 'Rakka provided.'

"It was then that I, too, left in disgust, and their calls of Infidel! and Damned! followed me out.

"I was glad to be gone from that place, for they listened not to simple reason, looked not at the world about them, sought not the truth, believing instead in the literal words of ancient tales—truths, history, parables, myths, legends, fables, and facts intermingled and recorded on their 'infallible' scrolls."

Aravan and Faeril rode along in silence for a mile or more, but at last Faeril spoke. "I would ask two questions of you, Aravan: First, is there not some truth in their tale of the flood? Second, do not we also say, 'Only Adon knows'? How is that different from saying, 'Only Rakka knows'?"

Aravan laughed. "Ah, Faeril, now thou seek what I can only speculate at, yet will I try to answer all.

"As to the truth of the flood: There are many legends from around the world of a great deluge. Some of these legends come from places where now and again mighty waves race over the ocean to flood the hindering lands in their path. Other tales come from places where island realms have sunk beneath the sea. Still others come from places where vast cyclones spin inward from the ocean, driving rain and great tides before them. Some legends come from lands below the mountains above, where all rain is funnelled down the slopes and into the vales, and when a great storm strikes and lasts for days, their world is flooded. Lastly, there are rivers which heavy storms cause to overflow their banks. At times, massive rains upland and down will swell these streams beyond what has e'er been encountered in the living memory of Mankind.

"As to the desert Kingdom, I suspect that long past a catastrophe occurred in the Avagon Sea. A great shifting of the earth, a sinking island, a detonating firemountain, who can say? In any event, mayhap waters from the sea rushed o'er the land, slaying nearly all in its path. Perhaps a family *did* escape the destruction, fleeing to a high cave, taking the best of their stock with them—ram and ewe, cock and hen, bull ox and cow, buck goat and doe, mayhap more than these few, mayhap less. Taking, too, seed grain and vegetable stock. And when the flood subsided, they emerged safe and whole and gave thanks to their god.

"If I am right, then this example or something just as plausible is the basis of their legend. And like many self-centered peoples, they believe that what has happened to them must have happened to all of the peoples of all the world, and that it was their god, angered by the sins of his people, who caused it."

"Then, Aravan, if you are right, they have taken a legend, caused by some natural catastrophe, and have attributed it to Rakka."

"Oh, wee one, I did not say that it was a *natural* catastrophe . . . only that it was a catastrophe. Natural or not, I cannot say. Yet I *do* say that it was not worldwide, regardless as to the claims of the priests of Rakka-who-loves-you."

Faeril nodded. "*Hmm.* No matter what they say about Rakka's beneficence, it seems to me that he rules through fear rather than love."

"Exactly so, Faeril. According to the priests, Rakka expressly says, '*Fear Me and obey Me, for I am the Lord of all.*' Yet I say of any god who uses fear to cause obedience, he is no better than the Great Evil, Gyphon Himself!"

"All right, Aravan, I accept that. But what about my second question? I mean, we say, 'Only Adon knows.' How is that different from the refuge taken by the desert Kingdom's priests when they say, 'Only Rakka knows'?"

Aravan laughed and clapped his hands, declaring, "Faeril, thou have answered thine own question."

Again Faeril twisted about to look at the Elf. "How so, Aravan? How so?"

"Just this, wee one: When the priests said, 'Only Rakka knows,' they were indeed taking *refuge* behind their faith, letting it protect them from a search for the truth, using that answer to keep hard questions at bay, giving distorted meaning to the saying, 'My faith is my shield.' For to hide behind doctrine and words recorded in ancient scrolls means refusing to look at alternatives wherein a believer would have to explore new ideas or speculations or facts which run contrary to hidebound literal orthodoxy. They believe that to search for truth is to question the god himself and demonstrates an appalling lack of faith, and that the Evil One is directly at the root of a curiosity that questions the tenants and tales of the 'one true way to salvation.'

"Yet when *we* say, 'Only Adon knows,' we are admitting an ignorance of the moment, believing that somewhere, can we just ferret it out, we can discover the truth. We believe that Adon encourages curiosity and upholds the search for truth, no matter where such a search may lead, for He has nothing to hide."

Faeril threw open her hands before her. "Oh, I see," she exclaimed. "In the one case, the saying is used to shield a person from discovering a truth that might cause him to reevaluate his faith, perhaps overturning his entire set of fundamental beliefs; whereas in the other case, the saying is used as a jumping-off place for the search for truth to begin, regardless as to what changes in faith its finding might bring about."

Aravan reached down and squeezed Faeril's shoulder. "Exactly so, Faeril. Exactly so."

The rain that had fallen upon them days past had left wide pools of water standing on low-lying hardpan, and the companions took every opportunity offered to replenish their canteens and goatskins as well as to drink deeply themselves, but only after assuring themselves that the water was fit, for some they found was not.

As they travelled through the renewed desert, the camels grazed every night, and in those places where the growling, grumbling beasts even though hobbled might wander far, they were staked out on long tethers 'mid the vegetation.

Still the days were hot and at times they would travel among barren dunes. Yet always they managed to find suitable grounds to camp. And inasmuch as it was now December, the nights in the desert were cold and the morning dew rich.

Five days after leaving the watering hole, they arrived at their next goal, a well, late in the night.

The following day they spent resting, and that night, Year's Long Night, beneath the moonless stars they stepped through the solemn Elven ritual celebrating the winter solstice, Urus joining Riatha and the others in the stately dance.

The following day they set out for the next goal, a well a hundred thirty miles hence.

In mid of day on the fourth day of travel they came to where the map proclaimed the well to be, yet were found nought but dunes thereat. Aravan again sighted on the Sun and looked at Riatha's map. "Either the marking on this chart is wrong or the well is gone . . . or mayhap it never was."

Riatha glanced 'round at all the sand. "Mayhap, Aravan, the well is indeed here but buried 'neath the drifting dunes."

"It matters not," rumbled Urus. "No well, no water . . . yet we still have plenty. I say we press onward for the oasis beyond."

And so they continued forth, now heading for the first of the three remaining oases marked on the map on their zigzagging route to Nizari.

Down they went through the desert, the nights cold, the days hot. The wind began to blow once more, and as they went, the greenery and blossoms wilted, and in mere days were turned brown. Yet there was forage for the camels, and the first oasis they came to and the one after were shaded and green and thriving.

As they drew nigh in the morning to the last oasis before Nizari, they saw a caravan leaving, heading into the Sun. And when the companions came in among the palms, there breaking camp was a young Man anxiously peering easterly after the distant receding silhouettes.

All five dismounted, and Aravan stepped to the Man and spoke to him. Clearly the Man was unnerved by Aravan's tilted eyes, and he held his right hand on the hilt of his curved knife in its scabbard, the fingers on his left hand curled in a sign of warding, his gaze nervously darting at the other four. Yet he answered Aravan's questions; both were speaking in Kabla, the tongue of the desert.

Finally, Aravan stepped away, and the Man loaded the last of his goods and mounted up. And crying, *"Yallah! Yallah!"* while whacking his camel with a long riding stick, he galloped off, his dromedary *hronking* loudly in protest at such ill treatment, the camels of the companions groaning and turning their heads and malignantly eyeing the five suspiciously, as if expecting some dastardly deed.

Gwylly, his emerald eyes aglitter, asked, "What did he say, Aravan?"

Aravan glanced about at the others. "The Man was frightened, not only of us but of the Red City, or of something which preys upon the dwellers therein. People are disappearing—"

*Stoke!* exclaimed Riatha and Urus together.

"Mayhap," continued Aravan, "yet not only are people vanishing, the city guard seems to be stopping everyone, asking after their identity, wanting to know their skills, their place of trade. It goes hard on those who cannot prove who they are or what they do, those who cannot get others to vouch for them."

*"Akka!"* spat Riatha. "They will never capture Stoke that way."

"Perhaps it is not Stoke they are after," suggested Gwylly. "Perhaps instead it is they, the guard, who are causing these 'disappearances.' It could be that Stoke is not in Nizari at all but somewhere else entirely. After all, we do not know that the city of Faeril's vision is indeed the Red City. It could be another place altogether."

Faeril looked back at Aravan. "What else did the Man say?"

"That he had left because he was afraid he, too, might 'disappear' one night. As well, he detested the guard . . . which leads me to believe that this young Man was not an upstanding citizen with a worthy trade.

"He also said that Nizari was some seventy-five leagues west southwest, which agrees with our map."

Urus crossed his arms over. "Was he telling the truth, do you think?"

Aravan nodded and laughed. "I believe that he was afraid to lie, else the evil *Djinn* before him would summon over the huge *Afrit* to tear him to tiny shreds."

Forty days and forty nights after setting out from the Ring of Dodona, from the crescent gorge of the Kandrawood, just after dawn they topped a ridge and came into sight of Nizari, the Red City of Assassins, crimson buildings clutched against dark, ruddy mountains, a high red wall encircling the town entire. And as the rising Sun glanced off the dome of the scarlet citadel above the city, Faeril turned to the others and softly said, "This is the place of my vision."

# CHAPTER 35

# Nizari

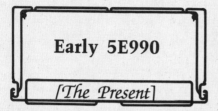

**D**own from the ridge rode the five, their eyes focused on the crimson city in the distance, fiery in the rising Sun, vivid against the iron-red rock of the mountain slopes behind, as a brilliant ruby set in bloodstained stone.

Riatha called out so that everyone could hear: "I would remind ye all that in the Great War of the Ban as well as in the Winter War, the peoples of Hyree were among our foe. They did then worship Gyphon, and some may still. Fair warning: be wary."

Gwylly turned in his saddle and peered up at the Elfess. "How about the K'affeyah people? Were they foe as well?"

"I think not," replied Riatha. "Even though Modru declared it a *jihad*, a Holy War, the nomads of the desert are a stubborn lot and would not be easily swayed. The Word of Shat'weh is what they live by, and he had said nought concerning the War between Gyphon and Adon."

"Well then, if they didn't side with anyone, it seems to me that this Red City, being on the edge of the desert as it is, mostly of Karoo rather than of Hyree across the mountains, it seems to me most likely that the city remained neutral, too."

"Thou may be right, Gwylly. Yet heed: this *is* the City of

Assassins, and in those days many were in service to the Evil One. For selfish gain, 'tis true, yet still in his hire. Hence, 'tis best that we ward 'gainst treachery within."

Long they rode and closer they drew to the city, and now individual structures could be made out: low, flat-roofed buildings for the most part, though here and there taller buildings stood. Jutting up among the structures were scattered high, slender minarets or soaring obelisks—at this distance they could not tell which. The whole of it seemed to follow no regular pattern, as if the city streets twisted and jinked throughout.

But dominating all was the adjoining citadel, its scarlet, onion-shaped dome rising to a tall spire. The dome was set in the center of a massive rectangular building, and its position was such that the five speculated it sat in a wide courtyard. The fortress was walled about with mighty battlements, and one of the high ramparts abutted against and towered above the southwest wall of the city.

The city itself sat at the foot of a rust-red mountain, the bastion guarding the mouth of a pass running through the range to the west. And *this* was why the Sultans of Hyree claimed Nizari, for it sat across the principal trade route through the Talâk Mountains.

It was mid-morning when the five came to the camel grounds outside the city walls, for here, as in all cities ringing the desert, because of their stench and their offensive habits, camels were not permitted into the town except to deliver or pick up goods. The five dismounted and led their groaning, growling, sneering camels through the lot. The beasts already staked there eructed and malignantly grimaced in return, but the companions were by now so used to the creatures that they did not notice the horrendous stink, and they dodged spat cuds without a second thought.

When they located the yardmaster, Aravan spoke with him to arrange for the boarding of the camels. As with every other encounter in this realm, the Man nervously eyed the companions, noting the strange eyes and the huge one's size, readily agreeing to *anything* that this *Djinn* asked of him. "*Jamal, Jamal,*" the yardmaster called. Two young Men popped out from the large tent nearby. *"Dabbir matrah lidd-wâbb!"* The young Men ran forward to care for the string of camels, though Aravan stopped them long enough for the companions to take from the cargo what they would need in the city.

As Gwylly retrieved the knapsack with his clothing and a few personal items, he looked about, noting that the helpers were just as afraid of the five as the yardmaster seemed to be.

While Aravan spoke further with the yardmaster and gave him a few silvers, the young Men unladed the rest of the goods and tack, stowing all in a small tent to one side, then led the beasts away.

At last Aravan returned to the other four. When they were well away from the ears of the lot workers, he said, "The best caravansary seems to be the Green Palm. Taking up residence there strengthens our pose as northern merchants seeking trade agreements. If dealing with the merchants of the city fails to bring us the knowledge we seek, we can move to the Golden Crown, a low to middling inn in the less elegant quarters of the city, where information can be had for a price."

Aravan looked at each of them, receiving nods from all. "The Green Palm it is, then."

As they approached the gate through the city wall, Gwylly asked, "Aravan, the yardmaster called *'Jamal, Jamal,'* to get his helpers to come to take away our camels. Yet I thought that *Jamal* means *camel.* Why would he call out 'camel, camel,' to fetch the young Men?"

Aravan laughed, then replied, "Gwylly, they deem we are demons. And thou must never let a demon know thy rightful name, else he will steal thy soul. To keep a demon, then, from knowing a loved one's Truename, call out *'Jamal'* instead."

Gwylly smiled at Aravan's answer, and on they strode toward the entryway into the city, a high and wide portal through a bulwark made of massive blocks of cut stone, red rock quarried from the mountains above. The wall itself rose vertically some twenty feet, and it had a wide overhang to thwart all but the best of climbers. Laid back against the stone blocks were great ironclad gates, a huge beam set to fall into place should there be a need to defend the city against invasion. In all, the wall and portal were the most formidable barriers the five had yet seen; not even Pendwyr had defenses such as these.

At the gates, a crowd of complaining people were lined up—the Women veiled, the Men bearded and turbaned—clamoring for entry into the city but held up by guards in red fezzes ornamented with long black tassels, the warders closely questioning each of those who were inbound, although people leaving the city seemed less hindered. The five fell in behind the crowd, Urus towering above everyone. The Man just ahead turned to protest the wait, saying *"Mâ bhibb id— Waugh!"* He leapt aside, his hand outflung in a warding gesture. Others turned to see what was amiss—and as if parted by a sword, the way before Aravan and Riatha and Gwylly and Faeril and Urus suddenly became empty of people, a corridor opening to the fore.

Laughing, Aravan led the way, and the five walked to the watchmen posted at the gates. Clearly, they, too, were shaken by the visages of the *Djinnain* and the *zrâr Djinnain* and the huge *Afrit*, yet in spite of their superstitions they stood firm.

Behind the five, the corridor closed again, the crowd surging closer, but not too close, clearly torn between their strong desire to enter the city and their equally strong desire to flee.

Beyond the gates and inside the city, others turned to look as well. Some hurried off, others stepped quickly into buildings, still others simply stood and stared. Gwylly noted one Man in a yellow turban and tan cloak who came forward to look closely, then turned and ran swiftly away, jostling through the crowds.

Gwylly tugged at Faeril's sleeve and pointed, saying in Twyll, ["If they are all as is that fleeing Man, then how will we ever get to talk to the people of this town?"]

She shook her head. ["I know not, love."]

The captain of the watch, a small, rotund Man with a golden crescent on his fez, came and spoke to Aravan in the Kabla tongue. The Elf in turn translated to his companions

in Sylva what he and the captain said, and Gwylly, lifted up
by Urus, translated the words into Baeron.

["What is your business in Nizari?"]

["We are merchants from the far northern lands and come
to strike trade agreements with the merchants of Nizari."]

["And your names . . . ?"]

Aravan smiled, his white teeth glistening. ["Shall we trade
names, Captain, thou and I?"]

Gwylly laughed as he translated this last to Urus.

["Harrumph, it will not be necessary. Where will you be
staying?"]

["We have heard that the Green Palm has much to offer.
Have thou another suggestion?"]

["The Green Palm is a caravansary noted for its elegance.
Many merchants stay there. You have chosen well. I will
send an escort with you to show you the way."]

["Most kind of thee, Captain."]

The Captain glanced up at the scarlet citadel. ["You know,
of course, that you must obtain the Emir's permission to
trade within Nizari. In fact, any and all trade agreements
made within his emirate need his approval."]

["Naturally, Captain. Naturally."]

The captain turned from Aravan and called out, *"Jamal,
Jamal!"* Gwylly whispered into Urus's ear, and the big Man
and the wee Warrow broke out in laughter.

In moments, escorted by two guards, they were on their
way through the winding streets of the city, the red brick
roads twisting this way and that, lanes and alleyways shooting off at odd angles, jinking 'round sharp corners to disappear beyond seeing, the whole of it a maze, like runs in a
rat's warren. Wending among buildings, they saw for the
most part that red tile and brick and ruddy stone made up
the structures, giving the city its crimson hue.

Up long stairways and down they went, past merchants'
shops and through bazaars, along alleys reeking of garbage
and sewage, across open squares, past community wells,
among dwellings rising high to either side. And everywhere
they went there was noise—shrieking children at play; arguing, haggling storekeepers and customers; strident moth-
ers shouting for sons and daughters; drovers cursing pack

camels, the beasts *hronking* in return; merchants hawking their wares—the city awash in a hubbub.

Too, they passed minarets, the slender towers seemingly fallen into ruin, loose bricks lying about upon the ground at the foot of the abandoned spires. And Faeril thought she could see that the cupolas at the top had suffered damage.

And all the time they traveled, southerly they fared, in the general direction of the citadel. At last they came to a more elegant section of the city, the streets wide and straight, the shops uncluttered, the dwellings large and spacious, the noise a subdued murmur in the distance. Here, too, were small city plazas where trees grew—acacia and fig and others—with benches in the shade below.

At last they came to the Green Palm, a large, three-storey inn behind a low wall. Through an open archway they went, entering a courtyard filled with date palms. To one side stood a brick stable for horses.

The city-guard escort led them through arched doorways and into an elegant foyer, where they were met by the hotelier. "Welcome . . . Green Palm. I talk good Common, yes?"

"I say, Faeril, did you get the idea that the manager was expecting us?" Gwylly held his foot above the suds and vigorously scrubbed it with the soft brush. "I mean, without a by-your-leave he began speaking to us in Common, even before he could have seen we were not native to this region."

Faeril nodded, soaping her hands and face. "Perhaps the gate captain sent a runner ahead . . . but why would he?"

Gwylly shrugged, ignoring the fact that Faeril's eyes were now closed against the sting of soap. "Here, love, let me do your back."

It was mid-afternoon when Gwylly and Faeril emerged from their chambers and made their way downstairs to the tea room. There they found Aravan sitting alone, sipping tea and eating small slices of date bread.

"Where is everyone?" asked Gwylly.

"They all ran," said the Elf, smiling. "Six merchants when I walked in, but they left . . . hurriedly."

"No, I meant Riatha and Urus. Where are they?"

Aravan laughed. "They are no doubt in their room, Gwylly, making up for lost time."

"Oh," murmured Gwylly, glancing at Faeril, and both Warrows blushed simultaneously.

Faeril climbed up into a chair and helped herself to some of the bread. Glancing about at the empty tea room, she asked, "How are we ever going to ask questions concerning the disappearances, concerning Baron Stoke, if everyone runs when they see us?"

"Oh, wee one, everyone doesn't run."

Faeril and Gwylly both cocked an eye.

Aravan gestured over his shoulder. "One of the guards who escorted us here is posted out front, across the street. The other guard is in the alleyway behind. In the entrance hall at a desk sits a Man who seemingly writes, yet he has not jotted one word but instead watches all comings and goings. On the occasions when I have passed through, he studiously looks away."

*Why?* asked Faeril and Gwylly simultaneously.

"Why? I know not. Yet heed: we are being observed, wee ones. Watched. As if someone wishes to keep track of our whereabouts."

Faeril settled back in her chair, a pensive frown on her face. But Gwylly looked about. "Say, what's a fellow got to do to get served around here?"

Prior to sundown, a force of fifty Men, dressed in maroon uniforms with gold turbans and gold sashes and armed with curved tulwars, marched into the Green Palm. The *jemadar* in charge found his quarry of five in the inner courtyard gardens. Approaching Aravan, he bowed and spoke in the Common tongue. "My master, the Emir of Nizari and all the lands beyond, bids you welcome to his Realm. He asks that you join him for dinner."

Aravan turned to the others, speaking in Sylva, a tongue not likely to be understood by the *jemadar*. ["I deem it is the Emir who is behind this spying on us. Why? I know not. Regardless, what say ye to this invitation?"]

Gwylly rapidly translated Aravan's words into Baeron for Urus.

Urus replied in the same tongue, Gwylly now translating into Sylva. ["I say we go. Firstly, given this armed force, we can hardly refuse. Secondly, who better than the Emir to speak of the 'disappearances' in his Realm?"]

Gwylly nodded his agreement even as he translated the Baeran's words.

Aravan looked at each in turn, receiving like nods, then he turned to the *jemadar*. "We are honored to accept. Yet we are ill prepared. Our clothing is yet being laundered."

The *jemadar* smiled. "Raiments will be provided. If you would follow, please." His words were not a request.

Amid an armed escort, up to the scarlet citadel marched the five, Faeril and Gwylly trotting to keep pace. They came to the crenellated wall, twice the height of the city rampart. Midway was located another massive steel-plated gate. Through the portal and into a red-stone courtyard they went, and Faeril gasped, for the building before them was enormous, its sides and dome clad with scarlet marble. A huge portico ran more than half the width of the frontage, tall crimson columns supporting the ornate roof. To left and right were other buildings, dwarfed by the main structure, and except for the stables nearby, what these other buildings housed was beyond knowing, though Faeril surmised that some were barracks while others held places of crafting: smithies and armories and carpenter shops and leather shops and the like. Yet she caught only a glimpse of these other buildings, for across a red-stone courtyard and up the steps they tramped, entering through an ogee-arched doorway, its onion-shaped vault mimicking the form of the great dome capping the building above.

They were escorted in through a high-vaulted gallery and across a marble floor, up a broad, curving staircase and along wide carpeted corridors, passing by wood-panelled doors, some closed, others open, the chambers beyond containing offices of state or collections of art objects or ornate rugs and gilded furniture. The companions were taken finally to two separate bathing rooms, the females to one, the males to another.

An hour later, bathed, perfumed, and clad in silks and satins, Riatha and Faeril veiled, the five were escorted to the

Emir's private dining hall. But ere they entered the guarded door, the major-domo said, "You must leave your weapons here, for except for his personal guard, arms are not allowed in the presence of the Emir."

Urus glanced at the others, then said, "These weapons are never out of our reach. However, we will submit to peace-bonding them."

The major-domo was adamant. "This is not permitted. Long past did an Emir allow such, and he did not live to see the light of morning. You must leave your weapons here."

Urus spoke in Baeron. ["If it comes to it, the Bear can fight while all others retrieve their arms."]

Gwylly translated into Sylva.

Aravan stepped forward, his crystal spear in hand, a dark look on his face. His teeth ground together, and he gritted at the major-domo, "Heed, this weapon and the others are precious to us. *Touch them not!* If aught happens to any, it will be *thou* who will not live to see the light of morning."

Reluctantly, one at a time, each gave over his weaponry—crystal spear, starlight sword, silver and steel throwing knives, steel and silver bullets and sling, iron morning star—all placed on a long mahogany table down the length of which ran a broad strip of red velvet fringed at the ends.

The shaken major-domo had backed away while the five disarmed themselves, but still Riatha turned to the Man, ice in her silver-grey eyes. "Instruct these guards to ward these weapons as they would their own Emir, else there will be Hèl to pay."

The major-domo stuttered out commands to the guards as Aravan carefully listened. The Elf then nodded to the others, and finally they came into the presence of the Emir.

The dining chamber they entered was enormous—some thirty paces long by twenty wide. Red velvet drapery covered the walls, a golden fringe along the top and bottom edges. The floor was marble, deep red and shot through with filaments of gold. The arched ceiling above was the reverse of the floor: gold streaked with red. In the very center of the room was a long, low, gilt platform set with dishes and cutlery and laden with fruits and breads and meats. On the floor about were scattered satin pillows.

At the head of the table sat the Emir. A large, portly Man, he was, and dressed in gold-trimmed black silk. Black was his hair and his close-cropped beard, and dark eyes looked out from beneath black brows. His skin was pale and his hands soft, his fingers pudgy. At his left side and slightly behind sat a youth, a smooth-cheeked boy, his clothing black-trimmed gold, the reverse of the Emir's. Ranged along the walls to left and right stood ten guards, five to each side, while behind the Emir stood four more.

As the five entered, the Emir looked up from his conversation with the boy, the Man's eyes intent upon his guests. Led by the major-domo, the companions paced across the floor, stopping some five steps from the Emir. Flourishing an elaborate bow, the major-domo said in his flawless Common, "Most Exalted, your guests."

Following Aravan's lead, the five bowed stiffly from the waist, forgoing any embellishments. The Emir smiled at them, yet Faeril noted that Aravan's fingers silently signalled <Shark>; the damman grinned and glanced at Gwylly, noting that he grinned, too, both Warrows struck by the incongruity of a shark living in the desert.

"Welcome, travellers, to my Kingdom." The Emir's words in the Common tongue were but slightly accented. "It is long since I have set these eyes upon Elven Folk, and never have I had the honor of entertaining your Kind." He gestured at the pillows strewn to either side. "Please, be seated, for I am famished, and though it cannot compare to your Elven dishes, still, honeyed quail awaits us."

Not only was there quail upon the table, but sliced roast oxen and mutton as well; three kinds of soups; a variety of stewed vegetables; pomegranates and dates, fresh peaches, oranges from Thyra, white grapes, and other succulent fruits; and sweet breads and cakes.

Faeril wondered just how she could possibly eat with this gauzy veil across her face, but then she saw Riatha unfasten hers, and so the damman did likewise, smiling at the Emir.

Throughout the meal, the Emir kept up a string of inconsequential chatter, asking after their travels, surprised that they had crossed the *Erg* from Sabra—". . . for it is told that the central Karoo is cursed . . ."—and inquiring as to what their purpose was in coming to Nizari, and what they might wish to obtain in the city for trade in the North.

The boy at the Emir's side served his master, sampling each dish ere passing it on to the Prince, the Emir ever watching the youth closely for any reaction to the food before tasting it himself.

Throughout the meal as well, Aravan danced a complex dance of conversation, circling slowly but ever closer to what they wished to know. The Emir laughed at Aravan's description of their entry into the city, of the crowd's reaction to his Elven eyes at the gate, of the merchants' reactions at the Green Palm, the Emir saying, "Ah, but they are an ignorant, superstitious lot."

Now and again one of the others would join in the conversation, Gwylly telling of hunting with Black, Urus speaking of the reach of the Greatwood.

But it was Faeril who brought an unexpected comment from the Emir: "I noted," she said, "when we came through the city, that the minarets were abandoned, fallen into ruin. Can you tell us what happened?"

The Emir looked at the damman and then turned to Riatha. "Your daughter and son, madam, are a delight, and full of curiosity as are all children."

Realizing the Emir's mistaken assumption, Gwylly started to speak up, but then fell silent at a gesture from Urus.

Riatha smiled, nodding. "Aye. They give me much pleasure."

The Emir spoke to Faeril. "In my grandsire's time, at last he overthrew the *imâmîn*, the clerics, for they hewed to a false prophet instead of the true god, and had done so for nearly nine hundred years. They were punished accordingly, and the mosques and minarets cleared of the vermin and their followers, and we returned to the old ways, the true ways."

Faeril started to ask another question, but Riatha smoothly cut her off. "Have thou some of this sweet bread, my darling," her fingers signalling, <*Danger.*> Faeril took the proffered pastry, falling into thoughtful silence.

Again Aravan took up the conversation, and as they came to the end of the meal, the Elf finally closed in on what they had come to hear. "As we came through an oasis north of here, we spoke with a traveller from Nizari. A young Man, he was afraid, and he told us of disappearances in and about the city."

The Emir nodded. "It is true. People are missing. Men. Women. Children."

Aravan, now at the heart of their quest, asked, "Know thou the root of this evil?"

"Oh, yes," answered the Emir. "But first . . ." He signalled to his taster. The boy stood and fetched a tray on which was a crystal flask filled with a ruby liquid and six crystal cups, two of them small, the other four larger. Turning to Aravan, the Emir said, "It is traditional to drink a toast at the end of a guesting feast. And I can assure you that you have never tasted a cordial such as this. Will you and your wife and children and your companion join me in such?"

At Aravan's assent, the Emir smiled and splashed a dollop into the small cups, and a greater measure into the others. "Here, wee cups for the wee ones, large cups for the larger."

Aravan signalled, <Wait,> and watched as the taster sipped from the Emir's cup, then passed it on to his master. The Emir raised the crystal vessel. "To the success of your mission," he said, then downed the drink in one gulp.

"To the success of our mission," responded Aravan, downing his own, and they all followed suit, finding the liqueur sweet and aromatic and strong.

And when each of the five set their emptied crystal cups to the table, the Emir began laughing, signalling the guards. The door opened, and the major-domo and ten additional warders marched in, each guard bearing a crossbow, cocked, quarrel in place. They ringed 'round in an arc flanking the Emir, deadly bows aimed at the five.

Aravan began to protest, but the Emir silenced him. "Fools!" spat the Man. "Know this: that you are in *Nizari*, the Red City of Assassins, and *I* am the High Assassin, the Assassin of Assassins.

"Pah! Of a certainty do I know your *true* mission. You are here after Stoke! And heed me! He knows of your coming . . . for he has directed me, *me*, to intercept you. And I have done so.

"Why do you deem my guards at the city gates escorted you to the Green Palm? As a favor? Nay! It was instead to watch over you and to keep you till I was ready.

"Merchants, faugh! A flimsy tale at best. Thin. Oh no, not merchants. Instead, you are hunters, and Stoke is your quarry, just as you are his prey.

"You must be powerful enemies indeed for him to fear you. Yet he, too, is a dangerous foe. But if he thinks to order me about at his whim, then he is mistaken."

The Emir clapped his hands, and the major-domo stepped forward bearing a basket, handing it to his Prince. "I will aid you to bring him down, but you must hurry, for even now one of his spies may be rushing to tell him of your arrival. *This* one we caught."

The Emir pulled the lid from the basket and pitched its contents rolling down the table. As it flopped to a stop they could see it was a Man's head, in a yellow turban. Gwylly gasped and turned to Faeril. "The Man at the gate, the one who ran." Faeril nodded and averted her eyes, refusing to glance again at the head.

Riatha looked at the Emir. "If thou know where is Baron Stoke, tell us. We will run him to earth, this I promise."

"Oh, madam, I *know* that you will go after Stoke to slay him, for *I* have taken steps to guarantee your full-hearted cooperation. You see, I have poisoned your children and only *I* have the antidote"—he held up a small crystal vial filled with a blue liquid.

At these words Gwylly's heart clenched, and he reached out to take his dammia's hand. But Urus roared in rage, starting to rise. One of the bow-bearing guards barked a command—"*Hâdir!*"—and Aravan cried out, "*Urus, no!*" The Baeran looked at the trained crossbows—two aimed at Gwylly, two at Faeril, two at Aravan, two at Riatha, and lastly, two at himself—and slowly, growling, he settled back.

"Fools!" sneered the Emir. "I saw you delay, waiting to see if the cordial was poisoned. Did I not tell you that this was the Red City of Assassins? It was the two small crystal cups that were lethal—not the drink.

"Now heed me! You have but one week to find Stoke, slay him, and bring his head to me. Else the children will be dead of the poison. . . ."

The Emir nodded to the major-domo, and at his signal, four guards stepped forward, slipping a cord about each Warrow's wrists, and leading them away.

"In the meantime," continued the Emir as the Wee Ones were taken from the room, "we will care well for them."

Riatha, Aravan, and Urus watched them go, frustration and rage in their eyes.

Riatha turned to the Emir. "Where is Stoke?"

"In a mosque in the mountains one day's hard ride from here. He has been there for nearly two years now, taking my people from me. No matter that he is favored by the Sultan, Stoke's depredations have gone on much too long. Too, he thinks to tell me, *me*, what to do, as if I were subject to his will. Well, then, we shall see about *that*, my friend. We shall see about that."

Urus yet fumed, but Aravan said, "We shall need a map, horses, our weaponry, some supplies, our own goods, and whatever information thou have concerning Stoke's strongholt."

The Emir gestured at the major-domo. "Abid will see to your needs. You may leave me now, but by all means hurry, for your time grows short, and the lives of your children spill out as does swift-running sand spill through a glass."

Surrounded by guards, the major-domo escorted them out, while behind sounded the crowing laughter of the Emir.

The trio retrieved their weapons as well as Gwylly's sling and bullets and Faeril's throwing knives. Abid informed them that their belongings had already been brought from the Green Palm and from the camel grounds to the Scarlet Citadel in anticipation of their "cooperation." He led them to the room where their goods were stored. Riatha rummaged through her belongings as well as those of the Waerlinga, retrieving the necessary items: long-knives, daggers, a bow and arrows, herbs and potions, and other such. Aravan and Urus also took up what they might use in the days ahead: lanterns, ropes, climbing gear, crue, flint and steel, and the like. Except for the weaponry, they packed all in backpacks and changed into their desert garb, taking as well their leathers. Too, Riatha packed a bit of extra clothing.

"Abid," barked Aravan. "We will need horses, for camels

walk softly but make too much noise, whereas horses' steps are louder yet rarely do they complain."

Urus added, "A large horse for me, little Man, one with the strength to bear my weight."

Abid called to one of the guards and issued orders, the Man leaving for the stables.

Riatha at last turned to the major-domo. "I am ready. Yet first I would see my children one last time, to bid them courage and kiss them farewell."

Abid glanced at the others and nodded. "Only you, madam, and you must go without weapons, and you must speak only the Common tongue."

Riatha handed over Dúnamis to Aravan, giving him her long-knife and dagger as well. "I shall return shortly, Aravan."

The major-domo led Riatha to a room in the citadel. The entry was warded by two guards. At a gesture from Abid, they stepped aside and the major-domo tugged open the door.

Gwylly and Faeril were standing next to a barred window, shutters open. As Riatha entered, Faeril turned and ran to the Elfess, Gwylly coming after. Riatha knelt and embraced the damman, and peered into the face of each Waerling. They looked pale, wan. "Courage, my children," she said. "We will return for you." <*Soon,*> she signalled in the silent hand code.

The Elfess carried Faeril back to the window and set her down. Peering out, she said, "It is time for me to go."

Kissing both and embracing them one last time, Riatha turned to Abid. "I am ready," she said, and he led her away. Her last sight of the Waerlinga was of the two standing and watching her leave, their arms about one another. And then the door closed.

Back to Aravan and Urus she went, and thence unto the stables. There waiting were three saddled horses—two mares and a large stud—and they laded them with the gear.

Mounting up, the trio rode clattering across the courtyard and out from the citadel, following after a soldier guide. And behind them the massive gates of the mighty fortress swung shut.

\*     \*     \*

Faeril hugged her forearms across her stomach. "I don't feel well, Gwylly."

Pallid, Gwylly reached out and stroked her hair, tears filling his eyes. "Neither do I, love. Neither do I."

"Perhaps if we lie down . . ."

They clambered onto the bed.

A time passed, and the door opened. A guard came in and looked about, then stepped back from the room.

The Emir entered, smiling when he saw the pale, trembling Warrows lying on the bed. "Well now, did I not tell you that I was the Assassin of Assassins? It seems as if the poison works on Elven children as it does on Human get. You will be dead by dawn.

"What's that? You actually believed my tale that you would last a week? Oh my, but you *are* silly children.

"I will leave you now, for I do hate to see suffering. And believe me, it will shortly become much more painful, my darlings. But you may scream all you wish, for each of my chambers is sealed against sound.

"Yet before I go . . ."

He took the tiny liquid-filled crystal flask from a silken pocket and stepped to the bedside, holding the vial up for the Wee Ones to see. He uncapped the crystal and slowly tilted the vial, pouring the blue liquid out onto the carpeted floor.

Gwylly croaked a protest, his words but a whisper, and he struggled to sit upright but had not the strength.

"Oh, child," said the Emir, "worry not. This is not an antidote. This is nothing but colored water.

"Fools! There is no antidote for the poison running in your veins."

# CHAPTER 36

# Extrication

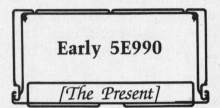

**Early 5E990**

*[The Present]*

**D**own through the twisting streets of Nizari rode the trio, down and away from the Scarlet Citadel, following the soldier riding before them. Night had fallen, and the guide bore a lantern, though here among the lighted dwellings and shops in the Red City its luminance was not needed. Urus rode stiffly, his knuckles white on the reins, his fury but barely held in check. Beside him, Riatha rode in grim silence, her lips compressed in a thin white line. Aravan, lagging after, gritted his teeth in frustration, the muscles jumping in his jaw. Although they followed the guard, their thoughts were back in the citadel, where entrapped and poisoned were Faeril and Gwylly, held in the clutch of the Prince of the city to warrant the death of Stoke. And so down through the tangled streets they rode, their thoughts churning in rage.

At last they came to the city gates, and at a word from their escort, on through they rode, past the warders there and beyond the high city walls.

Westerly they turned, bearing southward, heading into the Talâk Range, the walls of the pass steadily rising about them, looming upward toward the stars. Now the soldier's lantern cast a swaying light on the stony way, its glow pressing back the shadows as into the gloom they rode.

Onward they forged into the pass, the path curving, meandering, the walls closing in here and falling back there, in places a furlong or two apart, in other places mere yards between. The steady pace of the horses devoured the ground and within two hours they reached their goal: a narrow crevice splitting off southward from the main pass.

The soldier leading them drew up, his eyes wide with fright, and waited for Aravan to ride to the fore. ["This is your way,"] the guide said in the Kabla tongue, gesturing up the slot. ["The place you seek is miles beyond at the end of this arroyo: a downcast mosque of the false prophet. Here I leave you with a message from my Emir. I do not understand the meaning of his words, yet he bade me to repeat them: 'Remember, your children's lives run like swift sand through a glass. One week, no more, is all you have.' "]

As the guide fell silent, Aravan gritted, ["Say this to thy Prince: We will return within the sevenday, Stoke's head in our possession. Yet heed! Should aught happen to either child, then thou will discover why Stoke feared us so."]

Aravan turned his horse and into the notch he went, Riatha and Urus following after. The soldier sat listening to the footfalls of the steeds, sweat running in rivulets down his face—his dread of this haunted ravine nearly overcoming his sense of duty. When he could hear the horses no more, quickly he turned and rode swiftly away, his mount running at a dangerous pace through the enshadowed pass.

The soft cry of a Jillian crow echoed up the canyon.

"He is gone," said Riatha, prodding her horse into motion. Urus grunted and followed, and back down the ravine they rode, Aravan's mare on a tether trailing behind the Baeran.

When they reached the narrow opening and rode beyond into the pass, Aravan stepped from the shadows into the starlight, and Riatha and Urus dismounted.

Riatha was the first to speak: "Two courses of action lie before us: we can go on to Stoke's holt, slay him, and return to Nizari with his head; or we can ride back to Nizari now, free our companions, and then proceed to Stoke's mosque."

Aravan's eyes glinted in the starlight. "I trust not this 'Assassin of Assassins' to keep his word. Even should we bring him Stoke's head, still he may betray us.

"There is this as well: should we fail, or even be late, the Waerlinga's lives are forfeit.

"Nay, Riatha, going after Stoke with them yet in the clutches of the Emir entails considerable risk to Faeril and Gwylly. I would rather go back and free them now, this night."

Riatha nodded. "I do not trust this 'High Assassin' either, for when I went to see the Waerlinga, they were wan, pallid, the poison already at work upon them."

Urus spat upon the ground. "Can you find this place again, this room where they are held?"

"Aye, I looked well out that window. If they have not been moved, they are on the third floor above an ornamental garden. Outward, to the left of the window, to the right as we look inward, in garden center stands a statue of a Man on horseback. . . . The window, however, is barred."

"I will deal with the bars," said Urus. "I am more concerned with the poison. How will we nullify it?"

"Gwynthyme."

"Will it counteract this venom of the Emir's?"

"I have not known it to fail."

Urus grunted. "Still, it is a risk. The Emir claimed to have the only antidote, and should we take Faeril and Gwylly from the citadel and the gwynthyme not work, then . . ."

"Then we will yet have some days to contrive to get the antidote."

Aravan glanced at the two of them. "If he indeed has an antidote."

Urus growled. "Garn! The imponderables mount up."

"Aye," responded Riatha, "yet imponderables or not, we must decide."

Aravan's fingers strayed to his throat. The blue stone amulet held an edge of chill. "I say we go now, for I deem they are in danger. Too, Riatha has mentioned a thing that could thwart all of our plans, and it is this: what if they move the Waerlinga to a different place?"

Without another word they mounted up, spurring their horses into a canter back toward the Red City.

As they drew near the entrance to the pass, the waning gibbous Moon rose, shedding its yellow light slanting across the land, sharp-edged mooncast darkness streaming from rock and ridge and pinnacle. Ahead they could see the city clutched against the mountains, and as they had planned while returning, they angled their horses up the rocky slope, keeping to the shadows, aiming for the southwest corner of the wall surrounding the citadel, deeming that perhaps there would be less vigilance at the rear of the fortress.

They came to a shallow gully a quarter mile from the wall, and there they tethered the horses to the gnarled growth. Taking up their climbing gear and weaponry, and crouching low and following the deep ruts and furrows of the land, they made their way toward the citadel and farther up slope, seeking a place where they could look down on the ramparts.

At last they reached a high ridge, and in the moonlight they watched as the guards slowly made their rounds: there were but two, walking together, patrolling the walls above. Yet at each corner stood a sentry viewing the 'scape below, though whenever the two roaming guards passed, they would stop for a while and chat.

"Hèl!" spat Urus. "Given the placement of the sentries, it seems we will have to go up the wall midway between corners."

Aravan grunted his agreement. "Then let us climb the westernmost wall, for there the moonshadow is deepest."

Riatha sighed. "The room holding the Waerlinga faces east, where the moonlight is brightest."

"We've no help for that," rumbled Urus. "Let us go now."

Back down among the folds in the land scuttled the trio, heading for the westernmost wall.

"The crevices between the stones are mortared, the seams narrow and shallow," whispered Riatha. "The fingers of neither of ye are as slender as mine. I will climb."

Urus started to object, but Aravan cut him off. "She is right, Urus."

"When I reach the top, I will lower a rope. Wait for my signal ere climbing. I will tug three times when it is safe."

Up went the Elfess, slowly, free-climbing an offset join where abutted two columns of the massive blocks, jamming fingers and feet into narrow crevices, keeping three points anchored while shifting the fourth, making certain of her support ere moving on. The distance to the openings in the castellated wall was some forty feet above, the very top some five feet beyond. And it took her an eternity to travel those forty feet.

Just ere reaching the top, Riatha paused and listened, hearing nought. Carefully, she clambered on up the merlon, and when she could, she stepped into the crenel.

Again she listened . . . silence. She risked a quick look, then ducked back. The patrol was just leaving the southwest corner, coming her way.

Quickly, carefully, Riatha sought to regain her hand- and footholds on the merlon, racing against time yet moving slowly, small bits of loose mortar falling into the darkness below. At last she discovered her former holds and moved back onto the wall.

There she held—it seemed forever—yet at last the guards scuffed past. When they had moved sufficiently beyond, back into the crenel she stepped. Shaking with tension and fatigue, the Elfess uncoiled a rope, and after another quick look, anchored the small grapnel by two tines over the top of the merlon. Down she payed out the line, and when she felt the tug from below, she returned the signal with three quick pulls.

Urus came up first, the big Man haling hand over hand, stepping into the crenel beside her. "There's a ramp downward just across the banquette," whispered Riatha. "Go when it is safe."

Urus peered out at the corners opposite, then risked a glance at those adjacent. Moving in swift grace and silence, suddenly he was across and down.

Again Riatha tugged on the line, and up swarmed Aravan, as a sailor would swarm up rigging.

While the Elf unhooked the grapnel and recoiled the line, Riatha slipped across the walkway and down the ramp.

In quick succession, Aravan followed.

Down in the moonshade behind the outbuildings the three gathered. Following the wall, they glided through the dark, heading 'round the back and to the opposite side. Several times they paused, while soldiers passed in the moonlight. At last they circled to the far wall. Passing between buildings, they came to the flagstone pave. Across the way and slightly toward the rear of the citadel, they could see a garden, several palm trees scattered among the low-lying shrubs. In the midst of the trees stood the statue described by Riatha—a Man on horseback. Above and to the left, three storeys up was a dark window, barred. "There," hissed Riatha, pointing. "There is the chamber where last I saw Faeril and Gwylly."

Aravan looked across the bailey. "We will be in open moonlight as we cross over, and the wall we must scale is illumined by the silver beams."

"Nevertheless," growled Urus, "we must cross and climb."

"What of the bars?" queried Riatha.

"Just get a rope 'round them," responded Urus. "The Bear will take care of the rest."

Aravan's eyes widened, then he looked at Riatha. "Thou stay on the ground with the Bear, Dara. This time it is I who will climb."

"If the stone permits," amended the Elfess.

They waited until the patrol above had passed to the far side of the central dome. No one was in sight in the courtyard, and the corner sentries seemed to be watching the 'scape beyond the walls. Across the flagstone and into the garden they scurried, and they crouched down behind the broad pedestal supporting the statue, listening for calls of alarm; none were sounded.

The sculpture they hid behind was carved in the likeness of the Emir, somewhat more heroic than the tall, portly Prince, yet recognizable.

Hearing no challenges, they made their way to the wall of the building, finding only hairline seams between the red marble slabs cladding the side of the building, nothing that would permit free-climbing.

"*Vash!*" cursed Aravan. "We cannot use rocknails; the pounding will bring the guards." He stood back and gazed upward. "A grapnel, then . . ."

"The noise," warned Riatha.

Urus began ripping cloth from the hem of his shirt. "We will muffle the tines."

They wrapped fabric about the hooks and haft of the small

grapnel, and waited until the patrol had passed from sight again and the corner guards were looking outward. Aravan then made the toss, the grappling hook catching on the bars the very first cast, a faint muffled thud the only sound.

Aravan reversed his cloak, for although its color did not match that of the stone, the shade of the inner cloth more closely resembled the tone of the marble. "I will signal when I am ready."

Again they waited until the patrol passed from view, then up swarmed the Elf. At the window he looked into the room, and by the pale moonlight shining inward, he could see a bed and two small forms upon it.

Holding onto the heavy ornate grille Aravan loosened the grapnel, reaching under the frame and through and resetting the spikes to catch the sill beyond. Then one-handed, he looped a slipknot in the line, fixing a snapring therein. The ring he clipped to his climbing harness, and after making certain that the hook would hold, he let the line bear his weight.

Doubling a second line and tying it about the bars, he payed both ends down to those waiting below.

And he held his breath and did not move as the patrol on the ramparts slowly paced into view.

They stood and spoke with the corner guard for some time, then laughing, slowly moved on. They made some remark in passing to the next corner guard, and he, too, burst out in laughter as the pair on patrol continued their stately pace.

Aravan let out a sigh of relief as they moved beyond seeing.

And down below, beneath the trees, from the midst of a shimmering darkness emerged the Bear.

Quickly Riatha fashioned a simple rope harness and looped it about the Bear, the beast uncooperative, snuffling among the flowers, digging up bulbs to eat. At last all was ready.

"Urus, pull!" hissed the Elfess.

The Bear looked at this two-legs standing beside him, her hair pale in the bright night. Then he swung his head about, peering over his shoulder at the ropes arcing up through the trees. "*Whuff.*" He ambled forward several paces, until the ropes grew taut. And then he leaned into them, pulling, the lines stretching . . . to no avail.

And whispering in his ear was this two-legs, urging him on.

Harder he pulled and harder, knowing that *something* was supposed to happen, but whatever it was, it *wasn't* happening. Instead it was *defying* him.

*RRRAAAWWWW!* he roared, angered beyond his limits—

—the mighty bellow echoing throughout the courtyards, crashing among the buildings and walls of the citadel— *RRRAAAWWWW!* . . . *RRRAAAWWWWW* . . . *RRR- aaawwww* . . . *Rrraaawwww* . . . *awwww* . . . *www* . . .

*Spang!* snapped the anchoring rods supporting the cage of bars at the window, frame and all bursting outward, arcing down into the garden below, the Bear whirling and growling and biting at the now slack rope, the two-legs beside him hissing *"Urus! Urus!"* in his ear.

Above, Aravan whipped up and over the sill and into the room, drawing up his climbing rope after.

And on the walls, guards shouted—their own cries a confusion of echoes—and whirled about, peering outward into the moonlit 'scape, and inward at the courtyard below, unable to locate the source of the horrendous sound.

Barracks doors slammed open, and a clatter of running footsteps was heard, soldiers erupting into the bailey, their weapons in hand.

"Urus, change!" called Riatha in the Bear's ear as the beast found the rope slack, lifeless, slain, and stopped growling.

The Bear looked at the two-legs, then sat on his rump. And a dark shimmering came upon him, and swiftly he *changed*, Urus emerging.

"Garn!" he cursed, remembering all, slipping out from the rope harness, Riatha hissing, "Quickly, we must hide."

They scuttled behind the pedestal of the statue, Urus hauling in the rope and pulling the window bars to him, unfastening the line from the iron.

In the bailey, guards raced past, heading for the front of the building.

And in the room above, Aravan stepped to the bed, finding Gwylly and Faeril lying unconscious, their breathing shallow, each Waerling's pulse rapid and thready.

The Elf looped the rope under Faeril's arms and about her

chest, then picked the damman up and bore her to the window. Peering out, he could see warders racing past, running toward the front wall, as if expecting an attack, their shouts echoing in the sidecourt. Upon the ramparts, other warders stood, looking outward, seeking foe.

Momentarily the side yard cleared, and swiftly Aravan lowered Faeril down into the garden. In the darkness below, Riatha scurried to the damman's side, taking loose the line, casting it free, Aravan snaking it up and in.

Moments later, down came Gwylly, and as soon as the buccan touched the ground, Aravan swung over the sill, pausing only long enough to pull the inside shutters to, then he slid down afterward. As Urus bore Gwylly to the base of the statue, Aravan flipped loose the grapnel from the window above and followed.

"I like this not," said Riatha, raising her ear from Faeril's breast, then feeling Gwylly's pulse. "These Waerlinga are dying. We must get them to a safe place where we can treat them."

As more guards rushed past the garden, the Elfess withdrew a packet from beneath her cloak, drawing out two gwynthyme mint leaves. She put one in her mouth, handing the other to Urus. "Here, chew but do not swallow. Spit the liquid into Gwylly's mouth."

As Urus followed her directions, Riatha did the same for Faeril, buccan and damman both reflexively swallowing.

"Now the pulp," Riatha directed, placing the tiny cud inside Faeril's cheek, Urus following her example, tucking the pulp into Gwylly's.

"Now we must hie from here," declared Riatha, "yet we cannot simply bear the Waerlinga in the open."

"Under our cloaks, then," suggested Aravan, "strapped to our backs. Urus with Gwylly, Faeril with me."

Aravan rigged a rope harness, a simple boatswain's chair, passing a line around each of Gwylly's thighs and about his waist and chest, fixing the buccan's rigging to Urus's climbing harness. The unconscious Waerling was now borne by the Baeran much the same as a low-slung backpack, or as some Folk bore their babies. Turning to Faeril, Aravan repeated the process, and Riatha aided him in strapping the damman onto his own back.

Throwing their cloaks over the Waerlinga, Urus and Aravan signified they were ready.

"Then let us away from here," said Riatha. "In this confusion, I say we walk in the open."

Urus nodded. "To the ramp and up and over the wall, then. Three ropes. Grapnels. Sliding down."

Aravan grunted his agreement, fastening his scarf across his face, hiding his features, cinching on his climbing gloves, Urus and Riatha following his example.

And the three stepped forth from behind the pedestal.

Of a sudden, hindward shouted a voice. *"Shû 'ammâl ta'mil?"*

Whirling about, the trio saw a gold-turbaned Man at the garden edge. Urus and Riatha started to reach for their weapons, but Aravan hissed, *"No!"* The Elf gestured widely at the garden, calling out, *"Fattish 'ala a'âdi, Jemadar."*

*"Taiyib! Kammal!"*

*"Na'am yâ sîdi."*

As the Man strode on past, Aravan made a great show of searching the bushes, Riatha and Urus imitating his example. When the *jemadar* was beyond earshot, Aravan whispered to his two companions, "Continue to the far end of the garden, for he may look back. I told him we search for enemies."

"I gathered as much," rumbled Urus.

As soon as the Man vanished beyond the far corner, the trio left the garden and walked swiftly 'round the rear of the building and headed for the central ramp up to the battlements. Along the way, they passed several groups of soldiers hastening on errands of their own, and each time they steeled themselves for discovery. Yet none took notice of the trio hurrying through the pale moonlight.

Up the ramp they went and to the walls, now manned heavily, soldiers scanning the countryside. Even so, most were congregated near the corners, and the trio saw three open crenels nearby. Aravan looked at his companions and gestured, indicating which each would take, and they stepped to the openings.

Snapping open the tines on the grappling hooks, Riatha, Urus, and Aravan set the grapnels. Then, as if leaning out to look, they dropped the concealed ropes straight down.

Glancing at one another, "Hai!" called Aravan, and as one they leapt into the crenels and were over the wall and sliding down, sentries on the battlements gaping at the three. *"Waugh!"* cried one in astonishment, then, *"Jemadar! A'âdi!"*

It was forty feet down, yet in a trice they were on the ground and running, dashing through the pale moonlight over the broken terrain, racing for the gully where were tied the horses, cries of alarm mingled with shouted orders coming from behind. They had run a hundred feet or so when the first arrow struck among the rocks to one side. None of the trio risked a glance behind, and onward they hurtled, yells and shouts following.

Now several arrows shattered into the ground nearby, some glancing away before them. And though the moonlight was pale, on they raced, trusting to Elven eyes and the eyes of a BearLord to see the way.

They came to a shallow fold. Here Urus stopped, crouching down, calling to Aravan. "The Waldana!" he shouted. "We cannot use them as shields." But Aravan was already in the ditch, and like Urus, unbuckled his climbing harness to swing the Waerling into his arms.

Behind, Men slid down the ropes, coming in pursuit.

Up leapt Urus and Aravan, running again, bearing the Warrows before them to shield the Wee Ones from the hissing arrows. Swiftly they pounded beyond the range of an accurate cast, yet still shafts clattered about, the archers trusting to fortune to guide their missiles.

Riatha, racing ahead, came to the gulch, and her heart leapt into her throat, for she saw no horses! Left she looked, her eyes following the gully up slope. *There they are!*

"This way!" she called, dashing uphill.

Now Urus and Aravan followed, each cradling an unconscious Warrow.

Behind, Men shouted and ran toward them, some stumbling and falling in their haste, not blessed with the vision of Elvenkind.

And then Riatha came riding up and out from the gulch, haling Aravan's and Urus's steeds trailing after. Holding the Warrows, up the two mounted, and crying, *"Yah! Yah!"* down into the gulch and away galloped the three, bearing their two precious burdens, outstripping the hue and cry.

*　　*　　*

After a short sprint through the gully, down its length and out, the three slowed, for the ground was rough, and it would be disastrous for a horse to fall in this rocky land, to perhaps break a leg.

Yet soon they reached the road of the pass and increased their pace to a canter, heading into the mountains.

"We must stop and tend the Waerlinga," called Riatha.

Aravan looked back toward Nizari. "Not immediately, Dara, for the Emir's Men pursue."

In the near distance they could see a troop of mounted horsemen come bursting out from the gate to thunder toward them.

Now did the trio kick their mounts to a gallop and raced ahead in the shadow-wrapped defile.

And the hammering pursuit relentlessly followed.

Shattering echoes of pounding hooves shocked throughout the defile, the trio of steeds sounding as would a cavalry as they plunged headlong among the twisting turns, the silver Moon shedding light for the steeds to run by, though often they hurtled through pools of blackness.

In the lead Aravan rode with Faeril, Urus and Gwylly on his heels, Riatha coming last. Now and again the Elfess thought she could hear the sounds of riders behind, though among the reverberations she could not be certain.

A mile or more they galloped, perhaps two in all, before Aravan slowed his horse to a trot, calling back to the others, "We cannot keep up a full-running pace, else we will kill the horses. If any are to slay their steeds, let it be our pursuers."

From the rear Riatha spoke: "I deem we are yet two leagues, nearly three, from the way to Stoke's mosque, a ravine our guide seemed disinclined to enter. Mayhap those who follow will feel the same, can we reach it first."

"Winds of Fortune," rumbled Urus.

"Thy meaning?" asked Aravan.

"That Men pursue even though we ride where the Emir would have us go."

"Winds of Fortune, indeed," responded Aravan, "for we would deal with Stoke regardless of the Emir's schemes."

"Aye," said Urus. "Would that the Bear had not roared; we would not likely be fleeing now."

Riatha rode up beside Urus. "Mayhap, love, yet I ween that had the Bear not gotten angry, the bars would not have come down."

On they rode—Urus cradling Gwylly, Aravan holding Faeril—the miles consumed by trotting steeds. Yet now from behind they of a certain could hear the clatter of following hooves. How near or far, they could not say, for the echoes strengthened and faded.

At last they came to the slot cleaving away to the left of the pass. But ere they entered, Urus halted his horse. Dismounting, he handed Gwylly up to Riatha, the unconscious buccan still swaddled with rope and attached to Urus's loose climbing harness. Too, Urus handed over the reins of his horse to the Elfess. "Here, love, take Gwylly and my horse. I have yet one trick to play to shake off our pursuers."

A stricken look washed over Riatha's face, yet unquestioningly she took the buccan and the reins of the steed. "We will ride the gulch several furlongs and wait. *Vi chier ir, Urus.*"

"And I, you," he replied, softly touching her hand. "Now go."

And the hooves of the followers clattered toward them.

Aravan leading, into the slot they rode and from sight. Urus listened to the sound of the pursuers a moment, then stepped into the shadows of the notch.

["Jemadar, we come to the haunted defile. Surely those we chase will not enter there."]

["Who knows, Kauwâs? Who knows? We know not even who it is we pursue . . . or what they were after in the citadel."]

["Aiee. I have just had a most calamitous thought, Jemadar."]
["And it is . . .]

["If they were mad enough to attempt to invade the citadel, then they are mad enough to enter the haunted canyon."]

In the moonlight, the Men riding after the *jemadar* and the *kauwâs* glanced uneasily at one another, whispers rippling down the column.

Yet onward they rode, coming at last to the dreadful notch. The *jemadar* reined to a halt, stopping the column, the *kauwâs* beside him nervously eyeing the ebon gape. The horses snorted and skitted in fear, and it was all the Men could do to control them. But above the clack of their own steeds, the *jemadar* and *kauwâs* could hear the clattering echoes of riders moving up the gulch.

Grimly the *jemadar* gripped the reins of his dancing, frightened mount. The Man was preparing to speak, to issue orders. But in that very moment—

*RRRAAAWWWW!* A horrendous sound split the air, slapping and echoing among the crags, and lumbering out from the notch came a huge, walking monster, arms raised up high to strike.

*"Waugh!"* shrieked the *kauwâs.* ["Demon Afrit!"] Horses reared and belled in fear, bolting away, Men screaming, kicking the steeds for greater speed, pandemonium and panic reigning. Up the pass they galloped, down the pass as well, fleeing blindly, not caring which way they ran, only that they did so, for each knew that the dreaded *Afrit* was after him and him alone.

In moments they were gone.

The Bear dropped back down on all fours, having once again proven his might.

Then the Bear thought of Urus, and a dark shimmering came upon him.

Two furlongs or so had Urus walked within the gulch ere from above came the soft call of a crow, and he looked up to the east rim to see Aravan silhouetted against the dim sky. The Elf gestured to a wallbound ledge pitching steeply upward, running from the floor of the gorge to the lip above.

Up this path trudged the Baeran, entering camp just as Riatha, kneeling among rocks, placed a small pot of water to boil on a tiny tripod above a meager fire. And as the Man strode in, she stood and embraced him, clasping him tightly to her, and Urus kissed her gently.

To one side, Aravan began washing each Waerling's face with a wet cloth, chill in the night, Faeril's first, Gwylly's after. And as he washed the buccan's face, Gwylly moaned, his eyes fluttering. Momentarily he looked at the Elf, and he feebly pulled Aravan unto him, his voice whispering, Aravan listening closely. Then the buccan closed his eyes and did not speak again.

Riatha looked at Aravan. "What did he say?"

A stricken look filled Aravan's eyes. "He said, 'No antidote. Dead by dawn.'"

Riatha gasped, her own gaze flying to the early light even now beginning to pale the distant eastern skies.

# CHAPTER 37

# *Sanctuary*

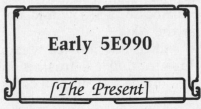

The eastern skies grew bright, dawn arriving, though the morning Sun was yet hidden behind the crests of the intervening mountains.

"There's nought we can do now but wait and see," said Riatha, setting aside the vessel, emptied of its gwynthyme tea.

Before the Elfess lay the Waerlinga, their breathing thready, their faces pallid.

Behind sat Urus by the fire, his forearms across his drawn-up knees, his hands lax, his head down, his eyes focused . . . elsewhere—or perhaps on an unseen point deep within the earth.

Aravan stood off by himself, watching the early skies.

Riatha came and sat beside Urus. "Urus, I am frightened for these Waerlinga. Even though they have taken gwynthyme, they teeter on the verge of death . . . would have been dead by dawn."

Urus's hands clenched into fists. "The Emir never intended for them to live. The week he gave us to bring him Stoke's head was a lie."

Riatha reached out, taking his hand, unclenching his fist, smoothing his fingers with hers. "If what Gwylly whispered is true, the Emir lied about the antidote as well. Perhaps he has no antidote at all."

Urus looked into her silver-grey eyes. "I feel so useless, so helpless."

Riatha sighed and kissed his hand. "So do we all, my love. So do we all."

Aravan whirled and strode to his horse. "I feel nought but rage. Yet heed, for this I swear: should I survive our quest, the Emir of Nizari will pay dearly for this deed he has done."

The Elf mounted up. "We and our steeds will need water and forage a goodly while, for the recovery of the Waerlinga will take time. Two doves I saw winging easterly, and in land such as this, at dawn and dusk they are the best guides to water.

"Too, we need move our camp away from this canyon. I deem there is cause for it to be feared so, and I would not have our sound and scent so near the edge.

"I go now to follow the doves, and to find a place where we will be safe, for there is nothing, *nothing!*"—frustration filled his voice, but then his gaze softened as he looked at the Wee Ones—"nothing I can do here."

Aravan turned his horse eastward and rode away.

After a moment, Riatha said, "Adon, I am weary."

Urus cradled her against him. "Sleep, love. I will wake you should there be need."

In mid-morn, Aravan rode back into the campsite. Urus knelt at the fire, feeding it twigs of thornbush, a pot just beginning to boil upon the tripod.

Riatha lay slumbering beneath a rigged shade, Urus's cloak roped above her.

The Waerlinga, too, lay in shade, a blanket fixed overhead.

Aravan dismounted and tied his steed to a branch of scrub, taking the biscuit of crue held out by Urus.

"Luck?" asked Urus, his voice hushed.

"Aye," answered Aravan in kind. "A league or so from here. Difficult to find. In a fold of stone. But the doves led me to it."

Urus set the steaming water aside and crumbled tea leaves into the liquid, covering it over to steep. Aravan looked at the Waerlinga, then cocked an eyebrow at Urus. "No change," said the Baeran, answering the unspoken question.

They sat in silence as the tea steeped, its fragrance filling the air.

Riatha stirred and opened her eyes. Groaning, she sat up, then stood and stepped to the side of Gwylly and Faeril. She knelt and watched their breathing while she took the measure of their pulses. Too, she rolled back an eyelid on each, gauging the response of the pupil to the light of day. She shook her head. "There is no change." Standing again, she walked into the brush to relieve herself, saying, "Set more water to boil. We will try gwynthyme again."

They moved their campsite in mid-afternoon, Aravan leading the way, Faeril in his arms. Riatha came after, and Urus rode at the rear, the Baeran cradling Gwylly. Some three miles easterly they fared, toward a convoluted massif of stone, long perpendicular folds running down its height, high, shallow cavities here and there. When they came to the face of the butte, Aravan rode straight at the barrier, as if he would ride under the very bulk of the mountain itself. But at the last instant, rightward he turned and disappeared, and Riatha, who followed, gave a small gasp of astonishment. Yet she, too, disappeared, and Urus riding last found a narrow opening doubling back to the right, the stone lapped vertically, a narrow passage behind the wall. Yet even when he looked directly at it he knew that without guidance, none could see the way, for the cast and flow of the stone curtain itself provided an illusory appearance of solidity.

Urus *chrked* his tongue, and the stud moved forward, twisting inward and to the right, entering a narrow, high passageway behind the rippling wall. Ahead rode Riatha and beyond her, Aravan.

The passage curved back to the left, and after some twenty yards debouched into a moss-laden covert beneath an immense sweeping loom of overarching stone. Shafts of sunlight stabbed inward through high openings in the outer wall, striking rock, diffusing downward to light the interior of the great hollow. Forward they rode into the cavity, their eyes filled with wonder at this haven. The air within was cool and fragrant, filled with the faint odor of sweet mint. Toward the rear, some thirty or forty yards away, water ran in rivulets down a broad band of stone and into a shadowed pool. And beside the lakelet stood a broad tree, the girth of its trunk mighty, its branches reaching outward above and beyond the darkling mere.

A profound stillness rested o'er all, the faint sound of trickling water seeming to deepen the stillness rather than to break it.

"Did I not know better," whispered Urus, his voice filling the chamber, "I would say that the tree is an oak. Yet oaks grow not in Hyree."

Aravan turned in his saddle to the Baeran. "Thine eye fools thee not, Urus, for in this wondrous place indeed grows an oak."

Riatha dismounted, stepping to Aravan to take Faeril from his arms, the Elf alighting afterward.

Urus, too, dismounted, yet cradling Gwylly.

While Riatha and Urus prepared a resting place for the Waerlinga, Aravan unladed the horses and led them to the pool, where not only was there cool water to drink but also succulent grasses growing, supplement to the rations of grain.

Urus followed the passage back outside, where he gathered hardened scrub, returning minutes later, his arms laden. "For the fire to make tea," he said as he piled it nearby. "Wait till I gather rocks for a fire ring."

Several trips later, he and Aravan had set rounded stones into a ring, and Riatha kindled a small blaze. The moment the fire caught, a sigh of wind sounded throughout the cavity, as if the hollow itself lamented at seeing the flames, the branches of the massive oak stirring in agitation.

Aravan stood, facing the interior of the cavern. "It is necessary," he called out. "We have no choice." To whom he directed his words, neither Riatha nor Urus knew.

Stillness returned to the cavity, though the trickle of water seemed somehow perturbed, disquieted.

Aravan turned to Riatha. "When the tea is made, extinguish the blaze."

Riatha nodded, setting the tiny pot upon the tripod.

"Still no change," said Riatha, placing Gwylly's hand across his breast.

Urus stirred. "How long has it been?"

Aravan held up a thumb and two fingers. "I make it three days—one upon the rim and two more here within this hollow."

Riatha turned to Faeril, putting her ear to the damman's breast. "It yet beats, but without strength. I fear the gwynthyme has merely held at bay the harm of the Emir's poison. When we exhaust our supply of the golden mint, then will the venom resume its fatal course."

Urus interlaced his fingers and gripped hard, his knuckles white. "Surely there is something we can do. . . . Perhaps the Emir *does* have an antidote after all, and can we get it . . ."

Aravan shook his head. "Nay, Urus. Gwylly knew. The Emir has no antidote."

In the night, Aravan sat watching over the Waerlinga. To one side, Urus and Riatha were curled together asleep. The cavern was dark, yet not completely without light, for starshine glimmered inward through the high openings above. The Elf sat atop a poolside rock, watching the rivulets glisten as they slid down into the pool. Why the pool did not overflow, where the water went, he did not know . . . down through the earth below, he surmised.

Aravan glanced at the Waerlinga, so still, so pallid, so near death.

And he knew that Riatha was coming to the end of her supply of gwynthyme.

The Elf calmed his mind, composing himself for prayer to Adon, as he had done every night since entering the hollow.

Aravan prayed even though he knew that Adon had pledged never to directly act in matters of the middle world. Elsewise, Adon had said, the hands of the Gods would destroy that which They had created, for Their power is too great, and those They sought to help, too fragile. Too, Adon told that were the Gods to interfere, it would fetter free will.

Even so, Aravan prayed, hoping against hope that the High One would intervene.

This night he held the blue stone amulet in hand as he cast his words unto the Allfather. "Adon, if it be Thy will, then take Thee the souls of these tiny Waerlinga unto Thyself. But if it not be Thy plan to let these wee ones lapse into death, then send aid. Send aid. For we are desperate, and little time remains."

Nought but silence answered him.

Aravan turned dejectedly to the great oak, remarking, "O tree, it would seem that Adon will yet keep his pledge. Would that you had the power to aid, for I would call . . . I would call."

A darkness seemed to gather high within the branches, and Aravan drew in his breath. Quickly he glanced up at the stars that he could see. They still glimmered brightly—no cloud intervened—yet among the leaves of the oak, shadows mustered.

Like a wisp of dusky smoke, the darkness coiled down and about the massive trunk. Aravan took his spear in hand but did not Truename it, for the blue amulet was still warm to the touch, not chill.

The Elf's eyes widened as <Friend,>echoed a voice within his mind, speaking the tongue of the Hidden Ones.

["Friend,"] answered Aravan.

<I did not recognize thee until thou spoke through the stone.> The mental voice seemed vaguely feminine, though that was by no means certain.

["I did not know the stone had the power to summon."]

<Nay, it does not have such power. Only to speak to one such as I, that is a power it *does* have.>

The shadow reached the moss at the base of the trunk and coalesced into an indistinct apparition some eighteen inches high. It moved across the ground, coming to a stop before the Elf. Aravan thought that he could see a vague darkness within the shade, as if the true being before him was even smaller and cloaked within folds of dusk.

<Thou called for aid.>

["Aye. We are in sore need. The two Wee Ones are dying of a poison, and we have no remedy. We can only arrest their death for a while. Yet soon we will have no more power to stay the Dark One's hand."]

<Is it not the fate of all mortals to one day die?>

["Aye, it is. Yet I would have it be a natural way of passing, and not this undeserved end."]

<What matter a few years more or less to mortals? They pass as swiftly as the mayfly, regardless.>

["What matter a few years? Why, just this: it is all they have and no more. I would not have their brief lives shortened by one jot."]

<Thou are persuasive, Aravan.>

["Thou know my name? How?"]

<Thou yet hold the stone, Elf.>

["What may I call thee?"]

<Thou may call me Nimué, though it is not my Truename.>

["Can thou aid, Nimué?"]

The shadow glided across the moss-laden ground, moving to Gwylly and Faeril. Long did Nimué pause at each, then the shadow stepped to the packet of gwynthyme, again pausing long. Finally, timorously it seemed, Nimué moved to Aravan, briefly touching the amulet in his hand before hastily backing away, as if afraid to stand too close to the Elf.

Aravan repeated his question. ["Nimué, can thou aid?"]

<Mayhap, yet what I offer is a two-edged sword, cutting both ways, fraught with danger.>

["Danger? . . ."]

<Aye. It will cure or kill, I cannot say which.>

Aravan fell into thought. Long moments later he said, ["Without aid they are dead regardless. Better a single chance in thousands than no chance at all.

["Speak. I will listen."]

<There is a flower which blossoms only at night: the *Nyktohrodon*—the Nightrose. Mix one petal of the flower with each leaf of the golden mint; it will be as if the subtle powers of night were commingling with the bright strength of day.

<Brew a tea from such, one leaf of each for each victim. Dip the amulet within as the liquid steeps, for I have touched the stone and it will now aid in the amalgamation.

<Let the afflicted ones sip such for three nights running. Then wait five days and do it once again.

<Yet heed: this treatment will render much agony, and therein lies its two-edged nature—the pain alone may kill the mortals.>

["But the blended tea may also cure."]

<Aye.>

["Where will I find this *Nyktohrodon?* What is its aspect?"]

<West lies a narrow canyon. . . .>

["I have been there."]

<Within, but nigh the rim, blooms the Nightrose.>

["And its color? . . ."]

<Moon white.>

["Is there aught special I must do?"]

<Pluck not the flower itself. Instead, take only that which thou need—eight petals, from eight different blossoms . . . in the darktide ere the Moon rises, for no moonlight must fall upon the petal, else it loses its potency until next its bloom opens in the moonless night. Neither let the Sun shine upon thy pluckings, or they will be rendered powerless as well. Wrap the petals in a dark cloth to bear them hither. Keep them enwrapped in such until ye would use them. And then do so only in the dark of the Moon and the Sun.>

["Is there aught else?"]

<Aye. When thou go in the night to fetch the flowers, beware, for ill things move through the canyon dark.>

["Things of Neddra?"]

<Most. Not all.>

["I shall be wary.

["Is there aught thou would ask of us?"]

<Just this: when thou are done, the mortals well or dead . . . I would that ye burn no more flames within my demesne.>

From behind came Riatha's voice. "Aravan, do thou speak to Faeril or Gwylly? Are they awake?"

Aravan glanced aback at the Elfess struggling up on one elbow, peering toward the Waerlinga. Quickly the Elf looked forward once again to Nimué, but the shadow-wrapped being was gone, fled. Aravan's gaze flew to the great oak, and he thought he saw a darkness swiftly vanish up among the branches high.

Urus shaded his eyes. "The Sun sets."

Aravan stood beside the Baeran and gazed down into the canyon below. Krystallopŷr was slung over his back. "It will be dark within the hour. The Moon will not rise until halfway 'tween mid of night and dawn. We will have some nine hours or so to find the blooms of the white Nightrose."

Each was fitted with his climbing harness, though it was planned for Aravan alone to clamber down within the canyon to gather whatever petals he could, while Urus stood above paying out and anchoring the line.

Dusk washed over the mountains, quickly followed by the nighttide, and soon only the stars cast their glimmering light upon the two below.

Along the rim of the gulch they moved, peering down within, seeking white blossoms.

"When will they open, I wonder?" murmured Urus.

"I know not," responded Aravan. "Nimué did not say."

An hour passed, and Urus hissed to Aravan. "Look there."

On the canyon wall some three yards below Urus's feet a white blossom had turned its face to the starlight, as if seeking the scintillant gleams.

Quickly Urus snapped the rope to Aravan's harness, and backward over the lip and down walked the Elf.

When he reached the flower he inhaled its fragrance. "Its smell is somewhat like that of an ordinary white rose," he softly called to Urus, "yet more subtle."

Taking care, Aravan plucked a single petal, wrapping it in a soft dark cloth, stuffing all in his jerkin pocket. Then up he swarmed, coming again to the rim.

They placed a small cairn of stones upon the lip above the Nightrose, marking it so that they would not pluck from this one's blossom again.

On they searched, roaming the canyon brim, peering down into the shadows below.

Once again Urus espied a blossom, and as Aravan plucked a petal from its bloom, in the distance he saw a third Nightrose.

Two more hours passed ere they saw the next white blossom, and as Aravan was down within the canyon he softly called up to Urus. "The blue stone, Urus, it grows chill."

Swiftly Aravan clambered up to the rim, and he and Urus lay on their stomachs and watched the shadows below. At last they heard the clip-clop of an oncoming mount, the sound echoing such that they could not tell which way it approached. Finally, 'round the bend and heading southward came a rider. Corpse white he was, with jet black hair. He wore a heavy dark cloak over his clothing, and in his hand he bore a cruel-barbed spear. A tulwar was girted at his waist, and black breeks and boots clad his legs and feet. He wore no helm, but around his neck was a spiked steel collar, wide and thick, as if to protect against beheadment.

The mount that bore him was horselike, but no horse this. Instead it was hairless and had cloven hooves, and as it passed below, the two on the rim could see that it had a snakelike, scaled tail. And a foetid stench drifted up to the watchers.

Of a sudden the beast squealed and stopped, its nostrils flaring, head casting about as if attempting to scent something or someone. The rider glared and gritted words in Slûk, harsh and guttural, yet he, too, looked about, searching.

Aravan and Urus slid back from the rim, out of sight, and the Elf clasped his blue amulet tightly, his eyes closed.

Heartbeats passed, and then they heard a glottal command and the sound of hooves pacing away. After a moment, cautiously, Urus peered over the brim, watching as the rider and steed moved onward, around a bend, disappearing from sight, bearing southward in the direction where Stoke's strongholt was said to lie.

When the rider was beyond hearing, Aravan breathed, "Ghûlk! And Hèlsteed, too!"

Urus glanced over his shoulder, eyeing his and Aravan's horses tethered to brush some distance back from the rim, knowing that if the mounts caught full scent of the Hèlsteed, riderless they would bolt in panic. The horses shifted about uneasily at the faint trace of malodor reaching them, but settled as the drift of air carried it away.

Urus turned to Aravan. "Think you that the Hèlsteed caught our scent? Is that why it stopped? If so—"

Aravan shook his head. "Nay, Urus. I deem instead that it sensed the warding of the amulet; some creatures are more sensitive to it than others. I tried to use the stone to will the creature on its way. Mayhap I succeeded, mayhap not. Regardless, the beast and its rider are now gone."

"Even so, that Ghûlk and Hèlsteed are here is ill news, for I thought all perished in the Winter War."

Urus grunted. "I know nothing of this Winter War but that which I have been told. Yet I *do* know of the Guula. A dreadful foe. Nearly unkillable. Wounds do not harm them unless they come from silver or a special blade."

Aravan nodded. "Aye, but there is this, too. Wood through the heart—stake or spear or e'en arrow—beheading, dismemberment, fire, the light of day: these will kill the Ghûlka as well."

Urus stood. "Even so, Aravan, if Stoke is drawing these allies unto him, then we will face dire foe."

"Aye, Urus, and forget not the Hèlsteeds, for they are deadly on their own and should not be underestimated."

Urus took up the rope still attached to the Elf's harness. "What other enemies, I ask, will we meet in Stoke's mosque? Rutcha and Drōkha of a certainty, Guula and Hèlsteed as well . . ."

As Aravan walked backward over the lip, he added to Urus's list. "Forget not the Vulgs, Urus. And if Stoke is collecting our enemies of old, then he perhaps has Trolls, too."

A grim look came upon Urus's visage and he muttered, "Ogrus."

Bearing the eighth and final petal, Aravan clambered up over the rim. Urus glanced at the sky, trying to judge the depth of the night. As Aravan unbuckled his harness, he said, "We have yet one hour ere the Moon rises, Urus. Mayhap enough time to start treatment this very nighttide."

The Baeran slung the coiled rope and his own climbing harness over his shoulder. "Then let us ride."

Swiftly they strode to their horses, untethering the steeds and mounting up, spurring them into action, riding for the sanctuary within the stone. The terrain was rough and they could not gallop or even canter, though here and there they could go at a trot. Even so, they covered the three miles in less than an hour.

Into the dim interior of the stone passageway they rode, emerging once again in the hollow behind, Elven eyes and those of a BearLord adequate in the glimmer of starlight seeping in through the high openings above.

As Riatha stood and stepped toward them, "Light the fire, Dara," said Aravan. "We were successful."

In mere moments a tiny blaze sprang up, its faint light but barely illuminating the interior above that of the stars shining in.

Urus unsaddled the horses as Riatha and Aravan spoke of the treatment yet again. The Baeran curried the beasts, finishing with one as the water came to a boil.

Setting the pot aside from the flame, Riatha carefully shredded a Moon-white petal of the Nightrose into the steeping water, quickly followed by a golden leaf of gwynthyme. As she fragmented the Nightrose, "Lily, mountain laurel, and rose," she murmured, describing the combination of scents drifting up from the white petal.

Aravan took the blue stone from his neck and, dangling it by its thong, immersed it in the hot liquid, stirring slowly.

Riatha repeated the shredding, another flower petal and mint leaf joining the first ones.

They sat fretting, Aravan stirring, now and then reversing direction. At last Riatha said, "We have but a quarter hour till the Moon rises," relying on her Elven gift for knowing at all times where stands the Sun, Moon, and stars.

Aravan continued to stir slowly. "It will be on the other side of the range, Dara; yet even so, I too would that we be finished with this first treatment ere the Moon broaches the horizon beyond."

Finished with the horses, Urus came and sat to one side.

Aravan leaned over the steeped tea, inhaling its fragrance, then he held the pot out for Riatha to smell. "What think thee, Dara? I can no longer sense the gwynthyme alone nor the smell of the Nightrose."

Riatha gently inhaled. "Aye, it is ready."

Pouring two cupfuls, Aravan took one and knelt at Faeril's side, Riatha moving to Gwylly's. Carefully, a few drops at a time, they spooned the warm liquid into Waerling mouths, Faeril and Gwylly reflexively swallowing.

Slowly the liquid diminished, yet the desperate Elves did not hurry, even though it was but minutes until the waning quarter Moon would break above the unseen horizon.

At last, "I am finished," said Riatha, wiping Gwylly's mouth.

Moments later, "So am I," said Aravan, setting his cup aside.

"Not an instant too soon," said Riatha, settling back on her heels, "for the Moon rises even . . . now."

That's when Gwylly began screaming.

So, too, did Faeril.

Over the next three days, Riatha, Aravan, and Urus took turns stepping outside to escape the dreadful pain within, yet unable to flee from the wrenching at their hearts.

And one at a time Riatha clutched each Waerling to her breast, singing softly and rocking, tears streaming down her face as the Wee One in her arms writhed, the pain beyond all endurance, their mouths stretched wide in silent agony, screaming without letup though they emitted no sound, their voices lost in the first hour of shrieking.

After the second treatment both Gwylly and Faeril opened their eyes, yet their gazes were wild and unseeing. And they thrashed about and clawed at themselves, and would have fled if they could have, their silent words shrilling into the hearts of those who tended them. *It burns! It burns! Everything burns! Oh, Adon, Adon, it burns!*

Urus suggested that the two be immersed in the pool, but that only seemed to make things worse. And so they held the Wee Ones to them, trying to comfort them but failing, their endless raw screams crying out and piercing the heart even though there was no sound but hissing air.

When came the third dose of Nightrose and gwynthyme, Gwylly looked into Riatha's eyes, his own gaze mad, frantic, the faint remnants of his voice crying out, "Oh, Adon, why do you hurt me so?"

And when Riatha tried to get him to sip the tea, he violently shoved her away, his whispers shrieking, "No, no, no . . ."

It was all they could do between them to hold him still and force down the tea.

And they wept as they did so.

Then they turned to Faeril, her own eyes mad with pain.

And Aravan shouted for all the world to hear, "Emir! Bastard! For this thou are dead!"

Throughout the following day the whispered shrilling slowly diminished and just ere dusk ceased altogether. Riatha put her ear to the breast of each Waerling. "Oh, Adon, they hang but by a thread," she said, her eyes flooding with tears.

Aravan glanced at the oak tree. "Nimué said it was a two-edged sword, cutting both ways. Life or death, we know not which it will yield."

The stillness in the sanctuary fell upon them all, only the soft trickle of water echoing within. "Sleep," said Aravan at last. "I will watch."

Exhausted, Urus and Riatha did not argue, and immediately fell aslumber.

It was three hours ere dawn when Faeril stirred, rolling over to see Aravan's silhouette against the starlight. She tried to speak yet could not, her voice gone.

Aravan swiftly knelt beside her, feeling her pulse, then clasped her to him, kissing her on the brow, his eyes filled with tears of relief.

Again she tried to whisper and failed. Even so, Aravan sensed her needs, giving over to the damman a cup of water and a crue biscuit. But the Waerling fell back to sleep before she could finish either.

Some two hours later, Gwylly awoke, his pulse strong, and Aravan hugged him and kissed him and gave him water and crue as well. The buccan managed to consume both biscuit and drink before collapsing again.

The following day Aravan slept, Riatha and Urus now watching over buccan and damman.

In mid-afternoon, again Gwylly awakened, and as he took more water and another biscuit, Faeril came around, too.

Gwylly managed a smile at his dammia, and she wanly smiled back at him. He inched his way to her and gave her a kiss, whispering in her ear. A great grin washed over her features, and she would have laughed, but her voice was gone. Even so, she motioned to Urus and whispered in his ear, and his great rolling laughter echoed throughout the sanctuary.

Urus turned to Riatha. "Gwylly says, 'This adventuring, some fun, neh?' "

Again the cavern rang with laughter.

*     *     *

The days passed slowly, Riatha, Urus, and Aravan swiftly recovering from their wretched days and nights, Faeril and Gwylly recuperating much more slowly.

Aravan told the buccan and damman what had befallen: of their rescue and flight, of the finding of the sanctuary, of Nimué and the Nightroses, of the Ghûlk and Hèlsteed, of the treatments.

Urus told of the Bear roaring twice: the first time imperiling the rescue; the second time routing pursuit, the Warrows silently laughing over this latter, their voices not yet recovered.

Riatha reminded all that there was one treatment yet to be administered, and soon.

It was in the dark time before dawn when Gwylly swirled the tea. Then he turned to Faeril and raised his cup. "I love you," he rasped, swallowing the drink in one prolonged gulp.

"And I, you, my buccaran," replied Faeril, her own voice nought but a rough burr, downing her drink as well.

Almost immediately, "I feel . . . hot," said Gwylly, Faeril nodding.

"Oh, oh . . . oh, it burns. It burns. Everything burns." Gwylly reached out for Faeril's hand, his eyes filled with pain. She reached for him, yet each began shrieking before their hands could meet, and both Warrows thrashed about in agony.

Riatha scooped up Faeril and Urus took Gwylly, and they held the screaming Waerlinga and rocked them gently and wept.

And Aravan paced back and forth, unable to contain his furious rage.

In the hour before mid of night, a shadow came down from the oak, creeping unto the sides of the silent Waerlinga. Long it paused at each of the Wee Ones. At last it returned to the tree. Aravan paced to the poolside below, his stone in hand.

["Nimué . . ."]

<This time the sword has cut one way; the next time it may well cut the other.>

["Tell me, Nimué, has the sword driven away Death or instead destroyed Life?"]

<These two mortal friends of yours, Aravan, they must come of a hardy stock, for I deem both will live.>

Aravan sank to the ground, his face in his hands, the sound of his weeping waking Riatha.

# CHAPTER 38

# Restoration

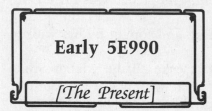

"It was as if every fiber of my being was on fire," whispered Gwylly, his throat raw, his voice all but gone. "Yet my body does not *remember* the pain, only my mind."

Riatha reached out and touched the buccan's hand. "It is well that thou cannot feel the pain of the past, else thou would die from the mere memory of it."

"Why did it hurt so, Riatha?" asked Faeril, her own voice but a whisper as well. "Why was the remedy more painful than the affliction?"

"I cannot say for certain, Faeril, yet I ween that ye both indeed were on fire, that the amalgam of Nightrose and gwynthyme sought out the Emir's poison and burned it away. It was long between when ye drank the poison and when we could begin treatment. Hence, the venom permeated thy entire being, and so the cure was burning everywhere inside ye as well."

"All I know," said Gwylly, "is it hurt like blazes."

Faeril smiled. "And 'blazes' it was, Gwylly, 'blazes' it was . . . or so it felt."

Urus growled, saying, "Damn the Emir! He sought to force us to do that which we had already taken as our sworn quest."

"And for that error he will pay," added Aravan.

Faeril whispered, "Perhaps we aided in his blunder."

Riatha's eyes widened. "How so?"

"Just this: had he known that Gwylly and I were Warrows, then perhaps he would have seen we were warriors on our own ... and not children of Elvenkind, younglings who might burden the quest. Perhaps, then, he would have heard us speak our pledge, rather than trying to force you three to go and slay Stoke while he held us two hostage."

Aravan leapt to his feet and paced back and forth. "Nay, wee one, I deem iniquity was always in his heart. He knew of us, of our coming. How? I cannot say. Yet it is of certain that in some fashion Stoke discovered our relentless pursuit and enlisted the Emir's perfidious aid.

"As to holding ye hostage, pah! His pledge was false from the beginning.

"Even so, he wishes Stoke dead, and sought by his wicked ploy to achieve that end."

Gwylly reached for a biscuit of crue. "If he wishes Stoke dead," whispered the buccan, "then why doesn't he simply send his army to the mosque and destroy the Baron? Or even go with them and kill Stoke himself?"

Aravan stopped his agitated pacing and sat back down. "First, Gwylly, the Emir would never go himself. Why, that would place him in danger ... and we know that he is a dastard, fearing death at the hand of an assassin. Did thou not see the way he wards himself about with guards? Too, he takes no food or drink without a taster's testing. Nay, he would not go with an army, preferring instead to work his will through others.

"Second, he would not send an army, for he said himself that Stoke has the favor of the Sultan of Hyree, and the Emir would never overtly go against the Sultan.

"Yet heed! By sending us, his hands are clean of any traceable act of rebellion. Should we succeed in slaying Stoke and the Sultan take him to task for it, the Emir will claim that we were merely strangers passing through, and there was no reason to be suspicious, no reason to think we were out to kill the Baron.

"And, had the Emir's scheme run its course and we had

succeeded in the mission, when we returned to redeem ye two, he would have slain us without compunction, so that he could tell the Sultan that he had executed the killers.

"Likewise, had we followed his scheme and gone to the mosque and failed, the Emir would have simply claimed to Stoke that we had escaped his hold, but at least he had slain ye two.

"But now that ye have been rescued, he will merely claim that we all escaped, should we fail and Stoke succeed."

Aravan fell silent, and Faeril shook her head in rue. "Wily and treacherous is this Emir. No matter whether we succeed or fail, he has an answer for the Sultan or the Baron, whichever one asks the questions."

"Lor, what a remarkable place is this," hissed Gwylly, Faeril nodding in agreement.

On across the moss and under the oak trod the two. Faeril looked up among the limbs, hoping to see Nimué, but only broad branches and dark green leaves did her eye perceive. "I hope she doesn't mind," whispered Faeril as she and her buccaran shed their clothes and slipped into the water.

"What makes you think Nimué is a she?" asked Gwylly, shivering, watching his skin turn to goose flesh in the chill water.

"Oh, I don't know. It's just that this wondrous hollow seems more suited to a she than a he."

Gwylly ducked and came up blowing, shaking the water from his eyes. "The bottom is sandy, and since we have no soap, this will have to do." He held out a fistful of beige grit to Faeril.

Using sand, they scrubbed their skin and hair, diving under to rinse off and to fetch up more clean grit. At last Gwylly moved to Faeril, saying, "Here, love, let me do your back."

Faeril smiled and drew up her hair from the nape of her neck, turning her back to her buccaran. "Every time you do my back, you know where it leads."

"Indeed I do, my love. Indeed I do."

Moments later, in the moss below the sheltering oak, someone whispered, "I do hope that Nimué has the decency to look the other way."

*　　*　　*

Two more days passed, the Warrows continuing to recover. On this day Urus and Aravan, not having the heart to kill the doves that came to the pool, had gone out hunting and had managed to bag several desert mountain quail. And when the late afternoon wind blew up the mountain slopes, Urus built a small fire outside the haven and roasted the birds.

It was the first meat they had had in the past seventeen days.

As they sat and ate, Gwylly, his mouth full, his voice raspy and breaking, asked, "Riddle me this riddle: Why would a monster such as Baron Stoke gain the favor of the Sultan of Hyree?"

"Only the two of them know of a certain," answered Riatha, "but mayhap there are clues pointing. List to this thread:

"In the Great War of the Ban as well as the Winter War, Hyree stood on the side of the foe.

"In both of those times they worshipped Gyphon, the Great Deceiver.

"When we came through Nizari, we saw mosques abandoned, minarets fallen into ruin. When Faeril asked why, we heard from the Emir's own lips that in his grandsire's time, the *imâmîn*, the clerics, had been overthrown, for they hewed to a false prophet instead of the true god, and had done so for nearly nine hundred years.

"Heed: nine hundred years back of the Emir's grandsire was in the time of the Winter War, when Hyree hewed to Gyphon.

"And after the War, the desert religion of the Prophet Shat'weh became dominant in Hyree. Hence, these mosques and minarets were those of Shat'weh, whom the Emir called the false prophet.

"The Emir then went on to say Hyree had returned to the old ways, the true ways. And that can mean but one thing—"

"Gyphon!" interjected Faeril. "Oh, Riatha, just now do I see why you stopped me from asking the Emir further questions about the mosques and minarets, about the false prophet and the true ways. . . ."

Riatha nodded. "Aye, for then we knew not of the treachery to come, and I did not wish him to believe that we would know enough of their Gyphon worship to carry word back to Pellar, back to the High King."

"This portends ill for Mithgar," said Aravan.

"Another War for supremacy, do you think?" asked Urus.

Aravan spread his hands, palms up. "Who can say? But there is this: When the Great War of the Ban ended, there were yet some mortals in Adonar, and when they returned to Mithgar—"

"But I thought the way between the Planes was sundered *before* the War ended," put in Gwylly.

"Not for Mithgarian blood, Gwylly. The way to Mithgar was yet open for them, still is for that matter, though it is closed to Elvenkind; just as the way back to Adonar is yet open to Elvenkind, but closed to mortals."

"Oh, right," said the buccan. "I forgot."

"In any event, the mortals brought with them their account of what had passed when Gyphon suffered Adon's judgement. The Deceiver was banished beyond the Spheres, but ere he fell into the Great Abyss, he said, 'Even now I have set into motion events you cannot stop. I shall return! I shall conquer! I shall rule!'

"The Myrkenstone was one of these events Gyphon had promised, and it brought on the Winter War. Yet who knows what other schemes he may have set into motion?"

"*Ooo*, that sends shivers up my spine," said Gwylly.

"Mine too," agreed Faeril, then cocked her head. "But what has this to do with Stoke?"

Urus spoke up. "The Sultan would favor Stoke only if he saw him as a powerful ally. Know this: Stoke draws Foul Folk unto himself. Perhaps the Sultan thinks Stoke will give him an army of these creatures. An army to rule the night."

"Lor," breathed Gwylly, "could this be preparation for another War with Gyphon? If so, how soon, I wonder?" The buccan looked 'round the circle, but none had any answers.

"If we succeed," said Urus at last, "at least we will have eliminated Stoke from the ranks of the foe."

The Baeran stood and looked at the sky. The Sun was setting beyond the range. "I will get the shovel and bury the fire and quail bones, for night comes and I would not have their scent lingering on the air."

"We were told the mosque was a hard day's ride from Nizari," said Faeril, her voice fully recovered. "Yet the Ghûl you saw on a Hèlsteed was moving at a walking pace. That can only mean one thing: somewhere along the way is a place of safety for those who suffer the Ban—a crack, crevice, or cave . . . a place where the light of day cannot reach."

Urus nodded and looked at Aravan and smiled. "We could have come to the same conclusion but did not, Aravan. Clever people, these Waldana . . . at least this one is."

Faeril grinned in pleasure. "I had good teachers," she said.

"Nay, wee one," responded Aravan. "Cleverness is a trait we cannot instill, and can only enhance slightly."

"Go on, Faeril," urged Riatha, "what would thou suggest be our course of action?"

"Just this," answered the damman. "If it is truly a hard day's ride to the mosque, and if we ride through the daylight hours, then we will arrive as night falls. And in the nighttime, Rūcks and such are at their strongest, for then they do not have to fear the Sun.

"Yet we cannot ride through the night hours—in particular, we cannot ride through the canyon in the night hours, for then is when the Spawn themselves use it.

"In fact, I think we should not ride in the gulch at all, else we will leave spoor for Vulgs and such to follow . . . especially if there is a way station for the Foul Folk down in the canyon—or somewhere nearby—for then on occasion they are likely to patrol its extent, and I would not have them find us within it. Instead we should try to choose a route that will avoid the ravine entirely, thus leaving no trace they are likely to stumble across.

"So this is what I suggest: that we ride the rim in the day, staying well back from the canyon, especially at night, for then we must hide from the foe.

"And when we find the mosque, if at all possible we should wait until daylight before entering. That way, if we are pressed beyond our limits, we can fall back to the Sun."

Faeril fell silent, and none said aught for a while. At last Urus rumbled, "See? I *told* you these Waldana were clever."

As the others nodded and agreed to the plan, Gwylly hugged his damman and kissed her, whispering, "And you are mine, all mine."

On the twenty-second day after entering the sanctuary, the five prepared to leave in the early dawn light.

A week past, Faeril and Gwylly had sorted through the things brought out of the citadel for the Waerlinga by Riatha, finding most of what they would need in the days to come: weapons, clothing, climbing gear, and other such. As they had taken inventory, Riatha had said: "E'en when ye were removed from us by the Emir, I knew that we would come back for ye. We retrieved thy weaponry from the table when we took up our own, and I packed away all else against the rescue to come. Had the warders been alert, they would have seen that we did so and would have stopped us. Yet they did not, and so, here is what we saved."

And now came the time to take up the mission once again, the time of recovery and planning at an end.

While Riatha, Urus, and Aravan saddled the steeds and laded them with their goods, Gwylly and Faeril girted themselves with bandoliers and bullet pouches, with throwing knives and sling, with daggers and long-knives. And they were dressed in their desert gear, leaving behind the Emir's silks and satins—the clothing they had been wearing when rescued—the garb clean and folded and placed under the oak, the rich cloth a gift to Nimué. Finally all was ready, and they took one last look at this wondrous refuge, and then turned to go.

Urus and Riatha led their horses out, and Gwylly and Faeril came after, but Aravan stayed behind, his blue stone in hand. And when his companions were gone, his voice quietly echoed throughout the great hollow:

["Nimué, we thank thee for the use of thy haven, a sanctuary sorely needed. Yet e'en more so, we thank thee for the lives of the Waerlinga, for they are precious to us and the world a better place with them in it.

"We go now to right old wrongs and rid the world of a monster. Should we survive and there be aught we can do for thee . . ."]

The Elf fell silent, and only silence answered.

Aravan turned and led his horse to the fold of stone leading outward. Just ere he entered the passageway—

<Friend.>—came the silent voice.

["Friend,"] responded Aravan, pausing expectantly . . . but there was no more, and so he walked on out to where his companions waited in the early light of day.

Southerly they rode, Gwylly sitting before Riatha on the withers of her steed, Faeril likewise ensconced before the Elf, Aravan.

The land they entered was rough beyond their expectations, but Urus saw this as an advantage, for, ". . . Stoke's minions are unlikely to come this way, preferring instead the easy passage of the gulch below." And so, across sharp-edged ridges and shattered plateaus and scree-laden slopes they fared, now and again coming to crevasses that they detoured long to pass around, or jumped if they were narrow—the Warrows swinging 'round behind their riders and hanging on tightly, the horses running and leaping, soaring, landing.

They rode throughout the day, stopping often to give the horses a breather, sometimes dismounting and walking. And as the Sun began to near the western horizon, they scouted the terrain for shelter, finding a narrow dead-end slot riving the face of a nearby bluff.

They judged that all in all this day they had come but five leagues—just fifteen miles total.

They took turns standing watch, the warder on duty holding Aravan's guardian stone. The chill on the amulet waxed and waned, growing cool and cooler, then warming again, never becoming frigid.

At mid of night, a nigh full Moon sailed silently overhead, and the 'scape was lighted nearly as bright as day. Even so, when the stone grew chill, still they saw no foe, each warder concluding that the enemy patrolled down in the distant gulch.

The second day was much the same as the first, as through a broken land they travelled, staying within sight of the canyon, using it to guide them to the destination. Just where was the mosque, the Emir's major-domo had not known,

". . . somewhere near the ravine, I am told," had said Abid, and no more.

And so, above the gulch they rode, keeping it well off to the right; and from the ridge tops and high ground their eyes ever searched the distant reach ahead, watching for minarets, for domes, for spires . . . searching but locating none.

As evening drew nigh, they came across a rivulet running down the mountain flank. Turning upstream, they discovered it issued from a crevice, yet they did not stay within, for it clove into the mountain far beyond their exploration. "This has water and could be a Ruchen bolt-hole," murmured Riatha, kneeling and refilling a goatskin upstream from the drinking horses, "and I would not hide where the *Spaunen* may come. Let us away to elsewhere."

And so, as the Sun set and night came, a mile beyond they settled for the darktide among a jumble of massive boulders.

Their order of watch was the same as they had kept before: Aravan, Gwylly, Faeril, Riatha, Urus.

It was nearing dawn when the stone grew chill and Urus saw the silhouette of a great, dark flying *thing* flap across the face of the Moon, winging southward.

"*Stoke!*" he hissed.

Then it was gone.

The Baeran did not waken the others.

All that day they rode among great boulders, twisting a tortuous route inching southerly. At times they would gain the open and check their bearings, keeping track of the whereabouts of the gulch. But occasionally, when they had ridden long without coming into the clear, they would stop, and one or another would climb onto a boulder to see where the gully lay, and to call out its course to the others below. And once they unexpectedly came upon a rim to find themselves peering down into the gulch itself, for it had taken a wrenching turn and had cut diagonally across their path. Quickly they had retreated, and had swung wide to pass 'round the bend.

They finally left the boulders behind and came to a foot of a long ridge sloping upward. And as they topped this ridge, suddenly, there before them in the distance high upon the mountainside, gleaming in the afternoon Sun, they could see a large, walled mosque, the building a sandy red, its dome a pale orange. And off to one side towering upward stood a slender minaret.

Gwylly's heart leapt to his throat, and his pulse hammered in his ears. He looked to Faeril and found her eyes on him, and they were grim. Then once again his gaze swung to the mosque afar.

They could see no movement in the distance, yet there was no doubt among them—

Somewhere inside a monster lay.

# CHAPTER 39

# Mosque

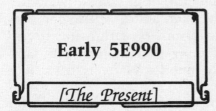

**Early 5E990**

*[The Present]*

Urus looked at the descending Sun. "I do not think there remains enough daylight for us to reach the mosque and complete our mission ere darkness falls. No matter that I chafe at the bit, Faeril's plan is sound—the temple itself must wait till morrow's dawn. Hence, we need find cover for the night. Let us take to the high ground for a place to hide, somewhere closer and above the holt, so that we may look down on it and lay our plans by what we see."

They scanned the mountainside, locating potential sites, finally choosing a cluster of crags on a horizontal ridge slightly higher than the plateau on which the mosque sat.

Up they rode and up, here and there dismounting and walking, sparing the horses the burden. As they climbed the slopes, the Sun sank in the west.

"Hah," huffed Gwylly, trudging upward, "the place is farther than it looks."

"Aye," agreed Urus. "Mountains are deceptive with their distances. Something to do with their huge size."

"Like a mirage? Like an illusion?" asked Gwylly.

"More like a *delusion*," put in Faeril, clambering up over a ledge.

Now and again as they climbed upward they would peer

at the mosque and its surround, yet no glimpse of movement did they see. Still the Sun descended, staying not its ceaseless course, copper rays now streaming through dark peaks to the west.

"Oh, lor," exclaimed Gwylly, "I've just had a horrid thought: what if the crags are infested by Foul Folk?"

"Then we are in for a fight," said Aravan.

"Nothing or all is the risk," added Urus. "There is no middle ground."

"We will soon know whether our choice was wise," said Faeril as they climbed up the last of the grade, the horses following.

They came in among the crags, stone pillars jutting up like great lithic sentinels surveying the slopes westward, ruddy rays of the setting Sun glancing from their unyielding flanks. A maze of sloping passages ran among them, open to the sky, widening into roofless chambers within the stony grove. Weapons in hand and leading their horses, into the labyrinth fared the five, and they found a relatively flat place where they could tether the steeds.

Riatha turned to the others. "Let us go back to where we may see the ground below and plot our course for tomorrow.

"I would remind ye all to hide that which might glimmer—Faeril, cover thy daggers; Aravan, thy crystal blade— for I would have no last stray glint from the setting Sun reveal us to watchers below. I would not have them come upon us in the dark of night, nor we to walk into a trap on the morrow's dawn."

A pulse of doom ran through Gwylly at these bodeful words, and he reached out for Faeril's hand and found her trembling. Swiftly he hugged her, whispering, "I love you," and together they followed the others through the winding crags, the damman pulling her cloak over her bandoliers.

Swiftly they came to the place where they could look down on the mosque, a half mile away and some two or three hundred feet lower down. The sinking Sun cast long shadows, yet the comrades could see well enough by its dying rays. And as they stood concealed among the pillars and peered downward, Aravan began speaking, drawing their attention to detail, detail that would perhaps be vital to their plan:

"I gauge the height of the mosque to be some one hundred feet or so from the courtyard below to the tip of the spire above, the width of its dome the same. The main building I would judge at fifty feet high, and its length mayhap at three hundred, its width slightly less.

"The wall surrounding is fifteen or twenty feet high, and it runs nigh twice the length and width of the mosque, say six or seven hundred by five.

"The minaret looks to be the same height as the mosque, a hundred feet or so. And see the two balconies evenly spaced up its sides, along with the one at the top 'neath the archways holding the cupola.

"Behind the mosque, inside the wall are three—"

"*Hsst!*" hissed Faeril, her voice tight with tension. "I saw movement in the yard: the far left corner."

Gwylly's heart hammered.

In the shadows beyond three large outbuildings along the back wall, there was a stir of motion.

" 'Tis a horse," said Riatha at last. "A paddock and stable is there."

"Probably for food," rumbled Urus. "Rutcha eat horses."

The last of the Sun dipped below the horizon, the building now in dusk. Aravan rushed to complete his description, for in this part of the world, darkness came swiftly upon the heels of twilight. "The plateau on which all sits is small, its sides steep, the mountain behind formidable.

"See, too, that the gulch swings nigh, and a twisting road leads up to the front gate, the only way that we can take our steeds."

"Are we taking the horses?" asked Gwylly.

Faeril nodded. "We should, for we may need swift transport—to pursue . . . or to flee."

Aravan laughed. "Aye, wee one, fight or flight."

Urus growled. "I do not intend to flee."

"Nor I," added Riatha.

Even as they looked on, night fell and stars winked into being. Somewhere beyond the mountains to the east a full Moon rose, its pale beams glancing through the high cols above.

"Well, Aravan," commented Faeril, "except for the minaret and the onion-shaped dome, why, this could be a fortress."

"Likely it is, wee one," responded the Elf. "A fortress, that is. Heed, as the Prophet Shat'weh's temples of worship were being built, oft they were attacked by the believers of the old ways, Gyphon's followers. And if this mosque was made in that time, then as with others I have seen, the walls will be thick, the windows barred, shuttered within, and the gates and doors difficult to breach. The outer wall will have banquettes for warriors to stand on, and arrow slits to fire on the foe. And the passages will have murder holes to rain death from above."

"Huh," grunted Gwylly. "Look, if you ask me, it's not much of a place of worship, not much of a holy place, if it was built to kill others."

Aravan clapped a hand on Gwylly's shoulder. "That, lad, I do not deny."

Faeril interlaced her fingers in Gwylly's, then turned again to Aravan. "How is it likely to be arranged on the inside?"

Aravan gazed back down at the starlit enclave. "The main hall of worship will be under the dome. Cloisters to the sides. Living quarters on the outer walls and in the back."

"Perhaps chambers below," added Riatha, "basements and sub basements."

"Oh," exclaimed Gwylly. "Like the monastery above the glacier. Almost all of their quarters were below ground."

"Aye," answered Riatha. "Mayhap."

"*Look!*" hissed Urus.

Below, a broad shaft of yellow illuminated the forecourt, as if the monastery doors had been thrown wide and light shone out. But where the comrades were ensconced, they could not see the front of the building, only the northern side and rear. That the doors had been opened became apparent, for out into the courtyard marched a squad of torch-bearing Rūcks, a Hlōk overseer at their side.

His heart pounding in his breast, Gwylly squeezed Faeril's hand to reassure her, and she did the same.

Aravan whispered, "If we did not know for certain that Stoke was below, I suspect that we do know it now."

While some of the Spawn readied to withdraw a great bar

from the front gate, others swarmed up the ramps to the walls to stand guard, the Hlōk among them.

In the still mountain air, sound drifted up to the crags, unintelligible murmurings for the most part. Yet when words did sound clear, still they could not be understood by the five, for the foe was speaking Slûk.

"I see no Vulgs," said Gwylly.

"Let us hope there are none," replied Riatha. "There is precious little gwynthyme left."

Urus shifted his stance. "If I know Stoke, he will have Vulgs about. Thrice have we met him—four times if you count the bolt-hole nigh the glacier—and each time he has had Rutcha and Drōkha and Vulgs in his train."

"And now, mayhap a Ghûlk and Hèlsteed," added Aravan. "Mayhap more than one."

"Beheading, wood through the heart, silver blade, fire, dismemberment," recited Gwylly, "those are the ways to kill a Ghûl, but what about a Hèlsteed?"

"Like a horse but not a horse," responded Aravan, "they are most dangerous. They have a hairless hide, tough as boiled leather, hard to cut. Too, they are savage, and their cloven hooves deadly. Their bite, if it does not kill outright, still may kill days later. Not poison, yet lethal if not cleansed.

"I have heard some say that their snakelike tail cuts as would a whip," added Riatha, "though others say 'tis but a rumor."

"Whip or not, get ye from behind them," said Aravan, "for their kick is nigh fatal."

"Yes," agreed Gwylly. "But how do you kill them?"

"From a distance, if possible," answered Urus, "spears, arrows, slings, quarrels. Even traps—deadfalls, pits, and the like. Up close, any weapon will do, *must* do, if you can avoid being slain by the beast first."

"Sounds worse than a Ghûl," replied Gwylly.

"Nay, Gwylly," answered Aravan. ""A Hèlsteed is merely savage and has not the cunning of a Ghûlk."

They fell silent for a while, watching the Foul Folk—setting up torches to ring the walls, opening wide the gates, as if expecting visitors.

"I wonder," murmured Faeril, "what other foe might await us down in the mosque below."

"Well," said Gwylly, "about the only thing we haven't named are Krakens and Ogrus and Dragons."

"There are other vilenesses that could await," said Aravan. "Things worse than Rucha, Loka, Ghûlka, and Trolls."

"Gargons," suggested Gwylly.

Both Aravan and Riatha sucked air in through clenched teeth, and Aravan said, "Gargoni, aye, they would be worse. Other things as well . . . yet I think none of these are likely to be in Stoke's sway."

"Unlikely, aye," agreed Riatha, "yet not beyond the realm of possibility. Recall though, as it is with all *Spaunen*, daylight will kill each and every one."

"But first," rumbled Urus, "you must lure them into the light of day."

A band of torch-bearing Rūcks marched out through the front gate, disappearing from sight on the far side of the wall. Behind them, the Rūcken warders swung the gates shut once more, sliding the drawbar back across. Beyond the fortress the marching squad came into view again, tramping down the road toward the gulch.

"Mayhap they go to patrol the canyon," said Aravan.

"Or to relieve the guard at the way station," added Faeril, "that is, if there is indeed a Rūckish bolt-hole somewhere along the ravine."

The squad marched into the gulch, turning northerly, and even though the band could not be seen down in the gully, still the five could follow their progress by the flickering glow seeping upward from their burning brands.

Finally, Urus turned to Aravan. "Alert me if anything untoward happens. I am going to care for the steeds."

"I suggest that we all return to the horses," said Riatha, "all but the one on watch. We need be rested for the morrow and cannot do so if we all of us stand ward together throughout the entire night."

Faeril said softly to Aravan, "I'll bring you water and crue."

Leaving the Elf behind, the other four slipped back and away from the ridge, following the twisting corridors among the adamant crags until they once more came to where the horses stood.

A full Moon sailing overhead, the blue stone amulet about his neck, Gwylly sat watching the mosque below. The buccan had not been able to sleep, his mind and heart seething with tomorrow's possibilities. And now he sat on guard duty, peering down at the torch-lit fortress afar, wondering what the morrow would bring.

Rūcks patrolled the high stone walls, making rounds, and occasionally indistinct voices would drift up to Gwylly from below.

The blue stone was chill but not frigid, yet when a pebble rattled behind, Gwylly jumped as if arrow shot, whirling about to face . . . Faeril coming through the crags.

"*Oh!*" hissed Gwylly. "You gave me a start, dammia."

"I couldn't sleep, Gwylly. Too many . . . possibilities."

"Hah! I know what you mean, love. All night my brain's been churning with what if's and could be's and I don't know's."

Faeril sat down beside Gwylly and took his hand in hers. "I keep thinking that the odds against us are so very great. I mean, there are just five of us, and who-knows-how-many of them . . . or even what kind? And there they are, holed up in that fortress below, Stoke's strongholt, and we don't know the arrangements of rooms, where he is within, or what traps he might have set for the unwary, or—"

"Oh, Faeril, those are the very same things I've been fretting over."

Faeril caressed his fingers. "They say that this is the calm before the storm, this time of waiting, yet I am anything but calm."

Gwylly put his arm about her shoulders, and they sat in silence and watched the mosque below. Still the Rūcks and such stood on the walls and scanned the land about, while the fulgent Moon crept up to the zenith.

Gwylly reached up and stroked Faeril's hair, her silver lock shining in the bright moonlight. The buccan smiled. "Riatha said to cover all things from which stray glints might gleam, and your silver tress—"

Faeril gasped, her hand flying to her hair. "Oh, Gwylly, do you think? . . . I had forgotten."

Gwylly pulled her to him and gave her a quick kiss. "No, love. I was just teasing. I don't believe—"

"I'd better cover it anyway," interjected Faeril, slipping her cloak hood over her head. "I wouldn't want to betray us."

Mid of night came, the Moon straight above. "Well, my buccaran, now it is I who ward and you who should go back and get some rest." Faeril held out her hand.

Gwylly took the blue stone from around his neck and handed it to the damman. "Here's your badge of office, love. But as for me getting some rest, I think instead I'll sit here with you awhile."

Taking comfort in each other's company, they sat and held hands in silence, watching.

A time passed, but then Faeril pointed. "Look, Gwylly, at the canyon. There."

Following her outstretched arm, Gwylly saw a wide band of reflected torch-light gleaming from the far lip of the steep-walled gulch. Slowly it moved toward the opening where lay the road to the front gate. And riding through came a Ghûl on Hèlsteed, accompanied by a torch-bearing Rûck on foot, and after came a file of prisoners, shackled to a long chain and flanked by Foul Folk bearing burning brands.

As Gwylly's heart hammered in his breast, Faeril gripped her buccaran's hand, tears brimming in her eyes. "Oh, Gwylly, they're bringing victims for Stoke."

"Yes, love. Men, I would say, though from here it is hard to tell."

Behind the chain of prisoners, skitting and shying, now came saddled horses and cargo-bearing camels, herded by a pack of Vulgs, the horses and camels near panic from the stench of Hèlsteed but more frightened of the black Wolf-like creatures running at their sides.

"Lor!" exclaimed Gwylly. "They *do* have Vulgs!"

"And a Ghûl and Hèlsteed, too," added Faeril.

A horn blat sounded on the still air, and as Rûcks inside ran to open the gates, raucous cheers drifted up from the walls.

"They've captured a caravan," said Faeril, wiping her eyes. "Quick, we must count what we see."

Carefully, Faeril talking, Gwylly grunting his assent, they numbered foe and prisoner alike. "One Ghûl; one Hèlsteed; one, two, three ... fourteen prisoners; seven Vulgs; nine Rūcks; three horses; eighteen camels; seven Rūcks on the walls; and—"

Suddenly Faeril fell silent. Then she hissed, "The minaret, Gwylly. Someone in the shadows."

Gwylly's gaze flew to the top of the spire. In the darkness within the crowning pavilion, a vague form could be seen, silhouetted by the torch-light beyond. But then in an ebon swirl, the figure disappeared.

"Stoke, do you believe?" whispered Gwylly, his heart racing again.

Faeril nodded, her lips drawn thin. "Yes. . . . Maybe we should waken the others."

Gwylly shook his head. "I would say not, love, for there is little we can do tonight. The fact that we may have seen Stoke changes nothing."

"Right," agreed Faeril. "Besides, if our companions sleep, rest is what's wanted, not more worry."

As the prisoners were driven through the gate and into the mosque, the horses and camels were herded 'round back to the paddock and shut within, the Rūcks began unlading the cargo from the camels and bearing it into the nearest outbuilding.

The Ghûl then rode the Hèlsteed through the sidecourt and to the cornermost outbuilding along the back wall, a Rūck opening the door, the Ghûl dismounting and leading the 'Steed inside.

Once again the front gates were closed.

A short time later, again the gates were opened and a squad marched out. Down the road and into the gully they went, their torch-light heading northward. "I counted twelve," whispered Gwylly. "Off to join the others, I suppose."

"No Vulgs went with them," said Faeril. "They are still inside the mosque."

Eventually, the Ghûl walked back through the sidecourt and entered the main building.

Another hour passed, the Moon slowly arcing across the sky, the vault of stars wheeling westward as well. Finally,

Riatha came through the shadows to join them. "Gwylly, thou should be resting, sleeping, not sitting watch with Faeril."

"I know, Riatha, but I couldn't sleep," said Gwylly, shrugging.

Faeril took the blue stone from her neck, handing it to the Elfess. "Riatha, we saw Stoke, we think. In the minaret. He watched as prisoners were brought to him. Men. A caravan, or so it would seem. Horses and camels, too."

Riatha glanced down at the distant mosque. "Was that what the horn announced?"

"You heard that, did you?" asked Gwylly. "You are not sleeping either, neh?"

Riatha smiled. "None are, I deem. Resting, aye; sleeping, nay."

The Elfess turned to Faeril. "How many prisoners? How many foe?"

"Fourteen prisoners; three horses; eighteen camels; one Ghûl; one Hèlsteed; seven Vulgs; nine Rūcks in the escort; seven Rūcks on the walls."

Gwylly added, "And afterward, twelve Rūcks marched down into the gully, heading north . . . like the others, going on patrol or to a hideaway somewhere."

"The Hèlsteed is stabled in the northernmost back building," said Faeril, "but as far as we know, the Vulgs are inside the mosque; none went with the patrol."

Riatha gazed at the mosque, a resigned look on her face. "I expected Vulgs to be within, for therein dwells a Vulgmaster."

The Elfess turned to the Waerlinga. "Go now. Rest. The morrow will come soon enough without our wakeful urging."

Faeril leading, Gwylly following, back through the stone corridors they went, back to their fireless campsite. The horses stood dozing there among the crags. To one side, Aravan appeared to be resting in the Elven state of meditation, sitting against an upthrust rock, his spear across his lap, his eyes glittering in the moonlight. Urus, too, sat leaning against a crag, his eyes closed.

Gwylly and Faeril spread out their blankets and snuggled down together, trying to get comfortable on the stony ground, and neither thought that sleep would ever come . . .

. . . But moments later, it seemed, Riatha gently wakened them.

Dawn was pale in the sky beyond the eastern mountains.

They watered the horses and fed them grain, and then took a quick meal of their own. Gwylly, his heart thudding, picked at his crue biscuit until Urus said, "Gwylly, on a campaign or when readying for battle, heed the warrior's creed: 'Eat at opportunity, for you know not when you will feed again.' "

The buccan took a large bite of the waybread, chewing without appetite, consuming it nevertheless.

"Are the Vulgs still inside?" asked Faeril.

"None left during my watch or Urus's," replied Riatha. "None came from the canyon either. And now the gates are shut and barred."

Gwylly swallowed. "So the mosque is still filled with Foul Folk: Rūcks, Hlōks, Vulgs, and a Ghûl."

The buccan took another bite of his crue. "And a Hèlsteed out back."

"Aye," replied Riatha. "Yet heed: Our task is to get in, find Stoke, slay him, and get back out. We are not on a mission to kill Foul Folk. And so, stealth and cunning is called for, and not the slaughter of *Spaunen.*

"They will disband soon enough when their master is dead."

Aravan looked up. "If Stoke is the one *I* seek, the Man with the yellow eyes, then there is the matter of the Dawn Sword. It may be hidden within the mosque, and if so, I would recover it."

"I will aid you in that event," rumbled Urus.

Aravan looked at the others, and each nodded. "We need sail that sea only if we come to it," said the Elf.

"What about the prisoners?" asked Faeril. "We can't just leave them caged."

Urus grunted. "If captives yet live, we will free them. But I do not hold hope that any survive."

"Beyond the mountains the Sun now lips the unseen horizon," said Riatha. "Let us go."

They led the horses out from the crags and down the slopes till they came to where they could safely ride. Mounting up, Gwylly before Riatha, Faeril before Aravan, they headed for the point where the road came up out of the gully, for the road was the only way to reach the surface of the steep-sided plateau by horse.

Slowly down the grades they fared, the stony ground rough and canted. And off to their left rose the mosque, its ruddy sides and orange dome dark in mountain shadow cast by the rising Sun beyond.

They passed the plateau and moved on toward the gulch, until at last they came to where the horses could lunge up the bordering slope and onto the surface of the road. Turning back easterly, toward the red walls they climbed, following the road through several switchbacks and up. Leftward at the corner, the minaret spiked upward, its cupola a hundred feet above the wall. In wall center stood the gate, huge iron-clad panels. Beyond the gate they could see the upper floors of the mosque and the dome above.

As they climbed toward the structure, Gwylly took a deep breath and then turned to Riatha. "Riatha, why is my heart racing so? I mean, I've trained for this mission, and yet I find that I am not prepared."

Riatha smiled at the buccan. "All of our hearts are pounding, Gwylly. No training I know of steels one against a hammering heart. It is a consequence of facing the unknown. Believe me, though, thou are prepared, for when comes the time to act, thou will find thy hands and heart, body and mind in total concert, as thou were trained to do."

"I hope you are right, Riatha. I hope you are right."

At last they came before the barred gates and dismounted.

"I will climb the wall and open them," said Urus, handing the reins of his steed to Aravan, then uncoiling a line and hook.

Casting the grapnel across the wall and taking up slack and setting the tine, Urus scrambled up and over the barrier, some twenty feet high. Soon they heard the sound of the drawbar being pulled, and moments later, protesting on its axles, the rightmost gate swung wide, Urus pushing it outward on its concealed hinges. Through the opening a hundred feet past they could see part of a portico, and beyond stood a great bronze door set in building center.

Aravan put a finger to his lips and said softly, "E'en though it is day, when the Foul Folk sleep, still I caution quietness, for inside closed chambers of this fortress, some *Spaunen* may stand watch during the sunlight hours."

Weapons in hand, into the forecourt they went, leading the horses, and all was eerily silent but for the clip-clop of hooves.

Now they could see the full front of the mosque, a great facade running its width. Bell-shaped openings were spaced evenly across the breadth of this facing, echoed in kind up three tiers one above the other. On each tier ran porches the full width, porches reaching back perhaps fifty feet in depth ere fetching up against the main building. In the center stood the largest opening, fully fifty feet wide and reaching up all three floors, the great bronze door beyond. The remainder of the openings stood but twelve feet high, past which they could see heavily barred windows on each tier, their sills deep in shadow, showing only darkness within.

They tied their horses to the ring posts embedded in the facade flanking the main opening, and then stepped up through the arch and onto the wide porch, crossing over to come to the bronze door. To either side of the portal were arrow slits, deep and narrow, and Gwylly could see back in the recess, iron shutters on the inside of the building, sealing the slots tight.

Urus tried the bronze door, pushing and pulling. It would not open. "Barred."

"The windows, too," whispered Aravan. "Metal shutters on the inside as well."

Across the width of the porch they went, finding the other windows barred and shuttered, too.

They found steps leading up to the porches above, yet no entrance did they find open, doors of bronze locked tight, windows barred and shuttered.

Back down they went and around the building, past the paddock with its camels, though of horses they saw none. But no entry into the mosque did they find, though they tried all doors and peered through all windows and arrow slits, doors and windows barred, iron shutters slammed to and locked.

And the Sun rose above the mountains, though the fortress mosque yet stood in the shadow of the slope of the mountain directly behind, and would do so until nearly midday.

Circling on around, toward the front they went, Faeril fretting. "Surely there must be a way in." As they passed one of the smaller doors, she asked, "What about the Bear? Could he break down one of these?"

Urus shook his head. "Perhaps. Perhaps not. Yet I would rather we find a different way, for it is as Riatha said— stealth and cunning is wanted here, neither of which is a strength of the Bear. I would rather go in as a Man, for as we saw at the citadel during your rescue, the Bear is too unpredictable."

"Nay, Faeril. Now is not the time for the Bear to come calling upon Baron Stoke."

"Something has been nagging at the back of my mind," said Gwylly, "but I can't quite— Hoy, now, wait a moment, it just flitted past.

"Look, when we saw Stoke in the minaret, he disappeared downward—"

Faeril clapped her hands. "And didn't cross the courtyard! Oh Gwylly, you are a marvel!" She grabbed her buccaran and kissed him.

"There's got to be an underground passage," said Gwylly, grinning over his dammia's shoulder. "And if it is open . . ."

They crossed the yard to the minaret. A small bronze door stood at the base . . . barred. "If we choose to break down any door," said Urus, "this will be the one."

The Baeran eyed up the sides of the spire. Two ring balconies were evenly spaced up its height, two balconies between the courtyard at the bottom and the cupola at the top. "Five spans to the first, five to the second, five more to the top."

"Spans?" said Gwylly.

"Fathoms," answered Aravan. "Six feet to a span."

"Oh."

Again Urus uncoiled his rope and grapnel. "Stand back. I might miss."

He did not, and up he clambered, coming to the first balcony and over. There he found another barred door.

Casting the grapnel again, up he went to the second ring balcony, and the door there was barred as well.

When he reached the top, he disappeared a moment, then leaned back over the railing and waved.

Long moments passed, and of a sudden they heard the bar on the door being set aside, and it swung open, Urus grinning. "There was only an unbarred trapdoor at the top," he said, then gestured in and downward, "and we will need lanterns, for there is a way below."

Aravan and Faeril went to the horses and took three tiny hooded lanterns from the saddlebags. When they returned, Aravan said, "I suggest that Faeril, Riatha, and Urus bear the lamps. Gwylly and I need two hands for our weaponry."

Riatha nodded and took a lantern, lighting it with the spark igniter on the side. "To avoid discovery, keep the hoods shielded. Enough light will seep out to show the way."

Into the minaret they went. A spiral stair wound upward to the cupola above, daylight shining down from the open trapdoor aloft. Before them a dark opening gaped, and they could see a straight set of stairs angling down and under the courtyard in the direction of the mosque.

Through the opening and down the stairwell they went, Urus in the lead, Riatha coming after, then Gwylly and Faeril side by side, Aravan last.

Again Gwylly's heart hammered, and to distract himself he began counting his footsteps, measuring how far they had gone.

Thirty steps they descended, coming to a landing where a portcullis barred the way, the sharp teeth of the grille bottomed out in sockets, holes drilled in the stone. Beyond the grate a narrow corridor stretched out before them, running straight, continuing toward the mosque. Along one wall a distance away stood the barway windlass. Urus and Aravan tried lifting the portcullis, to no avail. "Down and locked," Urus said softly.

"How can we open it?" asked Faeril. "I mean, is there a key or some such?"

Riatha pointed at the winch beyond. "See that lever behind the windlass? That is the key. Throw the lever, and the barway can then be lifted."

Faeril pressed her head against the bars and looked.

"I say," said Gwylly, "if those rods were set just a bit

farther apart, or even bowed a bit, I believe Faeril and I could slip through."

Aravan looked at the bars. "Too heavy to bend by hand, even for someone such as Urus, but if we had a large enough lever . . ."

"How about the bar from the door above?" asked Faeril.

Aravan shook his head. "Too short."

"Then a heavy rail from the paddock fence," suggested Faeril.

Several minutes later, Urus and Aravan carried the post rail down the steps and to the portcullis. They slipped it between the bars at the midpoint between floor and ceiling, where the give would be the greatest. Then together, Urus on the end, Aravan next, then Riatha, they threw their weight and strength against the lever, straining mightily. Slowly the bars gave, but then the end of the rail fetched up against the wall.

"Try it now," said Urus, lifting Gwylly to the bend in the bars. But the Warrow could not get his head through. "It needs more widening," said the buccan.

"Here, let me try," said Faeril, slipping out of her bandoliers and doffing her cloak, unbuckling her long-knife and dagger.

With Urus holding her, Faeril, hissing at the pain as she scraped against bars, managed to force her head through the gap. Then contorting her body and wriggling, she pressed on past, alighting at last on the floor beyond the barrier.

And suddenly Gwylly's heart was hammering again, for his dammia was there and he was here, and should Foul Folk come at this very moment— Gwylly shook his head to clear it of these dire thoughts, but still his heart raced in his breast.

"Here," said Riatha, passing the bandoliers through the bars.

Taking the belts of knives in hand, the damman ran lightly to the lever beyond the windlass, and struggling, managed to throw it, unlocking the portal.

Urus now slid the fence rail under the grille and lifted, iron protesting as it squealed up the track. Gwylly was the first to slide through the gap below the exposed iron fangs, embracing Faeril the moment he gained his feet. Riatha quickly followed, with Aravan immediately after. Aravan tested the use of the windlass to raise the portcullis, but even with a slight turn they knew that the clacking of the ratchet and squealing of the iron grate along its tracks would make entirely too much noise. And so, as Aravan, Riatha, Gwylly, and Faeril used the rail to lever the complaining portcullis upward, Urus slid under.

Faeril donned her weaponry and cloak and nodded to the others.

Along the narrow stone hall they trod, stepping softly, the daylight seeping down the stairwell behind fading as they went. And Gwylly thought that he could hear muttering in the distance.

"Riatha," he whispered, "do you hear murmurings?"

"Aye," she replied. "Echoes of distant voices."

Soon they were treading through a blackness pressed back only by the dim gleams leaking from the hooded lanterns they bore. But then, far ahead they heard the tramp of feet and a grumble of voices, and saw a growing glimmer of light. Shielding their lanterns under their cloaks, they flattened themselves against the walls.

In the distance a band of torch-bearing Foul Folk marching along a cross hall shuttered past the corridor, voices and light piercing the shadows. And Gwylly turned his eyes aside, not wanting their reflection to reveal the presence of the five.

Swiftly all the band passed 'cross, the light and sound fading as they tramped onward.

Gwylly exhaled, and only then realized that he had been holding his breath.

"Let's go," hissed Urus, and forward they slipped through the gloom, their lanterns leaking tiny beams past the metal hoods.

Soon they came to a junction, perhaps two hundred and fifty feet from the minaret by Gwylly's reckoning, though he wasn't certain at all, having lost count when the Spawn had marched past in the distance. Corridors angled off to left and right, doorways and archways opening into these halls. Voices could still be heard in the distance, and some archways dimly glowed with faint light, as if torches lay somewhere beyond.

Across the junction, the narrow passage continued straight ahead, silent and dark. "I deem we are in the basement of the mosque," breathed Riatha, "below the outer cloisters. Angling to the right is a passage under the front of the mosque; to the left, the north side of the temple. Ahead should lie the main chamber beneath the dome."

"If there is a chamber under the dome," whispered Urus, "then that is where Stoke will be—in the center of things, surrounded by his lackeys."

Riatha nodded, agreeing.

Peering left and right, seeing no torch-lit marchers, one at a time across the intersection they silently flitted.

They continued onward, travelling but another twenty feet or so ere coming to the bottom of a set of stairs rising upward to a closed door. Up these steps—thirty-two in all—went Urus ... Riatha, Gwylly, Faeril, and Aravan following.

Behind them again sounded voices and the tread of ironshod boot. Shielding their lanterns once more, they stood silently in the dark at the top of the stairs. Another squad marched past in the corridor below.

When it was gone, Urus at the doorway looked back at the others, receiving a nod from each and every one. Slowly the Baeran turned the ring post. With a soft *snick* the latch opened, and pushing gently, Urus gradually swung the door wide, the hinges squealing faintly.

From beyond, torch-light shone in and down the stairs, accompanied by a mutter of echoing voices. Urus peered outward and then stepped through, Riatha on his heels, Gwylly and Faeril and Aravan coming after.

They entered the main chamber of the mosque, the hollow dome high in the shadows overhead. Torches burned in room center, at the corners of a dais there, casting wavering light into the gloom. The hall was empty of Spawn, though their voices murmured throughout. The room was huge and square, a hundred and fifty feet along a side. But for the torch-lit dais and altar in mid room, centered under the dome, the chamber was completely barren of all furnishings.

Midway along the front wall stood an archway, and archways yawned at the midpoints of the side walls as well.

Gwylly pointed. "There I think is the way to the front entrance, but these others, I cannot say where they might lead . . . to the cloisters, I suppose."

"Where to now?" asked Faeril.

Urus looked toward the far back of the chamber. There a fourth archway stood. "In the monastery above the glacier, the sacristy was behind the main chamber. Beyond it and down, we found Stoke."

"Let us go," whispered Riatha.

Along the wall they scurried, the tramp of Rūcken feet and mutter of *Spaunen* voices rising and falling as the five slipped through the shadows. Just as they reached the side archway, suddenly, looming through came a monstrous figure. Huge it was, hulking, fourteen feet high, looking like a giant Rūck but no Rūck this; instead it was an Ogru.

"Troll!" shouted Riatha.

And right behind came a squad of Rūcks and Hlōks.

Surprise flashed on the Ogru's features, then rage. *RRRAAAWWW!* the monster leapt at Urus, its massive hands outstretched to crush this intruder.

Urus sprang aside and swung his morning star with all his strength, and the spiked iron ball crashed into the Ogru's stonelike hide, jarring the creature back, the Troll roaring in pain and rage.

Boiling inward came yawling the Rūcks and Hlōks, cudgels and scimitars in hand, their charge bearing Riatha and the Warrows backwards into Aravan.

"*Krystallopýr*," whispered Aravan, Truenaming his spear, leaping forward, attempting to win through the press to aid Urus, but a tulwar-bearing Hlōk came between the Elf and the Troll. Aravan parried the Hlōk's edge with the haft of his spear, then cut sideways with the crystal blade, the burning point searing through the foe's abdomen, entrails spilling forth. The Hlōk shrieked and fell dying, but two others took his place, charging at Aravan, their weapons raised for slaughter.

Gwylly let fly with a sling bullet, the missile crashing into the skull of a charging Rūck, and Faeril threw steel to bring down another. Yet the remaining Rūcks overbore Faeril and Gwylly, but Riatha hurled them back, Dúnamis singing of death.

Somewhere a horn blatted, its raucous call summoning aid.

Again Urus leapt aside and hammered the Troll with the morning star, a bone breaking in the monster's rib cage, the Ogru bellowing in pain. Risking a glance at his companions, Urus yelled, "Get to a place of safety!" But in that same moment the Troll swept up Urus and clasped the Man to him and squeezed, the creature's huge arms bulging with effort, Urus attempting to hammer at the Ogru, but he was unable to bring his weapon to bear. Perhaps as the Bear he could have resisted the Troll, even slain it, yet there had been no time for the transformation, for the Ogru was upon them ere any choice could be made. And now Urus dangled in the monster's awful grasp as would a child dangle in the grasp of a grown-up, his struggles futile, feeble.

"Urus!" shrieked Riatha, and started forward. But once more the Rūcks charged the Waerlinga, and again Riatha leapt to their defense.

Gwylly hurled a bullet at the Ogru, and it cracked against the Troll's skull, only to glance away from the granite-like bone. And then a yowling Rūck was upon the buccan, cudgel whistling down. A steel knife sprang full blown in the Rūck's throat, driving him back, yet even as the foe fell dead the bludgeon struck with force, knocking Gwylly from his feet, stunning him.

In that same moment there came a horrid cracking sound, the Ogru crushing Urus's bones, the Man slack, lifeless, blood bubbling from his mouth. Then the Ogru hurled the Baeran against the wall, Urus's broken body smashing into the stone and falling with a sodden thud, the Troll leaping after and pawing at Urus's frame, making certain the Man was dead.

Faeril stood above her fallen buccaran, a knife in either hand, shrieking a warcry in Twyll: *"Blūt vor blūt!"*

Aravan yanked Krystallopŷr from the chest of a Hlōk and closed ranks with Riatha, his crystal spear ready to pierce the foe she battled, but Riatha's starsilver blade, slashed through the enemy's throat, the Ruch staggering hindward clutching his neck, then crashing to the stone.

The remaining Spawn wrenched back, fear standing in their eyes.

Riatha now saw Urus's body, the Ogru looming above. "Urus!" she screamed, starting forward, but Aravan barred her way, clutching her, holding her back.

"There is nought thou can do, Dara!" his voice cracked out sharply. "'We are too late."

"Urus!" she cried again, struggling to break free.

"No, Dara," grated Aravan. "Instead we must heed Urus's last words and get to a place of safety."

The Elfess shook her head to clear her tears, her gaze shifting from Urus's body to the Ogru pawing the lifeless form. "Not until I kill the Troll," snarled Riatha, gripping Dúnamis, trying to push past Aravan . . . but he yielded not.

"The Waerlinga, Dara, the Waerlinga. Now is the time to protect the living and not to avenge the dead."

Riatha looked at Faeril above Gwylly, the buccan just now floundering to his feet, then at Urus and the Troll.

Behind shrieked a screech of metal, and Riatha turned in time to see a portcullis crash down *Blang!* over the door they had entered.

And still a *Rûptish* horn blatted an alarm.

As Gwylly shook off the last of the stunning, "The front entrance," gritted Riatha.

Even as she spoke, the Troll turned from Urus and started toward the four, Rūcks and Hlōks howling in glee.

Whirling in their tracks, toward the gaping arch in the front wall they ran, racing for their very lives, and above the yowling of the Spawn and the blaring of the horn, they could hear the thunderous tread of the Ogru hammering across the chamber at their heels, the Rūcks and such coming after.

Ahead of the Troll they dashed through the archway, coming into a vestibule some twenty-five feet wide and fifty feet long. Somewhere in the shadows ahead lay the door, but there, too, was a portcullis, down and locked, butted against the outer door, the portcullis clamping the crossbar in place.

"No!" shrilled Gwylly when he saw the barrier, the buc-can turning to look for the winch and lock, as Aravan and Riatha whirled about to meet the charge of the Troll, the monster just now stooping to enter the vestibule, Rūcks and Hlōks in his wake.

Gwylly's gaze darted left and right; there was no winch, no side doors either. Overhead, he saw machicolations—slots above—murder holes through which to rain destruction down upon invading foe. Over the archway back into the main chamber was a long slot, and the fangs of a raised portcullis could be seen, the vestibule a death trap for any who entered.

A death trap *they* had entered.

But death did not pour down from above. Instead it took the form of a great Ogru, flanked on either side by leering Rūcks and Hlōks.

Desperately, Gwylly spun about and began hammering on one of the iron shutters covering an arrow slit.

The Ogru struck at Aravan, the Elf ducking under the blow as Riatha sprang forward and slashed Dúnamis against the Troll's flank, but the starsilver sword merely glanced from the Ogru's hide. The monster roared and backhandedly slapped the Elfess aside, smashing her into the vestibule wall, Dúnamis lost to her grasp, skittering across the stone.

A Hlōk leaped toward the fallen Elfess, but Faeril hurled a steel knife, felling the *Rûpt*, the other Spawn recoiling.

Aravan stepped under the Troll's grasp, thrusting Krystal-lopŷr up and in, the burning blade piercing deep into the Ogru's abdomen, the monster yawling. With a wrenching motion Aravan drove the blade sideways, the crystal yet deep inside the creature's gut. Wide flew the Troll's eyes as Ara-van thrust upwards, stabbing deeper, Krystallopŷr bursting through the monster's heart, the Troll staggering backwards, Aravan jerking the spear free, the crystal blade blazing. Several steps the Ogru reeled hindward, black blood spilling out onto the stone, rock sizzling and popping where the ichor fell, dark smoke rising. And then the monster crashed dead to the stone floor.

And in the archway beyond stood a Man.

With yellow eyes.

Stoke.

And snarling Vulgs stood at his side.

"*Balak!*" he shouted, and with a shrieking of iron the inner portcullis thundered down *Clang!* plummeting into the sockets in the floor, a sharp *Clack!* sounding as somewhere above a bolt shot home, locking the grille in place.

"*Gluktu glush!*" he commanded, and the Rūcks and Hlōks within the vestibule surged forward.

And in that same moment Gwylly finally got the latch on the shutter free. "Take *this*, you *skuts!*" he shouted, the buccan wrenching the hinged cover aside, the panel screeching open, daylight streaming in through the narrow slot.

The Spawn caught directly in the light only had time to look up in horror as they collapsed and crumbled to dust. Those to the side turned to flee, but instead fell shrieking, and they withered and shrivelled, their limbs twisting grotesquely, their ribs collapsing, chests falling inward, their screams chopped short as if by a blade. The body of the slain Troll crumbled to dust, a massive skeleton momentarily appearing, and then the ligaments and cartilage in the joints crumbled, and the heavy bones separated from one another and clattered to the stone. From above, shrill cries pierced downward through the machicolations, along with a grim tattoo of creatures thrashing in agony, and then nought but ash sifted downward.

And beyond the portcullis, as the Vulgs collapsed, Stoke howled in agony and jerked back and aside, a hurtling silver knife flashing past, grazing his ear, blood flying, the blade clanging to the floor in the darkness far beyond as Stoke disappeared in the shadows.

And silence fell, grim and complete.

Faeril turned to Gwylly to see that he was all right. Then she knelt at Riatha's side, placing her ear to the Elfess's breast. As she did so, Riatha stirred, and Faeril began chafing the Elfess's hand, calling out, "Riatha. Riatha."

Aravan stepped past the Troll bones and knelt beside Faeril and swiftly examined the Elfess. "She is but stunned and even now recovers."

Gwylly came and stroked Faeril's hair. The damman

looked up at him. "I threw and I missed," she said, "missed Stoke. And he escaped."

"Stoke was here?" blurted Gwylly. "I didn't see him. That shutter . . . I almost didn't get it open."

"But thou did, Gwylly," said Aravan, smiling, "saving us all, I deem."

Tears trickled down Riatha's cheeks, the Elfess weeping even as she regained consciousness, murmuring, "*Chieran. Avó, chieran.*"

Tears sprang to Faeril's and Gwylly's eyes, and Aravan stood and walked to the barway. After a moment he said, "We must find a way out of this trap."

Gwylly, wiping his eyes, stepped to the inner portcullis beside the Elf, and they both looked back into the main hall of the mosque. Beyond the reach of the daylight streaming in through the open shutter, one of Faeril's silver daggers lay in the shadows on the floor, its blade glittering in the torchlight from the altar. Against the far wall lay Urus's lifeless body. Swiftly Gwylly looked away, for he knew that now was not the time to grieve.

The buccan cleared his throat and attempted to swallow his sorrow, yet his voice broke as through brimming eyes he examined the grate before them. Wiping his tears on his sleeve, he said, "Mayhap we can bend these bars as we did the others. We will need a lever, though."

The buccan turned, his sight flying to the Troll bones. "Perhaps the thighbone . . ." He stepped to the femur and tried to heft it—"Oof!"—the bone nearly four feet long. Yet its weight was more than the Warrow could lift, though he did get one end up off the floor somewhat. "Lor, but this is heavy."

"Troll bones and Dragonhide," said Aravan, stepping to Gwylly's side. "Mayhap it is because they are so solid that they are impervious to Adon's Ban." Aravan lifted the thighbone, grunting with the effort, bearing it to the portcullis, where he dropped it thudding to the stone floor.

Riatha stood and wiped her eyes with the heel of her hand. Faeril retrieved the starsilver sword and gave it over to the Elfess, Riatha sheathing it in the shoulder harness.

Together, damman and Elfess stepped to the portcullis,

Riatha's bleak gaze drawn to Urus's crumpled form lying in the shadows afar.

"Dara, we will mourn later," said Aravan, his voice gentle. "Now we must strive to escape this trap, for we must do so ere the Sun goes down."

Unable to speak, the Elfess nodded.

"I deem the lock and winch somewhere above," said Aravan, looking at the machicolations overhead. "Can we find the way up, then we can raise not only this portcullis but the one barring the outer door as well."

Gwylly stepped to the femur. "Then let us get to it."

"The bone, it may not be a long enough lever, Gwylly," said Aravan, "yet we will try."

"How can we help?" asked Faeril. "I mean, Gwylly and I. If you put it up where the bars are easiest to bend, then we cannot reach it. And you will need our strength, for Urus is not—" Faeril's words chopped off.

No one said aught for a moment, but then Aravan spoke: "First Riatha and I will try. If we cannot warp the bars, then we will loop a rope about the lever and through the bars and back for ye to hale upon."

"*Hsst!*" hissed Riatha. "Someone moves above."

They heard the scrape of footsteps overhead, and a rolling sound as of a glass bottle. Suddenly, down through a murder hole a glittering sphere dropped, shattering on the floor. Bilious green fumes whooshed forth.

"Hold thy breath!" shouted Riatha. " 'Tis gas!"

Gwylly gasped in a great breath and pressed his mouth shut. Another sphere plummeted into the vestibule and shattered, and more yellowish-green vapor billowed forth.

Aravan gestured to Gwylly and Faeril and Riatha, and they lay on the floor with their faces at the portcullis, where the way was open to the large chamber beyond.

Behind them, more glass spheres dropped through and shattered.

Gwylly could now see the sickly vapors drifting past them and into the altar room. And he gripped Faeril's hand and held his breath, clamping his lips tightly, his lungs screaming to breathe, his abdomen heaving, his body desperate for air, blackness swirling at the edges of his vision, sucking at his consciousness. *No!* his mind screamed. *I will not breathe! . . .*

. . . And yet in the end he could do nought else, and with great gasps he drew in the yellow-green fumes and his mind spun down into the boundless dark.

# CHAPTER 40

# Vengeance

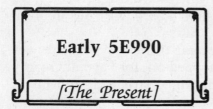

**Early 5E990**

*[The Present]*

*F*aeril stood in a graveyard, in a slaughter house, in a charnel house, and watched as Lord Death, as a butcher, as Baron Stoke, swung his deadly scythe, sledged cattle, slaughtered Humans, Elves, Dwarves, Warrows. Rūcks stood back and jeered, blood slathering down their arms as they plunged their grasping hands into the carcasses of slain horses, rending and wrenching free dangling gobbets of raw meat, gore oozing. Flies buzzed incessantly and a ghastly stench of death hung over all. Somewhere high above, there where the light dimly glowed, she could hear Gwylly calling her name.*

*Moaning in dread and lunging against the shackles, slowly Faeril struggled up through the ebon shadows and toward the light, dragging great, long chains behind, horrible images in the darkness all about—blood flying, bones breaking, intestines spilling, some images hideous beyond description, the mind refusing to comprehend what the eyes had seen—the damman struggling toward her buccaran's voice as Gwylly called . . . and called . . . and called . . .*

Even as Faeril regained consciousness, she could hear herself groaning in terror, the nightmare clinging. A foul, putrid smell overlay the air. And she opened her eyes to find herself

lying on a stone floor of a dimly lit chamber. She could hear
Gwylly calling from behind, and she rolled over to see the
buccan kneeling a short distance away. And now she saw
that he was fettered, iron cuffs about his wrists, chains anchored in the stone wall.

Faeril groaned and sat up, her vision swimming with the
mere effort, and found her own wrists ironbound, rattling
links connecting her to heavy studs embedded in rock.

A look of relief mingled with anxiety washed over Gwylly's face. "Oh, love, are you all right?"

Faeril took a deep breath and shook her head, trying to
clear it of the dizziness, trying as well to clear it of the
remnants of the horrid dream. "I'm a bit lightheaded,
Gwylly."

"That'll pass, love. The green gas, you know. . . . You have
the right of it: deep breaths help. Through your mouth,
though."

Faeril breathed in and out several times. "Where are we?
And where are—" Her words chopped off, for beyond Gwylly
and shackled as well lay Aravan and Riatha, Elf and Elfess
unconscious. "Are they all right, Gwylly?"

"They are breathing, love. And I've seen them move."

Gwylly lifted a hand and gestured outward away from the
wall. "As to where we are . . . well, my dammia, some kind
of Hèlhole, I would say."

Faeril looked into the gloom and recoiled, a moan escaping
from her lips. Corpses were strewn throughout the darkness—grinning jaws agape, sightless eyes staring, their flesh
a horrid dark red, as of dried blood all over. . . .

. . . And then Faeril saw that they had been *flayed*.

And *impaled*.

Split from crotch to navel, abdomens burst open, entrails
spilling out.

*I am still trapped in my nightmare!*

But no nightmare this; instead it was horribly real.

Faeril covered her face with her hands, but still she could
see the images. And smell the putrescent stench.

"Oh, Gwylly . . ."

Gwylly's voice came softly. "I know, love. I know."

Not looking at the dead, Faeril crawled to the limit of her
chains toward her buccaran, haling up short. "They're not

long enough for prisoners to reach one another," said Gwylly.

Faeril examined the fetters and links. Made of iron, the shackles were key locked, and they gripped snugly about the wrists. The chains themselves were perhaps five feet long, anchored in the wall some three feet up from the floor.

For long moments Faeril sat gathering her nerve, bracing herself for what she knew had to come next. *All right, my dammsel dear, you can't plan an escape if you don't look to see what's here.* Faeril gritted her teeth and stood and forced her gaze out into the shadowed chamber, her sight sliding over the decaying corpses.

The room was illuminated by a small chain-hung oil lamp in chamber center, but it cast enough light for her to see that the huge room itself was virtually square, some sixty feet or so to a side and perhaps sixteen feet to the ceiling, from which hung other oil lamps, unlit. Centered about the middle of the room, four stone pillars stood at the corners of a twenty-foot square, supporting a structure of heavy beams crisscrossing overhead.

Beside each pillar sat a long, narrow table, and with a sinking heart Faeril could see that each was bloodstained and fitted with straps for holding prisoners down.

Beneath the lamp sat another table on which were tools, implements, and except for the tongs and thin-bladed knives, Faeril could not identify any.

In mid-room as well, chains and shackles hung down from the overhead beams, the dangling fetters some eight feet above the floor.

Against a far wall, what Faeril had first taken for a corpse in the shadows instead were saddlebags and bedrolls and their weaponry, all heaped in a pile. Faeril's heart clenched at the sight of Urus's morning star, but she shook her head— *I will grieve later*—and wrested her thoughts back to the task at hand.

Located at the midpoints of the walls were shadowed wooden doorways, closed. And except for where each door stood, manacles and chains were studded at regular intervals around the room, enough to hold sixteen prisoners in all, four along each flank, two on either side of a door.

Faeril and Gwylly were anchored next to one another,

Faeril closest to a doorway, Gwylly between her and the nearest corner. Riatha lay 'round the corner adjacent to Gwylly, and Aravan beyond the Elfess.

As Faeril's gaze lingered on her companions, Riatha stirred and opened her eyes, the Elfess breathing deeply, trying to rid herself of the dregs of the gas.

And while Riatha slowly recovered, Faeril continued her survey of their prison, now forcing herself to look at the dead, glancing swiftly from one to another. *Thank Adon, Urus is not among them.*

Again she looked at the corpses, the bodies splayed, arms and legs akimbo. Stripped of clothing, all were armed as if for battle, and some wore helms or vambraces or greaves, the metal strapped against raw meat and bones of head or arms or legs. Some of the slain were obviously long dead, while others seemed freshly slaughtered. All had been flayed and impaled. Faeril counted: nine rotting, their flesh decomposed, sloughing away; fourteen newly killed, butchered like cattle, not yet falling into decay. *Nine old victims. Fourteen new. Now where—?* Faeril gasped, realizing, *The fourteen caravan prisoners: Stoke has murdered them all!* Faeril wrenched her eyes away, unable to look upon this butchery any longer.

Riatha now sat with her back to the wall, her silver gaze taking in the chamber and its horrid occupants.

Aravan began to stir.

Faeril searched throughout her clothing, looking for anything that might be used as a picklock, though she had no skill in such. "Nothing," she said at last, glancing up at Aravan.

The Elf looked at Gwylly. The buccan shook his head, *No.* Aravan turned to Riatha, the Elfess gazing across the room at Urus's morning star. She, too, shook her head, *No.* "I thought not," said Aravan. "They have stripped us of all that could do so."

Gwylly slumped back down, then looked up. "Have you your amulet, Aravan?"

Aravan nodded. "Aye, and it is chill. Like as not Stoke's lackeys fear it, will not touch it unless driven so."

The Elf turned and braced his feet against the wall and took up the slack in the right-hand chain. Not for the first time, he strained to break a link or pull the stud from the stone—to no avail.

"Some pickle, neh?" said Gwylly.

"Wha—what, Gwylly?" asked Faeril. "I didn't hear you."

"I said, it's some pickle we've gotten ourselves into this time, is it not so?"

The damman looked at her buccaran. "And one we are not likely to get out of alive either."

Though they could not touch, Gwylly held his hand out to her. "Ah, love, we yet breathe. And where there's life . . . what I mean is, we must be ready to seize any chance to get free. If even one of us survives, then there's still a possibility we can bring down Stoke—and speaking of Stoke, he may already be dead, killed by daylight."

Riatha shook her head. "Nay, Gwylly, I think he survived the light of the Sun. The glass spheres that dropped through the murder holes, Stoke used such once before."

"I know," responded the buccan. "I read it in the journal of the Firstborns."

"What is the hour, I wonder?" asked Faeril.

"Nearing sunset," answered Aravan, his Elven gift unimpaired by his imprisonment.

Faeril's heart thudded in her breast at Aravan's words. "I expect that we will soon know, then, whether or not Stoke yet lives."

It was nigh mid of night when the clack of bolts being shot and the clatter of key in lock and the clank of a bar being set aside announced the arrival of Baron Stoke.

The door swung open and in he came, accompanied by an escort of a half-dozen dusky Hlōks bearing cudgels and tulwars, the long curved blades glinting red in the lantern light. And in the shadows behind Baron Stoke came a Ghûl. Too, inward scurried two Rūcks, the swart *Rûpt* scuttling about the chamber to light oil lamps, driving back the shadows.

And Stoke bore with him a long golden stake, triangular steel blades glittering down its length.

Stoke paused a moment at the table containing the devices, as if to assure himself that all were present. Pallid he was and tall, with black hair and hands long and slender. His face was long and narrow, his nose straight and thin, his white cheeks unbearded. Dark humor played at the corners of his mouth, and when he smiled, long teeth gleamed, the canines sharp. He appeared to be in his thirties, though his actual age was nearer sixteen hundred years, a thousand of which he had spent trapped in a glacier. And then he looked up at his captives; his eyes were a pale amber—yellow, some would say.

Faeril shrank back against the stone wall, and Gwylly stood and stepped toward her, as if to come between his dammia and Stoke, yet his chains would not allow.

Riatha now stood, her silvery-grey gaze fixed upon this kinslayer before her, her eyes filled with bitter hatred.

Aravan's shoulders sagged, and he spoke in Sylva. ["Although he resembles Galarun's killer, this is not the yellow-eyed Man I seek."]

With care, Stoke lay the golden spike among the other instruments, and then came and stood before his prisoners, his fists on his hips, his yellow eyes gloating.

Immediately behind him stood the Man-sized Ghûl, dead black soulless eyes glittering in pasty white flesh, a red gash of a mouth filled with pointed yellow teeth, a cruelly barbed spear in his hand, a wide, spiked steel collar about his neck. Yet one side of his face was hideously blistered, as if he had been burned, and the hand gripping the spear was scalded as well, knuckles flame charred, wrist and forearm seared.

And he looked upon Gwylly with hatred in his eyes, as if he would murder the buccan, a hollow snarl growling deep in his chest.

Yet Stoke paid the Ghûl no heed, and instead one by one he gazed long at each of his captives, his eyes widening slightly at the sight of Faeril and Gwylly. Then his mad glare settled upon Riatha, and he spoke in a whisper that made Faeril shudder with the sound of it. "It has been long since I have had the pleasure of *harvesting* an Elf"—his yellow eyes flicked in Aravan's direction—"much less two."

Riatha stood in grim silence, her fists clenched.

Stoke's gaze swung to the Warrows and then back. "I am

surprised that these two yet accompany you, Elfess, for I did not know their Kind to be this long-lived, and they will please me much."

Faeril glanced at Gwylly and then back to Stoke. *Adon! He thinks we are Tomlin and Petal.*

Stoke glanced at the far wall where lay their weapons, then turned once more to Riatha. "Too bad about my old foe, Urus, for it would have delighted me to hear his howls as I flensed him of his skin. Yet though I will not have that pleasure, he will serve me nevertheless: this morning I had his corpse borne into the repository"—Stoke gestured at the door he had entered—"and later tonight he will join the ranks of my unconquerable army."

Riatha ground her teeth in rage and would have stepped forward but for her chains. "Urus is slain and will never serve thee, Stoke!"

Stoke laughed wickedly at her reaction, saying, "Not serve me? You fool, you know not even of what I speak."

Stoke made a sweeping gesture at the corpses in the chamber. "When you were first chained, I would have left you in the dark, but I wanted you to see my . . . handiwork . . . so that you would have sufficient time to admire it, to anticipate and relish your own fate to come.

"Yet merely by seeing the fallen dead you cannot fully appreciate your destiny, no matter how beautiful they are, no matter the exquisite way in which they died.

"Nay, I must show you what you will soon be, how you and yours will serve me, Baron Stoke."

Stoke turned, facing into the room. He stood in silence for a moment, as if gathering his strength, his will. Then his voice lashed out:

"*Ô nekroí!*"

The arcane words seemed to hang on the air, as ice would silently cling. And the Rūcks and Hlōks peered nervously about and edged toward the door, as if they would bolt from the room.

"*Egò gàr ho Stókos dè kèleuo humás!*"

A chill seeped into the chamber, and Gwylly shivered, glancing at Faeril, the damman's arms hugged about herself, her eyes wide with apprehension.

*"Akoúsete mè!"*

Aravan's hand crept to his throat, the blue stone frigid.

*"Peísesthe moi!"*

In the flickering light, from the corner of her eye Faeril thought that she saw faint motion among the dead. Her heart hammering furiously, she wrenched her gaze in that direction in time to see a black beetle drop from the gaping jaw of a corpse and scuttle away. *Oh, Adon, did it come from the mouth?*

Then Stoke's harsh words rolled out into the chill:

*"Stánton!"*

As if from ten thousand throats, a ghastly sigh whispered through the chamber, and now Faeril was certain that she saw a corpse move, head rolling to one side, dead eyes staring at Stoke, or staring at Faeril herself!

*"Stánton!"*

Now ten thousand anguished groans wailed, and corpses began to shift, dead arms and legs levering, lifting, a ghostly weeping filling the chamber, and now the Rūcks did run, disappearing into the shadowy hall beyond the open door.

Up jerked the corpses, lurching to their feet, weapons in hand, entrails dangling from burst abdomens.

When they all stood facing him, Stoke gestured toward the dead, his hand clawlike.

*"Léksete!"*

Ten thousand voices moaned throughout the chamber, groaning forth from slack jaws: *M'alim . . . Kibr . . . Kûman-dân' . . . Mîr . . .*

Now the Hlōks bolted from the room, slamming the door behind.

But the Ghûl stood fast, his blistered face split in a malevolent grin.

Stoke turned to Riatha. "See? This is what you will become. A soldier in my unconquerable army.

"Do you hear what they call me?"

Whispers and groans hissed throughout the chamber, the spectral voices of the dead ebbing and flowing as would a ghostly tide.

Aravan answered. "They speak the language of the desert, and name thee Master, Greatness, Commandant, Prince, and more. Yet heed, Stoke, thou are evil to delve into such matters, to visit such foul calamity upon these dead ones."

"Pah!" replied Stoke above the hideous murmurings. "I have surpassed—"

Suddenly he broke off and whirled toward the corpses. *"Hesukhádsete!"* he commanded, and the chamber groaned to silence.

Stoke turned once again to Aravan. "—I have surpassed the skills of my mentor, Ydral, he who showed me the pleasures of the harvest, who even now would like to know my secrets.

"But should I give such power to another? Nay, for it is mine and mine alone to wield as I will. What matter that he is my true father, for he would raise an army to rival my own."

Aravan's question came softly. "Where is this sire of thine?"

Stoke's eyes widened, but ere he spoke— "Why?" shouted Faeril. "Why do you need such a foul army? A legion of the cruelly slain."

Stoke laughed and turned to the damman. "Because with it I can rule the world. Think of it, runt: Where I march, swift fear will run before me. Weapons will not harm those already slain. Adon's Ban holds no sway over these soldiers, and with them I will conquer all.

"Pah, the Sultan of Hyree thinks I raise it for his use, my army of the dead. Yet he does not know what I truly intend.

"Let him fight his religious War, his *jihad.* I have bigger things in mind."

Again Aravan repeated his question. "Stoke, I asked, where is this sire of thine? Where is Ydral?"

Baron Stoke vaguely gestured to the east, then his eyes filled with rage. "Fool! Am I my father's keeper? I am not here to be questioned."

Agitatedly he paced back and forth, looking at the captives as if they were chattel. Then a slow, cruel smile spread over his face. "Instead, I am here to indulge in my . . . simple pleasures."

Now Stoke stepped before Gwylly. "And you, runt, you will suffer the most.

"Did you truly think that sunlight would kill me? Bah! I am a werecreature and will *never* die, for none is clever enough to kill me. And unless I am slain by silver pure, or by starsilver rare, or by fire, or by the fangs and claws of another such as I, I will live forever.

"Elves are not the only immortals.

"And as to your feeble attempt, I was in my present form in which the Sun can only cause me pain . . . and for that you will pay dearly.

"Heed, I suffer not Adon's Ban, unlike my *jemadar*"— Stoke gestured at the Ghûl—"who will die in the light of day. See what even a distant dimness did to him, there where he is charred, scalded, burned. He was well back in the chamber when you opened the shutter, and only a faint glimmer of the light fell upon him, yet it seared as a fire until he fled beyond its reach."

"Too bad," replied Gwylly. "I should have waited until he was closer."

Stoke murmured a word in Slûk and the Ghûl leapt forward and smashed a fist into Gwylly's face, sending the tiny Warrow crashing back against the stone wall and sprawling to the floor.

Shrieking, "You bastard!" Faeril leapt toward the Ghûl, only to be jerked short by her chains.

["Faeril, no,"] called Gwylly in Twyll, scrambling to his feet, blood runnelling from his nose. ["I am all right, and I would not have you hurt."]

The corpse-white foe stepped back, his red gash of a mouth split in a vile grin. Again Stoke murmured something in Slûk, and the Ghûl, still leering, stepped to the nearby stone pillar and drew forth a key from a carven slot.

Stoke turned to Gwylly. "Obviously, fool, you are fond of the female runt, and now I see just how I will make you suffer."

The Ghûl seized Faeril's wrists and unlocked the manacles, the damman struggling and kicking to no effect as he dragged her among the still standing corpses and toward the center of the room.

"Stoke! You *skut*!" shouted Gwylly, wrenching at his chains. "Leave her alone, murderer!"

In grim silence Riatha and Aravan haled against their own fetters, but the iron yielded not.

Stoke smiled, turning to watch as the Ghûl lifted Faeril up by one arm, fastening it into a dangling manacle mid-chamber. Then he did likewise to her other wrist, the damman kicking and shrilling curse words in Twyll.

Stoke beckoned the Ghûl to him, then turned to the buccan. "Ah, fear not, runt, for I will let you watch from close by."

With a terrible strength the Ghûl grabbed Gwylly by the jerkin, snarling at the Wee One who had caused him so much pain, slamming Gwylly back against the wall, stunning the buccan. Swiftly the Ghûl unlocked the shackles and dragged Gwylly to room center, hefting him up and chaining him dangling diagonally across from Faeril.

Behind, Riatha and Aravan began singing a deathsong, for there was nought they could do to prevent such, and so they sang a cant to Adon, asking that He receive the souls of these small ones unto His bosom.

As the Ghûl returned the key to its niche, Stoke stepped to the nearby instrument-cluttered table. And there he took up a vial filled with a blood-red liquid. Back he came to stand before Faeril, and he held the flask up to the lantern light. "You must drink, for I would not have you swoon from pleasure. This elixir will keep you alert to the very end, magnifying the exquisite sensations I will visit upon you . . . as I did these others." Stoke's hand swept in a gesture toward the standing dead, their unblinking eyes open and staring, their jaws gaping in hideous jape. "Your comrades in arms."

Stoke held the vial up to the damman, but she turned her head aside, clamping her lips shut.

"What? You do not trust me? Why, this is not poison . . . see." Stoke put the flask to his own lips and drank a swallow. "No more than a gulp is needed."

Again he held it up to Faeril, but she jerked her face aside.

Stoke motioned to the Ghûl, and he held the damman while the Baron forced liquid into her, as Gwylly shrieked in hatred, swinging on his chains, kicking out, trying to reach them, to no avail.

They turned to the buccan, and the Ghûl doubled his fist and slammed it into Gwylly's gut, driving the air from him, stunning the Wee One with pain, Stoke quickly pouring the liquid in the buccan's open mouth, forcing him to swallow.

Now the Baron stepped again to the table, setting down the flask. And then he took up the golden stake, some three inches in diameter and thirty inches long it was, tapering to a blunt point on one end, four blades set thereon, other razor-thin triangular steel blades glittering down the shank, blood-stones embedded here and there, the shaft butted against a polished steel plate on the opposite end.

Stoke stepped before Gwylly, the buccan yet gasping from the blow to his stomach. "How will I make you suffer, runt? Merely by allowing you to look and listen as I tend to your sweetling."

Stoke turned and moved to Faeril, his voice soft and gentle, his cruel harshness submerged. "Heed, my lovely. First I will remove your clothing so that I may see your fair skin . . . then I will remove that also, starting at your feet."

Her eyes widening in terror, her heart hammering, feet flailing, Faeril struggled against her fetters, chains clanking as she jerked to no avail.

Stoke smiled at the effect his words were having, and he said solicitously, "Oh, fear not, the elixir you drank will not only heighten your senses so that it will be exquisite beyond your wildest imaginings, but you will remain aware throughout and feel every excruciating moment."

Now Faeril began groaning in horror, and behind, Gwylly shouted in rage, while against the wall, Aravan and Riatha sang the deathsong.

Stoke raised his voice to be heard. "And when I have taken your skin from you"—he held up the hideous shaft, turning it in the light, gold gleaming, steel glinting—"*this* will be your *next* reward."

Laughing wildly, Stoke stepped back and set the stake to the floor where Faeril could see it, the instrument resting on its buttplate, the horrid bladed point stabbing upward, razors glittering.

Then the Baron took a swift stride to the table and seized a thin-bladed knife, coming back to Faeril. Motioning for the Ghûl to grasp her kicking legs, Stoke wrenched her boots from her and flung them aside. His hands trembling with eagerness, he set the blade in the shrieking damman's clothes, slicing upward, rending the cloth from her.

Soon Faeril was stripped naked, and Stoke turned to Gwylly. "Now, runt, experience the pleasure of seeing your loved one die an agonizing death."

Gwylly closed his eyes and turned his face upward, refusing to look.

And just as Stoke set his razor-sharp knife to the sole of Faeril's foot, from the hallway came a commotion, and inward darted three Rūcks, slamming the door behind.

Gwylly opened his eyes, looking upward, his gaze flying wide.

Angered, Stoke whirled, shouting invectives in Slûk. But his voice was lost beneath a deafening roar—

*RRRAAAWWWW!*

—and the door was shattered by a massive blow, the panel crashing inward, smashing down upon the Rūcks, and atop the wreckage stood a huge beast.

The Bear had come to call.

Stoke whirled about and snarled to the standing corpses, *"Ekeî eisìn hoi polémioi hoi emoí!"*

Corpses oriented upon the Bear, unblinking eyes staring. Others turned toward Riatha and Aravan. And yet others wheeled in the direction of Faeril and Gwylly.

"Faeril! Faeril!" shouted Gwylly, climbing up his right-hand chain.

The damman looked at her buccaran, and then overhead. Then she, too, began hoisting herself upward, toward the beam holding the hooks anchoring her chains.

*"Thanatósete autoús!"* shouted Stoke.

The ghostly howl of ten thousand ghastly voices fading in and out of gaping jaws, forward trod the ranks of the undead, scimitars and tulwars and cudgels upraised, the slain coming to kill the Bear, to kill the Elves, to kill the Warrows.

The Bear knew these two-legs were not *Urwa.* Still they challenged him! And roaring in rage he charged into the shuffling undead, his great claws sweeping left and right, rending and smashing and battering.

Gwylly fetched up against the wooden beam, and reaching

over, he slipped the topmost link of his left-hand chain up to the tip of its anchoring hook, and jerking and jerking, he wrenched it through the gap.

He looked over just as Faeril came to her beam. Grim determination reflected in her face. She glanced at him and said, "Gwylly, get the key and free Aravan and Riatha. I will get our weapons."

And below, the Bear roared and slashed the ranks of the undead, slamming them backwards, hammering them to the floor, great claws gashing their cadaverous flesh in devastating blows that would slay the living. But these soldiers were already dead, and so they rose up to attack again from wherever they had been whelmed.

And the howling dead came upon Aravan and Riatha, the Elves limited by the chains embedded in the wall. Even so, with a turning, thrusting kick, Riatha slammed her heel against the knee joint of a shuffling corpse, the leg breaking with a sharp *crack!* The Elfess snatched free the tulwar from the fallen undead, and with a chopping hack she decapitated the creature, then spun in time to parry a strike whistling at her.

Nearby, Aravan at the last instant stepped aside and let a massive blow rush past, seizing the corpse's arm at the wrist and breaking the elbow across his knee, wrenching loose the cudgel from the grip of the dead one. The Elf hammered the iron bar into the skull of another of the undead, the cranium smashing like a rotten egg.

And in room center, a dark shimmering came upon Baron Stoke, his shape altering, changing, dropping down to all fours, coalescing into a new shape, and where he had been now stood a huge black Vulg, virulent fangs adrip.

Above, Gwylly grasped an adjacent chain, taking the strain from his own right-hand fetter, and he hoisted the topmost link to the tip of the anchoring hook and jerked it loose as well.

Eight-foot chains dangling from his manacled wrists, the buccan was now free. But below stood undead soldiers, ghostly channelled voices keening, weapons in hand.

As the Vulg charged to battle the Bear, Gwylly slid partway down the chain he grasped and, swinging, managed to reach another chain, the undead shuffling after. Again

Gwylly swung, building up momentum, and at the height of his arc he released his hold, flying through the air, hurtling out and down, crashing to the stone floor. He struck hard and rolled, pain shooting throughout his entire body, the effect of the elixir hideously magnifying the impact. As he leapt to his feet, intense agony flashed up his left leg, his mind screaming in torment. Hobbling, each step harrowing torture, through tear-filled eyes Gwylly glanced back and up at Faeril, the damman even now beginning her own descent to the open floor below. Although the corpses had followed him, some now began to swing about, shuffling toward his dammia.

Standing, the Bear slammed a whelming blow against the skull of the great black Vulg, hammering the leaping beast aside, for he had fought *this* Urwa long past and it had nearly slain him. Roaring a challenge and ignoring the slashing tulwars and scimitars and pounding cudgels, the Bear charged toward the downed Vulg, knowing that this black four-legs was his enemy true.

Riatha hacked gaping wounds into the undead soldiers, yet they came shuffling forward regardless, a headless corpse now stumbling among them, striking out at random. The Elfess knew that the only way to stop them was to cut their hands and arms from them so that they could not grasp weapons; cut their legs from them so that they could not walk; cut their heads from them so that they could not see. And she set to this butchery, knowing that in the end they would overwhelm her, for she was chained to a wall.

On her flank, Aravan crushed skulls and broke arms and legs, corpses crashing down and rising up, only to be felled again by the Elven warrior. Yet he, too, was shackled to the wall.

Faeril dropped the last eight feet to the stone floor, crying out in agony as she struck, magnified pain lancing throughout as she crashed to the stone, smashing down to hands and knees. Corpses struck at her with wicked blades and iron bars, yet in spite of her agony she managed to roll aside and spring to her feet, and trailing her chains behind, she darted among the undead and toward the weapons against the wall alongside the broken door.

As the Vulg sprang upward, the Bear smashed him to the

floor again and leapt upon the back of the downed black beast. Grappling, tumbling and rolling, they crashed among the undead, battering them aside, the Vulg unable to claw, to bite, for the Bear had him in a crushing grasp from behind.

Gwylly gained the stone pillar and, reaching up, blindly felt within the niche for the shackle key, his fumbling fingers falling upon it. In triumph he grasped it, jerking it free, turning, to be smashed back by the haft of a barbed spear, the buccan crashing hindward against the pillar and collapsing in agony.

Such a blow would have rendered Gwylly unconscious in any other circumstance, but he had taken Stoke's elixir, and not only did it magnify Gwylly's pain, it kept the buccan from passing out, his mind awake and aware.

Through anguish-filled eyes Gwylly looked up to see the Ghûl standing above him, the red gash of his mouth gaping in a wide grin, pointed yellow teeth showing, his burned face sneering in triumph, savoring the moment of his revenge, and he raised his spear for the final blow.

Yet the Ghûl had not counted on the incredible quickness of the Wee Folk, and in spite of his pain Gwylly rolled aside even as the iron barbs struck stone. Scrambling away and leaping to his feet, the Warrow took a grip on the two chains shackled about his wrists. Whipping the fetters about his head, with all his might Gwylly lashed the chains into the Ghûl, bones cracking as iron links smashed into them.

But the Ghûl just grinned, for he was impervious to such.

Again Gwylly smashed the links into the Ghûl, yet this time the foe was ready, and he caught up the chains and slowly drew the struggling Warrow toward him, the barbs on his spear glinting wickedly.

Darting among the corpses, Faeril reached the pile, snatching up Riatha's sword and Aravan's spear, dodging aside as one of the undead struck at her and missed. The damman leaped back to snatch her bandoliers, yet she could not find Gwylly's sling or the long-knives and instead grabbed up her Elven dagger for him to use.

Now the Bear stood, his jaws clamped in the muscles of the Vulg's shoulders, his arms reaching 'round, claws embedded in the howling Vulg's chest, the massive grasp crushing ever tighter. And the Bear lifted the Vulg from the floor.

Gwylly wrenched back and forth, yet the Ghûl jerked him close and slammed the buccan facedown to the stone and smashed him down with a foot. Raising his wicked spear, he plunged it into the buccan, Gwylly crying out in agony as the barbs thrust through him, striking the stone floor below, and then were jerked back out.

Fetters snaking after, Faeril darted across the room, dodging blows, leaping aside, bearing the weaponry toward the wall where were chained Riatha and Aravan in desperate combat, both Elves wounded by blade and cudgel. Yet at last the damman came to the battle and managed to dart among the undead to thrust the haft of the spear into Aravan's hands—but she was driven back and could not reach Riatha.

Hammering a corpse hindward, *"Krystallopýr,"* whispered Aravan, Truenaming the spear, striking out, and where the blade pierced, the dead fell dead, never to rise again. "To me, Riatha!" he yelled, his weapon long enough to reach beyond her and protect them both.

And scrambling clear of the mêlée, Faeril turned to see— *"Gwylly!"* she shrieked as the Ghûl plunged the spear through the buccan again.

And again.

Dropping all but her Elven dagger, screaming in rage, Faeril ran shrieking across the space between her and the Ghûl. Leaping upon the creature's back, she plunged the blade into him time and again. Yawling, the Ghûl dropped his barbed spear and clawed hindward, clutching at the damman. But she was naked, having been stripped by the Baron Stoke, and he could not grasp her. Around and around the Ghûl whirled in agony, for the blade was silver pure, and it pierced him in pain.

Chains trailing after, leaving a long, bloody smear behind, Gwylly dragged himself across the floor, his life swiftly leaking from him. Yet he remained conscious and in hideous agony, for Stoke's elixir yet flowed. Ahead he could see Aravan and Riatha, undead striking at them, felled dead at their feet.

And he knew he had to reach them.

Blackness leached at his vision, and a terrible coldness filled him. He was so tired, so very tired, and he knew he could not go on, even though he must.

A sissing roar filled his hearing, and although he could see Riatha, and she him, he could not hear what she was calling.

But he knew he must reach her. He had to travel those last few feet.

For he still held the key.

And reaching out with the last of his strength, he felt her take his hand in hers, and he smiled.

And then the blackness took him.

And behind, at last the Ghûl clutched Faeril's hair and wrenched the damman up and over, holding her out at arm's length, his burned features distorted with rage.

"You bastard!" she shouted, and spat in his blistered face.

The Ghûl grabbed her by the throat and jerked her to him, and she plunged the silver blade into his heart. His dead black eyes widened in horror as he realized what he had done, what she had done, his hollow voice yowling, and then he collapsed.

Flayed corpses closed in to slay her, but ere they could strike a single blow, crystal spear and starsilver blade slammed into them. Aravan and Riatha were unchained at last.

In room center, whirling 'mid the undead, the Bear crushed his massive arms about the black Vulg, teeth rending fur and flesh from its back. And then the Bear glimpsed an auric spike standing on the floor. He raised the Vulg up high and drove the beast downward onto Stoke's own golden stake, slamming him clear to the stone, steel razors slicing, bladed blunt point bursting in and through and out, entrails spilling forth.

*Oooo* . . . moaned ten thousand ghastly voices, and corpses backed away.

The Vulg howled and tried to bite the horrid thing piercing him. But he could not reach it, and every time he moved the blades slashed within.

And a dark shimmering came over the beast, its form altering, shifting, changing, growing larger, elongating, widening,

and where had been a Vulg now flapped a huge, hideous
wingcd *thing*, its flailing pinions leathery and black, a single
scimitar-like spur at the forward bend of each wing, its beak
filled with jagged teeth, the claws of its feet clutching and
grasping at the air, *skrawwing* in agony, for it, too, was
impaled.

Once again came the dark shimmering, the altering, the
shifting, the shape growing smaller, compacting, wings drawing in, becoming arms, legs forming, beak shrinking, head
rounding, and where the *thing* had been, now was Baron
Stoke, shrieking in horrendous rack, for he was impaled, his
abdomen burst open, his entrails spilling out.

And the elixir magnified his agony and fended shock from
him, kept him awake and aware.

Yet he could not die from impalement, for he was a
werecreature.

The Bear stepped forward to slay him, claws raised.

But in the last moment he did not.

Instead, the Bear looked over at the female two-legs, the
one holding dark metal filled with stars.

"*Whuff!*" the Bear called, and backed away . . .

. . . and Riatha stepped before Stoke, her sword in hand,
the Baron screaming, his eyes wide in hideous pain, razors
inside slashing with every movement no matter how
slight.

Voicing an endless howl, he looked up at the Elfess. "This
is for Talar," she said, drawing back Dúnamis, tears streaming down her face. "For Gwylly. For all the others."

And with a dark silveron sword, the starlight blade glittering as it swung through the lantern light, Riatha took off his
head.

Corpses collapsed to the stone, the dead no longer undead.

The Bear sat down and a dark shimmering came upon the
beast. Riatha stepped forward as swiftly it *changed*, altering,
losing bulk, gaining form, and suddenly there before her sat
a giant of a Man, a Baeran: it was Urus.

And she knelt beside him and took his hand and kissed it
and held it to her cheek, tears flooding down her face.
"*Chieran. Avó, chieran.* I thought you dead."

Urus embraced her and kissed her gently.

But then his own eyes filled with tears, for over her shoulder in the shadows he saw a grieving Aravan standing ward above Faeril—the wee damman sitting on the stone floor, rocking and keening, her slain buccaran in her arms.

# CHAPTER 41

# Wings of Fire

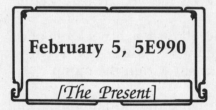

Urus stood, drawing Riatha up after, the huge Man blinking the tears from his eyes. "We cannot stop to mourn," he gritted, "for we have yet to fight our way free. We must grieve for Gwylly later.

"And you are wounded, my love, by Rutchen blade ... and so too may be Faeril and Aravan. We must clean and bind such, for the weapons of Wrgs are often poisoned, and the wounds they deliver can slay you days after."

Riatha nodded and wiped away her own tears, then turned toward the pile of goods. "Stand ward by the broken door for the foe may yet mount an attack, while I search among our belongings for any herbs and simples they may have overlooked. Bandages, too, as well as clothing for Faeril."

The saddlebags were yet buckled and the bedrolls bound, and as Riatha unclasped the leather pouches and began rummaging through, Urus took up his iron morning star and stepped to the portal and stood guard. He did not clear away the wreckage, or the dead Rutcha beneath, instead leaving it as loose rubble to slow any attack.

Quickly the Elfess found the medicine kit and Faeril's spare clothing and a white jerkin to be torn up as dressing for their wounds.

Too, she found their canteens and, sloshing them, discovered that they yet contained water. Riatha uncapped each and sniffed, then opened her pouch of herbs. She selected a white powder and dropped a small pinch into each flask, listening, capping them after. Pitching a canteen to Urus and shouldering the other four, "Drink," she said. "It is safe."

Riatha threaded her way among the fallen corpses to come to Faeril and Aravan, retrieving the damman's boots along the way.

"Here," she said, handing Aravan a canteen, setting all else to the floor. "Drink. It is safe and there is enough. Enough to cleanse all wounds as well."

The Elfess knelt beside Faeril. "Wee one, we must ready ourselves to leave. There may be foe yet about." Riatha looked up at Aravan.

"The stone is chill," said the Elf, "though not as it once was. Foe are nigh. What they may be, I know not, yet it is certain that Loka and Rucha remain within the mosque. As to Vulgs, others, I cannot say."

Faeril sat clasping Gwylly in her arms, stroking her buccaran's hair, tears flowing down her cheeks. She did not look up as she shook her head. "There are no Vulgs. They would have come at Stoke's howl had there been any. Gwylly killed them all with the daylight. He killed them all—"

"Even so, Faeril," responded Riatha, "were Gwylly here now, he would urge that thou not cast thy life away needlessly. He would tell thee to ready thyself for that which remains before us."

Riatha took the key and unbound the shackles yet fettering Faeril's wrists, casting the chains aside. The damman looked up. "Gwylly's too," she insisted, and Riatha unlocked those as well.

Then Riatha took Faeril's face between her hands. "Come, wee one, stand and let me bind thy wounds. Too, thou must get dressed and armed, for we have yet to fight our way out from this place of death, and we need thy aid."

Long did Faeril pause, looking from Riatha to Aravan to Urus. Last she gazed down at Gwylly, then gently lowered her slain buccaran to the stone floor. She stood and let Riatha examine her, the Elfess turning her about. Except for where the manacles had rubbed her wrists raw, the damman was unscathed.

Riatha gave her a canteen. "Drink, and then dress."

Faeril's throat was parched and she drank her fill, for she as well as the others had had no water in the long hours past, not since they had begun their descent down from the crags in the early dawn.

As the damman donned her garb and looped her bandoliers over her shoulders, Riatha washed and bound Aravan's wounds, applying a salve here and there. Then Aravan did likewise for her.

Riatha took a long drink from her canteen, then said, "Aravan, stand ward at the broken doorway while I attend to Urus."

When Urus came to the Elfess and was examined, lo! his wounds were already closing, some merely red lines upon his flesh. "I have always done so," he said. "It is my nature."

"Silver pure and starsilver rare," murmured Faeril. "They are all that may harm you. That and fire . . . and the fangs and claws of another so cursed."

Riatha looked at Faeril and then at Urus, wonder in her silver-grey eyes. Thoughtfully she cleansed Urus's cuts, applying salve, binding one or two.

As the Baeran dressed, Riatha said, "Now we must decide our course, decide where to spend the remainder of the night, for the dawn is just over five hours hence."

Urus growled, "I say we need reach the outside now, for the closer it comes to daylight, the more reluctant the Wrg will be to attack. Whereas should we remain here, day or no, they may mount a charge at any time."

They looked up at Aravan, who had been listening from beside the broken door. "I stand with Urus," he called. "The sooner out, the sooner safe."

"Even outside, they can come at us as long as it is night," said Riatha. "Hence, we will need a place of safety till first light."

Urus nodded, thinking, staring at the floor. At last he looked up. "'The minaret. At the top we can close the trapdoor . . . and even should they attack, they can come at us but one at a time."

Riatha nodded. "Let us be gone, then."

"Wait," cried Faeril. "I cannot, will not, leave Gwylly here in this"—she gestured about—"this charnel house, in this hideous place of death."

Riatha knelt and hugged her. "Oh, wee one, we would not leave him behind here among these—these obscenities. Nay, I will bear him myself."

"Wait," called Aravan. "There is yet that which I must do." And while the others sorted among which of their things to take with them, the Elf stepped to each of the corpses and began the grisly task of piercing each of them through the heart with Krystallopŷr, the spear burning the dead, Aravan making certain that they would not ever rise again.

Seeing this, Riatha stepped to the Ghûlk slain by Faeril and, striking below the steel collar, decapitated the creature and then dismembered it. When she was finished, she retrieved Faeril's Elven knife, pulling it from the Ghûlk's heart, returning the silver dagger to the damman.

Faeril girted herself with her long-knife and slipped the silver dagger into its scabbard. Too, she located Gwylly's sling and bullet bags, as well as his other weaponry, and she gathered them up along with her bedroll and his, too. Strapping hers onto her back, she untied Gwylly's blanket and enfolded her buccaran within.

Finally, laden with saddlebags and other goods, they stepped through the broken doorway, Urus leading, Riatha coming after and bearing Gwylly's blanket-wrapped body, Faeril next, and then Aravan.

As they passed from the chamber, Urus roared, imitating the Bear, and Faeril could hear footsteps scuttling away in the shadowed hall.

Urus led them to a spiral stair, and up this they went, emerging through an open trap and up onto the altar dais in the central chamber, torches burning at each of the four corners, brightly illuminating them. The hall was devoid of distant voices murmuring, unlike the time when they first had entered.

Down from the dais they stepped, Faeril's heart pounding, for any minute she expected black-shafted arrows or crossbow bolts to come winging out from the shadows.

Faeril saw something gleaming on the floor, and she stepped to it; it was the silver throwing knife she had hurled at Stoke, just missing. Quickly Faeril slipped the blade into its scabbard. Most of her steel knives were gone, having been cast in battle, but both silver blades were now housed in the bandoliers.

Now they started across the floor toward the way they had previously come into the hall, but the portcullis was yet down across the corner door, and so Urus changed course, swinging back toward the doorway through which the Ogru had come.

They entered a short corridor and came to a cross hall stretching away into shadows left and right. Straight ahead stood a stairwell, steps going upward as well as down. "This I ween will lead below, where lies the passage to the minaret," hissed Urus, and down they went.

No enemy did they meet in the hallway beneath, and swiftly they came to the tunnel. Taking a burning torch from its bracket, down the length of the underground passage they hurried, coming to the portcullis yet unlocked, the pole from the paddock yet lying against the wall. Urus spun the lifting wheel, *Clack! Clack! Clack!* the ratchet clattering and chains rattling as the protesting iron squealed upward.

As the others passed through, Urus propped the pole under the raised grille, then strode to the mechanism and, using his morning star, broke loose the lifting chains and shattered the spokes and ratchet. Then the Baeran stepped through, and with a grunt he heaved the pole free. The grate squealed down, *Clang!* the portcullis teeth slamming into the sockets below.

Up the stairs and to the ground floor of the minaret they went, finding the courtyard door yet open. Bright moonlight shone through. "After our 'invasion,' the Wrg perhaps never came here," breathed Urus, setting down his burdens. "Even so, some may be above. And though the squealing portcullis banging and clanging has announced our presence, they might think we are merely other Rutcha. I will go first in case Wrg lie in wait. Aravan, quench the torch and come with me. Riatha, stay here with Faeril . . . and Gwylly."

Taking his morning star in his left hand, up the spiral stairs went Urus, Aravan with his spear coming behind.

Faeril's heart raced as up they went, and she heard their soft steps ascending, but only until they were beyond sight, and then nought but silence.

Gently, Riatha lay Gwylly's body down. Then drawing Dúnamis, she stepped to the doorway and peered out, standing ward.

Faeril drew her long-knife and waited in the shadows.

All was silent, the front of the mosque dark, and of their horses there was no sign.

Long moments passed, endless moments, but at last Urus returned. "All is clear."

As Faeril went up the steps, Riatha came after, bearing Gwylly. Below, Urus closed and barred the door to the courtyard, then scooped up all remaining gear and followed.

At the top of the minaret, Aravan stood in the shadows, peering outward through the archways of the crowning pavilion. The Moon was two days past full, and it stood nigh the zenith, shedding its pale light down on the mosque and courtyard and the surrounding terrain beyond the fortress walls.

Faeril and Riatha came up through the trapdoor, followed by Urus. The Baeran dropped gear to the floor, while Riatha prepared to lay Gwylly down. "In the moonlight, Riatha," said Faeril, tears glistening. "Gwylly always said that moonlight was special."

As the Elfess placed the buccan on the stone where struck the silvery beams, Urus disappeared back down the spiral stairs. Faeril sat beside her buccaran and took loose the blanket and held his cold hand in hers, softly weeping.

Moments later Urus returned, and he had with him the paddock pole. The Baeran closed the trapdoor and then wedged the post athwart it, sliding one end far through a drain port, then haling it partway back to jam the opposite end under the anchoring arch of a stone table. "There," he said. "That ought to—"

A distant clank and clatter sounded.

Aravan cocked his head, listening. "A portcullis being raised," he hissed.

Faeril stood, drawing her long-knife. "Below?"

"Nay." Aravan pointed. "Yon. The front entrance, I deem."

Riatha unsheathed Dúnamis, her voice grim. "They come."

Next sounded a metallic *dnng* of a heavy brass door fetching up against stone, and wavering torch-light shone out from the front portico. Seconds passed, and suddenly five Hlōks scuttled across the space to the front gate, one bearing a torch, the others scrambling to draw the bar and open the leftmost portal, shoving the gate out just enough to squeeze through. Down the switchbacks they ran, fleeing toward the canyon below. Ere they reached it, three Rūcks came bolting out after, pounding through the bright moonlight, trying to catch the Hlōks ahead.

Aravan clutched the blue amulet and laughed softly. "There is yet a chill on the token, but even now it warms. I ween that they were the last of the Foul Folk, all but one left behind.

"Mayhap they think the Bear is yet inside, and that is why they fled."

"Even so," gritted Riatha, resheathing Dúnamis, "let us not cast lots with Fortune. Dawn is but five hours hence . . . then can we leave our aerie."

Aravan watched as the *Rûpt* entered the canyon and fled northward. Then the Elf turned to Urus. "My friend, we thought thee dead. Tell us, what passed?"

Urus sat down on the stone, drawing Riatha after, motioning Faeril to sit at his side, deliberately guiding her away from where she could see Gwylly. "When the Ogru had me in its grasp, I, too, knew that I was slain, for I could feel the monster crushing the life from me, bones breaking, blood bursting from my chest, filling my throat, choking me. Then all went black.

"How long I fell in the darkness, I could not then say, for when I wakened, all I knew was that I had been . . . 'dead.'

"Mayhap Faeril has the right of it, and only by silver pure or starsilver rare can I be slain . . . that or by fire, or by the fangs and claws of another so cursed.

"Regardless, when I awoke, I was strapped to a table. Yet I was fully alert, and I knew that my Ogru-given injuries had by this time healed, for breathing pained me not and blood no longer filled my throat and lungs. Knowing that I was whole, I looked about; beside me there were horribly mutilated dead, their chests laid open, their skulls split, legs and arms flayed to the bone, muscle and tissue and organs splayed about, as if some madman had been at work—Stoke. I was in his foul laboratory.

"I tried to break free, but the heavy straps were beyond my strength, and I knew that only the Bear might be able to rend the bonds.

"And so, I fixed my mind on but a single thought, telling the Bear to find each of you and set you free if you yet lived, and then I began the transformation . . ."

In a dull rage at being trussed, the Bear shattered the bonds and rolled off the ledge. Dead two-legs were in the room, strapped to other ledges. Snuffling each, none of these were the two-legs he sought, and he growled low, for he knew that his two-legs comrades were in danger.

Out from the chamber the Bear stalked, verging into a corridor. To one side lay other doorways, some open, some closed. To the other side it looked the same. Having no better choice, the Bear turned in the direction of his darker paw, nose in the air, seeking scent of his companions. Finding them would be difficult, for the two-legs cave was filled to overflowing with the stench of death.

Moving along the hallway, the Bear peered into every room, bashing open doors when they stood in the way. The chambers held arcane devices he could not fathom: some were iron cages hanging from the ceilings, dead two-legs inside; others were iron doors, dead two-legs mashed between; still others were long ledges, dead two-legs tied atop, ripped apart, arms over there, legs over here. None was a companion of the Bear, but even so, he knew that he had to find the comrades before some such thing happened to them.

Behind one shattered door the Bear found the lair of an old enemy, one he had fought long past, the scent like that of an *Urwa* but not an *Urwa*. Inside was his foe's rumpled bed.

And about the den was the smell of two-legs blood from a kill no more than a day old.

Again, it was not from one of the two-legs companions he sought.

*Whuffing* to clear his nose of the stench, the Bear stepped back into the hallway, only to confront three *Urwa*.

*Waugh!* they shouted, leaping back, turning, fleeing.

*RRRAAAWWWW!* roared the Bear, charging after. Ahead fled the *Urwa*, shrieking in panic.

But above their cries of terror, the Bear heard other sounds, other shouts and screams—and he recognized them as coming from the small two-legs he had befriended.

Now the Bear no longer pursued the *Urwa*, even though they ran before him. Instead he raced toward the cries of his comrades.

The *Urwa* ahead leapt through a door, slamming it after, and it was behind that very same door that the Bear could hear the screams of the small two-legs. Rearing up, and charging forward, into the door whelmed the Bear, the portal crashing inward before him, smashing down atop the *Urwa* and shattering.

And as the Bear stood upon the wreckage, he heard the cries of his comrades and saw them hanging from chains, and he scented his old foe—the-*Urwa*-not-*Urwa*—and he heard his enemy's voice, and he saw dead two-legs turning to attack . . . and he was enraged.

". . . And you know the rest," concluded Urus.

Aravan turned from his vigil. "Blessed be the Bear, Urus, for he came in the nick of time." Then Aravan's eye fell upon the tiny body wrapped in a blanket.

Beside Urus, Faeril began weeping again, and the huge Man enwrapped her in his arms and rocked her gently and stroked her hair as she sobbed in utter desolation. What he murmured is not known, but he did hum softly, a deep rumbling in his chest. And the exhausted wee damman in his arms cried herself to sleep.

Dawn came, the Sun beyond the mountains. Down from the minaret descended the four, Riatha carrying Gwylly. They made their way to the back of the mosque, and there they found camels in the paddock. Of their own horses there was no sign. "Slain by the Rutcha, I would think," said Urus. "Unless they are well trained, steeds cannot abide camels, their stench, their eructions. I would think that the Wrg slew our mounts rather than put up with their panic or rage. Too, they would look for any excuse to get at horseflesh."

"Horses or not," said Aravan, "a long journey lies ahead. We will need food and water, and tack for the camels."

Faeril spoke, her voice trembling. "You three search. I will remain here with my love. Yet I remind you, we need a funeral pyre for Gwylly. That is what he wanted."

The building nearest the stable once had been a smithy, for there they found a forge and bellows and mauls and tongs and anvils and other such long unused. Therein they also found plunder piled high, booty from raids, cargo from caravans: silks and satins; carven goods of ivory and ebony and semiprecious stone; spices and seasonings and flavorings, packed in tins and jars; small crates of crue; casks of tea; kegs of oil; chests of unknown contents; brass lamps and bronze and other such; woven rugs; other treasures scattered in piles. They searched among the jumble and located camel tack, though they did not find any of the double saddles fit to carry a child . . . or Faeril.

In the next building, a warehouse, they found more of the same, as well as a stair leading down. And as they stood above the steps—"*Hist!*" whispered Riatha. "I hear the trickle of water below."

Beneath, they found a cistern, water seeping from the stone of the mountain and running in. Too, there was an underground passage leading back toward the mosque. Urus scooped up a cupped hand of water and smelled then tasted it, nodding.

"Now we have all we need to leave this place behind," said Aravan. "Water. Food. Camels."

Riatha turned to the Elf. "Back by way of Nizari? Then across the Karoo? It will be dangerous."

Aravan agreed. "Thou are right, Dara: in the Red City they seek our death, and we are not likely to slip past unnoticed, even at night. Instead we can turn west from here and fare into Hyree, then head north along the west flank of the Talâk Range, posing as caravaneers. Northward, too, is the port of Khalísha along the Avagon Sea, where we can book passage to Pellar."

Riatha held up a hand. "If we go into Hyree, we will need guises, for if they are readying for a *jihad*, they will take us for spies lest we hide our nature."

Aravan nodded, glancing at Urus. "Then let us get on with it," said the Man.

They bore water to the camels and let them drink their fill. Then fitted them with tack and laded them with water-skins and food and cargo taken from the store of plunder.

When that was done they took apart the paddock fence, stacking the poles into a funeral pyre, covering over all with silks and satins.

And they washed Gwylly, cleansing him of blood, and clothed him in his Elven leathers and laid him thereupon.

During these ministrations, Aravan walked away, the Elf with tears in his eyes. Yet there was something he had left to do.

He bore with him his spear and a cask of oil and a heavy maul and paced to the third building. A foetor, a miasma hung upon the air, and he could hear the squeal of an angered beast behind the closed doors. He flung the portals wide, letting the day shine inward; an enraged scream chopped to silence, the Hèlsteed now dead, fallen into ruin.

Aravan clutched his amulet and nodded, all chill now gone from the stone. He strode to the front entrance of the mosque and flung the remaining portal wide, the bronze door fetching up against the inner wall with a massive *dnng!*

Inward he stalked, past the Troll bones and into the main chamber, daylight streaming after. To the north archway he went, and there in piles of dust he retrieved steel throwing knives, shoving them into his belt.

Next, Aravan went to the central dais and down the spiral stair and into the chamber of death where Stoke lay. He thrust Krystallopŷr into Stoke's torso, the spear burning through the heart. Then he jerked the golden, steel-bladed impaling stake free, and with the iron maul he hammered it to ruin upon the stone floor. He dragged the shards of the wooden door to the center of the room and flung Stoke's remains thereon, head and body. Then he poured oil over all and set the heap afire, the dry wood exploding in flames and burning furiously, Stoke's corpse blazing up, skull afire, the heat searing. "May thou burn forever in Hèl," gritted Aravan.

As he left the inferno behind, he took up the Ghûlk's head by the hair as well as the cruelly barbed spear, and back up the spiral steps he went, coming to the daylight. And there the Sun turned the Ghûlk's head into dust, the spiked steel collar clanging to the stone.

"Now, Gwylly, it is finished."

When Aravan returned, he gave the knives over to Faeril, and he cast the steel collar and barbed spear of the Ghûlk to the foot of the funeral pyre, the shaft broken in two, the Elf saying, "The weapon and armor of his enemy should lie at his feet."

Faeril, weeping, placed Gwylly's sling in his hand, a silver bullet in the leather. Then they poured fine oil over the silks and satins and wood.

At last all was ready, and Faeril gave her buccaran one final kiss. "I love you, Gwylly," she whispered, choking on her grief.

She stepped back, and Urus, bearing four torches aflame, handed one to each of them.

And together, standing at the cardinal points and weeping, they ignited the pyre.

And with voices of silver, Riatha and Aravan sang Gwylly's soul up into the sky.

They rode out through the gates, a long string of camels behind. As they passed beyond the walls, a white dove flew past, winging northward. "An omen of safe passage," murmured Aravan. "Let us hope it is true."

Down the switchbacks they rode, toward the canyon below. And just ere they entered, Faeril, riding before Aravan on an improvised saddle, looked back toward the mosque. A pillar of grey smoke climbed into the sky, turning gold as it emerged from mountain shadow and ascended in the morning Sun.

Her vision blurred with tears, Faeril whispered, "Rise up, my love, rise up to Adon on the golden wings of fire."

# CHAPTER 42

# Passages

**Late Winter to Early Autumn, 5E990**

*[The Present]*

Northerly through the canyon they rode, stone rising steeply to either side, hemming them in, binding them. And even though the gorge twisted and turned, wrenching left and right, still they moved at a goodly pace, for they wished to be free of the gulch ere nightfall some nine hours hence, the opening into the pass forty or so miles ahead. For the most part the caravan jogged in silence, the riders lost in their thoughts, though now and again a camel would *hronk* an idle complaint. There were eighteen camels in all, fifteen bearing light loads of cargo, three bearing riders, all bearing water. Aravan with Faeril rode in the lead, five camels trailing after. Next came Riatha and finally Urus, five camels in each of their trains as well. And northward through the twisting canyon they passed as the day first waxed then waned.

They had ridden some four hours or so, the Sun having passed overhead, when Aravan held up his hand and called back to the others, "The stone grows chill."

Onward they went, Faeril's heart racing, but then, "It's daylight," she said. "Surely we have little to fear."

"Aye, Faeril," responded Aravan. "There will be no attack unless they have Men among them—a most unlikely coupling."

Onward they rode, passing by a dark opening in the eastern wall, a crevice cleaving the stone. "There, I ween," said Aravan, pointing. "There is their bolt-hole."

Faeril looked into the shadowed slot, but it twisted away beyond seeing. "How far have we come?"

"Some seven leagues."

"Twenty-one miles," reckoned Faeril. "Then this is where the Ghûl and the Hèlsteed stayed when first you and Urus saw them, and the place where last night the Rūcks and Hlōks did run."

"Aye, Faeril, I deem thou have the right of it."

On past the crevice they went, Aravan's blue stone growing warmer as they rode away.

"I feel we are leaving a task undone," said Faeril, "a pest hole that needs to be cleared out and stoppered up."

"Mayhap, wee one. Yet the *Rûpt* are now leaderless, not the threat they once were. Left alone they will hide in the mountains and squabble among themselves."

"Do you mean, Aravan, that the raids will stop?"

"Nay, Faeril, raids will yet occur, though infrequently, and with much less success. For without a cunning mind to guide the *Spaunen*, travellers and steaders and dwellers in towns have much less to fear."

Four more hours they trotted northerly, debouching at last into the pass, leaving the gorge behind.

Leftward they turned, westerly, riding toward Hyree. An hour of daylight remained, yet when evening fell, they did not stop, for they wished to put more distance between themselves and the Rūcken bolt-hole.

And so they rode onward, twisting among the mountains of the Talâk Range, stars shining overhead. The gibbous Moon rose, glancing rays from the yellow globe casting long shadows. And as if impelled by the pale beams behind, eighteen camels pressed westerly.

They made camp at mid of night, there in the depths of the pass, some seventeen leagues beyond the bolt-hole, some fifty-one miles in all.

As Riatha changed the dressing on Aravan's wounds, Urus studied by firelight one of Riatha's maps. "This day alone we have travelled seventy-two miles or thereabouts—a pace the camels cannot sustain."

Aravan groaned. "Nor can I sustain such, Urus, at least not my backside."

Riatha tied off the last of Aravan's bandages, then turned to Urus.

"We will not press nearly as hard in the days to come," continued Aravan, rolling down his sleeve, "now that we are well free of the gorge."

Urus grunted. "I make it nearly one hundred fifty miles till we leave the pass, and then I measure another thousand or so to the port of Khalísha."

"Remove thy shirt, *chieran*," ordered Riatha.

Urus unlaced his jerkin and pulled it over his head.

"Aye," said Aravan. "Another month of travel should see us to the sea."

Urus nodded in agreement, as Riatha unbound the bandage on the Baeran's shoulder. Only a faint pink line showed where Urus had been wounded. In the other two places—wrist and rib—not even a line showed. "Thou are wholly healed, Urus," breathed Riatha, wonder in her eyes.

Urus grinned. " 'Tis my nature, love."

Riatha turned again to Aravan, handing him the salve and bandages, pulling off her own jerkin. As the Elf changed her dressings, he said, "On the morrow, thou and Faeril need don the garb thou found in the plunder at the mosque. And I will ready my own ruse, Urus likewise. Then should we come upon any soldiers, they will not know that we are aught but what we claim: caravaneers."

Aravan looked at the others, Urus and Riatha in accord.

But Faeril sat to one side, gazing at the fulgent Moon, tears running down her cheeks, the damman thinking of other times, other places . . . other Moons.

Thinking of Gwylly.

The next morning, Riatha and Faeril donned *thōbes*, the black veiled garments hiding Faeril's jewellike, tilted eyes and Riatha's Elven eyes, hiding as well Riatha's golden hair, the robes covering from head to foot so that nothing showed except the hands, as is the custom for females of the desert.

For Aravan's part, he lightly stained his face and arms and

hands to an ecru brown, and he wrapped a headband about his brow, capturing his pointed ears beneath his black hair, the cloth ready to pull down over his eyes. He donned a white *kaffiyeh*, the headdress held in place by a beaded *agāl*. Last, he cast a light blue *jellaba* over his shoulders, the cloak long and flowing.

Sun-bronzed, Urus used a stain to darken his hair and beard, and he replaced his iron morning star with a wide-bladed scimitar, sliding the curved weapon down through a broad blue sash about his waist. He fitted a blue turban 'round his head, pulling the face cloth into place.

Now all was ready, and they set out to fare through Hyree.

Late on the fifth day after leaving the mosque, the caravan came down from the pass and into the Sultanate of Hyree. There at the outlet was a small garrison, manned by border guards. Two warders stepped from the roadside station and halted the camel train.

["What news from Nizari?"] queried the guard, speaking in Hyrinian. ["How does the city fare?"]

["The city endures,"] responded the blind caravan master, his wholly veiled daughter sitting before him, ["growing rich on the tolls they charge."]

The other soldier walked the length of the train, looking over the goods as if to see what the caravan bore, glancing up at the *thōbe*-clad wife, then passing beyond. ["Any trouble at the haunted gorge?"] he called.

["None,"] replied the caravan master. ["Of course, I paid dearly for an escort from Nizari to see me well beyond."]

["Did you see any strangers on horses? Three Men and possibly two children? Or perhaps two Men and a Woman? Or the graves of children?"]

["Why, no,"] replied the blind one, gesturing at his bandaged eyes. ["But then, I see very little."] He broke out in laughter.

The other soldier snorted, smiling. ["Khassim, you have the brains of an ass. That happened a Moon ago. Those fugitives are either gone or dead by now."]

["We were told to ask,"] protested Khassim. ["We were told to ask."]

["Then stop, I tell you. No one can live near the notch

through even a single night, much less an entire Moon. They are no doubt dead, slain by the monster of the haunted gorge and eaten long ago."]

The blind master turned in the direction of his mute body-guard near the rear of the train. ["Jula,"] he called, signalling with his hands, ["find suitable gifts for these fine soldiers."]

Within a fraction of a sandglass, the caravan moved on-ward, the soldiers behind admiring their new *kaffiyehs*, trad-ing the headdresses back and forth, trying to select between silken white and holy blue, using each other as a mirror.

Northward fared the caravan along the western flank of the Talâk Range, this side of the mountains covered with greenery, for here the crests stole the rain from the sky, leaving for the most part nought but dry winds to blow on beyond, out over the mighty *Erg*, over the sands of the vast Karoo.

On the third evening of the northerly trek, Aravan sat with Riatha, the two speaking softly in the moonless night.

Aravan added a branch to the low-burning fire. "Dara, once apast as we sailed down the coast to Pellar, I asked thee who thou would defend if it came to a choice—thy lover, or those mayhap more in need. . . . Riatha, twice, mayhap thrice, thou were put to the test, and each time did thou leap to the defense of the Wee Ones. I beg thee to forgive me for my doubt."

Riatha shook her head. "Thou were right to question, Ara-van. For I did not know myself until came the time. . . ."

She glanced over at the sleeping Baeran. "Ah, would that I had known then that Urus takes wounds with little lasting effect. It would have saved me much consternation."

Aravan, too, looked at Urus. "Dara, how old would thou say he appears?"

"*Aro*, Aravan, I am no judge of a mortal's years."

"I would say . . . young," mused Aravan. "Lord Hanor at Caer Pendwyr guessed his age at no more than thirty years."

"What are thou driving at, Aravan?"

"Just this, Dara. Baron Stoke said that Elves were not the only immortals, and in that he was right . . . the Hidden Ones are immortal, as well as the Gods and others.

"Stoke claimed that he was immortal, too, saying that he could only die by silver pure or starsilver rare, by fire, or by the fangs and claws of another—"

"So cursed!" interjected Riatha, her heart hammering in her breast, hope soaring. "Urus is so cursed. Oh, Aravan, do you think . . . ?"

Aravan raised his hands, palms upward. "We can only wait and see, Dara. Urus may be immortal, or long lived but mortal . . . or neither. Yet this we know: time will tell . . . time indeed will tell."

They travelled by day and camped at night—the blind master, his wife and daughter, and his huge bodyguard—occasionally stopping in foothill villages to spend a day resting in a suitable inn, seizing the opportunities to bathe in private, to sleep in beds, to take on supplies.

And along the way they saw evidence of the casting down of the religion of the Prophet Shat'weh—minarets fallen to ruin, abandoned temples and mosques, the absence of morning and evening prayers. Too, now and again a troop of soldiers would ride past; whether this was commonplace in the back country, the foursome did not know, but even so it did seem somehow significant.

On two separate occasions rain fell: the first time gently, but on the second occurrence it was driven before a harsh wind. Days after, they forded swollen streams flowing down from the mountains above.

For nearly a month they wended northward, but there came a day—the twenty-ninth after leaving the mosque—when they topped a rise to stare out on the azure waters of the Avagon Sea. Below them lay the port of Khalísh, and out in the bay plying the waters fared lateen-sailed dhows. At sight of these, Faeril burst into tears, and when Aravan asked, she said, "Oh, Aravan, do you recall the mirage? Ships like these sailing the desert? Gwylly was so happy then. And so was I . . . so was I."

Keeping but few items unto themselves, they sold the caravan goods in the city, including the camels, the blind master haggling skillfully, haggling well, obtaining a fair price for all, the huge, mute bodyguard with the great scimitar weighing out the silver and gold.

They booked passage for Arbalin since no ship from Khalísh fared to Pellar, and nine days after arriving at the port city, they set sail in the morning on a three-masted dhow—the *Hilâl*—running out on the ebbing tide.

Across the Avagon they fared, coursing day and night, the ship crewed by dusky sailors, wiry and small. Through waters plied by rovers they ran, seemingly without fear, for Hyree and Kistan had strong ancient ties in commerce and combat and religion. And so they ran at night with lanterns lit, and lurid red sails in the day, announcing to one and all alike that here was a ship of courage, here was a ship of *Men*.

Although the captain had his cabin and the crew quartered on the cargo below, the blind master and his huge slave slept in the open, while the wife and girlchild shared a small deck tent. These female passengers remained enclosed in their canopy during the day, stretching their legs only after dark, as was the Hyrinian custom for Women aboard ships. It was during their nighttime exercise that Riatha and Faeril—soft Elven step and silent Warrow foot—came upon the steersman, his face to the stars, praying to the Prophet, for they heard the word *Shat'weh*. When the sailor saw that he was observed, he fervently pleaded with the *thōbe*-clad "Women," but what he said, they knew not, for neither spoke Hyrinian. Yet they stiffly bowed in silence and continued their stroll, while behind the shaken steersman plied the tiller and watched them walk on, anxiety in his eyes.

The very next eve was the night of the vernal equinox, and Aravan stepped to the same steersman and spoke softly to him. And in the wee hours, the sailor watched in wonderment as the four passengers stepped the stately paces of the Elven rite celebrating the coming of spring, Riatha and Aravan softly humming the ritual hymns.

When the dance was done, with tears streaming down her face behind her veil, Faeril said, "I must stop weeping at every little thing. Yet how can I stop, how can anyone stop remembering times past when there was another standing at hand, a love now gone."

Urus knelt and hugged the wee damman in her robes. "You must not even try to forget, Faeril. Not ever. Instead, relish those good times you had, for as long as we remember, something of Gwylly yet lives."

The seas were calm, though it rained several times, and the wind in the main blew briskly. Still in all it took some twenty-one days for them to reach the Isle of Arbalin, running in on the afternoon tide.

And that evening ashore, once again appeared two Lian Elves, a wee Warrow, and a huge Baeran—the blind master and his mute bodyguard gone forever in the suds of a bath, his wife and daughter vanished with the doffing of *thōbes*.

They were fortunate and booked an early passage on an Arbalina vessel—the *Delfino*—a carrack sailing for Pellar within but two days. And on the eleventh of April, they weighed anchor on the tide of dawn.

Along the shores of Jugo they sailed and past the mouth of the mighty River Argon, and now the land to the ship's port side was the Realm of Pellar. Beyond Thell Cove they fared—there where the *Eroean* was hidden in a grot—continuing easterly along the Pellarion coast.

They sailed into Hile Bay on the midday tide, the cliffs of Pendwyr towering above. Faeril was relieved to be once again at the city, though everywhere she looked, the despoiling hand of Mankind was evident: sewage stains running down the sheer stone bluffs from Pendwyr above, the waters of the bay unclean.

They put ashore in the early afternoon and clambered up the stairs of the cliffs, making their way through the noisy, crowded city, the odor of middens thick, the effluvium of sewage wafting.

At the caer they were welcomed by Commander Rori and ushered to suitable quarters. Later word came from Rori that he had arranged for them to see Lord Leith, Steward, on the morrow, for King Garon and Queen Thayla were of course in Challerain Keep, having fared north in early spring, not to return till early autumn.

In the darktide as Faeril lay down to sleep, she reflected

on how good it was to be back. But even better would be going home . . . wherever home might be. When she thought about it her mind did not conjure up a vision of the Boskydells, but instead she saw a cote in Arden Vale, where buccan and damman had lived on the hill above the River Tumble.

That night Faeril cried herself to sleep.

"Damnation!" exclaimed the portly Man, crashing a fist to table. "Another *jihad* now? Will they never learn?"

"My Lord Hanor," soothed Lord Leith, "it was not said that there would be a *jihad*, only that the mosques of the Prophet had been overthrown, and that is not news. Our spies have—"

"Military movements, that's what I heard. What else *can* it be if not preparation for a *jihad*?"

The steward turned to Commander Rori. "What say our spies about such, Rori?"

"It seems to be on the increase," answered the Realmsman, "as if something is afoot."

Aravan cleared his throat. "Mayhap the Sultan's schemes have been set back, for with the death of Stoke, any plans for an army of corpses have gone aglimmering—the secret of such died with that monster."

Lord Leith sighed. "Perhaps so, Lord Aravan. In any event, King Garon must hear of this. I will dispatch a rider to Challerain tomorrow, giving him your news."

Silence fell among those gathered. At last, Faeril turned to Rori. "Commander, did Halíd return? Last we saw, he set out across the desert for Sabra, to intercept Captain Legori and the *Bèllo Vènto*."

"Aye, that he did," replied the commander, glancing at the silver lock in the damman's otherwise black hair. "Came here back in December. Said that he was almost hanged as a horse-thief in Sabra.

"He stayed here but a day, leaving the very next morning for Darda Erynian . . . and in early April he and two Elves—Silverleaf and Tuon—appeared here in Pendwyr and set sail for Sabra, heading for that well in the Karoo where the creature dwells."

"Uâjii," murmured Aravan.

"Aye, that's it," said Rori, "the Well of Uâjii. They went to kill the wyrm, to avenge Reigo. You missed them by—let me see . . . why, just eight days."

"Fiddle-faddle I say to this monster down a hole in the desert," grumbled Lord Hanor. "A bigger monster sits on the throne of Hyree, and something must be done about it—an assassination, perhaps—else we may have a *jihad* true."

Aravan's sapphire-blue gaze took in the advisor. "The Sultan a monster, thou say? We brought only suspicions. Have thou proof of monstrous deeds?"

Hanor clenched a fist. "Pah! I need no proof, Lord Aravan. My suspicions are enough. I say that he is a monster, and like all monsters everywhere, he should be killed."

Aravan's gaze grew icy. "We met several monsters on this journey, slaying the greatest of them, though not the one I seek. Yet many more are left in this world, and if thou would hunt them all down, Lord Hanor, thou will have taken on a task thou cannot complete, for more are in the making even as we speak.

"Mayhap thou are right and all deserve to die, and surely they will if they are but mortal. Yet neither thee nor anyone else I have met can pierce the veils of time, and thou have only suspicions of vile deeds to come; none have yet been committed. I ask thee, Lord Hanor, would thou slay everyone thou suspect might commit perfidious acts sometime in the future? And this I ask thee as well: if thou could slay every one of them on thy suspicions alone, who would be the monster then?

"Mayhap thou would be right to seek the deaths of those who can cause the slaughter of innocents, yet I think that in the main, other ways are available to thwart their vile schemes."

Hanor snorted. "You are one to talk, Elf, for you seek the death of another. And what is the motive? . . . Revenge!"

"That I do not deny, Lord Hanor. Yet in many ways, vengeance is the purest motive of all, exacting just retribution for an unjust deed done, and at the very base it is the sum and substance of thine own manmade laws."

Lord Leith held up his hands, palms out as if stepping

between the Elf and Man. "Let it lie, m'Lords. I will say this, though: Lord Aravan, your point is well taken; we must indeed exact retribution for foul deeds done . . . but as to those we merely surmise *might* be done in the future, who knows precisely the foul deeds yet to occur? Had we this knowledge, then we could prevent such acts, but alas, we do not."

Lord Hanor ground his teeth. "I know in my heart that the Sultan of—"

"Hanor, I said let it lie," snapped Leith.

Hanor fell silent, clearly choking on his own words.

A long, uncomfortable moment passed, then the steward stood and stepped to Faeril, taking the tiny damman's hands in his. "Mistress, I am most saddened to hear of your loss. Yet know this: your Sir Gwylly was a hero, and the world is a poorer place without him."

Faeril's eyes brimmed with tears as Lord Leith kissed her hands. She had no words to return to him.

Three days later, Faeril, Aravan, Riatha, and Urus rode away from Pendwyr, heading northward, returning home. Six horses were in their train: four riding and two pack animals.

Up through the Glave Hills they rode and beyond, coming into the Greatwood, Urus leading the way, Faeril's horse on a long tether after. Behind followed Riatha and then Aravan, a pack animal trailing each.

Spring was on the land, life quickening, buds opening, pale green leaves sprouting, yellow grasses turning verdant, flowers bursting up and out from the soil. Faeril found that she had nearly forgotten how very green were the High King's Realms, for the ocean voyages crossed deep, dark waters, and the Karoo had been a deadly dun brown. Even the green of the Talâk Range seemed thin and lacking by comparison to the verdure now in the surround.

And as they wended through the awakening forest, birds returned from their long journeys and sang the four awake at every dawning. Animals scurried among the trees, and occasionally she saw a deer bounding away, and in the evenings they were serenaded by piping frogs.

The spring rains came, and they rode for days through a

forest awash or adrip, their storm cloaks fending the water from them. At night they made camp wherever they could, at times beneath hastily constructed lean-tos, at other times below hollow bluffs, and at rare times in a woodsman's shack or crofter's barn.

When it was not raining, they camped in the open, and many were the discussions 'round the fire.

Faeril remembered one in particular, the night she sat on the briar:

"Ow!" The damman stood, the others looking her way. "Hmph! Look here, mister thornbranch, I mean to sit on that log."

Faeril rummaged through her saddlebags, finding and donning her climbing gloves. Then she took hold of the long stem, haling upward to pull it free of the earth. It did not budge.

Again she tried, to no effect.

Urus, waterskins over his shoulder, stepped to her side. "Come, wee one, let us pull together."

Faeril again haled with all her strength, and Urus added a bit of his own, and out came the briar, root and all, and the root was nearly as long as the branch itself.

Faeril looked up at Urus and grinned, and the Baeran grinned back, then he and Riatha headed for the stream. The damman's gaze followed them a moment and then she glanced at the crescent Moon and smiled. She turned and cast the thornbranch on the fire and sat and watched it burn, lost in her thoughts.

After a while she looked up to see Aravan regarding her. "Would that all our problems were so easy," said Faeril, gesturing at the briar.

Aravan nodded and then said, "Some problems have entangled roots that go very deep."

"I've been wondering, Aravan—I mean, after the argument between you and Lord Hanor back at the caer—will Mankind ever get to the roots of his problems? That is, like the Elves seem to have done?"

Aravan smiled and shook his head. "Ah, wee one, Elvenkind has not solved all problems besetting them."

"But you . . . I mean, Elvenkind does not despoil the land.

And from discussions past, you no longer seek to conquer all, to dominate."

"True, Faeril, we have solved many of the more thorny issues, but there are many that remain. Yet I know what thou are asking.

"Will Mankind ever get to the root of his problems? . . . I think Man might not live long enough to do so.

"There are those among Elvenkind who have lived through all. They are the ones who brought about change by seeking out and dealing with the roots of our problems. Even so, we found down deep that the roots were all entangled with one another, just as are Mankind's. He will find that when he pulls up one by the roots, he will merely expose another, and another, and others thereafter.

"Yet Mankind is short-lived. He is too occupied in sating his reckless appetites, too busy breeding—one day I fear that there will be too many Humans plundering the world. Who among them will set aside his lusts and ponder the effect of Man upon the earth? Who among them will endure long enough to accumulate the knowledge needed to reach enlightenment?"

Faeril stirred the embers of the thornbranch. "Aravan, you once said that the children of Mankind provided links from the past to the future. Couldn't Man work in concert to gain that knowledge, and then pass what is learned from one generation to the next, the new generation building upon the knowledge of the old, generation after generation, until wisdom is gained?"

"He could, Faeril, but heed: to learn, thou must listen . . . and Man is too busy shouting to hear."

Faeril slowly shook her head. "Well, just as Urus and I worked together to uproot the briar, it seems to me that only by working together will Man ever resolve his problems. By getting at the root causes and pulling them into the light of day and examining them, then perhaps he can turn thornbranches into flowers, briar patches into gardens. Otherwise he simply prunes back a problem a bit, and more thorns will spring from the very same roots. Look, Lord Hanor wanted to kill the Sultan of Hyree, and perhaps he should be slain, yet isn't that merely pruning? Won't other despots spring from the same roots?"

Aravan smiled at Faeril. "Ah, my wee one, thou are now beginning to struggle with the same problems that our Elven philosophers dealt with long ago."

"Then, why doesn't Elvenkind just give Mankind the answers, Aravan?"

"He does not listen, Faeril. Mankind must recognize the consequences of his acts ere he will understand that he needs to change, and even then he might not have the fortitude to do so. Remember the lemmings—they know not of their collective rush to destruction. And should thou try to stop them, they will merely run over thee on their way to oblivion. Let us hope that Mankind realizes his own course ere it is too late, and then has the strength of will to do what must be done."

The Greatwood was a mighty timberland, some seven hundred miles long and two hundred and fifty wide. Yet Urus seemed to know every inch of it, and he rode unerringly toward where they were bound. Finally in the midst of the forest, they came to a vast glade known simply as The Clearing, so broad that the woods beyond could not be seen, some thirty miles afar.

Suddenly Faeril recalled, "Here it was that you came, Riatha, with Tomlin and Petal a thousand years ago, to sing of Urus's deeds."

Urus looked at the Elfess, a question in his eyes. "Yes, love," she said. "Thou were made into a legend that day—Tomlin telling of thy deeds, I singing of them."

Urus growled and shook his head, but Faeril could see that he was pleased.

Out into this open space fared the four, riding for the distant edge, and in the late May evening they came unto a woodland village hidden among foliage green just beyond the far rim.

They stayed in that Baeron hamlet for a full month, waiting for Year's Long Day, waiting for the Gathering. For then would all the Baeron come together in the Greatwood, in The Clearing, to engage in contests, to sing songs, and to tell of great deeds done. And this was why Urus had been pleased to hear of Tomlin's and Riatha's feat, for it was among the greatest of honors to have your tale told and a song sung of your deeds done at the Baeron Gathering.

But on the day when it finally came, it was Gwylly's tale that was told and Gwylly's song that was sung of Gwylly's deeds done that enthralled the gathered Baeron and nearly broke their hearts. And not an eye was dry when Riatha finished her song, the last note ringing long from the harp and into the quiet forest air.

They travelled on northward, crossing the River Rissanin at Eryn Ford, entering Darda Erynian, also known as the Great Greenhall, and as Blackwood of Old.

Through this vast woodland they fared, escorted by Dylvana Elves, the kindred of the Lian though somewhat smaller in stature.

And the long summer days and soft summer nights passed seemingly without number, yet within two weeks they had reached the Landover Road and had forded the mighty River Argon.

There the Dylvana left them, and the four rode onward, now headed up toward the Crestan Pass there in the Grimwalls.

Two more days elapsed, as up into the high country they went, with its brawling streams and waterfalls and pine forests and tranquil meadows covered with the wildflowers of summer.

Across the pass and down they fared, another two days going by, reaching their goal at last, arriving in Arden Vale on the ninth day of July.

And they were greeted with open arms, and with tears when Arden Elves heard what had come to pass.

Faeril groomed Blacktail and Dapper, the ponies having been returned to Arden from the port town of Ander on the Boreal Sea in Rian nearly three years agone.

Riatha came to the stables smiling. She held in her hand a folded parchment. "Faeril, see here."

"What is it, Riatha?"

" 'Tis a letter from the Adonite priests of the monastery above the glacier. It is dated two years past, is addressed to

Aravan, and just this day arrived. With it was the letter written by Aravan to Alor Inarion a year further back, when Aravan was in the monastery with Urus recovering.

"When Inarion received it, Aravan laughed, saying that 'twas good that urgent plans hinged not upon its arrival.

"As to his own letter from Doran, Aravan thought that all of us would like to see the words of the Abbot, and he gave it to me to read and to bear it to thee and thence to Urus." Riatha handed the letter to Faeril.

*My dear Lord Aravan:*

*As you advised, when came the summer, Gavan and I made our way down to the grasslands where the ren herds graze, and there we found the Aleutani. They were grieved to hear of the deaths of B'arr, Tchuka, and Ruluk at the hands of the Foul Folk, and they sent an expedition into the Grimwalls, to no avail.*

*As autumn arrived, they escorted us back unto the village of Innuk on the shores of the Boreal Sea.*

*Gavan and I waited long for a ship of the Fjordsmen to come, and one has arrived at last. Yet some two years have passed since we came to this village. But now we can send your letter on to Arden Vale as you desired.*

*I have also written to the Patriarch of my own Adonite order, telling him of what has passed here as well as in the abbey. As you suggested, I advised him that should he desire to once again occupy the monastery, then let it be with warrior priests, for such is needed in that perilous place.*

*As for Gavan and me, we have found a calling in ministering to the Aleutani, here in Innuk as well as in other villages. Yet they are an exceedingly stubborn lot, insisting that all good things flow from Tak'lat of the Snow rather than from Adon, or from Shuwah of the Sea, or from Jinnik of the Air, or from . . . well, it seems they have a thousand deities, more or less—crow gods, fish gods, seal gods, whale gods, tree gods, snow gods, ice gods, fire gods, water gods, rain gods, and more. Whatever there is on the face of the earth or*

*under, and in the sky or above, and on the sea or below,*
*real or imagined, material or immaterial, known or un-*
*known, or living or dead, the Aleutani have a god for*
*it.*

*I do hope that Gavan lives a long life, for the work*
*will not be finished in my own time.*

*I trust that this letter will find you well, and that*
*your quest has come to a satisfactory end.*

*Yours in Adon,*
*Doran, Abbot*

Riatha and Urus were married in an Elven ceremony on the
night of the autumnal equinox, Inarion voicing their pledges
to one another, there in the bright Elven hall. Riatha was
radiant in a pale green long-sleeved silken gown trimmed with
satin ribbons of gold, and pale green ribbons twined in her
golden hair, and a single band set with golden beryls fixed
about her brow. Urus was resplendent in dark velvet brown,
tan insets in the puffed shoulders of his long sleeves, tan
ruffles at his wrists, a tan lace ruff down his chest.

Many wondered that Riatha would take vows with a mortal, even though he looked youthful in spite of being more
than a thousand years old.

And Faeril wept as if she would never stop, for her heart
sang with joy; and she wept as if she would never stop, for
her heart flooded with grief—just five years past on the very
same night in the very same place with the very same vows
she and Gwylly had wed.

As October arrived, Faeril said her good-byes to Riatha and
Urus, the wee damman journeying back to the Boskydells,
the Elfess and Baeran sad to see her go. Too, she said farewell
to Alor Inarion as well as others, fast friends of hers in the
Elven vale. And ere she left, Inarion said to her, "Should
there ever come a need, thou are welcome to dwell here for
as long as thou desire." Faeril hugged him and kissed him
and said that if indeed there ever was a need, she would
come to the vale gladly. Then she and Aravan set forth down
the gorge, she riding upon Blacktail, with Dapper as a pack
pony tethered behind, Aravan mounted upon a rust-red roan.

Within two days they came out of Arden, riding beneath

the thundering falls, coming to the Crossland Road and turning westerly. Autumn was in the air, the days cool and growing short, the nights crisp and growing long. And Faeril found a memory in every hill, a remembrance in every stream, an image in every tree of happy days long past when another rode at her side.

And often she had tears in her eyes.

The days passed swiftly, the nights slowly, as they journeyed west. Across Arden Ford they fared, wading the River Tumble, entering into the Drearwood in the Land of Rhone.

Days later they crossed the Stone-arches Bridge above the River Caire to come into the Wilderland there between Harth and Rian. Among the Wilderness Hills they travelled and across the plains beyond, coming at last within sight of Beacontor, there where the Black Foxes had overthrown the Spawn.

Beyond Beacontor, Faeril and Aravan turned north, heading for Orith and Nelda's, Gwylly's Human parents, there on the edge of the shaggy Weiunwood.

Evening was falling when at last the farm came into sight, and as Faeril and Aravan rode into the yard and dismounted, Black came dashing from the house, barking and racing 'round.

And Nelda stepped onto the porch, peering through the twilight, Orith right after. Their eyes widened in wonder at the sight of an Elf Lord, and then Faeril walked 'round from behind.

"Oh, child, you've come home," cried Nelda, running down the steps and embracing her, weeping for joy.

She held the damman at arm's length. "Let me look at you. My, my, what a pretty sight."

Her gaze then swept beyond Faeril, searching through the twilight. "And just where is that wayward son of ours?"

And Faeril burst into tears.

Seven days they stayed at Orith and Nelda's, telling of all that had befallen, speaking of Gwylly—Orith or Nelda with tearful eyes telling of his finding, of his childhood, Faeril speaking of their lives together, and Aravan describing the quest, their voices soft, reminiscing.

And all the while they talked, Black lay by the door, his

sad eyes fixed on Faeril, raising his head at every little sound from outside, as if expecting Gwylly to step in at any moment.

Early on the fourth night after her arrival, as Faeril washed her face readying for bed, she saw Orith sitting on the porch in the chill twilight, autumn now gripping the land. Wrapping a blanket about herself, she stepped out to see if aught was amiss, to find him staring at a thin crescent Moon riding low in the west, clouds racing across the silver arc, driven by a cold wind.

"Once," said Faeril, "when we were deep in the desert, Gwylly looked up at the rising yellow Moon and he sang of a cow and a cat and a dog, and he sang of a fiddle and a dish and a spoon. . . . I laughed. Oh, how I laughed. And I asked him where he had learned such wonderful nonsense. And you know what he said?"

Orith looked at the damman, his eyes streaming tears. "I taught him that song. It was his favorite."

Faeril threw her arms about Orith and kissed him on the cheek. "Yes. Exactly. That is what he said."

Seven days after they arrived, Aravan and Faeril set out from Orith and Nelda's, riding again for the Boskydells. Black followed a short way, then stopped at Orith's whistle. Ere she passed beyond the bend, Faeril looked back and waved goodbye, and the last she saw of the two, Orith had his arm about Nelda as they turned and walked toward their solitary house.

The Weiunwood was clad in yellow and gold and scarlet, and along its flank they rode, the shaggy forest on the right, a low range of hills on their left. Southerly and then southwesterly they fared, camping in the hills that night.

Just ere dawn, a cold drizzle began, and they plodded in a miserable chill, coming to the Crossland Road, the track slowly turning into a mire.

West along the route they rode, now and then dismounting and walking, giving Aravan's roan and Faeril's pony a breather.

In late afternoon they came in through the east gate of Stonehill, passing down the cobbled streets to come to the

White Unicorn, Stonehill's finest inn. Dismounting at the stables, they turned their steeds over to a wiry lad, and they entered the warm, cheery common room of the hostel. Maltby Brewster, their host, and Murium, his wife, welcomed Faeril back, for five years past she had come through Stonehill, seeking a Gwylly Fenn . . . and both were saddened to hear that the buccan had been slain. They were surprised as well to discover that the damman was travelling with an Elf Lord, yet they arranged suitable quarters for each.

News of these visitors travelled swiftly through Stonehill, and folks came to the Unicorn to have an ale and a meal and to get a look at this Elf Lord, to see him for themselves. Aravan did not disappoint them, taking up a six-stringed lute and regaling all with songs of the sea, some soft and lorn, others bright and gay, still others wild and bawdy, full of hearty laughter.

That night they stayed and all the next day and the next night as well, waiting for the weather to clear.

Yet the following morn was fair, and as Aravan and Faeril readied to leave Stonehill, neither Maltby nor Murium would accept any coin, saying that Aravan's barding had paid for all.

And so, out from Stonehill they rode, a chill morning fog curling among the trees. Northward they turned onto the Post Road, which ran from Challerain Keep in the land north to Caer Pendwyr far to the south, the very same route taken by High King Garon and Queen Thayla on their journeys between.

The road curved westerly ere swinging northward again, arcing 'round the flanks of the Battle Downs, a place of War long past. And along this way plodded horse and pony, placidly bearing Elf and Warrow, first westerly, then northwesterly, then north, faring by day and camping by night. At last they came to Two-Fords Road, down which they turned.

Now straight toward the Boskydells they rode, their course carrying them west, and on the third day after leaving Stonehill, they sighted the formidable Thornwall, the barrier beringing the Land ahead. Left and right it stretched as far as the eye could see. And up into the air it reared, some fifty feet or so. A massive barrier of Spindlethorn, in places it was as wide as a mile but in no place less than a quarter mile across. So thick that even birds found it difficult to penetrate, this wall had fended friend and foe alike, for in but a few places could travellers and others pass through.

Spindle Ford was one of these places, and here it was that Faeril and Aravan fared. Yet when they came to the tunnel through the thorns, Aravan halted his horse, saying that he would not enter. Instead he dismounted and stepped to her pony, his eyes level with hers, and this is what he said:

"Faeril, thy Land is for the Wee Folk, and only in great need would I come within.

"Thou are now safely delivered unto thy Realm, and I have a vow to keep. And after I have fulfilled that pledge of retribution, then must I continue my quest. Somewhere in the world is a yellow-eyed Man—a sword stealer, a friend slayer. Mayhap it is Ydral, mayhap not; regardless, my quest is not done.

"And so I now will leave thee, yet heed: should thou ever need my aid, send word and I will come, for I do love thee, my valiant friend, and I will remember thee forever."

Faeril's eyes filled with tears, and she embraced and kissed the Elf Lord. ["And thee, Alor Aravan,"] she said in Sylva, ["I will remember thee for as long as I shall live as well."]

Aravan remounted his horse, and with a cry of *"Yah! Yah!"* spurred away, galloping back the way they had come, up the road and over the rise, and then he was gone beyond sight.

Faeril turned her face toward the Thornwall tunnel and urged Blacktail ahead. And into the gloom of the barrier they went, Dapper plodding behind.

That night she spent in Thornwalker quarters, there at the Spindle Ford station, the one Thornwalker assigned to the crossing glad for her company.

The next day she set out, the Thornwall on her right flank. All day she travelled, passing Hob's Cairn in the morning and turning her ponies westerly along the Upland Way. By evening she had reached the fringes of the Northwood, where she camped for the darktide.

*     *     *

The next morning she awoke to frost, the land about covered with the white rime, a small taste of winter to come. Breaking camp, into the 'Wood she rode, now faring for her home, yet some fifty miles hence. All day she rode, and part of the next, coming in the late afternoon to the place where she had been raised.

She rode into the tiny yard of the tiny cote and found her sire chopping wood. He dropped his axe when he saw who she was: his dammsel, some five years gone. And he hugged her and kissed her and ushered her into the house, shouting for all to come and see what he had found. Lorra dropped what she had been doing, hugging her fiercely and kissing her as well, saying, "Welcome home, oh my Faeril. Welcome home at last."

And as her brothers rushed into the room, Faeril hugging and kissing all three, the wee damman looked about, tears in her eyes, knowing in her heart of hearts that although she was back with those she loved . . . this was not home at all.

# CHAPTER 43

# Retribution

**C**losing the well-guarded door behind and bearing but a single candle, the Emir of Nizari entered his darkened bedchamber. Widely he yawned, for he was sleepy, sated from the dalliance with his latest smooth-cheeked boy. The candle cast a glowing halo as he moved across the room, a feeble yellow light flickering, pressing back the blackness from a small circle 'round.

The first that the Emir knew he was not alone was when that dim light was reflected from a pair of icy eyes like sapphires, tilted, peering at him from a cloaked, turbaned figure, face covered by a dark cloth.

["Who . . . ?"] the Emir asked in Hyrinian, holding up the candle, backing away.

Slowly the figure raised a hand and plucked away the cloth.

"*You!*" hissed the Emir.

Perhaps he screamed and screamed as he died, but none will ever know—or say, for all the rooms in the Scarlet Citadel are sealed against sound.

All that is known is the next morning when the majordomo Abid went to waken his master, the Emir was dead—run through by some burning weapon, or so it was surmised, for the wound was cauterized, as if a red-hot spear had been thrust through the master's body.

Who had done such a deed, none knew—though it was speculated that only a *Djinn* could have gotten past the guards unseen.

# CHAPTER 44

# Auguries

**Two Years Later . . .**

*. . . And Beyond*

The snow had melted at last, water runnelling everywhere, spring stirring throughout the Boskydells. In a small cote in the Northwood, Faeril and her sire and dam and her younger brother sat before the fire, taking their afternoon tea and speaking of things gone by and of things that were and of things yet to be.

Faeril's sire rocked in his chair. "You are set on doing this thing, child?" he asked.

"Yes, Dad. I feel I must."

"Oi, Faeril," said Dibby, sitting cross-legged on the floor, "leaving the Bosky for good, going to Arden Vale . . . well, I just don't know."

"You won't be with your kind at all," added Lorra, turning the embroidery hoop in her hands . . . turning it about . . . turning, not sewing . . . instead fighting back the tears.

"But, Mother, I was so happy there."

Her father slowly shook his head. "You can't go back through time, my dammsel."

Lorra set the hoop aside and took up her teacup. "She knows, Arlo. She knows."

The day outside was drab and wet. Water dripped from the

eaves, some to run down the window panes, streaking the wan light seeping inward, wavering shadows joining those already mustered within the room. The fire pressed back the dark and damp, its ruddy glow shining from Faeril's silver lock, chasing it with copper.

Faeril stared long into the fire. At last she said, "I believe we were camped at the ford on the River Hanü when Aravan said that which I did not understand until just now. He said, 'Auguries are oft subtle . . . and dangerous—thou may deem they mean one thing when they mean something else altogether.'

"Not one of us down through the years truly understood the meaning of Rael's prophecy concerning the Eye of the Hunter. Yet I do now . . . I do now."

Lorra's voice took on the cant of a chanter.

> *"When Spring comes upon the land,*
> *Yet Winter grips with icy hand,*
> *And the Eye of the Hunter stalks night skies,*
> *Bane and blessing alike will rise.*
> *Lastborn Firstborns of those who were there,*
> *Stand at thy side in the light of the Bear.*
> *Hunter and hunted, who can say*
> *Which is which on a given day?"*

"Aye, Mother"—Faeril's voice came softly through the dimness—"that was the prophecy."

"Where, my dammsel, where was it misinterpreted?" asked Lorra.

Faeril wiped the heel of her hand across her cheeks, drying them. "It isn't that it was misinterpreted; instead, it was not fully understood. The total of its extent eluded us, but now it is clear:

"We had always believed that the term *Lastborn Firstborns* meant the latest in a long line of firstborn dammsels and firstborn buccoes. But it meant more than that: it meant the very last in the line of Firstborns, after which the line would be broken—

"Oh, Mother, I never loved anyone as I loved Gwylly, and I never shall . . . I never shall."

Faeril began weeping, and Lorra moved beside her and comforted her.

Dibby looked on helplessly, not knowing what to do, and Arlo took a handkerchief from his pocket and dabbed his own eyes. Though none of her family had ever met Gwylly, they knew that Faeril was heartbroken, and they hurt for her.

At last Dibby said softly, "Dad, I don't understand."

Arlo looked at his son. "This is the way of it, Dibs: Some of us love but once and never again. Your sister is one of these. She will never remarry, never have any children of her own. After her the line will be broken—there will be no more Firstborns. She and Gwylly were truly the Lastborn Firstborns—just as the prophecy foretold, though no one knew what it meant in the end, until now. She is the last, the very last."

Dibby began to cry.


"When d'you think you'll be leaving?" asked Arlo, his hands continuing to ply the knife shaping the carving.

Faeril glanced out at the rain falling again. "In late spring when the weather comes warm."

"Well, dammsel, this time I'll turn out to say farewell."

Arlo augured the knife, twisting the point against the wood, making a hole. "I watched you go last time," he said quietly.

Faeril looked up from her stitchery. "You did?"

"Aye. Your brothers, too. Secretly, through that window." Arlo pointed.

"Why didn't you come out?"

"Well, I knew that should I step out to kiss you good-bye, I would beg you not to go . . . but I knew as well that you followed your destiny, and I would not thwart that."

Faeril sat in silence a long while, water pattering on the roof, her father's knife going *shkk, shkk*, curls of wood peeling. At last she stood and stepped to her sire, kissing him on the cheek.


Lightning flared and thunder hammered and the rain came drenching down. And as the four sat at supper, above the brawl of the storm came the thud of galloping horses and the flare of a horn cry.

"What the . . . ?" Dibby leapt to the fogged-over window, rubbing a hole in the wetness, peering out, Arlo at his side, but both Faeril and Lorra stepped to a bedroom.

Again came the horn cry, closer now.

Faeril hurried back into the room, her knife-filled bandoliers settled across her chest, the damman girting a long-knife about her waist.

Lorra, too, was accoutred in throwing knives.

Dibby turned. "Lor," he breathed, seeing the weaponry. "D'you think there's like to be danger?"

"Mayhap, Dibs," answered Faeril, and her brother rushed to catch up two knobbed staffs, one for himself, the other for his sire.

Now a rider thudded up to the cote through the driving rain, trailing a remount behind, water and mud splattering.

" 'Tis a Man," muttered Arlo, peering through the rain-streaked pane, the vision dim, distorted by water.

But lightning flared as the rider dismounted and cast back his hood. "Nay," said Faeril, "not a Man but an Elf instead! . . . 'Tis Jandrel from Arden! Something is amiss!"

She rushed out into the downpour. "Jandrel! Jandrel! What is it? What is wrong?"

A great smile burst across Jandrel's wet face and he caught up Faeril and whirled her about, water cascading down over both. "Wrong? Wrong? Why, my own sweet Faeril, what could possibly be wrong? I have come to fetch thee, back to Arden to witness the miracle. The first Elven birth in Mithgar ever!

"Dara Riatha is with child!"

"You mean, she's had a baby?"

"Nay, she is pregnant! She carries Urus's child. Isn't it wonderful?"

"But, Jandrel, that is impossible! Elves cannot get pregnant on Mithgar. And even if they could, Humans and Elves between them do not bear children."

"Aye!" Jandrel grinned. "Did I not say it was a miracle?"

Jandrel set her down. "Riatha sent me. Can thou leave on the morrow? She wishes thee at her side when the child comes."

Cold rain hammered upon the two. "Is it that quick? When is she due?"

Jandrel laughed, his face lighted with joy, and he spread out his hands, palms up. "Ah, wee one, no one knows. We have no experience with miracles at all. The last any Elf saw an Elven birth was more than five thousand years agone, on Adonar, ere the Sundering.

"And with Urus being the father, who can say when the child will come?"

Dibby and Arlo came splatting out in the rain, carrying Faeril's all-weather cloak with them and casting it about the damman's shoulders. "Your horses are too big to fit in my pony stable," called Arlo, "but they can take shelter in the byre yon." The Warrow looked up at the Elf. "And like your horses, you yourself are too big to walk through my door, but if you don't mind crawling in, we've got supper on the table, and there's plenty for you as well."

The very next morning—the tenth of April, 5E993—Faeril and Jandrel readied themselves to go.

'Mid the tearful good-byes, Arlo came to his daughter and kissed her and said, "I would beg you not to go . . . but I think that this is still your destiny. Take care of yourself, dammsel of mine."

Dibby, too, stepped forward. "When they get back, I'll tell Finch and Hawly your good-byes."

Faeril hugged him, saying, "Go see Lacey and tell her as well, Dibs. She likes you, you know. And tell her . . . tell her I will write."

Lorra embraced her. "I think your father is right—this is all part of what was meant to be. Even so, we will miss you dearly."

"I will miss you too, Mother. Yet I will write often, can I find couriers coming this way; mayhap two or three years will not elapse between missives."

Jandrel led the horses nigh, and with a final kiss for sire, dam, and brother, Faeril mounted up, the Elf lifting her to the saddle. And in the damp morning, running at a good clip they set out for Arden Vale, the Elf galloping in the lead, the damman mounted on the tethered horse coursing behind. And ere they raced beyond sight along the eastward trace, Jandrel lifted his horn to his lips, and the Northwood rang with his farewell call.

\*     \*     \*

Four nights later, they spent the darktide in Stonehill, and the very next night at Orith and Nelda's. And just five days after leaving those quarters, they came to the entrance of Arden Vale there at the waterfall. And on the following day amid calls of greeting they rode into the Elven settlement in the north part of the gorge. Fifty or more miles a day they had ridden, seventeen to eighteen leagues, Jandrel varying the pace so that the steeds would last, covering the nearly six hundred miles in but eleven days.

Riatha was radiant, and Urus beamed.

Faeril's intent gaze studied the Elfess. "They said you were with child, but I don't see . . ."

Riatha laughed. "As best as can be determined, the child is not due until autumn . . . October, mayhap."

Faeril mentally counted. *Five months, or six.* "How can this be, Riatha? I thought that Elves bore no young on Mithgar. And that there was no issue between Humans and Elves ever."

" 'Tis remarkable, true. Yet Urus and I deem it is because of his nature. He is something beside Human."

"A Cursed One," rumbled Urus, "or so I always thought, till now."

Faeril eyed the Baeran. "And now . . . ?"

"Now I am a Blessed One," replied Urus, grinning, embracing Riatha.

Faeril moved back into the cote where she and Gwylly had lived, there above the River Tumble, the place kept for her by Inarion, for it seems he knew that she would at last return.

And over the next weeks and months, marvelling Elves from throughout Mithgar came to be present at the birth.

Inarion and Urus sent representatives to the Great Greenhall to fetch a Baeran midwife, for the Elves had little or no experience in such—certainly not of late. And when she came, she was a strapping Woman, some six foot one or two. Yet her way was gentle, and her name was Yselle, and she and Riatha became fast friends.

And in the crafters' halls of Arden, workers of precious

metals and gems and ivories and other worthy stuffs began fashioning gifts for the child, even though they knew not whether it would be male or female.

Among these workers was a wee damman, learning the art of fine chain crafting, for Faeril would prepare a birthing gift with her own hands. And she fashioned a crystal pendant on a platinum chain, the stone remarkable for the figure within—that of a bird, a falcon, wings unfurled as if ready to spring into flight. Why she chose platinum over gold or silver or even starsilver, Faeril did not know, yet when she had touched the metal, she knew that this was meant to be. And all during the crafting, an elusive thought slid 'round the corners of her mind, always just beyond seeing, always glimpsed but not recognized. Yet on the day she finished the crafting, chain glittering, crystal sparkling in the bright sunlight, suddenly she remembered the words of Dodona, there in the Kandrawood ring:

*The eld Man seemed to look elsewhere, as if seeing something beyond the circle of trees. "Yes, child, your comrades are most worthy. You travel with a Friend; this I know, for that stone at your neck is his and not yours. Too, you travel with a BearLord, and I know whence he came. You travel with one who is to bear the hope of the world, and she is worthy. You travel with one who will aid in ridding the world of a foulness, though not the one you seek. And you travel with one who loves you, one whom you love in return. All of these companions are indeed honorable."*

Faeril caught her breath. *"You travel with one who is to bear the hope of the world, and she is worthy."*

Whelmed by the thought, Faeril sat down, staring at the crystal in her hand. *Could this be what Dodona had meant? That Riatha is to bear a child who will be the hope of the world?*

Suddenly Aravan's words sounded in her mind: *"Auguries are oft subtle . . . and dangerous—thou may deem they mean one thing when they mean something else altogether."*

Faeril kept her thoughts to herself, wanting to ponder Dodona's words longer ere sharing her insight. And oft she gazed at the clear crystal, the one with the bird inside.

And as if a floodgate had been loosed, visions and phrases inundated her mind as she recalled her first dangerous journey down into the depths of that transparent stone:

*Of a sudden she glimpsed an Elfess—Riatha?—she could not say, and standing behind was a huge Man. Next came a rider—Man or Elf?—on horse, a falcon on the rider's shoulder, something glittering in his hands.*

*And she shouted out words in Twyll:*

> *"Ritana fi Za'o*
> *De Kiler fi ca omos,*
> *Sekena, ircuma, va lin du*
> *En Vailena fi ca Lomos."*

*Words that meant:*

> *"Rider of Impossibility,*
> *And Child of the same,*
> *Seeker, searcher, he will be*
> *A Traveller of the Planes."*

For days upon days, Faeril's mind returned again and again to those visions, to those words:

*Rider of Impossibility, Child of the same.*
*Child of the same . . .*
*Of the same . . .*
*Rider of Impossibility . . .*
*Child of Impossibility? . . .*
*Riatha's child: the impossible child.*

Faeril's heart hammered in her breast. *That's it! Riatha's child is the impossible child! Seeker, searcher, he will be the traveller of the Planes!*

Her mind awhirl, Faeril prepared a pot of tea, and then sat without drinking as it grew cold, lost in her thoughts, lost in possibilities.

*Falcon on his shoulder, something glittering in his hands . . . the Dawn Sword?* Faeril held up the pendant, the crystal she had borne across much of Mithgar, seeing the falcon inside. *Does this have aught to do with the falcon on his shoulder?*

And again Aravan's words echoed in her mind: *"Auguries are oft subtle . . . and dangerous—thou may deem they mean one thing when they mean something else altogether."*

On the first day of October, among the visitors who came to be in the vale at the birthing were two slender Elves, one bearing a black spear, the other an Elven bow. 'Twas Tuon and Silverleaf, both of Darda Erynian—Tuon with the spear called Black Galgor, Silverleaf with the bow of white horn.

And with them came a dark, wiry Man, a Gjeenian, a Realmsman—it was Halíd.

Halíd sought out Faeril, and he spoke softly of Gwylly, expressing his sorrow, ". . . for I loved him, too."

And when Faeril asked of his mission, Halíd said, "Let me tell you of the wyrm in the Well of Uâjii, and *aina'àm!* of Silverleaf's *wonderful* plan that nearly got us all killed. . . ."

Faeril and Halíd walked off through the pine forest, Halíd speaking animatedly, his hands flinging back and forth in wild gestures, Tuon and Silverleaf strolling behind, laughing along with Faeril at the Gjeenian's outrageous words.

On the ninth of October, 5E993, at the mid of day, Riatha was delivered of a boychild. Faeril was at her side during the birthing, Midwife Yselle and two chosen Elfesses aiding in the delivery.

But after they had cut and tied the cord and had washed the child, it was Faeril given the honor of bearing the yowling newborn out to Urus, the Man pacing as if caged. And when she handed him up, Urus took the tiny child in his great arms, gentle as a waft of air. Urus lifted back the soft blanket covering the babe, and looked long at his son, the tiny face wrapped 'round howls. Turning to Inarion, he said, "Looks somewhat Elvish, somewhat Mannish, but squalls like a newborn cub."

Together they stepped to the porch of the great hall, out where all had gathered, and Urus raised his child overhead, toward the new Moon clasped in the arms of the old. And he called out to the waiting assembly, "On this day is a miracle, for on this day Riatha has delivered a child. Our son is born."

And a mighty shout flew up to the sky.

\* \* \*

The celebration went long into the night, wine flowing, shouts of joy, trills of laughter, wild dancing, feasting and drinking, bards singing and telling tales. . . .

That night, too, at the child's side someone left an exquisitely carven stone ring, set with a gem of jet, sized to fit a Man's hand. Whoever had left it had gotten in and out without notice. How? None knew. Yet on that very same night the celebrants heard foxes barking in the woods.

Aravan came the next day, riding in from the south, bearing a suitable gift: a gold-encased, glass-covered tiny arrow that always pointed north. He bore with him as well the news that someone had slain the Emir of Nizari . . . and Urus smiled fiercely to hear the Assassin of Assassins was dead.

On this day, too, in the glade of celebration there was an Elven naming ceremony, presided over by Inarion, the Elf Lord speaking in Sylva. And to this sacrament were gathered all the vale's occupants, for none had seen or heard the words of the rite in more than five thousand years.

And Inarion sprinkled the crystal water upon the newborn's forehead, intoning, ["Water!"] and touched the child's tiny hands and feet to clean earth held in a clay vessel ["Earth!"] and with a branch of laurel wafted the fragrant smoke of burning eldwood shavings over the babe ["Air!"] and illuminated the sleeping newborn's face with the light of a burning branch of yew ["Fire!"] and touched a lodestone to his wee hands and feet and temples and heart ["Aethyr!"]

At last Inarion turned to Riatha. ["And what shall be his name?"]

Riatha looked up at Urus and then down at the child. ["He shall be called Bair."]

["Bair,"] whispered Inarion in the babe's right ear and then in the left, and then he turned to the gathering. ["Ladies and Lords assembled,"] announced Inarion, ["from this day forward he shall be called Bair!"]

*Alor Bair!* rang out the response, thrice altogether.

The child yawned and nearly wakened, but did not. And on this day, the day of his naming, Bair was one day old; yet no matter his age, his life was just beginning.

\* \* \*

A week after, Aravan came seeking Faeril. And she sat with him and told of her suspicions concerning the auguries, reminding him of his own words as to the dangers of such. Even so, he said, "I deem thou have guessed the right of much. Mayhap Bair is indeed the Rider of the Planes, the Dawn Rider. Yet I cannot abandon my own quest for the finding of the Dawn Sword, nor for the yellow-eyed slayer of Galarun, for I am sworn.

"Have thou said aught to Riatha, to Urus?"

Faeril shook her head, *No.*

"Then I bid thee .to share what thou have guessed, for keeping it unto thyself may have consequences dire."

"Just as may the sharing," responded Faeril. "What I say will surely color the way he is raised, for ill or good, who can foretell? . . . Not I, Aravan. Not I."

"Nor I, Faeril. Yet heed: in knowledge lies strength; in ignorance, weakness. 'Tis always better to know even part than to know nothing at all."

Faeril slowly nodded, heeding his words.

They sat in silence for a while. At last Aravan said, "I leave on the morrow."

Faeril sighed. "Whence bound?"

"Easterly." After a moment he continued. "When Stoke nearly answered my question as to the whereabouts of Ydral, he vaguely gestured east."

"But, Aravan, there is a whole wide world to the east."

Aravan shrugged. "I have time, Faeril. I have time."

The next day Aravan was gone southward, and after they had waved him good-bye, Faeril turned to Riatha and Urus, the Baeran holding Bair in his arms. "Come," said the damman. "Let us sit awhile. I have something to tell you . . . something to unfold."

Throughout the following years, Faeril continued to live in Arden, in the cote that she and Gwylly had shared. Her life, though not as long as those of other Warrows, was gentle and filled with love.

And through the years as her long, dark hair slowly changed to blend with her silver lock, many friends came to visit with this golden-eyed damman, this last of the Lastborn Firstborns.

She was eighty-eight that final summer's eve, the eve of the autumnal equinox. And after the ceremonies in the glade, after the festivities in the Elven hall, after saying good night to one and all, she came back through the dark green pines and across the meadow to sit before the cote in the soft night, listening to the crickets, the stars wheeling above, the full platinum Moon overhead.

And as the silvery Tumble gurged quietly in the gorge below, Faeril thought she heard a soft footstep and looked up to see—

"Oh my buccaran, I knew you would come for me." And she reached up and took his hand.

*"Will they remember us, Aravan?*
*Will Mankind remember us at all?"*

*"Mayhap, Gwylly, mayhap.*
*Mayhap in their legends and fables.*
*Mayhap in nought but their dreams."*

# About the Author

Dennis L. McKiernan was born April 4, 1932, in Moberly, Missouri, where he lived until age eighteen, when he joined the U.S. Air Force, serving four years spanning the Korean War. He received a B.S. in Electrical Engineering from the University of Missouri in 1958 and an M.S. in the same field from Duke University in 1964. Dennis spent thirty-one years as one of the AT&T Bell Laboratories whiz kids in research and development—in anti-ballistic missile defense systems, in software for telephone systems, and in various management think-tank activities—before changing careers to be a full-time writer.

Currently living in Westerville, Ohio, Dennis began writing novels in 1977 while recuperating from a close encounter of the crunch kind with a 1967 red and black Plymouth Fury (Dennis lost: it ran over him: Plymouth 1, Dennis 0).

Among other hobbies, Dennis enjoys scuba diving, dirtbike riding, and motorcycle touring—all enthusiasms shared by his wife.

His critically acclaimed, best-selling novels include THE IRON TOWER trilogy, THE SILVER CALL duology, *Dragondoom*, and now *The Eye of the Hunter*. And forthcoming soon, the story collection, *Tales from the One-Eyed Crow*.